SHIFT

BOOK 1:

STAG'S HEART

S. L. THORNE

Shift

Text Copyright © 2019 SL Thorne

All rights reserved under International and Pan-American Copyright Conventions.

First revised paperback printing.

No part of this book may be reproduced or transmitted in any form or by any means, graphic, electronic, or mechanical, including photocopying, recording, taping, or by any information storage or retrieval system, without the permission in writing from the author.

This book is a work of fiction. Names, characters, places and incidents are products of the author's imagination or are used fictitiously. Any resemblance to actual events or locales or persons, living or dead, is entirely coincidental.

ISBN: 9798358787179

ACKNOWLEDGEMENTS and DEDICATIONS

First, and foremost, to my husband, for putting the bee back in my bonnet, and being so supportive. You have no idea how much having you walk in the door and hearing "how much have you got?" means to a writer. (Also, the inner giggles from hearing a grown man protecting 'story time'.)

For Laura, who was a giant help. With whom, with any luck, Liliwyn's story might get told.

For Gabriela, for telling me the story that led me to this one, and for letting me tell it my way.

For all those who supplied the bits and pieces, know it or not: I confess to nothing.

Finally:

For Scott Young:
Who gave everything for what he had and deserved so much more time than he got.

You will forever be my Marrok.
I hope the Mother cradles you tightly, gifts you abundantly, and gives you back to us eventually.

"I give you the ability to Become, that you might understand the world and your place in it. I give you Understanding, that you might be one."

-Caelyrima, Mother Chimera

1

She rode north west for the first time in her life. She had been north, into the Mistwood, more times than she could count, but never on the King's Road. And, most certainly, not with such an entourage. Hunting was a different matter, with different accoutrement; a different kind of wagon entirely, for holding camping gear and returning with fresh meat for the castle. Hunting was a matter of a week's roughing it deep in the Mistwood just a few miles from her beloved cliff side home in the Mistwood Reach, sometimes farther if the hunting was not as good. This... this was almost a travesty: three wagons holding furnishings and numerous trunks, plus two handmaidens currently riding in a carriage lady Petra felt certain she should be riding in. However, so long as lady Petra was in that carriage and it was not pouring rain, Lady Caelerys Maral would not be in it.

Lady Petra was an old friend of her father's, one of those stern and nosy widows that were affable enough with her late husband's friends, but with inflexible and distasteful ideas of how young women should comport themselves. The only daughter of Duke Elyas Maral, Caelerys had ideas of her own and they did not mesh with some of the more rigid, new philosophies of the Elder Church; of which lady Petra was a devout supporter.

Caelerys was fair skinned, pretty in an oval way, with eyes of the most vivid, deep sapphire. Her hair was the almost black of the northern blackwood, but glints of deep red could be seen when the sun finally shone upon it. Mostly it flowed freely down her back, drawn from her face with combs. She wore a split skirt and riding leathers, as if this were an ordinary ride, even though she knew it was not. At least for a little while still, she could pretend. Beneath her, Wraith sensed her shifting mood and danced sideways.

The silver buckskin mare wanted to run. She was tired of this lacklustre pace. Riding was serious business, not this drudgery which seemed, to her, to have no purpose. Caelerys loosened her knees and wrapped the reins once more around her gloved hand, leaned forward and gave the mare a pat on her neck in apology. Soon, she promised.

She looked behind her. Four days back, past the trailing wagons and the small army of men, lay Taluscliff, her home. A home she might never see again. Already she missed the cool, salty wind off the cliffs of the palisade, the rust-brown basalt columns that rose in sweeping spires by the sea; the northern moors where she would ride and hunt small game with her falcon, Tempest, who was overhead, somewhere. Already she missed her father, the occasional visits of her uncle, and even her rather brash, youngest brother, Vyncet.

It occurred to her that, at a more reasonable pace, it would only take her two days to get back.

With a sigh, she turned forward again, settling back into her seat and casting her mind to the city that lay ahead. Not just any city: the city-DragonsPoint on the King's Bay. The largest gathering of humanity in Elanthus. The prospect overwhelmed her. She could face a charging boar and keep her wits about her, but unknown people terrified her.

At least there were two people in DragonsPoint she would know: Willam, her eldest living brother and father's heir, and Janem, Master Smith and Maral subsequent. One she barely knew, the other she missed sorely. Willam had gone to Court when he was ten, hostage to the King's Justice after their eldest brother, Landyn, had attempted a mad rebellion against the crown in father's absence. She barely knew Willam, and Landyn had been killed the year she was born. Janem... she smiled, thinking warmly of him, with his flashing dark eyes and dark brown hair and ready smile. She had grown up with him.

Mace rode up along side her, a smile on his lined face. He ran a hand through grizzled hair where it rebelled against the loose queue he wore it in. "It is good to see you smile, little bird."

Mace was the Master Bowman of House Maral and he had been calling her 'little bird' since she was five. She smiled more in spite of herself. Of all her father's men, Mace was her favourite. He had taught her all she knew of the bow and the hunt.

"It won't last," she warned.

"I'll take it even so, my lady." He signalled some of the men behind him and one of them galloped past and out of sight. "About a mile ahead, around that bend, is an inn where we will stop and eat and ready ourselves for entrance to the city. If you wish to stretch the fidget out of that filly, now is the time."

Caelerys did not wait for further invitation, but pressed her knees against the sterling hide and tore off down the road. Mace kept pace a length behind and she could hear the hoof-beats of at least two more speeding up.

It was a short gallop, but exhilarating after four days of wagon pace. Tempest stooped, levelling out at the last and flying smoothly between the riders, the tips of her black-flecked wings deliberately brushing Caelerys's ear.

She was laughing as they reined in, prancing to a halt in the packed dirt courtyard of a pretty little stone inn. She and Wraith both had needed that. As she swung over and dropped from the saddle, a woman in a crisp, starched apron rushed out to meet them. The woman seemed momentarily surprised by the unladylike dismount, but carried on as if nothing were amiss, as though she had seen all sorts upon this road, and had long ago learned to pretend everything was as it should be.

"I have a room ready for you, my lady, as yer man asked. A bath bein' drawn as we speak and a dinner on the way up."

Caelerys's spirits fell almost immediately. This was it, the final stretch. If she ran now... she could throw herself into the saddle and be away before her men could remount, ...but Mace would find her. And her family was counting on her. This was far too important and no Maral had ever fled a battle. Retreated intelligently, sued for peace when the costs were too great, aye. Run in cowardice? Never. She would not be the first.

She thanked the goodwife politely and followed her into the comfortable establishment. The Mist's End was like any other inn, like the one at the opposite end of the road at her end of the Mistwood: a busy common room with fireplace and bar, stairs to one side and a row of rooms above. Several people eating in the taproom looked up at her entrance but went back to their food, curiosity satisfied. Only one watched her for any real length of time. The proprietress led her up the stairs to a modest room.

Caelerys seated herself at the small table and allowed a plump maid to serve her a light meal of stewed capon and warm bread. Two other maids came and went carrying water to fill a brass tub near the fire. She was almost finished with her food when lady Petra blew in the room with a scowl of disapproval.

She stared imperiously at Caelerys from the door for a long moment. Cae remained unintimidated. She had long ago lost her fear of the widow. The dame decided to pick her battle. "That is that last meal you will eat that has not been tasted first. Do you understand?" she demanded frostily.

The heel of bread fell from her suddenly nerveless fingers.

Lady Petra's eyes narrowed in triumph. "Yes, Lady Caelerys: Tasted. You are entering into a viper's nest of intrigue where the physical dangers will not necessarily come from a man charging you with a sword. Death will come unseen or in the night, at unprotected moments."

"But why would anyone..."

She stepped into the room and allowed the girl's handmaid and her own lady in waiting to enter. "Because you stand in their way. Because you became friends with the wrong person. Because you wore the same colour gown to the same function as another lady and looked better in it."

Caelerys was horrified.

"Good. I see I have finally managed to instil fear in you. You will be living among wild animals, exposed to every element and predation with only your wits to defend you. Some of these beasts will be benign. Some openly hostile. Others will seem harmless and even friendly, only to turn on you in a moment if it suits them. You must learn the difference."

Cae pushed what remained of her meal away, no appetite remaining. It was a brutal analogy, but one she understood. The cold pit in her stomach at the thought of dealing with strangers grew larger. Mutely, she allowed Fern to draw her to the small bath tub and wash the dust of the road from her body without getting her hair wet.

Lady Petra bustled about, directing the maids what to pull from the trunk that had been brought up. "Now, as much as I feel a lady should ride, demurely unseen, within a carriage, in this case I agree with your father..." She was interrupted by a large white falcon, as Tempest sailed through the open window and landed on the edge of the tub. A black peppered feather landed in the water and Cae giggled, reaching up to stroke the blue beak.

Scowling, lady Petra continued. "You should ride in state at the head of the procession. That bird should be on your wrist and properly hooded and jessed..." This earned her a glare from both girl and bird. The way the fowl's dark eyes bored into her made lady Petra feel as if the beast understood far more of what was said than was natural.

Cae found her back-bone again. "No. There will be no hoods and no jesses. She is far too well manned to need either. The last time she wore jesses, she got hopelessly tangled and nearly eaten by a wildcat."

"And if she gets loose and someone finds her? How will they know she is not a wild bird for the taking?"

Caelerys fingered the gold band around the bird's ankle, engraved with her name and house. "This. And I would be surprised if any one could catch her. And no one else can fly her."

"That is because you have spoiled her," she sniffed. "I swear that bird is more pet than hunter. You've ruined her."

Cae laughed, stroking the white breast feathers, admiring the scattering of black. "She should be, but she isn't. She protects me."

Lady Petra sighed, turned back to the task at hand, aware she would never win this fight. "You will ride side saddle, the hawk on your wrist..."

"Falcon."

"You will... what?"

"Falcon. Tempest is a gauvan, a very rare falcon, not a common hawk."

The brown eyes narrowed. Cae gave a tiny shrug of her head, rose from the water and stood to be rinsed.

Lady Petra watched as Fern poured a last ewer of warm water over the girl's nubile young body, assessing her while she had the chance. Caelerys was a woman flowered, she knew; but she also knew many young girls who flowered before they bloomed. The dukes' daughter however, was blooming. She had the height of her family, tall for a girl of just seventeen, but with the appearance of petiteness, and none of the coltish awkwardness one expected at that age and height. There was silent strength in her arms and legs, a criminally athletic body for a girl, but she was healthy and curving and soft, ...and still growing.

As the girl accepted the towel Fern wrapped around her, rubbing herself dry, lady Petra nodded to herself. She would gain maybe a few more inches in height over the next two years, still acceptably shorter than most men, and there would be no need for padding her bodice, or corsetry for trimness and posture.

The old dame continued. "You will ride at a sedate pace through the street of DragonsPoint up to the castle where you shall meet your brother Lord Willam. You will be courteous."

"Always," Cae said, began dusting her naked body with a small fur wand with a glistening powder from a little leather bag. The warm scent of honey filled the air.

"You will not speak unless spoken to and you will comport yourself as the eldest daughter of a Great House should. Now, the coronation of King Rorlan will be in seven days. Lord Willam will present you before the king and bring forth the gifts your father has sent with you. You will then mingle with the members of court, making yourself presentable and noticeable."

"What's the point if I can't talk to them?" came the muffled voice from within folds of heavy blue silk.

"They will speak to you if you approach. Your father says you are to make a list of your impressions of the men," she added, her tone conveying her true feelings about the idea and Caelerys's capacity to intelligently comply. "You and I will go over that list before it is sent on to your father, and I will inform you which of the men are, in fact, eligible. You are to convey to the new king your father's condolences upon the untimely death of his brother and generally make yourself available. You are here to make a suitable match to the advantage of your House."

Caelerys sighed, running her hand across the silk bodice with its high collar, embroidered silver netting and seed pearls. It was the finest dress she owned. "I know what is expected, and I know my duty, lady Petra. Father has already told me what he needs of me. I may be young, but I am not so foolish or silly as you seem to think me," she said firmly, sitting to allow lady Petra's lady in waiting to dress her hair. "I have no intention of falling in love with the first pretty face or kind gentleman to pay attention to me. I will look for a suitable match, and withhold my affections until such time as negotiations are done. Only then will I consider love."

Caelerys had very firm ideas of what she was looking for and what she would settle for, but she kept these to herself. She knew that for every nursemaid and bardic tale of love against all odds, there were ten that ended in tragedy and heartache. No, she kept her heart locked tightly away and would not give it lightly.

Lady Petra studied her, seemed satisfied. "You might do after all." She softened, nibbling upon what was left of Cae's lunch. "This is not to say that you won't come to love your husband. The Eldest knows I hated mine at first."

Caelerys turned to look at her. "Then why did you agree to light the candle?"

"Because it was what my family required. House Reynelds is a knightly house at best, and House Petra a minor but impoverished one. My family had the money, Petra had the status. I came to love him in the end. Even his more noxious habits became dear. I am a creature of comforts, my lamb, and my mother was ambitious. ...Leave a little hanging around her temples, Marigold. It frames her face nicely." She smiled, a surprisingly warm expression. "Don't worry, little one. Your father will not likely marry you to someone loathsome."

The air had chilled a little by the time Caelerys was as ready as she could be made, and a fog had begun to rise out of the Mistwood. When she finally descended the stairs, everyone in the common room stopped to stare. What had slipped upstairs had been a bright cheeked, rough young girl. What had come down was a beauty. The silk flowed after her like a cloud, the perfect shade of blue to bring out the jewel-tone of her sapphire eyes. The collar encircled her throat like a necklace of metallic lace and pearl, expounding her innocence. Not even the white leather pad strapped to her left shoulder detracted from the vision of the demure Lady of Court.

Outside, the rest of her entourage had caught up and were taking a short rest. Cartyr, the head of the cadre, was dividing the men between the caravan, which would follow later, and the Lady's honour-guard. Even the aged Mace caught his breath as Caelerys stepped out of the door into the courtyard.

A stable boy led Wraith to a mounting block and held her. The mare had been brushed until she shone like metal and stood there with her head and ears up. Her saddle had been changed to the dreaded side-saddle, and Caelerys allowed Mace to take her hand and lead her over. Wraith tossed her head as she approached and Cae noticed that tiny silver bells had been attached to her bridle by sapphire ribbons. Cae strongly suspected Wraith was playing with them, dancing rambunctious just to hear them ring. Mace handed her into the saddle and Cae adjusted her skirts. Tempest waited until she was settled before dropping onto the leather pad. Thankfully, she refrained from picking at her hair.

The men who were to ride with her mounted quickly as Cartyr shouted. Two of them took their places just ahead of her, the Maral banners at stirrup. A breath of wind lifted the deep blue fabric, unfurling the rampant white stag of her House and Caelerys took a deep breath. This was it. Cartyr took point, his men falling in behind the lady, and Mace rode beside her, bow in hand. She knew he would drop back when they came to the great bridge, but she took comfort in his presence whilst she had it.

The mist held onto the day as they rode out of the wood an hour later. It trailed after them, cloaking the procession in an aura of mystery and fey pageantry, as if reluctant to relinquish them from its enchanted grip. The few people on the road made way for them, and even the low estates, bringing in livestock or tending fields, stopped to watch them pass. The standard bearers' mail gleamed in the afternoon light, and the lady herself seemed to float across the ground on a horse of brushed silver.

They paused at the top of the hill which gave Caelerys a moment to absorb the sight before her. Mace stepped his horse up beside hers, spoke softly, "DragonsPoint, little bird. Jewel of the Western Sea. The centre of humanity in Elanthus."

"It looks like it houses half of it," she breathed. She tried to take it all in, and couldn't. The green hill sloped a little less than gently down to the river, though the road wound more softly against the side of it. The broad river was filled with barges and small boats and spanned by a bridge the size of a village. The bridge was massive and towered, guarded by two stone dragons that held up the front gate, and by two smaller bronze ones on the city side. Beyond that she could see the curve of King's Bay and the masts of a sea of ships breaking up the skyline. The city itself curved along in between river and bay and rose in an uneven sprawl. The walls were high and of a pale, greenish stone and pierced by one or two smaller gates, which had what looked like drawbridges for docks. At the far end of the city, upon a hill, rose a castle in a dark green stone with white slate roofs and many coloured pennants.

Whatever Cartyr had been waiting for had occurred. At a signal from him, her escort began moving forward and Mace dropped back behind her. The road was cleared all the way to the bridge, and what people were there stared without shame. They drank in the pageantry, feasting on the details to sustain them in their small hours. Caelerys caught the wide eye of a young child and smiled. Tempest half spread her wings, giving a shrill cry of pure pride, much to the child's delight. Cae turned her eyes forward to the bridge dragons, feeling overwhelmed and doing her best not to show it.

The guards at the first gates saluted the banners as they passed unchallenged. And then Caelerys was beneath the arch of stone claws thirty feet high and feeling the difference in the sound beneath Wraith's hooves. The world seemed unrooted suddenly, the sound of it different, almost hollow. She was surprised to see narrow buildings lining the length of the bridge. They seemed to be small customs offices and barracks, among other things.

And then she was out the second, bronze gates and in the city proper and she thought, for a moment, that her ears would burst. The noise was immense. On her shoulder, Tempest cried, stepping closer to her neck and spreading her wings protectively around Cae's head. She shifted her shoulder minutely and the bird began to settle down, though still complaining. Even Wraith did a twisting side-step as they entered the wall of living sound.

Two of the men-at-arms rode up beside her, just far enough back that she could be seen, but not enough that anyone could take advantage of the opening. People paused only a breath to stare, getting out of the way of the horses, but otherwise going about their business. Caelerys had to force herself to calm down. Wraith was beginning to sense her unease and tossing her head. The bells could barely be heard over the mass of voices and people. She tightened her grip on the reins and stared straight ahead, focusing on whatever she could to get her mind off her fear.

There were so many bodies. And, if lady Petra was to be believed, any one of them could decide she had offended them and try to kill her. By the time they were approaching the green gates of the castle she had decided the idea was ridiculous. By then, she had something else to occupy her thoughts; like the sheer size of the building.

Greenstone Citadel was easily three times the size of her family's great keep, a spare eleven acres across. It rose in mossy stone high above the large inner courtyard that was almost a village market of its own; with a blacksmith, wainwright, large carriage house and stable, and a three storied barracks. Broad, sweeping steps led up to the massive front doors, stained green with delicate, flat, golden dragons fastened to it, their bright claws slipped into the crack in between as if ready to pull them open upon request. There were just as many people in deep green and yellow livery as were not, and Caelerys noted a young woman emerging from one out building with a basket of fresh bread upon her head who deftly avoided running into another young man from the building next to it who was laden under smoked hams as easily as if this happened everyday.

In all, though the scale was beyond her, it was not that different from home. The parts of the village important to a castle's upkeep were just within the castle itself and not at its feet. When she looked up, it almost reminded her of looking up at Taluscliff from the beach, only with more spires and peaked roofs, and smoother walls. She was just taking note of trunks and furniture being moved in through a side door when a vaguely familiar voice hailed them.

She turned to look for the source, saw a tall, broad young man with dark curling locks that fell to his shoulders calling for his horse. He strode over to her with all the solemn, noble grace of an emperor stag. While Wraith was a dainty mare, she was not short. Even so, the man's head came to her waist. She looked down into the dark blue eyes, set in a handsome, strong face and recognized traces of the slender young man she had last seen two years ago at Harvest. "Willam?"

He quirked a smile, "Little sister."

She reached to be lifted from the saddle but he shook his head. "Now is not the time, Lady Caelerys," he said with unusual formality. He stepped back and took his reins from the approaching stable hand, turned to address Cartyr. "We head to Stag's Hall now." He threw himself into the saddle of a broad warhorse, a rich brown with heavy, white feathered legs and a broad blaze on his wide nose.

Caelerys frowned, reluctant to re-enter the noise of the city proper. She held her tongue though, knowing from experience that he would not explain right now. She rode sedately beside him, and wondered about this brother who was nearly a stranger.

"How was the ride?" he asked civilly.

"Boring," she replied.

He chuckled. "Plenty of excitement here," he conceded. "Maybe not to your tastes."

She cast her eyes over the packed road and milling people, and, even from the elevated place where the castle sat, all she could see spreading below her were buildings and people. "I will miss riding."

"There are places to ride," he said. "Just beyond the castle there is a training ground and a small wood, fields. They have an army to keep in shape, after all. The tourney will be held there, which is why the streets are so crowded. People coming for the King's Tournament. There will be events the ladies can enter, if you like. Equestrian and Archery, for instance."

His sister lit up as he had known she would. "Would I really be allowed?"

"Encouraged, even. Granted, not the jousting or the grand melee, though there is rumour of a woman slipping into the lists. The council is battling as to whether or not there should be any rule against it, and of course the church wants there to be."

Caelerys was suddenly grateful for this brother she did not really know. She realized that he had put her at ease in spite of being surrounded by hordes of strangers. It began to dawn on her that there was no need to worry about dealing with them, because she was just another anonymous member of the press. Well, not anonymous, but certainly nothing was expected of her in the way of social interaction. The mention of the church reminded her of something unpleasant though. "Will lady Petra be staying with us?"

Willam shook his head, and Caelerys thought there was a hint of relief at his reply, "No. She has her own place in town. She will be visiting often though, to make sure you are properly attired and briefed on courtly manners and that your maids know what will be expected of them." He hesitated a moment, gave her a sidelong look. "How do you feel about this... whole thing?"

She took a deep breath before answering. "I know my duty to the family. I will do my best to find the best choice for household alliances while still trying to find someone I can deal with. I would like a friend if nothing else. Have you found a bride, yet?"

Willam seemed confused a moment, then caught what she had asked. He cleared his throat and concentrated on the road ahead of him. "I haven't had the time. DragonsPoint has been chaos this last month."

Her eyes slid over the pale grey slate of a stately building, an actual anvil standing at the top of the marble steps: the symbol of the Eldest and the Divine Right of Man. The place did not engender comfortable thoughts. "What exactly happened? I had not heard."

This surprised him. "Father didn't tell you?"

She rolled her eyes skyward, "Lady Petra," was all she needed to say.

Willam laughed softly, clearly a noise he was no longer used to making. He gestured to an impressive, walled residence off to the right. "Lady Caelerys, welcome to Stag's Hall."

Two liveried men threw open the dark wooden gates to admit them to the little courtyard. It was a great deal smaller than home, but of good size. Three stories, a decent stable and small forge. As she rode inside, the sounds of the city muffled again; still there, but less intrusive, not unlike the background hum of a forest full of life, just different beasts. The building itself was grey stone with dark wood shutters on its narrow windows. Before she knew it, Willam was lifting her down from the saddle and she had to cling to him a moment, letting her legs uncramp from the unnatural pose she had been holding for hours. When she was ready, he took her arm and led her into the house.

It was nice. Not structured in a way she knew at all, but then, she had lived in a fortress all her life with occasional stays in a hunting lodge. There was a large foyer (not unexpected), a solar and a study off to the side and a wide staircase leading to the upper floors. Between the stairs and the study was a corridor that led to other parts of the house and he took her down this way first. There were hallways here, leading to the kitchen and servants' quarters, but what was of greatest interest to her was a door braced in iron shaped like roses just past the dining room. It opened into an inner courtyard complete with a broad kitchen garden and a trellis against one wall where roses had been recently planted. The late afternoon sun shone against one wall and glinted off broad glass windows, and nearly all of the third story rooms had balconies that overlooked the courtyard.

A decent sized aviary took up one corner, filled with the soft chirring of nesting toomi, the dull brown and grey little birds used for carrying messages. Caelerys had always been fond of them. They mated for life, and so complete was their devotion that the male would find the female no matter where she was, even if she was sent to a different aviary, even one he had never been to before. The wives were kept safe in household aviaries and the husbands were delivered to the various places where urgent messages were likely to be sent from. Once released, message tied to their leg, they headed straight for their wives. If you wanted to silence a house, you killed the females. The males, strangely, would never return to the nest, either losing their way or out of instinct. Somehow they always knew, and very often did not survive long themselves. The unattractive little birds were used as the symbol for lasting marital unions, and were often given as wedding gifts.

Willam stood back and watched his sister tour the garden. He had been told she was a fairly accomplished herbalist, and hoped the garden would be to her liking. He had ordered the roses planted because he wasn't sure if she would be happy with nothing pretty to look at. In fact, beyond that she was pretty, shy, well-read and a more than decent huntress, he knew next to nothing about this dark-haired girl who was now his responsibility. She had stopped to examine the roses, peering under a few of the leaves and frowning.

"We can have whatever you wish moved out to make room for more flowers," he told her. "Just make a list. We have not had a lady in residence in a very long time, so all we have had need of was a kitchen garden."

"Who tends it?" she asked.

"We don't have a gardener. The kitchen staff have been maintaining things, since they are the ones using it. They asked permission to use the space and I granted it."

"And now you are taking it back," she said, the slightest hint of reproof in her voice. "No. No need. It will suit my purposes as is. If I could have this patch over here for some specific, more medicinal flowers and herbs, I will be happy. But you might want to consider a dedicated gardener, or at least one who's main responsibility is the garden with light duties elsewhere. Some of what I'll want require a knowing hand. And they need to stop dead-heading the roses," she said, fingering a cut stem. "I know it makes them produce more blooms, but the hips are too useful."

It was moments like these that one found it hard to remember how young she was. "As you wish, little sister. Just give a list of what you want done to Fennel. She's been managing this end of things. Any other changes you want, tell her. She'll ask me if she feels it needs approval." He gave her a long look, not wanting to say it but feeling the need, "Just don't turn the house upside down."

She looked over at him, frowning. "Why would I do that?"

He looked uncomfortable. "Because girls... want things and need them a certain way, need to feel in control of a house and this one runs smoothly right now..."

She set her hands on her hips and tipped her head in that bird-like way he remembered from the few times he had come home. "And what, pray tell, gives you that idea?"

"I've seen it happen. Woman moves into a house, no matter her age, and sweeping changes are in the offing."

She decided to be uncharitable. "I'll let you know." She lifted her head, looking over to the aviary. "Jelma, tyet!" she called sternly in Old Vermian. The falcon lifted her snowy head guiltily, launched herself from the top of the tall cage and sailed easily back to her leather-cased wrist. She landed gingerly, being careful. She bobbed and twisted her head in apology. Caelerys sighed and relented, stroking her in her favourite places. She looked up to realize her brother was frowning at the bird. "What?"

"I had forgotten about her. I can have a mews built, but it'll have to be in the outer courtyard if she's going to bother the toomi."

"If that is all that's bothering you, don't worry about it," she smiled. "She sleeps in my room. I brought her stands. She'll likely be tagging along behind me no matter where I go anyway. And don't worry about the toomi. She will leave them alone," she said the last directly to the bird who sighed.

Willam shook his head and reached for his sister's free hand. "Let me show you the rest of the house."

2

William had not been overly present in the last week, was in and out of the house all day, and Caelerys wondered where he went. He did not always ride out, most days he walked. During one of the few family meals she managed to have with him that had not included lady Petra, she got him to tell her what had happened with the king. All she knew was that it had been violent. Willam was reluctant to talk about it, but he had finally realized she would need to know and would not rest until she did. Best it came from him.

"He went mad," he began bluntly.

"Why?"

He scowled, stabbing at his meat. "Who knows why men go mad? He became convinced the queen had lain with Jynn Halbourne, that all their children were the seed of another man. It was a slow maddening, it seemed. As the Southern Moon turned his face to the world, he began seeing treachery and shadows everywhere. There might have been a physical poison involved, because I remember him scratching at his arms until they bled, as if he were uncomfortable in his own skin." Willam went still in the telling, his eyes unfocused on the candle in front of him. "Then one night he went into the nursery and set it on fire. He barred the door on the infant twins, with their ten year old brother and elder sister, plus two young nurses and listened to them screaming. I found him leaning against the door, listening, feeling the heat grow. I called to him, and when he turned to look at me, there was something terrible in his eyes. I've never seen eyes like that on a man. They glowed. There was madness in them. He said.... 'now for the eldest and his whore mother, then the whore-monger himself.' And then he ran."

Willam seemed to break out of whatever reverie he was in and look down at the food on his plate. "I was torn. I knew he was going to do more damage, so when lord Mambyn Asparadane turned up, I sent him ahead to find out what, while I battered the door down. The king was his responsibility anyway as one of the Royal Guard.

"The bar had gotten so swollen I could not move it. By the time I'd gotten it open, death was a mercy to those children. We managed to get the fire out before it could spread. By then everything else had happened.

"Mambyn claimed the king had ripped out the throat of his eldest son, stabbed lady Caena Lutret twice, though not fatally, and the queen seven times. He also claimed that the king seemed to be ripping out of his skin. Lady Caena could not corroborate this. He said he tried to stop the king, bent on still further murder, but had no choice but to kill him. He had the furrows of what looked like claw marks on his arm, though how they were made I cannot profess to know. There was nothing in that room that could have been used to make them. They were deep."

He took a deep, cleansing breath, fortified himself with ale. "The king's brother, Rorlan, was found living in the Garden District; not far from here, actually. He was informed by the council that he was the next living heir and needed to come with them. So, in less than a week we will have a new king and royal family, and a tournament to celebrate. And all the Great and Noble Houses must come to kneel and give their oaths of loyalty to the new king, and present our unmarried children to forge fresh alliances for the security of this realm."

He left the table then, disturbed and unwilling to talk further. Cae did not see him for two days.

The kitchen staff had not begrudged the lady of the house a small portion of their garden for her own uses. A young man had been found to tend to the gardens as a whole, who happened to be good with toomi as well. This was a blessing, as the old man who previously had their care was getting too arthritic to manage them. Caelerys was glad to get someone who knew what he was doing, because some of the plants she was bringing in were dangerous if handled wrong. A lot of medicines were poison in the wrong doses or in conjunction with certain other things.

The household was thrilled to learn that not only was it to be a healing garden, but that she was skilled in the distilling arts as well as the use of the medicines she made. She was no physician, and made no claims to be; but the minor hurts and small emergencies of a keep and household she could handle well. She knew enough to keep a man's life until a physician could be called, and to tend to matters too minor to bother with one. It was one of those things her mother had told her before she died that a young lady needs to know. It helped that she could keep a level head in a crisis. Panic came before, or when it was all over; never during. Caelerys often wondered why she was that way. Most of the girls she knew, and a fair number of adult ladies, always panicked right in the middle, when the emotion did the least good and the most damage.

Once assured by Mace that she knew what she was doing, Willam had given over the keys to the still-room. It was currently being used to make small ale for the household and cold press ciders, and, when Cae informed them that they could keep half the room for said purposes provided they left her distillations alone, they were happy enough to clean it up for her.

A scant week after her arrival, Caelerys sat once more under the ministrations of lady Petra's handmaiden, Marigold. Only this time the woman was talking to Fern throughout, explaining what she was doing, how and why, talking hairstyles of the courtly. It was surprisingly restful. She had spent the week having her wardrobe gone through and adjustments made, additions ordered, being pinned and measured and criticized within an inch of her composure. Thankfully, lady Petra was not present this time, giving Cae time to think. Getting the still-room and gardens ready and working had been hard work but was actually relaxing compared to everything lady Petra brought with her.

She had been drifting with thoughts of flying and the sea when her reverie was interrupted by the sudden, looming presence of lady Petra. She opened her eyes and caught the woman's look in the mirror. There was something of a sneer of distaste for a brief second as the woman studied her, then some smug light sprang up and she actually smiled. "You, my dear, are a vision. Marigold, what made you style it this way?"

"Nothing else seemed to fit, my lady," the woman replied. "Any of the fancier styles just made her look... lumpy, or bald and compensating." The two exchanged a knowing expression that told Cae that last comment had been aimed at someone specific.

"Is it not appropriate for court?" Caelerys asked, suddenly dreading the thought of sitting through more pulling and braiding and pinning. She looked her reflection over in the small, silvered glass mirror. Her hair had been drawn back from her face, twisted loosely and pinned artfully in a coronet. The back had been painstakingly tucked up in spider-silk fine, silver net and felt almost heart-shaped.

"It is not a courtly style, no. It is too simple. But somehow, you make this simplicity the supremacy of elegance. It is neither pretentious nor too sophisticated for your age. It is, in short, perfectly you. You will shine, my lamb," she sighed like a happy, brooding hen. "But it is not complete. It needs... something..." she mused knowingly. She waved her hand and Fern opened the door.

Caelerys looked around the woman's bulk to see a tradesman enter the room carrying a small box. Strangely, the box drew her attention less than the man carrying it. He was broad of shoulder and deeply tanned, his dark, rust-brown hair pulled back in a queue, and he wore the thick, glossed fabric of a blacksmith: off-white shirt and leather trousers, though the quality was high. She stood, taking a step towards him, tipped her head to look up into his lowered face. Merry, brown-gold eyes laughed at her, and she squealed, throwing herself into his thick arms. "JANEM!"

He managed to catch her in an embrace, lift her up and spin her around, all without dropping the box in his hand. "Cae," he sighed.

It had been two years since she had seen her subsequent brother and she had missed him intensely.

There had been fourteen years between the birth of Landyn, Father's eldest son, and Willam. Their mother had despaired of being able to provide him with enough children. She had lost several in various stages after Landyn. Finally, she had encouraged Father to take a mistress or a paramour, but such was his love for her that he had settled for a concubine. She was a local girl, fairly pretty and solidly built and he had provided well for her ageing parents. Before she could bear him a child, Mother had gotten pregnant with Willam. Two years passed and she was convinced she had no more in her, and he again turned to Rosemary. Four years after Willam was born, Rosemary gave him a son: Janem, and he had grown up in the house with Elyas's precedent children. Two years after that, Mother had Vyncet, and two after that, Caelerys. But at forty, another child had proved too much. Mother had never really recovered. She died when Cae was six.

Willam had been sent to DragonsPoint just after Cae was born, and only came home for occasional holidays, so she knew little of him. Janem had been four when she was born, lived with them, played with her, teased her. She would sit in the forge to watch him work while she embroidered or read to him, translating old Vermian texts for him. When Janem reached eighteen, the Taluscliff smith could no longer justifiably keep him, and he had left for DragonsPoint to complete his journeymanship. Word had reached home that he had made Master within a year.

Janem set her down and she held on to his arms, feeling the corded iron beneath the cloth.

"You have grown into a bear!" she laughed.

"A naked bear," he chuckled ruefully. "I'm not hairy enough. But you, sister," he said, holding her out from him and giving her a little turn. "You have grown into a beauty."

She blushed. "Stop teasing."

"Stop traffic."

Her cheeks grew hotter. She distracted herself with the box still in his hands. "More bodkins?"

"Later. This is more important." He drew her back to the dressing stool and sat her down, knelt in front of her and opened the box.

She gasped. Nestled in the velvet-lined incensewood was a tortoiseshell comb surmounted by a set of silver antlers so realistic she could feel the ridges and natural rings. They had ten delicate points tipped in star sapphire. She lifted it from the box and was surprised by the lightness of it. She smelled it, her mouth slightly open like a cat. It smelled like silver, but it was beyond luminous. It had that untarnishable light that gold had. "Janem," she breathed, "what... what is this made of? It... tastes of silver but it's too light."

He beamed with pride. "Moonsilver."

Her mouth fell open. "You ...you found the secret?"

He nodded. "I found the secret. You helped, little sister."

"How?"

"All those stories you used to read to me in Old Vermian. I found a book and I made myself learn to read it. There were things in it... and I... just figured it out. Old Master Illet had a broken moonsilver sword. No one could fix it and the family never came to claim it so he saw no harm in my playing with it. Eventually I did it. It was my Masterpiece. I am due to present it at the coronation to the king. But this piece... this one I made for you. A symbol of our house."

He took the piece from her hands and passed it to Fern, who very proudly and carefully slipped it into the top of the curls gathered at the back of her head. It was the perfect, crowning glory.

"I didn't know you made jewellery."

He shrugged. "There are things a jeweller cannot do, and for that they come to me. When I need stones set, I go to them. Daph and I have a great working relationship. He agrees with me that there will be no other like this. Now, I have one other thing for you, and then you must get ready to go or lady Petra will turn me to a statue of ice where I stand."

This got the stifled giggle he had been looking for and took one last thing from the box. It was a small round pendant of normal silver, artfully blackened in the crevices to make the design stand out. It was her own personal seal: the Maral stag's head in profile with a single rose nestled in the curve of the antlers, denoting a lady of the house. What was odd about it were the tiny notches that ran all the way around the medallion. Something gleamed in between them. Janem pulled a piece of thread from a pocket and held it between both hands, brought it down into a notch and the thread fell in two pieces.

Cae picked up the cut thread, examining it. It had not frayed. The cut was cleaner than the best scissors she owned. Janem ran the medallion's edge across his palm, showed her that it had not cut him, then slipped the long silver chain around her neck. She hugged him again, her eyes threatened to tear up. "You are too good to me," she breathed.

"And you me," he countered, then whispered in her ear, "I am slipping the book into your care. No one will suspect it is here, and once it is known what I can do, it won't be safe in the forge."

She nodded, let him go. He stepped back, took one more admiring look at her before making an elegant leg and bowing out.

Cae now confronted her reflection and turned to try and see the comb. She could just glimpse a spike of silver and blue rising from the nest of curls and silver net. Her sleeveless overdress was a deep blue velvet, clinging to her growing curves as it fell to the floor in a dark bell. The collar was high, but open just to the hollow of her throat, though it only revealed a sliver of milky skin. Her underdress was a nearly sheer shift with broad flowing sleeves in a pale silver. The embellishments were simple embroidery at the hems in a grey-white silk. She presented a vision of subtlety.

Willam met her at the bottom of the stairs. He looked sharp in a long, black, sleeveless cote with gold braiding. His under shirt was also black, fastened at the throat with a silver stag's head pin. His dark blue eyes sparked approval as she took his hand. He kissed her fingertips. "The little sister has grown up."

She blushed, not sure exactly how to behave with him and unused to praise.

He chuckled as he led her out into the courtyard to where the horses stood waiting. "Just give a tiny nod or suggestion of a curtsey if you don't know what to say. ...Blushing is very becoming, too."

As she turned to berate him for teasing her, he seized her waist and lifted her into the saddle effortlessly. He let her hold on to him to steady herself while she settled her foot into the stirrup and her knee on the brace. "You will be fine, Caelerys. No one is going to bite you."

"You might," she growled, but smiled.

As Willam threw himself into the saddle, Tempest flew down from the balcony and landed on Caelerys's saddle horn. She sighed, drew the bird carefully onto her hand. The falcon stepped gingerly, nuzzling her fingers with her beak. "No, Tempest. You cannot come this time." The bird opened her beak, shrilled a response. "Jelma, tyet. Kata."

Tempest's eyes went wide, her entire body seemed to wilt. She gave a tiny cry, as if begging it not to be true. She saw her mistress firm and sagged on her hand. She gave Cae one last, loving peck, then flew up above the rooftops.

Willam watched the bird fly out of sight, frowning. "Will she be here when you get back?"

Caelerys shook her head as she gathered her reins. "I'll be lucky if she doesn't find me before I get home. She'll be here. She is very fond of ham."

"You spoil her."

"So I've been told."

Caelerys had not had much time to be afraid on the way to the castle. The streets were overflowing and it seemed the whole city had turned out to watch the various nobility on parade. Alvermian banners hung from upper story windows, deep green with a profiled dragon in gold, wings addorsed on the downstroke, and many of the second and third estates crowded those windows waving ribbons and throwing petals upon the travellers below them. Wraith took the cheering audience in stride and was fairly prancing by the time they reached Greenstone Citadel. There they dismounted and joined the flow of nobility up the broad marble steps and through the golden dragon doors.

On his arm, Caelerys trembled. Willam set his other hand upon hers, willing her strength. Cae reminded herself that she was a Maral, a proud family as good as any other here. Only the royal family stood higher than they, while most of those present were of lower rank. She could be terrified inside all she wanted, she just would not show it.

Willam guided her into the throne room, finding them a place with the other three Great Houses not far from the dais. In the centre of that platform stood two thrones, both ornately carved giltwood, padded in buttoned velvet, though one was slightly smaller and less ostentatious.

Willam kept her mind off her fears by identifying individuals in a low voice, telling her their names and ranks where he knew them. He didn't know everyone, but knew a goodly portion. He did not give her his opinions of people for several reasons, the first being that he did not want anyone else to know them. The second being that father had asked him not to, wanting to test her judgement.

She watched with glittering eyes, awed by the wealth being so baldly displayed. She had thought her gown extravagant in the extreme, and her hand played self-consciously with the velvet. There was one lord near them in a thick, blood red velvet more plush than hers, sewn with pearls large enough to have made a decent necklace. The gold thread embroidery and beading was so heavy across the shoulders one could barely see the fabric. Another lady, set a little back from where they stood, wore what looked to be cloth-of-gold with sable trim. And the hair... Caelerys shuddered at some of the styles.

Most of the men wore their hair like Willam, combed back but loose about the shoulders. Others queued or braided, and bound in gold or copper rings. Still others wore it shorter, about the ears. Nothing outlandish there. But the women! One lady had a tower built out of her braids. Another's was twisted into great wings sweeping back from her face. Yet another into a conical cap into which had been placed jewelled birds and gilded flowers. No one wore it loose.

The rustling in the room grew, then began to settle as the last arrivals hurried to enter the room and find a place before the doors closed.

Just off the dais, across the deep green carpet, Caelerys noticed a family. There was a nursemaid in a pale green gown with a white apron holding an infant in a deep green tunic. A slender, golden maiden a little younger than Caelerys stood beside her, built like a gazelle with rusty gold hair and the most startling, wisteria coloured eyes that seemed to observe everything around her. Behind her were two tall young men in matching black coats with gold and green embroidery. Both men looked similar of face, though the one on the left was slightly more solidly built and broad, while the other was more lithe and alert. Their hair was an antique gold and fell in soft, loose curls about the ears of the quiet one who stood staring straight ahead, almost at attention, and half way down the back of the slender one who was flashing a broad smile to any lady which caught his eye. The matriarch was a petite woman of middle age, with wide, round eyes and a bemused smile. Her hair was covered by a wimpled veil in an amber silk shot with gold, and her gown was simply cut and flattering to her slightly plump frame, though trimmed richly. There were subtleties in her choices which said wealth in an unconscious way, and she carried herself as if her embellishments were mere cotton and glass.

A tall, imposing man in an iron grey robe strode the length of the green carpet, carrying a small, symbolic anvil. Caelerys had not noticed him until he crossed her line of sight, but when he had passed, she found herself looking into the small woman's merry eyes. The woman gave the slightest tilt of her head then smiled, an expression which took her entire face, before sedately looking away and paying attention to the clergyman now standing on the dais. Confused, and feeling something stirring inside her that was altogether uncomfortable, Caelerys turned with the crowd to face the great doors which had opened again.

Striding down the path was a man almost completely swallowed by an enormous, emerald velvet cloak. It hung to his toes in front, trimmed in a golden fur, that seemed to be dusted with real gold, and spread out behind him to swallow the whole of the aisle. The man himself seemed unimpressive and small within its folds, though he had to be strong to pull that great weight behind him. As he drew up to where Cae stood with her brother, she could see that he was of average height, and possibly build, with short, dark gold hair beginning to thin at the brow, and warm green eyes that seemed a little stunned. Caelerys suddenly felt for this man who had never expected to be a king, and smiled shyly and with her deepest sympathy.

The man mounted the steps to where the priest still stood, holding his anvil out in front of him as if it were a crown itself, intoning an invocation to the Eldest and expounding on the Divine Right of Man as ruler of all he surveyed. Caelerys partially tuned out the sermon, began to suspect that the anvil couldn't be real or solid for him to be able to hold it at that angle for that length of time. What if he dropped it?

Finally, the man lowered the anvil and turned, walked to the throne and set it down at the foot. His brocade robes rustled as he executed another precision turn and stepped back to where the king-to-be waited. He bent, unfastening the gold ropes that bound the cloak about his throat and stepped aside.

Rorlan Alvermian continued his climb up the steps. The cloak remaining behind him, splayed across the broad stairs and ten yards past them, revealing itself the banner of his house. A great dragon was sewn into the deep velvet, of gold scales and thread with an emerald the size of a toomi egg for its gleaming eye. Caelerys tore her eyes from the banner and up to the dais in time to watch the man Rorlan kneel before the priest and the heavy gold crown be set upon his head. Then King Rorlan the First stood and faced the room, standing just above the symbol of his House. He now looked every inch a king, a little taller and broader than a moment before as he adjusted to the weight of responsibility. Everyone bowed.

The king stood there a moment, as his family mounted the dais and took their places. He turned, strode to the throne and sat. The merry woman, his queen, sank into the smaller throne beside him and his sons took up flanking positions, the lithe one by his mother and the stern one by his father. The princess drifted up beside her brother on her mother's side, taking the baby from the maid, and a smaller boy Caelerys had not seen earlier crossed to stand beside the other brother. She noticed a subtle hand set upon the child's shoulders and gently guide him back a half-step into place. He couldn't have been more than eight.

A narrow herald stepped to the top of the stairs and cleared his throat, his voice ringing through the room even over the murmuring that had begun as people stirred. "Presenting His Royal Majesty King Rorlan Alvermian the First, King of Elanthus and the Eastern Isles, Lord Protector of the Realm of Men. Queen Sigrun Echo, his queen and Mother of the Realm of Men, mother of his children: the Princes Valan, Balaran, Janniston and Verlan and the Princess Syera."

Caelerys jumped as the room erupted in cheers and shouts loud enough to deafen people in the courtyard. Somehow, she could hear bells pealing.

Four discreet servants slipped out of the crowd and began to gather the 'robe' which would be taken to the balcony above the main doors and hung as a banner for the length of the tourney. "Hear ye, hear ye! The first court of his Royal Majesty, King Rorlan Alvermian the first will now begin. His Royal Majesty will now accept the oaths of fealty from his vassals." With this he stepped to the side, drawing a scroll from his sleeve as another servant placed a set of cushions on the floor at the foot of the steps. "The Crown calls House Griff."

Caelerys watched as the man in the over-wrought coat stepped forward with a delicate young lady heavy with child at his hand and two men, less ostentatiously dressed, behind him. Caelerys noted that Duke Griff had a full griffon embroidered and beaded upon his tunic. What she had seen on his shoulders had been the wings. It was almost gaudy. The two men, one late twenties, the other of middle years bowed and remained bent, as their father attempted to assist his wife to curtsey. The king lifted a hand and he stopped, knelt himself while the girl gratefully stood, her head bowed.

The herald announced them. "Duke Avondyl Griff and his lady wife Duchess Maerinna Lutret. His sons, the Lords Rorik and Avondyl the younger."

Duke Griff remained on his knees and intoned, "I, Avondyl, Duke of House Griff of the Western March, do hereby swear the fealty of my House to King Rorlan Alvermian as long as he shall live, and unto his heirs."

He was signalled to rise with a nod from the king and a liveried servant in red and gold stepped forth, bearing a small casket. The servant stopped at the foot of the steps and opened the chest. A royal page stepped down, peered in and bowed, taking the casket and carrying it, open, up to the king who seemed impressed by its contents. The box was closed and taken away by an armed man.

"Your fealty and gift is accepted," intoned the king.

Duke Griff rose, bowed again, and led his family past the dais and out a side door.

The herald consulted his scroll. "The Crown calls House Maral."

Caelerys felt her body go cold. Willam's hand tightened on hers as he drew her out to the carpet and to the cushions at the foot of the steps. She curtsied, sank to her knees upon the cushion, the dark velvet pooling about her with a flick of her wrist. Willam went to a knee beside her, and she felt the sudden presence of Janem bowing behind them. As the light struck the comb in her hair, a murmuring began which was quickly silenced by the herald.

"Lord Willam, heir to the House of Maral, son of Duke Elyas Maral; his sister, Lady Caelerys; and their subsequent brother: Master Janem."

Willam's voice was rich and carried well in the crowded room. "I, Lord Willam Maral bring to you the fealty of my father, Duke Elyas Maral, and his House, and pledge to you his armies and the fruits of our fields from this day forward, so long as His Majesty shall reign."

A House servant strode forth with a slightly larger box than had been presented by Duke Griff. The page descended and looked in, frowning slightly, but took the box and carried it to the king. Willam raised his voice again. "If it please, Your Majesty, what lies within the box are mere representatives, themselves intended as amusements for the young prince." The king reached into the box and lifted out a figurine of a golden horse with a mane and tail of spun silver. After looking it over, he handed it to the boy beside him, much to the child's delight. "The actual horses are within your stable, Your Majesty: four, perfectly matched for carriage."

"We are pleased," the king said. "Your fealty and the gifts of your House are accepted."

"Also," Willam added, still on his knee and waiting for the king's acknowledgement. He continued with the royal nod. "Our brother comes to you, both of his own and of our House with a gift."

There were whispers at this, as a boy in plain clothes, no livery, began to walk down the carpet carrying a long, narrow box. Janem took a half step forward, partially straightening only to bow again. Caelerys thought he might be more uncomfortable than she was. "Your Majesty, I bear this gift not only in the name of my House but of my former Master, Illet, and The Singing Forge.

"Some years ago, the psion of the Noble House Spel brought Master Illet a sword. It was a family heirloom, a moonsilver blade that had been broken. It was left in his care for years, as no one could manage the mending. As the late Lord Spel died with no issue, we wish to return the family's blade to the care of King and Realm until you deem another worthy of it."

Janem stepped aside and allowed the folk boy to pass him. The young man stepped gingerly between Willam and Caelerys, not even coming close to treading upon her skirts though he did not look down. Head held high, but eyes respectfully lowered, he opened the box. Before his page could move, the king himself stood and descended the steps. Caelerys held her breath, and Janem bowed more deeply as the king drew the bright, unbroken blade from the box.

Light reflected off the length of it, casting patches of brilliance upon those kneeling at his feet. It was a simple arming sword, with a well worn and sturdy grip and only simple embellishments upon the hilt itself. The blade seemed unblemished until the king twisted it in the light and the delicate tracery of webbing became visible. Still holding it in his hand, he looked down at the bowed heads before him. "And which smith in Illet's forge claims this feat? No one has been able to work moonsilver in over a hundred years."

Janem had the grace to blush. His reluctance to confess was heard in his voice, which was lower and less clear than before, when he had been praising his house and forge. "It was my masterpiece, if it pleases Your Royal Majesty."

The king set the sword back in the box, gesturing for a soldier to take it away. "It pleases me, Master Smith, to see more of you and your work. Such arts should not be lost."

"Thank you, Your Majesty," Janem said quietly, humbled and dreading what this would mean.

Willam repeated the gratitude, and the king returned to the throne. Dismissed, Willam rose, lifted Caelerys to her feet and the group strode from the throne room even as the herald was announcing, "The Crown calls forth House Cygent."

The family breezed out of the throne room and off into one of several small side chambers where Caelerys all but collapsed onto a padded footstool. Janem looked a little the worse for wear and the folk boy who had carried the gift handed him a flask without a word. Janem took it and drank deep. "By the Mother," he swore.

Willam laughed, accepting the flask as it was passed and taking a more modest swallow. "You don't do things by half, do you?" He pressed the flask into Caelerys's hand. "Just a sip. It will calm your nerves."

Janem gave Cae a look of shared pain. He understood her anxiety. He watched as she sipped the liquor, barely flinching from the taste. "I didn't want to, but Master Illet felt it would be good for the forge as a whole, and he is right," he conceded reluctantly. "I just wish it didn't have to be me."

"Had to be you, Master," said the boy, taking a swallow of his own from the flask before it disappeared somewhere on his person. "Master Illet wanted to thank your father for sendin' ye ta him, and givin' some a' the glory ta yor House was a way o' doin' that. Through you a'course."

"Yeah, doesn't mean I have to be comfortable with it," Janem growled. He crossed to his sister and bent, placing a kiss on her cheek. "Stop traffic, little sister. And be careful. I wouldn't trust half of these courtiers further than I could throw Willam."

She blushed, kissing him back. She was feeling the liquor a little.

Willam frowned. "Leaving?"

"I've got work to do," he scowled. "Gonna have more than I can handle after this, you watch."

"Is that such a bad thing?" she asked him, allowing Fern to ply her with a strong tea.

"It's not the work I mind," he replied and took his apprentice and left by a side door.

No sooner had it closed behind them, than a tall, lean man of red hair and grey eye came in through the other. He was surprisingly well muscled for all his lankiness, and wore a grey, wolf fur mantle and looked around the room in disappointment. "Has he left?"

A voice came from behind him as someone shoved him out of the way. "Looks like it, doesn't it?" The second man was identical to the first, even to the sound of their voices. He rolled around his brother and approached Willam, hand offered. "Lord Edler Marrok, and this is my brother Reled. He's the rude one," he chuckled. Reled grinned and shrugged, also offering a hand.

Willam accepted both. "Welcome to DragonsPoint. Saw you two ride in yesterday. Cut it a little close, didn't you?"

They laughed. "Had a little trouble on the road."

"That wasn't really any trouble at all."

"Kinda fun actually. Broke up a really boring trip."

"Hey, is your other brother with you?"

Cae watched the exchange in confusion. She had seen which one had introduced the two, Edler, but still wasn't sure which was which once they started talking. They were a half a head shorter than Willam, with merry grey eyes and deep red hair. They wore closely trimmed beards, against cultural fashion, and were identical down to manner and dress. She quietly rose, forgotten for the moment and decided to explore the little solar.

"Which one?" Willam was asking.

"Well, the smith for starters."

"And Vyncet for finishers. Haven't seen him in a year or two."

"Brought something for him."

Willam groaned. "What'd he leave behind? Drinking bills?"

One of them waved his hand dismissively, "Pff. Those were settled. Naw, a tidy little bit from Woodbine sent a token with us."

"Begged us to remember her to him."

"I hope for her sake, he does," Willam sighed. "But no, Vyncet is still back home. Maybe after the tourney a little trip might be in order? It's only a couple days away at a good pace. As for Janem, you just missed him. Though after court, you might find him at the Galley. I don't know if he prefers the food or the company, but he dines there most nights."

The twins chuckled suggestively. "Might be the cook, heard she's a right sorceress in the kitchen. We ate there last night."

"But might be the proprietress, she's a right firebrand. Half the bar is sweet on her."

Caelerys was dutifully tuning the conversation out as she perused a small selection of books left on a side table. They were in Old Vermian. Something must have gone on behind her in pure look and gesture, because the next thing she heard was her name. She turned to find all three of them looking at her.

"My lords, my sister, Lady Caelerys Maral."

Still clutching one of the books in her hand, she crossed back, curtsied lightly, holding out her empty hand. "My lords."

They took it in turn. "Ah, a most beautiful..."

"...And breath-taking lady."

Cae blushed. "Thank you," she stammered. She concentrated on their hands as they bowed over it, to distract herself. There was a difference, she noticed. One of them had a scar on his palm, just at the base of his fingers. She met his warm grey eyes. "Your pardon. Reled or Edler?"

"Edler, my lady," the man grinned without taking his eyes from hers. "Brother, I think she has us."

The other man's brows went up. "Has she now," he also grinned.

There was something wolfish about them at that moment, though it did not make her feel like prey. There was mischief in those roughly handsome faces.

"Yes, I think she might."

They were interrupted by others drifting into the chamber and they stepped out of the doorway. She sketched the tiniest bow and backed off as they turned to greet the new-comer. There was something about the short, broad-shouldered man that entered that she did not like. She never even heard his name as she drifted away, slipping out the door Janem had vanished through.

She found herself in a servant's hallway with no idea where to go from here. She had seen the size of the castle and was suddenly terrified of getting lost. Thankfully, she was immediately rescued by a young girl in a faded green servant's gown. The girl had come out of a room across the way and seemed startled to see her.

"My lady?" She took in the book clutched to Cae's breast and the door behind her and a look of understanding crossed her pleasant face. "Escaping is you?"

Cae nodded gratefully.

"Well, them's not finished with the throning stuff, so you can't go back in there as yet. But there be other chambers for milling afters. Bigger places with more escape routes," she winked. "I'll take you. Gots to be careful with someo them highborn men," she said companionably as Caelerys fell in beside her and was led down the corridor. "Someo them low too." She chuckled, "Someo the low tryin' to be high be the worst though. Not as likely to try an' touch a highborn such as youself, my lady, but they sure as can make you uncomfortable or bore you to death-like."

Caelerys giggled. "Thank you, miss. I will take it under advisement."

She stopped at a broader door than the last. "Here you go, my lady." She stopped, her hand on the door handle. "Wait. An't you brought a handmaid with you? Sweet lady like youself shouldn't be without one. Not even here."

Caelerys looked back the way they had come. "Oh! I must have given her the slip, too. She might still be in that room with my brother."

"I'll bring her. Body get lost here they don' know the ways. What's be her name?"

"Fern. She's in blue."

"Deep or pale?"

Cae's smile was genuine. "Deepish. Thank you. What is your name, dear?"

The girl sketched a curtsey. "Rue an' it please you. You need anything, ask fer me. I work these lower floors. Now, in you go, my lady," she said, swinging the door open. "An' stay away from the walls. Back against may be fine fer fightin' men, but bad fer us females. Heres anyhow."

Caelerys nodded and entered the room, slipping in and off to the side quietly. She stood there observing the room as the door closed silently behind her. It was a rather large room, less than half the size of the throne room and almost as large as the great hall back home. Lords and ladies of all types mingled here. There were refreshments along one wall, attended by servants, and another where a cluster of pages and handmaids stood, keeping their eyes on their respective masters in case of need. There was plenty of seating, chairs, couches, liberally salted with small tables upon which to place one's drinks and still keep an eye upon it.

There was a larger number of people in here than she had expected. While not as tightly packed as they had been in the throne room, it somehow seemed more crowded. She felt the cold rising in the pit of her stomach that she had always felt when there were guests to the keep. She did what she always did, took a deep breath and ran a few lines of her favourite Vermian poem through her mind. Still unconsciously clutching the book to her, she stepped out of the shadows by the door and into the room proper. Her slippered feet were quiet, the leather soles softer than what she normally wore, so she only made the whisper of velvet as she moved. She had developed the habit of keeping harder leather soles quiet, so the soft kid was easy. It also allowed her to feel every joint and imperfection in the flagstones beneath her feet. Somehow it was more uncomfortable than it would have been crossing it barefooted.

She drifted past on the fringes of conversations, remained largely unnoticed and she was content with that. Most of the little groups were gossiping about things that had happened in the throne room. Not much of it interested her. Women were chattering about clothes and hair and jewels; the men, about the coming tourney and who had given what to the king as a coronation gift. One group was discussing the actual oaths taken; who had pledged their Houses to the heirs as well as the king and who had not. She took note of who was in this group as well as the list they named: Duke Griff and his eldest son, Lord Rorik, two other men Caelerys did not know, though one had a bird of some sort worked in rose upon his collar. There was a woman with them, her chased silver goblet curled up by her pale cheek. She wore a black gown in crushed velvet, heavily embroidered in copper thread and amber beads and she wore her almost silver-blonde hair in a braided cone from which spilled the rest of her hair in ringlets and copper ribbons. Cae could just make out her earrings, which were copper serpents coiled around a gold tree. There was something very unfriendly in her pale eyes.

Somewhere behind her, Caelerys heard a loud, boisterous and familiar voice. She turned, seeking its origin. As she moved away, she did not see those pale eyes fall on her.

She moved around the milling nobility until she found it, appropriately near the refreshments. The source was a mountain of a man with a fierce countenance and a voice that sounded like it came from the bottom of a barrel. It was appropriate, considering his chest was a barrel. He had his back to her as Cae slipped up quietly and merely stood beside him, paying attention to the conversation as if she had been there all along. He was telling a war story with an ale in his hand to three men on whom Caelerys turned her attention.

They were striking. Two of them were similar in feature, brothers perhaps. Their skin was a deep brown and their eyes equally dark. Their noses were a little more broad than most she had seen, and they had high cheekbones. There the resemblance ended. The older of the two was shorter and more rotund, with hair that fell in tight, oiled curls and heavy gold earrings that ran all the way around the rims of his ears and hung to his brightly coloured shoulders. His eyes were the lighter of the two, but there was something in them, behind those full lips, that made Cae uncomfortable. The younger was taller, and slim but well-muscled. He stood almost at attention, every inch a warrior, and there was arrogance in his black eyes. His head was shaved and he wore a golden, black-spotted pelt draped over his shoulder. He looked as if he would be more comfortable with a shield on his arm and his weapon at his side as he stood against the wall, watching everything, including her. Not liking him either, she let her eyes slide over him and up to the man next to him.

This one was a giant, a little taller than Willam and blacker than either of the others. His skin looked like oiled night and his head, too, was shaved. He had lighter eyes, almost golden, but his face was a little more friendly, even though he was slightly more imposing in his armour. Looking closer, she realized he was only wearing a decorative breast-plate. The tunic beneath it was blood red and fell to his knees.

Caelerys was just deciding she rather liked this dark man when the one standing between them finally noticed her. "NEICE!" he bellowed in surprise, foisting his drink upon his tall friend to sweep her up in a bone-crushing hug that lifted her from her feet.

Caelerys laughed, returning the hug. "Uncle Jehan."

He set her down and held her at arms length to get a good look at her. "Sweet Mother's Milk, but you have grown!" he swore, causing a blush to rise on her cheeks.

People were beginning to stare.

SHIFT: Stag's Heart

He turned her to face his companions. "Let me introduce you. This is my niece, Lady Caelerys. Which means my nephew Willam is about somewhere," he added, looking around. "Caelerys, these are the princes Kyleth and Cyran Onkelan of the Kingdom of Alumet in the North," he said, indicating the shorter one first. Both of them bowed slightly. Neither reached for her hand. "And this is my old friend, lord Tume Ca'than. We've fought together."

Lord Tume bowed more deeply, held out his hand in the Southern manner. She delicately set her fingertips on his and returned the courtesy. "Your highnesses," she said softly, "my lord."

"My prince," sneered Prince Cyran, correcting her.

She looked at him. His eyes were full of anger and disdain. "Your pardon?"

"The proper address is 'my prince'."

"But you're not."

She had not thought those eyes could grow darker. "What?"

"You are not 'my' prince," she said gently. "You may be a prince in the North, and to those sworn to you, you would be 'my prince'. But here, you are just Prince Cyran, or Your Highness, as our princes would be to you. To take insult because of differing customs is rather silly, don't you think?" she asked, turning to the older of the two.

The older prince chuckled, his eyes dancing with greed as he assessed her. "Indeed, Lady. Jehan, are all Southern women so bold?"

"Not likely," Jehan laughed, taking his tankard back from lord Tume just as the man was raising it to his smirking lips. "She's a Maral. Even our does have antlers!"

She rewarded her uncle with a swat to his arm. "No, we just know when to stand up for ourselves because our men are such rutting oafs."

Even lord Tume laughed at this, though Prince Cyran continued to scowl.

Caelerys gave Tume her attention. "Are you a member of my uncle's Free Legions?" she asked.

He chuckled, getting his own tankard from a servant at the table. "We are hardly 'free', my lady. Our services are expensive." His accent was lighter than his princes', but still round and exotic.

It was a joke she had heard often. She laughed softly as she turned back to the royals. "Tell me, what is this creature upon your device? May I assume the pelt upon your shoulder, Your Highness, is from one of these animals?"

Prince Cyran's long, slender hand reached up to caress the pelt. "It is a ca'theryn. The symbol of our family, a great spotted cat. We use them for hunting, like you Southerns use wolves."

She frowned thoughtfully. "If you keep them as companions and pets, why do you wear one's pelt?"

He sneered at her ignorance. "I have honoured the cat. She served me long years. She was my first. I outlived her. It is to her honour that I chose to wear her pelt."

"Oh, I see," she said, genuinely interested. "Do you also drink the blood of your enemies or prey in the same way?"

He looked at her with widened eyes, as if trying to decide if he was offended or merely disgusted.

She realized how it must have sounded. "It is the way of our House that we must taste of the blood of our first kill when hunting. It honours our prey and brings us closer to that upon which we depend for our survival."

Lord Tume stepped in. "And have you been through this ritual, lady?" he asked.

She smiled with a faint blush, nodding. "I have tasted the blood of the stag, my lord."

"Bugger was an eight-pointer, too," Jehan crowed proudly.

It was Prince Cyran's turn to look confused. His brother said something to him in their flow-and-hitch tongue, explaining perhaps. The prince nodded, still not impressed until lord Tume said something, holding his hand out flat at about five feet from the floor, at about the shoulder height of her first stag. The prince looked at her again with renewed respect.

They were interrupted by a servant who came to Jehan and bowed to the company in general. "My lords, my lady, forgive my intrusion, but the king has requested your presence, lord Jehan. And you as well, lord Tume. Your highnesses are welcome to join if you've a martial mind, though it is but a small matter."

Caelerys looked the man over, and got the distinct impression that it was not a 'small' matter at all, but that he was being diplomatic. From her uncle's reaction, he had understood the same thing.

"Where?" was all Jehan said.

"Green door to the left of the throne room, by the gallery staircase. If you will excuse me?" and with a bow he was gone again, speaking discreetly with another group.

Jehan was placing a kiss upon her temple. "Forgive us, sweet niece, but duty calls."

She nodded. "One piece, uncle."

He returned the gesture, promising to return so. "One piece. Come on, Tume, let's go crack some heads." He stalked out of the room with Tume at his heel, both men handing their tankards to the first servant they passed. The taller of the two princes, Cyran, followed them. Caelerys suddenly realized this left her alone with the elder of the two and she did not like the way he was looking at her. She glanced around the room and saw a man and a slightly older woman talking a little ways off. There was something merry in the woman's eyes that she liked.

She turned to the prince. "Please forgive me, Your Highness, for abandoning you as well, but... I see someone I must speak with. Father would not forgive..." she began leadingly.

"Of course, Lady," he smiled, bowing with a wave of his oiled hand. "Far be it for me to prevent you from appeasing your Lordly father."

Cae sketched a brief curtsey and crossed to the couple, though she could still feel the prince's eyes upon her. The pair seemed rather easy with each other and looked up as she approached. "Please forgive my interruption, but... I was just left alone with a very uncomfortable man and made speaking to you my excuse. Might I ask you to serve me as chaperone for a few moments? At least for a polite interval?"

The woman laughed, reached out to take her hand as if she'd known her for some time. "Nonsense!" she exclaimed, loud enough to be overheard. "How is your lord father?" she guessed.

"Duke Elyas Maral is well, my lady," she replied, providing the woman with a clue as to who she was dealing with. "Are you sure you do not mind?" she added softly.

She drew Caelerys down on the couch beside her, looking up at her companion. "We don't mind at all, do we, Avondyl?" she told him.

SHIFT: Stag's Heart

He gave the broad smile of the long suffering. "No, no we don't. Most charming company."

Cae suddenly recognized him as the younger son of the duke in the gaudy griffon embroidered coat. His own was rich, but more subtle and in far better taste. He held out his hand for hers. "Lord Avondyl Griff, the younger. This is my... old friend, lady Sigourney..."

The woman in question smiled, cutting him off. "I am with the Lord Mendicant, Lady Caelerys," she explained. "And you are welcome to our company. We'd just finished our conversation anyway and a young lady such as yourself should never be unchaperoned. Not even here." There was a look that went between them, full of pain and meaning, that told Caelerys that only the lady had wanted the previous conversation at an end. Lady Sigourney patted Cae's hand with a smile.

She was going to have to get used to strangers knowing who she was. After all, everyone had still been in the throne room when she was presented. "Please do not allow me to interrupt. I am very good at not listening to things I am not supposed to hear," she said shyly, clutching the small book.

Lady Sigourney waved her hand dismissively. "Pff! We were merely speaking of the King's Tourney. The first round of jousting is tomorrow and the day after that, the equestrian. I, for one, can't wait." Her brown eyes lit up, the corners crinkling pleasantly. "Do you ride?"

Cae smiled. "I do. My brother said I would be allowed to enter. I want to enter the archery, too."

"Good. Give ol' Bristlebritches a run fer his money!" she crowed.

"Bristle...?" Cae began.

"An obnoxious twaddle who almost always wins and lords it beyond his right. Never you mind me," replied Sigourney.

Lord Avondyl smiled. "Have you given your name to the herald yet, Lady Caelerys?"

She shook her head. "No, my lord, I haven't. I was not aware of what to do and haven't really had the time yet."

He nodded knowingly. "First time at court. Always a little overwhelming. Well, let's see..." He looked around, giving Caelerys time to study him.

He was not unattractive, with a rather unremarkable face and hazel eyes. Mid-length, mid-brown hair and a relaxed, almost irreverent manner. She did not dislike him at once, nor did she really like him, the way she had taken to lady Sigourney.

"Alas, Morlan isn't in the room at the moment. Look for a harried little man in a green tabard with a gold trumpet on it. But for now... let's educate you a bit, shall we?" he grinned with fiendish delight and came around to sit on the back of the couch behind lady Sigourney's head. He reached his hand behind him and a servant refilled his wine. "That delightfully curved woman in the orange dress, the red-head, is lady Caena Lutret. She is Queen Sigrun's Lady of the Chamber. She was the Lady of the Chamber for the late queen as well and knows Greenstone and its intricacies more intimately than she knew her late husband. Fairly personable, though the First Born know how she's even walking around right now."

Cae remembered her brother telling her she had been stabbed a month back when the old queen and her children had been killed.

"The gentleman she is talking to is no gentleman at all, but the eldest of a bad lot." Sigourney reached back and smacked his thigh, which made him no more than sigh and smile. "That would be Lord Remlock Kaladen. And you would be well to beware of his whole House. They're trolling for brides, I hear."

Caelerys shuddered. She was familiar with the name Kaladen. Her father had cursed it often enough, usually followed by the word 'pirate'.

"Oh, there's someone pleasant," he crowed cheerfully. "Copper gown, green trim, hair plaited like a mane: lady Aileen Pardet. Very easy going. She was fostered with Lord Cygent's eldest daughter, Lady Liliwyn. Almost never seen the two apart," he mused.

"Lady Liliwyn is not here," Sigourney informed him.

"Small wonder," he frowned. "Tragedy what happened to her."

Another slap to his thigh silenced him, but Cae was curious.

"What tragedy?"

Lady Sigourney sighed, lowering her voice. "She was betrothed to the late crown prince, Naeden Alvermian."

She did not have to say anything more. Cae had already heard what had happened to the former crown prince. "How terrible," she breathed.

Sigourney changed the subject by verbally pointing out a young lady who had just walked into the room. "The one in the amber gown, red trim."

"Rich brunette?" Cae asked to clarify, catching sight of the pretty young thing with her hair done up in a nest with small jewelled birds.

"That's the one," Sigourney smiled. "Lady Fayra Tyre."

Avondyl picked her out as well. "So it is. Rumour has it she is going to wed lord Jens Brock, third son of the Brock House, definite move up for her."

"She is," Caelerys smiled, recognizing the name and pleased to know something.

He turned his eyes to her and grinned like a greedy, well-fed cat. "Is she now?" He tutted, "Oh, right, they are both vassal houses to your father. I take it he has approved the match?" She nodded. "Ooo, rich! Do me a favour and keep that titbit to yourself for a mite? I want to torture someone with it for a little while."

Sigourney glared at him. "Behave yourself, Avi."

"I am behaving," he simpered, sipping his wine.

Sigourney cast her own eye over the crowd. "Ah, there is Duke Callowen Cygent, swan lord."

"And isn't he looking mighty pleased with himself?" he commented.

Sigourney nodded. "Well, he should. I heard his tribute was a mated pair of rare black swans for the queen's gardens and she is well pleased with the gift. He is a nice enough man, though a little stuffy. Married, mores the pity."

"Oh, we're looking with that in mind, are we?" he smirked. "Well, then. My brother Rorik is available. A little old, mind, but still serviceable," he said, pointing out the older man who had stood beside him in the throne room. The brother was in his early forties at the least, but was still a handsome, fit man. "Though you would reap the benefits of the diamond mines, he has heirs, so your children wouldn't inherit. Not sure if he's looking just yet, though, with Jayla just less than a year in the ground. There's Sir Hayden Trent," he added, directing her attention to a golden man laughing with a small group of young women in silver and lavender. "He's quite the catch. Lesser son of..." he racked his mind for the name.

"Josai Trent, vassal house to Halborne is the information you are looking for," Sigourney said. "He's a little beneath you, dear. Fine to look at, charming as hell; made knight on his own merit but not yet landed. He's better off looking at the Roshan girls, far more reachable. He's an excellent choice for Lady Balyra, though. She's the heir of her house, you see. Her father has sired no sons, not even on his concubine."

"Which his wife had to make him take," Avondyl interrupted.

Lady Sigourney continued as if he hadn't. "If he marries her, she's the stockier one with her hair in that absurd tower, he'd be able to take her name and become the heir of Valenwood. Her sister, Onelle, is the slightly thinner one beside her."

"Both pretty buxom," he commented.

Sigourney nodded in agreement. "Very true. Onelle's a mouse, though. Understand she has a pet owl."

"Ooo, there is two you want to steer clear of, my lady," Lord Avondyl said, directing her attention to a woman in a dark purple gown and hair that seemed more blonde than nature permitted and her companion, the woman in the crushed velvet.

Caelerys looked both women over. The silver-blonde she had noted before and thought prickly. Further study of her lovely, full lips did nothing to dispel her impression. She was casting her pale eyes upon one of the Roshan girls and the smile on her face was vicious. The other woman was softly shaped, quite voluptuous, and tightly bound about the waist. The corset binding that many women wore discreetly beneath one's gown to slim and shape, she wore boldly on the outside. It was deeply boned into an hourglass figure, and made from a rich, aubergine brocade with gold and red embellishments. She did not seem unfriendly or even as vicious as her friend.

"Poppy, lady Robyne and Lady Semelle Asparadane," said lord Avondyl. "And a more vicious viper never crawled the earth."

Caelerys frowned, being careful not to look directly at them. "I understand what you mean about Lady Asparadane. She gives me chills just walking past her, but her friend? And isn't Poppy a name of low estate?"

Lady Sigourney smiled. "Yes, it is," she said pointedly. "But that's not why you should avoid her company, my dear. She's nice enough, so I've been told. Married well, even if he was a fifth son of a minor house, and her no better than she should be."

Caelerys did not get the reference, turned to look at lady Sigourney. She did not want to have to reassess her opinion of this cheerful and helpful woman. "I frankly do not understand."

She patted Cae's arm, "Let us just say she is inappropriate company for a virtuous young maiden and leave it at that."

Lord Avondyl chuckled. "She's head seamstress in a house of seamstresses and not a needle among them," he said pointedly.

Caelerys suddenly understood. "Oh. Perhaps when I am married it might be safe to make her acquaintance."

Sigourney laughed at that. "If you so desire," she chuckled. "But beware her associates in any case."

Caelerys sat back against the couch and sighed. "So many people to remember. I'm beginning to wish I'd stayed in the throne room for the entire presentation."

Sigourney shook her head, and Avondyl seconded it. "Not enough wine in the kingdom," he exclaimed.

"You would have been bored to tears, dearling. You only get one chance to leave, you see. You leave when you're done or you're stuck for the whole dreary thing. And who really cares to watch it all? You want to know what everyone gave? The lists will be published soon enough and available for anyone to peruse in the Great Library."

This caught Cae's attention. "Library? For anyone to use?"

"Well," she began, fanning herself with a small lace fan she'd pulled from her sleeve. "Not really. If you have access to the castle, you have access to the books, though taking them out of the library requires royal dispensation. But if you can get in, you can sit and read. There is a public records office, though, in town and not far from the Hall of the Eldest. Anyone can go in there and ask to see any of the records. Helps to grease palms though, especially if you can't read. The low estates can get letters written and copies can be requested of anything, but you have to pay for those. Scribes make good money in DragonsPoint."

"Scribes can make money most anywhere," said a new voice. "That's the advantage for scraps who manage to learn to read."

They looked up to see a tall, lean man in a black velvet coat. He had cold grey eyes and a sharply handsome face, and Cae did not need to see the sinuous sea wolf embroidered at his breast to know him for a Kaladen. His hair was dark, of no real colour, neither black nor brown nor grey, and fell in one long, thin twist to his waist. Even his manner was narrow. He smiled. "Lord Aldane Kaladen, heir to Alden and the Eastern Isles." He held out his hand to Cae. "And you would be the Lady Maral," he said, seeking confirmation.

Caelerys set her hand to his fingertips, reluctant to touch him but more reluctant to be rude. "That will be my sister-in-law, my lord. I am merely Lady Caelerys of House Maral," she said quietly. She found she had trouble looking him in his flat grey eyes.

"There is nothing 'mere' about you."

Sigourney jumped to the rescue, forcing him to take her hand and release Cae's. "Lady Sigourney, and this is Lord Avondyl Griff. Pleasure." Her tone of voice said it was anything but; she had seen the greed in his eye at what Cae wore in her hair.

"The pleasure is all mine," he smiled, nodded to Avondyl. "So Master Janem is your brother," he began, turning his attention back to Cae. "He has made quite a name for himself here in DragonsPoint."

She took a breath. "He is my subsequent brother. My father's son. And yes. He is a Master Smith. I have known this a long time."

"He is hardly the only Master Smith in town," Lord Avondyl droned, waving a lacklustre hand. "Iron Alley is full of them."

"Ah, but none who can work moonsilver, nor craft with the delicacy I have heard tell of…" he began, his eyes rising to her hair.

Caelerys could see where this was going to go. Fortunately, lady Sigourney set a hand on hers, drawing her to her feet. "Oh, I see Morlan now. If you will excuse us, my lord? I really must get this young lady on the lists. Come along, dear, before someone else snatches him away."

Caelerys gave a brief, apologetic curtsey and allowed the woman to whisk her away towards the man in the green tabard.

"I do not think I need to warn you about that one?" she asked when they were out of earshot.

"No, ma'am," she said emphatically.

"Worse shark than his father. Just oilier," she said, shaking herself.

Cae giggled.

They caught up with the herald fairly quickly, got Cae's name put upon the lists for both the archery and the equestrian, as did lady

Sigourney. "You ride the day after tomorrow," he said. "Archery is in four days. Jousts will run throughout the next four." He paused as he consulted the lists. "Maral... we have two entered in the jousts and the grand melee, which is the last day of the tourney. Brothers?"

She smiled, "One is my uncle."

He nodded, closing the book on his papers once the ink was dry enough. "Well, my ladies, you are well and truly entered and good luck to you both."

"My thanks," Cae nodded.

"Thank you, my lady, for your patience. It has been a harrowing week and like as to get worse by the end of things. My deepest gratitude for getting with me early. There will be many who will wait until the last minute and then cry insult when they are called out of rank order."

Lady Sigourney winked at the man, setting a fond hand on his shoulder. "My gratitude is not a light thing, my boy. I would see you again to add fond words and fonder actions."

Lady Sigourney smiled as she led Caelerys away. Cae looked back, watched the man take a swallow of water brought to him by a servant and then nearly choke on it as the full implications of what the lady had said to him sank in. He stared agog, flush to the throat. When lady Sigourney gave him a knowing smile and a nod, he grinned and walked away with a lighter step and more firm voice as he approached someone else regarding the lists. Cae covered her mouth and giggled. "I suppose there are some advantages to being a widow," she smiled.

Lady Sigourney seemed a little startled. "Huh? OH!" She chuckled, "No, I never married, dear."

Caelerys stopped, confused. "But, you... I..." She shook her head, schooling herself. "I am sorry, I am being rude. I didn't mean..."

Lady Sigourney looped her arm through Cae's. "I forgive you. It is understandable to be confused," she said, continuing their walk. "There I was telling you that Poppy Robyne was unsuitable company and she a widow, and here I am, a spinster making assignations, ...with the second estate no less." She lowered her voice. "I was ruined a long time ago. I was, in fact, supposed to marry young Avondyl once upon a time. Things happened. Once the incident had occurred, well... his father wouldn't hear of it. Shame," she glanced over her shoulder at where Avondyl still sat on the back of the couch. "We would have suited one another."

"Did you love him?" she asked softly.

This made the woman laugh. "Mother, no, child! I said we suited. Not the same thing at all! One can hope and wish for love all one wants, but as soon request the moons. Many get lucky, find the love match that one's parents approve of, or come to love the one they wed. Too many are stuck with a harridan or a lout and nothing to be done but stick it out and put up with each other. Marriage becomes a duty and a chore, which is a crime really, and one makes do with paramours. The best you can hope for is someone you'll suit."

"A partnership," Cae said softly. "A friend. Someone you can work with."

Sigourney turned to study the girl's profile. She smiled. "You understand. Good. I had hoped you were not the tiresome type who dream of the 'knight in shining'."

Caelerys smiled, "The armour that shines has never been in a fight."

Sigourney laughed again. "I forget, you are a Maral. You would understand such things." She spied someone across the gallery and stiffened slightly. "Oh dear, lady Petra."

Caelerys froze. She had hoped not to encounter the woman again today. Alas, she came sweeping up the gallery in her dove grey dress and held out her hands to take Cae's. Fortunately, she was smiling.

"Ah, my dearest child," she beamed. "You have done marvellously so far. Your name is on the lips of many today."

Caelerys felt her guts quiver at that, but managed a shy smile. She knew a lot of that had to do with her brother. "Thank you," she all but whispered.

Lady Petra turned her attention to her companion. "And Sigourney! It has been a long time since I've seen you in the capitol." Caelerys was not exactly sure in what way lady Petra had meant that.

Sigourney returned with a controlled smile. "Well, the Lord Mendicant is in town for the King's Tourney. Where he goes, I go."

"How is the old charlatan?"

Caelerys frowned even as lady Sigourney was saying, "Very well, thank you."

"Your pardon, ladies but... who or what is this Lord Mendicant?"

They looked at her, surprised, then at each other. Lady Petra set her hand on Sigourney's arm. "I forget. She's been locked away in Taluscliff all her life. The Lord Mendicant's never come her way. Not much does."

"We have what we need," Caelerys said, feeling the need to defend her home. "We have our entertainments."

"You have nothing on the Lord Mendicant," Sigourney said firmly. "He is an artist! He used to be a great lord, but he stepped down in favour of his younger brother, who was... just better at it than he was, in all honesty."

"There was something else," lady Petra mused. "But I cannot recall..."

Sigourney just kept going. "He was always an excellent performer. Specializes in sleight of hand and illusions and fancy stage tricks. Really impressive show. He always attracts the best performers to his troupe."

"What do you do, lady Sigourney? You said you were with him."

"Harp, a little acting, light singing..."

"Light?" exclaimed lady Petra. "Signy, you make birds envious." She turned to Caelerys. "I shall make certain your brother takes you to at least one performance before the tourney is over. But if you will excuse us, I really must speak to Sigourney about something in private."

"Absolutely, lady Petra," she said with a tiny bow.

Sigourney set her hand on her arm. "Are you sure you will be all right, dear? Oh, good! I see your handmaiden has followed us. She is yours, yes?"

Cae looked over her shoulder and saw Fern standing discreetly by the wall. "Yes, she is. I will be fine, thank you. I think I know who to stay away from at this point."

"Good," Sigourney smiled. "I'll leave you to it then. If you keep going down this gallery you should end up in the courtyard of the royal gardens. Just don't wander too deeply in just yet. And certainly not alone."

She nodded and watched the two women heading off. She shook her head. From lady Sigourney's reaction, she had thought the two had not liked each other, but one would never think it to see them now. Fern looked at her in askance and Cae gave a light shake of her head, not really wanting the company. Fern nodded and step back to follow at a discreet distance.

SHIFT: Stag's Heart

Finally alone, Caelerys looked around her. She was in a long gallery hall with paintings and tapestries displayed upon one wall, but she could smell a garden not far away. She decided to save the artwork for another day and drifted further down the hall in the direction lady Sigourney had advised. It did not take her long to find the garden courtyard.

The gallery opened through a set of double doors that stood propped open. The courtyard was paved with flagstones of a milky white with pale green veins in a circular pattern radiating out from a large fountain. The stone centrepiece was a marble dragon twice the size of a man with down-spread wings that trailed into the water as if it had just launched itself into flight, and its open mouth sprayed water straight up. Scattered about the courtyard, there were marble benches flanked by raised beds spilling with flowers of all sorts, and men and women in courtly garb milling aimlessly about. She could hear the low buzz of conversation, maidenly giggles and low voices, and the snapping of lace fans.

Caelerys strode thoughtfully across the courtyard, sparing a moment or two to admire the fountain, before heading a little ways into the gardens themselves. Most of it was in raised boxes, at least up here by the walls of the castle, but reaching the apex of a small hill, she could see lawns spreading out below with more natural beds and shade trees. Just about every kind of flower to be found in the country was represented in these gardens, and on their best display. She wandered for several minutes, taking note of various plants. While all of them were clearly chosen for their beauty, she noted, a goodly number had other uses. This was good for cough if you made a tea from the dried petals; this one, a poultice from the fresh leaves relieved rash and itch; that one was merely beautiful; this one: a tisane in minuscule doses slowed rapid heart-rate, a little more and it could stop it completely. Still another, lovely to behold, but thankfully set back and out of easy reach behind unpleasant smelling but insect repelling orange flowers, was a trumpet flower whose pollen could cause hallucinations. There were some medicinal uses for that trumpet, but at the moment she could not remember them.

She was passing within the shade of a wisteria bower, taking intense delight in the light fragrances, when she smelled salt in the air and heard the sound of the sea. She followed her instincts, rounding the corner to find herself on a little patio that over-looked the mouth of the Desiter River. She crossed to the low stone wall and looked down and out. Below were jagged rocks, wet with ocean spray, and a few of the hardy scrub trees that thrive on the edges of salt water, all twisted and gnarled. She smiled. To the left were miles of open sky and sea, dotted here and there with the sails of ships. To the right, the opening of the great river and the dragon gates that permitted passage down river and to the ports below. Some might consider this a security risk, having such easy access to the ocean from the castle, but Caelerys knew that the waters below would be unpassable, even to small, shallow craft. She could see all manner of rocks rising from the unruly surf.

She sat down upon the edge of the wall, clutched the book to her stomach and gazed out on the waves, suddenly longing for home and familiarity. So many dangers, so many strangers, and a goodly, unknown number of them wanted something of her. She was not entirely sure she had it to give.

She had no idea how long she had been sitting there when she heard them, the sounds of armoured footsteps and the rattle of swords in their sheaths against chain-mail. She looked up to see the queen and one of her sons coming down the path. She slid from the wall and into a deep curtsey, waiting for them to pass. They did not pass her by. With a friendly, but calculating smile, the queen came straight towards her and stopped.

"Your Majesty," Cae said softly, thankful that she hadn't stammered.

"Rise, my dear," came the queen's gentle voice. "Mother knows that is a torturous position to hold for long."

Caelerys obeyed and looked up at the queen, careful not to meet her eyes. Her assessment of the woman at close quarters was quick and concise, and matched her first impression. This was not a woman born to great wealth or pomp and circumstance, and not greatly changed by it. Her dress was well made, of high quality cloth and flattered the body which had obviously borne several children, and her hair was likely beautifully dressed beneath the veil and wimple she wore. But there was nothing glamorous about her, nothing truly 'queenly' beyond the light crown upon her brow. And she wore the heavy silk brocade as if it were farmer's cotton. Nothing about her said 'royalty', not even her manner, which was jovial and open. And though Cae could tell there was something calculating behind her hazeled eyes, there was nothing unfriendly about her.

"You are the Lady Caelerys Maral, are you not?" asked the warm voice.

She gave a shallow bob of acknowledgement. "I am, Your Majesty." Cae was surprised when the queen held out her hand. Uncertain, she reached up, placing her fingertips upon the monarch's. The woman did not take it as most did in greeting, but ran callused fingers across Cae's palm and fingertips, examining the hand by feel more than by sight. Her smile broadened as she found the various callouses upon Cae's own, dainty hands, soft and sure for the most part, as a lady's should be, but they also bore the marks of industry: reins, sewing needles, the pen. The queen's hand was also not the lily white delicacy expected of women of quality.

"Allow me to introduce my son, Prince Balaran." She released Caelerys's hand only to place it in her son's.

Not even this hand was as Cae expected it to be. The callouses were in all the wrong places for a man of action, and while she could feel the strength in his fingers, they were wiry and agile. They were fingers that would have no difficulty dancing across the reaches of harp strings, though there was no hardening at the tips as there would have been. There were callouses and the faint staining of ink on his thumb and first two fingers which told her he was a scholar more than a swordsman.

"My lady," he said, bowing low over her hand with a very feline smile. His dancing blue eyes did not leave her sapphire ones even as he placed the lightest kiss upon the knuckles just below the opal ring her mother had left her. She suppressed a shiver from meeting that gaze, offered a belated, "Your Highness."

He was beautiful for a man, breathtakingly so. Were he a woman he would have started wars. As it was, he still might. There was mischief in those eyes, though, and that delighted her. When he finally released her hand she found breathing a little easier, but not so talking. Thankfully, he rescued her.

"So... reading at court?" he smiled, his eyes on the book in her hands.

She frowned slightly, not understanding, then followed his gaze to the tome, which she suddenly realized was not one of her own. "OH! I... I am terribly sorry, Your Highness," she said, holding the book out to him. "I... hadn't realized. It... reading calms me. I was going to look at it in the room where I found it, but then.... I didn't even realize I was still in possession of it."

He chuckled, but did not take the offered volume. "And are you nervous?"

She gave a shy smile and leaned forward slightly, holding the book to her body again. "Petrified," she confessed in a whisper.

"Well, far be it for me to remove anything which might make a lady's visit to my home less terrifying. Though that is heavy reading."

She gave a little frown, looking the title over. Translated, it was 'A History of Elanthus with a Treatise on Culture and Religion throughout the Known Ages'. She mused on it a moment, taking into account the thickness of the volume as well as the title. "Not really, Your Highness. Depending on the rains, four days at worst, two if I do naught else. It might prove interesting as well as educational."

He looked a little surprised. "You read Old Vermian?"

She smiled, shifting to the tongue. "Fluently. I actually prefer it. There is more poetry in it, and it has the power of turning even the most ordinary conversation into a thing of elegance and beauty, while actually having less chance of being misunderstood. Even Vermian metaphors are clear."

His grin was almost predatory, as he responded in kind. "Ah, beauty and intelligence, a rare and delightful combination."

Caelerys felt her cheeks beginning to burn and suddenly remembered there was another person attendant on the conversation.

She turned to the queen, hoping it would banish the blush. "Your Majesty, my apologies," she said with a token curtsey, shifting back to the common tongue of modern days.

The smile was deep and genuine in her lightly lined face. It was a merry, weathered visage, and Caelerys decided she liked it. "Why apologize? I brought him over here to speak with you, and you are engaging him quite nicely. I couldn't be more pleased."

She blushed a little more in spite of herself. "How does the pageantry suit you, Your Majesty?"

The queen dismissed it with a little wave of her hand. "Meh, it is necessary. The estates need it. It provides formality and colour. Beyond it, life will go on much the same for me. I will raise my children, and care for my husband and his people."

Caelerys smiled, "Only now 'his people' are in greater numbers, yes?"

The queen smiled again and there was something shrewd and noticing behind it. "There is that."

"I do wish you well of it all. I imagine the period of adjustment will be a little stressful, but the royal family is strong. My condolences, by the way," she added, turning a little to include Prince Balaran, "on your losses. It was a shocking tragedy."

"Everyone gets their share in their lifetime," the prince responded. "We do what we can with it. Life soldiers on in spite of it."

"Yes, Your Highness. That it does."

The conversation promised to get awkward quickly, as Caelerys could think of nothing else one could say to royalty when the prince rescued her, yet again. "So tell me, my lady, what do you like to do other than read difficult books in ancient languages?"

"Well, I ride. I hunt when the weather is good. I have my own falcon."

"Oh? What kind?" he asked brightly.

"She's a gauvan."

He arched one dark golden eyebrow. "Really? Those are rare birds, ...royal birds."

"They are also allowed to higher nobility," she reminded him softly. "Your late uncle gave father dispensation for me, considering... how I acquired her," she added, blushing furiously. Again.

Prince Balaran gestured towards a bench in a little nook, and Caelerys went to it obediently, still clutching the book like a drowning man clings to a rock. She waited until the queen sat before sitting beside her. The prince perched on the curved wall where he could see them both. "This is a story I must hear," he grinned.

Caelerys took a moment to collect herself. It wouldn't do to stammer or fumble with the story because of her shyness. Besides, it was Tempest she was talking about. "Well, I was about ten, I think. I was out riding with my brother Willam and I thought they were being too slow. We weren't hunting so there was nothing wrong with a bit of a gallop. Willam hadn't been home in a long time and didn't know I was a more than capable horsewoman. I had ridden by the cliffs for years with never a problem. And there wouldn't have been but for an eagle..."

"An eagle?" asked the queen.

"Yes, Your Majesty." This was a subject close to her heart and made talking easier. "You see, gauvan nest on cliff-side ledges. And there was a nest below... with a new hatchling. An eagle decided to make a meal of them, but the mother was having none of it. Where her mate was, we never discovered. He never returned. But she was fending the eagle off admirably. Trouble was, she chased him up the cliff just as I was riding past. My horse took fright. She was just some placid little mare my brother had brought me and insisted I ride, not my hunting horse who would have taken it in stride. It was a 'proper ladies' mount'. The side-saddle didn't help matters," she groaned with a slight roll of her eyes. "I would have refused to ride her at all and had my own horse, saddled properly, but I hadn't seen him in a long time and he looked so... pleased with the gift... I didn't have the heart to insist on my own mount. She was pretty enough, just ...empty headed."

"Let me guess, she threw you," the prince grinned.

She nodded. "Yes, Your Highness. She did. Have you ever ridden side-saddle?"

Now it was his turn to blush, though it was faint. "No, my lady, I cannot say that I ever have." There was a mischievous glint in his eye that told her he might being trying it in the very near future.

She pivoted on the bench, so that she was sitting perfectly side-saddle. "As you can see," she held up her hands to hold imaginary reins, "there is nothing to hold onto accept the reins and the horn. There is a knee brace, like a secondary horn here," she tucked one hand beneath her knee, "but while it will hold you in the saddle under normal conditions, if the horse rears it is no protection. I have never been thrown riding astride.

"So, on that fateful day, I was actually thrown for the first time in my life. Luckily, my brother Janem had insisted that I get falling practice. I learned how to land before I learned how to ride." She giggled at the memory, "He either tossed me or tipped me backwards off a short wall into a broken down hay rick. I think there was more hay in my hair and dress than in the horses' mangers for about a week." She blushed a little as the prince smiled at that. She could not see the queen's reaction.

"So your first real fall," he prompted as she faltered in her telling.

"Aye, Your Highness. It wouldn't have been so bad if only... we'd not had a recent storm and I not been so close to the cliff-side. The path is no more than a warhorse's length from the edge, and not normally a problem. I landed a little roughly, but I had managed to gather my wits quickly enough to tuck my shoulder and roll when I landed. I was lucky, I could have broken my neck. Instead, I rolled... too close to a too soft edge. The storm had weakened it and it crumbled beneath me. I scrabbled for purchase, but slid right off."

She heard the queen gasp.

"It took long enough that my brother and his men had seen what happened and where I had gone off. The Mother was kind. There was a ledge below, wide enough for my feet... and a falcon's nest."

A light went on in the prince's eyes. Clearly, he could see the good and the bad in the situation.

She smiled shyly. "Aye. I believe the rustics refer to it as 'out of the pot and into the fire'. While I was safe from the rocks several hundred feet below, I was now a second threat to the mother gauvan. She alternated between attacking the eagle and flying at me, then, when they arrived, attacking my brother and his men. In the end, in order to be able to save me, my brother ordered her shot. Oh, how I wept for her," she sighed. "I didn't care that she had torn my arms bloody and nearly tipped me off my ledge twice. I only knew she was dead because of me, and her baby... ah, then I thought about the baby. It was only a few steps away, and there was a scrub tree growing near which anchored the nest and would give me something to hold onto. So... I sidled over, held onto the tree and scooped the eyas from her nest and tucked her into the warmth of my bodice."

She heard the queen giggle softly and even the prince wore a smirk. "By the time they had lowered Mace on a makeshift harness to me... he is lighter than my brother and strong enough not to drop me... I'd stowed the hatchling and was ready. We were pulled up, I was briefly checked to make sure I didn't require immediate bandaging, thrown into the saddle in front of Willam and rode almost recklessly back to the castle. And I had thought riding side-saddle uncomfortable," she laughed softly. "It wasn't until they were putting me into a bath so they could more properly see my injuries that they realized I still had the eyas.

"Well, father, of course, threw a fit. Not about the bird, but about the whole adventure. I waded in to defend the birds who caused it all, though I confess, I did not much defend the horse. I only said it wasn't her fault she wasn't trained to ignore birds bursting suddenly from nowhere. Even father was a little shocked that I had been riding side-saddle, though he did fuss for my riding ahead. I was ten... I complained that my brother had thought we were on parade, not a relaxing ride. Willam argued that he had kept that pace for my delicacy which caused the whole room to collapse in laughter."

She did not have to see the queen to feel the arched brow and look she was sure she was being given. "I was... a bit wild as a child. I hunt with my father and my brothers and I have been taught the bow by the best. I could pass for an acceptable son but for my other, more lady-like, pursuits."

"My lady," he said gallantly, "trust me. No one would ever mistake you for a son."

There was something else behind the prince's grin that Caelerys decided it was best not to understand.

She blushed, not sure how to respond to that. It was the queen who saved her this time. "And the bird?"

"Oh, because it was my fault it was orphaned, I begged to keep her."

"Truthfully, it were the eagle's fault," the queen suggested.

"Aye, Your Majesty, but were it not for me... and the eagle was only doing as eagles do. It was the interference of men. And that was my fault. But father said that if I was going to keep her, I had to care for her completely, be mother to her. Then, when they showed him the feathers of the mother, he paled a little and said that when she was grown, we would have to see if I would be allowed to keep her. I did not know that he had even written the king until word came back from DragonsPoint. Thankfully, the king agreed that I had earned the right to keep her by virtue of my own blood spilt, and that if I proved worthy of the responsibility by getting her to adulthood, I should be granted the right to fly her. I have the dispensation at our manor in my things if the new king wishes to see it." A horrifying thought crossed her mind and she turned to the queen. "You don't think... his majesty would revoke it, do you?"

The queen smiled one of her motherly smiles and set her hand upon her arm. "No, my dear, I think he won't. He would need a great reason to revoke any gift or privilege granted by his brother."

Cae relaxed, smiled softly and nodded her thanks.

"So, you ride and you shoot," said the prince, recalling her attention.

She turned to face him. "Aye, Your Highness. I do. It is the one thing

I will miss living here."

"Ah, but you don't have to give it up," he laughed. "We have a full training ground for archery and a small wood with plenty of places to ride, all perfectly safe." He grinned as she lit up. "So is it safe to assume my lady has entered, or will be entering, my father's tourney in those categories?"

She nodded. "It is, Your Highness. I have already been put on the lists for both. And my brother will be riding in the joust and the grand melee."

"I am looking forward to your shooting, Lady Caelerys," said the queen.

"As am I," the prince's eyes danced. "I am also interested in watching your brother fight. I have heard things about that young mountain."

"Will you be participating?" she asked sweetly.

"Perhaps," he chuckled. "But my brother will be fighting."

Before Caelerys could respond, she noticed a well dressed woman in orange approach and wait discreetly where she would be noticed. She was perhaps late twenties, early thirties; pretty but not beautiful. She walked carefully. Cae remembered her as one of the queen's ladies that Lord Avondyl had pointed out.

"Yes, lady Caena?" asked the queen.

The woman curtsied deeply but gingerly, keeping her upper body perfectly straight. "Forgive my interruption, Your Majesty, but your royal husband requests your presence. And yours, Your Highness."

"Thank you, Caena," said the queen as she stood. She gave Caelerys a nod. "Another time, Lady Caelerys. I would see you gracing my gardens again."

Cae stood and dropped into a curtsey. "As you wish, Your Majesty. A good day to you."

"And to you. Come along, Bal."

The prince paused long enough to take Cae's hand and kiss it. "I will see you again, my lady."

Cae blushed as he drew her to her feet before turning on his heel and falling into step behind his mother. Caelerys remained where she was, finally opening the book in her hands. Reading the preface and the first page, she assessed that, had the book been written in the modern tongue, it would have been very dry. As it was, it soothed her, looked very promising. There was a whole chapter on the ancient faith and the new god and she decided she would keep this out of lady Petra's way. She had learned that the priests of the Eldest tended to frown upon study of the Others.

She had gotten through the first chapter when she noticed that the shadows around her had grown. Forcing herself to close the book, she rose and began to wander again. Her brother would be wondering where she'd vanished to. She meandered through the twisting paths, full of beautiful and useful things when she heard the familiar voice of her uncle. Lord Tume was not with him, and as she came around the corner of a floribunda rose, she saw him flirting with a maid with a tray of drinks. Crossing to him, she found herself in a more open area, set with pavilions and cushioned seats and milling people. Servants circulated with food and beverage giving the whole the effect of a garden party. Seeing Cae, the girl gratefully turned to her, offered her a drink.

Caelerys smiled, choosing a pale cider that promised to be mild. Without spilling a drop, the girl curtsied and slipped away. "Uncle, are you frightening the staff?"

He grinned, "Propositioning."

"Like I said," she replied with a light frown. She reached up and drew aside a lock of dark hair from his forehead to reveal a streak of blood. Thankfully it was no more than a graze. "Someone try to give you a haircut?"

He chuckled, fingering it ruefully. "Someone tried to shave my head. Luckily he was rather bad at it. We got the rotters in the end."

"What happened?" she gasped, shocked. "This is the king's coronation. Surely there is not that much unrest yet?"

"No, more like uprooting weeds of the old regime. Apparently, just before the coronation the king had ordered the book of accounts be brought to his rooms so that he might look over them tonight and know what he had to work with. Word came to the king's ear just after court that the Key to the Treasury had robbed his charge and was trying to flee upriver by ship. That's what we were called to go deal with. We caught him before he could reach the great fork, and let me tell you, I prefer my battles on solid ground," he laughed deeply.

"But you stopped him, did you not?"

"Oh, aye. But there'll be a need for a new Key."

"Why would he have..."

"Panicked," he shrugged. "We aren't sure, but suspicion is that he had been skimming. We'll know once the books have been gone through." He looked up as someone approached, called his niece's attention to the man with a subtle gesture.

It was the Kaladen heir. He smiled as he joined the conversation, reminding Caelerys uncomfortably of the sea wolves that were his house sigil. He bowed slightly. "My lady, my lord." He turned mostly to speak to her uncle. "Ah, but that was a magnificent sea battle, was it not? I had not expected to fight by ship at this tourney, but," he took a deep breath of sheer pleasure, "maybe we can convince king and country that it would be a wonderful addition to such events?"

Jehan looked a little green at the thought.

"Perhaps a boat race might be more practical," Caelerys suggested sweetly. "Ship battles are so much more likely to be... deadly."

"And the Grand Melee isn't?" he smiled, not seeing a difference.

"It is not supposed to be," Jehan interrupted. "Blunted weapons and no stabbing. Aye, men get hurt, happens when you take a battering, but it is more training than killing. Allow me to introduce myself," he added, holding out his arm and stepping slightly in front of Caelerys. "I am Jehan Maral, Lord Commander of the Sterling Company of the Free Legions."

Cae thought there was a touch of reluctance from Kaladen as he accepted the arm. "Sterling Company? That's... the second largest host of mercenaries in the Free Legions."

Jehan grinned wolfishly. "That's why it's the Sterling Company... and the best. Only the Iron Legion is larger. But they're less trained and worse armed."

"And cheaper," the man added.

"Most arrow fodder is," he grunted. "The Golden Battalion is smaller, but more noble of blood, being mostly younger sons in line for nothing but trouble. The Iron Legion is larger, but they're less trained and worse armed. The Sterling Company consists of both trained nobles and skilled commoners and is far more effective as a whole, especially since noble birth holds no bearing on your position in the Company. Only skill matters."

The man gave a short, tight laugh, either intimidated or impressed. Possibly both. He tried to turn the conversation back to Cae but Jehan would not relinquish his arm. He suddenly realized what the man was waiting for, introducing himself. As Jehan released him, he turned towards Cae. "My lady..."

"My niece, Lady Caelerys Maral," Jehan interrupted, reluctantly observing the courtesies.

"We've met," he said, reaching his hand for hers, his confidence returning.

"Really?" he asked, his voice growing more gruff and his body somehow wider.

Aldane withdrew his hand. "Aye, earlier this afternoon, before our excursion. She was with lady Sigourney and young lord Avondyl."

He glanced at his niece.

"Aye, lady Sigourney was gracious enough to play chaperone for me after you abandoned me in the company of Prince Kyleth," she smiled tightly.

"Ah," he said, sheepishly.

She smiled and kissed his cheek, laughing lightly. "You are forgiven, uncle. I understand the lure of the martial."

He laughed, "Aye, well..." He turned back to Aldane, pinning him with his eyes. "You arrived a mite late to that party, if I recall."

"...My father's man became lost in that labyrinth they call a castle."

"You were on that second boat, the one with the eyes painted on the front."

Aldane bristled. "Ship," he corrected. "And it's called a prow. Aye, the *Sea Bitch* is mine."

"What are the eyes for?"

"So she can see where she is going," he explained as if her uncle should know better.

Caelerys could see what her uncle was doing, resolved to stay out of the conversation, even if something that interested her was said. He was trying to keep the man's attention off of her and she was grateful. She tuned them both out and looked around this area of the garden. It seemed they were not that far from the fountain, as she could hear water tumbling nearby. The larch tree beside her was too tall to see the spray of water over, or she was certain she could have.

Just beyond Kaladen stood a cluster of the Kaladen family to judge by their appearances. They wore various shades of black, most of them fading, in styles well suited to hard islands and rough seas. What decoration they had was simple and not likely to catch on anything: rounded studs in repeating patterns, flat embroidery, small golden bands in the beards of those who wore them. Most had visible scars.

Two of them glanced over at her, and then she distinctly heard her name and the word bride, though nothing else of the sentence was understandable. She felt something cold run down her spine. She heard her name from another direction and nearly jumped. Turning, she saw her eldest brother approaching and wave her to him. She turned back, bobbed a negligent courtesy to lord Kaladen and kissed her uncle's cheek again. "I have to go, Willam calls."

"I'll see you at supper, niece."

She turned and whisked off before Aldane could do more than bow. Willam's face was stern as she glided up to him, taking the arm he offered her. His voice was low and quiet, aimed for her ears alone. "Why is the heir of Kaladen watching you walk away with such thirst?"

A shiver ran through her, "I am certain I have no idea. I do not think I have given him any reason at all to believe I would welcome it," a little stiffly.

Without another word, Willam turned at a flowering shrub which would cut them off from Kaladen's line of sight. Only then did he begin to make his way out of the gardens, on a course less direct than he could have taken. Cae relaxed a little.

"So what were you talking about?" he asked.

She detected no accusation in his voice. "I don't really know. The first time he spoke with me I was with lady Sigourney and lord Avondyl the younger, and I think he was trying to ask me about Janem." Her hand drifted to the comb in her hair. "It draws a great deal of attention, I think," she sighed.

"And the second?"

"Boats. Uncle Jehan distracted him by calling his ship a boat," she said with a faint smile. "What else they spoke of I do not know. I turned a deaf ear. I was far more concerned by what I heard his men say."

He paused for a single stride, covered his hesitation by bowing to passing courtiers. "And that would be?"

"All I heard clearly was my name and the word 'brides'." She trembled slightly at that, determined not to show how much that thought frightened her.

"Over my dead body," was all Willam said as he led her out into the dimming sunlight of the courtyard and to their horses.

3

The day after the coronation Willam took his sister to the tourney grounds early in the morning, promising her a chance to ride Wraith before the tournament began. They took Mace and two other men with them. They rode in silence, Tempest happily perched on Cae's shoulder.

The sound of the early morning city was startling for Cae. There were so many people bustling about, preparing for the day and yet they moved quietly. Well, relatively. It was about as noisy as home on a market day. She could see signs of last night's revelry being swept away, drunks tottering home, banners being mended and straightened. She still did not see why her brother liked it here, as it seemed he did. Maybe it was just that he had spent over half his life here.

They skirted the walls of Greenstone. It was a broad lane, lined on one side with some low growing plant that spread everywhere but the hard-packed road, though it did not attempt to climb the walls. It was peppered with pretty little yellow flowers. Caelerys smiled. She knew this plant. Most castles would not think to allow anything to grow against their walls, finding it a security risk. But this plant was Alarum, also known as Alarm Flower. It was pleasant and pretty to look at, even smelled fine, almost like a lemony mint ...until you stepped on it. Then it let up a horrendous stink that could be smelled for a hundred yards; more if the wind was up. Even most animals larger than a vole avoided it. The bed was wide enough that there was no way to lay a ladder against the wall or get a rope up without treading upon them, and the stink would have quickly risen up to the guards on the wall.

Cae looked up, saw a few armoured men walking the top of the wall, looking down upon the pretty little houses that faced the road, each with bronze bells hanging outside their windows to give the alarm should they see anything the guards missed. Rich men lived here. They would give alarm if they saw anyone skulking.

Then they were riding out of the city wall through a thick wooden gate guarded from both sides by four men. The guards nodded their heads as they passed. What lay before them, down a slight slope, struck her with awe.

It was only from here, at the wall, that you could see the whole of the grounds. It spread away between the city wall and the rush of rivers. The road wound softly enough, through a broad expanse of lawn which a few men with scythes were trimming in this early hour. But, to their right, the castle wall rose high and smooth at the top of a very steep incline completely blanketed with Alarum. A pair of gardeners were very carefully husbanding the borders of this patch, pulling what had begun to stray from designated beds.

The road ran down at the base of the slope to an area full of outbuildings. There was a complete tourney ground with permanent grandstand and a shaded royal box, and well tended sands for any number of activities. Lane dividers were being put up for the joust; long poles wrapped in ribbons of many colours and small flags representing the men who would be riding today.

Beyond that, facing the broad river, was an archery ground. Nearer stood a large stable, and pavilions striped with house colours for the fighting knights to prepare themselves. Just past all of this were broad, uncut meadows that lead into an ancient looking forest. In the southern half, the paths were clear and the undergrowth almost non-existent, at least at the edges, making it excellent for riding. The northern half looked to be a hunting preserve, and those meadows would have all sorts of game for hawking. Tempest was looking in that direction quite eagerly.

She reached a hand up to steady the bird, speaking in Vermian. "Easy, my sweet. Later, when we have permission."

Willam watched the bird nuzzle her hand, no longer on alert for prey, and had to wonder at their relationship, and not for the first time, either. He signalled Mace and the younger of the two guards to go with his sister. "There are bridle trails all through the wood south of the meadow. Enjoy yourself. But try to return when you hear the first trumpets, or before. You'll not want to miss the opening of the tourney or you'll find it hard to get a good seat. You should have an hour or so. When you return, take the horses to that stable. They'll be well tended until we are ready to leave the grounds."

"Where will you be?"

He waved his hand down to a smaller area she had not seen before as it was behind the stable and among the pavilions. There were already a couple of men in it practising at arms. "There. I promised to train my squire today. That's him in the dark blue, polishing shields and watching the fighting with hunger."

"He got here before you?"

He chuckled. "I sent him to get things ready. He spends a lot of time here." He pointed out another pavilion, between the grandstand and the stables, though this one had the sides rolled up. "Janem will be set up over there, if you want to drop in later. Just do it before the knights start arriving. He'll be very busy after that."

She beamed, glad to be able to see him again. Not seeing him moving around the portable forge his apprentices were setting up, she nudged her horse towards the meadows and the forest beyond. Tempest took flight, keeping up with her, but playing in the air currents between the tall trees.

The bridle trails were well tended and wide. The wood arched overhead in a green canopy, the trees well spaced. There was little underbrush, though some areas were lush with shade loving plants. She could see mushrooms and flowers and evidence of small animals, several patches of good herb. She could smell incensewood and needlewood, both of which guaranteed that Fallow would not leave this place a skeletal forest. There were sweetwoods and grandfather trees, a stand or two of silverwood and giltwood, combinations odd enough to make her believe this wood had been planted by intent rather than nature.

Somewhere she was sure there would be an orchard.

She amended her theory as the path entered an area that was wide open and yet almost dark, and the ground beside the path rose uneven and knobby. There was more undergrowth on the fringes here, keeping one from seeing most of what lay ahead. She slowed Wraith as she entered a dim clearing, awed to deep silence by what rose from the centre of it.

The tree was called 'queen of the forest', and with good reason. They took centuries to mature, and, though others grew near one, none ever rose past sapling level until the queen herself died, then it would shoot up majestically to the height of about twenty men and spread its canopy as far as it could, then slowly began to thicken in its mother's grave. Their trunks were broad and full of nooks and crannies, made both by a partly exposed root system and by the ruffled nature of the trunk itself. They were easy to climb if one were so inclined, due to their knobby nature, but the nearest thick limbs were high above. Thin, twig-like branches draped down, covered in long, feathery leaves referred to as the hair of the queen. There were only eight known in all the world. These trees were sacred, and to have one on one's lands brought prestige and good fortune. And naturally, when one died, disaster fell to those who lived nearby. There were two in the Mistwood, one in the Reach near her home said to be nearly a thousand years old, and one deep in the end here by DragonsPoint, though it was newer, its mother having been killed by lightning. It had died in the year of her brother's 'rebellion'.

She slowed to a walk as she followed the path around the edges of the dark clearing. Smooth though it was kept, it was never wise to rush around a queen, disrespectful. In fact, any animal or person who took shelter in one was protected, even from other animals. She could smell the spicy-sweet fragrance of her bark, and the faintest sound of sweet water. The wispy burble of a spring blended in with the hushed whisper of her leaves in the wind, interlaced with the tall branches of the trees that ringed her, almost silencing the sound of following hooves and the ringing of bridles and stirrups.

She looked behind her, saw the guards she had forgotten were with her paying attention to something else coming up the trail behind them. Her heart would have beat frightfully had she not been beneath the queen. Something about the fragrance of her calmed one.

Finally, they entered the glade, slowing to a walk just before it. The lead horse was a steely grey, dressed in green tack. His rider was just as smart as the horse, with a laid back manner of easy beauty. He wore a hooded jerkin of a blackened red with a trim so subtle you had to be close upon it to notice it. The hood was up, but the livery of the five men behind him declared him to be one of the royal family. At a signal from Mace, the other house guard turned his horse and fell back with him, bowing their heads. Mace guided his horse to the side, nearly in the surrounding wood, leaving Caelerys, while guarded, fully visible.

She sat there, still under the effects of the queen, pretty as a picture. Her split riding skirt was a dark blue with a tight, black leather, sleeveless coat she referred to as her 'armour'. Her hair was swept up and back for riding, and, though she did not wear the moonsilver comb today, it was held up with combs of similar design but carved of real antler. Her wits returned a few seconds later when Tempest landed on her shoulder, eyeing the party as if they were intruders. A twitch from her reins combined with a tap from her toe, and Wraith lowered herself into a pretty little curtsey and Caelerys bowed over her neck gracefully, though at an angle that would allow her to keep her seat.

At that the prince laughed and threw back his hood. His long golden braid spilled out upon his shoulder and his blue eyes danced. "My lady," he bowed. "Though I fear you have outdone me. That is not a trick I've taught Korizon here."

She signalled Wraith to stand and smiled at the prince. "Ah, but all ladies should know how to curtsey, Your Highness. And my Wraith, while spirited, is every inch a lady."

He chuckled at that. "Noted. Whereas my Korizon is certainly no gentleman," he added giving the highly arched neck a fond cuff. The horse was clearly posing for Wraith's benefit.

Caelerys took quick note of his behaviour, turned attention to her own mount. Her ears were starting to flick back. "He always like that? Or do I need to be concerned?"

The prince noticed his horse showing off and turned him sideways to curb his antics. "Just around pretty girls." He saw the mare's lashing tail and narrowing eyes and leaned to his stallion's ear. "She said no." The grey shook himself in irritation, but stopped showing off.

Wraith calmed down and pointedly looked away. Cae giggled. She made her sidle off the path onto the softer ground of the surrounding forest. "Please, Your Highness, do not allow me interfere with your outing."

He eyed her for a moment. "On the contrary, Lady Caelerys," he said finally. "Join me."

She bowed her head, "Certainly, Your highness. I would be delighted to have an escort who knows the wood."

As she turned Wraith's head to fall into step beside the prince's grey, Mace signalled her other guard to fall in as close behind her as the Royal Guard would allow. They permitted them to ride just behind his lady, though he was surrounded by the royal men. Mace fell to the rear of them, bow close at hand and kept his eyes on the distance as was his wont. The prince and Caelerys rode in the lead, several paces ahead of the guard, walking slowly around the majestic and jutting roots of the great queen of the forest.

She looked up into the branches, and Tempest's head tilted to follow her gaze. "It is breathtaking, isn't it?"

Prince Balaran chuckled. "Have you ever seen one before?"

"I've seen two, neither of which were set up like this, with a perfect bridle path and interlacing trees."

"Two?" he said, surprised. "Most never see one unless they are fortunate."

She smiled pointedly, "Or noble enough to be allowed to ride your wood."

He grinned, tipping his head in sheepish agreement, "Aye, or that. Which two?"

"I grew up in the Mistwood Reach," she reminded him gently.

He nodded. "The great Queen of the Reach. Five children, and herself near a thousand years old I hear."

It was her turn to be surprised. "You know your queens."

He smiled, pointing out a sapling near the back, nestled in the crook of the tree's knees that was no more than child's height, and thin as a reed. "There are two others in the outskirts, but there is our child, the one we expect is the heir should anything happen to her, the Mother forbid. What other, my lady?"

Her sapphire eyes danced with mischief. "Can you not guess, Your Highness?"

"Well, I was told you had never left the Reach, or your father's lands at the very least. And there IS one other queen in the Mistwood, but that is almost to DragonsPoint and well way from any road. I can think of few reasons you would have travelled so far and yet not come to the City. But it is the only option I can think of."

"You would be right. And you would be right that she is a long way from home. But I hunt, Your Highness, and when the family hunts we wander far and our family lodge is a bit south of the King's Road, nearer the heart of the wood. My brother would not let me get that close to a queen and not take me to see her. After all, she was crowned around the time I was born."

She could see the prince thinking. "Ah, yes, that would have been about the time of Landyn's tragedy," he said delicately as they followed the path out of the queen's presence.

She gave him a sad little smile. "Thank you for not referring to it as a rebellion, Your Highness."

He shook his head. "It wasn't. It did not have your father's will behind it and was the misguided plot of an unfortunate madman."

He noticed her hands tightening on the reins and watched her carefully schooled face. Her eyes were on the path ahead of them, but the bird was eyeing her with concern and starting to fluff up and turn accusing eyes on him. "I did not mean offence, my lady. But it is the kindest way I can..."

"Are you a student of history, Your Highness?" she asked quietly, taking a risk cutting him off. She had been worried about this very subject when she had first been told she was being sent to the capitol.

He seemed surprised at her daring, but found he could not be offended by her tone. "I am."

"Perhaps then you might educate me on matters my family will not speak of?"

He watched her more carefully. "You were never told?" She shook her head. He sighed. "I do not know if I am the best person to enlighten you. Surely your brother...."

"My brother tells me as little as he can get away with. He would never speak of this. I had to pester him to get him to tell me why your father needed to be crowned."

He arched one dark golden eyebrow. "And what did he tell you of that?"

"A tale of madness," she said softly.

He watched her for a few moments before he began. "No one really knows why he did it. Your father was away on a voyage, dealing with overseas issues, or so I was told. Your brother was in charge. I will not deny that your family was perhaps not dealt with fairly in the matter, but he could have handled it better. A royal ship had been wrecked off the Reach, carrying the tithes of the Southern coasts."

"I remember hearing about that. Bodies washed up for weeks. Some not found for days. There was a sickness that year."

He nodded, "Normally, your family has the right of salvage for anything they recover of wrecks off their coasts. A portion tithed to the crown, of course. Your father is normally very generous in these matters, offering any merchant who can prove possession of the cargo a percentage so they don't lose everything. However, my uncle..." he sighed. "Reports are conflicted. The courtier was supposed to try and convince your father to hand everything recovered back to the crown and accept the crown's normal portion for his own. Alas he was an ambitious man out to prove himself worthy of being a Royal Tax Collector. We believe that he presented things... more as a demand than a negotiation. And he wasn't dealing with a seasoned duke, but a young and brash Lord. Some say he demanded the full cargo be remanded and that there might have been a small reward for the work undertaken to salvage. Some said his manner was insulting, others his words. Some say your brother was the one who insulted first. Things got muddled and we'll never know at this point what the truth was.

"All we do know for sure is that your brother killed him and sent his head back to my uncle in a tithing chest. He then raised his levies and some of his friends and decided to unseat 'an unjust king' who 'had no respect for the ancient rights of the noble families'. He marched out of a raging, rainless storm, bellowing that he was the King of the Forest and one of the Second Sons and would bow to no one. Even his own men were second guessing him. He had antlers mounted on his helm and a wild look in his eye. In the end, by the time battle was enjoined in the fields below the road, the only men still with him were about twenty of his closest friends who were supposedly as mad as he."

He took a breath, shook his head and stole a glance at Cae. She was sitting on her horse staring at the path ahead, steady as a rock, but she was listening. "The story gets even more muddled from there. The only thing agreed upon was that most of his army remained on the ridge at the edge of the wood and would not ride further. Someone among them had sent a toomi to warn the king and to disavow his actions. Some say one of his friends ripped out of his own skin on the battlefield, turning into a giant, maddened badger and ripped three men apart with his bare hands, and one of them his own man. They also say that when one of Landyn's antlers were struck from his helm, they bled, that the fists he swung when his sword broke were as heavy as gauntlets, though his hands were bare. The battle was insane. None who fought and survived has been quite the same.

"When your father returned, he went straight to the king, disavowing his son's actions. And due to the unswerving loyalty of your family in the past, he was absolved of the action of a mad son. He even offered up the salvage whole but for what had already been paid to the actual salvagemen, and refused even a recovery fee."

Cae's voice was so quiet when she finally spoke that the prince almost didn't hear her. "He would have given a tithe ship back whole, though he would have accepted any reward the king would have offered him."

"Your brother should have known that. The gods only know why he didn't make that choice or held the collector off until his father returned. There is madness everywhere lately."

"That's when the queen died," she said. "In that storm. And my mother went into labour at the news of my brother's... folly. I was early."

"Hard way to come into the world."

"All ways are hard." She forced a smile. "Thank you, Your Majesty, for telling me. And for trying to be... objective."

"You are welcome. Mayhap one day we will know why your brother went mad and seventeen years later, my uncle. Because it had to be madness. Your family's loyalty to the crown is well documented."

SHIFT: Stag's Heart

She smiled ruefully. "We've only rebelled once in our entire history, and that over a stolen daughter."

He chuckled at that. "Isildar. I've heard that story. Your ancestor was well justified in his actions. And, famously, when he won, did not claim the crown as he could have, but demanded justice of the king for the actions of his son. It's almost a nursemaid's tale."

"One version in our library IS a nursemaid's tale. It said Prince Denan was a half dragon who stole the maiden and that the wolves of the south and the stags of the forest rose up and fought for her return. There is a picture in it that has a wolf in armour standing like a man, and you can see eagles in the air and a badger in the background with a dagger in paw. The story tells that she was brought out to her father in the form of a white doe with an iron collar around her neck, and when it was taken off she was disenchanted and became a girl again."

The prince was suddenly very interested. "Shifts? Is there more than just the one picture?"

She nodded. "There are a few. It is an illuminated book, very beautiful."

"I would like very much to see it."

"I brought it with me in an incensewood chest along with several other rare volumes. I would be honoured to loan it to you. But certain precautions must be taken when studying it. It is very old."

The prince nodded. "I have a few volumes of that nature myself. Send me the dimensions of the book and I'll have an incensewood case made to hold just it, and then you can deliver it safely to me yourself, if you will indulge me? Do not trust this to a courier."

Caelerys was pleased that he knew what he was doing, and, while she was reluctant to part with the book, it was an honour to loan it to the royal family. But something else occurred to her. "If you will pardon my question?"

He turned his jewel blue eyes on her. "Depends on the question," he smirked.

"Are you a follower of The Eldest?"

They rode in silence for so long, Cae was beginning to think she had offended him. "I... believe there is something out there," he finally said. "What that is I do not know but... I would never wholeheartedly follow any god that seeks to limit knowledge. Your book is safe with me, so long as we do not make a big deal of it. The page who will deliver the box will not be in royal livery and will not insist it to your hands alone."

Cae had an idea. "Oh, you are going to have it built?"

"Aye."

"Have the hinge and lock made by Master Janem. He works at the Singing Forge. He's actually here today on the tourney grounds. Have him deliver it."

He narrowed his eyes, obviously about to ask why having a master smith personally deliver something would be less conspicuous and then remembered, "Ah yes, your brother. No one will think twice about his repairing something for you and returning it himself. Clever. Then I will arrange for you to visit the royal library, and you can bring it with you."

She smiled, sighing with delight at the thought of the library.

"I will return it to you in excellent condition. It may take a little time, as I might wish to have it copied," he added.

"In your own time, Your Highness." Then she gasped as they rode out of the wood and stepped out onto a wide meadow that ended at the river.

She had thought the river was wide and imposing at the bridge. Here it was immense, nearly two leagues across. On a misty morning, one would not be able to see the far shore. She knew in her head that they were all the same river, that this was merely the second arm that cradled the delta. Both rivers flowed from the heart of the country in the mountains to form the broad and mighty Galen River. Then it split, forming the island upon which DragonsPoint sat. The two arms were both broad and deep, but only the slimmer, southern arm, the Desiter was in any way predictable. It was the calm brother, the reliable one upon which all trade traffic flowed. The northern arm, the Sinecar, was the wild one, broad and unpredictable, for all it looked like a plane of glass. There were places one could walk across, it was so shallow, but the sand below was so dark you could not tell where those places were until you ran aground. The currents were deceptive and vicious and ever-shifting, as were some of the great, jagged rocks it hid. The river could not be charted or crossed with any reliability, and so it made for an excellent 'castle wall'.

This was not to say it went unguarded. From where they stood on the narrow shore, allowing the horses a chance to drink from the placid surface water, they could see one of the small guard towers that safeguarded the shoreline. They watched for foolish ships and the occasional unfortunates who failed at the Great Fork. Sometimes they got to pull survivors from the water, but it was rare. It was more common that they watched the pikemen who were occasionally permitted to fish from the shore, and to make sure they paid forth the proper tithe of their catch to the castle.

She turned to look downriver and caught the prince smiling at her.

She gave a shy laugh, blushing. "What, Your Highness?"

He shook his head in denial, still grinning. "Absolutely nothing. Impressive isn't it?"

She took a deep breath. "I have never seen its like. I've seen broader waters, aye, but nothing so still."

He laughed, "Oh, don't be fooled, my lady. He is a true courtier, our Sinecar. He may look calm and placid on the surface, but underneath... you have no idea whose side he is on."

This, more than anything else, impressed upon her the nature of the world of which she was now a part. It terrified her even more. Wraith sensed the tension and took a step or two back from the water's edge. "At least here the water is clean, which is more than can be said for the Desiter." He glanced up at the sun, then back at the horizon. "We should head back soon, unless your ladyship will not be watching the jousts?"

She looked up. "Oh, aye, Your Highness. I should. My brother will be fighting. I had not planned on being out so long or ranging so far. I just needed to get Wraith limbered up and used to the amount of people so she won't be distracted tomorrow. I want her at her best," she said, giving her neck a pat.

"Smart. Tell you what, I'll show you the course on the way back."

"I would be honoured, Your Highness. Thank you."

He grinned broadly in what might have passed for a leer from a less charming man. "Oh, no trouble at all. What say we test your saddle skills a little now?"

She blushed without knowing why, turning Wraith's head to stand beside Korizon. The mare gave the stallion a glance that warned him to behave himself, and he pretended she wasn't even there with almost comic intensity. "Though a race would hardly be fair, Your Highness, with you knowing which path we will need to take and I having nary a clue. I have no choice but to follow you, thus letting you win."

Tempest, as if anticipating rough riding, leapt into the air, riding the air currents with joy.

"Not proposing a race, exactly," he shrugged. "Just a... swift and challenging ride. Can you jump?"

She laughed, tossing her head back and expressing herself freely. The sun glinted off her hair, turning it into a crown of dark fire, showing off the red like a sunset. "We've been known to jump unexpected cattle. And boar..." she added, ruefully.

He sighed dramatically. "Ah, another tale I shall have to wait to hear. Perhaps when you bring the book?"

"Perhaps," she teased.

With a sudden shout to his horse, the prince tore off down the beach, smoothly cutting across her path to place him on the forest side. Wraith was after him like a shot without any need for Cae to say anything. Behind them, the men valiantly attempted to keep up. Caelerys kept her mare just a pace behind and to the right of the prince's horse, to enable her time and room to react to anything he might suddenly do. A few moments and he veered off the beach and down a path into the forest a little narrower than what they had come down.

It was as vigorous a ride as he had promised, the path being less well travelled or cared for. Or perhaps it was left that way on purpose. There were long straight-aways, where Cae had to keep reminding Wraith this was not a race and she was not allowed to pass their guide; wide turns where the path sloped a little with the curve of the coarse, small streams to jump and large trees to slalom through. There was even an overturned tree that had been allowed to remain, with moss and vine growing along it. As she sailed over it, Cae glanced back, noting a small fox tucked in at the mouth of its den at the torn roots watching them ride by as if this was something that happened every day. Perhaps it did.

The path finally opened up on the far side of the tourney grounds and they shot out from the woods like arrows. There were men in the field now, planting poles with hooks on the end. The prince rode close by these, but not so near as to endanger the workers. Caelerys finally allowed Wraith her head and they drew neck and neck with the prince. It was clear neither horse wanted to give headway, even though they were tiring.

Both riders were leaned low over the grey necks, intent on the terrain, their mounts and which silvery nose was ahead of the other when a streak of white sailed out of the sky between them and skimmed ahead. Tempest glanced over her back at them and gave a cry as if to say 'I've beaten you both.'

They slowed the horses down, trying not to lose their seats from laughter and letting their men catch up with them. By the time they could finally speak, they had slowed to a walk and left the field, passed the sands and were approaching the village of tents and the sound of men-at-arms doing what they do. "That was enlightening, my lady. I cannot say I have enjoyed a ride more in a very long time."

She blushed a little deeper under the flush of exertion. "I find I must agree, Your Highness. It was a most exhilarating experience. Perhaps when the horses have cooled you can show me the course?"

"You just ran it, my lady."

She looked back at the men in the field, began to see the pattern emerging in the poles they were setting up. "All of it? Wood too?"

He nodded. "Wood too. Granted, it will begin over there," he pointed to a place just before the meadow. "Wide enough for early side by side. The path will be clearly marked and that portion will have ribboned rings you will have to capture. It curves around and joins just below that first stream we hit."

"I remember the fork," she nodded, picturing it.

"The rest of the course is the same. The field and beach will have the ribboned rings as well. The test is not only in speed but how many you collect of your own colour."

She nodded more slowly, musing, impressed. "It will be a challenge indeed. That tree will give some riders pause."

"That is why we will have squires and a Physician stationed there."

"Wise."

"Indeed. We mustn't lose any of the flowers of the kingdom before they can be properly plucked, now can we?"

She stared at him in shock, smiling all the while. "Your Highness," she chided gently, gave an embarrassed laugh.

He grinned wolfishly. "You understood me," he fired back.

Her expression changed to more of a friendly glare. "Have you met my uncle?"

He laughed openly at that. "Well said, my lady."

A page, sitting on a fence just a few yards away, jumped down as he saw the prince's approach. He walked up and bowed, taking the bridle when the prince nodded for him to do so. "Your presence is requested, Your Highness," said the boy in a clear, mellow voice.

The prince grinned at him as he dismounted. "You've stopped

squeaking, Tommet," he said, tousling his pale hair. "And nice tone, too. I might talk to Father about sending you to the heralds. Sounds like you'd make a good one."

The boy beamed. "Thank you, Your Highness. I think I would like that. I know mother would."

"I bet she would. Tell them I will be along shortly." He then turned to Caelerys. "Well, my lady. I wish to thank you for a stirring morning. Would you like aid to dismount now, or will you wait until you reach the stables to seek it?"

Caelerys knew she could dismount perfectly well on her own, and could see that he guessed that. She also knew it would not be prudent in the present circumstances. She could ride like a hellion if she was able, but in all other ways she had best be the perfect lady. She nodded to him, bringing her leg over the saddle and smoothing her skirt to allow him to more easily help her. She felt the faintest of shivers as he placed his strong hands up on her waist and lifted her down. She had been right about the manner of his strength. His fingers were long and lean and as strong as silk cable.

He set her lightly on her feet and slid one hand from her waist up the underside of her arm and down to take her gloved hand. He bowed over it and placed a kiss to the warm leather. "My lady."

She curtseyed as deeply as she could with one hand still in his. "Your Highness."

She watched him go as he turned and led his horse off towards the royal pavilion. Tempest landed on the saddle horn, squeaked for attention. Cae pulled a titbit of meat from a small bag on the saddle and fed her, as an apology for not allowing her to hunt. The falcon gobbled it greedily, not fazed in the least as Cae took the reins and began walking the horse towards the stables.

Inside it was darker and cool. The smell of hay and horses and leather rose pleasantly in the morning air and Cae took a deep breath of it. She sighed happily. Things were going better than she had expected them to go and she felt as ready as she ever would be for the equestrian tomorrow. She led Wraith deeper into the building, intent on finding the horses of her house and a groom to attend her, when she heard the sounds of an animal in distress.

She turned a corner and was startled as she nearly ran into a large man leaning over the wall of one of the larger stalls. She craned her neck to look up at him as he stood and recognized the dark face of her uncle's friend. He was even more massive in full plate. She sketched a quick curtsey. "Forgive me, lord Tume. I did not mean to disturb you."

There was a strain in his courteous smile, but before he could speak others arrived.

One was a handsome young knight, Sir Hayden, if memory served. He gave her a full, courtly bow, smiling with unashamed delight as he drank her in. "Ah, Lady Maral. What a beauteous morning it is, and how gracious the Mother is to place such a fair flower in my path this morning!"

Caelerys barely had time to turn and react as a man in rich clothing of foreign cut came up the aisle just past lord Tume, followed by a groom leading a very large, pitch black horse who began to show off the moment he noticed Wraith. In response, the mare put her ears back and glared at him. The stallion was either too dense to know better or had never been around a mare out of season. The groom had his hands full, but his master behaved as if he wasn't even there. The man eyed the three of them: Caelerys, flushed with recent exertion and sudden self-consciousness, standing in between the lord and the knight. The latter of which was bowing in a way that hinted at something more than courtly respect.

"Oh goodness," he said casually, "I hope I am not intruding." His expression gave lie to his words, as his eyes seemed all too eager to read all sorts of unsavoury things into this. Caelerys recognized the man from court yesterday. Only a half head taller than she and broad, with the arrogant stance of an ambitious man who believes everything is his for the right price.

Caelerys began to blush, uncomfortable with being the focus of so much attention. She tightened her grip on her mare, keeping her focused with a hand up near her ear. "I... I am sorry, my lords. I fear I might be the one intruding. I... was just bringing my mare in but..." She took note of the worried look in the black man's eyes and where his attention had been: what appeared to be an empty stall. She peered over the edge and a look of horror crossed her face. Lying in the straw, groaning, was a white warhorse; his mane and tail were a grey that faded to black at the tips as if they were dipped in ink and the arch of his nose delicately concave. "Oh, the poor thing!" she exclaimed. "Is it colic? Have you checked his feed? Has anyone..." She blushed more furiously as she realized she was babbling. "Forgive me, of course you've had someone look at him. Do they know what is wrong?"

The knight stepped up behind her to look into the stall himself, standing close enough Cae could feel the heat of his body. "Oh, I am sure the Master of Horse has the matter well in hand," he said dismissively.

Tempest apparently decided than the man was taking too many liberties with her lady and jumped from the saddle to Caelerys's shoulder, facing the knight and half-spreading her wings in threat. She gave a low shrill of warning until the man finally took the hint and stepped back.

Lord Tume sighed. "Aye, Lady. It is colic, I fear. Perhaps southern oats do not agree with him, or the wet in the not warm enough air. Either way, old friend," he added to the horse, "you and I shall not ride today. Unless I can find a substitute horse, I shall have to withdraw from the tourney. But where does one find a warhorse an hour before one must ride?" he shrugged.

Caelerys decided she rather liked the warm, honey flow of his voice and accent, for all she was intimidated by him as a whole. She wanted to know more about him, but that was impossible at the moment. Sir Hayden was standing as though claiming the rights to her attention as if he had arrived first, and the other man was watching the whole with a hunger that made her deeply uncomfortable. She made herself speak. "I... I would offer you my own mount, my lord, but that I know she could not carry you in full armour. My... my brother might have a spare to loan. It would not be your own mount, I know, but far better than withdrawing all together. I could ask him," she offered. "Or my uncle."

It was clear the man was considering the offer when the foreign man cleared his throat pointedly. They looked over at him, expectantly. "Or you could take the gift I brought you." He gestured to the black horse still tossing his head and grunting to show off.

Caelerys watched the Northerner's face go pale then dark, his jaw tightening. She stepped up, dipped a very shallow curtsey. "Forgive me, my lords. Where are my manners," she said prettily, introducing herself. "And you?"

The man set one leg behind the other and leaned back over it as he bowed instead of merely bending. He waved his left hand in a grand flourish designed to flutter his broad sleeve and show off the scarlet fabric within it. "Ah, forgive me," he said obsequiously. "I am lord Carlan Araan, of House Araan, and master of textiles both foreign and domestic. Surely you have heard of the Woven Garden?"

She shook her head lightly.

He looked absolutely martyred. "Only the best in the kingdom. A shop with every conceivable textile of only the finest quality. If it is woven, we possess it. If we don't have it, we can get it. If we can't get it... it is not worth having." His smile as he bowed again was all merchant.

The other two men introduced themselves.

Lord Carlan laid a hand upon the stallion's neck. "I had heard of your dilemma, lord Tume and I thought to mend the matter. A gift," he smiled. It was the smile of a man who does not expect to be refused.

Caelerys thought to herself that the whole situation was suspicious. Lord Tume was a foreign dignitary. His horse, an impressive creature and sure to give him an advantage in the jousts, falls sick the morning of the first round and, almost before word has gone very far, this man appears out of nowhere, not offering a loan or a rent, but with a gift... And one of such value. Cae thought the whole thing fishy, and from the look in lord Tume's eyes, so did he.

"I thank you for the offer," he said. "But you may be unaware that, in my country, black horses are extremely unlucky. And to gift one is to wish... all the worst of things upon a person."

The thought crossed her mind that gifts in general were tricky things and likely came with all manner of strings. This one especially. The man did not seem to understand at first that he was being refused.

"They soak up the luck of one's house like their coats soak the sunlight," Tume explained. "And when they die, or leave your possession for whatever reason, they take your luck with them."

It finally seemed to dawn on lord Carlan that he was being given the opportunity to rescind a terrible insult. He began waving his groom away with the horse. "Ah, this animal is too unruly anyway. I question his training. But alas, I have no other beasts to offer. This was the best of my stable."

This made Cae even more suspicious. The growing discomfort of the moment was alleviated by the sound of an approaching horse and a man in a well scarred breast-plate. Willam stopped at the sight of the crowd in the stable aisle, and his eyes narrowed at seeing Caelerys in the middle of it. "Sister?" he asked warily, eyeing the knight standing too close to her.

Caelerys all but melted as he came in, smiled in relief. "Willam!" she exclaimed. This only made him even more wary.

He handed his squire his horse and stepped up to take her hand, bowing properly over it. "Did you enjoy your ride?"

"I did," she said softly, breathing a little easier as Sir Hayden moved further away. Even Tempest settled down, though she still kept a wary eye on the young knight. "Do you know everyone?"

He glanced around, nodding. "I do, greetings all." Everyone gave polite nods, though Hayden gave a shallow bow. Cae was beginning to think stable etiquette was different for men. She needed to remember to ask Willam later.

The horse in the stall groaned and Willam stretched a little to look in without moving from his sister's side. "Oh, bad luck there, lord Tume. Nothing serious I hope?"

"It can be. But even not, it will be days before he is ridable," lord Tume sighed.

"Did you bring a spare?" he asked, taking Cae's arm upon his own.

Tume shook his head. "The distance was too great, and space limited for our ship. I have never needed a spare. I thought your uncle might have one, if you have seen him?"

Willam shook his head. "Not since last night."

A loud, boisterous voice rang through the rafters from somewhere in the stable as if summoned, and made the horses dance. "Hidey!"

Both the knight and the minor lord looked at each other in confusion. Willam closed his eyes in embarrassed pain, and Lord Tume gave an amused smirk. Cae just stifled a giggle.

When no one answered, he bellowed again, "HIDEY!"

Cae nudged her brother who groaned.

"Damn it, boy! I said HIDEY!"

Willam sighed. "Ho," he answered with no enthusiasm whatsoever.

The barrel figure of Jehan Maral all but rolled into view, roaring, "How am I supposed to find your scrawny ass if you don't 'ho' my 'hidey'?" He waved a half empty mug of ale, splashing some of it near lord Carlan who barely dodged.

"Because I am not eleven any more?"

He aimed his mug at his nephew. "Have you any idea how hard it is to find anyone in this place?"

Lord Tume caught his wrist neatly before it could be spilled all over him and Jehan looked blearily up at him. "Hey! Look who I found!" Jehan beamed. He set his free hand upon his friend's chest. "Hey, you remember that red headed tart in the Galley the last time we were in the 'Point? You know, the one with the moons in her blouse and absolutely no gag..." At that point he noticed Cae, blushing furiously and quickly amended what he was going to say, "...gling. I mean giggling... I... anyway I found her...."

Tume gave him a tolerant grin and patted him on the shoulder, taking the cup from him. "My friend, you are in no condition to ride. You aren't even in your padding."

Jehan waved his hand. "I'll be fine by tomorrow."

"Today is tomorrow. The jousts start today."

Jehan suddenly seemed to realize his hand rested on a breast-plate and glanced over at his nephew and the grinning knight, both in the beginnings of armour. Just behind him, Willam's horse stood waiting. Even the massive stallion wore plate. "The jousts are now?"

His answer came in the form of a trumpet blaring, to call people to begin getting ready. "Ah, fewmets," he groaned, looking up at Tume. "How long have I... I can't ride like this."

The northern man sighed, setting his arm on his friend's shoulder. "Neither of us will ride it seems. Come, your cup is nearly empty and we can't have that."

Jehan started to walk off with him when the impact of what had been said, hit him. "Wait, you're not drunk. Why can't you ride? You've been looking forward to this since it was announced, itching for a tourney for the better part of the year!"

A dark thumb called Jehan's attention to the miserable stallion.

"Damn, Tume! What is it? Bad tooth? Bad hay?"

"The cold and the food, more like, Uncle," Caelerys said softly. "And he has no spare," she added plaintively.

"What? Ridiculous! You're riding mine." Tume began to protest but Jehan wouldn't hear of it. "A loan!" he added quickly. "My horse is yours... unless you lose it. Then you're paying the ransom." He began to haul his friend deeper into the stables. "But I have money on you, so I'll make it up. And don't worry, I didn't bring the black bitch. I brought the brindle."

Lord Tume turned to sketch an apologetic bow to everyone, touching his forehead as he nodded to Caelerys and then was dragged around the corner. The silence in their wake was temporarily shattered by the drunken bellow of 'STERLING COMPANY!' and the complaining whinny of horses. Cae winced, and Willam tightened his grip on her arm.

There was an awkward moment. Sir Hayden seemed to be trying to decide if it was safe to resume his attempted flirtation and lord Carlan actually looked slightly embarrassed. The tension was broken when Willam's squire cleared his throat. "We should get you suited and mounted, my lord. The Procession will begin shortly."

He turned, grateful for the reminder. "Of course, Harlan. Thank you." He took note of Mace and the other guard standing just beyond his horse and nodded them over. "Mace, would you escort my dear sister to the stands? Rowan, take Wraith to our section and have the grooms attend to her."

The man-at-arms trotted forward immediately to take the reins from her. "At once, my lord. My lady," he added with a bow as she set the reins in his hand and he led the mare off down the aisle.

Willam pointedly set Cae's hand on Mace's arm before turning back to the two remaining men. "My lord, sir, if you will excuse me?"

Sir Hayden grinned, realizing he had been out-manoeuvred. He bowed to Willam, slightly deeper to Caelerys. "Of course, my lord, my lady. I really should be doing the same."

"Good luck, brother," she smiled as he walked past them, skirting the groom slipping into the sick horse's stall to tend to him.

Caelerys was aware that lord Carlan Araan remained behind to watch them all leave.

As soon as they were out of the stable and earshot, she spoke quietly to Mace. "How much of that did you witness?"

"Enough, little bird."

"And what did you see?" she asked casually, reaching up to stroke Tempest's breast.

He was quiet a moment, schooling his words. "A Telman trying to indebt himself with the appearance of generosity."

"He was a Telman merchant, was he not? Before he married Lady Araan?" Mace nodded. "Telman merchants do not give anything away. And he knew that, to the Northmen of Alumet, it is considered an insult to actually refuse a gift. Though I do question his arrival with a horse to fit the lord's needs when very few even knew he was ill. The timing is suspect; the colour fortunate," she smiled.

"Do you think lord Tume shares your suspicion?" he asked carefully.

"I believe he does. Though he gave him the opportunity to rescind the offer before true insult was given. I have this feeling that wars have been fought over less. And the princes would have reacted a great deal less... kindly."

He chuckled at that, "You may be right."

Caelerys caught sight of the blacksmith's tent and veered them towards it. "I wish to speak to my brother if he has a moment."

Mace nodded and led her in.

Janem was bent over his anvil, gently tapping a rivet through a greave to attach a new strap. He gave her a nod as he saw her. "Thought you might stop in. Expected you earlier, though."

"Busy?"

"A mite." He made the final stroke and set his hammer down, tugged on the strap to test it. Satisfied, he handed it to the waiting squire who darted off into the crowds to bring it to his lord. "Now I have a minute. Won't as soon as the first round is run, though."

He cleaned his hands on a rag and leaned in to place a brotherly kiss on her cheek, careful not to touch her clothes with his. "You look a little flush. Have a good ride with the prince?"

She blushed, reaching up unconsciously to make sure her hair was not in disarray. "How do you know I rode in with the prince?"

"By now, everyone knows," he laughed. "You two came in pretty hard and fast."

She fidgeted with the leather cross-strap of her shoulder pad. "I met him under the queen. He asked me to join him, so I did. He was showing me the course for tomorrow."

He chuckled, almost unkindly. "I'll just bet that wasn't all he wanted to show you."

She scowled at him. "Janem!"

He shrugged, picking up a bent pauldron and examining it. "Well, he has a reputation. I knew both men before they were princes. I'll tell you more later. Here is not the place."

"Come to dinner."

He looked out over the field of pavilions and the knights beginning to ride past. "Don't think I'll have the time. Not until the tourney is over. I will likely be up to the rafters in repairs."

"Then I will come to the forge and bring you dinner," she said stubbornly, crossing her arms.

Behind her, Mace covered a smile, gave Janem a look that said 'you know better'.

He sighed, tossing the pauldron to his apprentice. "Fine. But nothing long and drawn out. I will have work to do."

"A simple dinner," she promised, turning to leave. "Oh," she exclaimed, turning back. "I almost forgot. Someone is bringing me a box for storing old books, an incensewood case. It might need new hinges or a new latch. Would you bring it to the house when it's done?"

He looked at her in confusion, wondering why he was being bothered with such trivialities and saw something in her bright eyes. He aimed his hammer at her. "Fine, tit for tat. But I want Fennel to serve those roseberry tarts she makes."

"I will make sure she knows you are coming," she smiled, and allowed Mace to guide her out of the forge and down to the viewing stands.

Caelerys glanced over the crowd. There were a lot of people in bright colours and bedecked in ribbons, many waving coloured fans. The hairstyles were far more subdued today, certainly less tall, and the clothing more suited to viewing outdoor events. One or two even carried small falcons, hooded and jessed like feathered ornaments. They cast small, slightly worried glances at her unbound falcon until they saw Tempest ignoring them completely. Mace found her a place in the third tier near other ladies and sat directly behind her upon the servants' bench. He felt a little uncomfortable surrounded by handmaidens who spent several minutes giggling at him behind their fans.

As she settled on the cushioned bench, her eyes took in the crowded fence lines before them, pressed to the wood with the lower estates, wearing their finest and waving ribbons and flowers to cheer on their favourites. She felt a tremor at the thought that it would be so easy for this crowd to turn ugly and tear people apart. They craved excitement that much, that they were not particular of its form. A trumpet blared again and the low stands erupted in rabid cheering, a large mass of hungry people held back from frenzy by the press of flimsy wood and expectation. It grew louder as the procession began.

A trumpeter in green and gold livery rode before the dragon banner and paused to shrill his message again. He rode out to the centre of the field and stopped, turning to face the stands, out of the path of the procession. "Ladies, lords, assorted and specific royalties..." he glanced over his shoulder at the unseated throng with a disdainful grin, "... oh, and you lot," he rolled his eyes and got a laugh from 'that lot'. "I bring before you the cream of the kingdom and the spice of foreign Alumet. Not to mention one or two of our common boys hoping to make squire and one day earn his spurs!" The horses began to parade down the lists behind him as he named them.

The first in the parade was Prince Valan, on a silvery black steed with a high step and a loose mane that floated like smoke in the air. His armour was enamelled green and chased in golden dragons. He was followed by the more arrogant of the two northern princes, Cyran, on a small, golden horse barded in a spotted hide. His armour was of unusual design, lighter, with curves and points and only on his chest, arms and upper thighs. A red horse's tail flowed from the top of his helm.

Many followed, cheered and howled at by the crowd and giggled over by the ladies around her. Willam came fifth, sitting high on his bay, his armour not as shiny or fancy as those around him, but stronger and more functional. The only decoration upon it was a rampant stag etched over his heart and the small, symbolic antlers on his helm. The Marrok brothers both rode behind him, each with a wolf pelt draped over their shoulder. Not far behind them was lord Tume, riding her uncle's horse.

They rode a circuit around the field before lining up in three rows before the royal pavilion, the new prince alone in front. They bowed their heads and dipped their lances in respect and the king, standing, raised his arm to them. The crowd cheered again and the knights turned to ride back to their starting points. One of the herald's boys ran out to the tilt rail and hung two small banners from the centre of it, right in front of the king's box. They were the spotted cat proper on a blood field of Onkelan, trimmed in gold for the royal son, and the twin wolves of the Marrok brothers divided, sable on white. The sable wolf was on top, indicating the older of the twins, but which that actually was, Caelerys was not sure.

Cae was surprised when her uncle sat down beside her. He still smelled of ale but seemed a little clearer of head, ...and damp around the collar. She hid most of her smile. "Uncle," she said politely, her eyes on the field. Even Tempest chirruped at him.

"Niece... oh good, I didn't miss it! Edler's got a tidy sum riding on this," he said, paying the bird the attention she requested, though briefer than she desired.

Cae nodded. "So that's Reled riding?"

"Edler," he corrected.

She frowned. "He bet on himself?"

Her uncle laughed, "And on his brother."

"How are they scoring this one? I didn't get the chance to ask earlier."

"Five points. Upper body only. One point per hit, two for breaking the lance, three for unhorsing. In that case, of course, you win the horse, though you are supposed to allow it to be ransomed."

Their conversation was interrupted by a single blast of the trumpet, the thunder of charging horses and the roaring of the crowd. The impact was loud, even though Marrok's lance skimmed off the unusual armour of the Alumet prince. The prince's lance broke against his shoulder but Edler maintained his seat. They turned at the end of the tilt, the squires passing them both a second lance, and charged again.

The prince still rode with complete confidence and arrogance. The Marrok, on the other hand, seemed almost to shrink in his armour, tucking down as far as the metal would allow and leaning forward on his mount. The stocky red horse had a wild look in his eye as he ran, and a wilder noise began to rise from the field, slowly silencing the on-lookers and confusing prince Cyran. They met on the far side of centre, the larger horse moving faster than the sleek golden one, and before anyone could gasp the prince went flying to the ground, Edler's lance unbroken.

Beside her, Jehan jumped to his feet roaring like a madman, along with the gathered of the kingdom, and even Tempest shrilled and opened her wings.

The day wore on slowly, eventually breaking for an hour as the sun reached its zenith. The crowd of commons thinned out, moving among the erected fairgrounds to drinking tents and pie vendors and to view the fairings for sale. Jehan escorted her to her brother's pavilion, to share the light midday meal and talk over what had happened so far. Willam had already been eliminated, by Jehan's friend lord Tume, no less, though he had kept his horse. He had lost by the splintering of a single lance and seemed in good spirits about it.

He greeted his sister gently and his uncle more jovially as his squire removed his armour piece by piece. Caelerys sat at the small table, accepting the pigeon pie the page offered her and observed that this was one of the few times she ever saw her brother smile.

"Not sore, boy?" Jehan chuckled, accepting an ale before touching his meat.

"To lose to lord Tume? Nay. It was an education."

Jehan shook his head, "I meant the other kind of sore."

"He hits like a rutting ram," he groaned, rubbing his newly freed shoulder.

"So do you," Jehan pointed out, laughing.

Caelerys looked up from feeding Tempest. "Are you hurt?"

Willam shook his head. "Stiff, but I'll be fine for the melee. Tilting was never my sport. There was something about that armour though.... It's not quite like what his prince wears, more like ours, but there are touches to it like the Northern styles. Makes the lance tip more likely to slither aside. I want Janem to take a look at it, if he'll allow."

Jehan stuffed half a mushroom tart into his mouth. "If he's not already otherwise engaged, I'll bring him to supper tonight. You can ask him yourself."

Caelerys ate quietly, only half listening to them talking, occasionally slipping bits to the bird on her shoulder. Eventually, she rose, had the page assemble her a plate and a jug of small ale and carried it herself to the blacksmith's tent. She slipped in through the side, out of the way of grooms bringing horses through to be shod, and to the small back table where Janem's tools were laid out.

He was bent over his anvil, bolting a grand guard into place on a breast-plate. He did not take long, checking his work and testing the rivets before handing it to the waiting squire. He stopped long enough to write something down on a piece of wood with a stick of coal before cleaning his hands on his apron and stepping back to his sister. "You didn't need to bring me food," he complained when she removed the napkin to reveal his dinner.

"Have you eaten?" she challenged.

"No," he growled.

"Have you fed your apprentices?"

"Aye."

"Then eat. I brought things easily wolfed."

He sighed, tearing off a piece of the soft white bread. "You spoil me, sister."

"When I can," she agreed.

"Listen," he began, leaning in over his plate to cover the conversation. "Tell Willam to talk to the Griffs."

"About?" she asked softly, setting her arms on the table and fiddling with an awl.

"Griffin hunting," he said.

She frowned, turning the tool over in her hand. "Really? Who? He'll need to know more if he is to arm for a hunt," she answered evasively, aware of the movement of people around them and the level of the ambient noise.

"Sea-wolves."

"Will he understand with so little?"

He nodded, washing down his pie with a swig of ale and turning to a knight entering the tent. "How can I help you, sir?"

Caelerys slipped quietly out the back and headed back towards the Maral pavilion. They were finishing up when she arrived, and a nod of her head sent young Harlan running out to watch the flap. Once they were alone, she interrupted their conversation.

"Forgive me, brother, uncle, but this is important. Janem has apparently overheard something regarding our old enemies," she said softly.

They looked up at her. Jehan continued laughing, but spoke softly through his laughter, "Sharks?" utilizing the lesser used term for sea-wolves.

She nodded. "He said to make time to speak with the Griffs."

"He say anything else?" Willam asked.

She shook her head. The men looked at each other over their cups while Cae picked at a crust of bread. "Well, something about hunting," she said as if she were trying to remember. "Griffin-hunting," she mouthed.

Jehan slapped his hand down on the table in drunken joviality. "Why don't we go see what kind of ale Tume brought with him?"

Willam got up, nodding. "At least he doesn't have to tilt his own prince in the next session," he chuckled. "Edler took care of that rather neatly." He took Cae's hand and kissed the back of it. "Will you be all right with Mace?"

"Go, do what you must," she said with shooing gestures. "This is as important as what I must do, which is to return to the stands and socialize."

He nodded. Jehan bent to kiss her cheek and the two of them left together, with all the appearance of drunken consolation. As Cae stood to leave, Tempest declared herself tired by hopping to the back of a chair and giving a plaintive little cry. She smiled at the falcon, pouring a little water into a shallow cup from an ewer on the table and leaving her to her own devices.

When Mace led her back to the stands for the last half of the day's jousting, she found it a far more social scene. There was more mingling than earlier as the next group of knights prepared themselves. The Marrok lords were milling among the ladies, flirting and handing out brightly coloured ribbons twisted into roses around a wooden stem. Cae had no idea which brother was which at this point, as both had already fought and won their rounds, and they deliberately did not wear anything to distinguish themselves one from the other. As one of them bowed before her and handed her a white one, he made a show of wiggling his gloved hand playfully, grinning at having thwarted her. She smiled back, accepting the fairing and his teasing.

"I thought it were the women who gave tokens at a tourney, my lord," she giggled.

"Oh, aye, aye. But why should they have all the fun? Or feel left out?" He turned to the young woman who had moved up beside Caelerys, bowed as he offered her a lavender one. "My lady of Roshan."

She giggled as she accepted it, touching it to her nose as if it were real.

"Alas," he sighed. "They have no scent."

She smiled coyly. "A matter easily remedied, my lord. Thank you."

His brother called out to him as the herald strode back out onto the sands and he quickly excused himself, bowing over both their hands.

Caelerys glanced at the girl next to her and both of them burst into giggles. When they regained control of themselves, the girl gestured to the seats and asked, "May I?"

Cae nodded, smoothing her skirts as she sat, her fingers toying with the folded petals of the ribbon flower. She introduced herself, as there was no one there to do it properly.

"Lady Lucelle Roshan," the girl smiled.

Cae mulled that over a moment. "The heir or one with the owl?" she asked.

She waved the rose dismissively, "Oh, neither. I'm the cousin."

"Please forgive me," Cae said immediately. "I've never been to court before and I am still trying to learn everyone."

"I have been told it takes a while," she laughed softly. "You're not alone."

Caelerys looked her over. She was a tall girl, about Cae's age and slight of frame though she had ample hips. The amethyst material of her gown was just the right shade to compliment her creamy skin and light brown hair. Her eyes were brown and green and drank in the rush of horses charging each other below them.

"Have you given anyone your favour yet?" asked Lucelle.

Cae shook her head, thinking of the embroidered length of deep blue silk tucked into her sleeve. She had sewn the silver stag's head with the rose between its antlers with her own hand. "I was told giving one's favour is a serious thing, not to be done lightly. It shows an interest and I do not know anyone here well enough to have an interest." She blushed slightly, realizing that aside from her brothers, she knew the prince better than anyone else here. Still, she did not know him well enough, and he was not participating in the tourney.

She glanced up at the royal box, saw him flirting with one of his sister's ladies.

A shout from the crowd as a knight was thrown from his horse drew her attention back to the field and to her new companion.

Dinner that night was not the most pleasant she had experienced since leaving home. Willam had been in a rage and their uncle not in a much better mood. While Cae had wanted to take this opportunity to get to know lord Tume a little better, there was little chance of that, as the men spent the entire meal complaining about House Kaladen.

Janem had overheard a couple of the Kaladen men-at-arms jesting about their plans for the grand melee, wherein they planned to go 'Griffin hunting'. They had discussed the possibility of getting away with 'inadvertently' killing members of the Griff household in the fight. It was not unheard of for men to be killed unintentionally in such contests, but it was disgraceful to do so deliberately.

They had spent the better part of the meal roaring about it and then making plans to ally with the Griffs and one or two other households and band together in the beginning to battle the Sea-wolves and their kine.

Cae tried to keep up but beyond asking the single question, "How can you be sure this is what they intend and weren't just... dreaming aloud?", she really couldn't follow the conversation.

Even Janem got caught up early on in the planning, relaying things he knew about the Kaladen arms, as well as weaknesses in their allies that should be mentioned to them or shored up.

Cae left dinner early, excusing herself politely, which went almost unnoticed, and disappeared into the kitchen. This was not an uncommon occurrence for her. She had been at dinners at home where this was the case, but there she had the wives and daughters of whomever was at dinner to talk to. Here, she was the only lady at the table, as all the men present were bachelors.

Fennel looked up as she entered the kitchen, smiled at her as she curtseyed. "Everything acceptable, my lady?"

She smiled back, shook her head. "Everything but the conversation, for which I cannot blame you. No, I was hoping you might have some of those roseberry tarts I asked about?"

Fennel chuckled, going to a shelf near the oven. She pulled four of the tiny confections from beneath a cloth and put them on a plate. She lay a white napkin over the top of them and handed the plate to her mistress. "Master Janem tends to steal out the side door, through the garden."

Cae smiled her thanks and slipped out of the kitchen through the back and into the inner courtyard. She found a perch on the low stone wall by the roses and sat down to wait.

The night was quiet for the most part, and the Southern Moon well up and bright, though not quite full. She could hear bustling in the kitchen across the garden, and the muted sounds of the men still at dinner or at planning, one. When she heard those sounds get a little louder then quiet again, she slipped her hand under the cloth and took out one of the tarts, biting daintily into it. She was sighing with delight as she heard the courtyard door quietly shut and smiled.

"You are right, Janem," she moaned. "These are heavenly."

The figure by the wall started at the sound of her voice, then resigned itself and joined her. "I wondered why they were not brought to the table. I thought you had forgotten. Or there were no roseberries." He helped himself to one of the tarts.

"They're actually called rose hips," she laughed. "And Fennel preserves them."

"I don't care what they're called or how she makes them, so long as she makes them," he replied, popping half of one into his mouth.

"Now, you were going to tell me about the prince?" she prompted.

He sighed, "Balaran, right?"

"Either or both. I will need to know if the queen has her way."

He paused at that, then shrugged. "Not much to say about Valan. He used to be in the city watch, a captain. Good at his job, very focused."

She shook her head, "But... he was the king's nephew, son of the grand duke, why would he...?"

"Lower himself?" he chuckled.

She waved her hand, "Not exactly, but surely there were other duties expected of him?"

"Aye, but they had their own ambitions, and their father indulged them, saw no reason not to. The old king had three sons, the eldest due to be wed... next gold month, in fact. There was no reason to expect his sons to inherit anything but what he could give them. If Naeden had become king, Rorlan would have become the archduke, when Prince Feran became the grand duke, and, while he would have had council responsibilities, all that would have come to his sons would have been advantageous marriages in hopes of someday marrying back into the reigning line. So, they found other things to occupy themselves. Prince Valan had the ambition of becoming the High Commander of the City Watch, and so worked his way up from patrol in Cheapside to Captain of the Docks. He is very focused. Had a reputation of being unbuyable, but fair. Nothing bad about him."

"Have you ever met him?" she asked quietly.

"Why, interested?" he grinned, teasing her, helping himself to another tart.

She blushed. "I haven't even met him yet. Though the queen brought his brother around...."

"And you went riding with Bal," he nodded. He shook his head, "Sorry, Prince Balaran. Still getting used to them having royal titles."

"I take it you knew him personally?"

He shrugged again, "I've drunk with both of them. They would come into the tavern I like and most of Valan's equipment came from my forge. Bal used to flirt with the owner's wife something fierce, but that's a game everyone plays. They know she'd never run away with anyone but her husband. Balaran was a student."

"What did he study?"

"What didn't he study?" he exclaimed. "He talked about turning the Western Bastion into a University, a place for art and learning, but he never had the power to do anything about it. He was not interested in becoming a Physician, but Academics and Science..."

She felt a chill run up her spine. "So he is a follower of the Eldest?"

Janem shrugged. "Don't know. I don't know him well, and religion was never a subject he discussed. There was once a debate in the tavern about whether the Church should have a hand in the curriculum of the Bastion and he stayed pretty much out of it. But then, that could have had something to do with the lady on his lap," he added pointedly.

She looked up. "Not an uncommon occurrence for a tavern. I understand that virtue is not required of the lower estates."

"She was a lady, not a whore. Some knight's daughter, I think. I wouldn't know." He set aside the now empty plate and dusted the crumbs off his hands. "This is what I wanted to warn you about. He's... a charmer. Has a reputation for seducing young women, and the ladies love him. I don't think he is a man you can expect fidelity from. Devotion maybe. Fidelity...?" he shrugged. "He's a good man or so I hear. They both are. Just be careful and sure of what you want out of life."

She waved her hand dismissively, "It's not like I will have any real choice. What father decides, father decides."

He caught the hand as he stood up and bowed over it. "And you are a fool to think you will have no say whatsoever. You are father's favourite. And if you abhor a man or love a man, father will find an ironclad reason to force either issue. Just be careful, and use that head I know you have."

She smiled at him. "Good night, Janem. I know you have a lot of work to do. Thank you for indulging me."

"Good night, dear sister. And good night to you, too, 'pest."

Cae looked and saw her falcon sheepishly walking around the corner of the flowerbed wall, shining in the golden light of the Southern Moon.

Cae laughed and held out her arm. The bird chirped and flew up easily, careful to land on the leather bracer on her wrist.

Janem chuckled. "Still following you around like a puppy?"

She nodded, scratching the white head in just her favourite place. "Still. She was most put out about not coming with me to court the other day."

He reached out and stroked her breast with a finger, laughing softly as she made a great show of putting up with it even as she puffed her chest to make it easier. "Speaking of court, are you ready for tomorrow?"

"A little nervous, but ready."

"Good," he said. He leaned over her and kissed her forehead. "I will see you before the ride. I want to check Wraith's shoes."

She nodded. "Sleep well, brother."

"Sleep well, sister."

With that he was gone, letting himself out the sally port and making sure the gate keeper drew the bar after him. She could just hear him whistling down the lane.

4

The next morning dawned foggy, but Caelerys was up before the sun, as was her wont. There were no battlements here to walk and watch the dawn from, but she found a balcony on the third floor on the outer wall from whence she could look out over the city all the way to the King's Bay. She let Tempest fly up and out over the city, to stretch her wings and enjoy the morning air. She leaned on the rail, taking note that even here, fifty feet above the street, there were precautions taken for barricades and security. As the sky grew lighter, she looked out over her neighbours and noticed that their heights were staggered. They were closer together than she had ever seen houses, but no building was the same height as the one beside it. Stag's Hall was an three impressive stories. The next house was only two, though much wider. Beyond it stood a grand, four story building that seemed narrower than her own for all it lorded above it. All along the quarter it was like this.

"It keeps thieves and invaders from climbing to one roof and easily entering the one beside it."

She turned, only slightly startled to hear Willam's voice, or that he had guessed what had her attention. He stepped up beside her and set his large hands on the rail. He was still in his nightshirt, though he had put trousers on. He smiled at her. "I did remember you do this."

She smiled shyly in return. "It is a habit," she admitted. "Though I would have thought you might have gotten dressed before leaving your rooms," she added, looking out over the city to find Tempest just hanging in the air on a current.

"This is my room," he said. When she looked at him, he nodded his head to a half open door on his end of the balcony. "I left this part open for you, because I knew you would be looking for the highest part of the house. This is the master's room and that," he pointed to the door opposite his, "is the mistress's room."

She grinned, "So that visitation is discreet?"

"Of course. Forgive me for not putting you up in those rooms, but... maybe later. Right now they must be kept open for Father, should he come."

"Will he be here at all?" she asked. She wasn't insulted by her rooms. She was also aware that her safety had been considered in the choice.

He shook his head, "Not unless something happens. His business...." He sighed. "He's missed the coronation. Unless he has something to report personally, there is little point now."

She nodded, reaching out her hand as the bird called in a warning before landing neatly on her wrist.

Willam took note of the white leather bands, much scarred by the bird's talons. "Given up on gloves?"

She removed a loop of lacing from Tempest's claw. "Not entirely. But given her near constant presence, Mace thought these more practical. Not to mention more discreet."

He nodded. "You should be able to bring her today, though she cannot ride with you. You may have noticed some of the nobles carry them like they wear jewels, and yours says more about your place in this world than a strand of rubies."

She looked worriedly up at him, even as she fed the bird a titbit of meat. "Will she cause me trouble? Jealousy?"

"Oh, certainly. But far better to announce yourself with this subtlety. That you wear few jewels and your clothes are less ostentatious, yet carry a bird of her value tells the court that you are practical but of means as well as connected."

"And this is important?"

"Very," he answered solemnly. "Impressions are key. Now, you need to go get ready. You'll want time for your breakfast to settle before you go riding pell-mell through the wood."

She smiled and gave him a pert little curtsey. "Of course, brother." She turned with a sweep of her skirts and flowed into the house with the bird on her arm.

He found himself laughing softly as he turned back to his own rooms to dress.

Due to fog, the equestrian had been postponed until closer to noon.

The Maral contingent had gone to the tourney grounds early and spent the time waiting in Willam's pavilion. Janem had checked Wraith over and declared her fit, and Mace had gone over her tack personally. Lady Petra even joined them for a little light refreshment while they waited for the sun to burn off the mists. She turned up her nose when she discovered Cae would be riding astride.

"Ladies should ride side-saddle," she sniffed. "Lady Alten will be riding side-saddle."

"And lady Alten will lose," Cae said flatly, sipping at her water.

Lady Petra glared coldly. "It is unthinkable that women should be allowed to compete with men anyway. Ladies should not race horses."

"Nonsense," Willam declared, holding out his mug for a refill of his small ale. "This and archery is the one sport where women can compete. It is right that a woman be able to ride fast and hard, and shoot, Mother forbid that she has to. If ever her train is set upon or attacked, it is good to know that flight is an option. Besides, a sporting woman is a healthy woman." He caught her look and added, "And healthy women make strong children, and live long enough to bear them."

The dame had the grace not to say what was on her mind and let the matter drop. They ate the rest of the light meal in quiet speculation about who else would be on the field and which would be real competition. Not long after, the trumpet sounded, and a crier walked through the tents calling for riders to prepare and mount up.

Cae took a deep breath, confident in her ability, but nervous about the others involved. Willam set his hands on her shoulders and looked down into her eyes. "You will be fine. You are a good horsewoman," he said. "I know that now. You've been trained by the best. I have every confidence in you."

"But?" she asked, seeing one in his face.

"Be careful. This is a hunt like any other, just without a quarry at the end. They are taking precautions, but you can still get hurt."

She smiled, finding her resolve. "I know how to fall. And I don't intend to be close enough to any other riders to have to worry about that either."

"Good," he said, taking her arm and leading her outside to where his squire stood with Wraith.

The mare was itching to go. Caelerys paused to set her hand on the mare's neck and whisper to her in Vermian. The silvered nose nudged her and calmed down, ready to get to business. She then turned to Mace who stood by holding an antsy Tempest on a gloved fist. A few whispered words from her and the bird also settled. "She'll stay put," she told the bowman who bowed his head with a proud smile.

Willam handed her into the saddle, helping her to settle her split riding skirt and make sure all the last minute adjustments were made. He held the bridle himself and walked her along the tourney grounds towards the lists where the riders were to parade first. He gave her horse a last pat before leaving her to join their uncle in the stands.

Caelerys looked over at the other riders on the field. There weren't as many as she had expected, only a dozen, and most of them women. All three of the Roshan women were there: Balyra clearly wearing some form of trousers under her skirt, though Onelle was not and quite self-conscious of the fact, though both of them rode astride. Their cousin sat side-saddle, though she seemed confident in her seat. There were three men: a knight whose markings she did not know; a pale blonde man with a moustache in the clothing of the Royal guard, though without the tabard; and finally, a man in a black, hooded jerkin on a sterling grey. Cae hid her smile.

A boy in a herald's tabard crossed in front of them and gave them the order in which they were to parade past the royal box, instructing them in what they should do while a group of pages tied a set of coloured ribbons to the bridle of each horse. "Your order is not of rank," he announced, "but has been drawn by lot. You will line up before the box. My lord," he nodded to the unknown knight who was to be first, "you will stop and turn when you come even with the Cygent banner in front of the stands." The knight nodded. "When the last person is in place, you will bow as one to the royal box, and when dismissed, you will wheel and march to the open end of the lists, forming up right to left. When the signal is given you will ride."

At a trumpet blast from the field, he bowed and got out of the way, gesturing for them to proceed.

Cae was nearly overwhelmed by the roar that greeted them as they stepped out. Wraith pranced, taking delight in the adoration of the crowd. She was fifth in the line, which placed her before the edge of the royal box. The herald stood just below the box, facing them, and when they were all in place, he signalled them and they bowed in the saddle. Even Wraith performed her little curtsey to the pleasure of the mass of people.

The queen smiled at her and the princess hid a giggle behind her hand. Cae took note that only one of the princely twins was in the box with the king, which confirmed her suspicions about the hooded man. She would have her work cut out for her with the prince on the field. The herald stepped towards them at a signal from the king. "The course is clearly marked with wardens along the length of it in interest of fairness. When you enter the wood it is advisable to stay upon the path. On the field before and after the wood, there are staked markers, remain within them. At various points there are beribboned rings hanging from hooks. You will take only the rings that correspond to your own ribbons. Taking or knocking down the rings of others will be considered unsportsmanlike and penalized. This is not just a course of speed but also dexterity. The winner will be the one with the most rings and the fastest time. There are five for each of you. May the Mother grant you victory and safety." He raised his hand and they turned to march to the starting line.

Caelerys noted that her ribbons were blue and black. This was perhaps as random as their positions. She stepped to her place, adjusting her seat, and she felt Wraith settling in underneath her, more than ready for the call to the hunt. It came within a moment, a trumpet blare and the maddened shouting of the crowd. Wraith threw herself along the wide path, just ahead of her neighbours. She was by no means at the head of the pack, but easily in the top half. The first set of rings were set on opposite sides of the route and there was some scrambling as people had moved beyond their starting sides. Cae had remained on the right side of the field and slowed only a little as someone moved in front of her. Her ring was just ahead and she could afford to let them pass her to get theirs. A few seconds later and the black and blue ribboned ring was trailing in her hand and she spurred Wraith out of the way of a few more reckless riders.

She found a deep hook hanging on the front of her saddle by her knee and slipped the ring onto it, concentrating on the next set which was just before the edge of the wood. She saw she had a little bit of a straight-away as it began to narrow and clicked Wraith to close the gap. She let the mare deal with her footing and the running while she looked ahead for the next ring. Hers hung from a tree branch on the left side, just as they entered the wood.

She manoeuvred herself up and to the left, took note that these were too high to reach the ring itself, but not so the trailing ribbons. Still, she had to stand in the stirrups to reach, and had to time it carefully as the rings were within two hand-spans of each other. She caught the tail end in her hand and dropped back down, slipping the ring on its hook and settling in for the wood portion of the ride.

The first part was as the prince had informed her, wide and easy, a good place to get ahead of others. There were a few jumps, but nothing too difficult even for the side-saddles, though she witnessed a horse baulking at one of them. As she approached, a page was taking the lady's bridle and leading her into the wood around the jump. She noticed the lady was not released until she herself had flown past. She passed one other person, another side-saddle, before they burst out onto the river's edge.

As the prince had said, the path was marked, and she could see the ribbons blowing up river where the course turned back towards the wood. That would be the true test. Halfway down the course, she could see the hooked poles all on the river side and picked out where her ring hung. She gauged her competition and raced for it, knowing this was probably the last real chance to put some distance between her. Not far ahead of her, she saw the obnoxious black stallion from the stables the day before, ridden by the pale blonde with the moustache. Wraith saw him too and knuckled under in her determination. She kicked up speed, her lighter hooves not caring about the change in terrain from meadow to packed sand.

She pulled up even with him, on the inside between the beast and the poles. The man saw her coming and edged over, trying to bull her out of the course bounds and onto the wrong side of the hook so she couldn't grab her ring. Wraith was having none of it, and slipped through the narrow space between the poles so quickly the brute actually collided with his own post. She snatched her ring from the next one as the mare cut back onto the course so sharply Wraith's tail slapped the stallion in the face. Cae could not tell whether that was deliberate or not, but the mare settled down to cocky and satisfied as they pulled away.

Cae steadied her pace. The wood was coming up quickly, and she saw the prince's horse vanish into it just ahead of her. This was going to be the real challenge. There should be no more rings until the meadow, just hard, skilled riding. She thought quickly back at how many people were behind her and calculated that, at the moment, there were only two people unaccounted for. The prince, whom she had just seen, and the knight. She reached forward to stroke Wraith's neck, whispering Vermian words to her, "Easy, girl. This is the rough part. Steady wins this from here. If we pass them, we pass them. If not, we just have to make sure we get the last two rings."

The ride went as she remembered it: broad streams, winding path, occasional small trees and clear straight-aways. The only people she saw were the judges and lower estates who had come to watch. She did not see another rider until she reached the big jump where folk were clustered at one end. A horse was standing off to the side, favouring a leg. "Clear?" she called, not wanting to jump if there were people in the way. A voice bellowed back "Clear!" and she spurred Wraith for the jump. She did not look back, as the path began to wind here and she needed to concentrate. But the horse had been dark, not grey, so it had not been the prince who had taken the fall. She had noticed, however, a ring just past the tree, wrapped in red and blue, lost on the jump. Her hand went to her own collection without looking, her fingers counting three.

She relaxed and leaned into the ride. The woods were coming to an end quickly, with only the meadow, two rings and the prince ahead of her. At this point, it did not matter if he beat her to the line, so long as she got both of the up-coming rings.

When she burst out into the field, she saw the prince easily, sitting backwards in his saddle like a fool to the delight of the crowd. She ignored him, took stock of where the rings were. The first was on a high pole on the right hand side, and the last on a low pole on the left. The course wound a gentle s-curve through the field. She unwound the reins from her hand, leaving them loose in her glove and asked for a last burst of speed. She had heard the sound of hooves in the wood behind her, and the shouts of the watchers cheering them on. The fence of the field was packed with people, all screaming and cheering the last leg of the race.

She snatched the high ring in her right hand, set it onto her hook and swapped the reins into its place with one smooth movement. Then she bent low over the saddle, riding into the curve and leaning sideways, carefully balancing her weight. As the ring all but fell into her hand, she heard the crowd cheering the prince as he passed the fence to victory. She ignored it, rolling back up over Wraith's neck with the ring still in her left fist and barrelling through the finishing posts.

She slowed her horse down, turning her through an opening in the cheering crowd to a small side paddock where the prince was walking his horse. She made sure she was out of the way of the next people riding in and allowed a groom to take her bridle for the moment. One of the herald's men came up with his list, making a mark beside her name and requesting her rings. She handed them over as the blonde man on the black stallion came through, faster perhaps than he should have. She was glad she had made sure to be out of the way.

It did her no real good, however, as he trotted over to her and snapped at the herald. "I want her disqualified!" he demanded.

The herald looked shocked, glanced around looking for his superior. He waved the man over desperately. "My lord," he said to the blonde, "please refer such complaints to the Herald himself, as I am only to record rings and order. On that matter," he added, buying time for his superior to cross the grass, "how many do you have, lord Mambyn?"

"Four, thanks to that wench," he spat, tossing them down.

Caelerys stiffened in the saddle but said nothing. She had noticed the prince riding over, his face still obscured. She kept a tight grip on Wraith, both by knee and rein. The mare was starting to shake her head, irritated at the nearness of the ill-mannered brute. The stallion was still showing off and resisting all attempts of his rider to remain perfectly still.

"What is going on here, my lord, my lady?" Herald Morlan asked as he approached, keeping clear of the two horses. "Tetch, others are coming in, go record."

The man needed no second urging.

Lord Mambyn launched immediately into his complaint. "I want her disqualified, Herald."

"On what grounds, my lord?" he asked calmly.

"Riding a mare in season, for one. My horse gets uncontrollable around her. See?" he exclaimed as the stallion kicked up his back heels as he twisted his head.

Wraith's ears went back and she took a step backwards.

The Herald suddenly bowed deeply. "Your Highness," he said.

Lord Mambyn looked up as Cae bowed in the saddle when she saw the prince toss back his hood to reveal himself. He mumbled a hasty and belated "Your Highness," and bowed.

The prince was smiling, but Cae could see something dangerous behind it. "Are you claiming that your stallion is more virile than mine?" he asked with apparent casualness.

The man looked slightly flustered. "Of course not, Your Highness."

"Then she can't be in season or Korizon would be just as unruly. As would every other stallion in the race. Perhaps your horse just doesn't know how to behave around a lady."

Cae watched the man turn red from throat to ears and bite back the response he wanted to issue. "He is new, Your Highness. I have no real idea of his training," he admitted.

"Now, you had other objections?" the prince prompted.

This seemed to mollify the man and he launched once more into complaint mode. "She left the course. And in returning to it, cut us off so close my horse pulled back, and then she knocked my ring from its hook so I could not get it."

"Hmm," the prince mused. "Where was this?"

Cae remained silent. She would not answer the charge until she was asked to, not about to be drawn into an argument in front of the prince or the small crowd they had drawn.

"Down by the beach," he responded imperiously, convinced he was about to get his justice.

Cae became aware of Wraith's breathing, and of the dampness on her neck. "If you will excuse me, Your Highness?" Cae said softly, nodding her head to her horse.

He looked the mare over. "Of course, Lady Caelerys."

Cae dismounted immediately and handed her off to the groom with a pat on the neck and a kind word. She thanked the groom then turned to face the two mounted men and the herald, waiting patiently.

The Herald took his cue from the prince's look and waved over another of his servants. "Are the wardens coming in yet?"

"Slowly, sir. Some are in already, but not all of them."

"Inform me the moment the beach wardens are in, the ones by the rings."

The man nodded and bowed to the company before trotting off to delegate and obey.

Others were already riding slowly around in circles, winding their horses down. A great deal of attention was being paid to this off-centre little cluster, all curious as to how it would play out, which was making Cae uncomfortable but she was determined not to show it.

The Herald turned to lord Mambyn and gave him a slight bow. "If that is all your complaints, my lord, we shall wait upon the report of the beach warden at the rings. I will inform you when they come in. Your Highness, would you wish to be present for the report?"

"I would."

"Then if the lady and I may be excused, I will escort her safely from the paddock."

"Please do," he nodded, dismounting from his own horse.

The herald bowed and Cae dropped into a deep curtsey. The prince bowed over her hand. "My lady," he smiled. Releasing her, he nodded to lord Mambyn, "my lord," he said dismissively, then began walking his own horse.

Cae set her hand upon the herald's proffered arm and allowed him to lead her out of the paddock.

"I do apologize for the unpleasantness," he began.

She smiled, squeezed his arm lightly. "Thank you, but unnecessary. It is not you who has issued complaint."

"Is there cause for his complaint?" he asked gently.

She hesitated a moment. "There is cause *for* complaint."

He looked over at the ambiguous way she had put it. "Do *you* wish to issue a complaint, my lady?"

"Not at the moment, my lord herald. I am content to wait and see what the wardens have to say before I speak of the matter. It was a race after all. Things happen. Though for the record, Wraith is not in season and has warned that stallion before, yesterday in fact, that his advances are not welcome. Perhaps he is just young and never been around a mare before."

"Perhaps." He gave her hand a pat as he led her just past the crowd at the edge of the paddock. "I am afraid I must leave you here, my lady. I have work still."

"Perfectly fine, my lord herald. I need a little walk myself. I shall stay on the main thoroughfare between here and the blacksmith's when you are ready to summon me."

"Thank you, my lady."

She watched him walk away before turning herself and headed towards her brother's stall with slow, measured steps. It had been a hard ride, and she needed to walk as much as her horse and for the same reason. She heard the beat of wings just before Tempest landed on her shoulder, pipping her hello and nuzzling her hair. She smiled, stroking the bird as she walked. It was not long before she heard Mace's voice calling, "There she is, my lord."

A moment later, her brother and the bowman caught up with her. "Shall we go to my tent and wait, sister?"

She shook her head. "I promised the herald I would walk this path until he needed me. And I do need to keep walking."

He tilted his head. "Trouble?"

She shrugged, "Maybe not."

He frowned, but she would not answer.

They walked in silence, had nearly reached the cluster of blacksmith tents when a page wearing the herald's badge caught up with them. It was the boy, Tommet, from the day before. He guided them to a green and gold striped tent. Within were the herald and some of his men, the prince and one royal guard. Lord Mambyn arrived just after she did, glared at her and Willam but took his place beside her before the herald.

The herald bowed to all and cleared his throat. "The mare has been examined and she is not, in fact, in season. The stable hands claim the stallion reacts that way to all females. The warden on the beach has given his evidence, and it has been corroborated with two others strung along the same area. It has been assessed that lord Mambyn Asparadane has no grounds for complaint. Witnesses claim it was your own horse which knocked the ring from its post."

Caelerys noted the tightening of the man's fist, but he gave no other indication of his feelings.

"The Lady Caelerys Maral, on the other hand, has several," the herald continued. He turned to her. "Would you like to issue complaint, my lady?"

She glanced over at the man, then at her brother and finally the prince. "No, my lord herald. Distasteful as the act may have been...." There were other words for the act on her tongue, but she kept them there, feeling they would serve no purpose spoken so directly. "It was, after all, a race. Preventing me from reaching my goals was a strategy like any other. I was not harmed. I will not complain."

The herald nodded. "Then, if His Highness is agreeable, you are dismissed."

The prince watched her a moment, but nodded his assent.

"Very well then, keep yourself available. The decision will be made shortly and you will be called to the lists for the announcement."

Cae and Willam allowed lord Mambyn to stalk out ahead of them. As Mace was reaching to hold back the tent flap, they heard the herald sheepishly tell the prince, "You, as well, if it please Your Highness. You were a contestant after all, and appearances..."

Prince Balaran laughed. "Oh, nonsense. I should be disqualified myself. I was clearly showing off. It was... unchivalrous."

The herald glanced at his assistants. "Perhaps we should discuss that at length."

Willam led Cae out of the pavilion and towards the lists. She could feel the tension in him. Finally, he drew her aside at the entrance to the viewing stands. "Why did you not complain?" he asked tightly. "He was clearly trying to cheat."

She shrugged, "He only tried to force me off the course. He did force me off the course, tried to prevent me from getting my ring. He didn't take mine or knock it off intentionally, so it was technically not against the rules. He has paid for it by losing his own ring in the matter. While distasteful, it was not technically against the rules."

"But it was dishonourable," he protested. "He tried to disqualify you because he failed."

"And how would our House have been served by antagonizing him because of it?" she countered. "Think like a courtier not a big brother. He is already not our friend, I saw no point in making him our enemy."

He sighed, "And what, dear sister, makes you think you didn't anyway?"

She frowned, "I didn't press complaints he knew I had every right to press. Why would he dislike us more because of it?"

"You are wise in so many ways, Cae, and yet so naïve in others. You outshone him. You out-rode him, out-manoeuvred him and made him look like a petty fool. And in front of his prince, no less. He is a member of the royal guard. That the prince came to your defence..."

They were interrupted by the herald's trumpet. He escorted her to the end of the list and left her with plenty to think about before rushing off to join their uncle in the stands. As she moved out onto the sands with the other riders, she noted that Mace remained at the opening to wait for her. Some of the ladies smiled at her, and the Roshan girls surrounded her. She noticed the knight, aided by a squire, with his arm in a sling and a laughing wince on his face. She was glad he was not badly hurt.

When they reached the place where they had stood not long ago on horseback, they bowed as one before the royal box. When the king commanded them to rise, he called the herald to him, choosing to make this announcement himself.

"The four fastest riders were: Prince Balaran Alvermian, the Lady Caelerys Maral, lord Mambyn Asparadane, and the lady Balyra Roshan." He paused for the cheering of the crowd before he continued, "Only the ladies Maral and Roshan collected all five rings. Therefore, the first prize of a complete riding set: bridle, saddle and strap barding, is awarded to the Lady Caelerys Maral. Second, a length of velvet, to the lady Balyra Roshan. And the final prize of a silver clasp goes to my son, Prince Balaran Alvermian." The king then set aside the parchment and raised his hand and the crowd began cheering once more.

The fête afterwards was to be a grand affair, held in the gardens for the First Estate, and on the tourney grounds for the second and third. Caelerys imagined that party to be more of a country fair and was more than a little envious when her brother Janem informed her that was where he would be tonight. He kissed her and congratulated her, and promptly disappeared into the crowds with his apprentice, leaving a couple of journeymen to watch the forge whilst he fetched food and drink for those who would be working late into the night. She sighed and allowed the ecstatic Willam to escort her up to the castle gardens.

It was a long walk, almost a parade itself through the city gate and between the castle wall and the city. Those of the Middle Estate who were home, were hanging out second story windows throwing flowers and cheering. Cae clung to Willam's arm while trying not to appear to be. She had gotten a little used to riding through crowds, but walking among them still made her nervous. Tempest, while she had been nervous at first, was preening as if all the adoration was for her.

A buffet had been spread out in the garden, near the fountain: all manner of meats and fruits and other delicate things, sweetmeats and little cakes, tiny pies. Two great casks stood on barrel stands on one side, one of ale, the other of wine, though other drinks were available too. Willam helped her to fill a plate and acquired her a goblet of wine before taking her deeper into the garden to where open pavilions were set up over couches and seats. He seated her, placing her goblet for her on a little table within easy reach and whispered to keep her eyes on it.

"Why, where are you going?" she asked.

"To speak to men," he said, looking a little uncomfortable in the presence of all the women.

"You are supposed to be finding a wife, brother. You'll have to talk to them at some point," she added softly.

He leaned closer. "No, I just have to talk to their fathers."

She gave an exaggerated gasp and widened her eyes at the horrifying thought. "And not meet her at all first? What if she is absolutely horrid? Or spends money wastefully, or... Mother forbid, hates hunting?"

He laughed softly, "Those are your fears, little sister." He kissed her forehead, "There are steps to these things. The first is to find out who's available and from where." He left her staring after him as he bowed his way out of the milling nobility to find his friends.

She was left feeling very exposed for all of a minute, watching his retreating back. Then Tempest squawked a warning as several women descended upon her.

"That was some riding!" exclaimed Lucelle.

Cae blushed, "Not really, but thank you."

One of them, Balyra, gave a short, sharp laugh. "I saw you tangle with Asparadane. The brute tried to run you into the poles. That took some serious skill. I heard he claimed you knocked his ring off the hook?"

She lowered her eyes, nodded ever so slightly, "So he claimed. I did not see, so I do not know, but I was certain Wraith and I struck nothing. ...Well, she slapped his horse," she giggled, "but he was being impertinent."

The ladies giggled in chorus.

Balyra humphed, "Well, *I* saw it. I was certain you'd lost your ring, but that was quite the catch. That was so close I'm surprised she only hit him with her tail."

Cae could feel the heat rising in her cheeks, diverted herself by feeding titbits off her plate to her bird. "Heat of the moment. I've had closer calls hunting, honestly."

"Did you see the knight who fell at that last jump?" asked a slightly thinner girl sitting beside Balyra. Her mid-brown curls framed her heart shaped face neatly.

She shook her head, taking a sip of the wine for courage. "He had already been moved from the path when I passed. I am glad he was not badly hurt, though I fear for his horse. He was favouring a leg."

The girl tossed her curls, smiling, "Oh, he'll be fine. I saw him in the stables. The Master of Horse said it was only a sprain. He won't be able to ride him for the jousts though, so he may have to drop out."

Caelerys smiled knowingly, "That wasn't his warhorse. Though he will likely drop out due to his arm."

A third young woman whom Cae did not know spoke up with a tight, knowing smile. "Oh, he was already knocked out. My brother, lord Mambyn, beat him yesterday. Almost won his horse."

There were general murmurs of mixed response to that. "How did you know that wasn't his warhorse?" the thin girl asked Cae. "Do you know him?"

Lady Balyra sighed, "Onelle, it's simple. The horse he rode in the equestrian was not big enough to carry a man in armour. He was built for speed."

Caelerys saw the approach of a red brocade gown, glanced up, took note of the face above it and stood so quickly Tempest squawked a complaint and hid behind her skirts. "Your Majesty," she said with a deep curtsey.

The others looked as she stood, and swiftly joined her in bowing.

"Rise, ladies," she smiled. "I do not believe any of you have met my daughter, Princess Syera?"

"Your Highness," they chorused.

The queen affected introductions, beginning with Cae as the highest ranking among them. "The ladies Balyra and Onelle Roshan. Balyra is heir to the Valenwood," she added to her daughter. "And you know, lady Malyna Asparadane."

"Please to meet you," said the princess with a shallow curtsey. She blushed slightly, suddenly remembering she did not have to curtsey to anyone but her parents any more. She bowed her young head gracefully and her mother smiled warmly.

"Please do not let us interrupt the conversation," the queen said.

"Oh, we were only speaking of the day's competition, Your Majesty," lady Balyra explained. "Nothing of import."

"Oh nonsense. It is a shame about Sir Granyon though. I understand it was a most spectacular spill."

"None of us saw it, Your Majesty. I passed just after. I am merely glad neither he nor his horse was more harmed than they were," Cae said softly.

"Well, I hope you ladies enjoyed it, none-the-less." She glanced at lady Malyna, "those that competed. Will any of you be competing in the archery the day after tomorrow?" She looked directly at Cae at this, with a knowing smile that made her slightly uncomfortable.

"I will," answered Balyra.

"I'm more inclined to use birds than bows," Onelle confessed.

"Oh, I never could," Malyna blushed. "Mother would never approve." Her eyes flicked to Caelerys with either envy or remonstrance, Cae was not sure which.

The queen looked at Cae in askance as she stood silent. She flushed a little. "Aye, Your Majesty. I am looking forward to it."

"I am given to understand that you are quite good."

She felt the blush run to her throat. "I... I am better than my brothers," she offered.

The queen laughed. "That is not how I am hearing it told. I am counting on you, my dear. Young Avondyl and I have a small wager on you."

Caelerys did not know what to say to any of this. "I... I hope I do not disappoint Your Majesty."

The queen smiled knowingly, looking her over in a way that seemed to assess her to the bone.

The princess finally noticed Tempest. She gave an adorable little gasp. "How beautiful!"

The queen turned indulgently, moving so that her daughter had a clearer view. As all eyes turned on her, Tempest perked up.

The princess moved in front of her mother, careful of not moving too close too fast. Tempest turned her dark eye upon this creature in gold brocade. "What a lovely falcon," she whispered.

"Thank you, Your Highness. We are quite fond of each other, for all the trouble she gives me. Would you like to touch her?"

The pale lavender eyes lit up, turned briefly from the bird to her mistress. "Could I? Is she safe?"

Cae smiled, "I would not have brought her if she were not." She pulled her left sleeve back a little bit, exposing her bracer, and Tempest hopped eagerly to her wrist. "She will only attack if I am attacked or if I tell her she can. Unless of course you are a mouse. She just attacks those without question. Are you a mouse, Princess?" she asked with mock seriousness.

The princess gave her a shy, girlish grin. "Nay, my lady." Her mother's hand at her back made her stand up straighter. "I am a Princess Royal."

Cae turned to the bird. "Did you hear that, Tempest? She is a Princess Royal. Where are your manners? I know I taught you better than that. Jelma, teya." At this, the bird half spread her wings as if spreading her skirts and executed the prettiest little curtsey.

The princess clapped with delight and the ladies giggled or

murmured appreciatively. "Marvellous," she said and slowly raised her hand.

An unseen twitch from Cae and the bird stood, puffing her chest out. "Just there, at the breast."

The princess's slim hand reached out, softly stroking the breast feathers. "So soft," she breathed.

Lady Malyna watched the bird, fascinated. "She is quite beautiful. Is she heavy? She's so big."

Cae gave a little frown of concentration. She had never thought her heavy before.

"You get used to the weight," said lady Onelle. "You really do. Unless you got them grown. Did you train her yourself, Lady Caelerys?"

There was something knowing in the girl's eye that made her smile. "Aye, almost since she hatched. She's known no other mother or handler. Sometimes," she added, glancing at the princess with a conspiratorial eye, "if I don't take her with me, she'll walk behind me through the castle like a little hound."

"She walks?" asked lady Malyna with a frown. "Why wouldn't she fly?"

"Gauvan often run after prey along the ground, for surprising distances sometimes. Best way to catch mice in a castle where flying is narrow business," she replied. "Granted, she'd rather ride, but..." she turned back to the bird, scratching with a fingernail at the base of her neck, "I swear, one of these days, I'm going to teach her to carry my train if she's going to follow me like a lady in waiting," she chuckled.

The ladies laughed.

The queen set her hand on her daughter's shoulder. "Well, my dear, it has been lovely, and I am sure that Syera would love a visit from you and mistress Tempest," she added, giving the bird a royal nod, "but as much as I may wish to continue this conversation, there are other obligations."

The princess quickly wiped the look of disappointment off her face and became the image of the perfect courtier.

Caelerys curtseyed. "I would be honoured, Your Majesty, Your Highness. I promise I will let you hold her next time if you like?" She watched the girl's eyes light up. "But right now I am sure there are others who would like to make your acquaintance."

The queen nodded in approval and led her daughter away as the ladies dropped into curtseys.

They stood again when the royals were away and Lucelle immediately began gushing, "Oh, my word, we just had a conversation with the royal family!"

Her cousin Balyra elbowed her. "Oh, settle down, Lucelle. You're making yourself out to be some country bumpkin."

She tossed her head in frustration, "We live in the literal middle of nowhere."

"Or the middle of everywhere, depending on which way you view it," Cae grinned. This made Lucelle laugh.

"Point taken." She suddenly seemed to notice something. "How come yours isn't hooded like everyone else's."

"A very bad experience," she sighed. "When we were manning her, after she got old enough, we had her hooded in a busy room, so she would get used to the sound of people."

Lady Onelle nodded, familiar with the process.

"However, there was one young man, one of my father's wards, with a mean streak. He started to torment her when no one was looking. One day he frightened her so much, she tried to flee, ended upside down, flapping desperately to right herself and screaming blind."

The ladies looked on in horror and Onelle covered her mouth.

"We caught him, mostly because he still had one of her feathers in his hand. Father sent him home in disgrace. Ever since then, if you hood her, she'll do nothing but scream. It makes her panic, not calm. But she has learned to attack only what she is instructed to, or that attacks her or me, so there isn't an issue. You only hood when travelling, or you want to control what they see and react to, and sometimes when hunting to keep them focused only on the prey you want. Most raptors do not fear what they cannot see. Mine was taught to do just that."

Cae turned to Onelle, glad conversation had been turned to one of the few subjects she could discuss without her shyness getting in her way. "I understand you have an owl?"

The younger girl nodded vigorously. "Twill is a horned owl."

"Fairly large bird," she mused, sharing a smile with the girl. She was certain they had both heard the line 'Isn't that a mighty big bird for a small girl?' too many times to count.

"I got him when he was small, so I got used to him as he grew. Our falconer helped me to train him."

"Why didn't you bring him?" Lucelle asked. "Lots of people brought their birds. They just about wear them like brooches." She pointed out one lady who had a small sparrowhawk seated on her shoulder, with a golden chain from his ankle to a jewelled pendant at her breast. "See?"

Lady Onelle shook her head. "He's only just waking up. And the crowds... he doesn't like a lot of noise."

"Owls hunt by hearing, don't they?" Cae asked. The girl nodded. "That must have been horrible, coming into the city. For me, it was like hitting a wall of sound. Terribly frightening."

The girl nodded again with wide eyes.

"I've always loved that sensation, of coming into the city," said Malyna. "You come in out of the terrible quiet of the country and suddenly are surrounded by life on all sides. Humanity everywhere. No more loneliness."

Caelerys had something she wanted to say but thought better of.

Lady Balyra had no such reservations. "The country is teeming with life, more than in any city. You just have to listen for it. At any one moment, you are surrounded by a dozen small animals, lizards, frogs and snakes and more insects than you can count."

Lady Malyna shuddered visibly at the description.

Lady Lucelle blushed suddenly and looked shyly at the hem of her dress. Tempest looked just before Cae felt his presence. "The only difference is, that in the city, you can't hear the insects, only feel them, and the lizards and snakes wear human skins," chuckled a deep voice.

They looked up to see one of the Marrok twins bowing to them as he held his hand out to Lucelle. "My ladies, a thousand pardons but, the players have struck a tune and I would have a dance before the mummers begin."

She shyly placed her fingers in his and let him lead her away. She glanced back once to exchange a look of excited disbelief to her cousins before giving him her full attention.

"So was that lord Edler or lord Reled?" mused lady Balyra.

Cae watched them moving off. "I am not sure yet. They've been playing a merry game of it and are very careful around me."

Lady Malyna frowned, "Why would they be careful around you?"

"I know their secret."

Before the other girls could press what she could mean, a young man looking a lot like Malyna grabbed the girl's arm and dragged her onto the dance floor without even asking. He was followed quickly by the other Marrok and one of the Brocks who whisked off with both Roshan sisters. Cae glanced around, to see if anyone had an interest in her, but the only man she saw was the Kaladen heir and she turned to not be seen by him. She went to the buffet tables for food and found a place to sit to eat. She sat with her plate upon her lap, fervently wishing it were an embroidery frame instead, and nibbled delicately at her meal, feeding Tempest titbits. She was careful not to give her too much, but it would be at least the rest of the week before she could even ask for permission to go hunting, and the bird would cause less trouble if she were a little over-indulged.

She listened to everything going on around her. People laughing, their conversations. She had always been amazed at what people will say when they think they are alone. She observed the servants who were observing the nobility. Some seemed to merely watch for someone in need of them, attendant on their duty; others because it cruelly amused them, or they were being paid to hear these things.

She heard the queen's voice from somewhere behind her, a hushed admonition of "Go talk to her!" And a somewhat familiar voice snapping, "No," just as quietly. Then one of the princes stalked past her, actively ignoring her and disappearing into the crowd.

Cae did not know why she felt hurt by this. There was no reason for her to think it a rejection of her. She did not have long to ponder the matter as she noticed the other prince, Balaran, standing nearby awaiting her attention. She rose immediately, nearly dropping her thankfully empty plate as she sank into a curtsey. She just caught it. "Your Grace," she stammered, winced as she used the wrong address.

He laughed at her. "*You* are graceful," he countered, reached over to take the plate and set it in the hands of a servant. With a hand to her elbow, he bid her rise. She was blushing as she looked up at him, glanced off after his brother. "Oh, don't mind him. He's an ass."

She gasped, then laughed. "Ah, brotherhood. Was that about me?" she asked tentatively, glancing where the queen stood with her ladies.

"Heard that, did you?" he had the grace to look embarrassed for his brother. "Ah well, he's a blind ass at that."

"He doesn't even know me," she offered.

"Neither did I."

She blushed, glancing shyly away. "Chance meetings are not your mother thrusting you upon someone."

He grinned. "Who said anything about chance?"

She looked up at him in surprise, couldn't tell from his face if he was teasing or not.

"Sister?" came a voice from behind them. She turned, saw Willam looking upon the scene as if searching for impropriety. He bowed the moment he realized who she was standing with. "Your Highness."

Balaran turned, "Lord Willam," he nodded, waved him up even as he reached for Cae's hand. "I had just come over to deliver a message. My sister has requested you sit with us for the Lord Mendicant's Magnificence, my lady. I would like it if you would join us, Lord Willam."

He seemed surprised to be included. "We would be honoured."

The prince kept Cae's hand and Willam fell into step behind them as he escorted them to the section of seating reserved for the royal family. The princess lit up when she saw who her brother was bringing and restrained herself from clapping with joy. He bowed to her, "As you requested, dear sister. With extra treats."

She giggled at that, let her eyes glance over the large, handsome man bowing before her.

"Your Majesties, Your Highness," they both said, bowing to the king and queen as well as the princess.

The king impatiently waved them to rise. "Welcome. Please, be seated. I want the show to begin." He bent to the queen's ear and asked, "Do you think that fire-eater is still with them?"

She patted his hand and smiled indulgently. "We'll see in a moment, dear. You know he never tells."

Prince Balaran sat Caelerys beside his sister, waved Willam to sit beside Cae and took the seat next to him. Cae set Tempest onto the floor at her feet. The bird obeyed, but pecked at her knee for affection. She laughed as she obliged.

The princess looked down, adoring her. "Why did you put her down there?"

"She's too tall. She sits a head taller than I upon my shoulder and no one behind me will be able to see," she explained.

The princess glanced behind them, smiled indulgently. "The only people behind us will be standing and guards."

Cae looked. There were no seats behind them. It struck her then, her ignorance. No matter the performance, no one sits behind the royal family. She blushed. "You must think me such a country idiot."

The girl laughed, light and airy. The loops of braided gold that framed her face danced as she shook her head. "No, my lady. I think you considerate." She looked down as she heard the bird chirp.

Tempest was standing in between her and her mistress. She bowed when she had the maiden's attention, then lifted her head high and to the side, begging for a scratch. The princess giggled as she obliged. "She really is darling," she sighed.

"She really is spoiled," Willam growled under his breath. Cae elbowed him discreetly. Prince Balaran called his attention, speaking of the tourney and other matters.

The princess looked over in askance and Cae smiled and shook her head. "They don't get along," she explained. "She won't listen to anyone else but me, and I think he resents that. Thinks she's more pet than hunter, and he's right. But she'll do anything for me, including hunt. I don't know why."

"You are so lucky."

"Have you ever been hawking, Your Highness?"

"Kestrels. She'd be too heavy for me."

She smiled. "You do have very slender wrists, princess."

The girl blushed a little, looked at her and caught a glimpse of Willam on the other side of her and blushed more. Then there was a burst of smoke from the stage in front of them and everyone turned to see the Lord Mendicant standing in the clearing air seemingly out of nowhere.

He was brightly dressed in patchwork motley, artfully arranged from scraps of silks, velvets and brocades. His face was hidden by a half mask of black silk that covered his face from brow to cheek. His cloak was an unbroken black on the outside, but when he spread his arms, holding it open, a dozen multicoloured birds flew out and up, landing in various places around the stage to gasped delight. Tempest twitched at the rush of prey but Cae had not given a signal to fetch one and, as Tempest was full, she let them go.

The inside of his cloak was lined with feathers from every type of bird imaginable. He threw it back over his shoulders and bellowed in a voice that would carry across a crowded marketplace as he bowed. "My ladies, my lords, my Royal Guests. First but not greatest, I come before you on royal indulgence…" He hesitated, bowed to the king, "Nay, royal insistence…," he grinned, "to perform for one and all."

One of the birds who had landed on a short pillar behind him squawked a very clear, "Not yet."

He turned and growled, "Quiet you."

"Not yet, stupid," it yelled back. The audience laughed.

Another bird, a big red one, bent forward and shouted, "Fire Fire Fire!"

The audience clapped and cheered and some even took up the chant.

Centre stage, the Lord Mendicant sighed and lowered his head in mock surrender. He raised a hand and the crowd silenced. "Fine, fine. Bring out the dragon and the maiden!" he shouted and then stormed off stage.

A pretty young girl walked out on the stage leading a man on a long chain who was painted up to look like a dragon. His fake wings lay folded on his back, and he stalked forward on all fours, his front limbs almost as long as his back. Cae thought there was some trick to that, but it was hard to tell, so closely fitted was his costume and so convincing his paint. The girl herself couldn't be older than Cae, possibly younger, but carried herself with a confidence Cae was certain she would never have.

She felt a hand cover her own and turned, saw the princess had clasped hers in excitement, perhaps knowing what was to come. "Is she frightened of fire?" she whispered hastily.

Tempest looked up at Cae, wondering what was going on. She slid her feet forward a little and around the bird, giving her the protection of her skirts and Tempest leaned back into them. "She'll hide under my skirts if she feels the need. I deliberately fed her too much for her to care."

Their attention was immediately diverted by the girl on stage ordering the dragon up and through several tricks as one would a trained dog or dancing bear. Then she said a single Vermian word: Fire. Cae focused and Tempest slipped backwards under Cae's skirt, leaving only her head peeking out. The dragon-man did something and a gout of flames erupted from his mouth over the girl's head. Someone shrieked and the audience laughed.

The girl had a rope in hand with a black ball on both ends, and she began twirling them in the air. The dragon breathed at them, igniting them until she was dancing with spinning fire. The two danced together, doing fire tricks. The performance was entrancing until a tin knight strode out from the wings and proclaimed he'd rescue the maiden from the beast by slaying it. The dragon ran and hid behind the girl, then both of them comically chased the knight off stage.

The night was full of such acts. Lady Sigourney sang so sweetly the birds literally did descend to listen, then played a game of echoing melodies. She 'taught' each one a segment, then had them all sing together in one amazing, orchestrated voice. One comedic act had a fat man in foreign robes running from an actual, live ca'theryn. The sleek, spotted cat was about the size of a large wolfhound, and was magnificent. He caught and pounced on the man and ripped him open to the screams of the audience which swiftly turned to delight as his 'guts' turned out to be clouds of butterflies. Both cat and man seemed surprised at the development. When the cat turned up his nose and tried to scratch earth over him the audience laughed.

The highpoint was the Lord Mendicant himself. He dazzled with feats of impossibility and wonder, fast hands and faster bodies, which ended with him producing from his cloak each and every one of the night's performers, including the ca'theryn. Lady Petra had been right about one thing at least: it was a performance not to be missed.

Once the cat was off stage, Tempest crawled out from beneath Cae's skirts and hopped up onto her lap. Cae transferred her quickly to the leather wristband to save her dress. "That truly was...," she sighed, not having words for it.

The princess giggled. "I know. They'll do one tomorrow night at the fairing after the jousting, for the lower estates. From what I understand it's more... ribald," she whispered. "So, of course, I won't be able to attend."

The rest of the royal family began to stand to leave and Cae was quick to rise and curtsey. Princess Syera reached out and took up her hand. "You have to come see me in the gardens tomorrow morning."

"Of course, Princess. I would be delighted."

She looked over her shoulder at Willam. "Bring your brother, too, if you like," she giggled before slipping off in her mother's wake.

SHIFT: Stag's Heart

Willam held out his hand to his sister. "Shall we go home, Cae?"

She watched his eyes flick over her shoulder to the dwindling figures of the royal family and suppressed the smile that wanted to bloom. "If we must." As Tempest leapt to her shoulder, she caught a glimpse of several of the Kaladen men looking their way. One of them seemed to be pointing her out to his Lord. "Aye, home sounds safe right now."

He set her hand on his arm and escorted her through the gardens, muttered through his teeth. "Let me guess... pirates?"

"Aye."

He nodded to his squire who was just crossing to join them from where he had watched the performance with the servants. The boy immediately diverted and ran off to ready their mounts.

"On the other hand, your presence has been requested in the gardens tomorrow."

"Lovely," he said, his voice dripping with sarcasm.

5

Caelerys went alone to the gardens the next morning to meet the princess, followed only by Fern who stayed at her usual discreet distance. When the princess arrived, Tempest curtseyed with her mistress. "Good morning, Your Highness."

She noted the girl looking around, seeking something or someone out. She smiled briefly. "Forgive us, but my brother was unable to join us this morning."

The wisteria eyes turned to her, a little anger, a little disappointment, and an uncertainty of reaction flared in them. "He is well, I hope? Not over-indulged?"

Caelerys giggled briefly at the thought of Willam with a hangover. "No, Your Highness. We were all set to ride out when he received a message. He had to leave immediately. He did not look happy."

Concern won out. "Will he be safe?"

Cae smiled warmly at the princess, "I find it hard to imagine my brother not safe. Except perhaps in a room full of women with designs on him. But that is a danger of an entirely different matter."

The princess giggled. "Well, I have you to walk with me at least." She held out her arm and Cae obediently took it, and the two of them wandered through the gardens arm in arm, honey gold and brunette.

They talked of everything and nothing, as young girls do. They found a luncheon set up, waiting for them on a little patio overlooking the sea and Princess Syera invited her to eat with her. "I've arranged for us to go to the tourney grounds after this light repast."

Cae's brow rose at naming this a 'light repast'. There was more here than either of them could eat. Since none of the servants were in earshot, Cae leaned forward a little and lowered her voice. "May I ask you something... impertinent?"

The princess's eyes lit up, "Offensive or just rude?"

"Well, that depends on you," she said, thoughtfully feeding Tempest titbits. "I am trying to learn courtly ways and the question might help me."

She buttered a sweet, white roll and waved the knife for Cae to proceed. "Ask."

"This food. There is more here than we can possibly eat. But it occurs to me... do your servants eat what we will not?"

She nodded thoughtfully.

Cae sat back, thinking. "So, you order more than you can eat, knowing you are feeding your servants better food than they would know in the kitchens, thus keeping them loyal via their bellies. This is very wise, Your Highness."

The princess smiled. "Mama said you were smart. I actually hadn't thought of that last part. I was just doing what Mama always does and to be nice to them. They take such good care of me. ...It's something I'm not used to, people trying over-hard to please me. I mean, I've *always* been a princess. My father was the grand duke, but, being *The* Princess is very different." She reached out across the table and set her hand upon Cae's. "I've never really had a friend, Lady Caelerys. Ladies in Waiting aren't really friends, not when they are chosen for you and every one of them is hoping to gain something by it. In the end they are just servants... noble ones, but still servants."

She turned her hand to take the princess's. "Everyone deserves a friend. At least one loyal friend. And if you wish me to be that friend... you will have to start calling me Caelerys. Or Cae, depending on how informal you wish to be. I too, have no friends here, and I desperately need one who knows the terrain."

"Well, that I know. I would like that very much, Cae."

They spent most of the next hour learning about each other, their hopes, dreams and fears. Cae learned the girl was not so young of mind as she had first appeared, but only a certain shyness and uncertainty in her sudden elevation had made her come across so. The princess was sixteen, not the fifteen or fourteen she had come across as when they had first met.

"You know, Cae, you are not shy at all," the princess giggled over her glass of sweet fruit juice.

Cae blushed. "I am, too." The princess gave her a look that made Cae laugh uncomfortably. "All right, I'll ascede that right now I may not seem to be but... you tell me I have to walk into a room full of strangers and be polite and charming and actively seek them out and start a conversation... that has nothing to do with hunting or animals or reading," she added hastily, "and I'm stone cold terrified. But one on one, ...or about any of those subjects... that I can handle. I've had to play at the Lady of the House for years, but it still terrifies me. I'm so afraid of making a mistake and offending someone I shouldn't."

"I know what you mean. I've been a neglected princess for so long.... oh," she amended hastily, "I don't mean I was neglected in that way, just ...overlooked by important people. I mean, we were never expected to be here," she gestured to the palace in general, "so none of us were trained to it, beyond being psions of a Great House, so we were raised more like a family than a royal family. Only our parents ever went to court, and mostly only father. Bal was in and out of the castle for years poking through the library, staying with our cousins, and while he and Val were presented at one point, Val had other pursuits that interested him more. I've had a little more intrigue training than you, but I think that just makes me more frightened of mistakes. Especially now."

Cae nodded, "Certain people put me at ease, like Prince Balaran. Oh, I was nervous at first but he got me over that quickly."

There was something in her pale violet eyes, "Oh, he'll do that. But because I like you, I'm going to warn you. Give him a bite and he'll eat the whole roast and give you merely 'thanks' for all that," her eyes told her there was a secondary, less savoury meaning beneath it all.

She nodded with a faint smile as if they were speaking of something else all together more pleasant. "My brother has warned me. Apparently Janem graced the same tavern as both of your brothers in the past. I shall be careful with my favours. But tell me, is there anyone they are looking at for you? What do you think your prospects are?"

Now it was the princess's turn to blush. She nibbled daintily at a sweetmeat. "Well, I have favourites, but there are a few I know are looking to my father. I just hope the rest of you aren't being put on hold because some of them are hoping and holding out for me," she sighed, then brightened again. "I've been told both the Princes of Alumet are asking, along with Lord Griff for one of his sons. The Cygents, I think, have an unmarried son. I think some of the lesser houses are dreaming, but know there's not much chance."

"Ah, but who do *you* like?"

She giggled with a sudden shyness, "Well, I like your eldest right fine. Though I think he's shy, too."

Cae chuckled softly, "Only around women."

"The Marrok brothers are entertaining. Lord Selgan of Cygent is sweet faced and pleasant."

"Married," she sighed. "His younger brother, Galen, is the one available."

"Oh," she said, a little disappointed. "Oh, is he one your father has an eye on?"

Cae smiled, "I don't think my father has his eye on anyone yet. But he's been presented to me as an available person of interest. My father is waiting on me to give him a list of my choices."

Her wisteria eyes widened. "You'll be allowed to pick?"

Cae gave a soft shrug. "It is possible. Father wanted me to give him my opinions. I am certain that if I offer him a suitable choice he'll do his best to make the match, but I have no doubts that if I do not want a man he'll never hand over my candle to him."

"You are so lucky," she sighed.

"I am sorry your prospects have changed," Cae said companionably. "I am certain my lot would have been yours but for the madness of your royal uncle. Now the security of the kingdom could rest on your union. It's not fair."

She shrugged, "It is but my duty." Her eyes flicked over Cae's shoulder for a second, then she nodded. "Have you eaten your fill?"

"I honestly couldn't eat another thing. I've never had such a large meal this early," she groaned.

"Well, we should ride then. The tourney begins soon and my royal presence is required," she said airily. Their eyes met and both girls burst out laughing. "Come on," she said, rising. "That is, if you aren't too fat to ride," she teased.

"So fat my mare will despair to see me coming," she said with a hand dramatically pressed to her forehead. "But I think I can suffer the short ride to the tournament. Tempest, on the other wing, might be too fat to fly."

The two of them left the garden laughing.

At the tourney grounds, the princess insisted she follow her to the royal box and sit with her. Tempest opened an eye at the sound of cheering, talkative people, but once seated, she closed her eyes and went back to sleep.

They watched the parade of armoured men and commented back and forth on most of them, feeding each other information. When the black wolf of Marrok was carried by, the princess showed some interest. "I just wish I knew which was which," she groused. "I mean, I've learned little, subtle things to tell them apart, but I don't know which belong to which brother," she sighed. She caught Cae's sly grin. "What?" she demanded, accusing. "You know something."

Cae tipped her head in a very 'maybe' gesture. "Can you really tell them apart?"

"Can you?" she challenged.

"By one way and one way only. But knowing what you know, and what I know... we could tell them apart as easily as their mother."

The princess grinned. "I will tell you, if you tell me."

Cae leaned in close to whisper. "The next time you see them, make them take your hand. Edler has a small scar on his palm, just at the base of his fingers. When you know him, then tell me how to tell them apart by sight. I would rather associate the characteristics to the names from the first."

Her smile was almost predatory. "As soon as I know."

"And what are you two conspiring about?" came the mocking voice of Prince Balaran from behind them.

The pair of them jumped like startled mice and Tempest shrilled her annoyance at him for disturbing her nap. The princess laughed, but slapped his arm. "None of yours. Where have you been?" she countered. "At least five pairs have ridden."

He shrugged, sitting down on the seat behind them and leaning back. "Annoying Valan. Though if you want to see him ride, you need to turn around."

They looked, saw the prince's emerald enamelled armour approaching the end of the lists. His opponent was lord Tume Ca'than. The two wasted no time and the horses threw themselves down the lane.

The first pass was a miss on both ends, with the prince's lance just skittering off the curves of the foreign design. They did not wait for a second signal, but wheeled at the end and charged. This time they both struck, lances shattering.

They slowed this time, giving each other a chance to assess themselves and retrieve new lances. They waited until they were both ready, nodded to each other and then rode. This time the prince's lance caught the edge of a plate and instead of sliding away, caught hold of the metal and ripped it from the man's shoulder. They paused. A squire ran out and mounted the list rail to check the shoulder. The prince called for a fresh lance, though the other one had not noticeably broken. He waited until lord Tume nodded to him that he was ready.

They charged. The crowd held its breath as Tume rode without protection on his shoulder. The prince had to make a choice: aim for another target on his body or risk killing the man. In seconds, the choice did not matter as Tume dropped the shoulder in question and aimed for the prince's midsection, sliding past his shield, catching him up and flinging him from his horse. He pulled up and turned, lifting his visor to see if he had dealt an injury to a prince of this realm. Aye, even in his own country, a man is not held accountable, unless by dishonourable act, for deaths in a freely entered competition. But it would play almighty abyss with the politics between his country and this if he killed or maimed a Prince Royal.

After a few seconds, just as the squires were reaching him, the prince sat up. Behind Cae, she heard Prince Balaran breathe a sigh of relief. The princess was just thrumming with concern, and even the king had leaned forward.

Prince Valan threw up his visor, looking around. Then, after what seemed an interminable moment, he raised his hand in salute. Lord Tume dipped his lance to him, then turned to the royal box and did the same. The crowd erupted as Valan was helped off the field, his hand fingering the dent in his stomach plate.

"Oh, this is too much excitement," breathed the princess.

In the end, it was to be lord Mambyn Asparadane versus lord Tume Ca'than in the finals tomorrow after the archery competition. Then the Grand Melee.

The royal family left her to see Prince Valan and personally assure themselves of his well being. Caelerys felt a little nervous as she wandered alone towards the sea-side of the tourney lists. It was a breathtaking and distracting view of the rough seas, before which the archery butts had been placed. Any stray arrows would sail out over the water, endangering none but the fish. She leaned on the fence and studied the arrangement. It had been so long since she had shot a perfectly still target, she wasn't sure she really could any more. This was very unlike her own target practice at home.

Her father trained his yeomen to shoot wheeled dummies that were advanced upon the archers' position via a pulley and rope, or that hid partially behind bales and trees. He trained his hunters on swinging targets, and larger, rope drawn ones. Her father trained for practicality and real war. If he could safely manage targets that would shoot back without killing, he probably would have. As it was, he occasionally fired at his own castle and fields full of men with catapults loaded with small ragbags of mud, as much to train the horses as the men to handle themselves under fire, but that was the best he could do. The mud battles were some of Cae's favourites, as they were always held during the hottest days, for the river and shallows of the sea was welcome relief afterwards. The aftermath was always fun.

A boisterous voice crowed from behind her, "There's my favourite sister!"

She let her head sag a little, smiling. "I'm your only sister, Vyncet." She turned to see her nineteen year old brother striding up to her with Willam in tow, his dark curls bouncing as he spread his arms for her.

"And that changes things how?" he asked, taking her into a crushing embrace.

"Gently!" she squeaked. "I need that arm tomorrow."

He let her go, beaming. "So Willam was telling me. Going to win us a golden bow as well as a new saddle?"

"I don't know about that," she blushed. She swept her arm to encompass the field. "Not exactly the target practice I'm used to."

He glanced it over, frowned a moment, then dismissed it with a wave of his hand. "You've shot harder targets. I've seen you take a pigeon from a hawk without harming the hawk."

She gave his arm a sisterly shove. "That was not... I didn't see the hawk. This is... different. I've also never shot for prizes, and the queen herself has money on me."

"So have I... now," he grinned. "I understand the Marrok hellions are here. I'm sure I'll get good odds for you."

Willam shrugged. "Likely. Edler already has fifty gold suns on Mester Hayle."

Vyncet frowned. "Isn't that the Pardet subsequent?"

"Aye."

Vyncet turned back to Cae, "Speaking of subs, Janem brought an empty box by this morning for you." He grinned, "Anything I should know?"

"No," she glowered. "Nothing at all." She looked at Willam over his shoulder. "Is this why you didn't come this morning?" she asked, pointing at their brother. She had forgotten how easily he irritated.

Willam nodded. "Word came in that he was on the way. The bird was... damaged and delayed. I had to hurry if I was going to meet him at the gates."

She narrowed her eyes. "Hawk?"

He shook his head. "Something. Maybe. The new boy is tending him. He's got good hands."

Vyncet smiled broadly, patting her on the shoulder. "I'm sure it is nothing, sister. Now, how about we wander the fair and sample the local ale? Or we could go to that Galley place Janem spoke of?"

Willam stiffened immediately. "We are not taking Cae to the Galley."

Vyncet laughed, slapping Willam on the back. "Of course not, but I do like to see you choke on the thought." He held out his arm for Cae, "Come on, we'll get some small ale and maybe I'll buy you a fairing or two. Then," he added in a lower voice, pulling her closer, "we can get you home before Willam and I join Janem at the Galley, and you can show me this new trinket our brother made you."

She grumbled as she walked off with them. "It has garnered me too much attention already as it is."

6

Cae stood at the end of the archery field the next morning, nervously fidgeting with the tip of her bow. She was almost ashamed to note fraying at the end of her string, and the shabby nature of the wood itself. It was only the second bow she had ever owned, and had once belonged to each of her brothers in turn. It was handed down once it was outgrown or the current bearer proved to have no interest in archery. None of her brothers did. Willam she had never really known well, and Vyncet preferred hunting by dog, sword and spear. Cae was perfectly content to take her deer from the safety of horseback.

Her father had tried to teach her swords once. She could lift a light one, hold it in a convincingly threatening manner, even swing it if she had to, but, like Janem, she had no real aptitude for it. Aye, there was no reason for her to have even tried, but she liked knowing what she could do if she had the need.

The herald called for the archers to draw and she turned sideways to the distant target. She had three arrows in the ground before her and laid one to the string. Three arrows for the first round. She felt the wind on her cheek off the sea, and realized the one drawback to placing the field here. They had erected a wall on one side as a wind break, but it did not do her much good, out here on the far end. Those closer to the wall had the advantage.

The call to loose came and Cae held hers a moment longer than most, taking her time to adjust for the wind. Her first went a little wide, landing nearer the target beyond it, but gave her the information she needed to adjust. Her second hit the target and the last went into the red heart painted on the canvas covered bale. Hers was the last to hit and the herald called for his assistants to fetch and note the arrows.

Cae took the time to look over her competition. There were about twenty archers, a fair number of them women. The girl beside her was nearly in tears as she had missed every arrow. Cae put a comforting hand on her shoulder. "We have the wind here. There is no shame in missing."

The girl sniffled, getting herself under control. "You hit. And you're farther in the wind than I."

"I have four brothers," Cae smiled, shrugging. "I have to be better than them at something."

This made the girl laugh, even as the herald came over to tell her she'd been eliminated. She merely nodded to him, gave Cae a light curtsey and walked off to the stands.

The herald gestured for Cae to move closer to the centre with the rest of the remaining field. The younger of the Roshan girls was still in, as was their cousin, along with a girl of a knightly house whose crest Cae did not recognize. There were ten of them left, and only four of them women.

The front row of targets had been removed and the second set were half again as far away. Cae took her stance and gauged wind and distance. The wind was likely to be greater closer to the target. Her spare arrow was in the ground before her and her second on the bow, as they were only allowed two this round. The call to fire came and she loosed the first shaft. It struck the edge of the target and went through. She was clearly overcompensating. She drew the second and pulled farther, shifting at the last second to compensate for a burst of wind and nearly missed again, but landed near the heart.

She was certain she was going to be eliminated, but found herself left in a field of five of which she was the only woman. She sighed, embarrassed by how badly she was doing. It had been a long time, she realized, since she had shot from foot.

Two of the men were using longbows. This would be an advantage at the greater distance. The final targets were twice as far as the first, and still only two arrows to shoot. The crowd was hushed as they drew. The call to fire came and they loosed. Cae did much better, landing one in the heart, but was startled on her last as the man on the far end twisted and shot his arrow into the target of the man beside her, dead centre. Luckily, her arrow still hit the target, but the man beside her missed his last completely and turned to scowl at the other man. The offender turned to face him, smirked and gave him a sarcastic bow, turned to the royal box and gave a more sincere one before walking off the field. Cae noticed the king laughing quietly.

"Master Olen Alvermian, Master of the Hunt is disqualified," called the herald.

Cae turned to watch the man walk around the royal stands and where the spectators stood, to disappear, laughing into the woods. The golden tones to his light brown hair glinted in the sunlight and she realized that this was the king's subsequent brother. She glanced at the man beside her, young, handsome, arrogant and furious.

The herald consulted with his men, then approached the man beside her. "I am sorry, Master Kell, but you are..."

The man did not even wait for him to finish before making a cursory bow towards the royal box and stalking off. Cae raised her eyebrows in shock, meeting the herald's gaze. The man gave her an embarrassed smile before gesturing for her to move to stand with the last two men. She was genuinely surprised to find herself in the final round, but apparently the Master of the Hunt had disadvantaged everyone. Though only Master Kell had missed twice.

"Lady Caelerys Maral, Mester Hayle of House Pardet, and Mester Remmor of House Kaladen will compete in a final round. One shot each at one of four targets, a wand at forty paces, in order of precedence."

As he moved out of the way and Caelerys was told to step forward, she saw the four wands arrayed in a neat row just beyond where the standing targets had been. This would be the deciding round. Cae took a deep breath as she drew. She had never shot wands. She chose the second wand, aimed about a third down its length and fired. The arrow struck off-centre, taking a large chip out of the wood but not breaking it. The crowd cheered, but Cae knew it was not a winning shot. She bowed and stepped back, began fidgeting with the frayed end of her string, trying to twist it straight again.

Mester Hayle stepped up, eased his bow back and let go, taking the left end target out from the base. Again the crowd shouted happily. The man turned to walk back to the others and Cae nodded to him, acknowledging the better shot. He smiled at her, returned the nod.

The last man stepped up, took his time choosing and aiming. As the crowd started to get tetchy and complaining, he chose the far right wand and fired. The wand bent and waved as the feathers grazed it, but did not break or splinter. He swore as some of the crowd laughed and others clapped.

At a signal from the herald, the three of them crossed in front of the royal box and bowed while the crowd cheered.

The queen made the announcements this time, presenting Mester Hayle with the prize of a golden arrow. To Cae she handed an etched silver throat for her quiver, and to Mester Remmor, an oiled silk case for his bow. They stepped back and bowed again and the king announced that the final rounds of the jousting would be taking place shortly.

Cae started to unstring her bow to put it away when Mace came up behind her and took it from her hands. A nod and a nudge from him turned her attention to the approaching royalty even as he dropped into a bow. She curtsied before the queen. "Your Majesty," she breathed, blushing. "Please forgive my poor performance. I had no desire to lose you money."

"Who ever said I had wagered money?" she smiled.

Caelerys frowned for a second, puzzling things together, then gave a short laugh, bowed her head. "Then I hope I have not overly inconvenienced Your Majesty."

The queen dismissed the thought with a wave of her hand, nodded for Mace to go on with his work and looped her arm through Cae's. Mace discreetly took the prize from his mistress's hand as she was led off by the queen, smiling to himself as he took care of her equipment.

"So tell me what happened?" the queen asked.

Cae was nervous, strolling so casually arm in arm with the queen of the land, but there was a strong motherliness that wafted off the woman that served to keep it from getting too far out of hand. She shrugged. "I did not shoot well and Mester Hayle was better. There were others who were better but were disadvantaged by the strong winds at our end of the field."

"Why do you think you did not shoot well?" she persisted.

Caelerys thought about it. "Nerves, maybe," she surmised. "It was not a targeting set up I am used to. I more commonly shoot at moving targets, and often on horseback. This was my first tournament."

The queen gave her arm an encouraging squeeze. "You did amazing for a first tournament. That your favourite bow?"

Cae blushed again. "My only bow, Your Majesty. It was my brothers'. I've... never seen the need to ask for my own. I should have at least gotten a new string for the tournament, though."

"Don't worry about it, my dear. You are young. This is your first tournament and already you have placed second in a field of seasoned archers, and first in the equestrian. You have done very well. You are sure to catch someone's attention. And after a performance like that, it is not likely to be someone who will not appreciate such skills in a lady..." she added pointedly.

Cae looked up into her warm, inviting face and smiled. "Thank you, Your Majesty. You are too kind."

"Ah, here is your brother," she exclaimed, drawing Cae's attention to the two men standing near the steps to the stands. She held Cae's hand out to Willam as the men bowed. "Lord Willam," she smiled, "your sister is a delight. And so modest."

As Willam accepted Cae's hand and drew her to him, the queen's eyes fell on the man beside them. "Your Majesty," he said as quickly as he noticed, "please allow me to introduce our youngest brother, Vyncet."

Vyncet bowed over the queen's hand as she offered it. "My great pleasure, Your Majesty."

"Pleased," she smiled. "Will you be fighting tomorrow?"

"I will, Your Majesty. I would have been in the joust, but I, sadly, arrived too late."

"Perhaps next time. I wish you both the best of luck," she added with a nod and taking her leave to join the king in the royal box.

They bowed as she left, and the moment she was gone, Vyncet was hugging her. "Second place and a walk with the queen! Our little doe-eyed daisy is moving up in the world!"

She shrugged him off. "Ugh, don't remind me. I'm getting too much attention as it is. Though I like the queen. She's sweet. ...Reminds me a little of mother."

"Mother was taller," Willam said quietly.

She glared up at him. "You know what I mean. There's ...something about her..." She shook her head to dismiss the thought. "Let's get a good seat before they're all taken," she growled, waving them into the stands.

Vyncet offered her his arm to assist her up the steps. "So, have you given your favour to anyone?"

Cae shook her head. "I do not know anyone here well enough to do so."

"That never stopped anybody," Vyncet laughed.

She blushed, shoving him discreetly with her shoulder, "It is too late anyway."

"It's never too late," he retorted.

"Leave her be, Vynce," Willam growled.

"I can defend myself against this ninny, Will," she quipped. "I've had a great deal of practice."

Vyncet laughed, "More practice in getting even later."

She smiled wickedly, "Have *you* met any eligible young ladies yet, Vynce?"

He crowed, "A few..." He then coloured, remembering what the twins had brought him. "We need to worry about you first," he added as a distraction as he guided her to a seat, setting her between Will and himself.

Glancing back, Cae saw Willam actually smile.

They settled in to watch the final joust. As the last two contestants paraded before the Royal Box and the stands, Cae noted that lord Tume had repaired and replaced his pauldron. She leaned to Willam even as she glanced over the arrogant black stallion standing beside the Northern lord, tossing his head. "Did he go to Janem for repairs?"

"Aye. No one else could have figured it out. And yes, he was in a frenzy to look over the whole suit. Tume said he was going to try and talk his princes into taking their armour to him so he can study the original design. If he can make a better hybrid than Tume already has, he'll commission a new suit."

"Janem was over the moons, I'll wager."

He chuckled. "He's already looking over his current commissions and deciding which can be foisted off on the journeymen. He was right that he was going to be inordinately busy."

"I heard someone has a partial suit of moonsilver plate they're going to take to him," Vyncet added.

"Who?" they both asked.

He shook his head. "No clue. Heard it in passing. Or maybe it was a commission to make one, I don't remember."

Willam shrugged, "That'd likely be Duke Griff. Only one could afford it. Our brother is going to rich beyond our House soon."

Their conversation was interrupted by the blare of the bugle calling the fighters to position.

The two riders crossed to the opposites parts of the list, set their helmets and their lances. Their squires fled the moment weapons were in hand and shortly afterwards the signal was given to charge. Asparadane's black mount tossed his head and skipped a little before setting into his stride, throwing both men slightly off. Neither lance met target. They reached the end of the list and rounded the end poles. Mambyn charged again without pause and Tume had to spur his mount quickly. They met before Tume reached the middle, but it did not help Mambyn at all. His lance slid right off the flared shoulder while Tume's met him squarely in the chest and shattered.

Mambyn seemed to watch impatiently as his opponent's squire brought him a fresh lance. The moment it was seated he spurred the black into motion. This time Tume was ready and his borrowed horse shot forward. The lances met, Mambyn's shattering dead centre of Tume's shield while Tume's glanced off his shoulder.

Before taking a new lance from his squire, Mambyn adjusted his pauldron, glaring across the field. Tume waited patiently, watched carefully, and this time they charged forth simultaneously. They met, shattering both lances, bringing the bout even, and the herald waved that they should continue. They rounded the lists again. This time Mambyn went for the shoulder the prince had struck and stripped just days before. The impact was heavy, but the shape of the pauldron carried the tip up and off without breaking. The backward jerk of the strike threw Tume's lance off and he only grazed the shield.

They galloped around the end of the lists almost without slowing, Tume's mount all but pivoting on his heels whilst Mambyn's unruly black went a little wide. Tume let his shield hang a little lower, luring his opponent in for another attempt at the shoulder. At the last second he lowered his lance just enough and added an extra thrust, catching him in the centre of the belly and pushing him neatly out of the saddle. The crowd lost its mind. The yelling and cheering even from the noble seats was enough to make Caelerys cringe, leaning into Willam's bulk to shield herself as best she could.

When Mambyn rolled angrily to his feet and threw off his helmet, the dent in his armour was visible from the stands. His squire was momentarily torn between running to his knight or helping the two men trying to grab and control his horse. Eventually he went to his lord who railed at him as he flew to unbuckle his breast-plate.

Tume removed his helmet and rode to the centre of the lists in front of the Royal Box, bowing.

The king rose, but with everyone on their feet around them, Cae could not see what transpired. She barely heard the herald proclaiming lord Tume Ca'than Tourney Champion and presenting his award. When people finally sat again, she could see Mambyn making his own obeisance to the Royal Box.

"What do you think Tume'll do if Mambyn refuses to ransom his horse back?" Caelerys asked Will.

Vyncet looked confused. "Why would he not? It is a magnificent animal, worth a great deal I am told."

Willam answered for her, "Because it will take a great deal more training than he has the patience for to get him under control. I don't know. He might just refuse the animal outright. He'll not want to give away or sell his luck."

"That'll cause a stink," Vyncet murmured. Willam agreed.

This reminded Cae that Tume's horse was borrowed. "How is his own mount? Any better?"

"Why don't we go see?" Willam offered.

They joined the people beginning to leave the stands, though they did not head to the fairgrounds as most of them did, turning off towards the stables.

The barn was only moderately busy, with grooms coming and going, leading out horses to be boarded elsewhere that were no longer needed here. It was not difficult to find the white horse's stall, as it was the only one guarded.

A single, dark-skinned young man in what were clearly borrowed clothes stood watch at the door of the loose box. He did not stop them from pausing at the wall and looking in, though he kept a close eye on them.

Cae leaned against the box and looked in. The horse was still down, but no longer on his side. He looked worn and damp. He glanced wearily up at the faces peering in at him and apparently saw something he liked. He struggled to his feet, stood a little unsteadily for a moment, then slowly stepped to the wall of his box and sniffed Cae.

The guard moved at that, putting a hand on the small sword at his hip. "Onanan!" he snapped.

Vyncet held up his hands, shaking his head. "We're not harming him."

Cae tried to pull back from the horse, but he came closer, pressing his chest to the wall and straining to reach her. This caused the guard some consternation and no small amount of confusion.

She hesitantly set her hand on the delicately concave face, the tips of her fingers on a soot coloured spot between his eyes. She immediately shivered, feeling chilled and uncomfortable. She closed her eyes, trying to remember when she had felt this way before. She did not even hear the exchange of words between her brothers and the guard, nor anything else that was occurring around her.

It was not until she opened her eyes and looked into the horse's that she remembered. She had been twelve and caught a chill. When her fever had broken, she felt just like this, thirsty, chilled and over warm at the same time, fatigued. She set her hand on his neck and felt dampness. "Get him some water and a cloth. He needs rubbing down," she said suddenly.

"Tala valea, Saman, te," said a familiar voice.

She looked up to see lord Tume and her uncle facing them, and the guard, looking worried and chastened, running off. She blushed. "Forgive me my impertinence, my lord. But he is very thirsty and sweating. I think he is breaking his fever."

Jehan looked incredibly amused by the whole situation. Lord Tume looked both angry and pleased at the same time. He waved his hand to dismiss her worries, opening the stall door. "You have more sense than the boy. He was told to watch him, let no one unauthorized near, aye, but to care for him too."

A groom crossed the corridor with a pair of drying cloths, stepping inside and handing one to Tume. "Woulda done something an hour past, but he'd not have it. Nor even to bring water. Me an' the boys were talkin' of sendin' word soon ta get him seen ta, but you came. Nary a word was understood 'twixt us'n he."

Tume nodded his thanks and invited the man to help him rub the horse down. He noted that the horse refused to break contact with Cae. "My princes thought he might have been poisoned and set the guard. Only our own people were to have access. Trouble is, the man knows nothing of horses, and the rest of our people who do were in the lists with me." He growled at himself. "I was a fool not to notice, should have insisted someone stay back." He said soothing Northern words to the animal as he wiped the sweat away from sensitive parts.

He felt the animal move and looked up, laughed to see he had pressed his head against the lady's chest and closed his eyes. "Have him charmed, you do."

Vyncet leaned on the top of the wall and grinned. "He saw her and got up. Didn't care what that guard said or wanted."

"We are glad you came when you did," Willam added. "I am not sure what the man was going to do. She tried to back away, but the horse would not have it."

"Do all horses react like that to her?" Tume chuckled, working down the legs.

"Most animals," Jehan crowed proudly. "But only most. There are a rare few."

"Like that bitch your lieutenant keeps?" she quipped, rolling her eyes, remembering a particular brindle hound in her uncle's company.

He waved a hand in dismissal, "Yeah, but she hates everybody."

Finally the guard returned with a bucket of water. He looked unsure who he should give it to and unwilling to hold the bucket himself. Vyncet rolled his eyes and took it from him, handing it to his sister. She stopped stroking the pale head to grab the handle and hold it for him. He put his nose in the water, snorting a few bubbles before he began to drink gratefully. He nudged her with irritation when she pulled it away after a few minutes.

"Nay. You need to slow down," she chastised. "You need to eat too, you know. Drink too much you'll be sick again."

He flicked his ear in response, an annoyed acquiescence. She spent a moment playing with his black tipped forelock before letting him have more. He drank slower this time, less greedily and she let him have what he wanted. When he had nearly drained it, she looked at the guard and tapped the bucket. "More," she said. "Go," she said, pointing away, "bring more," she finished firmly, handing him the nearly empty bucket and not giving him an opportunity to refuse it.

He only paused to glance with confusion at his lord before obeying.

Tume grinned at her from over the wall, the rag hanging limp in one hand whilst his other rubbed the muscles of the great neck. "How'd you know he doesn't speak any Southern at all?"

She sighed, "Because the first words you learn in any tongue are usually 'no' and 'yes'. He did not."

He laughed, "Well, now he knows two words." He looked her over.

"Best watch yourself about my princes, my lady," he said with sudden solemnity.

"Why?" she asked, suddenly worried she had done something to cause issue.

"You are a contradiction of their expectations. One or both of them might take a liking to you."

"Would either be a bad match?"

"For you."

Willam looked over, "Explain," he asked.

Tume stood, taking his horse by the halter and gesturing for the groom to hold open the door. "Let's walk him," he suggested.

Jehan spoke up. "You're in good hands, Tume. I'm going to go see to my own horse. I'll meet you at the Galley later."

Willam tried to walk beside the horse's head, opposite his master, but the beast wasn't having it. He headbutted him, pushing him away and stretched his neck towards Cae. Resignedly, he moved to walk beside Tume and let his sister take his place. Only then would the horse let himself be walked.

Tume waited until they were away from prying ears before he spoke. "Prince Kyleth would treat you well, admiring your ...spark and way with wild things. I'd love to see you with some of our ca'theryn," he added aside. "But he already has two other wives and four concubines. Plus a paramour. So you would not be of any precedence in his house, and, as a new favourite and an exotic, you would draw the ire of the others. Our women can be ruthless.

"Prince Cyran..." He sighed. "He can be cruel. He is likely looking for a docile Southern wife instead of one of our Northern siroccos, though I doubt he would respect her. You are both of these things. You are delicate and docile seeming, but you are active like Northern women, fierce in your own way and I am thinking there is steel under all your petals, and a raging firestorm for any who make the mistake of exposing it."

Vyncet, trailing behind his sister, laughed. "You have her to a T."

Cae glared at him and 'accidentally' trod on his boot. He reacted with exaggerated pain, but failed because he couldn't stop laughing.

"You see my concerns," Tume continued, speaking directly to Willam, who nodded. "If they offer, be polite, tell them you will take the offer to your father and then come see me immediately. Refusing them, if you wish to, must be done with delicacy. You are the family of my closest friend, not to mention my commander. I would help you in this."

"Thank you, lord Tume. Your offer is most welcome, and I will come see you if such occurs. But would they not send the suit directly to father?"

He shook his head. "Not if the eldest son is physically here and the father is not. They would use you as proxy. If they surprise me and send a messenger to your father directly, treat him as a guest while you 'consider the offer' and summon me at once. If he asks, you are sending for a friend more knowledgeable in their customs to help with negotiations."

Willam nodded.

Something occurred to Cae and she asked without thinking. "You serve my uncle in his free legions, yet your princes provided you with a guard for your horse from their own men?"

He smiled, his white teeth flashing in his dark face. "Because I am the only of their countrymen here who has any knowledge of the South and their ways. While I am of the Sterling Company, they are still my princes. It would be unwise to refuse them such a small thing if I ever wish to return to my own lands someday. I am not labelled 'lord' here without reason. I am noble enough back home, for all I will inherit nothing. Sometimes it is good to spend time with one's countrymen. Even if they do treat you as beneath them."

"And if ever the Sterling Company is hired to work against Alumet?" she asked sweetly.

"Then I would be forced to choose my allegiances with great care." He looked her over a long moment before adding. "Though I doubt your uncle would make me choose. He would as likely hire me out to some other small task to put me out of the way."

"Sounds like him," she nodded.

The two men then fell to other conversations that interested her less. Even Vyncet eventually moved around to the other side to join them, as they spoke of the Grand Melee to be held the next day. She spent her concentration on the white stallion who followed her docilely. He was almost fully cooled and limber by the time she realized that he was following her and the men 'leading' him were just following where he walked, oblivious to anything but their conversation and who might be near enough to overhear.

She smiled softly, putting a finger to her lips in quiet conspiracy and began a slow arc to turn him back towards the barn. As she suspected, the men followed blindly and did not really realize where they were until they crossed into the shadows of the stable. She looked up at lord Tume demurely, "He was cool enough, my lord. He needs oats and rest now."

He glanced him over and thumped the white neck. "So he does.

Thank you, my lady," he said, taking the tips of her fingers on his in the Southern manner as he bowed over them.

Jealously, the horse pawed the ground, reached over and put his nose in her hand, severing the connection. This made them all laugh.

Vyncet crowed, "Another conquest, sister! Shall I have the Herald make announcements?"

This time it was Willam who chastised him, with a swat to his shoulder and a glower. Cae knew their next conversation was going to be harsh.

Vyncet only muttered a quiet 'ow' as he rubbed the impacted limb, but said no more.

Caelerys curtseyed to them all. "I thank you for an enlightening hour, my lords, but I have remembered another appointment I really should keep."

"Of course, my lady," Tume intoned, handing the lead to the groom who waited to take the horse into his box.

The stallion balked as Cae turned to walk away, whickering after her. She took a breath, turning back to him. "You, sirrah, are not mine," she told him. She glanced at his master. "What, pray, is his name?"

Tume smiled. "Walara."

"Wa-la-ra," she said carefully, keeping each syllable separate and saying each vowel identically as he had. She nodded her thanks, turned to the horse. "Walara, you need to eat and rest. Go."

He ignored her pointing finger and reached for her. She let him touch her with his soft lip, but stayed firm.

"No." She glanced around him to lord Tume. "What is 'no' in Alumet?"

"Anan."

"Anan," she repeated, this time to the horse. She softened just a bit at the hurt in his eyes. "I will come to see you later. But now, anan, go," she added, giving him a firm nudge in the proper direction. He hung his head, but went.

She turned and left before he could change his mind and never saw the looks exchanged behind her.

She met Fern in her brother's tent, waiting with the filled box and a tray holding a light meal. "Good, you remembered," Cae breathed with relief, reaching for the box.

Fern held it back and pointed to the tray. "You should eat something first, my lady. There is no telling when you will again have the opportunity. And I know you have had nothing between tournament and tourney."

As her stomach growled at that moment, she relented, not having realized how hungry she actually was. She sat upon the backless sling chair and picked up the pasty on the plate. Before she could take a bite there was a flutter of feather as Tempest flew up from the floor onto the table, chirping her request.

"You would show up when food was in the offing," she growled, taking a bite to spite her. "Where have you been all day?"

The bird only tipped her wings out a bit from the shoulders, an avian shrug as Cae had come to interpret it.

She relented and gave her a single nibble from the pasty, then finished it herself. As she washed it away with the water waiting by the plate, she dismissed the pitiful look the bird gave her that she didn't save her more. "You've been overfed the last few days. No." She stopped suddenly, glanced at Fern. "Um, it wasn't tasted?" she asked as she remembered no bite taken from it.

She shook her head. "No need, my lady. They were both acquired from common supply. Pasty bought amid a hundred others, the water from a barrel I watched others draw and drink from. Though I did drink a cup from the goblet before refilling it for you. Just in case someone got to the glass."

She sighed, "You shouldn't take such risks on yourself. I believe a taster has been acquired."

She shrugged, setting aside the dishes and taking up the box. "He was unavailable, my lady. But you should go. Though no set time was mentioned for this, this is the best opportunity for it, and his highness will know that. Though my lady has put it off long enough he may have found other game to occupy himself."

She relented, sweeping out of the tent flap the girl held open for her. "Really, I was beginning to think you'd forgotten," Fern added as she fell into step with her lady.

"There were horses," was all she could offer in response.

The walk to the Citadel took the better part of an hour, but before long she was striding up the steps to the open doors of the main building. Fern tipped her chin up and spoke clearly to the guards blocking their path. "My Lady Caelerys Maral to visit the Royal Library upon request by his royal highness, Prince Balaran."

The guards processed this silently before letting them pass. Neither of the women saw the bird following dutifully along behind Caelerys, though the guards allowed it, assuming it was part of her train. If they thought the bird walking instead of being carried odd, they did not show it.

The main foyer looked different from her first, grand entrance. There were less people, but everyone she saw looked busy. There were even a small team of men carrying a very large, covered piece of furniture up a broad staircase. Beside her, Fern caught her breath. Cae smiled, "You should have seen it the day of the coronation. It loomed both vastly large and yet not big enough all filled with people."

"I can't imagine, my lady." She managed to close her eyes and compose herself as befitted the handmaiden of a great lady. "Where do we go?"

"We don't. I need you to find me a maid called Rue. She works these lower floors. If any would know her way around here, it is she."

"Oh, I recollect her. She's the one that brought me to you when you fled... left the room after the coronation. I can find her easy. Will Your Ladyship be all right here alone?"

Caelerys glanced around at the guards that stood along the walls, protecting whatever lay beyond the archways to which they stood sentry. "I think anyone would be a fool to harass me here. Just be quick," she said, taking the box from her.

Fern passed it to her without complaint and strode quickly across to a hallway from which several servants came and went.

Cae looked around her, waiting patiently. The upper gallery was open to the main floor, balustraded by scrolled arches and fancy stonework. Banners of the various houses hung from the galleries that had been absent the day of the coronation. Her own hung beside Cygent and Griff and the royal Alvermian. While a handful of scattered courtiers passed her by, no one bothered or approached her until she saw Fern coming her way with a young man in green livery.

She curtsied as she stopped in front of her mistress, the servant bowing. "This is Roan," Fern said, a glow in her eyes that Cae had not seen before. "Rue introduced me, said that he knew the way to the library and would be glad to take us."

Cae looked the young man over, from his politely averted but lively blue eyes to his shock of red curls. Even with a splattering of freckles dusting his nose and cheeks he was a handsome man. She smiled as he bowed again, stealing a side-glance at Fern as he did. "Your Ladyship, will you be pleasing to follow me? The library is in the part of the Citadel for which I have responsibility."

"After you, Roan," she said graciously, trying to hide her smile.

He led them past the throne room and the side rooms where they had mingled the day of the coronation. They turned down several corridors, getting her thoroughly lost, before coming to a tall, doubled door at the very end of yet another hall. He opened both doors with an expansive gesture, stepping out of their way to watch their reactions.

Neither Cae nor Fern disappointed him. They stood there, just a few feet beyond the threshold and stared around them like a pair of backwoods country folk seeing the Capitol for the first time. There were a number of people here, but most seemed to be learned men and apprentices, scattered about the main room which was easily thirty feet long and nearly as wide, and swept upwards four tall stories. Balconies ringed the main room revealing floor to ceiling shelves every five feet, and from what Cae could see from the door, there were very few empty places on those shelves. The lower floor was filled with tables and chairs as well as more comfortable seating with ample lighting throughout. On the lower floor she could see that the stacks of shelves ran deep, and were lost in the shadows. She could not begin to calculate how many volumes these chambers held.

Cae turned back to Roan who was closing the doors quietly. "How do you find anything?"

"There be a system, my lady," he grinned. "The Master Librarian knows where everything be kept." He swept his arm up and to the left, "Records are kept this way, though them I'd be advisin' a guide for. That system be indecipherable to all but the Master and his worms. That way be fictional reading, upper floors bein' histories and other treatments," he added, gesturing to the right, "with reading nooks scattered throughout. Stairs be at the back and sides, and behind us here," he gestured to two curling ironwork staircases on the wall they had come in through, which curled up towards the ceiling with stops at each of the gallery floors. "The Master be keeping a desk near the back there and be's available if ye've need, though any worm be for the askin'. Just donna bother the worms at copying. Sets them all a bother."

"Worms?" she asked, confused.

"Yeh, as in bookworms, what they call the Librarian's apprentices," he smiled, glancing at Fern. "If ye've no need of yer handmaid, I kin show her a place ta rest and what. She's like ta git bored in here," he said, eyeing her with a look of hope. "She'll be within easy call, I promise. And there be no need of chaperone here. Too many worms."

When Fern gave her a shy, hopeful look, Cae nodded. "Learn what you can, Fern. We are in unfamiliar territory and I would have lady Petra's advice corroborated."

Fern blushed, brushed a quick curtsey. "Thank you, my lady. I will put the time to good use."

Cae smiled as she turned to face the room full of books once more and missed the look of surprise on Fern's face. She selected a young 'worm' loading a small stack of volumes onto a wooden basket suspended from the top floor by a series of ropes. She crossed to him and paused until he noticed her.

He started as he turned to grab the ropes, immediately bowed. "My lady!" even his startled cry was soft and not apt to travel far. "How may this lowly worm be of service?"

"I... my apologies. I was supposed to meet the prince here. I have a book he requested."

"Oh, of course, my lady." He turned to point to the staircase winding up from the right side of the now closed doors. "You'll be... you'll want," he corrected with a blush, "that case there. Last I've seen of his highness was on the second floor about halfway down, near the medicals. Might be there still."

"My thanks, young man," she smiled.

He straightened up, startled at being thanked. "We lowly worms are here to serve, my lady. No thanks needed."

She tipped her head slightly, in the suggestion of a shrug, "But helpful young men should always be told when they are so."

He leaned forward just a hair, placing his emphasis with pride. "But there be no 'young men' here, my lady, for all your pardon. Just Nobles, the Master and us worms."

"Ah," she nodded, now understanding. These young men took being called 'worms' with a great deal of pride. "And the less said...?" she asked.

He beamed, nodding. At a jerk on the rope from an impatient compatriot on the third floor, he began hauling away. She paused to watch the wooden basket rise slowly to the gallery above before turning to the staircase he had indicated.

She carefully climbed the iron spiral to the first opening on the second floor and began to slowly walk down the stacks. She inhaled deeply of the scent of dust and paper and ink and leather bindings. She had never seen so many books at one time in her life. The library at Taluscliff held maybe two hundred books upon its shelves, and thought that to be impressive. She had read every one of them, some of them many times. She felt she could remain on this one floor, on this one half of this library for the rest of her life and never read every book here.

She stepped into one of the stacks, her eye drawn by a familiar volume. She reached up with her free hand to caress the spine. Taluscliff had a copy of this one, though far more well worn. Beside it were other volumes of herbal lore she had never seen. She longed to pull them down and look through them, but she was not sure if it was permitted and she had no where to set the tome safely locked in the box on her arm. She sighed. "This... this is the real treasure of the kingdom," she breathed.

"That is why they call it 'a wealth of knowledge'," came a voice.

She looked down the end of the stack to see a golden head of cropped curls peering at her. It was a prince, but not the one she had expected. She dropped immediately into a deep curtsey, clutching the box tightly to her. "Your Highness," she breathed.

He slowly walked the length of the long shelf, stopping just a foot from the hem of her skirts before he spoke again. "Though there are those of my ancestors which begrudged the expense that went to build it.

Rise," he said, almost as an afterthought.

She obeyed, but kept her head still demurely lowered, almost afraid to look into the eyes of the man who had refused, even at his mother's behest, to speak to her. "Would Your Highness forgive me if I said they were fools?"

He was silent such a long moment she began to fear she had spoken too freely. Then he chuckled softly. His laugh was rough, a little gravelled, as if it did not get much exercise. "Why should I need to forgive the speaking of a truth?"

She dared to glance up a little, catching sight of his handsome face without looking him in the eye. His face was nearly identical to that of his brother, though it seemed rougher. There was a small scar that vanished into his hairline near his temple and his eyes were a darker blue, their colour almost black in the dimmer light of the shelves.

Then a quiet, short shrill from behind her made all colour leave her face. She turned, looked down to see the hooked blue beak and bright black eye peering at her worriedly from behind her skirts. "Oh, no," she breathed. "Please forgive me, Your Highness. I did not intend for her to follow me," she stammered, reached out her wrist for the bird as she dropped once more to a curtsey.

He caught the hand before the bird could reach it, arresting her obeisance. She looked at him, found her eyes locked with his. She could not read his expression, whether it was anger or amusement, but his grip on her hand was firm. "You did not hear her flying behind you?"

She caught her breath, feeling her cheeks flush. "She... she likely did not fly, Your Highness. She often runs along after me at home. It was not her fault but mine. I neglected to order her to remain behind." There was cold terror beginning to build in her belly.

"Walking?" he frowned. "Odd behaviour for a falcon."

She gave the tiniest shake of her head, "Not for a gauvan, Your Highness," she said in a small voice.

"A gauvan?" he asked in an authoritative tone.

"I... I have the dispensation at Stag's Hall, if Your Highness requires it. This will not happen again."

"If I wish to see it, I can have it pulled from the Records," he said dismissively. He drew her aside in an attempt to get a better look at the bird. To his consternation, the fowl followed her mistress, pressing herself between the bookshelf and her skirts.

Released from his eyes, she looked down to the bird, realized what he was trying to do, as Tempest followed her in a continuing circle. "You... you frighten her, Your Highness. If you wish to see her..." she braved, not daring to look up to his face again.

He stopped, standing uncomfortably close to her, giving her little choice but to look up at him again. "And do I frighten her lady?" There was something dangerous in those eyes... and something else.

She closed her own, took a deep breath, trying desperately to calm herself. "At this moment in time, under the current circumstances... aye, Your Highness," she all but whispered. "I fear for the consequences of my error."

His voice, when it came, was unbelievably soft. "There is no shame in admitting fear."

She opened her eyes, saw something different in his, but still indecipherable. "Only in failing to face it," she breathed. "Fear is what tells you when you are out of your depth."

"You tremble."

"Of course she's trembling, Valan, you've scared the wits out of her," snapped another voice.

The moment shattered like glass and the prince dropped her hand and stepped away from her, hardening in an instant as he turned to face his brother.

Balaran stood at the gallery end of the shelves, growling at his brother yet grinning at her. "I'd heard there was a white falcon following a Lady all the way to the library and I knew it had to be you."

Tempest crept out from behind her skirts to chirp inquisitively at Balaran. It was all Caelerys could do not to breathe a sigh of relief. "Truthfully, I did not intend to bring her into the library," she responded. "I forgot to tell her not to follow." She turned back to Prince Valan, though not meeting his eyes again. She couldn't bear to see the coldness she could feel in them. "I will take her immediately from here and warn her not to come to the Citadel again."

"What? And break our dear sister's heart?" Balaran chuckled. "Besides, I've seen a great many pretty birds carried as ornament by lesser ladies than you around here. It would be a shame to deny ourselves the company of one so beautiful and well behaved."

"The lady or the bird?" Valan sneered.

He shrugged with a grin, "Either. Take her to shoulder and let us take ourselves to a table to view the treasure you've brought me."

She found herself blushing again even as she bent to take the bird to her wrist. "Jelma," she chided, mostly to help calm herself and perhaps salvage some of the situation. "How do we greet royalty?"

The bird looked from her mistress to the two men and performed the bow she had made to the princess a few days back.

Balaran smiled and bowed back to the bird. Valan just stood there with his unreadable, near scowl. Finally, he merely nodded cursorily to her and his brother, "I will leave you to your plans." With that he turned and stalked back the way he had come.

Balaran only spared him a rolled eye before he offered his arm to Cae.

A slight lift of her wrist was all the signal Tempest needed to get her walking up Cae's arm to her shoulder. Caelerys then set her hand lightly on the prince's arm and allowed him to lead her to a nook at the far end of the floor. He guided her into a comfortable, padded chair and sat himself beside her in its match. She held the box out to him.

As he set his hands upon it, she hesitated, not yet releasing it. "You... you must promise me, Your Highness.... This will not be burnt? My father..."

He set one hand upon hers, looked deeply into her eyes. "I swear to you, no book, however blasphemous or dangerous, shall ever burn so long as I have a relative upon that throne. Hidden away, most assuredly, but none of my family believe in the burning of books. It will be returned to you in the same condition you have given it to me."

There was no doubt of the sincerity in his unblemished face. She was lost in that countenance a long moment, marvelling at the similarity of feature at the same time that she saw all the differences that set them apart. She also wondered why this prince set her so at ease while the other... was like facing some wild and terrible monster for all she felt drawn to that danger. She blushed as she nodded, letting the box go.

He gave her a disarming smile as he drew a small gold key from his tunic. She blushed again, having forgotten she had the key she had been given in her own small pocket. She should have known there would have been two and that he would have kept one for himself.

"I take it your family are not followers of the Eldest?" he asked casually as he dealt with lock and straps.

She glanced down at his hands, watching their nimble deftness as a distraction. "Not as he would have himself followed here. We have no priest and anvil. No church but the wild wood."

"Pontifex," he corrected. "They prefer the term 'pontifex'. While I laud your adherence to the old ways, you would do well to be subtle and quiet about it. The Eldest has insinuated himself everywhere thanks to my late aunt. It was she who made them so prominent, even to presiding over most important political events."

"And your immediate family?" she asked softly as he opened the box and drank deep of the incensewood's fragrance.

He gave her a devilish smile as he glanced sidelong at her. "My lady mother was once one of your father's vassals. What do you think?"

Thinking about it, she remembered the queen swearing by the Mother once. It struck her then, what she had missed the day of the coronation. 'Queen Sigrun Echo'. Echo was one of the Maral Vassals. The attentions the royal family had been paying her suddenly made sense. She sat back at against the chair, allowed Tempest to settled down in her lap as if she were a house cat. She took comfort in her weight and warmth and watched the prince's eyes light up as he lifted the book from its sanctuary.

It seemed silly to take such pleasure in his delight. It was only a book of children's tales after all, but he held the tome with such reverence. He opened the tooled leather cover and ran his hand across the smooth, polished paper bearing the title. It was beautifully illuminated, the colours still as vibrant as when they had been inked. Of course, thinking about it, she had never seen a book of children's tales so expensively presented.

"Show me the story of Isildar," he asked quietly, setting the volume on the table before them.

She moved the box out of the way and turned the book towards her. She opened it about half way, reaching over the bird in her lap as she carefully turned the pages to find the story she sought. When she came to the page with an antlered knight and his horse entangled in the vines that formed the illuminated drop capital, she stopped and slid the book back to him.

He read the story voraciously, setting the book upon his lap and turning the pages with reverence. When he came to the end of the tale, he turned back to the painted drawing that depicted the battle and return of the maiden. He studied it with an intensity that almost reminded her of his brother and the way he had looked at her.

She barely noted the worms moving through the stacks, refreshing lights, or the cat that had taken residence on the back of her chair until the tail curled down to brush her ear. She turned with a start, thinking perhaps some spider had descended onto her, waking the sleeping falcon. The cat simply looked at her with half closed eyes, only paying the bird half a mind. Tempest stood, fluffing up her feathers in jealous protest, but a hand on her back settled her down.

"That's unusual," said Balaran suddenly.

She turned to see him watching the three of them with curiosity, the book now closed in front of him.

"Which? That the cat has not made for bird or that Tempest stills at my touch?"

"That the cat is there at all."

She glanced back at the marbled feline lounging on the back of her chair. "I assure you, she is not mine, sire."

"Of course not," he said dismissively, still watching the cat. "It's one of the library cats. We keep them to keep the mice out of the books. But ...they usually only let the worms see them. I, myself, have only caught glimpses, and I've been in and out of this library for years."

She gave a thoughtful glance down at Tempest. "Hmm, yet another reason I should not bring her here. There might be territorial fights over the mice."

This made him laugh, which caused the cat to turn to glare at him. A cleared throat from nearby drew their attention. One of the library boys stood a few paces away, and bowed when they turned to him.

"Yes, worm," the prince growled through a grin.

The boy's grin was in his eyes but not on his face and he stood with stiff formality. "Her Majesty, the queen has requested your presence at table, Your Highness." He turned to Caelerys, gave another, half bow, "and there be..." he paused, catching Balaran's glare at the slip, "there is... a young lord on the first floor seeking his lady sister."

Tempest hopped to the table as Cae rose to peer over the balcony rail while the prince put the book into the box and locked it back up. Willam stood uncomfortably near the door with Fern at his side. She turned back to the prince as he handed the box to the worm.

"Make certain this gets into my bedchamber. Go now and stop for no one."

"On your study table, highness?" he asked as he accepted his literary charge.

"No, bedside." He stood and stretched as the worm darted off at once. He turned to Cae and held out his hand.

She reached out to set her fingertips on his. "Your Highness," she said, sketching a light curtsey. "My wishes for a good meal and a good rest go with you."

He smiled, bent to kiss her fingertips, never taking his eyes from hers. "My lady, I think you have most assuredly guaranteed I shall have no rest at all tonight."

She blushed, mildly shocked.

He had a devilish look in his eyes and a mischievous grin, "So much reading to do."

She let out the breath she had not been aware she had been holding, favoured him with reproachful glare.

He straightened, "Truthfully, my lady, what could you have been thinking?" he asked playfully.

She struggled to stop blushing, calling Tempest to her shoulder. "Truthfully, I do not know, Your Highness. There are those who have recently made more inappropriate insinuations with less wording."

His expression became serious as he offered her his arm. "Forgive me my fun, my lady. I had not meant to offend. Your reputation is above reproach. Please, allow me to at least see you to your brother's side."

Cae accepted his arm and allowed him to lead her to the spiral stairway halfway down the gallery.

"You missed it, sister," Willam said as he was handing her into her saddle for the return home.

"Missed what?" she asked idly as she took up the reins. There was much on her mind. She suddenly looked around. "Where's Vyncet?" she asked worriedly.

He chuckled at her response. "I didn't do anything to him. ...This time. He headed home nearly an hour ago, though he might have taken a detour. If he ran into the Marroks we won't see him 'til after dawn."

She settled herself as she waited for him to mount, mollified. "So what did I miss?"

"Remember that bad tempered black?"

Wraith and Cae tossed their heads almost together. "Aye. What of it?"

"Mambyn sent it by groom to the Ca'than lord."

She turned, mouth and eyes agog. "What did he do?"

Willam snorted, "Refused it, of course. Said that he would accept neither beast nor ransom."

"What did the groom do?" she asked, moving to follow him as they slowly rode out of the Citadel's courtyard.

"Protested, of course. It wasn't his place to ...something or other. Tume didn't really let him finish. He was in full heat and had drawn himself up to his full height. Now, I'm tall for a man, but he made me look below average."

Cae chuckled, "You're not tall for a man, you're short for a giant," she teased. "But I can see how the groom was terrified."

He gave his sister a sidelong glance. "Why do I get the feeling you wouldn't have been, even in the groom's shoes?"

She shrugged. "I have no idea. I highly doubt it if I were in the groom's shoes. But I do like him. Much better than his princes. But go on," she prompted, brushing her cheek against Tempest's breast.

"There is not much to tell, really. He informed the groom that to accept the beast in any form would be a greater insult than any dealt by refusing and that if his king wished to maintain fair relations with Alumet, his master would not press the matter further. And that if he wished to know why, he was free to ask Lord Araan. The groom wandered off in confusion after that."

"I don't know what to say. I wish I could have seen it."

"Well, you had pressing matters with Royalty, sister," he said in an insinuating tone.

"It was a matter of books," she insisted, feeling a blush rising.

"For you, that's practically flirting."

She took a swipe at him for that, and Willam laughed at her.

"So will lord Tume be on the list you send to father?" he asked.

She glared at him, but treated the topic seriously. "Everyone I know to be eligible will be on that list. I shall enumerate the virtues and failings of each along with my feelings. I will not hesitate to mention a loathsome man's advantages, just as I will not hesitate to inform father of why I do not like him."

"I expect no less."

"Father expects no less, Willam," she growled. "You, I think, expected a great deal less."

He sobered quickly as they turned down the street and into the courtyard. He studied her in the torchlight. "No longer, sister. And I pity the suitor who does. You have grown into a formidable woman, for all your terrors."

She sighed, remembering old lessons. "There is no courage where there is no fear."

He dismounted and crossed to her to help her down. "Your shyness is an asset, as is your steel. I only hope we can find a man worthy of both. Lord Tume I would mark as such a one. As Lord Rorik."

She held his gaze as her feet touched the ground. "And the princes?"

It was a moment before he answered. "I reserve my judgement on both of them. ...But Mother help the kingdom if either thinks he is," he added lightly, knowing it would make her smile. It did, but she still swatted him for it. That made him smile as he watched her go into the house.

That night Caelerys dreamt of flying.

Her dreams were full of the wind in her face, the rising sun on her cheek, and nothing but air beneath feathered arms. She looked down, seeking prey, saw a great stag running across broad meadows and dove, streaking right between the great antlers. Then she stumbled, caught her footing on the heath and felt the rhythm of great muscles pounding turf and stirring up the intense fragrance of clover and coltsfoot. She raced across the face of the earth 'til she reached a trifling stream, threw herself into the air to sail over and across it, but the sands that sprang up on the far side burned the pads of her feet.

She realised she was ravenously hungry, smelled the blood of fear in the air. Not far was a gazelle, unwary, its blood calling to hers, singing in her ears and pulling at her stomach. A short race and it was hers, hot blood spurting down her throat as her claws sank deeply, and they hurt, the pain blinding as teeth tore into exhausted flesh. The ca'theryn ripped her life from her once nimble body even as her struggles became less and she lay there, barely breathing as the beast feasted upon her. The last sight her eyes beheld before they closed forever was that of a great beast rising over the dune, scaled in amber and glinting like gold in the sun, breathing fire down upon everything.

7

Caelerys rose to a house full of excitement. This was the final day of the King's Tournament, and the day of the grand melee. Both of her brothers and her uncle had entered and even waking in a fright from her dreams well before dawn, she was apparently the last abed. There was no time to take Tempest to the balcony for a sunrise flight, and as she hurriedly dressed and rushed downstairs to breakfast, the bird ran along behind her like a faithful hound.

She had almost finished her sparse meal, as her kin had left very little behind, when lady Petra darkened the doorway. She tutted over the state of Cae's hair, even as Cae licked the last crumbs of a pastry from her fingers. "Really, this will not do. Fern, have you learned nothing from my Marigold?"

The girl bobbed a curtsey. "Forgive me, my lady, but I have not had time as yet. I thought to twist a simple braid circle and put flowers in it."

Lady Petra paused to look Caelerys over critically. "Hmm, that might do this morning for the grandstand, but it will not do at all for tonight." She turned back to the maiden under scrutiny. "Immediately after the melee, once awards have been granted, you will come straight back here. We will have a great deal of work to do with you if you are to be ready for the ball this evening."

Her cup slipped from her fingers as she tried to lift it up. Luckily it did not get more than an inch and nothing spilled. "Ball?"

Lady Petra smiled as she sighed with delight. "Yes! A grand ball to celebrate the tournament champions and the king's crowning. A chance to dance and mingle and display oneself to one's best. There will be no greater opportunity to catch the eyes of eligible men. Though I hear you have already caught the attention of nothing less than a prince." Her eyes narrowed. "Do not let that make you grow complacent. You are not the only maid to catch his eye, though you are the one who has been whispered about most. And catch his eye all you please, there may be others who are more strategically placed to cement the realm. Do not allow any one man to occupy all of your attentions, though they might well try."

Cae went from cold fear to maidenly blush to a furious one during the course of her effusive speech. She stood. "And what is it people have been saying?"

The dame waved her hand dismissively, gesturing for her to hurry upstairs to finish getting ready. "Nothing that is not to your advantage. But you have been seen over much in his company. One must be careful lest other, more eligible men think he has a claim on you. I am doing my best to counter that rumour wherever I encounter it. You have given no man your favour and none have laid a claim to you."

She allowed herself to be ushered back to her chambers, following the lady out of curiosity. "Who has been asking after me?"

Lady Petra gave a long suffering sigh, "Sadly, no one yet of consequences or hope."

"Allow me to guess," she said, calling the bird to her shoulder as she climbed the stairs, "Sir Hayden Trent?"

"Among others," she said. Try as Cae might, she could get no more out of her.

Whilst Fern hastily made more of her lady's hair, lady Petra began issuing orders to other servants for things that must be ready and waiting when the Grand Melee ended. Eventually Cae lost track of all the tiny details and just tuned it all out, made sure the straps for her shoulder pad were sound while her hair was being pinned.

Finally, she was allowed to buckle it on and leave the house, bird upon her shoulder, for her ride to the grandstand. By then it was too late for her to stop into the tents to see any of her family and lady Petra ushered her into the stands. Thankfully, she directed them towards lady Sigourney and very near the Roshan girls. She carefully transferred her shoulder pad to her thigh to protect her gown and set Tempest upon it. She knew the bird would obstruct the view of the people behind them and wished to be considerate. A few other ladies wore their birds upon their shoulders still, but they were dainty sparrowhawks, and trim little kestrels which impaired no one's view of the field.

Once settled, she observed the niceties with her neighbours, greeting lady Sigourney and the girls warmly. Sigourney set a companionable hand upon hers. "La, child, but your hand is like ice," she exclaimed. "Nervous?"

Cae turned to her from trying to get a good view of the tourney field. "Yes, my lady. I have heard some disturbing rumours regarding this battle."

Lucelle turned her head to look at her. "Oh?"

Cae immediately wished she had spoken more softly, having just noted the presence of black tunics trimmed in Kaladen grey very nearby. She lowered her voice and bent closer on the pretence of adjusting her shoe. "Sea Wolves seek Griffin prey, possibly lethally so. Stag has banded with Wolf and unknown others to deal with the matter."

Lucelle's hand drifted to her mouth to hide her small gasp. "That explains what Lord Vyncet was doing with my brother, Maddox."

Lady Sigourney's hand tightened on hers before withdrawing. "Well, we shall see soon enough."

Lady Petra frowned, "None of this is appropriate subject matter for proper young ladies."

"Then perhaps proper young ladies should not witness the fulminations of such topics," Cae said stiffly. "But then, this is practice for Life and to keep sharp required skills. Best we learn to handle and understand what we can of it while its lethality is curtailed and our own lives and honour do not rest in the balance."

Lucelle turned back around, stifling a giggle, and Cae felt her cheeks begin to warm a little. She was saved from any retort by the trumpet of the herald and the announcement of each of the participants. The melee was to be a last man standing affair, with numerous marshals wearing the most horrific orange and black tabards over their armour. Their helmets were the oddest Cae had ever seen, having an open face covered by a wire cage that gave them full field of vision whilst still protecting them from stray blows.

As the men were named in order of precedence, they moved to previously determined locations on the broad field, guided by the marshals. Cae hardly recognized it as the same sands upon which the jousts had been held just the day before. She saw her two brothers, armed with blunted swords and Willam hoisted a wooden war hammer on his shoulder. Her uncle was not announced until much later, with three other men from the Free Legions. He and lord Tume strode out together, followed by two men Cae had not seen before, but knew to be from the Iron Legion by their devices. Only the younger of the Alumet princes stood to fight. This did not surprise her, as the elder of the two had seemed more courtier than warrior.

The Sea-wolves were grouped near the lower stands and were indeed eyeing Lord Rorik and five other men in gold tabards trimmed in crimson with the rampant griffins in blood red.

Caelerys said a silent prayer to the Mother to keep her family safe even as the trumpet blared and the field fell to organized chaos. Even Tempest stretched her neck to watch with a worried chirrup.

Several groups of men, Maral, Marrok, the Free Legions and Roshan and all their vassals began to converge very quickly to the Griff position. Cae feared the Griffs would attack them, and it seemed, for just for a moment, that they would. But when backs were turned to them as they were loosely surrounded, they realized something else was afoot. Words must have been exchanged, as attitudes shifted immediately. Even unable to see faces, their bodies had all the expression needed. Cae breathed a sigh of relief before looking over the rest of the field.

Prince Valan was in the remaining muddle, clustered with four

Alvermian crests, along side six other men in black. Two of them were trimmed in silver, the rest in copper, and Cae only caught a glimpse of a copper viper, and none at all of the silver sigil. She recognized the tallest of the copper trimmed knights as lord Mambyn who had disgraced himself in the equestrian and nearly beaten lord Tume the day before. With such men as these behind him, she wondered if the prince stood a chance, but they seemed to be working together for the moment.

Her eye was drawn to the prince, who fought with a pair of blunted arming swords and no shield. She had seen her brothers fight before. Willam was a monster in combat, laying flat nearly anything unlucky enough to come within reach and Vyncet was nimble, fast and fierce. The prince was frightening. The twinned blades worked swift and glittering in a radius around him, both striking and shielding.

Her observation was interrupted by Onelle's confused question to her mother. "I thought the herald said it was every man for himself. Why are they fighting together?"

Sigourney was the one who answered. "Oh, it is not unusual in a grand melee. Often Houses and their vassals fight together, one group making allies with another for a common goal. Once that goal is met, or there is no one else on the field but for them, then they turn to deal with one another. Or something like that occurs," she commented dryly as one of the Asparadane turned on one of the Alvermian, taking him down before he even saw his opponent.

A marshal waved a flag at the struck man, announcing him beheaded and out of the fight. A glance and a word from the prince and the remaining of his men, as well as the two in silver on black turned and battered the offender until he held up both his arms, signalling that he, too, was 'dead'. A couple more blows rained in before the marshal could call it and make a path out of the battle for him.

Cae watched him walk past the man he'd 'killed' and saw heated words exchanged.

A shriek from Tempest turned her attention back to the battlefield. The Sea-wolves had realized their plan had been anticipated and countered and had, instead, split up and swarmed out into the general scrimmage and proceeded to sow as much chaos as they could. Often they would strike an opponent from behind and then go after his neighbour, half turning his back, luring his first victim into attacking the nearest person behind him, most often one of his own party. Or one would attack boldly from the front whilst one of his fellows slipped up behind to deliver a 'killing' blow.

"I'll say this much," lady Sigourney grumbled, "they are effective, however underhanded."

Lady Petra concurred. "I am just glad they are on our side these days. Watching them, I don't see how we managed to subdue them."

"Some would say we haven't really," Cae commented, remembering that many of the shipwrecks that washed up onto her beaches were their victims.

"We never subdued them at all," Sigourney said. "They turned on the Levitau like everyone else when they learned of their treachery."

Cae cheered as Willam clouted Prince Cyran solidly enough on the side of his helmet to send him sprawling. The four similarly attired warriors with him surged after Willam in rage, attempting to swarm him before he could get his hammer back around. Vyncet lunged in from the side, taking out two of them, one with his sword and the other with a shield to the face, only to get cut down by Cyran's still flailing blade. The nearest marshal ordered him to his knees if he would continue, which he did. The other two were blocked by Lord Rorik Griff, who took one at the shoulder with his sword and taking the blow of the second upon his side. The marshal did not call it, and Rorik finished him with a backstroke that made him stagger back.

Cae held back a scream as she saw a Sea-wolf slink in and make an attempt to drive his sword into Rorik's exposed armpit. Willam's boot to the man's hip interfered with his aim and made what could have been a lethal stab fall thankfully short. The crowd booed at the Kaladen man, cheering as Griff and Maral turned as one to put him down: Willam taking his legs out from under him and Rorik's blade following him to the ground with a 'beheading' blow to the chin that left him stunned on the sands.

The fighting was so thick and fierce in that cluster that the marshals had to give the order to 'hold' to enable three men, including the Kaladen on his back and the Alumet prince, to be removed from the field. Two others limped out with them, along with every one of the Northern warriors, 'injured' or not, as they followed their prince.

In the heat of the skirmish, Cae lost track of Vyncet and only found him again as he was aided, limping, off the field. His helmet was already in his squire's hand and he seemed to be laughing through his pain.

The Marrok brothers lasted almost to the end, fighting all comers nearly back to back and battling in perfect tandem. They were a true marvel to watch. Even when they took on two opponents, they fought like wolves, flanking their foes. Where one struck high, the other went low, working close so closely together that they should have been interfering with each other but were not. They would strike their own targets, turn, rolling against each others' backs to swap enemies. They were almost as graceful in combat as Prince Valan who managed to take one of them down with a cut to the hip even as the other took his left arm.

Tossing aside his left sword, the prince let that arm hang limply from his shoulder and deftly dispatched the remaining brother, who was so used to working with his brother that he left himself open. Two other opponents fell to the prince's remaining sword before he, himself was taken down by the combined might of Tume, Rorik and Jehan. It could not be seen who made the 'killing' blow, but that they all stood back as if in agreement as the prince stood with both hands up, declaring himself dead.

The three of them turned back to the field to find themselves alone but for Willam and young Terrel Alder, who Cae suddenly remembered was a distant cousin. They stopped, as they were all that remained of their original alliance, and stood in a circle facing each other, their hands held out in the centre.

"What are they doing?" Onelle asked.

"Dissolving the alliance, not doubt," Sigourney explained. "They came into this as friends with an agreement not to turn on one another until this moment."

"Some of them are kin and comrades in arms," Cae added.

"Oh? Who?" Lucelle asked excitedly. Cae noted that her elder sister said nothing, though she listened.

"The black skinned man and the barrel with the battleaxe are both in the Sterling Company of the Free Legions. The barrel is my uncle, Jehan Maral, and lord Tume's commander," Cae offered.

"Lord Tume is the dark, bald one, right?" Lucelle confirmed.

She nodded. "And the one with the war hammer is my eldest brother Willam, who must now fight his uncle... who taught him a fair piece of what he knows about combat."

"Oooh," Onelle groaned in sympathy.

Cae laughed. "Kin or no, Willam will not hold back."

"They're separating," Balyra said.

They turned to face the field and watched the five men turn their backs to each other in the circle. One of them called out a count, and they each took a step away at each number until it reached ten. Then they turned as one to the centre and held up their weapons in salute. At some signal unseen and unheard from the stands, the five of them roared and attacked their opponent of choice.

Willam tried to cross the circle to take on his uncle, by far the most dangerous opponent in both his and his sister's accounting. He was thwarted by Lord Rorik, who stood closest and chose Willam. The two tangled for several minutes before Willam's strength began to tell on the older man's endurance and an unlucky swing gave Willam room to side swipe his ribs with a cracking blow that had Rorik's fist in the air immediately as he tried to breathe through a dented plate. As marshal's aides rushed forth to pull the injured lord from the path of combat, Willam turned again to his true target.

Jehan had already dispatched lord Terrel and had bounced back from a particularly fierce bind with Tume when Willam engaged him. Jehan had to turn to block the incoming hammer and still keep himself protected from any attack Tume would make. Tume did not take the interruption well. He howled as he charged in, taking Willam from left thigh to right shoulder in a blow that sent up sparks from his blunted practice sword. This threw off Willam's block of the descending axe that skidded along his hammer's shaft to catch him on the hand and followed down to the top of the same shoulder. Cae flinched as her brother crumpled under the double onslaught.

There was a momentary pause as he fell. Tume's sword had caught the axe below the curve of the blade and carried it upward. They froze with the weapons above their heads to look down at Willam, say something inaudible in the frenzied roar of the crowd. They were apparently appeased when Willam's hand came up even as he tried to roll to his side to stand. Failing, he just waved them away to the laughter and appreciative cheers of the crowd.

The two remaining combatants disentangled their weapons and walked a few yards away to begin again.

Cae missed the rest of the fight, as she lifted Tempest from her lap and slipped past lady Petra, rushing from the stands as Willam was helped from the field. Once she was clear of the immediate press of people, she tossed the bird lightly into the air to fly ahead, and all but ran for the exit of the lists.

Willam was not so grievously wounded that he was taken to the Physician's tent, and was carried to his own. As his squire laboured beneath the weight of the practice hammer, Cae ran ahead to hold open the pavilion's flaps. She quickly gathered water and cleaning cloths, to have them ready whilst the squire moved to unbuckle the armour. When her hands were free, Cae helped him while Tempest sat on the table watching worriedly.

The Physician arrived as they were removing the cuisses from his thighs and tried to shoo Cae out. Willam did not protest, though she did.

"I am not done in or bleeding, sister. Though it is doubtful I shall be dancing overmuch tonight," he added with a half-hearted groan. "Why don't you go find Vyncet. If he is wounded and you haven't seen to him he will gripe about it for days."

Cae smiled softly, knowing it to be true. "Are you certain?" she asked, eyeing the Physician who was in the process of carefully peeling away his gambeson.

"Did you see any blood?" Will growled.

"No."

"Am I wheezing?"

"No."

"Then I'll live!" he snarled. "Go! And take that feathered dog of yours with you!" he roared as she slipped out of the tent, laughing.

She called the bird and held the flap open long enough for her to run outside. She stood there, hands upon her hips a moment as she thought aloud. "All right, Tempest. He should have been here and he's not. So, he's either hurt more severely than I thought and at the Physician's, which is possible if he broke the leg, or he's not hurt nearly as bad as he looked and is off drinking."

She looked down at Tempest who chirped a confused response. "Hmm, why don't you fly up and see if you can find him?" she suggested. "And I'll go look in at the Physician's."

Tempest piped an affirmative and took flight.

The Physician's tent was closest to the field for convenience. It was moderately busy, with those who were not tending injured carefully packing up what was not being used or would no longer be needed. Lord

Rorik was there, getting his chest bandaged for broken ribs. Cae politely looked away. There was an older squire getting his arm set and a few minor wounds being tended to and bandaged but no sign of her brother. She stopped to ask one of the apprentices who was packing his master's instruments.

"Excuse me," she said sweetly, getting his attention.

He turned, offered a cursory bow as he realized she was a lady and glanced her over. "My lady, are you injured or come you for another?"

"No, forgive me," she smiled, shaking her head in apology.

Strangely, he blushed slightly at that smile.

"My brother was all but carried off the field, a leg injury, but I do not see him here, nor is he in our pavilion. I thought I might ask if he had been seen to here?"

"Ah," he exclaimed, turning to put a roll of bandages into his bag to hide his expression. "A leg injury..." he mused. "Your house colours?"

"Argent on azure. Vyncet bears a stag's head."

He closed his eyes and flushed even further, took a moment to school his tightening expression. "Ah, yes, the younger Maral. Aye, my lady, he... he was here."

"Was he not so badly wounded as he appeared?" she asked, worry clear in her deep blue eyes.

He turned to her, his features more comforting now and his flush beginning to fade. "My lady can rest easy. His bone was luckily not broken, which is more than I can say for a great number of Sea-wolf victims. He was able to limp out of here some time ago. He was... complaining about his greave." Here, again, he blushed. "He was on a crutch when he left."

"Did he say anything that might tell me where he's gone?"

"He merely threw his greave at his squire and snapped something about seeing his brother," he said hastily as he returned to packing.

She took a step back, confused by his behaviour. "Well, thank you for your time. I will not keep you from your work."

Just before she could turn away, he seemed to remember his manners. "I wish you luck, my lady."

Again she thanked him before leaving the tent, only flinching slightly at the shout of the man having his arm set. She stood just out of the traffic flow for a moment, thinking. Clearly he did not go to Willam, but if he had been complaining about greaves he would have gone to Janem. Determined, she lifted the hem of her skirts just enough and set herself into the increased flow of people moving through the lane, headed for the armourers.

There were three blacksmith tents at the end of a little off-shoot from the main thoroughfare just before the fairgrounds proper. The area was fairly busy, with squires bustling back and forth carrying or carting their knight's or lord's armour for repairs after the fighting. Even if she had not known which tent belonged to the Singing Forge, she would have known it by the sound of Janem swearing, loudly and profusely. Smiling, she dodged a fleeing squire, and slipped inside.

She found both her brothers at the back near the work table where Janem threw the offending greave down with a spate of very creative Old Vermian invectives. Vyncet leaned back against the table across from him on his crutch, running one hand through his loose, black curls, trying to erase the marks of his helmet from them. "Tell me about it," he grumbled when Janem stopped to take a breath, not that he'd understood a word.

She slipped up between them and rest her elbows on the table and her chin on her fists, gazed adoringly up at Janem. "*Aye, brother, tell me about it,*" she smiled in the same tongue.

He pointed an awl at her, glaring. "Add to that a few more words whose meaning you shouldn't know," he growled.

She straightened up, laughing. "Willam is fine, by the way. Though he'll likely be giving you his whole uppers, pauldrons included, later."

He sighed, tossing the tool down. "Front or backplate?"

She thought about it for a moment. "Back for certain. Right shoulder, I think. Don't know about the rest. I saw sparks."

"Who hit him?" Vyncet asked, grinning.

"Uncle and lord Tume both at once. Tume up the back, Uncle down the shoulder."

Both men winced. "He'll be black and blue for weeks," Janem muttered

"Who won?" Vyncet asked.

She shrugged. "Have no idea. It was down to those two when I left. They had to help Willam up. I was too worried to stay for the finish. So, why were you calling the poor Physician's parentage into question?" she asked idly, picking up the discarded greave. She frowned at the deep dent along the side of the plate. It had a jagged cut along one side of it. "Did the weapon do this? How do you still have your leg?"

Janem reached across the table and took it from her. "No weapon did this," he snarled. "Lackwit apprentice took tin-snips to it!"

"What? Why?"

Vyncet snorted, "Couldn't get it off."

She looked at the perfectly sound leather straps. "Did he not know how to work a buckle?"

"I have no idea. I'd rather he'd cut the strap than the plate," he sighed, tossing the awl down.

She turned to look down at his heavily bandaged leg. "So what exactly happened? How bad is it?"

He pulled up, twisting so his leg was out of her reach just in case. "Never you mind."

She put her hands on her hips and gave him a deadpan glare. "Who do you think is going to be changing that bandage?"

"Fennel?" he offered.

Janem gestured absently at their sister. "She's better at it. Trust me."

He growled, giving in, but still tried to divert the subject. "So, can you fix it?" he asked Janem, pointing at his armour-piece. "Work your magic?"

Janem tossed it behind him into a pile beside the forge bellows. "Even magic can't mend that. I'll have to melt it down and reforge it. Which I can't do until your leg is healed and I can make certain of the fit." Vyncet looked crest-fallen but Janem ignored him. "So what happened?"

He sighed, gave in. "Blunted axe to the greave. Embedded the dent right next to the shin against the bone. Didn't even break the skin. They told me I was one lucky bastard."

Janem shook his head. "No, that's me."

Vyncet chuckled, "That's what I told him!"

"Haha, very funny. How long are you off it?" she asked, forcing him back to the subject.

"Crutch a fortnight, no riding for a gold moon. I'm supposed to stay off it and keep it up as much as possible. He said there'd be pain and swelling and we'll need to keep that down."

She nodded. "Simple teas and herbs for that. Cold compresses. Too bad it isn't Fallow. Snow packs would be just the thing. I also know a few pain remedies, because that is going to hurt. Did he tell you how to care for it?"

"I wasn't paying attention. You'll have to ask Marko."

She took a deep breath and let it out slowly. "And your squire is where?"

"Off to find me a way to get back to the Hall without walking or riding."

"Oh, you'll ride, just not a horse," Janem growled. "Now get out of here, I've got work to do."

Caelerys helped Vyncet to manoeuvre his way out of the forge through the open side walls, out of the way of the main traffic. She found him a stump to sit on until his squire returned.

Tempest found her rather easily, dropping from the sky to land on her shoulder, chattering incoherently at her. When she saw Vyncet, she paused in her rant, stretching her neck to see the length of white that was his lower leg. Cae stroked her breast. "He'll keep it. It's not as bad as it looks, but probably worse than he thinks."

This placated the bird who launched back into her tirade.

"My lord!" called a young, vaguely familiar voice. Tempest flipped her wings as if to say this was what she had been saying. Both Cae and her brother turned to see young Marko trotting over to them. "I have a cart," he panted as he came to a stop before them to catch his breath.

"A cart?" Vyncet exclaimed, horrified.

"Aye, my lord. And Lord Willam awaits you both in it."

Cae immediately moved to get Vyncet up and moving. The squire went to his master's other side and between the two of them, kept him from swaying too much on his crutch and prevented any collisions with other patrons.

As they stepped out of the little cul-de-sac where the smithies were, they found a small wagon waiting for them. The carter tied off the reins and moved to help them get Vyncet into the back where Willam sat.

Vyncet's reaction was immediate and loud. "Tell me you're kidding me!"

"Quit yer belly-aching and get in," Willam growled.

Cae stepped out of the way and let the two squires and the carter manage her brother before climbing up onto the tailgate with the boys, sitting closest to Willam.

"You sure you wouldn't rather ride on the front, my lady?" the carter asked.

She smiled. "I'll be fine, thank you. I'd rather sit with my brothers."

The man nodded and went around to climb into the driving seat.

The two squires immediately pulled apples out of their scripts and crunched into them, putting their heads together and talking something over earnestly. Cae smiled, flicked her shoulder to tell Tempest to fly, and turned to her brothers.

"So, Willam, I am certain you remembered what the Physician told you?" she asked as the bird took flight.

He nodded, holding his right arm stiffly against his body. "He gave me a balm and tincture for pain. I'll be sleeping on my belly for a while. If it would be no trouble for you to apply the balm? I should only need it for a fortnight or so."

"What's in it?"

"He gave me a paper," he smiled. "I asked. Harlan should have it in his script if he hasn't eaten it."

The boy looked up guiltily as his name was mentioned. "My lord?"

"You have the paper from the Physician?"

"Aye, my lord."

"When we are at the Hall and settled, give it to my sister."

"Aye, my lord."

He chuckled, looking back at his sister, "Satisfied?"

She smiled. "For now. So, you will not dance, but will you attend?" she asked Willam.

It was Vyncet who responded with a rousing, "Damn straight! Wouldn't miss it!"

She looked over at him. "I... I really don't think you should go. You need to keep that leg up and if you go...."

"I've already missed most of the Tourney and all the fun," he complained, running his sleeve over his brow. "I'm not missing the most important night!"

"Did the Physician give you anything at all?"

"No, my lady," answered his squire. "He was in too much a state over the ...tin-snips," he said, dropping his voice, "that they didn't give him anything before he left. I remember what we were told, though, and you have the right of it, my lady."

She nodded. "Good. I'll go over it with you when we get to the Hall. If you could write it down for me that would be marvellous."

"Aye, my lady."

Willam grunted a little as the cart wheels found a loose cobble and jarred them just a little. "You boys may attend, so long as you mind your places. Harlan, keep an eye out for me, in case I have need of you, but enjoy yourselves with the other squires and minor ladies. Tomorrow morning, though, I want both of you to go to the stables at the fairgrounds and bring our horses back to the Hall. You'll need an extra hand, as you'll be bringing back three of them."

The responding, "Aye, my lord," came in perfect unison and was followed by complaints from Vyncet about suborning his squire.

"By the way," Willam added as they passed through the gates into the city itself, "Uncle won."

When the carter pulled into the courtyard of Stag's Hall, lady Petra descended from the house like a harrier in full flight. Her pale blue sleeves even flapped in her wake like a harrier's feathers, her eyes were like chips of jasper. "My lady, I believe I told you to come home straight away after the Grand Melee. I searched for you, but you'd run off like some country knight's get!"

"Lady Petra," Willam interrupted, "she was attending to her familial duties. She will be with you shortly."

She stiffened, catching sight of Vyncet's leg and sweaty brow. "Of course, my lord. But she will need a bath and it will take time to get her ready. We shall be late."

Willam eased himself off the end of the wagon with the help of his sister and squire. "I dare say she would be late even if she had come straight home. It will take me a bit longer than usual to be ready." He glanced back at his brother. "Vyncet, I fear, will be staying here, want to or not."

There was only a modicum of protest from the party in question.

"Harlan, never mind me, go get Cartyr and tell him we'll need a stretcher. Sister, if you've anything for pain and sleep for him, you'd best fetch it."

She nodded. "Maybe something for the swelling and fever, too. And something mild for yourself. Harlan can apply the balm tonight."

He nodded his ascent.

"Marko, if you will come with me?" she asked as she went into the house, headed for the still-room beyond the garden courtyard. She quizzed him on the way for what the Physician had ordered for Vyncet and busied herself collecting what she had and what she thought might suffice in place of what she did not. She took him into the kitchen with her where she prepared a tray with a cup of wine into which she carefully added a tincture for the pain and swelling. This she handed the squire with strict instructions and sent him off to tend his master.

She then turned to Fennel. "I'll need you to brew up a pot of white waterwood tea. In a few hours, take a cup up to Vyncet and check up on him. If he's feverish, wake him and make him drink it. If he's not, just check up on him regularly and give it to him when he wakes. If he takes a turn for the worse, do not hesitate to send for a Physician."

"At once, my lady," she said, already bustling and ordering the scullery to put the kettle on the hob.

"Thank you. And as soon as it is ready, send a cup up to Willam. It will ease some of his pain without hindering him this evening. He's going to need it."

She was already putting a second cup onto the tray and turning to measure the tea into the pot. "I have this well in hand, my lady. Best you get up to your chambers to get ready. You've a bath waiting and lady

Petra's been in fits for an hour."

Dreading every step for so many reasons, Cae left the kitchen and hurried upstairs to her room.

Tempest was already perched on the edge of the bathtub and fussing at lady Petra, though she stopped the moment Cae opened the door, giving her a plaintive cry. "Not now, pet," she sighed as she entered and both Fern and Marigold descended upon her to help her out of her gown and into the bath. "And before you begin, lady Petra, I am truly sorry to have kept you waiting, but my responsibility to my brothers and the health of this house come before anything short of a royal order. I am only saddened that I have not had time to make up enough of the things we'll need in the coming months. The new herbs are only just setting in and are not ready for harvest and certainly not for distilling."

"Calm yourself, Lady Caelerys."

Cae stopped with one foot in the cooling water. The woman's tone had been different than she had expected. "My lady?" she said automatically, confused.

The dame's manner was calm and serene as she stood with her hands folded in front of her. "Your lady mother would have been proud," she said gently. "Now, in you go. You are mine now and there is still much to be done."

Still feeling bemused, Cae put her other foot into the tub and sank down into the water which was less than hot, but not yet tepid. She would have preferred it warmer, but it was her fault for keeping it waiting. As she ran the cloth over her body, cleaning off any traces of horse and sweat and whatever she had gotten herself into that afternoon, she watched the woman directing the maids and going through her small jewel box, picking out a few choice pieces and laying them out. It was then that something caught her attention about the water. It was a little heavier than she was used to, felt silky. She held the cloth to her nose and picked up the delicate fragrance of an oil. It had a hint of floral, lightly sweet but citrusy as well, with a hint of, dare she think it, leather under it all. It was calming and very her. It clung to her skin just enough to leave it feeling like the golden cream it resembled.

When she rose, water dripping, the maids both descended upon her with towels, patting her body dry instead of letting her rub herself as she usually did. Fern brought her bag of dusted honey and held it as Cae applied it beneath her breasts and under her arms, brushing just a hint across her face and throat to give her a light glow.

Then they began dressing her.

First came her shift and under things. Then an under-gown that felt like silk but looked like cloth-of-silver. The sleeves were close fitting and looped over her middle finger in a point. Over this went an over-gown of midnight blue sueded silk with trailing sleeves cut to the shoulder and buttoned with tiny silver roses from throat to waist to display the under-gown to advantage. The collar was a standing affair, about two inches tall, fastened over the hollow of her throat by a sapphire cut in the shape of a rose that braced the slight gap with antlers embroidered with silver thread. There was other embroidery at the hems and edges, but they were almost spiderweb fine traceries that caught the light intermittently.

Cae caught sight of the ensemble in the small polished mirror in her room and was stunned.

She allowed them to guide her to the dressing stool where they began to rework her hair with swift coordination. While she waited, she kept as still as she could while investigating the jewels that had been lain out. There was her sapphire ring to grace the other hand, opposite her mother's opal. There was no necklace, but the gown hardly needed anything at her throat. The collar button was jewel enough. The earrings were delicate cascades of pearls dripping from teardrop cut sapphires. Naturally, the moonsilver comb sat in pride of place between them. She sighed, fingering its delicate, cool antlers.

"I know, my dear," soothed lady Petra, "but needs must. If there is any night to wear all our best finery, this is it."

"I feel like I have borrowed a wardrobe," she sighed, slipping the earrings on without overly disturbing the maids working their magic in her hair.

"But all of these are yours, my dear. Your father has been planning for this for a long time. Some of this was your mother's even." Her long, bony fingers reached out to caress the dark silk and smooth down a fold on the sleeve. "This fabric for instance. She wore this while pregnant with you. Did the embroidery herself. Granted, some adjustments had to be made here and there, but it fits you like a glove."

Happy with her inspection of the hair, she picked up the comb and placed it herself, just at the crown of her head. She stepped back, pleased with the vision, from the dusty plum of the girl's lips to the cobalt slippers on her dainty feet.

Gingerly, Cae reached back to feel her hair. It was loosely twisted back from her temples, with only a few uneven curls allowed to 'cleverly escape'. The rest hung almost freely in the back but caught up in woven net of dozens of tiny, dark braids that hung to just below her shoulders. She turned her head to test the weight. It moved a little, felt like she were wearing a net snood. She could even feel tiny seed pearls gracing the joints. The comb rest just at the top of the 'basket'.

Finally she stood, took a deep breath. "I can do this," she whispered.

Lady Petra stood behind her, looking at her reflection over her shoulder as she rest her hands on her arms. "You can do this."

"I *must* do this," Cae added.

She looked down at the falcon walking along her dressing table, looking up at her in wonder. She laughed softly. "I know, Jelma. I do not look like myself. I don't even feel like myself."

"Maybe that might help, my lady," offered Fern kindly, knowing how shy her mistress really was, even as she gazed proudly at her.

Cae smiled. "Maybe. Well, I cannot put it off any longer. Jelma, tyetne, ketava. Fern will feed you and tuck you in. I will be home when I am home." She reached out to stroke the side of her cheek. The bird closed her eyes and leaned into the caress.

Fern approached, drawing on a hawking glove. "Come on, 'Pest. I think I heard a mouse down the hall last night, how about that?"

The bird reluctantly allowed herself to be picked up and sat on the girl's wrist trying to look dejected but ending up just looking tired. Finally, she chirped a goodbye and flew to her stand by the window.

Cae started to smile sadly at her when lady Petra ushered her out the door. "Oh, Eldest preserve us! You behave as if you were about to be put on trial instead of attending a royal ball! Most girls your age would be chomping at the bit to go!"

Below in the courtyard, a rented carriage awaited them. It was not terribly fancy, a simple black, covered coach with a driver on the front wearing a plain black cote and hose. Cartyr was just helping Willam inside. She watched the two squires, faces shining above their best tunics. She knew that they were both good, dark blue broadcloth with grey-white stags embroidered at their breasts; Harlan with a rearing stag, and Marko with just the head in profile. She could almost feel their excitement.

Cartyr handed her in, and Willam took her hand to steady her. She sat across from him whilst lady Petra took the space beside her. While there was still light from the courtyard torches, she looked her brother over. He wore an almost plain cote with straight sleeves, either black or blue, she could not really tell in this light, with an over vest that hung to his knees. This at least was trimmed in silver. His hair was brushed back, its dark, loose curls past his shoulders. A single ring glinted on his hand and a silver stag pin graced his breast. She also noticed that he was not leaning back against the cushions and held himself stiffly.

"Did you drink your tea?" she asked as the door was closed and the carriage pulled away from the Hall.

"Yes, thank you. It helped."

"It should last you a good bit of the night. I want you to tell me if it starts to wear off."

An eyebrow cocked in her direction. "You have more with you, hidden away in a pocket?"

"Don't be silly, Willam. If it starts to wear off we shall merely make our excuses and I will take you home."

"We shall see," was all lady Petra said to that.

Willam just chuckled. "Oh, the things I have forgotten about you, little sister," he sighed.

"Like what?" she quipped, feeling heat beginning to rise to her cheeks.

"Like how much trouble you are. How much of a frightened little mouse lives inside the ca'theryn that is you. And how much light you bring with you in spite of it all."

It was an unusual compliment and it rendered her silent almost the entire way to the Citadel.

They were late, but not so late that there were not still a number of carriages ahead of and behind them, as well as those who rode ahorse and several afoot who lived closely enough to walk. Alighting from the carriage, Willam took Caelerys's arm, whilst his squire, Harlan, offered his to lady Petra. Marko followed along behind, gawking at everything.

They slowly climbed the shallow steps through the open, dragon-braced doors. The king's banner, which had served him cloak for his coronation, hung above them, flapping darkly in the night breeze. The thin slice of the Eastern moon cast silver accents on one side of the golden thread, whilst the golden chunk of the Southern moon hung higher in the sky, picking out the golden dragon embroidered there, giving it the illusion of breathing.

Willam paused just inside the doors and Cae could feel the tension in his arm as he tried to ease his back. She did not ask, merely waiting patiently. It gave her a moment to view the entry hall in the different light of evening. Small braziers glowed along the walls, casting dancing shadows on the green stone. It surprised her that the ball was not being held in the throne room. People were being guided via guard and banner down one of the side corridors off to the left of the closed throne room doors. As soon as Willam had recovered himself, they followed.

The corridor was lit by translucent stone braziers in varied colours set just above eye level, casting the wide hall and its occupants in a rainbow of shifting light. There was a double row of white tiles on the floor that guided one towards a pair of open doors upon the inside of which were carved dancers reaching towards each other across the gap. When left open, they seemed to be trying to draw the viewer within to dance with them.

The hall spilled into a room that was slightly wider than the throne room but no less deep, though the ceiling was a great deal lower. It was sectioned off in multiple vaults that were sheeted in highly polished metal, reflecting the lights to greater effect and gleaming with the blurred swirls of colours of the people below. There was an alcove protected by a lattice screen on the far side of the room where musicians played, near but not too close to a dais where most of the royal family currently sat. Buffet tables with what seemed like a hundred servants lined one wall and to either side of the entrance was scattered seating. Opposite the buffet, it seemed the entire wall was simply a row of doors thrown open to the night and a garden patio she had somehow missed on her visits. Or perhaps she simply had not recognized the closed doors for what they were. These open doorways allowed a breeze to play through the room, alleviating the heat and inevitable odour of so many bodies engaged in exercise in heavy fabrics.

They had not fully entered the press of people yet, but already she could smell the mix of cloying perfumes and men who perhaps had not been so vigorous in their bathing. She felt her stomach seize, her limbs turning to lumps of metal at the thought of entering any further into that room. Her brother's hand on her arm reassured her, reminding her that she was not alone, and among people she knew.

He leaned down to her, speaking softly. "You got through the coronation, and its aftermath. You can get through this. Janem said to tell you that it's no different than the vassal dinners back home, except that you aren't the hostess." Surprisingly, this helped her to calm a little. "Now, antlers up, little sister. First the formalities."

He led their little party straight across the room towards the dais at least a dozen yards behind the group in front of them. While occasionally revellers crossed the centre path, none lingered there, leaving a loose aisle. Their group drifted forward until the way was clear, bowed or curtseyed before the thrones. The queen gave them her dreamy, knowing smile. Prince Balaran's eyes glittered appreciatively, though his nod to Willam was almost companionable. The princess's expression went from slightly bored to ecstatic at Cae to suddenly blushing shyly at Willam. Prince Valan nodded stiffly, barely seeing anyone. Cae noticed that, though his arm did not seem bandaged, he held it still. The king nodded graciously, and then they were rising and turning towards the musicians and away.

She breathed a little easier as they moved off to the side. A nod from Willam and the boys were just gone, bound for the food, no doubt. Lady Petra came around in front of them.

"Now, I wish I could stand chaperone all night, but I have other obligations, but I will not be very far if you need me. Lady Caelerys, do not go too deeply into the gardens alone, or with no less than two people, but you need to mingle, dance and generally be available. You are here to be noticed. Remember that. And that goes for both of you," she added with a glare up at Willam. "Your father wants you looking as well, you know, and if you put it off too late, the pickings will be …well, leavings."

Cae did not know how he managed to not roll his eyes or sigh at that. While he had been softening throughout the last few weeks, he was the former, stiff Willam she remembered from his infrequent visits home, once again heir to a Great House. For the first time in her life she began to wonder if he resented that.

"Right now, you both should get something to eat. I know you haven't and you will need your strength. Lady Caelerys, eat lightly, but frequently, and only from those tables. Do not let your plate out of your sight. Same with your drinks. There will be servants wandering with offerings, take none. Accept drinks only from the servants at the buffet poured from communal vessels, or from people you trust implicitly: family, myself, or your own servants, none of which you brought. Remember this and you'll be fine."

"You are scaring her, lady Petra," Willam said quietly. "She needs to be relaxed if she is going to be able to do anything tonight. She will be careful." At that he turned to her. "Do yourself a favour and for every glass of wine you drink, eat a sweetmeat or breadbit from the buffet. It will help keep your head clear."

She nodded, squeezing his hand. Thankfully, lady Petra seemed to think this enough and bowed out, disappearing into the crowd.

Willam guided her past the tables, picking morsels that caught their interest as they went. While the whole had the look of having been fairly picked over, there were still mountains of food all served in convenient bite sized pieces. Willam took mostly meats with a few breadbits and honeyed fruits, while Cae took only a few meats that looked interesting and mostly fruits and what few vegetables were on offer. Willam glanced at her plate and placed a honey glazed breadbit on it. "Trust me," was all he said.

She sighed and allowed it. They watched the servants pour their wines and drifted to find a place to sit and eat.

There was only a little trouble finding a place, as the early arrivers had already eaten and gone to mingle. They were not really surprised to find out how hungry they were. They did not speak a word until their plates were clean and Cae stacked the two together and out of their way. She quietly sipped her wine as she studied the people in the room.

The elaborate hairstyles were much in evidence again, and the clothes were as sumptuous as at the coronation but were less stiff to allow free movement for the dancing which had not started up yet. The processions had thinned out enough that the dancing was likely to start soon.

She tried to find signs of people she knew. Lord Rorik was standing near his father and brother, laughing stiffly, as if trying hard not to hurt himself doing so. "I think Lord Rorik broke ribs," she commented.

Willam gave a small grin. "I did hit him pretty hard. I'll have to have a word later. Oh, I see Uncle. Would you join us?" he asked as he rose gingerly.

"Wouldn't miss it. Where is he?" she asked, trying to find him.

Willam just took her arm and led her through the crowd to where Jehan stood with the other members of the Free Legions. None of the five men were Folk, each one a noble son at the very least. There were plenty of Folk and the Middle Estate in the Free Legions, but only those of the First Estate would have been invited. Though Cae did notice the mester who had won the archery tournament present in the crowd. She supposed that all the winners were permitted regardless of their Estate or position. There were even a small handful of the Second Estate here, and stiff Pontifices in their grey robes. She noticed one or two wearing finer fabrics with black embroidery, but all of them watched the crowd with a mixture of greed and suspicion.

She was gratefully distracted by the conversation they were entering.

"...We'd agreed we'd take him down together to save the crown's pride. Would not do to have a prince thought little of in combat, play or no. We were worried there for a minute that he might lose his mind though," Jehan was explaining to a man from the Golden Battalion. "I've seen that look on Halbourne and Brock just before they slip into battle frenzy. But he maintained his control."

"He was always a stickler for self-control," Willam offered as they approached, having gleaned the subject of the conversation.

Seeing his niece and nephew coming over, Jehan greeted them enthusiastically, but much more appropriately than he had at the coronation. He made introduction and asked after his nephew's health.

"Not sore, lad?" he asked with a gleam in his eye.

Willam actually laughed. "Oh, I'm sore all right. Will be walking carefully for at least a fortnight. But it were fairly done."

Lord Tume grinned, flashing white teeth in his handsome, dark face. "Well, you were cutting in."

He laughed, "Aye, I'll ask next time."

"How did your battle fall out?" Caelerys asked brightly. "I did not get to see the end. I only know you won, Uncle."

"It was a close thing," answered lord Finn, the man from the Golden Battalion. "A thing of beauty."

"He knocked my cursed helmet off!" Jehan exclaimed, rubbing his head.

Cae gasped, then looked confused. "Wait, how was that not a kill-shot?"

"I caught him with my hilt, not the blade," Tume answered ruefully. "He paid me back fair enough," he chuckled.

The man from Sterling Company grinned. "Threw the helmet at his legs, fouling his balance, caught his other ankle with the underside of the axehead and pulled him off his feet. Had the blade at the back of his neck before the marshal could even secure the helmet."

"I am sorry I missed it," she smiled, sipping her wine for courage.

"Occasionally I wish I had," Jehan chuckled, drinking deeply from his tankard.

"Ears still ringing?" Tume chuckled.

"Bit. Not as bad as your prince, though. *I* don't have a concussion."

There was a mixed expression on Tume's face as he held up his glass to drink. "My prince has a very hard head. He will survive. His temper might not," he added with a grin and took a sip.

Jehan suddenly noticed someone missing and looked around. "How's Vyncet? He didn't break that leg, did he?"

"He's very lucky he didn't," Cae responded. "I still don't see how. The plate got embedded alongside the bone. He'll be laid up longer than Willam."

"Should have seen it," said the lordling from the Golden Battalion. "He's on his knees, because of having 'lost' the leg, but he's still in the thick of it, taking advantage of his position. Shield held high, and his sword going at everything from the belly down. He took out at least three people, two of them Sea-wolves, when someone just bulled him over. He rolled to his back, but before he could get out of the way, one of those

Kaladen curs took a swing at him like he was chopping wood with those oversized boarding axes they carry. I'm surprised he didn't lose the leg. Couple of the 'dead' dragged him out of the way and carried him off field."

"That part I saw. He was laughing," Caelerys said.

"Sometimes, my lady, that is the best way to deal with pain," said the Sterling man.

"And sometimes, that is just my brother," added Willam, making everyone laugh.

"Was it just me," Tume mused, "or were there an inordinately greater number of injuries for a tourney?"

"Vastly," responded Jehan. They exchanged pointed glances with the other men, and expressions darkened as they drank.

As Cae tried to decipher what was passing between them, she heard a shift in the crowd around them, noticed the noise level drop to a murmur. She turned to look, and saw a breath-taking young woman with a cascade of honey-gold curls bound in real flowers and a shimmering gown of pale pink drift towards the dais on the proud arm of Lord Selgan Cygent. They were followed by his brother, Lord Galen, who had his sister-in-law upon his arm. Everyone was paying attention as they made their obeisances before the royal family.

"Is that...?" Jehan began, nudging Willam less gently than he had intended.

"Lady Liliwyn Cygent, aye," he said, stifling a groan of pain. "It was believed she would not be coming. But apparently Lord Selgan managed to convince her."

"She doesn't look...," Cae began.

"Like she wants to be here?" Willam offered.

Cae thought about the glimpse of face she had seen, the soft, downcast eyes above a bearing that while defeated, seemed to know nothing of submission. "Like she doesn't want to be anywhere," she said softly.

She watched the family turn aside from the dais as long as she could, until they vanished beyond the crowd and she was distracted by the closing of the ballroom doors. When she turned back to her brother and the lords to whom they were speaking, she found herself being stared at by a strikingly tall, dark woman standing next to lord Tume. She was nearly as tall as Willam, and lithe like the wands of the queen of the forest. Her skin was like Tume's though no where near as dark, fairly glowing like a highly polished darkwood. Her face was an angular oval with high cheekbones and large, almond eyes of a tawny brown. Her black hair was dressed in hundreds of narrow braids capped with gold that hung about her face and shoulders like a mane. She wore a gold and red patterned top that wrapped around her upper torso but left her midriff bare to show off a jewelled naval. The skirt seemed to be one long piece of geometrically patterned fabric in vivid reds, yellows and brown trimmed in gold that draped her hips with a long, tail-like scarf that crossed her back and breast and hung off the opposite shoulder. It left a good deal of her long, dark legs exposed. Her shoes were little more than a series of crossing straps from the soles to her knee. Her upper arms and wrists were graced with broad and ornate gold bracelets. Compared to the other women in the room, she was practically naked and perfectly comfortable.

Caelerys was so caught up by the shock of her look and presence that she almost did not hear lord Tume introduce them to her.

"...Princess Semiana Onkelan of Alumet."

The woman smiled briefly at the men as they were named and presented, but there was something distinctly predatory in the way she watched Cae. When she spoke, her voice was like warm silk slithering across velvet, only mildly coloured by the flow-and-hitch accent of her people. "I hear you are an accomplished horsewoman," she purred.

Cae felt the rising blush. "It is as much knowing one's mount as practised skill," she replied, barely managing not to stammer. While the princess carried herself much like the Onkelan warrior prince, the same fluid, warrior grace and intense pride, there was little of his disdain. Instead of Prince Cyran's perpetual sneer, she seemed to take fierce delight in everything.

Her response seemed to please the princess. "You were right, Tume. She has wisdom. Though I will reserve my judgement for a few days more, I do not believe I shall allow either of my brothers to ask for her. She would be wasted on them, I think."

She felt the blush shift to something more akin to anger than shyness, uncertain if she had just been insulted or admired. She knew she was saved in any case, as a match with either of the foreign princes had not appealed to her. Still, she felt challenged.

Before she had the need to formulate some kind of response, the princess reached her hand towards Willam, though she spoke to Cae. "I am going to steal your brother for a little while, if you do not mind. I wish to learn Southern dancing."

Faced with the stunning smile suddenly turned on him, Willam could not refuse, accepting her strong hand in his to draw her towards the space that was clearing out for dancing.

All Cae could think to say was, "Be gentle with him. He got between our kinsman and yours and they were less than kind."

Her laugh was open and ringing, "So I have heard."

Cae watched the two walk off, feeling a little lost. She felt her uncle's hand at her shoulder. "She has that effect on people," he chuckled.

The lord of the Golden Battalion watched the princess a few moments more, asked Tume, "Does she know how scandalous her attire is?"

"More's the question, does she care?" he quipped, drinking deeply of his wine. "She knows. But that is proper in the North, formal even, and, as an ambassador, she knows there is little anyone can say."

"I think she does it for that look right there," Jehan said into his cup as he watched the sour faces of the pontifices scowling in her direction.

"You could be right," Tume replied.

"I take it there are few servants of the Eldest in the North?" asked the lordling.

He shook his head. "Staunch believers in Mother Chimera, one and all. And as dutiful children, we do not worship her. We pay our respects, as we should, to her and all her children, but she never asked for worship."

Jehan broke up the conversation by shouldering his friend. "Well, I believe I shall ask for an ale instead of whatever this is. Was. Come on, Tume, a feast is no place for religion."

With a nod the two men wandered off to get refills and the remaining three excused themselves under various pretexts. Cae realized she was being remiss herself. She had spent entirely too much time in the company of unavailable men. She felt a little saddened that her uncle had taken lord Tume with him. She would have liked to have at least one dance with him.

She looked around, feeling suddenly very lost. People were mingling in and out of the open doors if they were not moving in the stately reels and turns of the dance. She did not see lady Sigourney or Lord Avondyl, and both the Marrok brothers were on the floor with the Roshans. She was hoping she might have a chance to meet Lady Liliwyn, but could not find her, either.

She started to go towards the food tables to refresh her drink when she saw Prince Kyleth speaking with lord Tume and her uncle. She turned the other way, determined not to be caught up in conversation with him and found lord Aldane Kaladen approaching her. A quick glance around told her she had no polite or viable exit. She decided to attempt to remain aloof and distant while still observing the courtesies, but to give him no real reason to linger.

He was smiling as he reached out and took her hand and kissed it. She stiffened slightly at his presumption, but simply withdrew her hand from his. "Lord Aldane," she said coolly.

"My lady. May I say that you are more breath-taking than you were at the coronation?"

"And if I decided you may not, what would be the point? It is already said," she replied before she was even aware she had thought it. She covered her own shock by standing a bit taller, trying to imagine how lady Petra would handle this matter. She wished she felt confident enough of her place to deal with it the way lady Sigourney would have, but she didn't have quite that much courage.

His grin was full of predatory delight, but he controlled himself. "I wish to extend the apologies of my family to you personally."

"For?"

"The injury to your brother. I did not see him arrive with you. I trust he is not grievously hurt?"

"We breed strong and hearty in the Reach. He will walk again, and fight as before," she said, hoping she didn't come off as stiff as she felt.

"I am glad to hear that. Again, our apologies. My men were a little... over enthusiastic. Hard for their minds to accept a battle that is not in earnest."

"I imagine you have a great many apologies to tender then."

"Such fire," he laughed. "One should not waste it on the sidelines. Dance with me?"

Caelerys hesitated. When she did not refuse, he took it for assent and drew her towards the dancers, slipping them into the pavane in progress. She thanked the Mother that it was one of the stately, arm's length dances, and not one of the more energetic reels or sarabande, though she would have preferred a quadrille or one that traded partners. Even Sir Halden Trent would have been preferable at this moment.

She concentrated on her movements and resisted his attempts at conversation, giving short and simple answers where she could not avoid it. He talked mostly of how his family had grown in wealth and power, that they had a great many ships without giving a useful number, how her father's men and unlimited access to the ports beholden to him could increase the worth of both houses. He said little of the beauty of his islands beyond that they were a hardy people. When he smiled at her she felt a chill, as his flat eyes were full of avarice, not admiration or any warm emotion.

"And where do your women stand in all this?" she finally asked, mostly to get him to stop talking about his 'Sea Bitch'.

"The scraps are as hardy and hale as the men, even to serving on ships sometime. But our daughters," by which it was obvious he meant only the noble women, "want for nothing. Nary sully their hands at land-bound labours."

"Nor keep a thought of their own in their empty heads?" she snapped to her horror. She had not intended to say it.

He merely laughed it off. "Our wives perhaps, but our daughters... they have thoughts and are not shy about sharing. Sometimes at knife-point."

The musicians ended the current dance with a flourish and Cae and Aldane ended facing each other. She curtseyed as was proper, but as he bowed over her hand, about to kiss it, he drew up. She could feel the sudden tension in his fingers and saw a flickering of expression in his flat eyes that she hesitated to call fear. He let her hand go and Cae turned to see her brother Willam descending upon them. She was certain that was the last look an enemy saw before the hammer came crashing down.

Willam was stiffly polite, fully aware of where he was and what surrounded them. He reached his hand for his sister's without taking his eyes from Aldane. "Sister, I would be remiss if I did not ask at least one dance this evening."

Aldane bowed again, watching Willam warily, "But of course, Lord Willam," he said, taking a step back.

Cae had the grace to hold her tongue, turning her back to the

Kaladen lord and walking a short distance with her brother. Only when she was certain no one else would hear did she speak, and then softly. "I swear to you, Willam, if father insists me there I will throw myself from the highest peak of Taluscliff."

"And I swear to you, Caelerys," he answered just as firmly, "that even were we destitute and broken and they richer than Griff, they would have nothing to offer that would make such a match reasonable. If you had asked in that direction I would have lost all respect and begin to believe you had taken leave of your senses."

She took a deep breath and slowly let it out with all the tension she had not been aware had been building to the levels it had. "So long as we agree. How did you know?"

"Harlan."

"Bless the boy," she sighed.

"Every day I don't curse him," he chuckled.

The music began a quadrille and he turned her to face the three nearest couples, which happened to be Prince Balaran with Lady Liliwyn on his arm, lady Lucelle and one of the Marrok brothers, and Princess Syera with Lord Rorik.

Cae relaxed. While she had yet to meet Lady Liliwyn and was as yet mildly intimidated by the older Griff son, this was still more pleasant than being caught in a partner changing reel with certain others, met and unmet. Lord Rorik was apologizing to the princess that he might be less energetic than the dance might request. There was a certain ginger stiffness to the way he carried himself and a faint bulk to his tunic that confirmed for Cae that he had indeed broken ribs.

"Is it wise to attempt the dance at all, my lord Rorik?" Cae asked as the couples faced each other with their hands all touching in the centre.

His smile was warm, in the way of an indulgent uncle yet still on the edge of flirtation, "If the flowers of Elanthus are gentle with a broken old warhorse."

This got him the reaction he desired, which was a smile and light laugh from the ladies as they began to slowly circle each other.

Once the music really got going, and the couples broke off from the circle to parade around each other, conversation died down. It was a long dance, well balanced with stately promenades, slower circling steps and more energetic interchanges where the women were passed from partner's hand to partner's hand as they wove around the circle. When they got back to where they started, the women then turned to the partner behind them and it all began again, only with different partners. By the time it was over, each woman had danced with each of the men, and ended with a different partner than she had begun. In the end, Willam ended up with Lady Liliwyn, lady Lucelle with Lord Rorik, and the princess stood giggling beside the Marrok lord. She gave Cae a wink when she caught her eye and Cae could only smile.

Prince Balaran turned to Willam and gave him a polite bow. "With your permission, Will, I think I'm going to steal your sister for something more... spirited."

Willam glared at the remark until the next piece began and revealed itself to be a saltarello. "If you mean to ask her to dance," he said pointedly, "I have no objection."

Balaran turned his intense smile upon her. "I have been remiss. Will you dance with me again?"

The tip of his head and look in his eyes gave him an almost plaintive look that made her have to try very hard not to laugh. "I would be honoured."

As he began to lead her out among the other couples beginning to space themselves out a bit more, she heard her brother speaking to Lady Liliwyn. "While I must sit this one out to rest, I would not dream of depriving you of the dance if you wish to find another partner. Though I would be delighted with your company."

She did not hear her reply, but caught a glimpse of the princess's face and read only disappointment.

The dance did not lend itself to conversation any more than the previous one had, but Cae began to enjoy herself. For all his scandalousness and reputation, she found she liked Balaran a great deal. She felt she could almost be herself around him without expectation or judgement.

Once the dance was over, she was more than ready for a rest, and the prince guided her to the refreshment table to get her a drink. She remembered her brother's advice and took a breadbit to nibble. "Is your sister infatuated with my brother, do you think?" she asked, and immediately could not believe she had dared.

He smiled at her, watching her blush.

"Forgive me," she stammered. "I promise you, it is not the wine that makes me so free with my words. You... I forget myself."

"In private, I encourage you to be as comfortable as you wish. Indeed, to ask me anything," he replied, his eyes flashing over his cup. "But elsewise ...mice listen to every word and carry more than crumbs back to their dens."

She nodded, taking a drink to keep herself from trying to explain herself into a deeper hole.

He leaned nearer to her ear. "Later you may ask me any impertinent thing you like. Once upon a tavern, your brother Willam has asked things far more inappropriate."

She smiled to try and cover the deepening of her blush.

A servant came up and requested the prince's attention. There was a brief, whispered conversation before he turned back to her, leaving his own drink in the servant's hands. He took up her hand and bowed over it. "If my lady will forgive my untimely disappearance? There is a small matter I must attend. I shall return. That was too much fun and I shall want another."

"Dance?" she asked pointedly.

He threw his head back and laughed. "Aye, my lady. A dance. You are almost too much your brother's sister for my comfort," he added and took his leave.

Cae moved away from the refreshment tables seeking a chair where she could rest herself and watch the people. She did not see Willam or lady Liliwyn at all, guessed that they had slipped out into the gardens. Princess Syera was dancing with some lord Cae did not know, and Princess Semiana was engaging lord Tume in something more akin to Northern dance steps. Her moves were more sinuous and suggestive as they circled each other, and Tume looked more like circled prey than predator.

She had not seen Prince Valan on the dance floor yet. He still sat in his chair upon the dais with his mother's head bent to him in earnest, though apparently one-sided, conversation. She wondered if his injury was what kept him to himself, but she dismissed that thought almost immediately. She had seen him move the arm, though carefully. There was too much tension in his posture of a kind that did not speak of pain, and a wariness in his eye as he watched the room. He clearly did not want to be here.

For a brief moment, he caught her eye. She felt it like a shock, causing her to catch her breath and wonder why she had ever thought she could survive this environment.

Then suddenly her view was blocked by a black velvet gown studded with topaz and the air filled with the scent of a heavy, cloying perfume of overblown roses and something musky. She looked up, startled, to find herself skewered by eyes nearly as pale as the cascade of copper bound braids that hung over her shoulder.

Gazing up into that unfriendly face, Cae felt an overwhelming desire to stand so she might have a chance to back away, but Lady Asparadane stood too close for that. The silver chased goblet in her hand drew her eyes to the long, slender fingers and the copper nails filed sharp. "Lady Asparadane," she managed. "How may I..." She found herself choking on her words under the weight of disdain in that glare.

"Oh, I just wished to finally meet the girl who out-rode my son." Her voice was pretty, smooth and sultry, but there was something cold to it that gave Cae goosebumps.

"Ah," she swallowed. "He rode well, Your Ladyship. Had he a better, more seasoned mount, he may well have beaten me."

Her smile was predatory. "A gift from a vassal. He has a love of fine, well bred animals, and the impatience of youth. As you said, a little seasoning and it will be a magnificent creature."

"Aye, he was a very handsome animal."

"Skilled horsewoman, fair archer, falconer, dancer," she listed. "A great many accomplishments for a young woman your age. Have you any lady-like pursuits? Though I suppose losing one's mother so young, I dare say your father over-indulged you."

Cae fought the rising flush. "I would you know, my lady, that my mother ensured I would be taught all that a lady need know to manage a Great House. I can sew and embroider, manage accounts as well as tend the minor hurts of the household."

She hummed with a dismissive arch of her eyebrow, "Again, self-sufficiency. Something I suppose is needed out in the lonely Reach, Great House or not. You are at Court now, my dear. I would not brag overmuch of such things. While in the outlying wilds it might make you highly desirable to smaller, country lords, but the Great Houses of the city and the like seek daintier qualities. That bird of yours, for instance, hardly appropriate to a girl of your age, much less your station."

"That bird was fairly gained with rights granted by the crown itself," she replied. "I could not be better guarded with her on my shoulder than if I had a wolfhound at heel."

The eyebrow went up again, remained there a moment longer than before. "Indeed."

There was a short length of silence that made Cae feel a little awkward.

"Still, guarded of body you might be with her, reputations are far more fragile things and hardly to be trusted to flights of fancy feathering." She paused to take a drink of her wine. Cae almost reached for her own automatically, but the butterflies in her stomach would not have been quieted by wine. She settled for merely turning the base of the goblet with nervous fingers.

"Have you yet been to service at the Hall of the Eldest?"

Cae knew immediately that she must be careful. "I have not yet had the time or opportunity."

"Nonsense, one must always make time for faith. My Malyna attends twice weekly and my sons every second Fourth Day. I should introduce you to High Pontifex Ulranel. He is here, after all. I cannot believe lady Petra has been so remiss in your education. I shall have to have words with her."

Cae felt panic rising in her breast as the lady turned to look over her shoulder, seeking some sign of the sour-faced priest. The Mother blessed Cae with the sight of lord Tume coming towards them instead.

His approaching bulk blocked any view Lady Asparadane might have had of her targets and caused her to turn to face him more fully. "My lord?" she asked prettily, though her eyes belied any pleasure at the interruption.

Tume held his hand out to her, giving her a short bow. "Lady Asparadane, could you see it in your heart to afford me a dance?"

Her hand drifted back towards the still seated Caelerys. "Surely a man of your youth and vitality came seeking younger partnership?"

His eyes glinted with mischief as they crossed Cae's only briefly. "There are advantages to the fully opened blossom," he said, catching up the slender hand, kissing the air above it.

Covering any reaction other than pleasure, she held out her silver cup to the servant that materialized from somewhere behind Caelerys's chair and accepted his request. Cae noted she did not even observe the courtesies of excusing herself, even though Caelerys outranked her.

She was relieved to see Princess Semiana coming over from a different direction. She stood, picking up her goblet with the intent of taking a calming draught of it. The princess reached out and took it from her, setting it firmly back on the table. "Forgive me, dear. That must be terribly warm by now. Allow me to get you a fresh one, and introduce you to the delights of our Northern wines."

There was something rather intent in her tawny eyes as she dismissed the half filled goblet that made Cae suddenly question the servant who had appeared from behind her. "While the spirit of the Great Stag guards and guides those of my house, I find myself grateful once again for more earthly and feline protectors," Cae said softly, allowing herself to be drawn away.

"Oh good, you aren't clueless," the princess responded with delight.

Cae blushed. "Not entirely, Princess Semiana," she answered. "Though no where near as attentive as I should have been."

"Semi, please. Ceremonies are fine in their place, but I detest unnecessary formalities," she said with a dismissive wave as she looped one arm through Cae's.

She smiled, warming quickly to the tall woman. "Then call me Cae."

"Done."

"So..." she ventured, making sure her words would not carry clearly beyond the princess's hearing, "you sacrificed lord Tume to rescue me?"

She laughed at that. "Well, if I had sent him to ask you, she would not have permitted it. She'd already run off three men seeking your attentions."

Cae looked back to where she had been sitting. "What? How? She never broke her conversation..."

"By her presence, little one. And with her sons. And don't fret that she tried to poison you, ...it might only have made you too ill to remain, or otherwise disgrace yourself," she breezed, pressing one of two goblets into her hand passed to her by a dark-skinned servant at the end of the wine tables. "Here, taste this."

Cae sipped the pale golden liquid as the princess drank deeply of her own. It was light, half sweet, half tangy and full of fruit flavours beyond the grape. It also did not threaten to go to her head. "Oh," she exclaimed. "I simply must get some of this for father! Is there anything I could..."

She shook her head with a great rattling of the gold in her braids. "Nonsense, I will have a barrel sent tomorrow. And one for your hall here."

Cae was startled. "Oh, that is too much! I couldn't impose..."

Her brow arched with a half smile, "Or fall under obligation?"

She was brought up short, ashamed to have implied it and that she had not considered it when she would have from most anyone else. "It is not that. But we are barely acquainted... and I would not have your brothers misthink that negotiations..."

She waved that off immediately, "My reasons are my own. I wish to know you and your House better. And my brothers have already been warned they are not to dare think it. Cyran would not entertain the thought and Kyleth has been informed he would be selfish to do so. No, I am courting more practical matters. Your spirit and pretty face has distracted Kyleth from his purpose, hence me."

Cae blushed, and not from the wine, which she drank more of. "Best your gifts be aimed at my brother then."

Her tawny eye gleamed. "Tending to your needs *is* a gift aimed at your brother. He and I have already come to our understanding. And of all the simpering, wilting flowers in this room, you are the only one with real thorns, and I like that. There, thrice refused, niceties observed, barrels to be delivered," she said firmly, aiming that last at the servant who nodded.

She turned Cae to observe the room. "Now, what do you see?"

Cae looked at the milling people and whirling dancers. Partners had changed out, and the dance was now one more a waltz of pairs than a promenade or reel. Lady Lucelle was dancing with the Marrok again, and her cousin with his brother. She noticed that lady Balyra was the better dancer of the two by far, though Lucelle seemed to be enjoying herself more. There was no sign of Liliwyn or Willam, nor even lady Petra, which surprised her. Lady Asparadane was engaging lord Tume in conversation as they danced near her uncle and lady Caena. Even the queen was on the floor with the king. Then she saw Prince Balaran dancing with lady Malyna. The girl was simpering and coy, and giving off so many mixed signals that Cae could not read her. She couldn't tell if she was merely trying to be shy and coquettish or if she really was that awkward. She also noted the mother's eye falling on the pair often.

"Ah, you see it," Semi smiled. "Watch both of them. I have dealt with Lady Asparadane in the past, and there are things about her which beg questioning."

Something occurred to her. "Why... I don't mean to be rude, but if I don't ask, I will never learn. But... hers is only a noble house, how is it you know of her at all so far North and why would she concern your kingdom?"

Semi's smile was predatory as she sipped her wine. "Lesser house or no, her sister was wed to the late king."

Cae could read what went unsaid simply by watching Lady Asparadane watching her daughter with the prince. House Asparadane was once wed to the crown, and it was clear she meant it to be again. Off to the side, she saw the young man who looked so much like Malyna dancing with Princess Syera as if already betrothed.

"I can see how that would be of interest to a neighbouring kingdom," she said softly.

Semi watched her for several minutes, catching the flickering emotions that ran across her face. "Are you certain you wish to swim in these waters? They are treacherous."

Cae sighed, drinking the rest of her wine. "I will do what my family needs me to do, and try my best not to shame them."

The princess leaned in with an intense smile on her face. "And you wondered why I might take an interest in your welfare?" She straightened, "That and Tume has spoken well of you."

The dance wound to an end and the princess turned to someone approaching, inclining her head regally. "Prince Valan," she purred.

"Princess Semiana," he responded, giving her a shallow bow before turning to her companion. "Lady Caelerys."

Cae was already sinking into a curtsey when she noticed he was holding his hand out to her. With only the faintest of trembling, she set her fingertips upon his. "My prince," she breathed, trying desperately to remain calm. Their last encounter had ended abruptly and left her in confusion. At the moment, she just did not know where she stood.

His hand slid against her palm, taking more of her hand onto his, and she felt a dry heat that threatened to burn her to her core. She met his eyes, blue to blue, and found she could neither read them nor look away. "I would have this next dance," he said.

"Of course, Your Highness," she replied, unaware of when she had risen from her curtsey.

Their palms pivoted against one another as he drew her to stand beside him, his own rolling so that hers rested, light as a bird, upon the back of his. Semi had apparently taken her cup from her unaware fingers. Unencumbered, he led her out into the midst of the dancers to await the musicians.

They stood there for an uncomfortable minute, eyes locked, completely unaware of the queen having hurried words with the players to alter their choice of music. What eventually played was another stately waltz. They began with bows before stepping closer, face to face, and he took her hand to his shoulder while keeping her other captive in his.

They had taken several steps and turns before she could bring herself to speak. "Have I offended Your Highness?"

"Why would you think that?"

She fought back her blush, succeeded in restricting it to a faint glow. "Our last encounter. The way you have avoided me as if my very existence were an affront."

"I am dancing with you," he said.

"Yes. Your mother put you up to it?" she dared.

She thought there might be a smile in his eyes, glowing behind his resentment. "Yes," he admitted, bluntly.

"Why?"

"Who knows," he responded.

She shook her head. "No, my prince. I meant: why do you not wish to dance with me."

It was a moment before he responded. "Because I am too dangerous right now for any one."

That said, she realized she could feel tension in every muscle of him where they were in contact. He was careful of his arm, but it was more than that. She made herself relax, to be the calm one.

"I may not be a warrior like the Alumet princess, but Maral women can hold their own."

He seemed surprised at the firmness of her response. "I have seen your shy and retiring nature. Aside from the saddle and the bow, you are a dainty thing, unfit for harsh treatment."

Now her resolve and calm were no longer feigned. "I have no place here, not yet. No purpose. Of course I am uncertain. Not knowing my place, I am at sea, adrift. Once I know what is expected of me, where I fit, I am as sure of myself as any. Yes, I am shy of strangers. I cannot let that stop me. I will not."

He studied her as they danced, her words turning in his mind and behind his eyes. "And what place is it that you desire?"

She sighed. "That, my prince, is a tricky question to answer. I desire what is best for my House and family. What is best for the people to whom I am responsible."

"For yourself? What do you desire for yourself?"

"In life? Or a mate?"

"Both."

He let her take a moment to think. "A purpose. I am not one of those idle ladies that is content filling her hours with meaningless entertainments and needless embroidery, chatting with her ladies, whose only real purpose is to breed children. I want to be a helpmate, to be bound to a friend if not a lover, who will accept me for who I am and what I can offer of myself, and not just what my family or dower brings. I need meaningful work. While I am no fair hand at cooking a meal or cleaning or other Folk work, I can lay a fire if needs must. And what I can do, I will. I need to be needed. I cannot stand idle. I am not an ornament."

He seemed surprised. "You don't want the faery tale? Love and complete devotion?"

She gave a dry laugh. "Faery tales are just that, stories. Pretty words. And while I love them for what they are, I know that they are not real. Vermian poetry makes my heart sing, but a real partner would keep it beating."

He let the conversation pause as they performed the great wheeling turns about one another that the dance required. As she came back in to him, taking up his shoulder and hand once more, she asked, "And what is it that you want, Your Highness?"

There was no hesitation. "My kingdom safe and happy. My people healthy and well cared for. Before my uncle's death, my goal was a well guarded city. Now I have an entire kingdom to think of. That would always come first."

"I, at least, would never ask for less. Not so long as I were allowed to help as I could."

"You understand duty."

"I also understand that one must never be allowed to become one's duty. No matter how many or well one's desires are met, it means nothing to a hungry soul. Eventually Duty eats everything until you can no longer fulfil it. This will not serve a kingdom."

He had been beginning to ease, the tension slipping away bit by bit, but now it returned. "There is a great deal going on that you do not understand."

"So explain," she said simply. "Share the burden. More hands halve work." He started to look away, his expression tightening. She moved her head to recapture his gaze. "If not me, then someone. Your brother, some other lady more to your taste. It matters not who, but that you can trust them to have only your best interests at heart."

There was more behind his dark blue eyes paying attention to her than was clearly apparent. "You wish to be the best king you can be," she said. "I wish you to be the best king you can be. I will help you in any way I can, ...even if it means I am not to be the one to do it."

"You are a confusing contradiction of fancy and practicality, lady."

She chuckled softly, glancing away only for a half second. "Of all the things I have been accused of, that one is new." She settled herself, taking a breath to think. "Yes, I have wants and needs and desires. Everyone does. But the fact of the matter is bald: for the security of the kingdom, both you and your brother must wed and well. Most of the people here are here because they need to make matches for the security of their Houses. Tell me the qualities you seek and I will do my best to find ladies who might meet those needs. Or at the very least, suggest those you should investigate for consideration." She caught his disbelieving look and smiled. "Oh, I am no matchmaker. I leave that to the likes of lady Petra, but... down amongst the herd, as it were, I might note some trait otherwise overlooked amongst my fellows."

The arch of his golden brow made her laugh, which teased a chuckle from him.

"There I go again," she sighed, blushing. "Talking too much."

"Not altogether a bad thing if what you have to say is worth the air."

"There is also value in silence," she groaned.

"Some silence."

They finished the final promenade and sank into their bows. There was a great deal wheeling about behind his eyes. He took up her hand again, the rest of his body returning to attention as he escorted her way from the dancing floor in the direction of the fragrant garden breeze.

The cloying scent of musk and roses struck her nose as Lady Asparadane came to a stop before them, bowing to the prince with her daughter in tow.

"Your Highness," she smiled. "My lady," she added as an afterthought.

"Lady Asparadane," he said, stiffly. Cae could feel all the tension from before creeping back into his arm beneath hers, felt the heat rising.

The woman drew Malyna more in front of her. "You remember your cousin, my daughter, Malyna?" she offered innocently.

Cae glanced at the girl who seemed both thrilled at the introduction and terrified of her mother.

"I do. It is good to see you again." His entire manner and tone belied his words.

Malyna curtseyed again, a faint blush on her pale cheeks. "It has been a while, Your Highness."

"You two have hardly had the time to get reacquainted, what between the tourney and the coronation ceremonies," Lady Asparadane continued, clearly angling for him to ask her daughter to dance.

"I have been remiss in my attendance upon my cousins, I agree," he replied stiffly, with a slight bow. Only Cae noticed the clenching and unclenching of his fist. "But you must forgive me. There are things I must attend to at once. You will excuse me."

If Lady Asparadane was taken aback by the dismissal, she did not show it, merely curtseying her reply, "Of course."

He turned to Cae before the other lady had barely begun to sink into her obeisance. He gave her a slightly deeper bow over the hand he had yet to release. "Good even to you, my lady. And thank you. I shall... consider the matters we have discussed."

With that, her fingers slipped from his grip and he was gone.

As Caelerys watched him leave the ballroom, she noticed her brother's squire trying to get her attention. She turned back to the two Asparadane women trying to fathom what had just happened and whether or not it was to their advantage. "Oh, please forgive me, Lady Asparadane, lady Malyna, but I must go. I believe my brother needs me."

She did not wait for either of them to respond, but worked her way through the crowd towards the boy. "Is everything all right, Harlan?" she asked, looking around for Willam.

"As right as it can be, my lady," he sighed. "He won't admit it, but I believe he's done in. If it would not inconvenience my lady, could you convince him to go home?"

She smiled, set a companionable hand on his shoulder. "It would not. I believe I have done everything that can be done tonight, and his needs come first in this."

"Bein' the only one to dance with the crown prince?" the boy grinned. "Yeah, not really much left after that."

She gave his shoulder a light cuff even as she smiled at him. "Where is he, you scamp?"

"By the fountain."

"Take me to him, then find Marko and have the carriage brought."

"Aye, my lady."

The squire brought her out onto the garden patio and down a short path to where the dragon fountain sprayed scented water into the air. Willam was seated upon a bench facing it, his back leaning carefully against the short wall of flower boxes behind him. Harlan scampered off immediately.

There were a few torches lit throughout the gardens, and Cae walked up to her brother and looked into his eyes. They were slightly glazed. He breathed a heavy sigh. "We are going home, then, aren't we?"

"Without a doubt," she said, sitting down beside him to watch the water with him.

"Did you...."

"I have danced with both princes since you rescued me from the Seawolf."

"Both?"

"Don't look so surprised. Apparently I have appeal."

He gave a pained chuckle. "You do cause traffic."

"Janem says I stop traffic."

"Which only makes it worse," he nodded.

"You are tired."

"I have not had enough wine."

"Speaking of wine...." she began just as Willam caught sight of Marko and waved him over.

"I know. I've had further words with Princess Semiana. Friends are good. High placed friends are better." He let the squire help him to his feet.

"You make it sound so mercenary."

"Our uncle is a mercenary," he reminded her.

She growled, helping Marko keep him steady. "You know what I mean."

They had little trouble getting him back inside and out to the courtyard. One of the palace servants saw them and lent a hand, taking them down the servants corridors to minimize distance and chances of jostling. The carriage ride back was torture, but he bore it mostly in silence.

The servants at the Hall helped to get him up to bed, and Cae checked in on Vyncet. He was already sleeping fine and without fever, so she left him to get something from the still-room for Willam's pain and to help him sleep.

It was well past the midnight hour before she managed to fall into her own bed. And when she did, she dreamed of flying.

8

Late as Caelerys went to bed, she was still up at dawn. Taking Tempest to the balcony on the top floor, she stood at the rail in her night dress and dressing gown and watched the bird stretching her wings over the city in the morning light. Her fingers idly unwound her nightbraid and she sighed happily in the gentle breezes filled with the smells of a city morning.

Her dreams had been disturbing, hence the reason she had not been able to sleep any later. The dragon had been there again, and had been so close to her that she could smell the warm, spicy musk of it, the faintest hint of ozone and char. This time the moons made an appearance: the slender silver sister, The Eastern Moon, watching, loving, blowing kisses to couples to draw them inexorably together, marking them for none other. Then there was the heavier, golden brother, the Southern Moon, full of righteous anger at something in the world below, lashing out with rays like spears, prodding and poking then finally stabbing at some poor soul until they went mad and were swarmed and killed by their fellows. This had seemed to make him even angrier, causing him to turn to another. He had just turned in her direction when the membrane of a golden wing blocked her view and swept away to reveal the pre-dawn grey filling her room and the dark beaded eye above a blue beak staring down at her.

She shivered as she thought about it, wrapping herself tighter in her dressing gown even though she knew the chill she felt had nothing to do with the coming Fallow. She suddenly realized she had lost track of the bird and shielded her eyes from the rising sun with her hand, trying to spot the flash of black barring in the pale sky. She heard her before she saw her, coming from behind her, over the roof of the house. She was shrieking in panic.

Cae leaned over the rail, trying to see. There were few birds that would attack her, and she had seen no eagles nesting in the last few weeks. The dream dragon flashed through her mind for an instant, just as the bird swooped down over the edge of the roof, twisting in the air to right herself before ignoring Cae's outstretched hand and landing on the rail. She continued to shrill, her wings partly spread as she half walked half hopped down the length of wood towards her.

The more she tried to calm the bird, the more she felt her own panic rising. Tempest was not injured that she could see, so that was not the source of her tirade. She was usually such a calm bird. In fact, the only time she could remember her doing anything remotely like this had been when a small band of robbers had been sneaking up on their hunting party in the Mistwood.

The uncomfortable feeling in her chest clicked into place and she just knew. She ran to the end of the balcony and began to pound on her brother's door. "WILLAM!" she yelled, striking the wood with the flat of her hand enough times to give him some warning before she just barged in.

Harlan was just coming in from the side chamber where he slept, with Willam's boots in hand, his hair tousled and a smear of bootblack on his cheek. "My lady?" he asked.

The curtains were still drawn on the bed, but the sudden and choked cry told her that Willam woken with a start and his body had retaliated.

"Harlan!" he choked.

The boy dropped the boots and ran to pull aside the curtains on the bed. Willam was on his stomach, fists clenched in the bedding as he stared out at his sister in her nightclothes, saw the bird running up behind her looking harried.

"What is it? Who's attacking?" he gasped.

"I don't know, but something is terribly wrong."

He struggled to move, fighting his body to enable him to get up to meet the foe whatever it was. "Is it fire? Riot?"

"I wish I could explain. But I know something terrible has happened."

Just as he was about to suggest she'd had a bad dream, through the open door he began to hear the screeching of the toomi in the inner courtyard. He cursed at himself, barked to Harlan to fetch the balm.

As the boy dashed to obey, Willam reached for the headboard to pull himself up. The covers slipped from his back, revealing a diagonal stripe of purple radiating down like a starburst from the blackened and swollen flesh of his shoulder. Her mind saw the Southern Moon again, shooting forth his golden rays in her dream.

He growled, swearing yet again. "Cae, go find out what is going on. Make sure Cartyr and Mace are with you, just in case. I'll be down as soon as I can... move," he gasped. Cae watched the muscle spasm ripple across his back. With a squeak, she turned and fled out of the room.

She raced downstairs, the bird gliding through the air behind her and landing on the newel post at the end. She didn't get much farther than the bottom of the staircase before the front door was opened for an out of breath and harried blacksmith's apprentice.

"Robin!" gasped Fennel as she held the door.

"Janem?" Cae squeaked.

The boy shook his head, leaned forward with his hands on his knees to get his breath. "Fine. Forge. Robbed."

"Anyone there when it happened?"

"Journeyman Hill has ... broken head," he gasped, tapping his own. "He'll live but... not... whole."

Fennel immediately began to take charge, ushering the boy down the hall. "All right, to the kitchen with ye. Water, then breakfast."

Caelerys started to follow them when the housekeeper stopped her with a soft look at her unbound hair and billowing nightdress. "Master Janem is not injured and the rest of the news will keep, my lady. Let me tend the boy for the moment. Best you get yourself presentable."

Cae clutched at her open dressing gown, suddenly remembering it. "Thank you. If you can have someone take the waterwood tea up to Willam and check on Vyncet? Willam's awake and in pain. I haven't peeked in on our other invalid yet."

She nodded and shooed both young people in opposite directions.

Cae found Fern already laying out a simple, russet gown for her. "Morning, my lady. Oh, you're in a state!" she gasped as Cae threw her dressing gown onto the nearest chair.

"Someone broke into the Singing Forge last night," she exclaimed.

"Mother preserve us!" the girl cried watching her mistress fighting her way out of her nightdress and having to battle the static of a cloud of dark hair. She tossed the gold shift in her hands onto the bed and moved to help, tutting, "My lady, this is why you don't unbraid until you're dressed."

She grabbed the length of it and twisted it into a hasty knot, pinning it in place with the first thing that came to hand. Only then did she pick up the shift and help Cae to get dressed, observing none of her usual morning toiletries. She tied off the russet laces and picked up the brush, guiding her to the stool.

"Just brush it out, Fern. I don't have to go to court today and I don't have time for anything fancy."

Fern merely nodded, making short work of the tangles and smoothing the static out of her tresses. Cae was up and headed for the door the second she was done.

"My lady," Fern called back.

Cae turned. Fern held up a simple metal fillet to hold her hair back from her face. Caelerys came back and let her slip it onto her brow, tucking the strands of her hair back.

When she finally left her room, Willam was dressed and being helped to the stairs.

"What's going on?" he called, bringing her to a halt at the top step.

"Janem's forge was broken into. His apprentice is down in the kitchen right now recovering from the run here." She pictured Willam trying to sit in the kitchen to hear the boy's report and decided it would not be a good idea in his condition. "Harlan, take him down to the solar and make him comfortable. I will bring the boy there."

Harlan nodded, and Cae did not give her brother time to protest or agree before she was all but flying down the stairs to the kitchen. She headed straight for the door to the still-room as she told Fennel what was going on and to have the boy and the tea brought to the solar. In the still-room, she checked her small collection of medicaments, selecting her distillates. She mixed a tincture of comfort root with mallow boiled in wine into a cup. She paused to check on her other distillations, adding a little water or an herb and making minor necessary adjustments, before taking the cup to the solar.

Willam was just being settled onto a padded couch when she arrived, and Fennel was setting the tray with the waterwood tea beside him. Cae handed him the potioned wine.

He stared down at the cup in his hand and the one at his elbow and glared at her. "So which is it to be and what are you dosing me with?" he growled.

She sighed, "Both, any order." She pointed to the tea, "That is for inflammation and to curb any fever." She pointed to the cup. "That is for pain and to calm the muscles and heal the bruising. Vyncet will be getting the same when he wakes."

"Fine," he grumbled, taking a sip. Once he figured out he wouldn't mind the taste, he set it aside, grabbed the teacup and swallowed it in a single gulp, making a face at the bite. "Robin," he pointed to a chair as he took a more substantial drink of the boiled wine. The boy seated himself as everyone else began to settle down. "Spill."

The boy then told them how they had found the forge that morning. "They had to be lookin' fer somethin'. They didn't take any tools 'r scrap metal. They just opened all the storage chests and threw everythin' helter skelter."

"Anything missing?"

He nodded. "Some jewels, a lot a papers, some of which fell inta the forge and damn near... sorry, my lady," he added hastily when Fennel glared at him from behind Willam's couch. "Very nearly caught the building on fire. They also got a breast-plate and vanbrace that were brought in late yesterday."

"Wasn't anyone in the forge to guard the place?" Willam growled.

"How did the place not burn?" Caelerys asked at the same time.

He shook his head. "I don't know, my lady. The Mother was smiling fer sure. But Hill was the overnight. His billet's on top of the valuables. They near killed him to take it."

"Broke his head, you said?" Cae asked for her brother's sake.

"Aye, my lady. Cracked skull, bled like a stuck pig. Hasn't got his senses yet so we don't know how many or who."

Willam's expression twisted. "Wait, you said they took a breast-plate and vanbraces?" The boy nodded. "Why? Whose armour did they take? And why only those pieces?"

Robin looked decidedly uncomfortable all of a sudden. "I have only the highest respect fer Yer Lordship and yer House. But I cain't answer that. You have to ask the Master. Like as not he'll tell you. But that's not news fer wild ears."

Willam nodded. "Are the City Watch there now?"

"They were when I left, my lord, but only just."

He turned to Caelerys. "I want to go, but I am not so much the fool. I can already feel whatever you put in this sapping my strength."

"It is not sapping your strength, it is relaxing those knots in your back," she protested. "The heaviness you are feeling is just a side-effect. Give the medicine time to work."

"I am not faulting you, woman," he growled, trying to set the cup on the table. "I am telling you that I am yielding to the Physician. I am asking you to go in my stead. Take Mace with you. Be my eyes and ears, little sister."

She took the cup from him, her expression softening. "I will. I am also small enough to stay out of the way."

"Done," he nodded, reached over to grab Harlan's arm. "Get me back up to bed. If anything happens or anyone needs anything, wake me."

"If I can," the boy snarked.

He gave the boy a good-natured cuff and turned back to his brother's apprentice. "Thank you, Robin. Is there anything else you or your master needs from us?"

"Not that I know at this time, my lord. I will not hesitate to return if there is," he nodded, standing.

"Do you have other errands or were you only tasked to inform the family?" Cae asked.

"Just the family, my lady," he responded with a bob of his head.

Cae stood, gestured Harlan to cease trying to get Willam off the couch. "Then I would ask that you go back to the kitchen and avail yourself of Fennel's spoiling and wait until we are ready to go. You can escort us to the forge."

"Damn it, lad, get me up," Willam growled, slurring just a little.

She turned, leaving the apprentice to Fennel's attentions and waved the squire at a pillow and lap rug on a chair nearer the fireplace. "No," she said firmly, pushing him back and over. "You might as well lie here for a few hours. Give the medicine time to work. That way you can be at the centre of everything should news come in and yet people can check on you easily."

He did not have the strength to fight her putting the pillow beneath his head and covering him with the rug. He stared blearily up at her. "You have to make Vynce drink that stuff," he mumbled as she bent to kiss his forehead. "Most quiet we're gonna have of him."

She chuckled softly and left him sleeping. She turned to the family's Bow Master. "Mace," she asked softly, "would it be better to walk or ride?"

He walked a little further away from the couch, keeping his voice low but not whispering. "It is not very far at all, little bird. Should be safe enough. Besides, the boys have not yet gone for the horses. They are still at the training field stables by the fairgrounds."

She nodded. "I shall get my walking shoes, then. Will I need anything else?"

"A dagger, no more. Your bow would be a bit much," he smirked.

"You think?" she smiled, shaking her head.

It did not take long for them to get ready and leave.

The marketplace was bustling with early morning traffic trying to get goods to stalls and set up, but a great many others were not out and about even though most of the Folk were awake and already working. Cae walked beside Mace with the boy leading and two other of her family's men close enough to prevent anything untoward but not noticeably hemming her in on guard. Tempest had flown on ahead as they left the market square and Cae felt a little bare without her.

The merchant district was in various states of open. Most stood with the doors ajar, being swept out for the day, some doing a brisk business even now, though some had their curtains drawn still and their doors barred. Just past a baker's they reached the mouth of the Iron Alley. The street was set a little apart from its neighbours, nearer the city walls than its heart, and surrounded on all sides by a channel the width of a narrow street, through which ran dark, bitter water. The air carried the heavy smell and taste of metal and fire and the ringing cacophony of numerous hammers pounding away at their craft.

They crossed the wooden bridge and entered the street proper. It was not really an alley for all it was named thus, rather a wide street lined with blacksmith shops and farriers and metalworkers of all sizes and skill. Anything that required a forge and fire to work was made here.

"They've noticed," Robin remarked with a frown.

"Noticed what? And how can you tell?" Cae asked.

"That the Singing Forge is quiet," he muttered. "They know something's happened, even all the way down here." He glanced back at her. "It's too quiet. Their rhythms are off."

"Why is it called the Singing Forge," asked one of the men with them. "I never understood that."

Caelerys smiled. "You've never heard my brother work."

"Come down here when Master Janem is at the anvil and you'll not ask that question," the boy crowed proudly.

"It sings?" he asked, disbelieving.

"Something very like," Caelerys responded. She began to notice apprentices and a few of the senior smiths all along the row peeking out to perhaps glean some information more than they already had. Most returned to their work, disappointed that it was only a noble lady seeking whatever caught her fancy. A few tried to hawk their skills, but a glare from young Robin silenced them.

It did not take them long to reach the Singing Forge, set back in one of the three largest buildings near the end of the alley. The front of the edifice was a neat shop with spun glass windows and a well framed door that now hung chipped and battered beside the lock. Inside was a fair sized room displaying items for sale, most made by the apprentices and journeymen of the forge, with a long counter currently manned by a rather vexed-looking young man.

"Rob! There you are! Master Illet needs you upstairs. Where've you been?"

Robin stiffened slightly, obviously getting his temper under control. "I was sent by Master Janem early this morning on an errand," he answered.

"Well, you were takin' yer time. Get up! I'll tend the customers."

"But... they're not..."

"No, buts! Go!" he snarled.

Taking a deep breath, Robin turned to Cae and gave her a bow of apology before darting behind the counter and up a staircase hidden behind a door.

The journeyman turned to face their group and gave them a tired attempt at a smile. "Forgive me, my lady, sirs. Apprentices will find any excuse, aye?" If he expected them to nod or murmur in agreement, he was disappointed.

Mace decided he would allow his lady to handle matters. Cae merely stood there, looking at the man.

"What might the Singing Forge do fer ye this morn?" he asked, trying to recover his composure. "I beg ye excuse us fer the moment, as we've had a... an issue last night. We aren't open fer work yet but if ye've an order ye wish placed, I kin manage. Though if ye're picking one up, ye'll have t' await one of the Masters."

"Are the City Watch still here?" she asked sweetly.

"The ...Watch, my lady? I don't..."

She gave him a tight smile, taking pity on him. "It might be best if you just inform Master Janem that his sister is here."

"Sis...sister?" he choked. "Um... right away, my lady," he gasped and darted through a curtained doorway.

A moment later she heard Janem's voice, "Of course she's here! That's her bird!"

Then the journeyman was holding back the curtain and gesturing for her to come through, looking thoroughly chagrined.

Mace held her back for a moment. "It might be too crowded if we go with you, my lady. We'll be about. I'll not be far."

She nodded, thanked the men and stepped beyond the curtain into the forge itself.

The first room was smaller than the shop portion, but with a higher ceiling. At the very top was a row of short windows through which the morning sun streamed, bouncing off curves of metal across from them to shine upon the tables which lined the walls. Their surfaces were covered by rows of boxes to hold the fine-work tools that were, at the moment, scattered all over the place. Two apprentices were busy sorting them out and recovering what they could of any fine-work that had been in progress on the tables. Tempest was here, under one of them, picking up small gemstones and bits of gold and dropping them into a bowl for the boys. She shrilled a greeting as she saw Caelerys, who merely laughed softly at her. "You can keep helping," she said. She took the small pouch of titbits she kept for the bird from her belt and handed it to the nearest of the apprentices. "When she is done, give her a bit from this. Just one or two, and then send her after me."

"Thank you, my lady. She's been most helpful," he exclaimed, accepting the bag.

"Got better eyes than we anyways," said the other.

The doorway leaving this room had neither curtain nor door and opened into a larger chamber filled with light. There were at least six anvils arranged in the middle of the space with a few scattered tables and places for tools to hang near at hand or rest in barrels. There were two forges, one on either side of the room, and the walls had been pulled up and fastened out of the way to allow in as much light and air as possible, as well as to provide quick access to water from the canal.

Janem stood at the edge of the building, leaning against the wall post with his arms crossed over his chest as he talked with a Watch Lieutenant. He nodded when he saw his sister, and Cae found herself a stool far enough from the left forge to not risk catching her skirts and sat to wait. Two journeymen were also in this area, trying to make some order from the scattered papers and pieces of armour littering the tables and floor.

In the corner by the doorway to the fine-work room, stood a full suit of armour on an armour stand. The only thing missing from it was the helmet, and that she assumed was the half-finished piece resting on the anvil nearest the far forge.

An apprentice came in and fiddled with a poker embedded in the coals. "Master Janem, you want I should stoke it?" he called.

Janem looked over, cast his eye over the rest of the forge and sighed. "Not as yet. Don't know if we'll get any work done today. If you're done in the fine-room, you can right and refill the charcoal bins."

The boy nodded and darted off to obey. The lieutenant finished whatever his business was and walked towards the front of the smithy. She heard his footsteps overhead shortly.

Janem came over to her and wrapped his arms around her, pulling her off her perch. She sank into the embrace, knowing there was more to it than just to cover a whispered conversation. "This is what I was afraid of, but Master Illet would not listen."

"He was right in any case," she replied against his neck. "It would not have been long before it was known and at least this way you have the interest of the crown."

He huffed at that. "We shall see what that is worth. You have it safe?"

"Aye, hidden in plain sight with my other books. Will you have need to refer to it?"

He shook his head lightly. "I know what I need."

"I should send it home then."

She didn't get to finish what else she would have said, as Janem suddenly pulled away and bowed to someone who had just walked in. She turned, saw a familiar hooded figure and sank into a curtsey.

The prince pushed back the cowl as two guardsmen stepped in behind him and took flanking positions near the door. Cae was a little surprised to realize that it was Prince Valan and not Balaran beneath the hood. He gave a soft chuckle at their expressions, pulling his gloves off. "I still have friends in the Watch, my lady. Master Janem," he said with a nod of his head, "are you willing to explain again?"

Janem straightened, relaxed just a little. "Of course, Your Highness. I trust your skills in the matter more in any case," he added with a sigh.

The prince smiled. "I do remember the case of a minor theft of something of yours a few years back. The boy still your apprentice?"

"And taking to this craft as well as the other," he grinned, turning to his sister. "You did bring Rob back with you, yes?"

She nodded, her expression a little tighter. "He was sent upstairs by the journeyman out front, and rather rudely. He was not given opportunity to explain my presence."

Janem's eyes darkened. "Would you call it abusive?"

She thought about it before shaking her head. "Not on the surface, no. But I got the impression that he listens very little to those below him and assumes they all shirk their work. Were I you, I would observe more carefully for a while."

He nodded, turning back to the prince among them. He started to say something and stopped, laughing ruefully at himself. "I almost called you Captain, Your Highness."

Valan's smile was genuine and warm. "Well, I was not that very long ago. There are moments when even I forget."

Caelerys found it hard to believe he forgot anything, but kept the thought to herself.

"Perhaps we should take this discussion upstairs?" Janem offered. "Kale," he called to the boy who was wheeling in a barrow of charcoal, "Illet still upstairs?"

He shook his head, gulping at the armed men now blocking his progress. "No, Master. I think he's out front talking with the lieutenant."

Valan gestured for them to let the child get on with his work and the men moved out of the way, though they kept their eyes on him.

"Shall we?" Janem asked with a wave of his hand.

When the prince nodded, he led them to the hidden stairway and up to one of a series of rooms. Valan ordered his men to remain below and moved with an easy grace in the narrow space. Caelerys felt a little self-conscious walking with the prince behind her, but Janem was leading the way and had yet to relinquish her hand. She did not know why the fact that she was in a more everyday gown with her hair practically unbound bothered her in the prince's presence, but it did. She was certain lady Petra would have hours of things to say as to how bad this was.

Janem gestured to a large, messy room full of beds even as he opened what looked to be a small office across from it. "As you can see, they even tossed the apprentices' room."

"They were unharmed?" the prince asked.

"They were not here, sire. Once everything had been brought back from the fairgrounds and the fair tent put away, they were given leave. They went to the fair and then to their families for the night. They've worked hard and deserved the holiday. Only Hill was here last night."

"Was that unusual?" he asked. He stopped in the doorway and frowned at the haphazard stacks of slates and papers that cluttered the desk instead of gracing the now empty shelves on the back wall.

Janem cleared a chair for Cae and all but deposited her in it whilst he sought to clear a place for his royal guest. "No. He has no family of his own, so he's the de facto guard for both forge and apprentices. He keeps them in line at night, gets them up early enough, fed and to work, etc. His room is at the back of the hall and his bed a pallet over the strongboxes. He was the only one here last night."

"Do you know if it was just a random robbery or were they after something?"

He shook his head. "I don't think this was random, Your Highness. I think they were after moonsilver... and they got it."

Cae watched the prince's posture change, saw that something unnamed ripple beneath his manner and presence, itching to rear its head.

"How much did you have here?"

Janem stopped trying to clear another seat when it was apparent the prince would not have taken it in any case. He leaned his hip against the front of the desk. "The raw ore? Not much. Only a little that I've managed to refine that was left over from the Spel sword ...and my sister's trinket," he added with a grin. She glared at him, feeling heat at her cheeks at being reminded of the thing. "It was enough to make repairs on the piece brought to us late yesterday. The rest of that commission was going to take me a gold month just to refine enough silver."

"So it is silver?" the prince asked.

Janem sighed, crossing his arms over his chest, far more comfortable in the royal presence than his sister was, but she guessed that was due to old acquaintance pre-royal investment. And while the prince stood with authority, there was little that demanded royal deference. At the moment he looked more like a watch captain. "At its core, aye. But there is so much more to it."

The prince held up a hand. "I respect the trade secret. So long as it will not be lost with you," he added.

Janem gave him a pointed, hooded look, lowering his voice so it would not carry. "Should anything happen to me before I have an apprentice trained well enough to impart the secret to, my family know what is to be done. I have taken precautions."

Valan glanced down at Cae, then gestured to the empty shelves. "So they sought the secret here and did not take it?"

He nodded. "Aye. I had already ...removed it from the premises."

"So what can they do with the ore they do have?"

Janem gave an amused snort. "Nothing. It's dead weight, a lump of bright metal suitable only to hold paper against drafts."

"It cannot be worked at all?" he asked, surprised.

"Not without the secret. Once refined, it requires a special process that no one knows to work but me. No, Your Highness, what will cause me problems is what else they took." Valan looked at him expectantly. "Yesterday afternoon, Duke Cygent brought in a breast-plate and a single vanbrace."

"Not a full cuirass?" the prince asked curiously.

Janem shook his head, "Just the front plate. The design is odd, since it doesn't look like it was meant to *have* a backplate. The duke wanted to commission a repair of the plate, and have a second brace made to match the first. I hadn't even had the chance to assess the job to give him a price. I was still out at the fairgrounds. Master Illet took the job in and promised I'd get back to him some time today. Two pieces of heirloom plate stolen and I don't think the forge can survive the cost of replacement."

"Surely the forge has done well, and other commissions will come in soon," Cae injected, worried for her brother.

He shook his head. "Word gets out that I've had such things taken and no one will entrust us with more. Even if I could find all of our records, complete and/or deliver every job we have current, it would not be enough. And some of those records burned. Tally sheets of approved costs, promises of payment and records of what belong to whom are scattered throughout the building, destroyed or are outright missing."

"Were records stolen you think?" the prince asked suddenly. "Or are they merely burned or lost?"

Janem sighed. "I fear some are stolen. Nothing was deliberately destroyed, I think. What we know burned happened in the struggle downstairs with Hill. All that is just records of current work and what prices were agreed upon. Up here," he gestured helplessly. "Up here would only have been records of past sales, shipping records, and any manuals of technique."

"Which are gone," the prince said flatly.

"Which are gone."

Caelerys had a cold feeling beginning to grow in her stomach. "Would... would the records up here... tell someone who might be in possession of valuable items?"

Both men looked at her. The prince studying her, and her brother with an expression akin to pride.

"People will have to be warned," she sighed.

"Discreetly, of course," the prince stated.

"If I only knew who was most at risk," Janem sighed. "Master Illet might remember most of it. The older things tend to cling to his mind more than newer information these days."

"Would there have been any records of who had moonsilver?" Cae asked quietly.

He shook his head. "Not likely, unless it was brought in for repairs. And there's really only been that one sword for decades. No one's been able to work it 'til now."

"Most families who have any pieces would have stored them or displayed them, fearing to damage them with use," said the prince, "as it has been centuries since the last known piece was forged. Some families probably don't even remember they have one. I cannot find any reference to any branch of the Alvermian line owning a single piece beyond the odd ring."

"I find that strange," Cae mused. "The Alvermian have been on the throne for a several centuries, is one of the most powerful of the Great Houses. How is it they possess no moonsilver? Our house has a helm, I think, and even our vassals, the Marrok, have a set of gauntlets."

The prince gave a small shrug with his hands, "I cannot explain it either. Of the first houses, the sons of the Firstborn, only Roshan and Griff are mentioned to have pieces. Alvermian and Levitau are never mentioned to have worn it."

"And of those Firstborn houses, only Dragon and Griffin are still Great Houses," Janem added. "Unicorn has fallen to the wayside, and Leviathan is extinct."

"Sea-wolves are bad enough," the prince commented, "Leviathans were worse."

Caelerys looked up at him. "They've been extinct a thousand years, how...?"

"Only eight hundred and sixty. And you've seen the library?" he added pointedly.

She blushed, remembering the encounter.

"Supposedly, House Griff has an entire suit somewhere, and Roshan might have most of one, if they gathered the pieces. Though there is no telling where they've all...." The prince's sentence drifted off to nothing as the door swung partly open.

They turned, Valan's hand falling to the hilt of his sword.

About twenty inches from the floor, a small white head peered around the edge of the door, saw Cae and piped a muffled exclamation. Tempest shoved the door open the rest of the way and ran over to her mistress, carrying the small bag of treats. She hopped into the air and landed on Cae's lap with a few flaps, and settled herself, pushing the bag into her hand.

Cae laughed softly as she took it, distracting the bird with one hand and sweet Vermian words whilst she fished a bit of meat from the bag to offer her. "There, you greedy thing," she said. "Were you helpful?"

Tempest chirruped an affirmative and gobbled her treat before settling down to preen herself.

Cae stroked the peppered back idly, looked up to see Janem smirking and the prince staring in placid disbelief. "Your Highness?" she asked softly, suddenly uncertain.

The bird looked over her shoulder at the prince, cocked her head a moment, then turned and gave a pretty little bow.

"Well she has manners, at least," was all the prince said.

They were interrupted yet again by the door opening fully this time. Master Illet entered the room with a bow to the prince. "Welcome to the Singing Forge, Your Highness. I am only sorry it had to be under such circumstances."

Valan gave the old craftsman a respectful bow and a half smile. "It is hardly the first time, Master Illet."

The old man drew himself up with a crack of his spine. "This is the first time *Prince Valan* has graced my establishment. Though I do seem to remember a Captain Valan who used to pop by from time to time. The sword still serve?" he asked.

Cae looked from Illet to the prince's sword to her brother. She had not known that her brother had already made weapons for the crown, even if they had not been the crown at the time.

"A sword crafted in this house never fails," he answered.

Master Illet had once been a broad man, and, though age had bent him and softened the corded iron that had been his arms, he still filled a room. When his knee popped as he shifted, Cae stood, giving the man a brief curtsey as she took the bird to her shoulder. "I wish you a better morning, Master Illet, but perhaps I should return home."

"Nonsense, girl," he blustered. "You are welcome here."

She shook her head. "I understand, Master Illet, but this room is small and there is no need for me to be here any longer and no room should I desire it." She turned to her brother, "I have what I came for and I have invalids at home that need my care."

Janem nodded, bent to kiss her cheek. "Be careful."

They traded a glance that said volumes and she gave him the barest nod and turned back to the craftsman. "Our brother has said that if you need anything, sent to us. A guarded place to store something, men to guard what remains... a place to bed apprentices. Name it."

He took her hand in gratitude and bowed over it. "I owe your House a great debt, my lady, and I mean to pay it."

She smiled and turned to Prince Valan, sinking into a deeper curtsey before him. Somehow, for all the informal air of the previous half hour's conversation, she always felt the need to observe the formalities with him. "By your leave, my prince?" she said softly.

He took her hand and bowed over it, watching her with his dark eyes and something more. "Of course, my lady. I would never stand between someone and their duty."

She felt the creeping heat of a blush, and swept out of the room as quickly as was meet, to hide it.

When she returned to the Hall it was just approaching the mid-day meal. She checked in on Willam and found him still sleeping. She left him quietly and went to the kitchen.

Fennel was making up a tray to be taken to Vyncet and asked if she wished to dine with him, or in the hall with Willam.

"Will is still asleep, but I have no problems eating with Vyncet. I'll even take the tray up," she offered. She turned to pass a titbit of meat down to Tempest and found her darting under the baking table after something. There was a clatter, a shriek and a squeak that ended abruptly. She looked under the table and saw Tempest trotting out with a mouse in her beak.

"Oh, you can just eat that down here," she said, putting the scrap in her hand away.

Tempest gave her a low whistle of offer.

"Yes, I am quite sure I don't want any. It's all yours," she insisted. "Mice are always yours."

She accepted the tray of food and allowed one of the scullery boys to run ahead of her holding open doors.

Vyncet was already awake and sitting up in bed. He had gotten dressed as far as throwing a tunic on, but was still beneath the covers with his leg propped up.

"How's my favourite sister?" he grinned, his eyes lighting up as he saw the food. "About time, too. Beginning to wonder if no one remembered me in this House."

From the other side of the bed, Marko rolled his eyes for Cae's benefit, silently telling her what he had been putting up with for the last few hours.

She laughed. "Marko, go get yourself fed."

The boy needed no second urging and rabbited out the door.

Cae set the tray down upon a worktable several feet away from the bed, and turned as Vyncet threw off his covers, clearly intending to come to the table for his food. She crossed the room and pushed him back down with ease. "No, you don't."

"But the food's over there," he complained, aiming a wild hand in that direction.

She deftly ducked, and set a hand on his brow. It was only a little damp and warm. "Good, fever's down. A cup of waterwood after lunch will do wonders." She then set a hand on his leg, gently, but exerting just enough pressure to get him to yield while also telling her what the swelling was like. She checked the top edges of his bandage and the toes poking out of the bottom. A little reddened, but not dry and hot and with no signs of lightning marks that boded extremely ill. "I will have to unwrap that and check it, but it can wait until we eat."

"I would rather not lose my appetite, thank you," he remarked.

She laughed as he hurried her with gestures to bring over his portion of the meal: cold, shredded fowl with carrots. "That you are ravenous is a good sign."

"That doesn't begin to cover it," he growled, snatching the small loaf of bread and tearing off a piece. "I think I could out-eat Marko and Harlan both."

"That would take some serious eating," she smirked. "And I would not advise you trying." She set her plate on the small night-table and ate far more daintily than her brother.

"So what goes on in the world that I have missed, sister dear? You two went to the ball and left me here to rot. Were there a lot of beautiful ladies?" he moaned around mouthfuls of food.

"Slow down or I won't tell you anything of what happened, last night or this morning."

He growled, but obeyed, and she gave him the highlights of the previous evening. He beamed at her small triumphs and bemoaned all of the beautiful women he was certain would be taken before he had a chance to even meet them. "And Lady Liliwyn was there? I have heard legends of her beauty."

Caelerys just sighed with a small smile, indulging him. "Well, I can say her sorrow has made her beauty even more haunting."

That seemed to sober him a moment. "Aye, they say her betrothal to Naeden was a love-match. I am surprised she even came."

"So was everybody else." She looked over at her brother's empty plate, glanced at her only half-eaten meal and gave him her plate. "But whilst we were dancing away the moons, someone was breaking into Janem's forge."

"What?!"

"I will tell you more when Willam gets up," she said, moving to unwrap his leg whilst he was still distracted with food.

He started to rail at her for being cruel to the invalid when something she'd said caught his attention. "Wait, Willam's still abed? He rises almost as early as you do."

"Whilst you lie abed until the sun is well on its way to its own dinner?" She adjusted the pillows to rest under his ankle to make removing the bandages easier. "No, he rose just after I did, when I woke him with the news."

"Then why is he sleeping?"

"Because our fair sister drugged me," growled a voice from the doorway.

Willam towered in the door frame, shifting only just enough for the returning squire to dart in past him.

"Don't argue that you didn't need it," she snipped.

Vyncet glanced from one to the other and commented, "She's getting feisty. What'd you do to her last night?"

"That question was always aimed at you, brother," he chuckled, crossing the room slowly, but not as ginger as he had been this morning. "And no, I am not arguing against it. I do feel a great deal better. Some warning would have been nice, however."

She shrugged to cover a wince as she peeled back the last layer of bandage, "Having never dosed you, I had no idea how it would effect you. Father can drink that dose in one gulp and still keep both wit and balance. It also depends upon how badly you need it."

Willam glanced over at the leg and made a face. "You going to dose him, too?" he asked, pointing without looking.

"I have no interest in sleeping all day," Vyncet protested, throwing the hard heel of his bread at Willam.

Will did not even look up, but batted it out of the air with ease.

"Since you'll be in bed all day for the next several days, it would probably go easier on you if you *are* sleeping it away."

He glared at her, "Stop making sense, dammit!" He tried to peek at the leg over his tray. "Howsit?"

"I may have to amputate," she remarked calmly.

"You're joking," he stammered, his face going white. He looked at Willam. "She's joking right?"

Willam just nodded at her. "I'll get uncle's axe."

"Don't bother him. Just get the axe for chopping firewood. I'm sure it's sharp enough."

"Now I know you're teasing, you monster!" He threw a pillow at her. "That is no way to treat an invalid!" When no one rose to the bait, he added, "Seriously, how bad is it?"

Cae did not answer him as she began rolling up the bandage, checking its length for soiling. "Marko, would you go get Colt from the gardens? Tell him I need comfort root for a compress and a rolling pin."

The squire nodded and slipped swiftly out of the room.

"That bad?"

At a nod from Cae, Willam took the tray away from him and set it on the table.

"It looks worse than it is," she answered. "I'll rewrap it over the compress when Colt brings me the comfort root. It will heal more swiftly then. But you are going to need to watch this and stay off of it for no less than a fortnight."

"So I'll be up and about in a fortnight? Dancing, women, fighting, women..." he intoned dreamily.

"You'll be in bed for a fortnight," she corrected. "It could take several months before you can put enough weight on it to even ride a horse, much less fight."

He threw himself back against the pillows and stared up at the canopy. "I am going to lose my mind," he groaned.

"Can't lose what you never had," Will quipped.

"You can get a lot of reading done," Cae offered, trying to divert the two. "You could be moved to the solar and have visitors, but you'll have to keep it elevated. You're lucky you're not being fitted for a peg."

"We could send you home," Will offered.

"Not for at least a fortnight," Cae countered before Vyncet could object. "He won't be well enough for travel, not even in a wagon for four days minimum."

"Give me the abyssal sleeping draught," he growled.

The door opened again and Marko walked in, his face solemn and white. He held the door for Colt, the young gardener who carried in his hands a toomi male. His expression was grave. He carried the bird to Caelerys and held it out to her.

Confused, Cae set the rolled bandage down and accepted the small brown bird, frowned as she felt something odd and damp on his side under his wing. She shifted it to one hand, holding it firmly whilst she gently spread his wing. There were two missing feathers and a line of partially dried blood on the underbody. Silently, Colt handed Willam the message the bird had carried.

"Arrow," she said. "He's from home," she added, glancing at the band on his leg.

She watched the expression on her brother's face range from fear to rage and back again. Numb, he sank onto the edge of the bed.

"What, what is it?" Vyncet demanded, vainly trying to reach the paper.

"Is it father?" Cae whispered, unaware of Colt gently taking the toomi from her.

"No. Raiders," he choked.

"Where?" Vyncet growled, then cursed, realizing he could do nothing.

Will drank the cup of wine that Marko handed him before answering. When he did, his voice was flat, "Benhurst. One of the Taluscliff toomi kept at Benhurst returned to his wife late last night. He carried no message. Father sent a messenger to investigate. He found nothing."

"Nothing?" Cae echoed.

"What do you mean 'nothing'?" Vyncet insisted.

"I mean nothing. Not a single villager or piece of livestock. Every toomi wife killed."

"Bodies?" she choked.

He looked down at the paper. "I don't know. It doesn't say. I think it would say if they'd been wiped out, all killed. I can only assume this means taken. I... I have to take this to crown. Father fears there may be more attacks coming. He bids me gather what can be and go. Two forces to ride from opposite ends, maybe we'll catch who's done this in the middle."

"Benhurst is on the coast of the Mistwood, halfway down the Strand, isn't it?" Cae asked, looking back at Vyncet. "We stayed there once when I got surprised by that boar."

"Aye, I think that's the place," he breathed.

She looked back at her eldest brother. "Willam, you can't go yourself. You shouldn't ride yet."

He stood, turning on her, angry now. "And what would you have me do? Hide behind my injury like some simpering courtier or malingering parasite while our people are being taken slaves? Fine things Father'd think of his heir then!"

"You don't know that's what's happening," she insisted.

"You're smarter than that, Cae. What the festering cess-pit else could be happening? A whole village just gone!" he ranted. "I would not be surprised to find that those puss-mucking, crab-bait sea-wolves have something to do with all this, and I cannot just sit around here with my feet up."

"The timing is suspicious," Vyncet threw out.

Willam paused in his pacing tirade to look at him.

"Think about it, Will," he said. "The 'Griffin-hunting', the unusual aggression in the melee..."

"The inordinate number of injuries," Will added.

"The attempts to actually kill Rorik Griff, their heir dancing with our sister...."

Willam suddenly turned to Caelerys, "What was taken from the forge?"

She was a little thrown off by the sudden shift of topic, but she ignored the rising chill up her back. "Moonsilver: a sample of the refined ore, and the breast-plate and vanbrace of House Cygent."

"Did they get anything else?" he insisted, stepping closer.

She took a breath, glanced around the room and saw Colt still standing nearby, holding the wounded bird to his chest and looking lost. "Colt," she said firmly, using it to calm herself, "the toomi will be all right. You can doctor him later. He's not really bleeding right now. But I need you to go get me the comfort roots."

"How you want 'em?" he asked, like her, mention of work was a calming focus.

"Crushed for a poultice. I'll need fresh mallow leaves, too."

"At once, my lady." The boy darted out the door, gratefully.

"Marko, go find Harlan and help him get things ready for Willam to go the Citadel at once."

The squire only glanced at the two lords before dashing off to obey.

Willam said nothing about her systematic emptying of the room and merely closed the door behind the boys. He then stood there, arms crossed over his chest, staring at her.

"No," she finally answered. "They did not get anything else, except for older records of purchase and repair. Though if they wanted them or not we do not know. For all we know they might toss them out when they discover they do not contain what they were after."

"Which was?" Vyncet prompted.

They both looked at him, spoke simultaneously, "Moonsilver."

"Worse," she added, "they wanted the secret. They took the ore thinking they could do something with it, and the armour bits, well, just because of what they are. But without the secret, not only can they not make more, they can't even do anything with what they have. There's a reason that no one's been able to even repair moonsilver in centuries."

"And Janem knows?" Vyncet asked.

"Have you really not been paying attention?" she asked, shaking her head. "He presented a repaired blade at the coronation. He practically admitted in front of all of Elanthus that he knows the secret."

"Is it written?" Will asked.

She sighed. "Not in so many words, no, I don't think so. But Jan found a book from which he deciphered... he figured it out from. I don't think it was a straight-forward manual, not exactly: 'add two parts iron, one part silver and smelt an hour at boiling point'."

"And this book is where?" Willam's expression did not change. "If they broke into the forge they will search his rooms next."

"It won't matter," she said, shaking her head. "I have it. I had decided today to send it home, but now that might not be terribly wise."

"No, it might not," he said flatly. "Nor might it be wise to keep it here."

"It's on a shelf with my books of faery tales and Vermian Poetry," she said with a half-cocked eyebrow.

"I wouldn't look there," Vyncet grumbled.

"I have other books, more important looking ones, set elsewhere," she added. "It doesn't look important."

Willam moved and she got the impression that his muscles were beginning to protest again. "I will leave at once to take this message to the citadel. I will return tonight with orders. Until then, I want you to have the hall fortified, and Mace prepare the men for departure. Those I choose will likely leave at first light." He gestured at Vyncet as he opened the door for the squire about to knock. "Dose him as heavily as is safe for tonight, but lightly as you dare until the matter is settled. I will want his senses about him even if he cannot rise to wield a blade. Harlan, you have been told what is going on?" he asked the boy standing there, wide-eyed.

"Aye, my lord. Benhurst," he swallowed. "That's where my sister lives."

"We will know soon enough her fate, boy. Find my uncle. He'll be with the Sterling Company. Thank the Mother for hangovers, else they would likely have left this morning. Tell him what is going on and that, if need be, I will foot the bill. Now fly."

The child was gone in a flash, trading places in the doorway with Colt who was carrying the carefully bruised and rolled out poultice of comfort root and mallow on a platter. He came in wordlessly and set it down on the bed beside the injured limb and proceeded to help Cae lift it onto the wound.

Vynce took a deep breath and exhaled slowly, feeling the near immediate relief of the cool concoction. He barely flinched as the pair of them began to wrap the leg back up in bandages.

"I'll be back," Willam said, turning to follow his squire out the door.

"Prince Valan knows," she said.

He stopped, turning back.

"He knows what was taken. He came to the forge after the Watch, spoke with Jan and me about what happened."

"I will seek him out first then," he said. "If you have the time, I would compose your letter for father. I will make sure it arrives."

She nodded, turning back to Colt. "You're very good at this. Have you ever considered becoming a Physician?"

He shook his head. "Nay, my lady. Not as I'd ever afford the schooling. They don't apprentice as most crafts. I like my birds, I like the garden. I'd like to know more how to use what's in it, though, if my lady'd a mind to teach," he added, glancing hopefully at her.

He was a gangly youth, with dark hair and eyes, about fifteen or sixteen. He had that rugged kind of good looks the folk tended towards when they were fortunate. She could see intelligence without real ambition lurking in his eyes. She smiled, tucking the pillow more fully under her brother's leg for support and pulling the covers back over it. "Well, then, come with me and I will teach you as we go," she said, and led him down to the still-room without a word to her brother.

Vyncet slept through supper, and Cae sat up in his room with her sewing. She left the door open so that she might hear anything downstairs as she carefully embroidered a dark blue tunic with silver thread. It was nearly the middle of the night when Willam finally returned home. Someone downstairs must have told him where she was, because she was only just putting away her threads when he poked his head in the door.

She gestured him to silence and slipped out into the hallway, closing Vyncet's door softly behind her. "What news?" she whispered.

"What news is a small army. What of our vassals are here are already making ready to leave soon after dawn."

"Uncle Jehan?"

"Half the Sterling company rides with."

She shook her head, "And the cost of that?"

"Surprisingly, that is all volunteer. The only cost will be expenses."

"Why?" she frowned. "I did not expect that of mercenaries."

He shrugged. "Some had families along the coasts, some have personal grudges with slavers and raiders. There are subsequent sons of the coastal houses in the company. They all have their reasons. As the Free Legions have no current wars to fight, or other call for their swords, they need to keep busy."

That made some sense. She guessed they might take plunder in the process, though that would be kept to a minimum. "What did the royal family have to say?"

"The prince and the king both are eager to see this matter put paid. The crown prince rides with us."

"Us?" she frowned. "Willam, you are not well enough."

"And neither is he," he said vehemently, though he kept his voice down. "Neither is Rorik Griff, but he's riding out, broken ribs or not."

"You're all mad."

"Aye, well, men do what needs must." He set a gentle hand on her arm, "We all know the risks. The king has insisted that the three of us are to lead from the rear or the middle at best. Our expertise is needed. We all know our roles, and we do not ride alone. Asparadane rides as does Halbourne and Trent. Haru and Alder ride at the head of Roshan, both Cygent sons, and Selkan and Lutret all field men. We ride out over a hundred strong."

"So few?" she frowned.

"Any more would be too bulky to move with any silence. And we do not wish our quarry to know that we are coming. Worry not. We will be enough men to handle two ships worth of raiders but small enough to move like wraiths through the wood."

"Providing they did not take immediately to ship with their prey," she sighed.

"And that is where the navy will come in. The king has ordered six vessels of war to follow the coasts all the way to the Reach, just in case. If they have taken to sea, they will be run down. Father and the men he manages to muster will likely be coming up the coast, along with salvage crews doing the same."

"Everything seems to ride on Fortune," she breathed, leaning back against the wall. "Will I be able to see you ride out?"

"If you rise early enough. We march from the Citadel at dawn."

She nodded. "I want to ride with you to the Citadel."

He sighed, "Be aware that if you do, you will not be able to leave until late. The queen has said she wished to gather all the young ladies of court together."

"For what? Did she say?"

He shook his head. "Commiseration is my guess. At worst she means to take your measure in crisis."

"I'll not show wanting there at least," she breathed. "Well, if you mean to ride, I shall have to prepare medicines for the road."

"Something for the tightness and the pain which will not cloud my head, please. Though I might wish for sleep tonight," he added pointedly.

"I'll give you a little of what I gave you this morning. Enough to relax and put you out but not enough to keep you abed longer than you wish. I'll bring an arnica balm as well, to speed the healing."

"Thank you. Then you best get to bed yourself."

She stifled a yawn. "Did they say anything about Janem's forge? About the loss of the Cygent armour?"

He shook his head as he headed for his chambers. "No, but I doubt that they will allow it to bankrupt them. There may be some concessions Jan will not want to make, but I believe they'll cover the losses. It is not like the thieves can sell it."

She gave him a light push down the hall even as she headed for the stairs. "Go on, I'll send the medicine to you shortly."

She went to the still-room and prepared him a much smaller dose than either of them had been given earlier and sent it up with a salve. Taking a wineskin which she marked by wrapping a red thread around the neck, she filled it with a tonic of waterwood and boxflower, with a splash of comfort root to ease pain, keep the muscles lightly loose and to speed healing. Only then did she head to her own bed.

9

By the time the sun rose, the hall had been a hive of activity for two hours. Horses were saddled and stood waiting in the courtyard with men filling saddlebags with last minute victuals and other necessaries. Cae had already packed Willam's scrip with her letter home, the balm and minor medicines.

She handed him the marked wineskin and made him drink some before she let him leave his room. "One good swallow first thing in the morning," she said, "followed by one at midday, or whenever you start aching again. One last swallow before bed. This should last you four or five days. I've put a small pouch of sweetmeats in here too..."

"Sister, I'm off to war, not holiday."

"No, you are off hunting, just more dangerous prey. They are spice root candied in honey to make them easer to take. Only eat them if you are in a lot of pain, or you start to spasm. And yes, this will mess with your head, but no where near as badly as what I gave you last night. It should only numb your sensations and might effect your balance. So you might want to eat one before bed the first night, before you run into anything serious, just to find out how it will effect you. Use your own judgement after that."

"You are trying to pack a whole Physician in to one small bag."

"If I thought I could, I would. Not that you would listen to one. Or me for that matter," she sighed. "My letter to father is in there, too, so don't forget. I've said very little baldly, just in case of interception, but be careful anyway."

They stood there a long moment, just staring at each other. Then she threw her arms around him and he curled her into a crushing embrace. "One piece, brother," she whispered, fighting tears.

"Aye. One piece." The sun was just beginning to rise over the edges of the city walls as they entered the crowded courtyard. Men on horseback were milling about with men not yet ahorse, gathering themselves into groups according to Lord Rorik who sat stiffly on the back of a steady, blood bay. He gave Willam a nod as he saw them.

Will paused beside her, leaning over to kiss her cheek. "I have to muster. Stay out of trouble if you can. And remember, the women of the court are more dangerous and certainly more vicious."

"Don't over do it," she warned.

He waved his men to gather in one group until he had a chance to speak to Rorik and rode over to confer.

Cae turned Wraith aside, trying to get out of the way. From her perch, she could see most of the royal family standing on the stairs leading into the Citadel proper. The queen looked worried, and rest her hands on the shoulders of her middle boy who stood watching almost blindly as he clung to one of the golden toy horses her family had gifted him. The princess stood almost hidden by her mother's skirts and looking very alone. The king and the two eldest sons were not to be seen.

Princess Syera caught sight of her and waved her to come over.

Cae made sure she had room and rode as close as she could before dismounting. She found a place to tie off her reins for the time being, and slid from the saddle, slipping in between the bustling people to reach the relatively empty stair.

They were standing on the top landing just off the side of the doorway, which was currently closed. The princess reached for her before she was even close enough, pulling her past the few guards and to her side. Cae had to wait to curtsey until she was in the small group.

"I'm glad you came with him," Syera said softly. "You couldn't talk any sense into him either?"

She shook her head, knowing they were speaking of brothers.

The queen looked worried, but wore it well, with a kind of serenity Cae was more than mildly jealous of. "You will stay with us whilst the menfolk are gone?" she asked.

She bobbed a half curtsey, "Aye, Your Majesty. I was told you desired us for the afternoon."

"Oh, no, dear," she corrected in a gentle, motherly tone, "everyone was asked for the afternoon. I was speaking of you staying here until they return."

She was taken aback by the offer. "Oh, I... I was not aware of the full extent of the request. I am afraid I cannot. I still have one invalid brother at home."

"Surely the servants can tend him?"

She gave a sheepish smile. "They can, but ...he will not be satisfied with them. They he can order to disregard Physician advice. I he cannot."

The queen smiled. "Bring him here, then. He will not be able to order about our servants."

"I am honoured by the offer, Your Majesty, but Vyncet cannot be moved for at least three more days, four would be better. If they are still away, I could accept then, but I would be remiss in my duty to my family if I agreed any earlier."

"Few would dare to refuse such an offer," the queen mused.

"It is not that I do not wish it."

"Oh, suredly." She waved the matter off. "I am merely surprised, though I shouldn't be. Four days then. You should be fine at least that long," she added, looking dreamily out over the milling host.

Syera pulled her further back, nearer the wall. "Don't ask, she can't answer you," she sighed. "But her instincts are good. Oh, do say you'll come as soon as he's well enough," she pleaded.

"I will try." She could not help but laugh at the princess's eagerness. "I understand how lonely it can get, being the only girl. Have you no ladies in waiting yet?"

She sighed, almost pouted. "There are some being considered, but they're not 'friends'. It's not the same. I have handmaidens," she shrugged.

They were interrupted by the opening of the doors and the arrival of the king flanked by his two eldest sons. There was a roar from the men in the courtyard and Cae felt buffeted by the sound which bounced off the castle behind her and echoed in the curve of the wall. The four of them bowed and Prince Valan crossed over to them. He bowed formally to the group, then came closer to kiss his mother and to hear any last whispered advice she might give.

Cae wanted to shrink back against the wall behind the princess and be completely overlooked, but she had something tucked into her sleeve she was desperately trying to mount the courage to offer. She decided to just stand back a little behind the princess and wait. If he acknowledged her, then maybe, but she tried not to appear to be waiting.

He bent to have words with his little brother, to hug his sister. Cae was still trying to be as invisible as a servant when Valan's eyes met hers and she froze. It took her a second to realize he was holding his hand out to her and to set her fingertips upon it. "Lady Caelerys," he said, his voice rumbling in his chest.

"Your Highness," she breathed.

"I have a request of you."

She caught her breath, but not in time to prevent the words which slipped out, "And I of you."

One golden brow arched, and the barest hint of a smile graced his lips.

She blushed. "What does my prince wish of me?"

"The day I saw you in the library I was researching something. Something delicate and very important."

"I take it to be a matter too sensitive for worms?"

He nodded once, something twisting behind his eyes.

"Surely if Your Highness has not found it by now?" she suggested.

"Oh, I found it, but as all treasure hunts go, one clue has led to another and now I have no time."

She took a deep breath, trying not to freeze or smile or giggle or any number of embarrassing things. "What prey does my prince wish me to pursue?"

"The moons. Find me all you can on the moons, the Southern one especially. I do not care how obscure or fanciful the reference. Compile me a reading list. If you are half the woman I have heard, you will know when you have found what I seek."

She lowered her eyes and bent her knees just a little, "As you wish."

He curled his fingers under hers, drawing them tighter against his hand as he bent and kissed it. His lips were warm and dry where they brushed her skin and she shivered. He glanced slyly up at her. "And what request had my lady for me?"

"Oh," she started, having momentarily forgotten. She held out her other hand, offering the length of midnight blue silk. Silver threads winked in the pale light of dawn. "If you like? A reminder of my promise to help in any way I can. A mark of my sincerity. A secret if you wish, between you and I. Indeed, I will have no promise from you in the acceptance but this: One piece."

He frowned slightly at her words. "One piece?"

She gave him a shy smile. "Ask my brother."

"Son," said the king, gently recalling him to his duty and the time.

Valan slipped the scarf beneath his breast-plate, once more kissing the hand he had yet to release. He pulled away then, moving with swift grace down the wide steps to his waiting horse.

Beside her, Princess Syera took her hand again and squeezed, giving her a delighted smile even as Balaran moved to stand behind them.

They watched the prince ride to the head of the host and lead the procession out the gates and towards the great bronze dragons of the bridge. Down at the docks, six ships of war would be sailing on the tide with much less fanfare. Once the last of the host had left the courtyard, the king offered his arm to his queen to escort her within.

The queen paused to smile at Caelerys, studying her for a moment before speaking. "Would you be a dear and keep Syera company in the gardens until the other ladies arrive? I will have a light repast set up on the terrace overlooking the harbour, so you can watch the ships sail out. Perhaps tonight, before supper, you can peruse the library, and at any time you feel the need. I will expect you at supper at the very least."

She sank into a curtsey. "Thank you, Your Majesty. You are too kind. Allow me to see to my horse and I will be there presently."

"Nonsense," said the king, waving his hand to a nearby page and gesturing to the mare still tied to a nearby balustrade.

With little excuses left, she fell in behind Balaran who walked behind their parents, arm in arm with the princess.

"Did you not bring Tempest?" she asked, disappointed.

Cae smiled. "I did. She is aloft. She will watch probably until they enter the Mistwood. Then she will fly back to me."

"How will she find you?"

She laughed, shaking her head. "Like a toomi finds his wife, I imagine. I do not know how, but she always does."

The princess filled her ear with all sorts of idle nonsense until they were out in the gardens and comfortably seated on the terrace. Awnings were up and there was plenty of room for at least thirty young women, though there was only food enough for five.

Cae ate lightly, having grabbed a quick bite before dawn, while the princess had her breakfast. "So how badly hurt is your brother?" she asked Cae as she peeled an orange.

"Which one?"

"Either," she shrugged, trying to behave as if neither were her real concern.

"Vyncet, the younger one," Cae began.

"The one you can't leave alone?"

She nodded. "The whiner," she chuckled. "He makes such a big deal of being laid up. Not that I blame him, I think I would chaff too, but I at least have some sedentary pursuits. He's not going to lose the leg, which is good, but it will take him the better part of the season before he'll be able to really be active again. It'll be well into Fallow before he can dispense with crutches."

"And Willam?"

She sighed. "Willam would have been fine in a fortnight or so. It is only a bruise, however hideous it looks. But it will take longer for the muscles to heal now that he is riding weeks before he was supposed to. No telling how long if he actually gets into combat."

"Or what else he'll hurt because he wasn't at his best?" she added cautiously.

She nodded. "Exactly. How bad is yours?"

"Valan?" she asked, a little surprised. She shrugged, "I think the arm is strained. I know they had to relocate his shoulder, but, he's at least as good with both hands, so it won't be any real hindrance. What is going on between the two of you?" she added slyly. "I thought you were more interested in Bal."

Cae blushed. "Nothing. And no. I am friends with Balaran, maybe on my way there with Valan, but... frankly, Valan terrifies me."

"He has been getting a little scary lately."

Cae played idly with a sweetbread, watching the girl. "How so?"

The princess leaned back, "Don't get me wrong, he was never what anybody'd call 'fun'. Balaran was always the jester, into everything, making jokes, playing with words. Val... Val has always been very aware that he's the firstborn, twin or no. That he was father's heir and was the one who would need to make something of himself once it became clear that Uncle Rorlan had heirs enough we didn't have to worry about this," she said with a rueful gesture at the Citadel behind them. "But lately...." She sighed, setting down a half-eaten pastry, not really wanting it any more.

"Every since uncle went... mad...," she whispered the word, "he's been prone to fits of anger. Again, nothing new. It's how he reacts to them. One minute, you think he's about to swell up and explode and then next he's hunched over, or splayed with his hands against the coldest wall he can find and just concentrating on his breathing. He has started to avoid things that could make him too excited. He won't even take wine that isn't watered. Not even small ale. And he's always in the library looking for things, or in a corner reading what he's found, but he's never satisfied."

"Have you tried asking him what's wrong?"

She shook her head. "He won't even talk to his twin. They used to be so close and now... now it's like he's suddenly fed up with how carefree Bal is. Bal's always been that way." She gave Cae a long look. "If you are getting him to confide in someone, I'm glad. Really. I just hope it's enough."

"I told him he needed to talk to someone, anyone, even if it wasn't me."

She picked up her drink. "And that right there might be the reason he's confiding in you. The question is, whether or not whatever's eating away at him is the reason he scares you."

"I don't know what it is. I mean, I'm always scared when I first meet someone. Most people terrify me. But, ...Balaran put me at ease fairly quickly, even though he was flirting. Valan... Valan makes me feel so formal. I am aware every second that he's the crown prince, whilst with Balaran I'm just with a person of similar interests."

"Speaking of interests," she said brightly, sitting up and determined to change the subject and brighten the mood, "what are Willam's?"

Cae grinned. "I knew it! You are sweet on him!"

It was the princess's turn to blush. "Maybe. For all the good it will do me."

Cae frowned. "What do you mean? My father would have absolutely no objections."

"No, your father wouldn't, but... there are political considerations in play and... mother has her eye on you."

Cae did not have a chance to ask her what she meant by that as the sound of other voices began to reach them.

Syera gestured for the servants to swiftly take away the remains of the meal and bring back drinks and titbits for the arriving guests.

The queen arrived shortly in the company of about twenty women, most of which were the unmarried young ladies of court, though some of their mothers and a handful of the married ladies were in evidence. Duchess Griff was there, with two handmaidens dancing nervous attendance upon her. Lady Liliwyn Cygent brought up the rear on Prince Balaran's arm.

Cae felt immediately out of place in her ordinary day gown. It was a simple overdress of deep blue linen, trimmed in broad ruffles of paler blue veiling material to compensate for the fact that she'd outgrown the length some time ago. It showed off her crisp white under-gown nicely, but compared to what the other ladies were wearing she might as well have been a toomi amid peacocks. Everyone else had dressed for court, with hair far more elaborate then her simple, braided crown and loose waves.

Greetings were exchanged in a gaggle of feminine chatter, and the women eventually settled themselves with about as much rustling and fluffing as a flock of birds. The Roshan girls found seats with Cae and the princess, with Lucelle sitting next to Cae. Malyna Asparadane fluttered over and was about to squeeze in between Caelerys and the princess when Tempest dropped out of the air with a shrill and landed on the back of the bench.

Malyna shrieked and jumped back, nearly upsetting a small table with a pitcher of refreshments.

The princess only squeaked a moment in surprise, but smiled with delight as the bird dropped down onto the few inches of space between them. The queen's eye crossed in their direction, but she said nothing. Malyna instead insinuated herself on the other side of the princess, presuming upon her relation, however much by marriage it might have been. She gave a strained smile and looked admiring as the princess made much of the bird.

"There you are!" Syera exclaimed with delight. "I take it our men are off safely?"

Cae laughed as the bird looked at her, begging for a treat as if nothing was amiss. She slipped the treat from her hidden pocket, but did not give it to her. "Ah, Jelma, first you say hello like a lady."

The bird actually sighed, hopping up onto her knee to turn to the gathering of women and bowed prettily. She snapped up the treat offered and settled down to enjoy whatever attentions and pampering were going to come her way.

"Does that mean yes?" Lucelle asked.

"If anything were wrong she'd be in a right state. I assume they've entered the Mistwood without trouble. Like as not they will see no action today. Tomorrow..." she left her words hanging, catching the glaring eyes of some of the matrons in the group at the topic. "So, Lucelle, tell me, is a lord of Marrok courting?"

The girl blushed and fluttered, trying to hide her giggles and excitement, nodded furiously. "Edler. He is so sweet. I just hope he talks to father when he gets back."

"Congratulations," the princess offered.

"Oh, it's too early for that," she said dismissively. "I mustn't jinx it."

"Oh, but of course," Syera nodded sagely, reaching out to pet Tempest. The bird, of course, allowed it. "Is it a match you desire?" she asked pointedly.

"She would be a fool not to," injected lady Balyra. "He is the heir to his House, however minor. It would bring her branch of the House great honour."

Cae forced herself to smile sweetly. "Marrok is a Lordly House in its own right. They are not one of the Houses Minor. They are directly beneath House Maral, above Brock and Tyre. If she likes him, as I think she does," she added with a genuine grin, "then I say may the Mother bless you with the union."

"Yes," said lady Malyna, "Blessings of the Eldest upon you for your fortune."

Lucelle sank back against the couch, "I'll take all the blessings I can get my hands on!"

That sent the group, all but her eldest cousin, into titters, and even Malyna joined in, though late.

"Has any one else had any luck?" Lucelle asked, redirecting everyone's attention off of herself.

The conversation went in that direction for some time, with the girls pointing out who they had seen dancing with whom. Someone brought up that lady Malyna had been dancing with lord Aldane Kaladen.

"Do you think he'll offer?" someone asked.

Malyna blushed and shyly looked down at her hands. "Oh, I doubt it. There have been so many offers already, with better positions, and mother has refused them all. I highly doubt his suit would be considered when others more worthy were not." She looked over at Cae. "Though I am given to understand he is quite smitten with you, Lady Caelerys. Perhaps you might be lucky enough to one day be Lady Kaladen?"

Cae suppressed a shudder, but not so completely that the princess did not notice. Syera gave her a concerned look. Cae gave a tiny shake of her head and answered as sweetly as she could. "It matters not whether he is or no, that is one suit my father will never accept. Not even were he the only man to ever ask."

"Why-ever not?" she asked. "He seems nice, and such a large fief. A number of islands, too."

Cae thought how best to express her father's opinion of the entire Kaladen line. There were very few polite ways. "Let us just say there is an ocean of bad blood in between their islands and my father's castle."

"A marriage is an excellent way to mend such breaches," Malyna continued. "Why a child of both houses would have the best of both worlds, serve to seal whatever happened in its grave, Eldest willing. You should be honoured to be considered."

"I do not think that our families are any where near ready to make that kind of overture," she said ruefully, taking a long drink of the weak pear cider that was being served in order to drown the word 'pirate' back from her tongue. "Besides, I am very unsuited to island life."

"How so?" asked young Onelle. "I know it is far to the South. Is it so much colder there?"

"Cold and rocky, or so I'm told. Little in the way of forest and hard press grazing."

Malyna shrugged. "So you would have to give up riding, surely you have other, more lady-like pursuits to occupy your hours?"

More than one lady looked pointedly in her direction. Cae noticed they were not just the women who had ridden in the tournament. It was Balyra who answered. "If the sacrifice was demanded of me by my family that there was no other option? Maybe. But you don't ride, you cannot understand what that simple freedom means to a lady."

"I ride," she protested meekly.

Balyra snorted, "Being led side-saddle on a fat, placid palfrey that wouldn't run if a snake bit it? That's not riding. Once you have the wind in your hair, all that power beneath you and you in complete control over where you go and how fast? You never want out of the saddle after that."

Malyna reached up to touch her hair. Today it was woven into a basket much like Cae had worn to the ball but tighter and more stiff. "But that leaves your hair in disarray and gives rise to all sorts of unpleasant rumours."

Cae remembered her own state upon her return from the ride with Balaran on the first day of the tourney and wondered if the girl was making reference to existing rumours

"Still worth it," lady Lucelle quipped.

"Surely there are other, more lady-like pursuits in the Reach?" Malyna asked. "Needlepoint? Music?"

Cae stroked Tempest's back to remind herself to stay calm. "Many. I sew."

"Oh, don't you just love needlepoint?"

Her smile was tight. "I do not needlepoint. What embroidery I do is to embellish our clothing, which I help sew."

"You... don't have women to do that?" she simpered.

"We do. We just help, especially in the Fallow months. And then I am making clothing for the poor children of the Duchy."

"Oh, that's nice," the princess said. "Something from your own hands means more."

"We give alms all the time, money and food, usually through the church," Malyna said. "The church of the Eldest back home is very active with the people."

"I would never trust another to deliver my largesse," Cae frowned. "After all, it is my duty to the people to see them well cared for. Though I will grant you there are far more in need here in the City than I have ever seen in my life. I know every cotter and villager in a hundred mile radius of Taluscliff. I have visited them with my father to see to their needs and collect our tithes personally. It does them good to see their Lord among them, seeing for himself their hardships."

"It is a lot of work, being head of a House," Balyra nodded. "I personally like it. Even the hard decisions."

"You are your father's heir, are you not, lady Balyra?" the princess asked.

Balyra nodded. "Aye, Princess."

"Oh, I am so glad I do not have the responsibility for so many lives," Malyna simpered. "I don't know if I could handle the stress. I mean, lives depend on you making the right decisions."

The queen's eyes fell on the girl at that, and Cae was certain the prince had heard as well, though he said nothing.

Cae turned to Balyra, "Do you know how to use any weapons?"

She shrugged, "I'm no where near as good as you with the bow. But my father taught me how to use a shield. Very effective weapon if you wield it right," she laughed.

Several of the women joined her laughter.

"Almost as effective as a mace, but with a much larger striking surface," Cae giggled.

"And you don't have to worry much about the delicacies of parrying," Balyra added. "You? You know anything beyond the bow?"

"I'm a fair hand with a knife, and if I had to, I could pick up a sword and make the unschooled think twice," Cae chuckled. "But not much more than that. I might have Willam teach me a little more, just in case."

"Just in case of what?" Malyna choked.

They looked back at her and saw the look of absolute horror on her face.

"In case I'm ever attacked?" Cae responded.

"But... that's what men are for! A lady should never have to pick up a weapon to defend herself."

"Or her home, or her cradle? Or her own honour?" Cae asked pointedly.

Lady Malyna seemed firm, setting her shoulders as if to convince herself as much as the others, "A true lady should never have the need to defend her own honour."

"So," said Balaran suddenly, appearing behind their couch, leaning his arms next to his sister's head, "your men are away at war and the enemy is at your castle gate," he proposed.

"It's not like I would be home alone, Your Highness," she protested. "There would be men-at-arms."

"But the enemy breaks in, kills the men-at-arms," he continued. "They are seeking to take you captive and kill the child in the cradle behind you. Now what?"

She sat up straighter, holding her shoulders back. "I take the child and run, hiding. Give it to a maidservant if I could not and would resist with lady-like dignity."

"I'd attack with a sword until they got close and then stab them with my dagger when they thought they had me," Balyra said, folding her arms.

Cae giggled, enjoying the game. "I think I would trap the room first, make it harder for them. Have the maid hide the child and then use every trick and weapon at hand. A lady should always be prepared to defend herself if caught alone."

"A lady should never *be* alone," Malyna said quietly, as if parroting her training and beginning to doubt it.

"Maybe at court," one of the other ladies said. "At home one wants a private moment now and again."

There were nods of agreement.

Lady Arran was sitting nearby, leaned on the back of her couch to enter the conversation. "Of all the houses that would value such activities in their women, I imagine Kaladen and the Northern kingdoms would be it," she said with an air of superciliousness. "The greater houses, such as Griff and Cygent, and any which reside in the larger cities would disdain you for such skills. It is something to consider if you wish as broad a market as possible for yourselves."

Cae caught the glimmer in the prince's eye and decided not to allow herself to be antagonized by the blatant bait.

"Well, the Northern peoples will most certainly look upon one the less if one wasn't capable of defending oneself, in one way or another," said Balaran.

"Not all of them are warriors," Malyna said. "Prince Kyleth is quite the courtier. Certainly not as aggressive as his royal brother."

"I'm glad you enjoyed his company, lady Malyna," Cae smiled. "I understand he is looking for another wife. It would be quite the catch for you."

She smiled until she caught a word, and her expression stumbled. "Another?" she squeaked. "What happened to his last one?"

Cae shook her head lightly. "Nothing. I understand she is alive and well."

"Set aside?" asked Onelle, scandalized.

Balaran gave a laugh. "I doubt she could do anything to get set aside. No, she is still married. They practice polygamy in the North."

She had not known Balaran knew so much of their Northern neighbours and ignored Malyna's expression of shock and revulsion to turn to him. "Tell me, does it go both ways or just one? I never got the chance to discuss the subject with Princess Semi."

He turned, smiling. "Mostly just the one, though it has been known for powerful daughters to take more than one husband instead of the other way around. It is rare though."

She smiled at the thought. "I would not doubt that Princess Semi is one of those women."

"If she took a fancy, I can see her doing it," he grinned. He reached over and stroked Tempest at the back of her neck, chuckling as the bird leaned into it. "Say, if I can tear you away from my sister and your invalid brother, would you like to go hawking with me tomorrow?"

Tempest turned her head at that, looking up at him with eyes bright and an excited chirp.

"Well, that's her answer," he smirked. "Will her lady be joining her?"

"She might," she smiled.

"Good. I think my subsequent uncle can scare up a peregrine for my use."

Lucelle smiled dreamily. "That sounds like a lot of fun."

He looked over at her with an indulgent smile. "Have you ever been hawking before?"

"Oh, no. My family doesn't keep a mews. My cousins do, but I've never flown one myself. I'd love to watch though. And the ride would be a delight."

"It would be a good opportunity for the ladies to get out," said the queen. "Some sun and exercise would do them all good."

"You are so right, mother," he beamed. "What better way to spend the morning than alone in the meadow with a bevy of beauty, basking in the plentiful pulchritude of feather and fair skin. And horses, mustn't forget the horses."

The ladies giggled at his wit, and all of them looked excited at the prospect except for Malyna. "Mother would never let me go," she sighed.

"Why ever not?" Balaran asked. "It is a noble sport, well suited for ladies."

"Hunting of any sort is not ladylike."

"So you don't hunt," he tutted. "Just ride. With hawks we are not likely to go for a wild gallop."

"I would love to, but... perhaps..."

He stood, dismissing her reluctance. "Stay or go, it is no matter. The rest of us will have a wonderful afternoon. Mother, could we have a lunch set up on the fairgrounds for when we return?"

"I do not see why not. Make the arrangements."

No one seemed to notice the conflict that danced across lady Malyna's face, everyone was too excited about the promised outing. And only she noticed the prince bending to Cae's ear just briefly.

"And after lunch, you and I can disappear amongst the worms and actually get some work done. I have things to show you," he whispered. "And maybe we can get that cat to pay us a visit again?" he added with a grin.

She only nodded slightly in acknowledgement as her eye caught sight of sails moving away from the harbour. "Oh, look," she exclaimed, pointing. "The ships are leaving! The tides must have turned finally. Aren't they breath-taking?"

"Only from shore," said one of the minor ladies ruefully.

Cae gave her a reassuring smile. "I've only been on shipboard in harbour, myself. I've never been on the open water. I've always wanted to do it at least once."

"There is a certain romance to it," Liliwyn sighed.

It was the first time she had spoken in Cae's company and her voice was just as beautiful as her face, even with the weight of her sadness. She smiled at her, trying to be comforting. "There is. Father has promised to let me go out to watch a salvage operation but we thankfully haven't had one since."

"Thankfully?" Malyna asked, confused. "If you don't want to go, why did you ask to?"

"Oh, I want to. I say thankfully because, for there to be a salvage job, someone's ship has to sink. And luckily we have had no bad storms or pirate attacks since..." she paused to think, "oh, Planting last year?"

"Wasn't there a terrible storm last Fallow?" asked Duchess Griff, glancing up from her embroidery.

Cae shook her head, "Yes, my lady, but thank the Mother and all the First Born that the only ship that was about in that weather made it to shelter in time. No ships were lost off our coasts, at least."

She nodded with a tightened smile. "Yes, thank the Mother," she breathed. "We only caught the edges of it, but we knew it was more severe to the East. I had wondered how you fared."

Cae watched her carefully as she answered, noticing something odd in the way she was breathing and holding herself. "A little wet, a little flattened," she answered, "but nothing not easily rebuilt. Our woodsmen and carpenters were busy for months. My lady, are you quite all right?"

"Oh, I'm f..." she fluttered, her teeth tightening suddenly upon her lip before the word got out, drawing a bit of blood.

Caelerys's eyes darted pointedly to the handmaidens above her. "My lady, I rather think you should lie down." She caught sight of something else and turned towards the queen who reigned a few couches over watching the ships with her son. "Your Majesty might wish to call a midwife," she said.

She set Tempest on the princess's lap and stepped over to the lady. "May I?" she asked, waiting for a confused nod before setting a hand on her belly. There was a great deal of movement.

The young lady beside her set her hand on the couch cushion between them to adjust her own position and gasped. "Oh!" When she held up her hand and shifted quickly looking down accusingly at the cushion, Cae knew.

She took Duchess Griff by the hand. "Squeeze as tight as you like. My brothers are stronger than you," she smiled. She looked over her head to the handmaidens staring cluelessly. "Ladies?" she insisted.

By this time, others outside of the small circle had noticed and come over, including the prince.

"Duchess?" he asked.

"Oh, I don't know," she fluttered. "It's been like this off and on all day. I've been assured it's normal."

Cae laughed. "Aye, it's normal, my lady. It's also now."

Balaran looked at her. "You sure?"

"Water's come," she said softly.

The prince shooed the girl sitting next to the duchess away and bent down, sweeping the woman up into his arms. He only paused long enough to bark at her ladies, "You, go get the midwife! You, follow!" he snapped, and marched off with several of the older ladies following.

Cae remained standing, watching their retreating backs as the rest of the ladies gathered closer to chatter over the impending birth. She noticed the girls next to the now wet cushion moved further away fastidiously, so she snatched it up from the couch and held it out to the nearest servant standing discreetly near the shrubs. "If you please?" she asked sweetly.

The girl took the cushion from her and bobbed a curtsey. "Of course, my lady. I'll bring another straight away."

Turning back to the gathered gaggle, she sighed. Malyna was now dominating the conversation with talk of babies and exclaimed prayers to the Eldest for a fine son for the lady. Beside Cae, she heard a quiet remark from Lady Liliwyn of, "I would rather think they would like a girl, as Duke Griff has four sons and no daughters."

Cae glanced at her. "I thought he only had the two."

Liliwyn smiled softly. "Now. He had four. One died young, the other he's disowned."

"Oh, how terrible. Why-ever would he?"

She shook her head demurely. "No one really knows, but there are rumours."

Cae smiled. "There are always rumours. Would you... would you like to take a walk? I find the subject matter... tedious."

Liliwyn looked her over a moment. "I would love that. But I would have thought you would have gone with the others to the birthing. You seem to know so much."

Cae blushed as she called Tempest to her shoulder, began walking deeper into the gardens with the lady. "There are others who know far more than I. I would only be in the way. Besides, the only births I've helped with are livestock and Folk. I understand Noble births are attended differently."

She gave a soft laugh and Cae decided she would like very much to hear it more often. "Aye, I imagine the Folk care little for the niceties and formalities. We have some odd customs and ideas," she sighed. "I imagine the Folk just get on with it."

"You've attended a noble birth?"

She nodded. "My sister-in-law. There was a great deal of... unnecessaries, I thought. But then, my sister-in-law is one of the Eldest's, so she insisted on a Pontifex as well as a Physician."

Cae spoke before she could stop herself. "They certainly are starting to poke their noses into places they have no business," she growled. "I take it there was no midwife either?"

"You would be correct."

She sighed. "You are right, Folk do it differently. If they are abed, there are no men allowed but the man who got her that way, and only if he wants or can. I've known Folk women to birth in the field, pick the child up and go back to working. And once, I helped one in the tide pools," she added excitedly.

"Seriously? Tide pools?"

Cae nodded, remembering. "There is one village, Kelpwood, I believe. Their whole lives revolve around the sea. If the tide is right, they try to birth in the tide pools. They say it's easier. Safer. And it must be because they have fewer problems with the mother after."

Liliwyn suddenly laughed. "And here we walked away from all that to escape this topic."

Cae giggled. "We did, didn't we? Well," she asked, taking a breath to banish the giggles, "what would you like to talk about, Lady Liliwyn?"

"Well, Lady Caelerys," she said with equal formality, "I suppose we could start with these magnificent gardens."

This started the laughter all over again. "All right, but in private, please just call me Cae. I'm not one of those stuffy dainties that insist upon observing the formalities even in private.

"Fine, then I am Lili."

She grinned, "Not Wynnie?"

She rolled her eyes, "Only to my brothers. And only when they are trying to be trying."

Cae giggled. "Vyncet used to call me Ri, to annoy me."

"Used to? How'd you get him to stop?"

Her smile was devilish, "First, I put toad slime in his boot shine."

Lili winced, "First?"

"Then I added salt to his favourite tart. Then I frayed his bowstring just enough so that when he was at archery it broke and caught him across his cheek."

"All this because he called you Ri?" she asked, incredulous.

"Oh, no, it was a lot of little things, these just happened shortly after he called me Ri. The last time I just punched him in the gut."

She laughed, "How long ago was this?"

"I was eight, I think. He hasn't called me Ri since," she shrugged with a grin.

"Being punched by your eight year old sister would do it."

"Please don't get the idea that I am a wild child who is unfit company for proper young ladies," Cae said suddenly, as if occurred to her that this gentle lady beside her would never have contemplated hitting her siblings.

Her smile was enigmatic. "Oh, of course not. You only win horse races, nearly win archery tournaments, can fend off an attack long enough for rescue to come and hunt with the best of them," she said with mock seriousness.

Cae blushed, realizing she was coming off as rough and unfit for court.

"Though for the record, I would have dusted his tart with slipwort."

Cae looked over, staring agape. "Oh, you are devious!" she breathed, trying not to laugh.

They both gave up and devolved for a few minutes in unrepentant laughter.

"Well," Lili gasped when she could breathe again, "we have to find some way to hold our own against brothers. They can be such monsters when we're young. And I most certainly could not get away with punching."

Cae grinned. "I only got away with it because he was too embarrassed to tell. So, you know your way around a garden?"

Lili's eyes lit up. "Would you like me to show you something?"

"Absolutely."

She led her deep into the gardens, down a twisting path that Cae had not noticed the few times she had been here. It led into a pretty little bower fairly dripping with white and pink cascades of bell-blossoms that hung like fat, fragrant grapes from the lattice frame above. At the far end was a white, curved bench just big enough for two, and all manner of shade loving flowers and lacy greenery thrived around them. Cae noticed that the path was not paved here, but carpeted with a fragrant herb that sent up light and delicious aromas when bruised by passing feet. Even Tempest left her shoulder to walk amongst the sweet carpet.

Lili did a little turn beneath the lattice, letting her skirts swirl out and taking in the complex scents now surrounding them. "Just smell that," she sighed.

Cae stopped and closed her eyes, taking it all in. "It is... like a feast for the senses."

She felt the silky velvet of a spray of blossoms that brushed against her cheek, noticed other nuances, subtle and otherwise. There were some fragrances that Cae had never liked by themselves, but coupled with everything else around them, they balanced perfectly. Almost every angle brought a new dish before her, each one more rich than the last and none that overpowered the other.

She heard a soft sound that did not mesh with the luxurious background and opened her eyes, turned to see Lili sitting on the bench curled in on herself, weeping softly. Cae rushed to her side, sliding onto the bench and folding the girl into her arms. For a little while Lili let her, resting her cheek on her shoulder and taking her heart's ease. But then she pulled away, fussing at the damp spot on Cae's dress. "I mustn't," she sniffled. "I will ruin your gown."

Caelerys's pressed a small square of linen into her hand to dry her eyes and ease the sniffling. "It's seen worse. Unlike everyone else here, I dressed in haste and in old clothes."

She frowned, looking the gown over. "It doesn't look old or that bad. It's not silk but, sometimes you don't want to overdo it. I mean, did you see lady Malyna's gown? Did she wear that to the coronation?"

Cae chuckled softly, glad she was feeling better, enough to gossip at least. "I wouldn't know. My family was the second to present and I don't think if I saw her I paid any attention to her specifically. But I highly doubt her mother would allow her to wear the same dress to court twice in a silver month's time."

"Try twice in a season," she giggled, drying her eyes. She took a minute to compose herself. "Again, forgive me. I had not intended to weep all over you. I just... I planted this for him," she said, gesturing weakly to the bower. "We only got to sit here twice before.... I didn't think it would hit me so hard."

"Scent is very powerful. You designed this marvel?" she asked, awed.

Lili nodded. "Everything carefully chosen. It took me months to find everything and to get the balance just right. It is a little off for a few weeks between Harvest and Fallow, but then the Fallow greens bloom and the whole symphony changes."

"It is incredible. I'm sure he loved it. And I'm also sure he would not want you to come to hate it just because he is not here any more. It may take a while before it stops bringing you pain, but there will always be joy just beneath it."

"I hope you are right."

"So do I. I would never want something I created to bring another pain. But then I don't have much to worry about as I have no skills that meet this."

"I'm sure you do," she protested.

SHIFT: Stag's Heart

Cae shook her head firmly, leaning back. "No. I'm not ashamed of that. This is …I just don't have enough words. What I bring forth is not a thing like this that can be held in the hand or touched. My way is …I suppose in provision? I mean, I sew, there is that, but that carries only a small sentimental value only to be enjoyed by the wearer. I have my animals, but they will hardly outlast me."

"You have your love," she said softly.

Cae looked at her in disbelief. "Oh, I have no love. I mean, I'm not in love with anyone, and I'm not sure I will ever be able to be."

"Nonsense," she insisted. "Tell me about your brothers."

"Which one?"

"Whichever."

She stopped to think but Lili grabbed her hand and drew her attention. "No, don't think about it. Just tell me."

"Well, there's Vyncet, the youngest. I've told you a little of him. He's the prankster, the fun one. I don't think he takes anything seriously. Then there's Janem, my subsequent brother. We grew up together. He's my favourite, I think. He's warm and kind and very talented. I used to read to him while he worked, and he learned how to make the anvil sing in time to any poetry I'd read. I'd bring him food because he'd get so wrapped up in working he'd forget. And then there's Willam. He's the eldest now, but I hardly know him. He was fostered with the old king when I was born because of…" her cheeks flushed.

Lili patted her hand. "I know Willam," she said. "We saw a great deal of each other the last few years. He often played chaperone for Naeden and me. He is kind and thoughtful. Steady. But you see, I listen to you speak of these men and I hear the love in your heart sing, like Janem's anvil. You can love. You may hold yourself in reserve all you want until a choice is made for you, but when you fall, you will tumble and never recover, I think. Like me, you aren't going to have a choice."

Cae studied the girls eyes, seemed startled to realize they weren't exactly a grey-blue as she had thought but a hazy shade of violet. "You truly loved him, didn't you."

"Yes. We were very lucky and we know it... knew it."

She put her arm around her shoulders. "I don't want you to ever think you cannot be yourself or break down in front of me. If you ever need someone to just let you cry, to comfort you in silence and cheer you back up when you are done, do not hesitate to ask me. Stag's Hall is not that hard to find, and I will always be home for you."

"That is kind of you. But you hardly know me."

She smiled. "Anyone who knows plants better than I do is someone I want to know better."

This made Lili laugh. "You keep a garden?"

She nodded. "Not like this, mind," she exclaimed, waving her hand, "not here, but enough. Stag's Hall's garden is small and mostly utility. I have roses and a few things that are also pretty, but just about everything else in my garden can be eaten or brewed for medicine. Taluscliff was more impressive and could provide both castle and village in a pinch."

"That's a valuable skill."

She gave a self-depreciating laugh. "Well, yes, but it isn't... a recreation of the garden of the Firstborn."

Lili blushed. "It isn't that impressive."

"I beg to differ," said Prince Balaran from the entrance to the bower. He waved his hand for them to remain seated when they moved to rise and bow. "This is undeniably my favourite part of the gardens. I had known you were talented. I had not known you planted this."

"It was a surprise for him. I didn't really want a big deal made of it."

"I can understand why. Certain people find out about this and you'll be swamped with requests and demands," Cae said.

Balaran's eyes narrowed even as he smiled, "You begin to sound like your brother Janem."

She laughed at that as he approached. "I suppose that was rather like him. I take it Duchess Griff is well in hand?"

"And underway," he said with a tone that said he did not want to think any more of the matter.

"And you are not dancing attendance upon the others why?" Lili smiled.

He leaned in closely, "They're still talking about babies," he shuddered. He stood straighter, moving out of Tempest's way as she chased a cricket through the thick ground cover. "Don't get me wrong, I will want children of my own, and I am not shy about handling my own infant brother, but... they go on and on," he groaned. "You would think that all they need do is express their desire to be a mother with an enormous brood to make themselves irresistible."

The two giggled, rising.

"Would you two ladies like to walk a bit more? Give me an excuse?" he asked, offering his arm to both of them.

"Why, of course, Your Highness," Cae smiled, bobbing and taking his left arm.

"As you wish, Your Highness," Lili blushed, taking his right.

When they finally returned to the main group, it had thankfully broken up a little, with only those trying hardest to curry favour remaining with the princess. The queen had left with the birthing mother. A luncheon was served out on the terrace, a great deal more substantial and broad a spread than had been offered for breakfast.

Cae stayed on the fringes of the conversations this time as they ate, not wishing to get embroiled in the religious discussion that was unfolding. Lady Malyna attempted to get some of the other girls to go with her to the temple to offer prayers for the departed men and the coming newborn. The others protested, claiming that the queen had wished them to remain within the Citadel for the time being. Balaran had countered this by telling Malyna that she was welcome to use the chapel the late queen, her aunt, had had built within the Citadel.

This caused her to blush with delight, then mild disappointment when no one else wanted to go with her but two of the married ladies. In the end, she stayed put.

When Caelerys had the opportunity of a private word to the prince, she asked if she might be able to slip away into the library for a few hours.

"My lady, the library is open to you at all hours. You might wish to see if Liliwyn wants to come with you. She is quite familiar with its shelves and might relish the quiet."

Lili was thrilled with the idea, though she spoke softly so as not to alert everyone's attention to what was clearly isolated privileges. "I used to love curling up on the third floor with that great calico on my lap."

Balaran scowled. "How is it that everyone else has seen those cursed cats but me?"

"Maybe you aren't mouse enough?" Cae giggled. He rewarded her with a playful glare, but it brought to her mind Tempest and that she probably shouldn't take her with them. "Jelma, go check on Janem."

Tempest gave a complaining chirp, and begged for a treat in consolation. Cae fed her a bit of ham which she gobbled happily, then flew off.

"Where's she going?" asked Lucelle, worriedly.

"Oh, I've sent her on an errand. She'll go home after."

"You trust that she'll actually go?" asked Malyna.

"I've trained her well."

Onelle piped up, pausing in her conquest of a sweetbread. "Falcons can be very clever if you train them right, though ravens are smarter. I've seen people train ravens to run errands. But that is very impressive that you can just tell her to go home and she will."

"I've never really thought about it," she responded softly. "It's just... we have an understanding."

"Oh, I get that. Twill somehow knows when I want him to ignore certain prey, or when I'm sending him to the mews, but we have to be close enough or he'll take detours. Especially if he spies a vole. Are we going early enough in the morning that I can bring him, Your Highness?"

"Absolutely," he said, stepping closer to block the view of Cae and Lili, effectively cutting them out of the conversation and taking everyone's attention onto himself.

Grateful, the two woman slipped away.

Cae let Lili guide her to the library, still not remembering quite how to get there. She asked her advice on where to look for books on the moons and was directed in two different directions. She chose scientific first, and spent a good couple of hours perusing dry treatises on orbits and physical influences of tides and the confluence with other heavenly bodies. She read what she could find and took note of one or two which might be helpful, but she left the stack feeling certain that nothing there was what the prince sought.

She had better luck amongst the other section devoted to flights of fancy, legend and poetry. There was really too much to go through in a single day, so she began at one end and skimmed through them one by one, setting aside any that she thought might need deeper assessment. When she noticed the worms moving about and lighting the balcony lamps, she realized it was very late. She tucked the three volumes she wished to study more fully under her arm and went to find her new friend.

Lili was indeed curled up on one of the chairs with the cat in her lap as she read. Cae was surprised to see she had tucked her feet up underneath her on the soft chair. Lili caught her smirking as she looked at her legs and suddenly, very self-consciously lowered them. "What?"

"I am sorry, it's just... I thought I was the only one uncouth enough to do that," she giggled. "I never expected it of you."

"Am I that stuffy?" she asked, a little hurt though she was smiling.

"Oh no, just... that lady-like. You are the epitome of grace and class," she said with a broad, melodramatic gesture, "as lady Petra would say. Luckily I have not seen her since the ball, or she would have worn out my ears extolling your virtues to the point I might not have been able to like you nearly so much."

Lili blushed, laughing softly. "Well, I am very glad I got to you first."

"My ladies," said the soft voice of a nearby worm.

Cae turned and Lili leaned to look around her. "Oh, good evening, Ward. Are we being too loud?" Lili asked him.

"Not at all, Lady Liliwyn. Merely that I was sent to locate you both. It is nearly the hour for supper and I am given to understand the pair of you are expected at the royal table."

"Oh," Cae exclaimed softly. "I had completely forgotten. Thank you for the reminder. Ward, is it?"

He nodded. "Aye, my lady. How may this lowly worm serve?"

"I need to actually read these three volumes and I have not yet had the chance to ask for permission to remove them from the library. Is there a place they can be set aside for me until I know or in case my request is refused? I will be by tomorrow to continue my search."

He held out his hands for the books. "Absolutely, your ladyship. Upon your return, simply ask for them. If you ladies will follow me? I will lead you to the door."

Cae glanced back at Lili as she handed her book to the worm and untangled herself from the cat. "Do I look that lost?" she whispered.

Lili smiled, shaking her head. "Courtesy when under request. The worms know the fastest ways out. I'll thank you to keep that for me, Ward. I'll want it this evening."

"Shall I send it to your chambers?"

"Yes, thank you."

And the worm led them out of the library in short order.

Supper was not as formal an affair as Cae had supposed it would be, and immediately felt better about the way she was dressed. The table was large enough to seat twenty with ease, but everyone was comfortably spaced out near the head. The queen sat at the king's right hand, as was custom, and Balaran was placed on his left in his brother's usual seat. The eight year old Janniston was seated beside his mother where she could keep an eye on him and Liliwyn was seated beside him. Syera sat beside Balaran and Cae was seated beside her. There was no one else at the table.

The meal was brought out in courses much like back home, and not in the stately way they would have been at a formal meal. Entire courses were laid out on the table at once and everyone helped themselves. This had very much the feel of a family supper, complete with the youngest exhibiting less than perfect table manners and conversation being punctuated by 'please pass the--'. Cae understood why Liliwyn was here, but could not begin to fathom why she had been included in this rather intimate affair; though she noticed the queen's eye upon her frequently.

"Is there word about the duchess?" Cae asked politely.

The queen smiled. "A beautiful daughter. She will be the jewel of her House's eye, that one. The mother is weak but will be hale enough in a few days."

Everyone breathed a sigh of relief and said various exclamations of blessings as they held up their wine.

"Semelle tried to insinuate an invitation tonight," the king said casually to his queen.

"Oh?" was all the queen said, unsurprised.

"I think she feels snubbed," he added as if it were no matter.

"She does? Well, she always was perceptive," she commented as she calmly ate her dinner. "Janniston, you have a fork and you know how to use it."

"She is going to wonder why," the king said.

"Then she is not half as perceptive as rumoured," she answered flatly.

"That was years ago, Sigrun. She understood."

The queen set her fork down. "She gave up her desire for you so that her sister could marry the crown. She married her cousin to keep matters in the family. Her mistake, not mine. Her husband and her brother are both dead. You are not. Her sister is now dead. You are king and suddenly she is thrusting both herself and her empty headed, useless daughter in front of you and she expects me not only not to notice but to accept her poison at my table? She's a greater fool than I thought. Or she takes me for an empty headed fool."

The king was quiet a moment as the queen resumed eating as if nothing were amiss. "Malyna is not useless. She is quite the accomplished young lady," he began.

"Father," Bal injected, "she expressed relief that she had not the responsibilities for the lives of other people, that she had no great, sweeping decisions to make."

"That... that would make for an unsuitable queen," he mused, going back to his food.

"Well, I won't have her," Bal said flatly. "Marry her to Janniston if you must, maybe she'll have matured by their wedding day."

The boy in question made a face at that.

"Marry her to Verlan, if you've the whim," the queen said without looking up from her plate as she spoke of her infant son, "but trust that, if you do, she'll be queen before he's old enough to feed himself."

The king looked at her, appalled.

"I don't think Malyna'd poison my brothers," Syera gasped. "She's too meek."

"There was never any proof," he protested, answering another accusation entire.

"There will never be any proof," she said pointedly. "She's too good." She turned to her daughter. "As for mice never presuming to kill cats, you are practically looking at her mother when you face the daughter. Semelle was just as demure and meek. It is all a façade."

Balaran made a doubtful face. "Maybe not yet. She's made too many blunders to make me think her smart enough to equal her mother. But, vipers are vipers, the whole family. Even her cousin turned on Valan in the melee, long before it was appropriate."

Cae caught Lili's eyes across the table and ate in silence, determined to stay out of what was obviously a family quarrel.

"What do you think of her, Caelerys?" asked the queen suddenly.

Cae looked up, startled. "Um, the daughter or the mother?" The look the queen gave her answered the question. She tried to think fast, feeling uneasy at being put upon the spot. "I... I think her mother is very hard on her and I can't decide how much of what she is trying to do is her or her mother."

"And what is it she is trying to do?" asked the king.

"Anyone can see her mother means to have another Asparadane on the throne. She would have her house rise higher than it is. She makes me uneasy... like being in a room with a venomous serpent and not knowing where it is or when it will strike, just knowing at some point it will. The daughter... just feels like a trap, like the bait. Please forgive me, I do not know much about court intrigues and the like and I have heard none of the rumours that seem to intimate she had a hand in the death of her husband beyond unspoken insinuations. I can only compare it to my experiences. But I think if there is any question, or there was any history between the two of you, that one should avoid anything which might cast shadows upon your association."

Liliwyn added in when the queen looked to her. "I agree. No matter what the truth is, right now the crown cannot afford the slightest implication. If it is discovered, and if it is to her advantage for it to be, it will be, that the two of you were once betrothed, then every private conversation you have with her is going to be questioned. You could just take her as mistress, which would alleviate scandal but cause the gossips to wonder what failing of the queen's has driven you to it. You could openly take her as a paramour, but that would shatter the kingdom's image of the loving royal family that everyone currently holds, which will make them wonder what else is just an illusion. That will cascade down to your children. And if Lady Asparadane were to fall out pregnant...," she said.

"And she will," Sigrun said quietly.

"It will not matter whose child it be, but it will be yours, with all the claims that come with that."

The king was quiet. Cae was not sure if there was anger underneath, but his grip was tight on his fork. "It is a long way for a subsequent child to come from unclaimed to a throne. There are five souls between him and it. More if I have my way."

"Your Majesty," Cae said very quietly. "I beg you to remember how you and your family came to be sitting where you are."

His eyes were piercing and suddenly she could see where Valan got it from. She felt horrible, and terrified she had gone too far. But she had said no more than the truth. She must have gone completely white, because Syera set her hand on hers under the table and gave it a squeeze.

The queen distracted the king by refilling his wine. "Stop petrifying the girl, Rorlan. She has said no more than bald truth. That is what I have always loved about the Maral line. You're blunt. Oh, you can make the truth dance if you've a mind, but when it counts...," her hand struck the table and made the tableware jump, "like a hammer. I don't think you can help it." Her gaze became more intent for a second. "In fact I am sure of it," she added, turning away. "That is the end of that, Rorlan. I will not have that woman in my house or at my table so long as I breathe. And if you tell her so, Rory, I promise you that will not be for long." There was something in her eye as she pinned him with her gaze that even the king did not want to question. "Now," she continued lightly, refilling her own glass, "tell me, Liliwyn, how have you been? Are you sure you are ready to be out and ...available? Because, if you're not, I will have words with Callowen myself."

Lili blushed. "There is no need to berate my father, Your Majesty. I agreed. My brother is right, sooner is better. I am not getting younger, and if I wait until I am ready I will be old and toothless. So long as the chosen husband is understanding, I shall be fine."

"Well said," the queen answered. "The best balm for Tragedy is Life." She looked across to Caelerys. "Lady Liliwyn is staying with us for the time being, until the men return. I thought of the poor dear cooped up in that house with her sister-in-law, never mind her mother tutting over her, and I couldn't bear it."

"Mother's not so bad," Lili offered, playing with her fork.

"I remember Nessa very well, thank you. She is a marvel at comforting minor hurts and the wounds of childhood, but real tragedy? She simply doesn't understand it, so how can she comfort it?"

"She *is* all about moving on," she sighed. "I appreciate the reprieve, Your Majesty."

"I made the same offer to Caelerys," she continued, still eating. "But alas, she must stay and attend her injured brother for a few more days yet. Three was it?"

"Four would be best, Your Majesty. We shall see after the third."

"Do not leave it too long."

The last course was brought out and Cae did not think she could bring herself to eat any more.

"I was meaning to ask, Your Majesties," Caelerys ventured. They looked expectantly in her direction. "There are some books I need to read more in depth, and I was wondering if I might take them home with me? For a few days?"

"I don't see why not," Balaran said to his father. "After all, she has loaned me one of her most precious."

The king looked from son to lady in surprise. "Has she?" he asked. Something in his gaze made her think Valan had told him that her family had the care of the moonsilver secret.

She blushed, "It was only an old book of obscure faery tales."

"And old Vermian poetry, and a few plays I have not heard of before," he added.

The king seemed to relax at that. "Oh, I do not see a problem with that, then."

A servant slipped up and bent to the king's ear. The king turned to look at him in confusion. "Well, there she is. Tell her, not me!" he exclaimed good-naturedly.

Cae suddenly felt a cold pit in her stomach, especially as the man came around her side of the table. "Yes?" she asked hesitantly.

"Your brother's squire is in the atrium, my lady. Said that the lord is getting out of bed and railing at the servants. Even your subsequent cannot keep him abed."

"Oh my," she breathed, placing her napkin beside her plate.

"Trouble, dear?" asked the queen.

"Only my brother being foolish. I have been gone too long, I'm afraid, and even Janem cannot stop him. Supper was absolutely lovely and I thank you for allowing me to join you for it, but, I must beg your leave. If I do not go..."

The queen nodded. "Do what you must, my child. And hurry, lest he damage himself irreparably."

The king looked at his queen in askance even as Caelerys rose from her chair. "What can she do that the smith cannot?"

"Drug him, Your Majesty," she answered as she curtseyed. "By your leave," she said, and followed the servant from the room.

It took all she had to restrain herself, and only the fact that she had no idea how to get to the atrium from here kept her from flying past the servant. Marko was on pins and needles himself, standing in the now empty front entrance. The poor boy was dwarfed by his surroundings. He looked relieved when he saw her coming towards him.

"Did you ride?" she asked without preamble, finally moving around the servant with a nodded thanks and hurrying out the door opened by a guard.

"Yes, my lady."

The horse stood waiting near the steps, held by a single groom from the royal stables. It was Vyncet's horse. Marko helped Cae vault into the saddle, heedless of her lack of a riding skirt. "Just go on without me, my lady," he said. "I'll be fine walking back. You need to stop him. He's not listening to Master Janem, who's too afraid to hurt him further to really force him."

She settled herself in the saddle and reached down for him. "Nonsense, Marko. There is room for us both."

Reluctantly he let her pull him up onto the saddle behind her and held on for dear life as she spurred the horse to go as quickly as she could get away with in the darkened streets.

A guard was left standing at the gates of Stag Hall, threw them open as he heard the oncoming hoof beats. He closed them behind her and someone ran out of the stable to take the reins even as Marko was sliding off the back. No one said anything about the glimpse of bare leg Cae flashed as she dismounted and rushed inside the house.

She had no problems finding the source of the commotion. Vyncet was cursing Janem and whoever dared poke their head in at full volume.

"Really? That's the best you've got?" Janem challenged as Cae entered the room.

She stood in the doorway and just stared. Janem was on the bed with Vyncet's back pressed to his chest, and his arms looped up under Vyncet's and his hands locked behind his neck. Vynce's hands flailed above his head trying in vain to reach his assailant. "Oh, and I suppose you can do better?"

"In three languages," Jan bragged. "Hell, our sister can do better than that."

"Don't tempt me," she growled, crossing her arms over her chest.

Vynce looked over at her and grinned, "Hey, if it isn't...."

She cut him off viciously. "Don't start!" she snapped. "I was at supper with the royal family, I'll have you know! A supper I had to leave before it was over because you can't follow orders. I've been invited to remain at the palace until Willam returns, but I cannot because I have to play nanny to you!"

"But... why can't you go?" he asked innocently.

"This!" she shouted, gesturing to the bed. "This is why I cannot! You cannot be moved yet! You cannot get out of bed."

"Not even to..." he began.

"Bedpan!" she snarled.

"But...." A glare from her silenced whatever he had been about to say. He tried a couple more times, with false starts, but ended before he even got a whole word out. Finally, "I'm sorry."

She started to relax.

"It's just... so frustrating. I'm home alone, nothing to do and I can't get up. I'm helpless," he moaned flopping his hands useless above his head..

She sighed, stepping closer. "If he lets go of you, will you stop trying to get out of bed?"

Reluctantly, he agreed, and Jan released him. He rubbed his shoulders as Janem got off the bed. "Where in the name of the First did you learn to do that?" he groaned.

"Will."

"Figures," he grumped.

"Have you eaten?" she asked.

"Yes," Vynce answered at the same time as Jan said, "No."

She took a deep breath, begging the Mother for patience. She pointed out the door. "Jan, go eat. I will meet you in the kitchen in a little while." She saw Colt lurking in the corridor and waved him in as her brother headed out. "Are you in pain?" she asked Vynce.

He shrugged. "Some. More now," he groaned, still working out the kinks in his shoulder.

Colt bobbed his head. "I would have given him fer the pain, my lady, knowin' what needs, but I didn't know the much."

"Wise to wait," she said gently. He pressed the bottle into her hand. "It depends upon the weight of the man. More needs more."

She moved to the small table in the room where the remains of his supper sat and poured a half cup of wine. She took the small measuring glass he handed her and poured carefully. "For most, it is one dram for each five stone, but some men require more, some less."

"How do you know which?" he asked as she poured the measure into the wine.

"By knowing the man. More importantly, how he handles his drink. With the grown you can err a little with no ill effect so long as their heart is sound. With children you have to err on the side of not enough."

"Understood."

She took the cup over to her brother and scowled at him as she held it out. He took it, drinking it down sheepishly. "And which am I, sister? More or less?"

"More to a point," she said flatly. "After that you are quite the bit less."

He looked hurt by that, then tried to puzzle it out in confusion. She took advantage of this to examine the bandages. There was no real change at the edges and no stains, so she did not bother to unwrap it.

"I'll redo that tomorrow. No," she said suddenly, straightening up. "Colt, you know what to look for, yes?"

"I think so, my lady. The lightning marks, redness, heat."

"Good. You check him in the morning. Freshen the compress for me."

"And where will you be that you won't even have breakfast with me?" Vyncet asked. "For the second day in a row," he added for good measure.

She gave him an imperious look. "Hawking."

"You can do that any t..."

"With the prince."

"Oh." He stared at her in silence for a long minute. "I... I think I'm going to sleep now. Good night?"

"Good night," she answered less gently than she'd intended. "And fair warning, I'm telling Marko to sleep in here tonight. He'll let me know if you try anything again."

"Will was right! You *are* suborning our squires!"

"For your own good. Marko, he's yours. And if he tries anything, poke him in the leg!"

As she closed the door on her brother's aghast expression, Colt looked unsure. "Do you mean him to really...?"

"No."

"Do you think he will?"

"I think Vyncet isn't sure. Which means he might actually behave."

"Remind me never to underestimate sisters, my lady," he chuckled.

"If you have one of your own, I think you already know that by now," she smiled.

"I have one, but she be new, my lady. Nice to know the expecting," he grinned.

She took the time to tell him what medicines her brother would need the next day and where to find her if he should have any questions or trouble, then sent him off to bed.

She went down to the kitchen where Janem was finishing up a roseberry tart. She sat down at the table and laid her head down on the scrubbed wood.

"That bad?"

She lifted her head just enough to look at him. "You were the one had him in a headlock."

"That was not a headlock. I think he called that a shoulder lock."

She groaned, pressing her forehead to the table again for a few minutes, before sitting up and accepting the warmed wine Fennel handed her. She looked at the housekeeper. "No one is to obey him if he goes contrary to Physician orders," she said. "Any problems, bring them to me. This is for his own good." The woman nodded and busied herself at the bread table preparing the dough for the morning.

A thought suddenly occurred to her and she blanched, groaning.

"What?" he asked.

"I'm to go hawking with the prince tomorrow."

"So?"

"So I left my horse at the Citadel. I rode in with Will, but I was in such a hurry to get back here I forgot completely. I just rode the horse Marko came in on."

He chuckled. "I'm sure we can send someone to fetch it tonight."

Fennel looked over her shoulder at them, nodding. "I'll send one of the men when I'm done here."

"So you set your bird to watch me again?" Jan asked, changing the subject.

"She found you? Where is she?" she asked, looking around.

"Probably in your room. I told her to bug off."

"Did she?"

He snorted, "She brought me here. Good thing, too. You've got your hands full."

She glared, "*My* hands? You're not going to help?"

He shook his head. "I've got too much work. We have a lot to recover."

She sighed. "Will you at least consider living here? Your rooms aren't going to be safe."

"Can't. I'm living above the forge now. Better for me to work anyway. *Moonsilver is night work*," he added in old Vermian.

"But there's no kitchen at the forge. What'll you eat?"

He shrugged. "There's a pie cart that comes round twice a day."

She was getting ready to fuss at him when Fennel set another tart in front of Janem and one before her. "If my lady wishes and allows it, I'll be happy to send meals around for him."

He sighed, looking at both women and knew he wasn't going to get out of it. "Fine. I'll send an apprentice by to fetch it."

"Send that young Robin, if you don't mind," Fennel said, wiping her hands on her apron. "He has sweet manners and I'll not mind feedin' him, too."

"Watch your heart there, Fennel. That scamp will steal more than pies, you aren't careful."

She swatted him with the apron as she took it off, draping it over the bread dough as she set it on the hob to rise. "It is late. You both should be abed yourselves," she said. "I'm that way myself unless ye've any need of me?"

They both shook their heads and the woman slipped quietly out of the kitchen.

"Hawking with a prince, eh?" he commented dryly, watching her as he ate his tart.

"It will not be just the two of us. Half the court will be going, I think."

"Good. Make sure you dress better tomorrow than you did today. You said farewell to a prince in that?" he mocked.

"He didn't seem to mind," she growled. She took a few minutes to catch him up with the day and hear what he would tell of his own. By the time her cup was empty, they were both ready for bed. "Be safe. There are brigands about," she warned playfully. "And I will still expect you to supper at least one night a week. Else I will be the one to bring it to you."

"Fairly warned," he nodded, paused to give her a hug before heading out the garden door.

Cae blew out the lamp in the kitchen and walked through the darkened house towards her room. She knew the way by now and barely needed the light of the twinned moons shining through the high windows. It was lovely, the quiet, soft light. The Eastern Moon was in a better position to reach this side of the house and her light shown delicate and silvery through her bedroom window.

Tempest was already asleep on her perch and did not wake when Fern came in with a single candle to undress her. When she was done and her hair twisted into her nightbraid, Cae lit the candle beside her bed and picked up the small, innocuous book Janem had given her to keep safe. Curling up against the pillows, she fell asleep reading.

10

Fern entered the room a little before the time that Caelerys normally rose, throwing open the bed curtains. The only light that came in through the opening was the light from the brace of candles she had brought with her. Cae rolled over, sitting up as the bedcurtains were tied back. "Is anything wrong?" she asked.

"Not unless you call lady Petra wrong," she whispered, bringing over a dressing gown.

Cae groaned as she climbed out of the bed. "She knows nothing of dressing for hunting," she sighed. On her perch, Tempest complained sleepily.

"I'll let my lady wage that battle, as it is 'not my place'," she said archly. "Though a present has come for you. Well, more than one, but I am certain my Lord Willam or your Lordly Father would be tempted to send the other to the midden."

"Oh?" she asked with narrowed eyes.

She shook her head, unwilling to spoil the surprise. "What gown would you like for today?"

Cae thought about it. "Did we bring that russet split skirt?"

"I believe we did. That one is nice. Ornate enough for a courtly outing, yet functional. Good choice, not that her ladyship will agree."

With a sigh, Cae went into the dressing room to find the lady laying out a sumptuous blue velvet gown.

"That will not do at all, lady Petra. Today we hunt. I will need something far more practical," she said without preamble, crossing to the dressing table where a light breakfast had been laid out for her.

"You are going to court, on an outing with no less than a prince of the realm. You must look your best."

She nibbled quietly on a pastry. "I wore one of my most plain and oldest gowns yestermorn to see the crown prince ride off to battle and yet still managed an invitation to sup with the royal family. I think I am doing quite well choosing for myself, thank you."

Lady Petra drew herself up, incensed, missing part of what she'd said. "I am trying to do my best by your lady mother, helping your father find you the best husband I can and you chose to disregard my advice..."

"No, lady Petra. I have appreciated your efforts, and I am sure there is still much I can learn from you. But I must temper my experiences and knowledge with both courtly expectations and my own capabilities, personality and limitations. I would do neither myself nor my future husband any service by letting anyone believe I am a simpering, dainty songbird content to sit on a perch and sing all day, serving only for breeding and decoration. I am like yonder falcon. Fair to gaze upon, aye, affectionate and useful and completely unhappy if I am not at least occasionally put to my use."

She crossed to let Fern help her into the unusual, three pieced gown. Lady Petra merely watched in heated silence as she traded her nightdress for a short linen chemise with embroidered sleeves and stepped into the soft wool skirt the colour of Harvest leaves. This was covered by a short coat whose half-length sleeves were split to show off the chemise and its thread-work, but which covered the waist of the skirt.

"I suppose that may do for a hunt," lady Petra snipped. "But when you return you should change into something more sumptuous. I know the crown prince is away, as is most of the more eligible men, but there is still the other prince and the mothers to impress.

"You really should come with me to services next Fourth Day. You can be introduced to all sorts of influential people as well as coming off as properly pious."

She sighed. "I might attend a single service to see what all the fuss is about, but my family do not bow to priests nor look to others to tell us how to honour the First."

"Worship of the First is so passé, my dear. Even the king himself was recognized formally by the church at his coronation."

There was a glint her eyes as she looked at the dame in the mirror. Thankfully, Fern soon blocked her view, began brushing out her nightbraid. Cae was tempted to tell her to leave it all loose, just to spite the woman, but she knew she had to be practical.

"I will not engage in a discussion of holy matters with you. You make me think of that Asparadane woman when you do."

"Matters of religion are not to be disdained," she replied. "And you would do well to court Lady Semelle Asparadane's favour, as she can make or break you at court."

This almost made Cae laugh, but she controlled herself. "You want me to gain the highest marriage possible, correct?"

"Of course, my dear. I owe it to your parents," she said, softening.

"Do you think that a prince might be in my future? Or that the queen herself taking an interest in me would do me greater good than the mistress of a mere Lordly House?"

"Well, anything is possible. And the queen's good will would be invaluable."

"Well, I know for a fact that if I have Lady Asparadane's good will, I will lose the queen's."

Lady Petra dismissed the thought with a wave of her hand. "Oh, they are both over that. That was twenty-five years ago."

"Tell that to the women involved." She handed up the things that Fern needed as she twisted and braided her hair back into the style she preferred for hunting, but managed to still make it attractive.

"You couldn't possibly know..." she began.

"I thought you had your fingers upon the pulse of the court? How could you not know that I had supper last night with the royal family and Lady Liliwyn? A private supper, not a formal one. At which meal the queen made her position on your vaunted Lady Asparadane known. I will grant you that the woman might be able to destroy me, but raise me up? I think not. All of the men I have told father would make very good choices have no love for that woman or her family."

"I told you we should go over that list together. You may very well have left off several qualified choices."

She shook her head slightly. "Oh, I listed everyone who is available, met them or not. I told him which I've met and which I haven't and what I've heard, observed and experienced of each. He will know my preferences and has been given sound reasons for me to deny each one I disliked. I even admitted where I was biased. I might have let you peruse it in case I forgot anything, but you were not here and it needed to be sent with Willam. Besides, I would not have allowed you to change anything."

"How can I help you if you will disregard me?" she exclaimed.

She sighed. "By stopping your attempts to make me something I am not, and by telling me useful things. Like why something is not done a certain way, who dislikes what, who likes what, who would be good to know and who would not. And please do not mention that serpent in my presence again. Even if she adored me and wanted only the best for me, she would cut my throat in a heartbeat if she thought I was in the way of her dainty daughter and her precious ambition, and quite truthfully, I think I am."

Tempest shrilled her irritation from the doorway, having walked in in the middle of the tirade.

She sighed. "You are quite right, my pet, I am getting myself worked up. And it will do me absolutely no good. Fern, if you are finished, you said there were gifts? It might be best if I saw to them before I ride out."

"Of course, my lady," she said, pinning a final blossom into the sturdy braid crown holding the rest back from her face.

Lady Petra tried to regain her composure as they waited for the gifts to be brought. "You are gaining confidence at the very least," she sniffed.

Cae sighed. "I am very confident when I am myself. It is only when I don't know what is expected and I am dealing with strangers that I lose that."

A man servant followed Fern back into the room carrying a long, narrow box, while she carried two boxes of lesser size. She handed Cae the top one, a small wooden casket.

Inside was a glass vial of perfume. Cae pulled the stopper for a sniff and nearly gagged. It reeked of rosemary and evergreen and some kind of mint. She closed it quickly and picked up the note tucked into the box with it. It was a gift from Malyna Asparadane with wishes of a good hunt and blessings of the Eldest, etc. Cae closed it back in the box and set it aside. "We shall decide what to do about that later," she sighed.

"Does she wish your ladyship to smell like a crone?" Fern whispered, wrinkling her nose.

"That was lovely of her," lady Petra said, admiring the box. "You should send her a thank you gift."

"If the scent pleases you, you may have it," Cae said.

A flash of avarice crossed her eyes which was quickly squashed. "That would be rude. It is a princely gift."

"No, that's the other box," Fern mumbled.

Cae's eyes lit up and followed her glance at the box still being held by the manservant. "Nonsense, lady Petra. It would be wasted in my possession. I do not wear scents. Not even my talc is scented."

Lady Petra forced herself to move away from the dressing table and the vial to gesture to the other box Fern held. "And this one?"

"From lord Aldane Kaladen," Fern announced.

Cae opened the flat box with caution, using only the tip of her finger at the corner. The lid fell back against Fern's chest as her eyes widened.

Nestled in a fold of rich, black velvet was a heavy necklace of worked gold, studded with rubies, the largest of which would have covered her thumbnail.

Lady Petra took a deep breath and released it with regret. "It is a pity your father would never accept his suit. You'll have to send that back."

"It is not a pity," Cae said, snapping the box closed. "It is a relief. Especially if he thinks merely throwing stolen gold at me will win me over. He could make me a dress of diamonds and I would not warm to him. He should make this offer to a woman of avarice." She nodded for her maid to take the offending trinket away.

"I will see to it, my lady" Fern said. "The other came by royal courier."

"Royal?" gasped lady Petra with some excitement.

Tempest hopped up onto the back of a chair near the box to watch eagerly. The case itself was a beauty, deeply carved with a tangle of briers and roses with small birds and butterflies hidden throughout. It was not incensewood, but nearly as good, a sweet smelling honeywood. She timidly lifted the lid and gasped in delight. Inside was an unstrung bow. It was a masterpiece, of a dark, polished wood with a hand grip and arrow rest inlaid with lapis trimmed in silver, with carvings of stags leaping away from the grip. There was a letter tied with a bowstring, and two extras at the bottom of the box.

Cae itched to hold the bow, but picked up the letter instead, slid the string from it and unrolled it. "It's from the queen!" she exclaimed. "'I thought it high time that an archer of your quality had a bow of her very own'," she read aloud.

"What else does she say?" lady Petra prompted.

"That's all she says."

"It can't be," she insisted, taking the letter Cae handed off.

Cae was too interested in picking up and admiring the work of art. It fit well in her smaller hands, but in all other respects felt like a man's bow. She quickly strung it, expected more difficulty from the beautiful recurve, but it only took a bit of effort to bend it enough to hook the string. She tilted it diagonally as she preferred and pulled the string back to her cheek. It was tight, nearly at her weight limit, but with practice her strength would grow to match the bow. She had a feeling it would fly true so long as her arrows were up to its standards. She eased the string back and unstrung it, setting it with care back into the box. She turned to the manservant still waiting beside Fern. "Place this in my bedchamber, if you please, next to my quiver. I may send for it this afternoon."

Lady Petra looked at her, stunned. "This is a costly gift," she breathed. "Perhaps this is only catering to the daughter of her former lord, or perhaps you are right and she has taken a great deal of interest in you."

"Former lord, my lady?" asked Fern, confused.

"Queen Sigrun was once merely lady Sigrun Echo, vassal to House Maral," lady Petra explained gently. "In fact, I think your father was the one who helped to arrange the union," she added to Cae, "after lady Feranda Asparadane married Ranlan. But we digress," she snapped, pulling herself out of wherever her mind was drifting to, "and you are going to be late."

Fern ordered the manservant coming out of the bedchamber to go and make sure that the horses were saddled and ready. She then pulled Cae's riding boots from the chest and helped her lady to don them. Cae asked lady Petra if she would check in on Vyncet and make sure that he took the medicine that Colt would be giving him. And perhaps she might keep him company for a short while? After all, he needed a wife as well and she might know someone suitable.

Lady Petra was only too delighted and Cae felt a little guilty as she strode out into the courtyard to find Wraith waiting as promised. She and Fern mounted up and headed out towards the Citadel with a single guard to ensure their safety.

Upon arrival, she did not even have to dismount, as most of the hunting party was already gathered out front and were in the process of mounting. Prince Balaran grinned as she rode up with Tempest balancing herself on the saddle horn. She bowed from the saddle and smiled, "Please forgive my tardiness, Your Highness," she said. "But there were matters which arrived as I was rising that required my attentions."

"How is your brother, my lady?" he asked, settling a hooded peregrine on his wrist.

She glanced about at the gathered ladies and took a chance, spoke to him in old Vermian, "*Still the same ass he always is.*"

Only Lady Liliwyn tittered at that remark, and the prince smiled broadly. "So none the worse for wear?"

"I left him to lady Petra's tender mercies for a few hours."

"Oh, you cruel woman!" he laughed. "Remind me never to get on your bad side."

"It would be most unwise, Your Highness," added Lili with a knowing smile. "Are we all here?"

He glanced around. "It seems we are, and even were we not, we are well past the hour set."

"Is the princess not coming?" Cae asked, not seeing her.

He shook his head. "Alas, it is just as well you did not stay for the dessert. Apparently quinces do not agree with my noble sister."

"Please tender her my condolences."

Cae's guardsman nodded to her as he drew Fern aside and helped her dismount. It was understood that the pair of them would be waiting for her here at the Citadel.

As they turned to ride out of the gates, they encountered lady Malyna on a fat little mare that did not seem fully aware of her surroundings. She was accompanied by a handmaiden and a man-at-arms. She was wearing a richly embroidered, velvet gown and jewelled slippers that could just be seen as she sat primly side-saddle. There was no bird in evidence.

"Decided to join us, lady Malyna?" the prince asked. "Or are you merely arriving to await our return?"

"Mother agreed to allow me to ride with the party, Your Highness. If I am permitted to ride but not hunt?"

"As it pleases you. Just do not get in the way of the hunters." And with that he spurred his horse to continue and waved the rest of the party to join him.

Struggling to turn her little group around, Malyna ended up towards the back of the gathering, with a pair of older ladies and the chaperones. Lady Lucelle rode just ahead of her with her cousins and all three of them rode astride with trousers hidden beneath their skirts. Balyra had a fierce little kestrel, and her sister carried the horned owl. Even Liliwyn had a pretty little sparrowhawk that Cae learned was a loan from the royal mews.

The Master of the Hunt led the group around the outer wall of the

Citadel towards the fairgrounds where a pavilion was being set up for their mid-day dinner. From there, it was a nice, pleasant ride to the great meadow cradled by wood where he assisted the various ladies who did not know what they were doing to fly their birds.

Twill was one of the first birds to fly, as the Master knew that the owl would only be willing to hunt for a short while. He managed to snare himself a small pigeon by snatching it out of the air. Lady Onelle was very pleased with him and gave him treats once the bird had been fetched back to her.

Cae waited patiently and Tempest sat quietly on her wrist. Every time prey was sited, she would glance at Cae, hoping to be allowed to fly, but did not grouse over much when another bird was unhooded. Eventually, the Master of the Hunt nodded to her to indicate the next prey was to be theirs. Tempest tossed her head happily, expressing only mild irritation at the delay. Cae held up her arm and let Tempest launch herself.

The bird did not go high into the sky, just enough to find a thermal to hang in as she scanned the meadow. One of the beaters scared up a partridge and Tempest started to go for it, but veered off suddenly and began flying after something else. After about twenty feet she rose and stooped at the edge of the forest.

There were some unkind titters behind her that the bird might not be as well-trained as claimed, but Cae ignored them. She merely dismounted and began walking around the edges of the meadow towards where the bird was dealing with whatever she had brought down.

She was about halfway to her when it broke free and started to run. Tempest ran after it with an angry skree and finally tackled it. When Cae arrived, she had a hare larger than herself pinned to the earth by the neck and was pecking at its skull to get it to stop kicking. Cae just stared at her for a moment until the bird looked plaintively up at her. "Would you like some help?" she asked.

She laughed as the bird seemed to think about it, then moved further down the twitching body so Cae could grab its ears. She pulled a small dagger from her boot and slit the poor thing's throat. That done, Tempest hopped up to the shoulder pad and crowed her victory. Cae merely grabbed the beast by his hind feet and started to walk back.

Other birds were flown while she walked, and only some of the ladies needed assistance. When she returned and handed her kill to the Master of the Hunt, the women who had made their snide comments were sullenly silent. She swung easily back into the saddle without aid.

"Well done, Lady Caelerys," said the prince, turning away from lady Malyna's attempts to engage him in conversation.

Tempest chirped at him in irritation and he laughed. "Excellent kill, Lady Tempest," he added with a nod.

Mollified, the bird nodded back and turned to pick at a flower in Cae's hair that was tickling her.

"And what has Your Highness taken?" she asked, having noted his peregrine in the air on her return walk.

"Pheasant."

"Good eating and excellent feathers," she smiled.

He chuckled. "Maybe we can have it for supper."

He was distracted by another bird taking to the air and Cae turned to Lucelle who had come up next to her.

"That was amazing," she gushed. "Does she always pick her own prey like that?"

"Hunting like this? Not normally. Though if she is given a choice, she'll usually go for the larger meal," she laughed. She reached up to stroke the bird, "She's a greedy little bit."

Lucelle smiled. "Maybe she just wants to fatten up her mother," she giggled.

"She probably does think I don't eat enough," she laughed.

Liliwyn moved over to her other side, tightening the hood on her little sparrowhawk. "I only got a little rock hen."

"Do not feel bad. Rock hens are delicious."

She smiled, "They are better in pairs."

Lucelle frowned. "In pears or groups of two?"

They laughed softly. "I've never tried them with pears. I might have to suggest it to cook," Liliwyn said thoughtfully.

"Sounds delicious," said lady Malyna, coming over to stand her sleepy mare next to Lili. "But then, I have a fondness for pears."

The wind shifted slightly and Wraith lifted her head, softly stepping forward a few feet and looked around Lucelle's palfrey. Cae turned to see what had caught her attention and saw a stag a few yards into the trees studying them. She held her breath watching him, sat as still as he stood. She could almost feel his sides quivering as he decided whether the horsemen across the meadow were a threat to him and his and if he ran would it provoke a chase. She could almost smell him. She was just beginning to lose herself when she heard Malyna's voice ask, "Wishing you had a bow?"

She forced herself to relax, not wanting the beast to go but hoping that he would just turn and walk away in safety. The stag lowered his head a fraction, took a couple of steps backwards before turning and walking deeper into the woods.

She realized a response was being waited upon and shook her head. "I am not so blood-thirsty that I cannot just bask in his majesty without wanting to kill him. I hunt only to feed myself and my people, never for sport. And today we are not hunting larger meat. I only hunt for rabbit when my house has no need for meat but my bird has a need to hunt, and then I gift the meat to those most in need in the nearest village. Most often houses with pregnant or nursing women. It helps my people and keeps them out of our crops."

"So you don't like killing?" Malyna asked.

"No, I don't. But I understand that everything must kill to eat. I respect my place in the scheme of things. I would more hunters did so."

"Admirable, my lady," said the Master of the Hunt from near their bridles. "A sentiment I agree with. Unless my royal brother objects, I would ask you to join the hunt the next time we go out to provision the Citadel."

"I would be delighted, thank you, Master Olen," she blushed.

"It will not be a formal hunt, like my eldest brother preferred. Just the acquisition of select prey for the table."

"That seems to be the way she prefers it," Malyna said quietly.

Cae nodded, then hesitated. "Would boar be on that menu?" she asked timidly.

He smiled, "I do not believe it planned. But were we to sight boar, I will send a group off to deal with it separately."

"There is something you do *not* hunt?" asked Lucelle.

She shuddered. "I still have the scar from the last one I tangled with.

My brothers like hunting afoot and boar just fine. I'll take my game by bow and ahorse, thank you." She glanced down at the huntsman. "Though if the hunt requires a bit afoot, I will not balk," she assured him.

He chuckled, giving her horse a pat on the neck. "I will bear that in mind, my lady. Now, if you ladies are done? Lady Caelerys, I believe you have only flown the once. Do you desire a second?"

She shook her head. "Oh, no thank you. I believe my Jelma has caught more than her share," she purred, rubbing her cheek against the white breast. Tempest nuzzled her back.

"Very well, my lady. Ladies, if you will follow his highness back to the fairgrounds I believe there is a dinner waiting. I will see to it that your kills are delivered appropriately."

They rode back amid general excited chatter. The prince eased his horse back until he was riding in the midst of the ladies and extolling their virtues. He took the time to speak to nearly every one, though he did not spend as much time with Cae or Lili. The two of them were content to ride side by side at the head of the little group, though Wraith was itching for a more brisk pace.

Finally, tired of the begging, she turned in the saddle and called back, "Your Highness, with your permission, I need to let Wraith have a little run. I would meet up with you shortly?"

He smiled, nodding, the look on his face proclaiming that he would love nothing more himself.

She set Tempest into the air and excused herself from Lili, letting the mare gallop a little ways ahead and then taking her in a broad circle away and back. She carefully timed it so that she was riding up as the others had already dismounted and begun to walk into the open sided pavilion. She passed Wraith to a groom to walk her and joined them.

"Feel better?" Lucelle asked, laughing.

"Much. Sometimes you just have to let her run the fidgets out," she smiled. "I haven't had the chance to give her any real exercise since the race." She joined them at the tables, making herself a plate.

Tempest flew in just as she was taking a slice of ham. The falcon completely ignored the bird stands against the only wall at the back of the pavilion, and chose to make herself comfortable on her shoulder. She laughed as she fed the bird small pieces.

"Your mare really is magnificent," said Liliwyn. "She has a really smooth stride."

"Thank you. You hardly feel her change gaits and she loves running. She doesn't care what the terrain is."

"Do I detect a hint of Northern blood in her lines?" she asked.

Cae smiled. "Very likely. My uncle gave her to me a few years ago and he spends a great deal of his time in the warm North. I've considered breeding her but haven't found the right stallion yet."

"My brother has a really magnificent stallion," lady Malyna offered. "If you like, I might be able to arrange something."

She looked over, "Do you mean that ill-mannered black Lord Araan tried to gift lord Tume when his horse got sick?"

She drew back a little, unsure. This was apparently news she had not known. "Maybe. Lord Araan did gift him to my brother at the beginning of the tourney."

She shook her head, pouring a cup of water from the pitcher in the middle of the table. "Thank you for the offer, but my mare has already refused his attention more than once. Like as not she'll kick him in the head before she lets him near enough."

Balyra laughed, "She's already slapped him once."

This caused a spate of giggles that settled down when Onelle said to Liliwyn, "I didn't know you knew so much about horses. I'd heard you were into gardens."

She smiled softly, "The Pardets and the horse clans answer to my House. In fact, lady Aileen fostered with us. And a woman may be an expert in any number of things. One never knows what will be required."

Cae nodded. "Be prepared for anything, that's what my mother used to say. Well, it's one of the few things I remember her telling me. I was rather young when she died. But she made sure my education would be diverse."

Malyna sighed. "You are an expert in so many things, how can anyone of us hope to compete?"

Cae frowned. "By being yourself, and being true to who you are, not who others want you to be. Besides, men compete. Women should cooperate."

"Collaborate," added Liliwyn.

"And collude," finished Balyra with a grin.

"But... we're all vying for the same pool of husbands," she protested. "How can we not compete?"

Cae thought she heard someone behind her mutter, 'poor deluded child'.

"*We* aren't competing," Liliwyn said firmly. "Our parents are, if you want to get right down to it."

"True," someone said.

Malyna looked confused and devastated.

"Listen, I had this discussion with lady Petra just this morning," Cae began, ignoring the fact that Tempest was helping herself to her plate, picking out the ham. One of the girls groaned at the mention of lady Petra. "What matters to our parents is what the match will bring to the family: wealth, higher station, access to resources, even alliances. Who we are isn't really going to influence that much. If we are lucky and something about us sparks an interest, a man will move mountains to win us. That's the faery tale. My father fought a duel for the rights to my mother, so I cannot say it doesn't happen. It's rare, but it does happen. But how fair is it to him if he wants and thinks he's getting a demure, meek little titmouse, only to discover she's a right harpy after they wed? No, I say be who you are. If it is what attracts them, all the better. If all they want is what you bring to the table at least there are no surprises."

"Right," injected lady Balyra. "Our aunt, our other aunt," she said seeing the look on Lucelle's face, "did her duty, produced several heirs and took a paramour. She has three subsequent children of her own."

Malyna and a couple of other ladies looked shocked. "How scandalous. I mean, it is expected of men..."

"And why not women?" asked the prince, finally speaking up. He had been sitting on the outskirts of the conversation for some time just enjoying himself. "You have needs, same as men. And in a loveless marriage, why should you not take your comfort where you can?"

"Because the Eldest frowns upon it. Fidelity is expected of women," Malyna insisted.

"But not of men?" he asked.

She drew herself up, quoting what Cae took to be church dogma.

SHIFT: Stag's Heart

"Men have needs and the responsibility of procreating. Women should be faithful and cleave to their marriage vows, that a man always knows that the children in his house are of his blood."

"And you are all right with a double standard?" he said pointedly.

She stuttered. "It's... it's not like that. Men have the means and responsibility to care for their subsequent children. Women do not, and it is wrong to expect her husband to support the product of her infidelity."

"Wait, marriage *vows*?" asked Lucelle.

This brought the subject back around as apparently most of the women had not known this.

Surprisingly, it was Liliwyn who answered. "Yes, marriage *vows*."

"Have you seen an Eldest wedding?" Onelle asked.

Liliwyn nodded, but Malyna interrupted. "Oh, isn't it the most beautiful ceremony?"

The women looked to Liliwyn to agree or disagree. She chose to explain instead. "The promised couple stand before the Pontifex and proclaim themselves before the god and community."

"And then they light her candle," Lucelle nodded.

"No." This caused an outburst. "First come the vows. He promises to care for her and keep her safe and to extend his protection to all of their progeny until one of the pair dies."

"Well, that's not so bad," Lucelle mumbled. "Not much different than the contract."

"Wait for it," Balaran muttered.

"Then the woman promises her worldly goods, devotion, obedience and fidelity in all matters until she dies," Lili finished, taking a sip of her water.

There were gasps and the outraged exclamation of 'obedience' and finally, "Wait, only until *she* dies?" asked Cae, catching the loophole.

"Aye."

"So?" asked Onelle, confused.

"So, she's bound to the rotter until she dies. Not him, her. He dies before her and she is still bound to a dead man." Cae looked over at Liliwyn, "Do I have that right?"

Lili's nod was barely perceptible.

Onelle turned to Malyna, "And you think this is a great idea?"

"Well, yes," she responded meekly. "It is the way the Eldest wishes it. He preaches about the divine rights of man." Balaran gave a snort of derision at that and she looked at him. "I am surprised that you feel that way, Your Highness. After all, what man doesn't want a loving, obedient and loyal wife to look after his children and worldly goods?"

"A man who desires a challenge," he answered flatly. "A man wants a wife like that may as well contract a concubine."

Malyna seemed to shrink from that, unsure what to think.

"So, the candle?" asked Lucelle. "No candle at all?"

Malyna made a face. "That is a barbaric and disgusting custom and the church is discouraging it. But for those families that insist, the candles are lit at the signing of the contract between the families."

"Disgusting?" Balyra gaped. "It's one of the few things that protect us!"

"How does making a candle infused with your first moons-blood protect you?" sneered one of the other ladies. "How does one even present that to a chandler without dying of embarrassment?"

"Magic," Cae said.

"Sorcery," she retorted as if that was the answer to everything.

"It is a symbol of the contract between two people and two houses," Cae insisted. "The written contract is the declaration of everything the two families offer in exchange. By affixing his sigil above that of her family, he is promising to uphold his end of that bargain. The contract is only valid once the candle has been lit."

"That can be done with just signing the parchment where the contract is written," Malyna said. "No need for the candle at all."

"Ah," Balyra cut in. "But there is. The contract stays with the family. The candle goes with the couple. If he decides he wants out, all he has to do is hand her the candle and send her home, though doing so requires him to surrender everything she brought into the marriage."

"If she's a good wife, there'd be no need to set her aside."

"And if she's barren?"

"That's what concubines are for," the lady sneered.

"And if he's abusive," Cae said, "and she needs out? She can just break the candle."

"Of course that leaves her with nothing and he gets to keep everything," Balaran said. "Better to petition the courts for the return of the candle."

"Also, a woman can't be forced to light her candle," Lucelle added. "It's bad luck."

Onelle nodded vigorously. "A woman can completely jinx a marriage if she's forced to it. Make a man unlucky, or even impotent."

"And that, ladies," crowed Balaran, "is why the church is trying to get rid of it."

"Of course," Malyna protested. "Sorcery is evil."

Cae kept her mouth shut on what she thought of the church at that outburst.

Liliwyn spoke quietly, but the sentiment was echoed by several of them. "Caelyrima would not have given us anything that was truly evil. If magic exists in the world, it is because Mother Chimera wished it to be so."

The prince stood, cutting off anything else the followers of the Eldest were going to say. "Well, ladies, I do believe it has been a lovely morning, but there are things that I, as a prince, am responsible for. So if you will pardon me, I am off. Stay or remain as it please you."

Almost as one, the ladies rose and curtseyed. For a moment, Cae thought Malyna might try to follow him, but in the end she did not dare. The rest of them milled about for a while longer, though Cae and Liliwyn rode out with the Roshan girls before too long had past. They saw the trio to the gates of the Citadel, from which they rode on, and Cae and Lili entered the gates.

Seeking out the library together, they ran across the queen's path. When they saw her ahead of them, she was standing at a cross corridor looking slightly confused. A handmaiden stood a little ways back from her, not offering to assist, just waiting patiently. When the queen saw the two of them coming towards her, she smiled as if she suddenly understood whatever was confusing her. They came to meet her and curtseyed.

She waved them up, "And how are you ladies this morning?"

"It was a very nice outing, Your Majesty," Liliwyn answered.

She reached out and took Lili's hands in hers. "And you?" she asked pointedly.

Lili sighed softly, lowering her eyes a moment. "Getting better day by day. It will be a long road, Your Majesty."

The queen patted her hand gently. "Not so long as you think if you just keep walking. One day you'll look around and realize you are truly happy." She turned to Caelerys, leaving Liliwyn's head spinning a little. "And you dear? Brothers well, house in order, everything arrived as it should?"

She blushed suddenly, realizing what she was hinting at. "I cannot thank you enough, Your Majesty. It is a princely gift."

"It was actually, or was intended to be some time ago. But the young man in question lost interest in archery before the gift could be completed. I merely had it... personalized. It will serve you well if you keep it near you," she said enigmatically. She took up Cae's hand in hers and frowned slightly, staring at it. She seemed to be feeling the texture of her skin. "I worry about you. But I'm sure you'll be fine. You are a Maral after all and I have armed you sufficiently. Your brothers have done the rest. How are they?" she asked suddenly.

"Vyncet had to be restrained last night, then drugged. I intend to return early to him today. I only must meet Prince Balaran in the library for a moment and to pick up the books I asked about last night, then I intend to return to him."

"Take your time, dear. And Master Janem?"

"Working again. He's decided to move into the rooms above the forge to better keep an eye on things. He is worried though that, between him and Master Illet, they will not be able to cover the loses from the theft."

The queen let her go and waved her hand as if to ward the thought off like a fly, "Oh, he shouldn't worry. Rory has spoken to the duke. And while I have told them it will be found eventually, he has promised to provide the materials for Janem to make a replacement now that he can."

"That will be a relief, Your Majesty, thank you. And I would thank you again for not gifting me a dainty bow more fit to a lady."

"It is not too strong for you?"

"Almost," she smiled. "But I can draw it with a little effort, and will gain the strength soon enough to draw it with none."

"Good. I hate for things to go to waste: gifts, talents, food..." Her mind began to drift off, but she suddenly recalled herself enough to smile, give the girls a nod and bid them a good day.

They watched her wander off with the maiden following helplessly along. The queen reached another junction and then suddenly seemed to remember what she was about and turned down another corridor with more determination. They looked at each other in wonder.

"I'd heard she was a little... off," Cae whispered.

"You have no idea," Lili breathed. "It's both scary and intriguing, and I've only been here a few days. She'll just do or say something and then wonder why, but only for a moment. She's rarely wrong, though."

"How rarely?"

Lili shrugged as they continued towards the library. "I've heard of it happening, but never experienced it. That's something you'd have to ask Princess Syera. Do you really have to go home soon?"

She sighed, "If I don't want to come home to what I did last night, probably."

Lili looked at her in wide-eyed curiosity. Cae told her.

They entered the library trying to suppress their giggles as Lili pictured Vyncet's struggles.

Once inside, they went their separate ways: Liliwyn wandering into the stacks and Cae going to the nearest worm to ask after the prince.

He looked up and smiled. "He's not here at the moment, but gave orders to be notified the moment you arrived. Someone's already running that errand. Would you like for me to fetch the lady's books?"

"That would be lovely, thank you, worm."

He grinned and trotted off to fetch the books. He returned with four and handed them to her.

Cae frowned. "I only reserved three."

He shrugged. "Ward must have found another one for you. It seems to be on the same subject. The prince will likely meet you on the third floor, where you were the first day you came."

She smiled and thanked him again, drifting across the main floor to the spiral stair. Here she encountered the one trouble with split skirts. It was nearly impossible to climb steep stairs with only one hand to hold up your hems. She managed the struggle and crossed to the alcove at the end of the balcony. She seated herself and began looking through the small volume that had been added to her stack. She was a few pages in with her lap being warmed by a random cat when the prince arrived carrying a heavy volume. She smiled and set her book aside, trying to curtsey without rising.

"I hope you don't mind?" she asked, clearly reluctant to disturb the queen sleeping in her lap.

"Mind?" he asked. "I think I would be offended if you did. She might leave, and I never get to see them. Maybe if they start seeing me while they're around you they'll approach me on their own," he chuckled.

"Surely you have access to cats if you wish?"

He shrugged. "All the ones at our old home were half wild mousers, and father was always more partial to dogs."

"Ah. Well, what have you found, Your Highness? You said you had something?"

He set the book on the table and began flipping through it. "It's more a reference to another reference, but it'll be helpful. Your book, (I'm having it copied, by the way) has a lot of stories I'd never heard, most of them having to do with various Firstborn and Second Sons, who ironically aren't all sons but modern translations of the Vermian word for child... it just became 'son' over time. Anyway, this one speaks a lot of the early faith, long before the emergence of the Eldest as a god. Which reminded me of this book, where I found this." He pointed out a passage that mentioned the constellations of the two generations of Mother Chimera's children and how they ruled over the fates of men. It referenced yet another book for a fuller explanation.

"What is this book?" she asked, attempting to take a peek at the cover without disturbing the cat.

"It's a history. Well, it seems to be half history and half fancy, because it speaks of magic and shifts and something called a sympath, but I have no idea with that is and less clue where to look. Did you know that the Houses were originally clans? All claiming descent from one of the First and Second. Claimed to live as one with their 'totem' it calls them. And that, at random, some member of the clan would be able to shift fully or partially into that creature. There was apparently no way to tell who would be granted that gift. There are arguments that it was whoever most embodied their clan guardian."

"Shifts," she said. "A gift of the goddess. It makes sense. 'I give you the ability to Become, that you might understand the world and your place in it. I give you Understanding, that you might be one'."

He looked at her curiously. "Where did you hear that?"

She gave him an incredulous laugh. "Did you just jump straight into the stories?"

"...Yes," he said uncertainly.

"It's right there in the front of the book," she smiled. "A caption on the first illustration."

"The woodcut?"

She nodded. "I'm surprised you didn't examine that in depth, considering it's the only one. All the rest are hand drawn and inked."

A light went on in his eyes. "Wait, if it was a woodcut, that means there are other copies of the image."

"Could be."

He managed to refocus himself. "Now we just have to find this book referenced here," he said, closing it and setting it down next to hers. "My, you have quite a lot of reading to do," he commented, glancing through the stack. "And here I was going to ask you to help me."

She gave a lazy smile as she sat back, stroking the cat. "Your brother beat you to it."

He looked up, "He actually asked you to help him with something?"

"Just before he left. I think he's testing me."

"He may very well be." He picked up the smallest book, the one that had been added to her stack. "Hey, this is the book I was looking for!"

She leaned forward as far as the cat would let her. "Really? Mayhap Ward put it in my stack instead of yours?"

He gave her a sidelong grin. "On first name basis with the worms now?"

"Lady Liliwyn," she said.

He shook his head, setting the book down. "But I didn't ask for any books to be set aside. This must tie into the research you are doing for my brother. The worms are good that way. Occasionally, if they remember some other reference they'll add it to those you request."

"Please, take it then," she offered.

Again he shook his head. "No, my lady. It was intended for you. I can read it when you're done."

"Your Highness," she sighed. "One, you outrank me, so you have precedence."

"Except where I choose to indulge a lady."

She nodded acceptance of that while still pressing her case. "Two, the book is small and will be a swift read. You see what else I must go through tonight? If I stop to really read, I'll be a couple days on these volumes alone. By the time I am ready for this slender thing, you could have finished it, and maybe tell me how relevant it might or might not be."

His eyes flashed. "Well, for that you'd have to tell me what my brother is researching."

She gave him a chiding smile. "Maybe after you've read that," she said. "Now, as much as I would like to stay, I really only came to get those and to see what you wished to show me. I really must get back to Vyncet." He started to protest. "I left him with lady Petra."

He swallowed. "Very well, go, have mercy on the man!"

She laughed quietly and gathered up the cat, turning to place her on the prince's lap. "There, stay still long enough and she might get used to you."

With that, she handed him the slender book, grabbed her own and curtseyed, turning as she rose. As she walked towards the spiral stair, she heard minor noises of pain from him as the cat began to knead herself a more comfortable spot on his lap.

Back home, she discovered that lady Petra had already left, and Vynce was sitting up in the bed reading. There was a game of castle set up on the small table, clearly in endgame. She smiled at him. "So, Colt says you behaved yourself today, and your leg is looking much better."

He glared up at her over the book, "You left me with lady Petra."

She had the grace to look sorry. "Well... you obviously needed looking after by someone you couldn't bully," she shrugged.

He dropped the book onto his lap. "I don't bully!"

"No, you badger, ignore..."

He held up his hands in surrender. "All right, I might have deserved it."

"I am sorry if she bored you," she said, sitting on the edge of his bed.

He shrugged, setting the book aside. "Actually, it wasn't too terrible. She's a mean castle player. I only beat her once and that by the skin of my teeth. She left just before dinner. So how was your outing? I know you've been dying to go hunting."

She smiled. "It would have been nicer if there were fewer people. I swear, aside from the prince, the Master of the Hunt and the beaters, it was all female, and only about half of them had ever hunted before."

"'Pest catch anything?"

"Almost had a partridge."

He looked crestfallen, "Almost? How'd she miss?"

She shrugged. "She chose other prey."

"What would have been better than a fat partridge?"

"To her? A hare. Bigger than she was," she smiled.

He sighed. "Rabbit, again? When I could have had partridge?"

She patted his arm gently. "Don't worry. When it arrives I intend to have Fennel cook it up for Janem."

He narrowed his eyes at her. "You know, he's a grown man who's chosen a profession. He can feed himself."

"And he still supports this House, looks after our interests and has no wife to cook for him."

"He didn't have those things before, not that I'm complaining really. But you didn't bring him meals then."

She sighed. "I wasn't in the city then, and the rooms he had were over a tavern were food was available. He's now living above the forge which boasts no kitchen. And as long as I have any say in the matter, the man will be fed at least once a day from mine."

"You'd feed the apprentices too, if you could," he narrowed his eyes at her, but she knew he was not angry about it.

"You're right, I would. I am rather fond of young Robin." She stood. "Now, I am going down to the kitchens to check with Fennel about our supper and his and then go to my room to read until it is ready. Will you be all right alone for a few more hours?"

He shrugged. "Have to be, don't I?"

She gave him a coy smile, "Well, you only have another two days of this. After that, if Willam and the others have not returned, then you will be moved to the Citadel where you can lounge in the gardens and be fawned upon by all manner of eligible ladies."

"Don't tease me, sister. Between the drugs and the boredom I don't think I can take it," he warned.

She only grinned and skipped out of the room.

She found Fennel in the kitchen dressing the hare. "Oh good, it was delivered."

The woman looked up and beamed, "Oh, so this largesse is your doing?"

"Tempest, actually. What, you accepted it not knowing?"

"When a messenger from the Citadel arrives bearing gifts of game, you do not turn it away," she said, punctuating her statement with a chop that neatly removed the rabbit's head. "What would you like me to do with it? I had planned something more fowl for supper, but I can cook that for tomorrow...."

Cae sat and rest her elbows on the well-scrubbed work table, watching her work. "Actually, I had intended the beast for Janem. Do you think you can get it cooked and ready by supper?"

"I can get the beastie well roasted and give him a share of the carrots and parsnips, too. This bunny'll feed more than him though, maybe even two meals."

Cae shrugged. "I figure Robin's still with him. I think he's moved the other apprentices to Master Illet's house for safety."

"Might be as it'll feed those too," she nodded. "I'll have something together and sent by the time I send up supper for the two of you. You will be supping with the young lord, yes?"

"If he needs me to. Actually, I'd like to take supper to the forge myself. I need to talk to him anyway."

Fennel nodded. "I'll have Mace ready to escort you by dusk. Your own supper should be ready to table by the time you get back if you don't dally terrible much. Just make sure Mace brings yesterday's dishes back, my lady, if that's not presuming."

She smiled as she rose, "Of course."

Cae went up to her room and started reading the books she'd brought. The first one turned out to be less than useful and she set it aside fairly quickly. She was absorbed in the other one when Tempest alerted her to someone at the door.

Fern answered the knock and returned, "Mace, my lady. He says Janem's supper is ready if you are willing to leave now."

"If we go now we should miss most of the evening traffic," Mace said, following Fern.

Cae nodded, setting the book aside and rising. She slipped into a cloak against the rising chill in the air and followed him downstairs where another man-at-arms waited holding the basket. She held out her hands for it. "I'll take that if it is not too heavy?"

He handed it to her with a little reluctance.

"You are supposed to be guarding me, right?" she asked, suppressing a grin. He nodded. "Much easier to handle weapons with empty hands."

Behind her, Mace laughed softly.

The walk was pleasant, as the streets were not too crowded. The people who were about were heading home from closed shops and in a hurry to get to their own suppers. Few people paid her and her escort any mind until the reached the little footbridge over the canal that surrounded Iron Alley. There were two of the City Guard standing on the land side blocking their path.

"Alley's closed, my lady," said the senior of the two. "You'll have to shop tomorrow."

"I am not here to shop but to deliver."

"Deliveries can be done in the morning. But if you'll pardon my saying, my lady, you're a little highborn to be a delivery girl," said his companion.

She smiled at them, "I understand this is new?"

They frowned, not understanding.

"Your job guarding the Alley is because of the break-in at my brother's forge?"

"We don't really know why just…" began one.

"Brother?" said the other.

Mace stepped up. "Yes. My Lady Caelerys Maral is here to bring supper to her subsequent brother, Master Janem of the Singing Forge. While my lady may not always be the one to make the delivery, someone will be doing so from our household from now on."

"At least as long as he continues living there," she added. "Now, if you do not mind? His supper grows cold."

Still a little confused, they allowed her to pass, watching as she began the walk up the curving street.

They did not get far before they could hear the melodic ringing of hammer on anvil. Cae smiled and sighed happily. Other forges were shutting down and banking their fires, but Janem was just getting started. When she had come the other day, the hammers of the neighbours had been harsh and purposeful, heavy. She would know Janem's work anywhere, had not realized until that moment how much she had missed it. The blows were light and brilliant, reverberant. They sang.

When she rapped upon the closed door of the shop, it was opened by Robin, who beamed as he bowed. He rose taking deep sniff, eyes wide with unexpected delight. "My lady, please tell me what I'm smelling in that basket is fer the master and me?"

"It is. If you will set up a place for the two of you to dine?"

"Oh, most glorious of women!" he proclaimed. "My lady is a paragon of virtue!"

"It'll get cold before you stop," Mace growled.

The boy jack-rabbited off to set up a place for them to eat and Cae let herself through to the forge.

Two of the sides were still open, helping to trap a little of the heat in the room against the slowly growing chill. It was going to be a nice evening, though it was clear that Fallow was not long away. Janem was at his anvil playing his melody on a band of silver. She just stood there watching him, the light of the rising moon shining down on his work.

Several minutes went by before he looked up, seemed surprised to see her. "Cae?"

She held up the basket. He groaned, setting aside his work and tools and crossed over. "You didn't have to bring it yourself. I'd have sent Rob, ...eventually."

"And that is why," she answered. "Rob is setting your table."

"Upstairs," he said. "Evening, Mace, Hollen," he said to the two men as he led his sister back to the front where the stairs were hidden. "Would you gentlemen mind keeping an eye out down here? I don't leave the forge alone if the walls are up. You can keep warm by the fire."

Mace nodded and led the two of them back into the forge.

"So what did you really want to see me for?" he asked as they climbed to the second floor where Robin had cleared off a table and set out cups and plates in the old apprentice's room.

She smiled, setting the basket on the table and beginning to lay out the feast. Robin's mouth was visibly watering. "How much are you feeding this runt?" she asked with a tilt of her head. "You'd think he's starving, or surviving only on sausage pies."

"Apprentices are always starving," he growled.

"We *has* been surviving on sausage pies," Robin injected.

"Well," she said, revealing the plate of roast hare, "compliments of Tempest and my hunting trip with the prince this morning."

Janem, in spite of his protests, began loading his plate eagerly. "Where is the feathered mongrel?"

"She was sleeping when I left. She had a busy morning. The rabbit gave her a little trouble."

She let them eat, filling Janem in on what she had been up to that day, including her conversation with the queen.

He took a deep breath at that. "Master Illet will be relieved. I've started already, but I've got to make the moonsilver first. That takes time. Time I can't spend on other things."

"That's what I'm for, Master," Rob piped with his mouth full.

"You are getting good, I'll grant you, but you're not ready to work this stuff yet."

He shook his head vigorously. "Naw, Master. I'm content watchin' ye fer a bit longer. Besides, I ain't got the hang of the rhythm yet. Maybe when I get that down. It's enough to be trusted with the secret."

Janem looked proudly at him. "You need a lighter touch."

"Maybe learn to play the drums?" Cae suggested. "It might be a good way to learn the rhythms."

"Not how I learned," Jan frowned.

She gave him a light cuff on the arm. "Yes, well, I don't think having someone reading Vermian poetry is going to do it for him. He might learn more from copying your patterns on the drum, then translate them to hammer and anvil."

He looked the boy over, thinking. "Might work. We can see about that tomorrow."

"By the way, did you know you have guards posted at the Alley bridge?"

"Do I, now? Some of the other smiths might have asked, for fear of being next."

"So what do they think was taken?" she asked.

"Jewels, gold, so naturally the gold smiths are panicking. I don't think anyone in the Alley knows yet about the moonsilver."

"It won't take them long," Robin said with his mouth full. "But not many have courtly contacts. Won't have filtered down sa much yet. When it does it'll explode."

"And Daph keeps his silence. I don't think even his apprentices know what he worked for me."

"Our apprentices may not be able to hold their tongues much longer," Rob commented. "Bein' at Master Illet's house'll give them more opportunity.

"Be that as it may," Janem shrugged. "It was bound to happen at some point. Rob, get the dishes from last night for my sister."

The boy wolfed down a last carrot and went to obey.

"What?" she asked him.

"You need to be careful."

"I am being careful," she said.

He glared at her. "No, you came here, at evening, with only two men. I appreciate the meal, really. But you can't do this any more. I promised I'd come by once a week. And if you really need to see me, send a page. The risk is too great."

"Jan," she protested. "I'm not under siege or attack. There is no threat on my life."

"That is what you do not understand, dear heart. You have attracted the attention of the queen, and both princes, from what I hear. There are families who will not hesitate to, if not outright kill you, at the very least make you ill enough or injured enough to give them a fairer chance. Or just manufacture a scandal. Anything to get you out of the way."

She sat back down, feeling that horrible sinking beginning in her stomach. He reached out and took her suddenly cold hand in his. "I'm not trying to scare you. Just make you understand the risks. There are too many boars and wolves in these woods for you to walk unarmed, and these wolves are not our friends."

"I... I will be more cautious. I suppose I could attempt to lower my sights..."

"No, little sister, you need to do the best you can, just be aware that there are those who want to see you trampled first."

Robin returned then, put the requested dishes and the current ones into the basket for her, setting aside what remained of the rabbit for tomorrow's meal.

Janem escorted her back downstairs whilst Robin fetched her men. He kissed her good-bye in the shop and returned to the forge, leaving the boy to lock the door.

They had not gotten past the neighbouring shop before the night rang once more with the melody of his hammers.

Returning to the house, she spent a few hours with Vince, eating supper and playing a game of castle with him before dosing him and retiring to her own bed to read more. When she finally slept, her dreams were scattered, flitting from one thing to another and none of them making any sense.

11

Cae rose at her usual hour, disappointed that she had found nothing in the books so far. She still had one more to look through before she would need to return to the library, but she simply could not make herself open it yet. A certain box was calling to her.

Tempest tugged at the hem of her gown, begging to go for her morning flight, but Cae had a different idea. "How about we go to the archery field this morning? You can fly over the estuary."

Tempest thought this over while Cae got dressed, putting on one of her less fancy split skirts and asking for Wraith to be made ready. When she came down, Tempest tagging along behind her, she found Mace standing beside a second horse. "I understand my little bird is going to practice," he said.

She smiled, handed him her new bow as she moved to give Wraith an affectionate good morning. "Ah, well, a new bow requires testing and adjustment, does it not?"

"It most certainly does," he said marvelling over the bow in his hand. "I heard you had received one as a gift, but did not believe it was as fine as Lathe said."

She smiled as he tested the pull and vaulted into her saddle.

"You are right, my lady, you are going to need some practice. Do not be discouraged if you are not immediately as accurate as you are accustomed to being. After all, you have only ever used the one bow with any regularity. You've never had to make the adjustment to a new one," he advised, handing it up to her.

"I've got to get used to the draw if nothing else," she grinned, getting her quiver and the bow settled as he mounted. Tempest waited until she was done before flying up to the pommel and getting comfortable.

The ride to the training grounds was a little more crowded than the morning before, as she was coming from a different direction and many people were busy getting themselves and their wares to the markets and shops. Most people gave way before a lady on horseback, but some either had no choice or were just stubborn. Eventually, they made it. There were already a few young men practising with older soldiers on the training ground, and some young squire being schooled with a jousting dummy, but no one was out at the archery field.

The temporary wall that had been erected for the tourney had been taken down, but there was not too much wind at the moment. She commented on it as Mace tied the horses off to the fence that prevented people from unwittingly wandering into the line of fire. "There are lulls in the wind at least twice a day, the first is in the morning. Good time to shoot. So shoot," he grinned, aiming a hand at the targets set up along the shore. "And don't miss. I'm not going swimming for your arrows."

She laughed and stepped into position. Her first few arrows fell short, but she was determined. Mace helped her to figure out the differences between her old bow and her new one and it did not take her long to make the adjustments. It was a marvellous weapon, and shot like a dream once she got used to it. She had been right about its accuracy. Mace set up wands for her to practice with.

"I realized during the tournament where I had been lax in your training," he said. "You've never had a need to shoot wands, but they are a good test of accuracy. Think of it as a bird's wing. The wand is the bone. If you don't hit it just on, you'll skim past, take a feather or two and the bird will fly off. Like the toomi with the message about the raids."

"That's a really good way of thinking about it," she said.

The sun was well off the horizon's edge and the morning fog beginning to burn off where it still clung to the wood by the time she could take the wands at any point he called off. She backed off another twenty-five paces for another round at the regular targets. "Too bad you can't roll them across the field," she chuckled.

"I'll see what I can do for next time. Maybe bring things to throw."

She took longer to aim this time, as the wind was beginning to pick up, coming in from the sea. Something caught her eye just beyond the target, out on the ocean just at the mouth of the Desiter. When she realized what it was, the string slipped from her fingers and the arrow sailed past the target out over the water.

Mace frowned that she had missed that badly, then saw her

expression a second before she began to run towards the shore. Above them, Tempest streaked over the water and snatched up the arrow before it could sink, proudly bringing it back to her mistress, who, for once, paid her no mind. Her eyes were locked on what she thought might be a sea battle, and the more she stared, the less she doubted.

"MACE!" she screamed, pointing.

He ran up to her, shielding his eyes from the sun and following her gaze. All that could be discerned clearly in the scraps of fog that still lingered were four ships tangled together, uncomfortably close. Three of the masts were barren of pennant, but the centre held the Griff flag. The red griffin fluttered desperately upon the gold field just a moment before the entire top quarter of the mast tipped and fell into the sea.

"Pirates!" he cursed. Without a word of agreement both of them began running towards the watch towers in opposite directions, screaming the word to attract attention.

Before long, bells were ringing from the towers all along the shores, with answering peals from the few warships that remained in the harbour. Once the alarm had been sounded, Cae drifted back to the targets, standing on the seaward side to watch the horror unfold. Mace joined her, placing an arm around her to steady her. She leaned back into him, her hand covering her mouth as the attackers moved away one by one. By the time the king's ships reached them, they would be long gone. The Griff ship was already sinking slowly.

"That was the Griff treasure ship, wasn't it?" she breathed.

"The timing would be right. It would be the Harvest ship, loaded with uncut diamonds."

They watched in horrified silence as the king's ships became rescue ships, having fought the headwind and tide just to reach the site. The three attackers had sailed off in three different directions so pursuit with so few ships was impossible.

Finally, Cae turned to Mace and asked him to take her home.

At the hall, she went straight to her room. Even Tempest followed her quietly. News had already reached here, but Mace played interference for her, explaining to the household what they had seen.

In her room, Cae set her bow on top of its box, and laid her quiver on the floor beside it. She did not even bother to unstring it. She sank into a chair beneath her window and watched the activity in the courtyard in silence. Tempest hopped into her lap and snuggled against her, crooning softly as Cae stroked her without even thinking about it.

When Fern brought in dinner, she made herself get up and eat and then be productive. She checked on her brother, replaced his compress and stayed to play a game of castle which she lost badly. Vynce complained she wasn't even trying.

"You're right, I'm not. I'm sorry," and went back to her room to read without another word.

She set her reading table up by the window and read until the light became too dim. By then it was time for supper, which she ate in her brother's room though she was poor company. Vynce tried to joke her out of her funk, but was surprisingly unsuccessful.

"Come on, Cae," he complained, "it's not like you were on that ship, or it was one of ours."

She glared at him. "No, it isn't. But it still makes me think."

"About what?"

"About how convenient it was that we had raiders in our lands, just a scant hundred miles from the City, of enough significance to draw royal assistance, and just days before the Harvest diamond shipment from Griff!" she snapped.

He closed his mouth and thought about that.

"Surely they won't blame us?" he finally said.

"Won't they? You think Asparadane isn't at this moment poisoning the king's ear with that very insinuation?"

"We've never had issues with that house before," he complained. "Why now?"

"Because I came to court when there are royal marriages to be made just when their own daughter was being presented. Lady Petra warned me. What's worse, I think Malyna might be genuinely trying to be friends without ever understanding why I cannot trust any overture she makes. I almost feel sorry for her."

"If she'd been fostered out she might have stood a chance."

Cae huffed over her wine. "I highly doubt that woman fosters any of her children. She wouldn't trust anyone else to raise them."

"Hey, even I was fostered with the Marrok for a few years. It was a great experience."

"I'm sure it was nice spending time with boys your own age," she consented.

"And it got around any awkwardness after mother died," he added ruefully. "I understand that father had to make some adjustments, and I was a handful while you and Jan were helpful."

"Also too young."

"Also that," he conceded. He set aside the tray. "Great Mother, now *I'm* depressed."

"Sorry. I didn't mean to share."

"When you hurt, everyone hurts. When you are happy it is hard for the rest of us not to be," he said, taking her hand. "You're our only sister and we've always felt that responsibility. You are the hub of this family, even more so than father, more than Will."

She shook her head, tried to pull away, not believing him.

He held on. "No, you are. You picked up where mother left off. You've kept in touch with all of us no matter where we've been scattered. You sent letters to Janem when some families would have just let him vanish into obscurity once he left the security of the House for a profession. Hell, you even keep in touch with Rosemary, reading her Janem's letters. Who pays attention to their father's concubine? Especially after she's left the house? Truthfully, I don't know what we're going to do when you get married. You'll have an new household to take care of. What's going to become of the rest of us, eh?"

She blushed, fighting back tears she couldn't explain. "Willam will be fine. He's been on his own for a while."

"He's still family and I know for a fact that you've written him too. Why do you think I'm not married yet?"

"Not mature enough to settle on one woman?" she chuckled.

He laughed with her but shook his head. "No, because I won't settle for less than you."

She pulled back, "What?"

He sighed, "I've said that badly. When I meet a young woman, I'm comparing her to you. Is she going to be able to hold my family together even when it's scattered to the winds? Can she stand up to me?"

"I don't know what to say."

He gave her a long look. "Well you can start by telling me which of your friends are up to your standards."

She gave a short laugh. "If all you want is a woman to stand up to you... I would like to introduce you to Lady Balyra Roshan. I guarantee you, you will not get away with anything with her."

"Really?"

"And you might actually get her to lighten up a little."

"Oh, you're going to settle me with some sour-faced old maid?" he growled, threatening her with a pillow.

"She's the Roshan heir," she offered.

"So you're going to settle me with Will in a skirt?"

That made her laugh. "I never thought of her that way. She does tend to wear trousers under her skirts when she rides."

They were interrupted by Colt bringing a message, followed by a servant to take the trays. "From a Taluscliff bird, my lady."

Cae accepted the message with thanks, unfolded it and read it out once she had skimmed it. "Father says that another village has been taken, Holtwell nearer the Griff boarders."

"That's a Lutret holding, isn't it?"

She shook her head. "I don't think so. There may be a few Lutret subsequents living there, but I'm fairly sure it's ours. Echo lands, I think. Father's men have also joined forces with the prince's host. They've dealt with one small band of brigands, but nothing major yet. Oh, and my letter arrived safely."

"That was important?" he frowned.

"Actually, yes. It fills father in on what's been going on in the capitol for the last fortnight. And there has been a great deal that is somewhat sensitive. I asked him to let me know when it arrived. Just in case."

"Oh."

"Also by this we know that Willam at least made it close enough to send a courier, is still in one piece and we have some idea where they are headed."

"It didn't say any of that, except where they might be going."

"Exactly."

Suddenly he understood. "Oh, he'd have mentioned it if anything..." he nodded.

She did one last check on his leg, gave him something mild for the pain with the usual comfort/mallow draught, before leaving the room with Colt. "Tell me," she asked the young man as the thought occurred to her. "Can you read?"

"Some, my lady. I mean, I knows a few words by sight, place names and such like," he shrugged. "I kin follow cook's notes."

"I'll have to fix that. I have a book for you when you can read. I don't have any primers here." She thought about it a moment, deciding that tomorrow she would either go to a bookshop or send someone to fetch one. "I'll take care of that in the morning. You go on to bed or whatever else you do after supper."

"Thank you, my lady. You really... really gonna teach me the reading?"

"And speak properly when you desire to."

He frowned. "Why 'when I desire?' I mean, wouldn't I's always want for speaking proper once I'm knowing the how?"

"Because there are some Folk who will not trust you if you speak like a noble servant," she smiled. "And I am not trying to change who you are, just help you get the best opportunities you can."

He gave his forelock a tug at that, started to actually blush. "Truly, my lady, the on'y opps I be wanting be never to leaving this House. Work town-wise be hard findin' fer Rustics and service here be bettering than all hope."

"I am pleased to hear you say that. But one must always be prepared for an uncertain future, even when we are content, even happy, with what we have. One never knows what storms may come."

He bowed. "Thank you, my lady. And goodly night."

He trotted down the stairs and Cae went back to her room. Fern had a bath waiting, which Cae had not requested but was grateful for. It helped to soothe her, both body and mind. When she was done, dried and dressed for bed, she was ready to sleep. She did not even bother moving the books away from the window where Tempest sat keeping watch on the night. She stroked the bird once and decided to leave the window open for her, and, in order to enjoy the cool breeze moving lightly through the room, she bade Fern leave the curtains only half closed.

She was asleep before Fern had blown out the candles.

Caelerys slowly came awake to Tempest on the bed and pecking at her. The bird was making a low, rapid kakakakak and pulling at her sleeve. When Cae did not immediately respond, she grabbed her hand in her talon and pulled. Cae came awake with a startled cry of pain, holding her hand as she sat up.

Tempest jumped back out of the way as her mistress rose, gave her warning cry again and flew to the open window. Cae followed her, looking out into the courtyard where the toomi were flapping restlessly, but not yet in alarm. Then she saw a shadow move against the wall near her roses, where stood the side door to the street that Janem preferred. The door was open and a handful of figures slipped in, one of them carrying a battleaxe.

Cae pulled back from the window quickly, lest she be seen, and whispered to Tempest to go wake the house. "Start in the stable," she said. "*Bell, Tempest. The bell!*" she said in Vermian and the bird flew out the window.

Cae ran into her dressing room and threw open the wardrobe, snatching out the thick leather coat she wore when hunting, what she mockingly called her armour. After the run-in with the boar, she had insisted on having it made. Fern came out of her side chamber sleepily, checking on the noise. When she saw her mistress buckling her armour on, she panicked. "My lady? What's happening?!"

"I don't know, but someone just broke through the side gate. Lock yourself in your room and don't come out until you hear voices you recognize."

"But what about you, my lady?" she squeaked.

"I'm going to do what I can," she growled. "Now go!" With that she ran back into her bedchamber, strapped on her quiver and grabbed her new bow.

Going back through the dressing room and out into the hall, she ran to Vyncet's room and opened the door. On the floor, a sleepy Marko rolled over on his pallet and looked up, blinking. "My lady?" he asked groggily.

"Barricade the door, grab a weapon and prepare yourself. We're under attack."

The boy was off the floor in a heartbeat, grabbing his arming sword. "Show me," he began.

She shook her head, pointing to the bed where Vynce was fighting the effects of his medicine and starting to stir. "I need you to protect him. I have the rest of the men to guard me."

"But my lady!" he began as she closed the door. After a moment, she heard the sound of something heavy being dragged in front of it.

Cae then ran to the head of the stairs. She could hear footsteps below, trying to move quietly through the house. There were men-at-arms sleeping on the first floor, but she would have to run past where she thought the brigands were to get to them. She did the next best thing she could think of: she took a deep breath and screamed for all she was worth, as loud and as long as she could.

There was an immediate response from the intruders, and a great deal of profanity, but she also heard the pealing of the fire bell in the stable going crazy. She nocked an arrow and aimed into the dimness below the stairs, waiting for a target. When she saw movement that was not clad in white night-cloth, she fired and was rewarded by another spate of profanity.

She managed to get another arrow off at one of three men charging up the stairs towards her, buying her enough time to turn and run to her rooms and slam the door, throwing the meagre bolt. She did not think it would hold them long, but it could be long enough. She dragged one of her chests in front of the door and backed almost all the way to her bedchamber. There, she nocked another arrow and waited.

From deeper in the house she could hear the sounds of struggle, metal on metal, fist on flesh. She tried to get her breathing under control, to emulate the battle calm she had seen her father and brothers fall into so easily.

Something large hit the door and tried to batter it open. Then she heard a rough voice snarl to someone to go help the others, followed by running footsteps. Further down the hall, she heard Willam's door being forced open and the room ransacked. Then an axe bit deep into the wood of her own door and she had to cover a yelp. She clenched her teeth together and forced herself to concentrate, telling herself it was no more than a boar in human shape, no less deadly but not impossible if you fought smart.

It took him a few tries to make enough of a hole for someone to reach through and unlock the door. She pinned the hand to the splintered planks with a single arrow, grinning at the howl it sent up. As she drew and placed another, she heard the sickening chop and scream as the hand suddenly hung limp and unattached from the arrow, spraying blood.

This time the hand that reached through wore a gauntlet and the arrow skipped off, not even biting into the door. The bolt was seized and drawn and a shoulder was shoved against it. Slowly it moved, the chest not having enough weight to provide more than token resistance. No sooner had he shoved his way in than Cae snatched up her powder pot from the dressing table and lobbed it at his head. It struck him right in the middle of the forehead, causing him to reel for a moment. The chalcedony pot shattered when it connected and talc went everywhere, most importantly, into his eyes.

He roared in pain and flailed wildly with the axe. Behind him, at least one man other than the handless one sobbing on the floor started to follow him in, only slightly more clear-eyed. He was struck from behind by a sword and turned to engage whoever had attacked him.

To Cae's horror, the man in the room with her appeared to get larger. The seams of his broadcloth tunic looked unable to hold him, as if his muscles were swelling in response to his anger. When he blinked in her direction, his eyes were a shade of red that could not be accounted to the talc. She felt everything grow cold. She had seen this happen only once, in her father when brigands had dared to ambush their hunting party. She knew that look, the mindless rage and battle fury that lay behind it, robbing a man of all sense but killing and granting him superhuman strength to do it. Bearsarkers did not stop until well after they were dead, as if whatever controlled their bodies were quite unaware of having died yet. She began to back away, firing arrows as fast as she could load them.

Glancing back into the room behind her, she saw a clear path to her window. If she could get him to charge her, she might be able to dodge and send him falling to the courtyard below.

Half-blind, he moved with surprising speed and closed the distance just enough to take a swing at her and keep her from firing again. The axe bit deeply into the door, coming so close to her head that she felt the chill of its steel as she twisted away. While he struggled to pull it free, she took the arrow in her hand and drove it into the pit of his upraised arm.

The bellow he gave off was not quite human.

Mace appeared behind him, stabbing him in the back. The man roared again, yanked the axe so hard that it tore free of the wood and swung wild, connecting the haft with the side of Mace's head. The old man went down in a heap.

Cae took advantage of the moment to run to the window, throwing a chair in her path to trip him up. She turned, raising her bow to aim for more vulnerable spots. As he swung back around and the thin, silvery light of the Eastern moon shone upon his face, she could have sworn she saw the face of a bull. The half helm he wore was skewed sideways by a pair of horns and the hands gripping the axe seemed to be trying to rip through the gauntlets he wore. She let the arrow fly, grazing his temple. He lowered his head and started to charge as her second arrow caught him in the throat. As he crossed the room, he tripped over the fallen chair and landed on his face, his momentum carrying him the rest of the way until he crashed into the table at her feet, knocking the books to the floor.

She put one more into his back to be certain, then leaned back against the window, ready to climb out if he moved again.

She was still standing there, breathing in short, quick pants, a dead grip on her bow when Hollen and two of the men-at-arms came in looking for anyone else. Hollen ran to pull the man away from her, to make sure he was dead, and when he grabbed him by the hair to turn his face to the light, he was no more than a man.

Cae could feel hot tears running down her cheeks, but ignored them. She gathered her wits quickly and stepped gingerly around the dead man, running to check on Mace.

The man-at-arms was helping him to sit up, but he complained of the room spinning and she bade him to stop. She began to check him over. Aside from a few minor wounds, which were clearly obvious on his nightshirt, there was only the head wound. She could not be fully certain he had not broken it, but she was positive he was concussed.

He glared over at the dead man, then at Cae and began to issue orders. He winced when he spoke too loudly. He gestured Hollen over. "Take over. Put her in with Lord Vyncet, and her maid if you can find her. Search the house for any more and barricade the side gate. Set guards. Send someone for the watch."

"You should not be giving orders, Mace," she growled. "You look to have a concussion."

"I'll send for a Physician," he growled back. "Threat's not over."

As Hollen helped her to her feet to escort her out, Mace reached up to grab her hand. "Quick thinking, little bird, both screaming and sending the falcon to rouse the stable. T'were the horses that woke us first, but your voice that spoke the danger."

"Will you just lay back and rest?" she retorted, trying not to blush.

He merely smiled at her and pulled himself up to lean against the wall. "Pail," he gasped to the man helping him, who went white and ran for the rubbish bin.

"Now I know you have a concussion," she said as she crossed the room.

"Aye, little bird. I know it, too."

Vyncet was sitting up in the bed with his sword across his lap when Cae was ushered in. She glared at the weapon. "And what were you going to do with that?"

"Stab whatever I could reach. Are you all right?" he asked, clear-headed now. "Why are you wearing your hunting coat?"

"I went hunting."

He glared at her. "You did what? Other than scream the house down?"

She sighed. "I screamed the house UP. I was trying to wake as many as I could."

He leaned his head back against the headboard with a groan. "What did you do?"

She shrugged, sitting on the edge of his bed. "Nothing, just killed a bearsarker."

His head came up as her looked at her. "Oh, that's all? I'm stuck in bed, helpless as a kitten and my baby sister takes on a battlerager with just a bow?"

"And a powder pot."

At that he just laughed the laugh of the mad. "Will is going lose his shit. And then Father is going to lock you in a tower until your wedding day."

"I don't think so," she humphed.

"You're right, he'll probably crow about it from now until Fallow next. Uncle will be over both moons when he hears. He's always bragging how Maral women have antlers." He took a deep breath, let it out. "So tell me. Leave out no detail, however gory."

"I think he was a shift," she said quietly, then told him what had happened.

"Are you sure?"

"His half helm was coming off, being pushed from his head by horns," she exclaimed. "I don't think I imagined that or the sound he made. His face was wrong. He got bigger, like the battleragers, but it seemed like he was breaking out of his gauntlets."

"And you decided to stand and fight instead of hiding with Fern?" he cried.

"Hey, I was trying to defenestrate him! I figured he was so blind with rage he wouldn't see the window and wouldn't have time to stop himself before he went out."

"So instead you shot out his throat at nine paces?"

Marko watched the siblings with a sense of awe, gazed at Cae as if she were some divine warrior being.

"Wait, he had gauntlets?" he asked suddenly.

"Yes, and a skullcap. No other armour I remember, though he carried an axe not unlike Uncle's."

"You know this is bad, don't you?"

She nodded. "It means they were sent by a noble."

"Could be Free Legion," Marko suggested.

Vynce shook his head. "No, they'd be better equipped. Not wearing such piece-meal, and they'd buy a breast-plate before gauntlets."

She looked at him. "Not if they were Iron Legion. Or lesser. There are a few outfits that have not the prestige or wealth to kit properly, or are desperate enough to take a job like this."

"Let's hope we got one of them alive," he mumbled.

She sighed. "None of the ones I saw were. Even the guy who had his hand chopped off bled out in the hall."

There was a knock at the door. When given permission, it was opened and Hollen stepped in. "Beg pardon, my lord, my lady, but there is a contingent in Alvermian green armed to the teeth. Say they are to escort the pair of you to the Citadel."

Cae rose. "I will speak with them, Hollen."

She followed him down to the front hall, pointedly ignoring the bodies being carried outside. Six men stood in the atrium, all in royal livery. Five of them snapped to attention and the senior of them bowed. "My Lady Caelerys, I have been sent by the queen to convey you and your brother to the Citadel for your safety."

"I thank you and the queen for your kind attentiveness, but I could not possibly leave until I have seen to my house. I have men who are injured, one I know with a concussion, and I still have not been informed of the extent of the damages to the Hall or its people. I could not in good conscience leave until then."

He gave another sharp bow. "My orders were explicit, my lady. But I can afford you a little time to get ready to depart, within which you might attend those matters," he conceded.

She sighed, glancing down at her bloodstained nightdress and bare, bloody feet. "I would need a bath at the very least."

"There will be one awaiting you at the Citadel, my lady. As well as anything else you may require. I was told to have you to safety within the hour."

"I want physicians to see to my injured. And I want a full report brought to me and, if it is not too much to ask, some extra fortification for the evening, at the very least?"

He gave her a stiff nod. "I will see to it personally, my lady."

"Your name, sir?"

"Minal Wren, my lady."

"I will hold you to your promises, Sir Wren."

His bow was less stiff this time, but no less meant.

Cae turned to go back upstairs. "I shall be down shortly. There are things I will not leave without. The least of which is my maid, whom I must go let out."

There was a curious and amused arch of his brow but he said nothing of it. As she headed for her chambers, she heard him issuing orders to the men he had brought with him.

Once in her room, she knocked on Fern's door, told her that it was safe to come out. "We have to leave now."

She unbolted and opened the door immediately. "What? Why?"

"Royal decree," was all she said.

"We have to get you dressed."

"I actually do not believe he will afford me that time. And I will not wish to change until I have bathed, which I have been told I certainly do not have time for. Just grab what we cannot do without."

With that the went into her bedchamber to grab the books. They had been scattered on the floor next to the bull-man's body. Gingerly, she bent to pick up the small but very precious book of her brother's and noticed something shining on the open pages. She crouched there, carefully turning the page in the moonlight. There was no doubt that there was something silvery written there in between the lines of neatly scripted text. It glittered in the light from the window.

She heard noise downstairs and hastily closed the book and grabbed the others.

"My lady!" exclaimed Hollen, entering the room. "You should not be so close to the corpse."

She stood, holding the books to her chest. "Why not? I made it." Even so, she moved away from the body and crossed to her slippers, lying forgotten by the bed. Even as she lifted a foot to slip into one, she realized she it was a bad idea. She would only ruin them.

She sighed. "Hollen, Sir Wren is taking over for the time being. I need you to make sure the rest of the House assists him. I want an assessment done of everyone and everything damaged. Make sure every hurt is attended however minor, and get a Physician here at once for Mace and anyone else who needs specialized care. Until he is well you are in charge of security, Fennel of the house."

"My lady, they are moving Lord Vynce now," Fern announced from the door. "They wish you to follow."

"Find Tempest."

The girl disappeared as Cae daintily stepped around the body.

She waited patiently in the hall for them to manoeuvre her brother down the stairs. It took some careful manipulation not to jar him. Standing beside her, waiting, was Marko, who looked her over and ran back off down the hall for a moment, coming back with her cloak and insisted on her putting it on.

"Tis a chill in the air, my lady. We cannot have you catching your death. Not after surviving this."

She allowed him his gallantry, and permitted him to fasten the clasp for her, not wanting to let go of her books. By the time he was done, they had managed to get Vyncet to the ground floor and Cae flowed down the stairs on her bloody feet with Marko trailing behind her.

Fern, who had gone down the back servant stairs, emerged from the hall that led to the kitchen with Tempest running after her holding one wing slightly away from her body, and chirping plaintively. "See, 'Pest, there she is," she said turning sideways to let the bird pass. "I am sorry, my lady, but she would not be carried."

Caelerys went to her knees and set the books on the floor beside her. Tempest ran to her, chattering her pain and showing her the damaged wing. Cae managed to give it a quick look, ascertained that she wasn't actively bleeding and put out her hand. Tempest walked as carefully as she could up Cae's arm to her shoulder, but even so, she winced once or twice. She swept the books back up and rose, following the noticeably impatient but infinitely polite Sir Wren to a carriage that stood waiting.

She was assisted getting inside, and sat across from Vyncet who was seated sideways with his leg stretched across the seat. After making sure his master had what he needed, Marko jumped out again and climbed up on the back of the carriage. Fern settled in beside her lady and Tempest hopped down onto the top of the books. She had to be held still when the carriage lurched forward the instant the door was closed.

While there was not enough light to examine the wing more thoroughly, Cae felt blindly along the bones, gently checking for breaks. She did not feel any, though there was a place near the blood that caused her pain. Cae laid her feathers as flat as she could and smoothed the wing. "You'll be all right, my sweet," she crooned. "We'll ask Master Olen if he'll take a look at you and you'll be right as rain."

The bird sat down on the books and leaned against her, rubbing her head against the leather with plaintive little chirps.

"And what about me?" said Vyncet. "Languishing away in utter boredom and pain and you spend all your efforts pampering a pet."

She could see his grin in the dim light coming through the curtains. "You're just jealous I got to fend off an attack on the house and you had to stay in bed like an invalid."

"Damn straight."

There was silence for a long moment.

"Who's going to tell father?" she asked softly.

"Mace most likely."

"Mace has a concussion."

"Hollen then," he sighed. "If there are any Taluscliff males left in our loft, he'll send one tonight. How long do you think before Janem knows?"

"Maybe another four hours? Less if Hollen thinks to send word," she sighed. "He's been working nights."

"Why?"

There was not time to answer him as they crossed the drawbridge to the Citadel and entered the well-lit courtyard.

Caelerys was brought out first with Fern, as Vynce would take a bit more effort. She was swept along up the steps and into the single open door, held by a guard as if they feared further attack. The queen stood in the atrium in nightbraid and dressing gown with a mildly worried look upon her face. She crossed to take Cae's hand immediately, looking her over critically. "Any of that yours?" she asked.

"No, Your Majesty," she stammered, trying to observe the proper etiquette and curtsey, but was hampered by bird, books and monarch.

"See, I told you that you would be fine. How did it serve?"

Cae blushed as she realized she meant the bow and that she had left it behind in her brother's room. "There was never any doubt but that it would, Your Majesty. It is a masterful weapon."

"Good. Now," she said, waving to servants who had begun to pour out of the side halls, "first things first, you have a steaming bath waiting. I took the liberty of ordering some lavender, camomile and rose petals thrown in, to help soothe you. It may not have hit you yet, but it will."

Cae turned to look at Fern but saw the girl being escorted off by a flock of maids that included young Rue who merely winked at Cae. "Your Majesty, my maid..." she began.

"Oh, you won't be needing her tonight. She has her own pampering in store. She needs a bath and wine and a rest, too."

Cae blushed, feeling that she had been selfish and thoughtless. She allowed the queen to sweep her up the stairs to the residential levels. She was careful to not step on the narrow strip of carpet that flowed down the marble, aware she was probably leaving bloody footprints behind her that someone would have to clean. She could feel the stickiness still, pulling at her skin as she climbed.

"How did you know?" she asked suddenly as they left the staircase for an ornate hall.

"What, my dear?" asked the queen. If she had noticed the suddenness or lack of courtesies in the question, she ignored them.

"That we were under attack? Word could not have reached you that quickly. You had an armed guard and a carriage in our yard before even the Watch arrived."

The queen gave a slow, enigmatic smile. "I do not really know that I knew," she said softly. "I woke from a horrible dream and I just knew it was tonight. I only do as the Mother bids. Her nudges are subtle and quiet and persistent. I just do and all comes clear."

"May I ask another question?" she dared.

"You may ask me anything you like in private. I cannot guarantee I will like the question or provide an answer, but you have permission to ask."

"Why me?" she asked in a small voice. "Surely there are others more worthy of your attentions?"

"Like Lady Liliwyn?" she countered.

"Aye, Your Majesty."

"Tut, and here I thought we were doing so well," she sighed. "So long as we are engaged in informalities and bordering impertinence, you may as well dispense with the honorifics."

"Of course, Y..." she stopped herself, took a moment to compose her emotions. The queen merely walked with a serene smile. "I am aware you have taken an interest in her. But am I in your sights because of old loyalties?"

"Oh, child," she breathed sadly, stopping before a door. "I am afraid that is one of those questions for which I have no answer. The Mother wants me to keep an eye on you, so I will. I have no idea why. I do not think, though, that it has anything to do with old loyalties. I've known you were in danger for some time, and I've been aware that some of it is my fault. Perhaps for that I may feel some obligation, but no more. I only know that if I do not act as I am guided to, bad things will happen. ...Though sometimes bad things happen when I do," she added, musing, "but those are always bad things the Mother desires to happen. I have learned not to question."

"Was marrying Grand Duke Rorlan one of those things?" she asked, feeling bold.

The queen smiled. "He was Prince Rorlan then, but bound to become the grand duke. And actually, not marrying Lord Avondyl Griff before the announcement of the betrothal of Prince Ranlan was one of 'those' things." She set a motherly hand on Cae's shoulder. "If you really want to know why, look deep into your heart at what makes you special, what makes you you, and then observe what happens or doesn't happen because of where you are. You'll eventually see it. I haven't gone looking, but then I have a great deal tugging me in all directions. But your bath will begin to get cold," she finished, opening the door and gesturing for Cae to proceed her into the room.

It was an opulent apartment with rich furnishings fit for a grand lady to entertain a small court. There was a comfortable chair near a window with an embroidery frame by it, seating for several others and a scattering of delicate worktables. The room had two other doors, one of which the queen directed her to, guiding her thoughtfully around a thick, rich rug of Northern make.

This second chamber was a dressing room not unlike her own at home, though more expensively furnished. It had no real personality, though, as if it were merely held in waiting for whichever occupant had the honour of spending the night. There were also four handmaids standing around a steaming tub, adding last ewers of hot water. There was a polished brass brazier at a safe distance keeping the room warm and the fragrance of relaxing flowers and herbs filled the air.

The maids moved to help her undress and Tempest shrilled, opening her one wing and warning them off. They shrieked and backed away. Cae felt mortally embarrassed. "Jelma! Tyet! They are only doing what Fern would do. No one is going to harm me." She turned to the queen and gave a little curtsey. "Actually, Tempest helped immensely in the fight and somehow was injured. I would like it very much if the Master of the Hunt could look her over? I don't think she broke anything, but the blood on her wing is hers and there is some pain."

"Of course, dear. Rosie, please go fetch him?"

Cae crossed to one of the tables and set the books down, made the bird sit on the table with them. Tempest looked around her body to stare at the large, claw-footed tub, then plaintively up at Cae. "No, you cannot sit on the edge," she laughed. "You stay here. And when the Master gets here, you will let him look at you."

There was a vocal objection and a twist of her head at that.

"Yes, you will," Cae insisted. "If my brothers must submit to the mercies of Physicians, so must you. He will be gentle, ketava." The bird gave a sad little whistle and nibbled her fingers, but let her go.

She began to unfasten the buckles across her chest holding on her leathers as she crossed to the tub. The queen was watching with a pleased and knowing look, and the maids were just staring. It took them a moment and the leathers hitting a chair before they gathered enough of their wits to help her out of her blood-soaked gown. One of them checked to make sure she did not need her hair washed, then pinned it up and out of the way before Cae stepped into the glorious heat of the bath. She sank gratefully into it. Behind her, she could hear the queen usher the maids out for the time being, bidding one to remain and make sure Caelerys did not fall asleep and to alert the others when she was ready to wash.

She very nearly did fall asleep. The heat of the water was delicious on muscles she had not been aware were tense, and the herbs brought a delicate, calm fragrance to her senses. She was more than content to lie back and drift until the water became tepid.

It had not quite gotten there when there was a soft knock on the door and one of the other maids entered. "My lady, the Master of the Hunt is here for your bird. Is she safe to approach?" she asked timidly.

"He awaits her in the other room?" she asked, sitting up. The girl nodded. She looked to the bird. "Tempest, can you get down?"

The falcon paced the table, found herself a chair which she hopped down to, and from there the floor. She ran over to the tub, stretching up for affection.

"I'm wet," she said, letting a few drops splash on her. "Follow, Rosie was it?" she asked, turning to the girl. She nodded. "Her name is Tempest, just lead her in and introduce her. She'll mind her manners," she added the last to the bird, who sulked for a second, then walked after the maid.

The other girl had come from her seat by the wall, bringing washing cloths and soap. "She is a very unusual bird, my lady."

"That she is. My brothers complain she is more pet than predator but she saved us tonight," she sighed, allowing the girl to help her with the bathing.

"She saved you?" she asked. "If... if I may ask, my lady?" suddenly hesitant.

Cae smiled. "You may ask me just about anything. I may not answer, but I will never chastise you for asking unless there are others who are offended. Be discreet, please."

"Of course, my lady."

"She woke me, alerting me to the invasion, then roused the stable and the men-at-arms by ringing the bell."

The other women came into the room and carefully closed the door before crossing to the tub, helping her out and to dry, then putting her into a new nightdress. This one was much nicer than her own, though hers was not cheap. This one was of a heavy silk with a fine spray of lace at the throat and sleeves. It made her feel positively spoiled. The slippers they insisted she wear were also silk, though the dressing gown was a heavy, red velvet.

"Would my lady wish to see the Master of the Hunt?" asked Rosie.

"She would," she responded, making sure she was presentable before walking into the antechamber.

Tempest was standing on a table with her injured wing stretched out and watching the man's every move. She shrilled at Cae as she entered and the man glanced up from his work.

"She was lucky," he said. "She only lost a pinion."

She came around the table, holding her fingers out to the bird's head to nuzzle. "They bleed that much?" she asked.

"Oh, no. She was cut, too. See the gap?" he showed her the column of missing feathers just below the cut he was gently dabbing with a wadding soaked in medicine. "Whatever caught her just missed the bone, but cut the skin. She's going to be awkward in flight for a while. I wouldn't advise hunting her." He finished his work and let her wing go, offered her a titbit from a pouch similar to Cae's own. "Here you go, beautiful," he said, and was shocked when the bird refused it, looking, instead, over her shoulder to her mistress.

Cae laughed. "Yes, you can have it. And thank him for mending you."

She turned on the table to face him, tipped her head and bobbed it with a light chirrup.

"Well, you are welcome, mistress Tempest," he said, then laughed as she then gobbled the meat.

"I take it she will not return to the mews with me, will she?" he added ruefully, watching the bird cross to her mistress for affection.

"You take correctly. I would not risk separation, especially not tonight. She's the one who woke me to the danger and roused the house."

"We shall have to speak of her training one day. I am very interested."

Cae stifled a yawn. "No secret, really, Master Olen. Merely raising by an inexperienced ten-year-old. I think I'm part mother, part hunting companion."

"That would only explain part of this. But I should allow you to rest. I am glad you and your family are unharmed, Lady Caelerys," he said with a bow and left the room.

Cae took a deep breath, looking around at the four maids still here and noticing the absence of the queen. "Has Her Majesty returned to bed?" she asked hopefully.

"I believe so, my lady. We are yours to command," curtseyed the oldest of them.

"Well, since Fern is being taken care of, and Tempest is taken care of," she said, wrapping a cloth around her wrist and hand and offering the perch to the bird, "and I am exhausted beyond reason... and you have been so kind... I suppose I should ask for my bed?"

The older one smiled and bowed with a wave of her arm. "Right this way."

The last door led to a room that was deeply shadowed, lit only by the candles held by one of the maids. But the bed they opened the curtains to and turned down the covers of, was larger than her parents' bed and half again as tall. She actually needed a pair of steps to climb into it. She set Tempest onto the headboard to get comfortable and sank into the depths of feather beds and down-quilted spreads. She was so tired that she did not even remember being covered up or the curtains closing. Fortunately, if she dreamed, it was not worth remembering.

12

Caelerys woke to a silent room, still wrapped in the dark of her curtains. Tempest had come off the headboard in the night and tucked herself up under her arm and snuggled close. As Cae stirred, the bird followed suit, clearly debating on whether or not to just go back to sleep. Cae, on the other hand, felt that it was high time she got up.

Tempest complained when she sat up, tried burrowing back under the covers. Cae tossed them off of her and picked her up. "No, you don't. These are not our sheets and I will not have you putting holes in them."

A chirped protest followed that remark and Cae stroked her back. "I know you don't mean to. You cannot help it and we are guests."

Cae opened the curtains and slipped out of the bed. She forgot how high it was and slid a little further than she had expected. She made a small exclamation and held Tempest out, not wanting to fall on her, but she kept her feet. She quickly set the bird on the floor and began to explore the room.

There were no windows in here, but she supposed that was a security measure. The fire in the grate was still banked, though slowly dying, but then, the room was still warm enough and it had not merited relighting. She found a taper and lit it from the dim coals and looked around. There was nothing of real significance in the room at all, for all it's rich appointments. There was a chair against one wall, she supposed for the benefit of any maid left on watch. There was a lamp that hung in the centre of the canopy and a small table beside the bed. There was a stand on another wall with a pitcher of water and washing bowl for quick ablutions, and a narrow door discreetly tucked between a pair of tapestries.

Curious, she opened the door to find a private necessary. Setting the candle on the shelf for it, she gratefully took care of her own needs. Upon emerging, she found one of the maids from the night before looking into the bed.

The girl heard the door and turned with a start. "Oh, my lady! You gave me a fright. I thought for the moment we'd lost you!"

"No," she smiled. "Though I feel like I may have slept well past my usual hour."

The girl curtseyed. "Forgive us, my lady, but we did not know your normal time and... truthfully, we were told to let you sleep as long as you would. You have had a terrible night. I was just coming to check on you."

"Well, I am up and well, thank you."

The girl seemed a little startled to be thanked. "Would my lady prefer to dress or dine first?"

"Dress. And is it dinner all ready?"

"Aye, my lady. If you will come with me we shall get you dressed, and your meal should be here by the time we are done."

She followed the girl through a door she had not found yet which led straight into the dressing room. Rosie and the other girls were there already. They stood and curtseyed upon her entrance. "At your service, my lady," they said in unison.

"Are you *all* assigned to me for the duration of my stay?" she asked.

The oldest curtseyed again. "Aye, my lady."

"Then I would know your names and if Fern is to be joining your number."

"I am Coral," introduced the eldest, "senior handmaiden. The redhead is Rosie, the plump one is Sorrel, and the young one is Pansy. As for this Fern, I do not know the maid, so I could not tell you."

"Fern is the maid I brought with me from my home. I will have her join me when she is recovered."

"Was she harmed in the attack?" gasped the blonde Pansy.

Cae smiled, "No. She spent the attack locked in her room, but when we arrived she was whisked off by Rue and a group of maids to be taken care of even as I was."

"In that case, it is quite likely she will be joining our number," said Coral. "Now, my lady's clothes have not been brought and you came in your nightdress, so we have a selection of gowns for you. I am aware that your House colours are silver on midnight but some ladies prefer not to wear their House colours all the time. We have a beautiful gown of dark blue velvet, though it is trimmed in gold, as well as a selection of russets and greens," she listed, opening a clothes press and pulling open staggered drawers to display at least eight gown in various colours.

She drifted over, finding herself spoiled for choice. She let her hands drift across the rich fabrics, finally settling on a soft, silvery green that reminded her of waterwood leaves. "This one?" she asked.

The woman drew the gown out and held it up to her, comparing the colour to her complexion. "Your hair is almost too dark for it, but I believe you can pull it off. You have chosen the plainest gown in the press, though," she said, making a small face.

"I like simple."

That seemed to settle her mind, and she sent the rest of the ladies into a flurry of activity. In short, efficient order, Cae was dressed and sitting to have her hair done.

"Does my lady have a preference for fragrances?" Pansy asked, sorting through a box of bottles.

"She does not prefer them at all," Cae answered, watching Tempest following one girl after another, curiously poking her beak into everything, and occasionally chasing after trailing things like ribbon. "I don't even perfume my talc."

"How... how does my lady prevent... odour?" Sorrel asked.

"Plain talc and powdered honey. Fern will explain when she arrives. For now, just no scents."

"As you wish, my lady," Pansy said a little sadly and put the box away.

Coral stood back and held up a small mirror behind Cae's head, reflecting the image of her hair into the larger mirror in front of them. "Will this please my lady's love of simplicity?"

The front was twisted artfully back from her face to form a coronet, and then done in an elaborate, single braid down the middle, leaving the rest of her hair free. "It pleases it greatly, thank you," she smiled. "You must teach Fern how to do this for me."

"If you wish."

"If it would not be too much trouble," she added pointedly.

Coral gave a slight bow, "Of course, my lady. Now, if you are ready, your dinner has arrived."

Cae was led into the sitting room where a meal had been lain out, complete with a plate of meat bits for Tempest. Once Cae was seated, Pansy brought over a smaller table for the falcon and her food. She still seemed a little nervous about the bird, but smiled happily to be so close.

What disturbed Cae was the obvious evidence that the food had been tasted. She knew it was deliberately done that way, so she would know. "Rosie witnessed the tasting, my lady," Coral instructed. "The young man is fine."

She closed her eyes and took a deep breath, hating this part of court life. Finally she began to eat. "What happened to the books I brought with me?" she asked, finding the meal quite delicious. Tempest was gobbling happily until she glared at her, then slowed down.

"They were brought into the bedchamber, my lady," Sorrel answered.

"The larger three need to be returned to the castle library. The smaller one I would like now please. It was a gift and I would not have it lost or misplaced."

The girl bobbed and disappeared into the bedchamber.

Cae was about halfway through her meal when a knock upon her door was answered to admit a page. The boy crossed to the table and bowed, waiting until Cae nodded for him to deliver his message. "There is a blacksmith insisting on seeing you, my lady."

She smiled. "Oh, good. Has he been to see Lord Vyncet yet?"

The boy seemed disconcerted by her attitude and question. "I do not know, my lady. Only that he's asked for you and is most... impatient? We were hesitant, my lady, not knowing if we should dismiss him out of hand or inform you. Should I call a guard?"

She laughed. "No, my dear. Please show him up immediately with all due deference. He is no ordinary blacksmith. He is a master and my subsequent brother."

He paled a little. "I'll bring him immediately, my lady."

Tempest had finished her meal and sat on her table preening when Janem was escorted in.

Cae looked calmly up at him and smiled. "I hope you didn't lose too much sleep," she said, rising to meet him.

He did not let her hug him, but held her at arm's length and looked her over. A couple of the maids tittered in the background and were silenced by Coral who sent the offenders into the bedchamber to clean up.

"I am fine," she laughed.

Tempest chirped at that.

"She says you aren't," he snapped.

"No, she said she was the one who got hurt."

The bird held out her damaged wing, showing the missing feathers.

Janem turned back to his sister. "Really, Cae? What were you thinking?!"

"You *have* seen Vyncet already."

"No, Hollen. I went to the Hall when I heard this morning. They said you'd been taken to the Citadel. What in the name of Caelerima's Children possessed you to attack a bearsarker with only a bow!?" he yelled.

"More like a bullsarker," she muttered. "I didn't have a choice, Jan! By the time I knew he was a battlerager he'd already gotten into my room!"

"Well," he stammered, still angry and yet stunned, "...damn!" he cried. "How many arrows did it take?" he asked when he got control of his emotions.

She sat down again and offered him food. He was so conflicted between worry and pride, he obeyed without really thinking about it. "I have no idea. At least four or five. Plus a powder pot."

"Powder pot?"

"My talc. If the stone box didn't stun him, the powder would blind him," she shrugged, refilling her cup of wine and handing it to him.

"Did it work?"

"No to the first, though he felt it. Yes to the second. That was when..." she glanced around at the ladies. "May we have some privacy, please?" she asked.

Coral reluctantly nodded and ushered everyone into one room or another of the apartment.

When they were gone, she told him everything she had seen. Before she was done he had to refill the cup and had drunk half of that.

"Do you think this was connected to the robbery at the forge?" he asked.

She shook her head. "Well, unless Hill has woken enough to describe his attackers?"

"He's awake, but doesn't remember. He's not... right. May never be right," he sighed.

She set her hand on his. "That, unfortunately, is the way of head wounds."

"He was a good smith. It's a shame he's ruined. Master Illet's going to take him into his own household if he's capable. Maybe just have him keep his eyes on the apprentices. And don't think I don't realize what you just did," he said, glaring at her over the cup.

"What?" she asked innocently. "How's Mace?"

"Better than Hill. Physician said he'll be fine by Fourth Day."

"Oh good. He took a hard knock. He also stabbed the bearsarker."

"Yeah, but it was your arrows that felled him. Nothing was taken?" he asked nervously.

She picked the book up from the chair beside her. "Other than this, I do not know. I am still waiting on Sir Wren's report. Unless they took one alive, I have no idea what they were after. I can't even tell you if killing me had been the bearsarker's original plan or if that was born of the rage."

"You hitting him with the pot's what triggered it, wasn't it?"

"Probably."

"You do have a talent for pissing people off," he smirked. Then he lowered his voice. "You are certain he was a shift?" he asked.

"To be honest, I am beginning to both doubt and think that the late king might not have been mad. Merely driven so by the shift. It would explain some of the things that Will told me about that night."

"Keep this to yourself for a while," he said. "Could start a panic until we know more."

She tapped the book. "I've also discovered what you discovered," she said pointedly, "all thanks to the bull."

He grinned. "Really? All of it?"

She narrowed her eyes. "There is more? I didn't really have time to read it, though I plan to tonight."

He looked over at the window and grinned. "Maybe I'll come see you in the morning before I crawl off to bed."

"Is that all it takes to get you to visit me?"

His look was serious. "You are our lodestone, sister."

She sighed, "Vynce said something to that effect last night. I still don't see it. Would you like to see Vyncet? I suppose I should check on him any way. Make sure he's not driving everyone to distraction."

He rose, offered her his hand. "I think I can spare the time."

"Coral," she called, loud enough to be heard through the doors. When the woman appeared, she informed her of their intent to visit their other brother.

"Of course, my lady. If you will wait just a moment." She disappeared to ask the others if any of them knew which rooms her brother had been given. She returned shortly with the young blonde. "Pansy will take you, my lady, Master."

"Thank you." She then handed the book to Coral. "Please put this somewhere safe. I would be heartbroken were it damaged or misplaced. I will want it tonight."

Pansy cheerfully went to open the door and startled the page who was preparing to knock. "Yes?" she asked, recovering more quickly than the boy.

"Sir Wren is here to present a requested report to Lady Caelerys."

Cae went to the door. "Oh, delightful! Your timing could not be better, Sir Wren," she smiled at the knight standing behind the page. "We were just on our way to visit my other brother. Would you join us and inform us all at once?"

He bowed and stepped back from the door. "As you please, my lady."

Vyncet was down at the other end of the hall. Their small party was admitted immediately. Vynce was propped up on a couch, fully dressed and with a pair of crutches leaning against the wall near at hand. He grinned as they were brought in. "Well, if it isn't my favourite sister!" he crowed.

"What am I, her shadow?" Janem growled playfully.

"No, that's on the floor next to her," he pointed to the bird tagging along. "Heard she got hurt."

"She'll fly like you'll walk," she retorted. "You remember Sir Minal Wren?"

Vynce studied his face for a long moment. "Oh, aye. The man who rescued me from the doldrums of my bedchamber. I must thank you, good sir. I thought this wretch would keep me locked up in there forever," he grinned.

Sir Wren merely raised an eyebrow at the commentary. "You... are welcome, my lord."

"He's come to give us the report I insisted upon," Cae said, finding herself a seat. Jan found himself a harder chair. Tempest settled on the floor between Cae's feet.

"Oh, wonderful. Carry on then."

The knight pulled out a scroll which he handed to Cae. Vynce scowled at that, but said nothing. "This is the detailed report of injuries and breakages. No one was killed or crippled, though there is one man-at-arms with a broken arm, and another with a nasty gash. Your senior man, Mace, I believe," he continued when she nodded, "has been confirmed to have a concussion, but should be fine in a fortnight. As for anything missing," he sighed. "Upstairs could not be answered for, as the personal servants responsible for those rooms were not present to make the assessment. If you could send the servants involved and get word to the Watch, it would make everything easier."

"Will be difficult for the master bedroom," Cae sighed. "I heard them break in, but Harlan's the one who would know and he's with Willam."

"And this Willam is where?" he asked politely.

"With the crown prince, routing a group of slavers," Janem answered.

Sir Wren's attitude shifted, not that he had been less than polite or respectful. "Ah. That will have to wait unless either of you would be able to tell."

Cae shook her head and Vyncet just grumbled. "He never let anyone else in there."

"I was in there once, but unless it was large, I'm not going to be able to tell you," Cae said.

"There was some broken furniture upstairs, the room on the other side of the outer balcony," he continued. "As for downstairs: some crockery, there's a kettle that got dented against one of the invader's heads."

Cae giggled, and Janem grinned. "Fennel, I'll bet," he chuckled. "You don't mess with her kitchen."

"The man found unconscious in the kitchen is the only one we've taken alive. He's been taken to the Citadel dungeons. We'll let you know if we get anything out of him. There's a list of foodstuffs that were ruined and will need replacing," he added, pointing to the scroll, "and a few other things the Housekeeper insisted you should know. You were very lucky."

"We were warned early," Cae said, bending to stroke Tempest.

"The only thing of value they could tell me was missing was a box containing a gold and ruby necklace."

"That means someone got away," she breathed.

"Do you know the value of the piece? Can you give a description, my lady?"

"It was probably stolen to begin with," she muttered.

This caught his attention and not in a good way. "My lady?"

"Forgive me, I... misspoke. I have no proof of what I said and speak only from many years of bad blood," Caelerys said formally, blushing that she had forgotten herself so much. "The necklace was a gift from an unwelcome suitor, and was to be returned. I care not for its whereabouts but that the giver knows that it was intended to be returned and now cannot be. It will make things awkward for a spell, but I will survive it."

"Lady Petra," Vyncet said. Cae and Janem both looked at him. "She would know how best to handle the etiquette of the matter."

Cae nodded and turned back to the knight, rising and offered her hand as would a man. "I thank you very much for your attentions, Sir Wren. Your assistance and interventions have been most helpful and we are grateful. I will make certain to mention your attentiveness to the queen when next I see Her Majesty. Is my Hall secure enough for the time being, should the invaders be foolish enough to try again?"

He accepted her hand and the firm clasp she gave him. He bowed, "You are well in hand, and a new gate should be in place by nightfall. I have left four of my men to supplement your own for the next day or so. But I would recommend hiring new guards and being extremely careful in vetting them."

"Would you have any recommendations in that matter?" she asked him.

"If I think of any, I will send you word, my lady. Good day, Lady Caelerys, my lords," he added, bowing once more before leaving.

Behind her back Vyncet and Janem were grinning at each other. "I told you," Vynce said.

"I knew it before you did, Vynce. I told you it would happen. It was already happening."

She turned and glared at the two of them, her hands on her hips. Jan had his arms crossed over his chest and just stared unabashed right back at her. "Told you what?"

"That you were turning into Mother," Vynce grinned.

"A right little Lady of the Manor," Janem added.

She threw up her hands and growled. "Oh, you two! Come on, Tempest, I need to go find our hosts and pay our respects," she snapped, striding out of the room.

"And there she is!" Vynce crowed.

"And there she goes," chuckled Janem. Before the door closed behind her, she heard Janem asking, "Was it really a bearsarker?"

"Why is that so hard to believe?" asked the squire, "My lady is fierce."

She closed the outer door on the men laughing.

Pansy fell almost unnoticed into her shadow as she started back down the hall to her room. When Cae stopped outside what she was certain was her own door without moving to open it, the girl dared to ask, "Is there somewhere else my lady wishes to go?"

She thought a moment. "I need to pay my respects to my hosts, but at their convenience. I suppose I should send word to the queen, but I also need to speak with Prince Balaran on a different matter. I need to check on Fern, and I would like to spend time with Lady Liliwyn and the princess if I could."

"Well, my lady could just go to the gardens. It is the most likely place to find the lady and the princess. The queen is prone to wandering and that is a place she usually ends up. His Highness would either be in the library or a number of haunts, but messages can be sent to his valet."

Caelerys sighed. As much as she dreaded the thought of walking into a garden full of the bevy of women that filled it of late, she knew it to be the best option. It would simply not do to send a message, not to the royal family. "I think I know where in the gardens they are most likely to be found. And sending a message to His Highness will not be necessary. If needs must, I know of a way that requires me to do nothing but show up."

Pansy looked at her in confused question.

"He has standing orders that if I enter the library, he is to be informed. At least I think they are standing orders. Please, lead the way. I do not know my way about quite yet."

Pansy shook her head even though she began to guide her towards the staircase, "Oh, no, my lady, the queen has left specific instructions that you are not to be left alone outside you bedchamber, at all. And there is a very short list of people with whom you may be left with."

Caelerys stopped in the middle of the stair. "What?"

SHIFT: Stag's Heart

Three steps down, Pansy turned, uneasy. "It... it is for your safety, my lady. Her Majesty is very concerned for you. And there are threats everywhere, even here."

"This list," she said flatly.

The girl counted them off on her fingers. "The queen and the princess, of course. The king, because who is going to tell him no? Your family without question, which was why there was hesitation until it was known the Master Smith was your brother. Myself, Coral, Sorrel, Rosie and your Fern if she joins us."

"And the princes?"

"Especially not the princes. She is protecting your reputation as well." She lowered her voice, "And at least one of them has a reputation of his own."

"There is a maid on the first floor I wish added to that list. I am aware she is perhaps not qualified to serve the upper floors, being one of the rustics, but I like her and she has proved very helpful to me. Her name is Rue."

Pansy looked uncertain. "I will see what I can do. But there is no guarantee. Will my lady go to the gardens now?"

Steeling herself, Cae nodded and the girl lead on.

When they reached the gardens, they had to step aside and curtsey as the king swept by speaking with one of his Keys. Cae was not sure which office the man served. The king and his guards went past without acknowledging her.

Once the retinue had gone by, they turned down one of the side paths that led to the familiar terrace where once again, canopies had been set up over refreshments. There was a cry as she was sighted and, in very short order, she was swarmed by the girls wanting to know how she was and how awful the whole ordeal had been.

It wasn't until the princess cleared her throat pointedly that they fell back and made room, curtsied.

Cae sank as well, grateful for the reprieve. Then Syera was hugging her tightly and whispering if she was all right.

"Aye," she whispered back. "I slept wonderfully, thank you," she added, at a normal volume. "I wish to thank your family for your generosity and hospitality."

The princess grinned, glancing down at Cae's dress. "It looks better on you than it ever did on me," she smiled. "I tried it on once, but the colour doesn't suit me. It makes you look like a dark flower," she added, fingering a curl of her dark hair and unwinding it to hang artfully over Cae's shoulder. "Don't you just hate it when gifts are given without careful consideration?"

She blushed slightly, aware that Malyna was not far away in the crowd. "I assure you that all of the gifts Your Majesties have given have been nothing but the most suitable and fitting," she said with a tiny bob.

Syera waved her hand, as if to dismiss the subject and guided Cae over to the seats, drawing her down beside her. "So, we are dying to know," she cajoled as the rest of the women found places to sit.

At Cae's feet, Tempest chirped, begging for a lift. "Ginger then," she told her, bending to offer her hand. The bird was very careful with her talons, and Cae lifted her to the back of the bench between herself and the princess, where she settled comfortably, feeling included.

Syera slowly reached up to stroke the bird's white chest. "I heard the poor thing was injured."

"Not terribly. She shouldn't fly for a few days. And she'll be awkward a while after that until the missing pinions grow back."

"So what happened?" asked Lucelle.

Cae once again told the story, though there was a great deal more reaction and interruptions than when she had told her brother. She did not, however, speak of the shift beyond that he was a bearsarker.

Lady Malyna and the three other women who had already shown themselves to be staunch worshippers of the Eldest looked more horrified than the others. "That is terrible. What is your father going to do now?" Malyna asked with wide, damp eyes.

"Nothing until he finds out who sent them. Then... I do not think well for their chances."

"Oh, of course, but... I meant about your marriage prospects?"

Cae frowned. "I do not understand. That has not changed."

"But...," she stammered, seemed at war with courtesy and concern, "you're... ruined," she finally whispered.

"What makes you think that? The man missed me." Her hand brushed the hair by her temple unconsciously. "I will confess he came close. I felt the wind of that axe, but he never touched me."

"He broke into your *bedchamber*," she insisted. "You were alone with him. Whether true or not, there is the appearance, and the question... will be whispered."

Cae's eyes darkened. "I was not alone with him. My father's man, Mace, was attacking from the hall. He took out the man's companions and stabbed the man himself."

"But he was knocked out," added another lady. "Anything could have happened."

Balyra turned on the small group. "Anyone who suggests or even insinuates anything of the kind is just being deliberately malicious. And I can promise you, Salera, even if Caelerys were sent home in disgrace, it would not help *your* chances in the slightest."

Liliwyn set a hand on Cae's arm. "No one is saying anything about ruin. You have proven what we were saying just the other day about being able to defend one's own honour and life. And you did so admirably. We can only hope we'd hold up to such horrors half as well."

Cae smiled gratefully. "Some of you have more spine than you display. One never knows what one will do until tested. I confess I am still a little shaken when I think about it. The man had murder in his eyes. My ruination was the last thing on his mind."

"It does beg the question, though," came the voice of Balaran from behind them. He stepped out from the cover of a tall, flowering bush. "Was his intent murder or ruin?"

Cae shuddered. "There is no way to know. Unless the man who was captured talks."

"That, I am afraid, is going to be difficult, seeing as he is dead."

Cae's exclaimed "What?" was chorused by various other exclamations in the same vein.

"Sir Wren said nothing about him being grievously injured," she insisted, feeling the cold pit in her stomach rearing its frigid head.

"Sadly, he wasn't. Nonetheless, he was found dead in his cell less than half an hour ago. My lady, would you take a walk with me?"

She accepted his hand and rose, bobbing a polite curtsey on her way up. "With pleasure, Your Highness."

There were envious expressions from some of the women, and

SHIFT: Stag's Heart

pleased ones from others. Lady Lucelle winked at her. Cae could not help blushing as she excused herself from the princess's company and turned away from the group. They had not gotten very far when Balaran leaned to her. "So, with pleasure or relief, my lady?" he asked with a grin.

She smiled. "Both actually." She glanced at Pansy who was following them a few paces back and saw Tempest running after them. She sighed. "Well come on," she called, as if to an errant puppy. "Pansy, would you give us a private distance, please?"

She curtseyed and stopped, "Of course, my lady." She waited there until they were far enough away to be out of earshot but not line of sight.

"She could just be sent away altogether," he suggested.

"Oh no, Your Highness. Your mother's orders I'm afraid," she grinned.

"Oh." He then set her hand upon his arm and settled in for a more proper promenade. "I wanted to rescue you and ask my own questions," he said. "Which is why I took you away from my sister."

"It is just as well, Your Highness, as I needed to speak with you also."

"On?" he asked.

She glanced up at him with absolute mischief in her eyes. "Can you meet me tonight? Somewhere discreet. I would not have what I am going to show you seen but we must, as I have so recently been reminded, make certain there will be no questions of my... virtue."

His smile was devilish. "Why, Lady Caelerys, I would never have thought it of you."

She gave him a sidelong glare. "If you do not wish to see what I have discovered..." she shrugged casually.

"Oh, I am interested. To what does it pertain?"

"I need two things."

"Name them."

"A place outside, again, where what I show you will not be observed, and the book."

He paused, "Which book?"

"The one I loaned you. Some place high would be best, where if we are seen it will be from below and not above."

"And you will not tell me what we are about?"

She shook her head. "I have heard the mice in this place gather more than mere crumbs," she grinned. "Let us just say, you are the person I think who will appreciate it most."

"I am flattered."

She blushed. "I... I consider you a friend. Someone with whom I have a common interest."

He placed his free hand to his chest in mock pain. "Ah, you wound me, my lady. Am I so succinctly excised from your consideration?"

"Don't be," she said, glancing up at him. "That is the first thing I want in any man, especially a husband, if that is your fear. It is not a bad thing, to befriend one's wife. Though please do not take that as a request for a proposal. I would not so presume. Just don't..." she sighed. "I should give up while I am ahead. I seem to have a knack for putting my foot in my mouth," she blushed.

He gave a soft chuckle as he set his hand on hers. "Tell me honestly, if you were told you could marry either of us you chose, which would you take and why?"

She studied his face for a moment, realizing he genuinely wanted the answer. It was not a mere test. "Right now? I do not know. I care for both of you, but for very different reasons. I could be happy in either direction, I think. You? I love spending time with you. We have common interests, and you are so light hearted and full of life you are a joy to be around. No matter where I am wed, I hope you will always be my friend."

"I think I can make that promise, my lady. And my brother?"

"He is... a conundrum. He sparks something... when he's... near."

"Something I do not?"

"It is akin to fear, so yes, it is something you do not. But it also feels inexorable. He is to be king, but I could care less for all that. What my father chooses is what my father chooses, but for my own choice? If I were to choose him it would not matter if he were still a Captain of the City Watch, and honestly, I would prefer it thus. But I want what is best for him and the kingdom and I understand duty. I think I might be coming to understand him and that frightens me even more."

"But if he frightens you why would you chose him?"

She gave him a long look, trying to understand it herself. "I... I'm not afraid he would harm me. Not really. I mean, at first... he was so cold and actually rude to me and I didn't know why, but I am beginning to think I do. And I think the fear I feel around him is his own."

He gave an abrupt laugh. "My brother? Afraid?"

"Oh yes," she breathed. "I am certain of it, ...now. He fears himself." This silenced him. "I would be happy, I think, with you. But I believe your brother needs me more. He needs someone. And if I cannot find someone better fit... and I am looking."

His eyes bored into her. "Mother said you understood more than you were aware of."

She blushed, turning away from his gaze. "Many insinuations have been made of my virtues, Your Highness, and I still have yet to see any of it. But Your Highness had questions?"

He sighed, continued their walk. "How about while we are in private, you dispense with the 'Your Highnesses?' Just call me Bal, or Balaran."

"How terribly informal of you," she said, trying not to grin.

"I do try."

"What do you wish to ask?"

"Oh, only what you didn't tell them."

She looked at him. "What do you mean?"

"There was something in the way you told your story to the ladies that tells me you left some things out. You were editing even as you spoke. I would know the rest."

She became a little pensive. "I have already begun to doubt what I thought I saw."

"Which was?"

"How much do you know of Shifts?"

He stopped, turned her to look at him. "More than I want to admit, less than I want. Do you think the bearsarker was a Shift?"

"That is not all I think. But perhaps these theories should be saved for tonight."

"A private audience after dark with an unmarried Maral lady," he teased. "Oh, how will I survive the scandal?"

"We shall not be alone," she said.

He glanced back to the trailing Pansy who was walking companionably with Tempest.

"Oh, not her," Cae said. "I will bring Fern with me. I know her and I trust my secrets with her. She will serve chaperone and tell no one what we discussed other than perhaps astronomy."

"Astronomy?" he exclaimed. "Well, I happen to know where we can find a telescope and the perfect place to use it."

"Perfect. When and where shall I meet you?"

"Outside the library after supper."

"I will be there. At some point I really need to speak with the queen. I must thank her for her hospitality."

"You can tell her tonight at supper."

"Is that an invitation?" she asked.

"That is a royal request, which in layman speak is an order," he answered stuffily. Cae giggled.

"Is my brother to attend as well?" she asked, almost hoping the answer was no.

"Well I have been told he must wait until tomorrow before he can wander far from his apartments. So no. Of course, tomorrow, we shall probably be setting the cat among the pigeons when he is allowed to sit in the gardens."

She frowned, "Are the ladies to gather there tomorrow as well?"

Ruefully, he nodded.

"Oh, then absolutely. Though it might provide relief for some of you."

He chuckled, "It might. Providing he does not pursue the wrong pigeon."

She cocked an eyebrow at him. "Oh? Have you an eye on specific prey?"

"I might," he said evasively.

"Am I so succinctly excised from your consideration?" she asked, turning the tables neatly.

He threw back his head and laughed, pausing to draw her hand from his arm and kissing it firmly. "No, Caelerys, you are never far from my mind, but you have given me food for thought, speaking of 'who needs me more'. Fear not, fair lady. I would bow to Northern custom and take a second wife before I allow you to be married off to a Kaladen swine."

Her eyes glittered at that. "You... you saw that? At the ball?"

His grin was almost predatory. "And have already heard that he has asked for you." He set her hand back upon his arm and resume their stroll. "My brother may be slated to become king, but he will need help. I shall not be my father and content to live out my life well outside of the court and know next to nothing should tragedy strike. I fully intend to be Valan's eyes and ears, to make sure he has all the tools necessary at his disposal."

"I was under the impression you two did not get along," she replied.

"That is more of late." He shrugged, "He is still my brother. And even if I came to hate him, which I might if he does not treat you as you deserve, but I will still be the only one he can truly trust with anything. He's my twin. I am everything he is not, and he is everything I am not. Together, we are a whole man. Hopefully, a better one that we are separately."

She smiled. "You are filled with philosophy today, Bal," she said, liking the feel of his name in her mouth.

"Oh, I am always filled with such nonsense," he chuckled. "But now I fear I must give you back to my sister, or she will pout and maybe slip frogs into my teapot again."

She laughed as he had intended, even as she realized they had come full circle and returned to the pavilioned terrace. He seated her with a flourish in an empty place near if not right next to his sister and bowed to all present. "If you ladies will excuse me, I needs must retrieve something from the copyists," he said, catching her eye deliberately.

She gave him a knowing nod, and tried to pick up the threads of the conversation that had been in progress.

Once most of the ladies had departed for the day, Caelerys returned to her rooms to seek out Coral. She was surprised to find the women in the dressing chamber, unpacking a trunk full of her things. Cae had barely made it across the sitting room when Fern came out of the room, tutting like an old hen. "I can't believe I let you leave home without these," she said, carrying Cae's white leather bracers. "That poor bird has probably worn her talons to the nub following you like a dog."

Cae laughed, drawing the woman into a hug. "It is good to have you back, Fern. Are you doing all right?"

She drew herself up. "Aside from being mortified at myself for neglecting you as I have? I am as right as you are, my lady." She began to slide the bracers on her arm and lacing them up. "I'll have your shoulder pad out as soon as I find it. Fennel had inadequate help packing. And before you ask, I've had my fill of pampering. Too much more rest and I'll start to be getting ideas above my station."

Cae smiled. "When you would much prefer a certain red-head from the lower floors?"

The woman blushed. "We'll not be chatting that subject here, if you don't mind? Oh, my word," she breathed. "I'm starting to sound like lady Petra! I told you all that cosseting was no good for me," she exclaimed, tightening the laces.

"I am relieved to be in familiar hands. I only hope there isn't any friction?" she asked pointedly.

Fern glanced back into the room where the others were still working. "Oh, I think we'll be fine. We all have a little learning to do."

"I have a meeting after supper with Prince Balaran," she said quietly. "Only you are to attend."

"Oh?" she asked, glancing up at her with suspicious curiosity.

"Nothing untoward. That's what you are to prevent. But I trust your discretion more with what will amount to family secrets."

"But you'll share them with His Highness?" she asked warily.

"He can help me with the matter. Janem already knows most of this, and Will... well, Will isn't here and it isn't quite his sort of thing. You'll see."

As she tied off the last bracer, Sorrel came into the room holding the leather shoulder pad. "Is this what we're looking for, Fern?" she asked.

"Yes," she exclaimed, taking it from her and showing her how to put it on their lady. Cae stood, quietly amused as she served dressmaker's dummy, and Tempest waited patiently on the floor. The moment they were done she began squawking to be picked up.

Cae bent, offering her wrist. Tempest was barely on the bracers than she was walking all the way up to the shoulder pad where she settled. She immediately began preening her mistress, fussing with a stray lock of hair, getting it out of her way and generally running her beak lovingly along her temple. "I love you, too, my Jelma."

Sorrel bobbed a curtsey. "Your pardon, my lady but... I thought her name was Tempest. Yet I've heard you often call her Jelma."

Cae smiled. "Jelma is the old Vermian word for storm, i.e., a tempest."

"Oh. She not only understands you speaking Elanthian but the old Vermian as well?"

"Mostly. She understands me more than others, though," she added. "Do you remember the book I had Coral put away for safekeeping?"

"Small thing, 'bout yea big?" she asked, holding her hands at roughly the right size.

"Yes."

"Oh, aye. Will my lady be wanting it now?"

"No. Make sure it is put in Fern's keeping as soon as possible." The woman bobbed a curtsey and dashed back into the dressing room.

Fern looked at her in askance.

"Remember the book Jan gave me?"

She nodded.

She lowered her voice. "I need you to find a very safe place for it. I will be supping with the royal family tonight." The girl's eyes lit up with excitement for her lady, but she held her silence. "Afterwards, I need you to meet me at the library door with that book. Keep it closed and the front cover held against your body."

"Why? Is it something forbidden?"

She shook her head. "I don't want to take any chances of ...something. You will understand tonight. Just don't make a big deal of it. It is 'merely sentimental'."

"Yes, my lady."

"Good. I shall leave you to deal with my things and make note of anything missing of any significance. Did they bring the comb?"

"Aye. Already locked in the jewel box with your other treasures. Coral gave me the key. Thought you might be more comfortable if I had control of it."

"She is a wise woman. I am going to go to the library to do what research I can before supper. I know you want to supervise this, so I'll take Pansy. Once you've got things settled to your satisfaction, you can take her place if you'd like," she smiled.

Fern looked back at the quartet in a whirlwind of taking things out and putting them away again. "It will be nice to have help, my lady. Though I do not begrudge the work at all. While I might chaff at Coral being senior and all, she knows how to serve at court and I think I need to learn all I can from her. I hope eventually to not need her, but..." she shrugged. "Whatever is best for you is best for me."

Cae smiled, gave her shoulder a squeeze. "How I have missed you, Pansy?"

The girl appeared from the bedchamber holding a nightdress. "Aye, my lady?" When Cae merely nodded to the gown in askance, she looked down what was in her hands. "Oh, would my lady like to wear one of her own gowns this evening or continue wearing the one the queen gifted you?"

This made Cae pause. "Gifted? These clothes are not on loan?"

She shook her head brightly. "Oh, no. The queen said to provide for you, and that anything you liked, you were to keep, even if you leave the Citadel."

Cae was struck by the generosity. "I... well.... I think I shall wear the one I wore last night then, thank you. You can put that one away. I will be going to the library momentarily and would like you to accompany me."

"Of course, my lady."

"And could you ask Coral to come see me, please?"

"Right away!" she called, disappearing back into the bedchamber.

"Fern, do you know how much spending money father has given me and how to access it?"

"Aye, my lady. What have you in mind?"

At that moment Coral strode up with Pansy in tow. "You asked to see me, Lady Caelerys?"

"Yes. I wish to order a gift for the queen, a small broach or pendant. Fern knows the financial matters left to me. I would like it very much if such a thing can be arranged."

Coral brightened. "Of course it can, my lady. Do you wish to pick the piece out yourself or designate one of us to do so?"

She smiled. "Actually, I would like to order it from Master Daph. A small, rose-gold bat with onyx eyes. Make sure that he knows it will be for the queen and that I am the one ordering it. He apparently has a very good working relationship with my brother Janem."

"I will see to it, personally. My lady, where would you like your bow and quiver stored?"

"It was brought?" she asked, suddenly relieved. "Oh, good. Somewhere close at hand, by the bed perhaps."

"Very good," she said as she curtseyed and turned to attend to it.

With a final nod, Cae left them to it and headed for the library with Pansy.

Cae was brought to the dining room for supper having spent the last three hours in fruitless search. She had gotten lost at least once, and had to be rescued by a worm.

Supper was not quite a repeat of the previous meal, as this time, in addition to Lady Liliwyn, Duke Griff and his lady wife were present and Prince Janniston was absent. This meal was more formal and conversation a little more structured. Cae was relieved when it was over.

Pansy was waiting for her, just outside the dining room, to lead her back to her chambers, but Cae asked to return to the library.

"Of course, my lady, but isn't it a bit late? You'll have to read by candlelight and the worms are particular about reading lights."

"It is not too late for what I need to do."

Fern was waiting patiently when they arrived.

Cae turned to the other girl. "Pansy, you may go now. Go get your own supper. Fern will not leave my side, I promise you. As for getting me to bed, she will handle the necessaries, so the rest of you may retire as well. Just leave a lamp burning in the sitting room for us."

A little confused, Pansy went away, pleased to be getting to eat early when she expected to sup late.

Fern handed her the book the moment the girl had gone. The pair of them waited in silence for Balaran, who arrived some little while later carrying the incensewood box that held her own tome.

"Evening, ladies," he grinned wolfishly. "Shall we hie away?" he gestured them off.

They moved through a great number of hallways, some of which were better lit than others; finally ending at a narrow stair on an upper floor. Both women were totally turned around as to where they were. The prince led them up a very long, winding staircase that had few windows and no doors until the top. There he handed Fern the lamp he had carried, and pulled an iron key from his pocket.

The door opened into a round workroom, in what was very clearly a tower. There was a table along one wall and another in the centre of the room which was heavily scarred. There were only two shabby stools and no other furnishings. Dust spiders danced in the corners in the wind of the opening door.

Cae looked the room over in the dim light of the lamp which he set on the table next to the book. "This won't do, Balaran," she said, disappointed. "We need to be under the open sky for this. There aren't even any windows."

He merely grinned. "Patience, Caelerys. Please, have a little faith."

If Fern thought their use of proper names without honorifics out of place or improper, she kept it to herself.

The prince crossed to a corner, brushing away the dustwebs impatiently, searching the ceiling for something. With a crowed, "Aha!" he dragged a stool over and climbed up on it, wedging his knife-blade into a crevice she had not seen. He levered into part of the ceiling and grinned as a hatch swung open and a folding ladder slid down.

"Very well, I will grant you a modicum of faith," she conceded, smiling as golden moonlight spilled through the opening.

Fern followed him up the ladder, stopping halfway up as Cae passed her first the lamp, then the book-box to hand up to the prince. Once the three of them were on the flat, crenelated roof, he closed the trapdoor behind them.

The tower was just over a dozen feet across and was overlooked only by a single spire several hundred feet away. There were marks on the green stones at several places, where a telescope once stood, but other than that the roof was bare but for the now folded ladder. The prince set the box across the rungs, adjusting it until it was stable.

"Welcome to the old astronomy tower. I am sorry I cannot offer you ladies a seat, but... I really did not have the time to clean up and provide," he grinned.

"Why was this place abandoned?" she asked.

He made a face. "Because my aunt was a staunch Believer, and the Eldest frowns upon the practice."

She shook her head, looking up to the sky in wonder. "How can he disapprove of such beauty?" she breathed.

His laughing eyes settled onto her upturned face, bathed in the golden light of the waning Southern moon. "Now, why are we here?"

She smiled, slowly uncovering the book in her hands. She looked down at the cover and saw thin lines of gold lettering that only half formed old Vermian words. Eagerly, she opened the book to the page she had seen before, marked by a few drops of dried blood. She frowned, looking down at it. The silvery script she had seen before was not there. Instead there were other words, also oddly spaced, in gold. "I... I don't understand," she breathed. "This isn't... the same."

His eyes caught the glimmer on the page and he looked over her shoulder, blocking the light from the page. The lettering vanished. "Wait, I saw something a moment ago..." he insisted.

She looked up at the moon, then down on the page. She reached out and gently pushed him back even as she took a step back herself and the writing was once more visible as the light fell upon it. "It's the moonlight," she gasped. "It was silver last night, because the window of my room faces East and was filled by the Eastern Moon. This is gold because only the Southern Moon is up yet!"

She laughed. "I'll bet that my window here faces South. That was what my brother meant!"

"But what does this mean?" he asked, as she handed him the book.

"It means, there lies hidden the secret of moonsilver as my brother found it. Hidden beneath secrets in a fading language." She turned to the book-box and knelt on the floor beside the ladder and pulling the book onto her lap.

She flipped immediately to the story of Isildar and Denan, to the full two page illustration. There were glimmers of half written words and things which made little sense. The image itself had subtle highlights, like the heraldic marks upon armour and shield. It showed her things she had never noticed before. Fern watched it all with wondrous eyes and held her silence.

The prince, meanwhile was flipping through the book in amazement. "This is marvellous, but... half of it makes no sense. Unless I'm mistranslating?"

"I... I don't think you are," Cae said. "I think we need to wait for the Eastern Lady."

He met her eyes over the books. "So, you only see the gold by the southern and silver by the east and both when under both? But how... that's what I want to know. How do you make an ink that is visible only under certain lights?"

"Maybe the hidden text will tell us. But this also means that this book is an original," she said, tapping her own tome. "Your copy is not going to be quite the same."

"Mores the pity."

"How long do you think until the Eastern Lady rises?" she asked.

Fern's voice came from the side of the battlements. "I'd say half an hour, maybe a whole, before she's high enough to read by."

They looked to where she was standing and saw the rising crescent of silver on the horizon. Cae secured the book and got up, crossing to watch with her. They became aware of the prince standing behind them.

While they waited, she looked up at the stars above them. "You know, I think I would like very much to actually see these stars through a telescope."

"I will have to find it, but I agree," the prince said.

Spread below them, lit here and there by flickering dim candles and rippling torchlight and braziers, the city was a wonder, glowing softly beneath the gilding moon. If she listened hard, she thought she could almost hear the ringing of Janem's forge on the wind.

Eventually, the moon rose high enough to shine over the edges of the battlements and Bal pulled the book out again. He turned it so that only the silver light touched it, and the silvery lettering glittered on the page. He tilted it so that the light of both shone upon it and both flared to life. She stood close to him so they both could read at once. There were notes written both between black inked lines and in the margins; diagrams drawn over the whole. Some made what was written in black make more complete sense. The current pages spoke of metallurgy and alloys and processes.

Cae turned and went to the book on the ladder, turned back to the illustration which now fairly glowed in the light. "Oh, Bal... you've got to see this."

SHIFT: Stag's Heart

He crossed to her, looking over her shoulder, caught a glimpse of the image and went to his knees beside her. "So that's what it's for," he breathed.

"Right?" she whispered, running a feather-light finger over the gleaming breastplate on the stag figure of Isildar's father. "You can't see the armour in normal light."

"Look, Lord Maral here as a man and here as the stag, the armour is still there. It changes with the body."

She sank back on her heels. "When the bull-man was shifting..." she began. "It looked like his hands were stretching the gauntlets. If they had been moonsilver..."

"They'd have shifted with him?"

"Maybe," she said. She began to look over the other figures in the images. "Look, almost everyone has something moonsilver except Prince Denan."

"Maybe the Alvermian..." He stopped cold, leaning closer. "Look... the badger's crest."

"House Brock. ...A badger. And here, Pardet, a horse... The crests..."

"Maybe Alvermian is too big?" he breathed. "That's why we don't have any."

"Isildar's collar when she's a doe is moonsilver, too, for all it looks iron by other light."

"Perhaps putting it on her while shifted prevents the change?" he guessed.

"That may be poetic license."

He shook his head, "I can't disagree with that. But this is still... revealing. I'm... going to be losing a lot of sleep," he sighed.

"You and me both."

He gave her a long look. "It will not be good for your reputation to be coming up here at all hours with me, maid or not."

It was her turn to sigh. "No, it will not. Nor is it safe to read these anywhere we can be observed. Perhaps if it were known I am spending time in the library..."

"You could read in your sitting room, my lady," Fern offered. "It has a window."

She shook her head. "I'll only get the Southern Lord there. For some of this I'll need both. And we both can't have possession of the book."

The prince rolled off his knees and leaned back against the folded ladder, thinking. "If I have a key made... a copy of this tower key," he began. "And we left the book up here, we could take it in turns. We'll just have to be certain that if one of us is up here, the other is very obviously observed elsewhere."

"And what, leave notes on what we've found?" she asked. "Will that be any safer?"

"For the time being, I have the only key. If I have your brother make the spare, then we can be sure there isn't a third copy running about."

"Either way I'll still be vanishing at all hours of the night," she sighed, sitting back on her heels.

"Library? If you are seen burning the midnight oil on whatever you are researching for Valan... then every other night or so disappearing into the stacks..."

"Do you know a secret way out of the library other than the front door?" she asked.

"I might," he said, thinking rapidly. "If we arrange it carefully... find a way to get you up here unseen, have your maid remain in the library? Maybe that bird of yours. No one will think you are not up there somewhere if she's about. I may even be able to convince a worm or two to help."

She looked doubtful. "The less people involved..."

"Yes, but Ward I trust. Squeek, maybe, but not immediately." He picked up Jan's book again, flipped back to the beginning as he made himself comfortable. "Give me a day or so. I'll see what I can find out. I still have a secret or two up my sleeve. For now, let us take an hour or two and read what we can."

She nodded, turning back to reacquainting herself with the book she had known since childhood.

In the end, it was well past midnight when she found her way to bed. Even Tempest was too sleepy to chastise her much. Her dreams were full of gleaming silver and the smiling faces of the moons.

13

Days had passed before Balaran sent her word that he had found something. Her days had been divided between the gardens with the princess and her ladies and the library trying to find what she could on the moons. She suspected her nights would be more fruitful on that subject, as she spent those at her sitting room window, re-reading what she could of the faery tale book.

She was seated on the terrace between the princess and Liliwyn, embroidering a pale green undergown as they talked, watching her brother milk his injury for all it was worth. She was highly amused at the following he had attracted. He flattered them at every turn, while somehow getting them to pamper him. She smiled. Vyncet was everything Willam was not around women.

"He is so unlike Lord Willam," the princess sighed, as if reading her thoughts.

"Not a bad thing," she commented. "He knows how to get want he wants, his only problem is that he hasn't decided what that is yet. Willam... Will knows what he wants and what he is going to have and understands they may not be the same thing. He's as braced as I on the matter of marriage. Better to not get your hopes up," she sighed. "Fall in love if you can after."

"Has there been any word?" Syera asked.

Cae knew she meant from Will. She shook her head. "But no worse news."

Liliwyn picked up a fallen skein of thread for her. "My brother has sent word that there have been a few skirmishes. They've been informed of the sinking of the Harvest shipment. I'm sure father will be tightening security on the grain caravans which should be leaving home next week. There should be a good herd of Planting foals as well. Might be fun to go to the horse market that week."

"If they let me leave the Citadel," Cae sighed. "I haven't even been allowed to go riding."

"Mayhap I can do something about that?" said Balaran, appearing behind their bench between her and Lili.

Syera jumped. She reached over to swat at him. "Will you stop doing that?"

"Doing what?" he complained innocently.

"Eavesdropping for one," she growled.

"I really can't," he shrugged. "It's practice. Anyway, I was thinking I could take the three of you for a ride tomorrow?"

"I know I would love it," Cae sighed.

"I would love to go," said Lili.

The princess seemed to be trying to decide whether or not to be mollified. "Maybe."

"Lady Liliwyn," he said, leaning forward over the back of the bench, "would you grant me a walk?"

She smiled shyly, and rose, curtseyed to excuse herself as he came around to take her arm. He bowed himself and started to walk away with her, then stopped as if suddenly remembering something. He turned back. "Oh, and Lady Caelerys, I want to thank you for your recommendation of that historical treatise we discussed last Fourth Day. May I return the favour?"

"You are most welcome and of course, Your Highness," she said, hiding her confusion.

"When you are in the library this evening, ask one of the worms to show you the volumes of Waller. I think you will find his grasp of the language exceptional and educational."

"I will, thank you," she bowed, suddenly understanding.

Several of the ladies looked at her in askance as the prince walked off. Some of them suspiciously, but Lucelle was always looking for a romantic angle. As soon as the prince was out of earshot she asked with suggestive excitement, "And what was that about?"

Cae shook her head, paying attention to her sewing. "Nothing, really. We've crossed paths in the library on occasion. Our reading habits merely coincide. Besides," she added, glancing after the retreating figures with a smile, "I think his eyes are turning in other directions in that regard."

Lucelle sighed wistfully, "I really do wish her well. She's had too much tragedy already."

"Both of them have," added Balyra.

"And has your Marrok sweetheart made any motions to becoming your intended?" Syera asked, knowing it would divert the topic for hours.

Lucelle was more than happy to comply.

As she chattered on, bouncing the conversation from one hoped for betrothal to another, Caelerys noticed that lady Balyra hardly participated at all, and kept glancing over to where Vynce was being fawned over by his four most recent 'nurses'.

"Tell me, lady Balyra," she asked, "do you play Castle?"

Balyra looked over at her quizzically. "Why do you ask? Do you play?"

Cae shook her head. "Oh, I am hopeless at it. Vyncet however is always in the market for a good opponent. He keeps wanting me to play, but I don't care for the game. I only learned because he was tired of playing father and forever losing," she chuckled.

Balyra smiled at that. "I am a fair hand," she finally admitted.

"Your Highness," Cae said, turning to Syera, "do you think we could have a board brought out?"

The princess caught the look in her eye and smiled. "Oh, I think it can be managed." She called over one of the waiting handmaids and sent her off for a board and a table to play it on.

"Mother says that Castle is as close to war as a proper lady should get," said Malyna. "I'm not bad," she added as everyone else turned to look at her.

The conversation dried up a little after that until the table was brought and set up among the ladies. Malyna immediately offered Balyra a game, which she lost in less than twenty moves. A couple of other women tried their hand, including the princess, but no one could really provide a challenge.

"How about you, Caelerys?" Balyra asked.

"Oh, no thank you," she said, just loud enough to carry. "Vynce says I'm absolute rubbish at it. I seriously doubt I could be more of a challenge than these noble ladies." Out of the corner of her eye, she saw that she'd had the effect she wanted: Vynce's attention. "Why don't you try my brother? I'm sure he's been dying for an opponent better than his squire."

"That boy is hopeless," he called over. "He crowns when he should consolidate and charges when he should corner," he growled.

"I do believe that to be a challenge, lady Balyra," Cae said casually. "Unless my darling brother thinks..."

"Don't finish that sentence, Cae," he snarled, grabbing up his crutches.

Balyra stood. "Please, do not get up, my lord. I will happily bring the table to you."

At that, two servants came in and picked the whole table up, game and all and carried it and a chair for her over to the bench where Vyncet had been ensconced.

Onelle and Lucelle watched the pair setting up their pieces.

"Very neatly done, Cae," Lucelle grinned.

Onelle looked slightly jealous. "Indeed. Would you happen to have any other brothers hidden away?" she added hopefully.

The others giggled at that. Cae merely smiled. "Alas, only my subsequent."

She shrugged. "There's no shame in a Master Smith."

"He is nicely put together," someone commented, which earned her frowns from the religious crowd. "Well he is."

Cae chuckled. "And he's well placed," she said. "Handsome, strong family ties, heir to a famous forge of his own and with a unique and highly in demand skill."

"There is that," Lucelle said.

"There is always that," Onelle complained. "Can't we like a man for himself? After all, that's what we want, isn't it?"

Cae sighed. "Yes, it is nice to want the man for himself and to be wanted likewise. But we are not Folk. The decisions will be made for us by men who may not take our desires into consideration. Therefore, we have to find these other reasons that make our desires acceptable. If we are clever, we can convince our fathers that the man we want is the man he needs. Alliances, money, assets, horses, land, men, ships,... I could go on forever."

"We also have to consider the other direction," Lucelle moaned. "I mean, it is clear Edler and I want each other, but will his father agree? Mine... there is no question, it is a great triumph for me and my family. The trouble will be convincing Lord Marrok that I am to be preferred over a more prominent House."

Cae thought for a moment. "If you could provide me with a list of assets your family might be willing to provide, things that would make you a good choice for them instead of, say Balyra or Onelle, who are part of the main House, I might be able to get my father to weigh in on the matter for you."

Her eyes lit up. "You would do this?"

"Why wouldn't I? If marrying you would make my father's vassal happy... it makes him a more effective vassal," she smiled.

"And if your father helps, he cements himself further into the loyalty of his vassal," Malyna added, nodding wisely. The others looked at her. "Well, it is. Edler's the heir, isn't he?"

Lucelle blushed.

"He is," Cae nodded. "There are many reasons why my father would help. We just have to give him reasons to give Lord Marrok."

Lucelle was aglow with hopeful excitement. "I'll write father immediately!"

Onelle sighed, watching her cousin chattering away, trying to think of reasons. "At least someone has some inkling of her future. What about you, Cae? Who do you think..."

Cae cut her off. "Oh, I don't want to talk about me right now. Everything is still so uncertain, with our men away."

This brought the conversation back around to the peril a good half of court was engaged in, and spirits flagged a little.

Cae remained in the gardens until dinner, when most of the ladies went their own ways. She had her own mid-day meal in her chambers and laid down for a nap, with instructions to be awakened for supper. If she was going to be up late hours, she needed to rest while she could.

She was awakened near dusk by the smell of food. Entering the sitting room, she found her supper being placed upon the table. The servant who was delivering it stood aside for the taster, and bowed to her when she came in the room. "The queen requests your pardon, my lady, but the family are supping separately tonight. The king has matters to attend."

"It is quite all right," she said, smiling, and trying very hard not to watch the taster at work. "Please send her my regards."

The man bowed again and left. Cae had no real choice but to look at the man sipping from her goblet and trying to discern any additives. It was a very real aspect of court life, and one she wished was unnecessary. But with people like the Asparadanes within the castle, she could not trust that they would not try something. She had an extensive knowledge of herbs and their flavours, which ones were toxic and in what doses. She had even taken pains to know which you could not mix without deadly results, so that she did not accidentally feed sages to a person who was taking beeslippers for their heart.

A thought struck her.

"Excuse me," she said to the taster, "but,... is it uncommon for someone to slip something into the food to make them ill? Or poisons which act only if mixed with something else?"

"The first is not common, my lady, but it has been known to happen. The other... I have never heard of it. Why do you ask?"

She gave him a long look. "There is more harm to be done to a person's food than kill. Things that you have just told me someone could add and no one would be the wiser."

"That is a terrifying thought, my lady," said Coral in a quiet voice.

"It is, isn't it?" she said. Cae turned back to the taster. "You might do yourself a great service by learning what these herbs are and what they taste like. And how their flavours can be disguised. It would make your services even more valuable than they currently are. Services for which I wish to thank you. I abhor putting someone else's life at risk to protect my own."

He bowed deeply. "If anyone wishes to harm you through your plate or cup, they will go first through me, my lady. I am feeling quite well, thank you, and the food is excellent. Though you may find the carrots to be a bit over salted. I have tasted the wine and the water as well. Please, enjoy your meal in good health." With that, he bowed out of the room before she could even ask his name.

Under his advisement she only took the smallest bite of the carrots and agreed with him, leaving them upon the plate. Everything else was to her liking.

As soon as she had finished the meal, she picked up the book in its box and headed for the library with Fern in tow. If any of the other ladies felt slighted at not being chosen to go with her, it was balanced by their relief at not having to stay up the extremely odd hours their lady was beginning to keep.

Once in the library, she found Ward quickly enough and asked him where to find Waller. He grinned and led her deep into the stacks on the third floor where he just left her with no further word. She found that odd, but began to search the shelves for the books by Waller. She had not been looking long when Fern stifled a yelp. She turned and saw her standing there, hand over her mouth now trying not to laugh as the prince peered around the edge of a bookcase that should not have been where it was. "No one ever really reads Waller," he grinned.

She set the book she had been glancing at back on the shelf and followed him behind the bookcase. He had a small lamp placed upon a shelf on the wall, and he showed her the mechanism for opening the hidden door. "Here, you pull it closed. Make sure you can."

She stepped up and pulled the handle towards her. The case resisted a little at first, but came easily otherwise. He showed her how to open and close the door from both sides. "Make sure you always check first, to be certain you are not seen," he added.

He reached up and collected the light. "Set the lamp here when you leave. If it's not there I will assume you are in the tower and go elsewhere." He began to lead them down a narrow passage.

"How did you find this place?"

"Oh, every serious castle has at least one. Usually just a siege tunnel, maybe a place to hide valuables."

"Taluscliff has a cavern below the castle to hide the women and children, as well as a hidden cove," she answered.

"See?"

She rolled her eyes. "Again, how did you find it?"

"Lots of exploration and experimentation with my cousins," he laughed. "We stumbled on part of them when we were kids. I'd found this one once, but it took me a little while to remember where it was. If you thought the Citadel's main halls were confusing? You best be careful in here. Naeden, Val and I found a skeleton in here."

Fern gave a tiny gasp. Cae studied him, trying to figure out if he was pulling her leg or not. It was entirely possible he wasn't.

He pointed out a chalk mark on the wall about a foot from the floor. "I've marked the path here. Horizontal line means keep going. Arrow line on the top means a left turn, on the bottom of the line it means turn right."

"And a vertical line through the middle?" she asked, pointing out one at the edge of a turn off.

"Don't go down there for any reason," he said seriously. "Either those passages are used, or are unsafe, or lead somewhere equally dangerous."

"These passages are used?" she asked.

He shrugged. "Some of them. There are only a handful of very trusted servants who know the secrets. Those would be passages of most use to them."

"Are there any of these that enter my chambers?" she asked warily.

He thought about that for a moment. "Maybe. I know of one in my rooms. I would imagine that all the royal apartments would have at least one that can be locked or blocked from the room, in case of invasion."

She shuddered at that thought. "If only Stag's Hall had been big enough to have something like that," she sighed.

A great distance and two staircases later, Bal paused at a section of the hall and held the lamp behind his back. He pulled a peg out of the wall and put his eye to the hole. Satisfied, he replaced the plug and held the lamp up over the door. He showed her the mechanism to do so, let her open it to make certain she could do this on her own.

Like the library passage, it resisted at first, but finally gave. He frowned at the noise. "Going to have to mend that," he mumbled, stepping into a narrow hallway.

Cae recognized it immediately as the end of the passage that led to the tower stair. She closed the passage behind Fern and looked it over, figured out how to open it from this side.

When they finally reached the astronomy tower, she noticed that he had been hard at work up here. The room was clean. There were stacks of paper and ink and quills for taking notes. A pair of bookends were on the table against the wall, and a cord had been added to the ladder, to make access easier. The upper level had recently been furnished with a reading table with a simple but still comfortable chair and reading weights.

He watched her as she took all of it in, pleased with her reaction.

"Only one chair?" she asked pointedly.

He grinned sheepishly. "Well, technically, we are not to both be here together. Not until I find that telescope. Your maid should more wisely wait in the library, in warmth and comfort. That way, if need be, she can come and 'fetch' you, claiming you were deep in the stacks."

"Aren't we clever," she smiled. "You know I'm going to search my rooms for a passage, don't you?"

"I would have thought less of you if you didn't," he laughed and pulled out the chair for her. "I've taken the liberty of making space to store the books in the room below. They'll be safe and we don't have to carry them around, putting them at risk."

"What about your copy?" she asked as she opened the book on the table.

He shrugged. "It will wait. It wouldn't be this volume at any rate, not the important parts, until we can find the key to this marvellous ink." He pulled Jan's book out of his doublet and settled himself down against the wall to read.

"Hoping to find it in those pages?" she grinned.

He just smiled and angled himself to get the best light.

14

Several weeks of this went by. Days were spent in the gardens or on one highly escorted event or another. Nights were spent alternately in the library or the astronomy tower. Their books of notes slowly grew. And Cae would frequently walk past the library windows with old Vermian books, hoping to find a spark. Either the books she was looking through were not old enough or not important enough for hidden script.

One rainy day, they were ensconced in the princess's sitting room. Even Tempest sat in the windowsill, looking morosely out at the rain. When the wind shifted, and the rain began to blow into the room, she gave a shrill cry and pulled the shutter mostly closed. She shook herself dry and put her eye to the opening.

The conversation was almost non-existent. Most of them were

engaged in sewing of some form or another, though Balyra, Onelle and Lucelle were playing cards with Duchess Griff, whilst the Eldest contingent pointedly ignored them. None of the remaining male courtiers had bothered to come, having found other occupations for a rainy day.

Cae was about to ask Lady Liliwyn something when Tempest shrieked and shoved the window open again, then jumped out of it.

She dropped her sewing and ran to the window to call her back and pull the shutter to, but stopped, seeing something in the grey light moving through the streets outside the Citadel wall. She ignored the rain slowly dampening her hair and sleeves, finding the flash of barred white hanging in the sky and flying a little lopsidedly towards the streets. Whatever it was, was beginning to draw a crowd in spite of the rain, and what were possibly cheers began to filter upward. She felt an unexplained, building excitement.

"Close the window, Caelerys!" Malyna complained, as she was sitting closest and beginning to feel spatters.

Cae ignored her and the questions of the other girls coming up behind her. She had seen Tempest circle then suddenly stoop into the street. Her heart soared with joy as she focused and finally saw the bedraggled pennants. "They're back!" she shouted, turning from the window. "The men are back!"

She ran from the room, heedless of the rain still coming in the forgotten window. Without thinking about her comportment, she ran towards the apartment at the end of the hall with the two guards standing outside it, yelling, "Your Majesty! They're back!"

She came to a halt before the guards, did not even try to get past them. "Please let her majesty know! The army has returned!"

One of them entered the room even as Cae was headed for the sweeping staircase. The queen appeared in the doorway behind her just as she reached the head of it.

"Where did you see them?" she called.

"They're coming up the hill!"

Cae was barely aware of the others on the stair behind her, trying vainly to keep up. She would have run out into the courtyard and out of the citadel to meet them, but the guards at the door stopped her. She repeated her news, but they still did not let her pass. They opened the doors only when the queen approached.

The queen placed a gentle hand on Cae's shoulder, whispered, "Contain yourself, my dear. They will be here soon enough."

She tried to restrain herself, even as she gasped, "Oh, never soon enough, Your Majesty!"

The gathering in the doorway grew as they waited. The atrium filled with a quiet, but excited murmuring not unlike the day of the coronation.

It was nearly impossible to hold back, but Cae managed until she heard the hooves on the gate planking. She took a step, stopped, scanning the figures parading through the gateway. The prince rode up front, of course, flanked by his two commanders. Her heart skipped a beat seeing him, but when she saw the bird sitting on the shoulder of his left hand commander she could no longer hold herself back. She ran out into the rain, heedless of what it would do to her blue linen gown.

Will barely had time to get off his horse before she flew into his arms, not caring that he was still in his armour. Tempest flew into the open door to dry off, her task done.

"One piece?" she asked as he held her up.

"More or less," he chuckled. "I would like to get out of the rain before I rust, though."

She let him put her down even as grooms ran out to take the horses. "And are you going in before your men are seen to?"

"Of course not."

"Then neither am I."

"Stubborn..." he began.

"Yes, you are." she answered flatly.

He sighed, drawing her off to the side and standing with his arm around her shoulders. His men separated out from the host and gathered behind him, as did all the others who had gone with them.

"Where's uncle?" she asked, not seeing him or any of the Free Legions.

"Headed to the Reach. They did not come back with us. He is hale and hearty, worry not."

They waited for the prince to dismount and finally climb the steps to the doorway to bow to the king standing in the light of the citadel's atrium.

"Well, did we win?" asked the king.

"We have, Your Majesty," he said formally. "There are matters to discuss, but first the men must be seen to."

"Of course," the king nodded.

"I will want to feast these men tomorrow, father. They've earned it."

"Tomorrow."

Valan bowed again, turned, his helmet tucked under his arm. "My lords, see to your men and your families, and your own immediate health. I would have the lords Griff, Maral, Cygent, Marrok, Roshan, Asparadane and Selkan return as soon as possible for a briefing."

With that, he dismissed the troops and turned to greet his own family, bending to kiss his mother and his sister.

Will started to lead them out of the gates towards Stag Hall, but Cae pulled him back. "Will, there is something you do not know about."

He looked down at her. "Can't it wait until we get home?"

"No, it can't," she insisted. "Because ...I can't go home. I've... been moved in here," she said gesturing back at the citadel. "I was brought here until you returned. The hall is empty but for the servants. Even Vynce is here."

"Why?" There was growing violence in his eyes, fuelled by worry.

"Send them to the Hall, and come inside. We'll get you dry and clean and then we can talk."

She could hear him grinding his teeth as he turned back to his second. "You heard her, take everyone to the Hall and have them seen to. No doubt Fennel has heard of our arrival and is preparing a feast. Make sure everyone is taken care of. I'll come by when I have found out what is going on and am free to do so."

The man nodded, and filed out of the citadel with the rest of the troops eager to get home.

Without another word, she lead him and his squire into the citadel and up to Vyncet's room. Vynce was not there yet, but Marko was, polishing his master's boots. Cae began issuing orders immediately. "Marko, help Harlan get Will out of his armour and see to it." She gestured to the man servant who entered from the dressing room when he heard voices. "Please have a bath drawn for Lord Willam immediately. I will bring him clothes shortly."

She turned back to the squires as the man left to put the order in for hot water. "Harlan, as soon as he is out of that, I want you out of those wet clothes and dried off. Marko, do you have anything that will fit him?"

Marko glanced over at the other boy, gauging how much taller and broader he was. "My shirts might fit him, but my trews an't gonna."

She nodded. "I'll see if someone can find something that will. You'll do Will no good if you catch your death, young man," she insisted when Harlan tried to protest that he should be the one to take care of the armour.

"Sister," Will said firmly.

She looked up. "Brother?" she mocked.

"You, too."

"Me too what?" she frowned.

"Get dry."

She looked down at herself, suddenly realizing that she was just as wet as they were, and laughed. "Yes, I think I shall. I'll send Fern with dry clothes for you."

"Why would you have my clothes here?" he asked.

"I made you new ones."

He rolled his eyes.

"Well, new shirt and trews, at least. I'm sure Vynce can loan you a jerkin or tabard. I will need to see you when you are done, before you go to the prince's meeting."

"I will not have much time."

"You will have more than you think," she said, heading for the door. "Everyone else has to go all the way home and all the way back."

In the hall, she found Tempest patiently waiting outside her own door. She smiled, opening it for her to discover a bath being readied for her as well. Fern looked up as she came in, drew her towards the dressing room and the waiting water. "The moment you ran out of the princess's apartments I came here to get this ready."

"It is as if you know me," she teased.

"Not at all, my lady," she said without a trace of the apparent sarcasm. "In you go."

In short order, she was bathed, dried and dressed and Will was in her sitting room as she sat with her back to the fireplace drying her hair.

The shirt and trews fit him well enough, and the subtle embroidery at the collar and placard suited his more austere nature. The jerkin, however, was snug and accentuated as much as it covered. He pulled over a chair and sat in front of her, accepting the goblet of warmed wine Sorrel handed him. "Talk," he said.

"You first have to promise to keep your temper."

"You know I cannot do that," he said, studying the contents of the cup even as he flexed his other hand.

"Well, then, promise not to yell or act upon anything until I am done or I don't say another word."

"I could just ask Vynce," he threatened.

"Oh, that's so much better," she glared. "Promise," she insisted.

He only nodded, though with reluctance.

She eyed the goblet in his hand, was relieved that it was metal. With as little embellishment as possible, she explained what had happened while he was away. She was impressed that he restrained himself.

"The only reason I did not move in right after you left was because I could not move Vynce yet. The queen asked that morning."

"Let me see the bow."

She glanced up at one of the maids near the bedchamber door and nodded. The girl vanished and returned carrying the strung bow very carefully. Will accepted it and looked it over, testing the pull.

"You can fire this?" he asked.

"Much easier now," she said, running her fingers through her hair to let the heat reach other strands.

"So, how did it feel?"

She glanced up at him. "The bow in general or killing a man?"

He just looked at her. She sighed, closing her eyes and pulling the drier strands over her shoulder to expose the rest. "It shoots as beautifully as it looks. And... hollow, if you must know."

"Good."

She looked up again. His dark eyes glinted. "It shouldn't feel good. Not for any reason. The day it does, worry."

"Even in battle? Against someone trying to kill you?"

"Sometimes even then. You have to ask yourself why are they trying to kill you? Because someone else ordered them to? That should never feel good. For those that made the choice... exceptions can be made. But your first... that should always affect you."

"It was almost like... killing an animal," she breathed. He watched her at that, and she could see it concerned him. "Not in that it was easy, but.... I know it was necessary. Like the boar, he'd have torn me apart had I not. But... I still felt pity after." She lowered her voice. "I'll explain later, or Vynce will, in private. I don't know if killing me was what he'd come for, or if that choice was taken from him."

"He still chose to invade our house."

"And he paid for that with his life."

He was silent a long moment while he alternately studied the bow and his sister. "A powder pot? Really?"

She laughed. "Whatever works! Never underestimate a lady's arsenal."

He handed her the bow. "Leaving it strung? Even here?"

"Even here," she nodded. "Forgetting to unstring it gave me time to put my armour on. Besides, it's a new bow. It can handle it."

She rose to rehang the weapon in her room. "You should probably go, see where the prince is going to hold his meeting. I'll see you back here, after."

"It could be very late," he said.

She smiled. "I'm up late these days. Send word for me at the library when you are free."

"Library? Of course. You and books," he groaned.

"Yes, me and books," she said, shooing him out.

As she hung the bow back on its pegs beside her bed, she sighed, feeling a deep sadness she could not explain. Not feeling in the mood for dinner, she laid down upon her bed for her midday nap. Tempest took up her perch on the headboard to watch over her.

It was late when one of the worms delivered a page's message that Willam was on his way to her rooms. She thanked him and left. By now she knew the way from the library to her apartments, and needed no guide, so she was quite surprised to realize she had taken a wrong turn and ended up down one of the servant's corridors. She stopped, about to turn around and backtrack, when she heard a sound around the corner. It came again, a dull thud and a grunt of pain and restraint.

Hesitant, she padded, nearly silent, to the corner and peeked.

Near the end of the hall, bathed in the light of the Southern Lord from a narrow window, was the crown prince. He was leaning forward, his forehead pressed to the cold green stone, a look of pain and concentration on his face. Once more he raised his fist and punched the wall.

Cae nearly turned again and fled, but something drew her forward. Terrified she was making a mistake, she tread carefully, walked slowly as if approaching an animal whose temperament was in doubt. When he raised his fist again to strike the wall, she gently placed her hand over it. She felt the tension in it, the Something Other rippling beneath the corded muscle that stopped the forward motion before he crushed her hand against the stone.

His words came out through his teeth. "Not wise, my lady."

She kept her voice soft, but did not release him. "Neither is your punishment of the wall, my prince. Whatever its crime may be, you are the only one feeling the brunt."

His head turned slightly, and she saw the nameless other peering from behind his deeply flashing eyes.

Feeling bold, she slid her hand off his knuckles and more to the side of his hand, applied gentle pressure towards her. He only resisted for a second, then allowed her to draw him out of the moonlight as she took a step back. She could not bring herself to break the contact. "Better?" she whispered.

His head now off the wall, he looked at her from beneath his wild locks that appeared nearly platinum in the golden light. He did not answer her, but he did not take his eyes off hers. Hesitantly, she reached her hand out to his face, still moving with frightened slowness, brushing the ragged tendrils behind his ear and her fingertips lightly across his brow and temple, smoothing away the tension. Only then did his eyes close and his breathing settle.

Beginning to feel she had dared too much, she started to withdraw, but his hand seized hers in a fierce grip. "It writhes within," he whispered.

"I... I can see it, my prince. Let it sleep. Let it sleep," she crooned softly.

"If only it would," he growled, drawing her hand back to his face, pressing it to his cheek and taking a deep breath of her wrist. "Honey and leather," he sighed. "Why do my dreams smell of honey and leather?"

"My prince?" she asked, confused. She was beginning to feel shivers in places she knew she should not allow.

"Always," he went on, eyes still closed, breathing deeply of her. "Whether they begin in fire and flight and blood, they always end in honey and leather." They snapped open suddenly, stared into hers and drew her close, pressing his cheek hard against hers and smelling the hollow below her ear. A shiver chased its way down her spine. "You are no dream, my lady," he whispered. "And I should not be alone with you ever again."

"My prince?" she asked again, feeling the tinge of fear returning.

He released her face and buried his fingers in the length of her still unbound hair. "Go, maiden," he said more firmly. "Go while I am still in control."

"I... I cannot. You still have hold of me," she said softly.

"Like chains," he said, drawing his hands away, still tangled in her tresses. "Raw silk."

"You... you need to rest, Your Highness."

This time he seemed to realize where he was and what he was doing. He abruptly untangled himself and walked away without a word, leaving her standing in the hall breathing heavily and frightened for no reason she could understand. She did not move until a servant happened upon her a few moments later, and seemed surprised to find her standing there.

"My lady?" he asked. "Are you lost?"

"Yes," she said too quickly. She took a breath to calm herself. "Yes, I am sorry. I thought I knew the way. I am on the guest floor."

"I will be happy to show you the way," he said. "May I ask what you were staring at? You seem so... frightened."

"Oh, I was... I thought I saw... something that wasn't there of course. Please, my brother is waiting for me."

By the time he had brought her to the room, she had gotten herself enough under control that she did not send up any further alarms in her brother.

He did not seem happy, standing staring into her fireplace with a goblet.

"How did it go?" she asked.

He shook his head. "Well and not well."

She frowned, pouring herself a cup of the wine. "Did you catch them?"

"Most," he sighed. "We rescued the survivors. Most are on the ships being returned to the village. Father is going to retire some of his castle garrison and scatter them throughout the affected villages to help should this happen again."

"Who were they?"

He shrugged. "Raiders. None wore Kaladen colours if that is what you are asking. Just whatever rags they could get hold of. Typical pirate raiders," he spat. "We didn't take any alive. Well, we did, but they died of the 'sleeping dagger sickness'," he snarled.

"Sleeping dagger..." she began, then understood. "Who? Who would do that?"

"That we also did not discover. One of them had a small knife on him. It has been suggested he slit their throats and then his own, but I have my doubts."

"But no proof?"

"Aye."

"Well, are you going to the Hall tonight or bunking with Vynce?" she asked, holding up the ewer to offer more wine.

"Vynce. Hall in the morning," he said, holding out his cup for a refill. She obliged. "You are to stay here until further notice."

"What?" she growled, setting the ewer down.

He shook his head. "Queen's insistence. And it puts you in a better position anyway. I want to see to the security of the Hall first, regardless,"

He drained half of the cup in one swallow.

"You look exhausted. We can talk tomorrow."

"Yes, we will talk tomorrow. There is to be a feast tomorrow night."

"I know," she said, taking his wine glass and guiding him towards the door. "I was there."

"I want you at my side," he insisted, though he allowed himself to be ushered out and down the hall.

"I will be there if I am allowed."

He stared at her, taking in her raw beauty and the flush at her cheeks which had little to do with the wine. "You will be. I want you looking like a Maral," he said. "Not whatever lady Petra has been trying to turn you into. I need the Lady of the House."

"Well, if you ask our brothers, I've pretty much already managed that." She opened the door and called for Harlan. "Put this man to bed," she ordered when he appeared. She then pushed her brother into the room and left him to the tender mercies of his squire.

Cae returned to her own chambers and sat at the window, watching the rain washed night. Her sitting room was just high enough to afford her a view over the Citadel and city walls. The Mistwood rose on the far side of the Desiter, tall and majestic and mysterious. Mists curled out of the wood and crept across the fields like a living thing in the moonlight, and she could almost imagine it a dragon as it flowed and billowed.

Before she even climbed into the bed and closed her eyes, she knew what her dreams would hold, and she was not wrong.

15

Cae was up by dawn, let Tempest out to stretch her wings. She knew that Will would be headed to the hall very soon, and intended to go with him. If any of the ladies showed up this morning, all they would be talking about would be the feast and what they would wear, etc. Cae just wasn't in the mood to deal with it.

When she entered her dressing room, her maids were already laying out a simple day gown for her. Rosie curtseyed as she came in. "Your brother left a message this morning," she began. "He said that he would be back after dinner to talk to you before the feast."

Cae sighed. "He's left already?"

Rosie nodded. "I am sorry, my lady. He was most adamant. You were to stay here."

Cae resigned herself to being subjected to the small court which had gathered around the princess. "Is that not rather plain for dancing court upon the princess today?"

Sorrel shook her head. "Oh, no one is paying court today, my lady."

She looked over at the maid. "Truly?" When she nodded, she breathed a sigh of relief. "Oh, wonderful. I can put together my report for his highness, then."

"Report?" she asked, confused as she helped her into the smoky grey daygown.

"Research he asked me to do for him. Nothing to worry about. I just have to go get my notes."

As soon as she was dressed and simply coiffed, Caelerys and Fern headed for the astronomy tower using the main hallways. The upper hall was rarely used, so no one saw her head up the narrow stair. She did not go up onto the tower roof, but gathered her collection of notes on the moons and their influences. They returned to her apartments as soon as she had them. They did not have to speak with anyone on the way, as everyone they saw were servants hurrying about on errands to prepare for the feast.

Hours later, she was finishing up her document when there was a knock at her door. Sorrel answered it, returning immediately to Cae's side to whisper hurriedly with wide eyes, "The prince is at the door, my lady. Asking an audience."

"And you left him in the hall?" She shooed her off, "Admit him at once!"

"He insisted on waiting," she explained, even as she rushed back to open the door with a deep bow.

Cae stood, prepared to greet Balaran with some smart remark about standing on ceremony, when Valan was escorted inside. She sank immediately into a deep curtsey, blushing even as she sank.

"Rise, my lady," he said.

She obeyed, crossing the room and standing awkwardly, not sure what was the proper etiquette. "How may I serve, Your Majesty?"

The smile was in his eyes even if not on his lips. "These are your apartments, my lady. Here it is I who pay court."

She felt her blush grow more heated and offered him a seat near the fire. "Please, be comfortable, Your Highness. And while these may be my apartments, 'tis your house and hospitality I am enjoying."

Aware of mutual awkwardness, they sat together, and Coral entered with an offer of refreshments. To her surprise, he accepted an offer of tea. There was a flurry of activity as maids were set to acquire, and Fern seated herself against the wall and took out her mending.

"To what do I owe this honour?" she asked.

"How very direct," he said with a half smile.

She took a breath, convinced her blush could not get any redder. "As I have been reminded very recently, I am a Maral. But if you wish to observe courtly niceties?" she asked.

He took pity on her. "First allow me to offer my condolences and admiration. I have heard why you are here."

"Oh," she said quietly, looking down at her hands. "I... thank you."

"Are you well?"

"I took no injury, fortunately, Your Highness. Unlike some of my house. Your mother's gift served me well."

His smile was genuine. "Ah, yes. I am glad it found service somewhere. Unfortunately, I never took to the weapon. I am glad it is not gathering dust."

Her breath caught in her throat as she looked up at him. "That was... *your* bow?"

"I thought mother told you."

"She said only that the original intended had lost interest."

He laughed softly. "And so I did. I was really only interested so far as knowing how to fight against an archer. Dare I suggest that, were you in possession of that bow for the tourney, the outcome might have been very different?"

"Oh, I cannot say that I would have beaten Mester Hayle, but yes, I would have shot better, I think. At least, I would like to think I would have." She paused as the maids brought in the tea and Cae served, taking the first sip before offering him the cup.

He watched her, but said nothing.

"And how did Your Highness fare on the excursion?" she asked. His eyes darkened at that. "You do not have to discuss it, if you do not wish to," she added hastily. "I... merely meant that you were injured when you rode out, and I wondered if you were better or were further harmed. My brother has not had the chance to tell me much."

"What has he told you?" he asked, a little frostily.

She sipped her own tea to regain her composure. "Not much. Only that you were successful, and that the surviving villagers are on their way home, and that those you captured alive were... disposed of before they could talk."

The anger in his eyes at that was not at her, and his chill manner warmed. "Aye. I, too, suspect that too convenient. No, my lady," he said. "I was not further injured. I am fully healed. Lord Rorik took further injury, however. We lost a few men, but not many."

"Did you get them all?" she asked.

"I do not know about the ships. There may have been one that slipped our nets, but none of those ashore escaped."

He set his empty cup down. "Before I left, I asked a favour of you," he began. "Have you had the opportunity to comply?"

She smiled, looked over at Fern who was already fetching the papers from her writing table. She curtseyed as she handed them to Caelerys. "Thank you, Fern." She passed the thin bundle to the prince. "There you go, Your Highness. Everything I was able to find so far. I only hope it is what you need."

His brow arched as he accepted it. "And do you yet know what that may be?"

She hesitated. "I am beginning to think I do."

His gaze was unwavering. "And are you afraid?"

"Oh, my prince," she sighed, "I am afraid of everything. But I back down from nothing."

There was a spark behind his eyes. "Even when you are wrong?" he asked.

She laughed, "Oh, if I am in the wrong, that is another matter entire. I can admit to mistakes. I make far too many of them not to; but, if something must be done... no, no matter how unpleasant."

"Like taking on a bearsarker with only a bow."

This time the secrets were behind her own eyes as she looked at him pointedly. "Your Highness should read my report. It will tell you, perhaps, more on many subjects. And after... if my prince has any questions... he might ask them one afternoon in the gardens," she said obliquely.

He looked down at the paper in his hand, then glanced back up at her. "And am I likely to have questions?"

"Oh, most certainly. A lady must be circumspect in her letters, lest they are read by her enemies. And as your brother once warned me, the mice here gather more than crumbs."

His expression was unreadable. Then he rose and held out his hand to her. She stood, curtseyed even as she set her fingertips upon his. He bowed over their hands, his eyes never leaving hers. "I shall look forward to it then. If you will excuse me, I believe I have some reading to do?"

"Of course, Your Highness," she said, curtseying again. Pansy slipped around the edges of the room behind him to open the door for him.

Once the door closed on his back, Cae sank back into her chair with her hand pressed to her rapidly beating heart.

"My lady, are you all right?" Pansy asked.

"Oh, I'll be fine, Pansy dear," she breathed. "I... I am just shocked at myself is all."

"Well," she said, fanning Cae with a kerchief, "you just had the crown prince in your apartments for a little chat like it was nothing, my lady. I dare say you're getting the hang of things just fine," she smiled.

Cae laughed at that. "I suppose I did. I guess if I can handle that I can handle dealing with the bevy of ladies at the feast tonight," she sighed.

Coral crossed the room to gather the tea things. "Oh, there will not be many other ladies present, my lady," she said. "Only the Great Ladies will be there with their husbands. The feast is more for the men who fought."

She frowned. "Then why am I going?"

Fern set her hand on her shoulder. "Because there is no Duchess Maral, my lady."

"Oh."

When Willam finally came to fetch her, Cae was already dressed in her blue velvet coronation gown and having her hair pinned. She had him admitted to her dressing room and looked him over in the small mirror. He was wearing his new clothes beneath his own knee-length vest and cote. His hair was a little longer than she remembered it, but it still curled stubbornly from the nape of his neck. "Any news?" she asked.

"Nothing was taken from my chambers, if that is what you are asking," he said, crossing his arms over his chest and drawing himself up. He looked every inch the Maral Lord. "A few things broken, but nothing irreplaceable. Everyone is doing well, and they miss you. Even Mace is his old self."

She watched him a moment. "So what happened while you were out there?" she asked.

"What do you mean?"

"Prince Valan was here today." This caught his attention. "And when I asked how he had fared, he grew cold, as if I'd insulted him. He wanted to know what you'd told me but you hadn't, so he calmed down. I want to know what happened."

"You aren't going to leave this alone, are you?" he said flatly, meeting her steady gaze.

"No, I'm not. I need to know so I don't make any more blunders."

It took him a moment to form his answer. "We were ambushed one night."

"How?"

"Probably the same way they snuck up on entire villages and took them wholesale," he growled. "I don't know how. But... the prince froze."

"How do you mean?" she asked, feeling something cold in her gut.

"I mean he froze. Well, it looked more like he was in pain. It might have been his injury, it might not. For all I know, he was blinded when the moon came out from behind a cloud. What matters is that he was not prepared to fight the man who nearly killed him."

Her eyes grew wide.

"You think I have a temper?" he said, moving to the other side of the room to look her in the face instead of through the glass. "Imagine mine and father's and Vyncet's all crammed into this jar," he said, holding up her new talc pot. "Only don't let it out. That's what's boiling inside that man. And he has better control than I do. Mother help this kingdom if he ever loses his grip on it."

"You... you think he's a bearsarker?"

He shrugged. "Maybe. If so, he's never let go. I don't think he could stop if he did."

"I thought you knew him. Why didn't you tell me this before?"

"Because I never fought with him before. Not like this. He killed one man and then froze, fighting it, I think. If it weren't for Rorik, we'd have been bringing home a royal corpse."

Cae lost feeling in her fingers for a moment, forgot to breathe.

Will set his hand on her shoulder as Fern slid the moonsilver comb into place in her hair. "We survive, sister."

She set her hand on his, feeling the small golden signet ring on his little finger. She took a deep breath and let it out. It would not do for her to show over much attention or concern for anyone outside the family right now. Finally, she nodded, opening her eyes and allowed him to lead her down to dinner.

The ballroom had been converted to a dining hall. The doors were closed and braziers burned in the corners. A long table had been set up where the state chairs had stood the night of the ball, and the walls were lined with trestle tables two rows deep, to accommodate the hundred men. A smaller table capped the head of each of these for the heads of the Lordly and Noble Houses who attended to sit with their wives and their men. The centre was kept clear for what entertainment there might eventually be.

Each person was escorted to their places at the table by servants, and the two of them were led to the head table on the dais. Duke and Duchess Griff were there, with Lord Rorik, seated to the immediate right of the royal family's place. To the left of the five state chairs, was a place set for Duke Cygent and his duchess. Caelerys and Willam were shown to the last two chairs to the left of the throne. It wasn't until the Cygents were seated and Liliwyn was not with them that she realized the order of precedence had been altered slightly. While she understood why she was here and Lili was not, and that Rorik had as much right here as Will, even though his parents were present as head of house, what confused her was that Rorik was seated closest to the royal chairs, instead of upon the end as he should have been. He had been placed above his father and the duke did not seem upset by the slight. In fact, pride shone on his ruddy face. Perhaps it was just because he was the one who fought and saved the prince's life, she told herself.

The fighting host was completely seated and sending up a dull roar of chatter when trumpets announced the entrance of the royal family. Everyone fell silent and stood, bowing or curtseying as appropriate. The king and queen took the centre places, Valan beside his father and Balaran beside the queen. Syera was seated beside Valan, placing her next to Lord Rorik. From the look on her face, she was as confused as Cae about the matter, though she hid it well.

The king then gestured everyone to sit whilst he remained on his feet. Servants flooded the room filling goblets.

Cae watched the parade, and noticed a dozen servants in slightly better Alvermian livery watching the servers like hawks, each one watching those closest to them. She surmised it was to watch for anyone slipping something into the drink.

Once the servants had stepped back to the walls, their ewers in hand, the king raised his goblet and everyone followed. "Here I give a toast to those brave men, and women," he added, nodding to the three females in soldier's clothing among the Marroks that Cae had not noticed before, "who went out to assist the kingdom in its hour of need. The people are our life's blood, high and low. A drink to our fallen, fighting and Folk. A drink to the rescuers and the rescued. A toast to the Free Legionnaires not now with us who gave of their arms for whatever their reasons. To one and all, I salute!"

There was a shout throughout the hall that would have completely deafened Cae had she not added her voice to the throng. It was a trick she had learned years ago, that noises were not nearly so loud if you were adding to them. Everyone drank.

SHIFT: Stag's Heart

When the king sat, more servants filed out of every available entrance carrying platters of food.

"I was supposed to go on that last hunt," she whispered to Will.

"Really?"

She nodded, "The Master of the Hunt invited me to the provisioning hunt."

"Why didn't you go?"

She sighed. "The queen said there was a safety issue. Too many knew I'd been asked. He's promised that the next opportunity I could go with him if I was willing to go in disguise," she smiled.

"And the queen?" he asked, glancing over at the monarch.

"She hasn't said no," she shrugged.

When a nearly whole boar of massive size was placed in front of the king, she felt a chill. Will chuckled. "Maybe it is just as well you did not go."

She elbowed him for that, but he laughed it off.

The meal was several courses, and Cae ate sparingly of each, as Will warned her. There was a great deal of conversation in the hall, at all of the tables, and the lower ranks were thrilled to be eating at a royal banquet with their betters. Entertainment was provided, though not as great as the Lord Mendicant, but the tumblers and troubadours were well received.

The whole evening reminded Cae a little of the entertainments at home during the bigger suppers for vassals. And she was enjoying herself until she realized that the troubadour was singing a song of her battle with the bearsarker. She blushed furiously as others began to realize it, too, and look up at her. She buried her face in her hands for a moment, peeked out enough to see the Marrok twins at their lower table both grinning like madmen and raising their cups to her. She shot them a warning glance which made them laugh, ducking their heads as if frightened, amusing their table even further. She did catch smiles and raised cups from the three women at the table and nodded to them.

When she thought she felt more royal eyes upon her, she blushed deeper and concentrated upon her plate.

Once the sweet course had been swept away, other servants appeared with ewers of wine and ale. The king stood again and all eyes fell upon him. Once the observers against the walls had seen that every glass was filled, they nodded to the king and he raised his goblet once more. "There were many moments of valour and bravery in the past weeks. But one stands closest to home and my heart and I wish it to be recognized."

Cae leaned forward to be able to see. Balaran and Syera waited with mild curiosity. Valan and the queen both stared straight ahead, goblets tightly in hand. Of all of them, only they and the Griffs seemed to know what to expect. Lord Rorik had an eager look in his eye, his grip on his chalice firm.

The king continued. "At a crucial moment during an ambush, Lord Rorik Griff, heir to House Griff, saved the life of my son and heir, the Crown Prince Valan Alvermian. He took a near grievous wound, ignoring danger to his own person, in order to block a blow to my son's unprotected back."

Beside her, she felt Will tense, but his face showed no response. She glanced back to the king, saw Syera turning a grateful smile to the man seated beside her.

"Without him I would be without a son and the burden of the impending crown would have been passed to his brother, as even as mine came to me. So, it is with great pleasure and relief that I offer to you," he said, turning to Rorik, "the hand of my only daughter, Princess Syera, in marriage, if you will accept."

Syera's smile froze and all colour left her face. Lord Rorik rose amid the cheers of the feasters and bowed, first to the king then to the princess. "How could I refuse such a rare flower? Will the maid be so kind as to accept my undying devotion?" he asked, lifting her cold hand to his lips, but holding off until she gave the barest nod.

The shouts of the room were deafening and all drank to the health of the couple. Cae put on her best smile, and lifted her brother's goblet with her own, pushing against him in order to nudge him discreetly. "Look happy, brother," she whispered. "Our enemies are watching."

He glanced up, plastering a fake smile upon his face as he caught sight of Mambyn Asparadane observing him from across the room. He drained the cup and called for more. Cae asked the servant to bring him ale instead. She kept at him for the rest of the feast, keeping him from drinking too much but poking him to keep up the façade. The end of the night could not come soon enough, and not just for House Maral. Prince Valan never once looked at his sister though she sat beside him. He glanced at Cae only once before his own departure.

After he left, the queen took the stunned Syera and drew her away. The princess paused and turned back. "Lady Caelerys, will you please join us?" she asked. There was pleading in her eyes and Cae was torn between her friend and her brother.

Finally, Cae nodded. "With your permission, I'll be along in one moment, Your Highness."

The queen nodded and drew her daughter off, leaving orders with a servant where to bring Caelerys when she was ready.

Cae went down to the lower tables, and bent between the Marrok twins. "My lords, I have a favour to ask."

"Anything for my lady," replied one.

"Lady Maral in all but name," grinned the other.

She lowered her voice to carry only between the pair of them. "My brother needs tending and I am called with the queen. Would you see him to his room or home, one? Some place his tongue will not need to be guarded."

They looked over her shoulder at their lord and nodded to each other, beginning to understand. "No one must suspect," she began.

"And no one will," said Edler as the other rose and headed with exaggerated drunkenness to the end of the head table.

"Lord Willam," said Reled, placing a hand on Will's shoulder to steady himself. "My brother and I have just gotten a cask of Wolfshead Ale, and we've been arguing over the quality."

His brother joined him, managing to get Will to his feet between them without seeming to be forcing the issue. "I don't think it's as good as last year's, but he insists it's the best it's ever been. Better even than old Barley's."

Cae, feeling relieved, followed the servant to the room where the princess and the queen had gone. It was not far away, a private and very comfortable retiring chamber for ladies who needed to catch their breath during long events like tonight. Syera was on the floor with her head on her mother's lap crying her eyes out. Cae crossed to her, heedless of etiquette and left the servant to close the door behind her. She sank to the floor beside her and set a hand on her back.

Syera turned to her, angry and in pain. "I thought you said he loved me!"

Cae's heart felt like it was breaking for her friend. "Oh, ketava, he cares very deeply. You have no idea how much he is hurting right now. It was all I could do to help him hide the fact. I warned you to guard your heart. Though it was unkindly done, him knowing and you all unaware," she said, glaring up at the queen, no longer caring that she was the monarch.

The queen's face was serene, but full of her daughter's pain. "It was how her father wished it, and I could not dissuade him." She sighed, tipped her daughter's face up to look at her, drying her eyes with the corner of her veil. "Oh, Syera, my joy. This is how it has to be."

"That I'm just a trinket? A trophy or chattel to be awarded to the man who saves my brother's life? Couldn't he have been given lands or horses?"

The queen kissed her forehead. "He is already heir to the wealthiest and highest title in the land next to the crown. What more can he give him but his most precious? And he asked. He had already offered for your hand before this. Sadly, it is politics."

"I hate politics!" she sobbed. "I don't think I can love him."

"Do you dislike him?" Cae asked softly.

"No, but... I ... I love... elsewhere," she said, refusing to say his name.

"He is not so bad. And I think he genuinely cares for you," Cae offered.

She turned a savage look on her mother. "How is he a good match for this family?" she challenged. "He is a widower with grown children and his own heirs. When he dies before me, his son will become Lord

Griff and I'll be left a dowager likely before I see twenty. Never mind what will happen to my children. Is father going to force him to make our children take precedence over his older issue? Because I won't have that. It's not fair to them or to me, to subject me to the resentment and hatred that will turn on me and mine."

She gave her daughter a soft smile, stroking her hair with one hand, even as she still held her chin in her other. "There is too much at stake. And this opens the rest of your siblings to more advantageous positions. The Mother knows best. I have looked, child," she said firmly when Syera was about to say something scathing. "Truly. I have prayed for you and this... and all its unpleasantness, ...this is the only way. Yes, this road will bring you to grief, but," she added, placing a finger on the girl's open mouth, "it is also the only road that will lead you to true happiness. You must have faith, my daughter. And take strength in the joys of others."

"And fake my own?" she sobbed.

"If needs must. He does love you."

A servant knocked on the door, entered when the queen called. "Your Majesty, the king requests your presence."

Queen Sigrun sighed, kissing her daughter once more before rising. She gave Cae a significant look and a nod before taking her leave.

The moment the door was closed again, Syera fell into Cae's arms, sobbing into her shoulder. Cae enveloped her in a crushing hug, knowing instinctively it was what was needed. It only lasted a few moments before Syera sat back, drying her face on a kerchief.

Cae just sat there beside her, waiting.

Syera reached out and dabbed her kerchief on Cae's shoulder, blotting at the damp velvet. "I'm sorry about that."

Cae shook her head, dismissing the thought and then laughed. "It just occurred to me, Your Highness. I have become your lady in waiting."

Syera frowned. "You are not my servant."

She shook her head, "No, you have handmaids for that. But here I am, waiting upon your needs. To see if you need another hug, or more time to cry." She reached out to adjust a hair pin that had gone askew. "And to make sure you are presentable."

The princess laughed at that. "I would rather you were just my friend. If you were my lady in waiting I would be able to resent you."

Cae frowned. "Why? Why would you want to?"

She sniffed, "Because in the back of my mind I know you are the reason I'm being given to House Griff."

Cae was dumbfounded. "What?"

"Oh, I know you had no hand in it, not directly," she sighed, beginning to pull herself together again. "But... I think they mean you for my brother. And if that is the case, I cannot marry into the same House. It would be bad politics." She shrugged, "Plus, they'll get more from you than they will for me." She took in her friend's shocked face. "You were the one who said to look at it from their side. What are we but pieces in an elaborate game of Castle?"

She set her hand on Syera's. "We are so much more than that, and you know it."

She shook her head. "Not until we are wed, we aren't. You were fortunate to remain a duke's daughter. You have more choice. I wish you the best. I will see my friends happy even if I am not to be." She shrugged again, smiled. "Who knows, maybe after I have given him a child or two I can take a lover. Provided the Eldest hasn't wiped out the practice by then."

"Stuff the Eldest in his brothers' hind ends," Cae growled.

This made Syera gasp in shock and devolve into giggles. Cae was not too far behind her. "Um... I didn't intend to say that out loud," she blushed.

"I'll have to remember that one. If I ever need it," she giggled. "Brothers?"

"Uncle," Cae replied, shaking her head. "One of his more... polite moments."

"I'd hate to hear it raw."

"Turn your ears blue." Cae laughed as the princess touched her ears to check. "Listen," she said, getting serious. "Your mother said this will make you stronger and promised you happiness in the end."

"She also promised grief."

"Yes, well, women are made for grief. We weather in silence pain that would bring men to their knees," she said. She stood, helped Syera to her feet. "I trust your mother."

"She has never been wrong," Syera replied. "Except when she tries to explain. She misreads things sometimes. And sometimes really bad things happen to those who do what she tells them," she added, thinking. "But never to those she says will be happy in the end. If she says it will be for the best, it usually is. I don't have to like it, but I can pretend to."

Cae took her arm in her own. "Why don't we take a page from my brother's book and head to your room, then drink ourselves into a stupor."

Syera thought about that, her free hand on her hip. "You know, I think Bal has a distilled spirit that is guaranteed to make one incredibly silly before passing out to sleep like the dead."

"Think he'll give us some?"

She humphed, began to head for the door. "I know where he keeps it."

16

Caelerys woke late the next morning in the princess's bed, with what felt like Janem's forge ringing in her head. She looked over at the princess, still sleeping beside her, her golden hair spilled out over the pillow. Cae reached up and fingered her own dark locks. They were not loose, but neither were they in the coif they had been when she had come to the princess's room. Cautiously she opened the bed-curtain. Light pierced through her eye straight to her brain and she was struck from behind by a pillow. "Close it, you cow!" Syera growled into another pillow.

Instead, Cae slipped out of the bed and closed the curtain behind her. She was in her underdress and the room was far too bright. She found the water pitcher without too much difficulty, and splashed her face. It did not help, so she filled a cup with the water and drank it. That did, though slowly. Groaning, she crossed to the window and pulled the curtains closed. She refilled the cup and went around to Syera's side of the bed. Opening the curtains, she tugged at the pillow.

"Come on, drink this, Sai," she said as softly as she could. "It'll help, promise."

The princess rolled over, peeked at her from under the pillow. "Caelerys?"

"Yes?"

"...Did I just call you a cow?"

She smiled. "Yes, you did."

Syera sat up, pinching the bridge of her nose. "Ow... I'm... I'm sorry. I thought you were Daia." She accepted the cup from her and sipped hesitantly.

"Daia?"

"Maid," she groaned.

"Why would you call her a cow?"

She sighed, drinking the rest of the water. "Because opening the curtains like that would have been deliberate. You saw the way she was looking at us last night."

"I honestly don't remember," Cae shrugged. "Everything's a little hazy."

Syera squinted at her. "What did you do to your hair?"

Cae's hands went up, felt the wild array of braids going every which way. "I didn't do this," she frowned. "I can't braid at all."

The princess held up a handful of her own, loose waves. "Obviously. You braided mine last night."

"Why were we playing with our hair?" she asked, leaning against the mattress.

"I don't even remember."

They were interrupted by the bedchamber door opening wide, spilling in more painful light from the outer room. A maid came in carrying a tray which she set upon a table and threw the curtains open again. "Good afternoon, Your Highness, my lady," she said. She had a clipped voice that grated on Cae's ears. "Your royal brother stopped by this morning with breakfast and a message."

Syera ducked back into the safety of the bed curtains. "What message?"

"It's on the tray with your breakfast. I am afraid it is cold by now, Your Highness," came the voice. "Lady Caelerys, I have taken the liberty of informing your own ladies of your location."

The two of them did not move until they heard the door close. "Is she gone?" Syera asked.

Cae peeked. "Yes."

"Please, close those curtains," she groaned, flopping back over onto the bed.

Shielding herself the best she could, Cae managed to get them closed again, blocking out the light. "Is she always that mean?"

"No," she mumbled from her pillow. "She's being nice today because you are here."

"Why haven't you asked for a replacement?" Cae asked, shocked. "Her attitude is appalling."

"She's been like that ever since I refused to go to the chapel with her that first Fourth Day."

Cae moved over to the tray to look over what was on offer. "Oh, one of the Eldest's," she groaned.

The tray contained two cups of some foul smelling juice cocktail, four slices of stale toast and a few pieces of a candied spice root. Those, at least, Cae could identify and ate one. It was spicy, almost too hot, but it soothed the stomach.

"So what does the brute say?"

Cae picked up the note, even as she heard her friend stirring herself out of the bed. "He says 'hold your nose and drink it down, quick as you can. Eat everything. Drink lots of water. There is a reason I hide that bottle'."

The curtain was batted aside angrily. "Why that annoying, cheeky... warthog!"

Cae grinned. "Getting better. You're still too afraid to really offend," she chuckled, picking up one of the glasses.

She sniffed it, nearly gagged on the conglomeration of smells that just did not mingle well. Some of them she recognized. A taste of it told her that there was waterwood bark ground in it. "Oh, this is going to be bitter," she groaned. She raised the glass to the princess in a toast, held her breath and chugged it down.

When the glass was empty, she dropped it onto the tray and doubled over, trying desperately to keep it down. "Oh, Sweet Chimera..." she gasped.

"Poison?" Syera asked, rushing over.

"I wish," she groaned, managed to reach up and grab another of the spice candies, swallowing it whole. "Go on, get it over with," she advised. "Eat one of those after, it'll help."

Syera obeyed, quickly joining her on the floor. Together they sat against the wall, slowly drinking as much water as they could stand as they waited until their heads and stomachs stopped trying to revolt. They even managed to choke down the cold toast.

"There is one thing to look forward to about married life though," Cae said.

"Oh, and what might that be?" Syera growled.

"You'll get an entirely new set of handmaids."

This finally made Syera laugh.

Hearing life from within the bedchamber, Daia entered followed by three other women. She headed back to the window but Syera's voice called her up short. "If you touch those curtains one more time before I wish them opened, you will find yourself on a narrow raft in the middle of the Sinecar."

The woman sniffed with disapproval, but left the window alone. A pair of baths were brought in and filled, and both of them sank gratefully into them. When Cae refused scented oils in her water, Syera asked her, "Why don't you like perfumes? I've heard you even asked for plain talc for your dressing table."

Cae shrugged, sinking a little deeper into the water. "I've never liked them. I don't know why. They smell... artificial I guess. If you put the herbs or flowers in my bath water, I'm all right with it, but I don't like the changes when they're distilled. Too mediciny? Also, if you are going to hunt an animal, it is best to smell like its environment. I'll sometimes rub myself and my horse with fragrant branches I find in the areas we're hunting in. It helps to not warn them you're coming."

"Never thought of it like that. Is that why father's dogs like to roll in unpleasant smells?"

"Could very well be," she mused.

When they climbed out of the baths, Cae found Fern and Pansy had joined the princess's ladies in the adjoining dressing room with a gown for her. The two women were dressed and brushed whilst they chatted.

"I guess this is what it must be like to have a sister," Cae sighed.

Syera smiled. "I wouldn't know, but I'd like to think so. I think you and Lili will be the ones I'll miss most when I leave here."

"We'll just have to come visit."

When they finally headed downstairs to the gardens, Cae took the opportunity to ask her something she had been meaning to, but wouldn't in the presence of her unfriendly maids. "Last night, you said that they mean me for your brother. What did you mean?"

The princess sighed softly. "I'm sorry I said that. You really aren't supposed to know yet. I told you a long time ago that mother had her eye on you. I am certain she means you and Lili both for my brothers. Father is suddenly resisting for some reason, but mother is steadfast."

Cae digested this, even as she thanked the Mother for the overcast day. "Why is your father resisting? I thought he liked me."

"He does, but... Questions keep getting brought up. So does Malyna's name," she added softly.

"Really? I suppose her mother is the one whispering in his ear," she sighed. "I'm surprised she wasn't pushing Malyna's twin on you."

Syera shook her head. "No, marrying me puts them too far from the throne. Only by marrying Val or Bal will they get close enough." She lowered her voice again. "She's brought up you and Kaladen again, trying to convince him to force your father to mend that breach with you. Mother stopped speaking to him for days the last time he mentioned it."

"Who is that viper after? Do you know?" Cae asked.

"I think she realizes she may not get Valan. So she's pushing Lili for

Val, claiming it will mollify her family who had expected to marry the heir to the crown. And Malyna for Bal."

"He won't go for it, though," Cae mumbled, remembering a conversation with the prince in question.

"Maybe. But will he be bold enough to defy father? I don't know if Val would even if father insisted."

Cae glanced around as they neared the terrace. "How do you know all this?"

Syera smiled. "I listen. Mostly in places I shouldn't. Another reason Daia finds fault with me."

Cae laughed softly. "I have learned there is no pleasing the servants of the new god."

They did not have the opportunity to talk more as they were now in among the courtiers milling about the gardens. There were a great many more people than had been here of late, and once more, Cae felt a little shy entering into the fray. Sir Halden Trent was on a bench flirting with a giggling young lady Cae had never seen, teasing her with a flower.

"Who is that with Trent?" she asked softly.

The princess looked over, "Oh, that's Liliwyn's niece, Vieva. Kind of empty headed."

"That's rather unkind," she commented.

"So is she." The princess sighed, "And I am still feeling a little ungenerous."

"More water," Cae advised just before they were greeted by a number of people, some of whom Cae had not yet met. All in all, it was not the best time for her to be trying to remember new faces and new names.

She saw Willam and Vyncet on a path with lady Balyra. Vynce was off the crutches, using only a cane to ease his gait. Willam was looking more dour than ever.

He stiffened as the princess led Cae over to them. Bows and formal greetings exchanged, Syera requested Willam's company for a walk. Cae could feel the tension and resignation roiling off both of them as they walked off towards the overlook of the river.

The three of them watched the pair go with trepidation. "I hope he knows what he's doing," Vynce sighed.

"Don't antagonize him over it," she admonished. "This is hard enough. They are both disciplined enough. There will be no scandal."

"Yeah, but his temper is going to be shorter than ever."

"So watch your mouth," she warned.

Balyra looked from one to the other in question, but wisely said nothing.

Cae put on a smile for Balyra. "So, what has the conversation been about?"

She turned, seemed grateful for the opening. "Oh, the usual: marriage. Several offers have been made this morning, apparently. Men returning from battles have their mortality in mind, I think."

"Not uncommon," Vynce said.

"Malyna's mother refused another offer last night, or so she says. She was also livid about having been left off the guest list last night," Balyra added, glancing at Caelerys.

"Oh, she would have found it barbaric," she grinned. "Very small, backwoods court style. Tumblers, troubadours, even a trio of dancing dogs."

SHIFT: Stag's Heart

"And of course the announcement," Vynce added. "Everyone's talking about that."

"Spreads quickly," Cae said, dryly.

"The Griffs are rightly proud," Balyra said. "And proud men have very loose tongues."

Cae smiled, glad that the rather stiff Roshan heir was beginning to warm up. "I am glad the two of you have found common ground."

Balyra smiled, but Vynce grinned, elbowing his sister. "I heard you and the princess found a little common ground last night. Are you walking with her for the wedding?"

She sighed. "We haven't even discussed the wedding yet. Though I am certain everyone else has."

She felt an unwarranted tension in the air just before Tempest dropped out of the sky onto her shoulder and began scolding her. Cae laughed softly, stroking the bird and trying to soothe her. "Please, softly, Jelma. My head."

This only set the bird to complaining about her hairstyle and trying to rearrange the braids so that they did not ruffle her feathers every time Cae turned her head.

The bird finally began to settle, only fussing quietly between nuzzling her temple and ear. The tension did not leave.

The group rounded a tree and Vynce guided them towards a bench so that he might rest.

"You were told not to overdo it," Balyra admonished.

Cae smiled secretly, trying not to be too obvious about things. Her smile faded as she saw Prince Valan coming down the path, two guards trailing along behind him. They bowed as he approached, stepping out of the way.

The prince stopped in front of them. He nodded to the other two, greeting them by name and formal title. "You are healing well, Lord Vyncet?" he asked.

"So they tell me, Your Highness," he grinned. "Not fast enough, but I will live. I might even sit a horse within a fortnight."

"I am glad to hear it. Lady Balyra, your father is well?"

She curtseyed again. "Aye, Your Highness. Thank you."

He then turned to Caelerys and held out his hand. She set her fingertips upon his and he bowed over them. "If my lady would accompany me for a walk? I have questions."

She bobbed a curtsey, nodding her agreement as she could not yet bring herself to speak. He set her hand upon his arm and strode down a more fragrant, less used path. The guards hung back out of earshot, but well within reach if there were trouble.

They walked in silence for a long while before he finally spoke. "I think I like it better loose," he said.

It took her a moment to realize he meant her hair. She blushed, keeping her eyes upon the passing flowers. "I think Tempest agrees with you."

He glanced over her head at the bird. "I hear that you are well chaperoned when she is with you. Is that true?"

"Usually, yes, Your Highness."

Another moment passed as they walked, the bird and prince trading looks. "Will she protect you from me, do you think?"

She glanced up at the bird, chuffing softly to her. "If you meant me harm, I think she might. If I felt unsafe, she might warn you off. Why do you ask, Your Highness?"

"I told you the other night that I should not be alone with you ever again."

His statement was flat and almost cold.

When she answered, her voice was soft, timid. "I had begun to think Your Highness had been sleepwalking."

"In a way I was. I do not remember everything, but... things stick. And they prick."

She shivered, unsure if this was a good thing and fearing it was not. She could not explain the tension she was feeling, especially when he slowed a moment, staring off down a lower path where his sister stood with her brother. The princess was facing the water as she spoke. Will stood facing her, his whole body rigid.

"May I speak frankly, Your Highness?" she asked softly.

"I would hope that you will always speak frankly. I value truth," he said simply, looking down at her.

"I mean freely, Your Highness. Bald," she answered, not meeting his gaze. "And before you answer, please know that you may not like what I wish to say."

"I'll live."

She half smiled at that, reminded of something her brother had said to her not that long ago. "We survive," she whispered to herself. "You feel guilty about what is happening to your sister," she said, before she could lose her nerve. She still would not look at him.

He stopped.

Her hand trembled on his arm. "It is true. But you should not blame yourself. What you are fighting...," she breathed. "And your mother assures her it is for the best. And maybe it is."

"And maybe it isn't," he said. Something in his voice made her look up at him. "But it remains that I am the source of my sibling's misery."

"And I mine," she whispered.

"Perhaps," he answered. His eyes glittered. "I fear your brother far more noble than I," he said.

"How so?" she frowned.

His hand drifted up as if to touch her face but stopped short. "I do not think I could walk away from something I wanted that badly, even for my sister's happiness."

"But you have," she said. He frowned. "You wanted to be the Captain of the City Watch. But you walked away from that for the security of the kingdom. And for the security of the kingdom, you too will do as she is and do as your father bids. Whatever that may be," she added, looking away.

He did not seem convinced, but turned and began walking again. "I have read your 'report'," he said, changing the subject. There was still a stiff formality to him and Cae did not know how to respond.

"And?"

"I had expected a list of books and references. Not the... treatise you have given me. Which is filled with yet more questions."

She took a deep breath, reaching out and fingering the petals of a fragrant vine that hung over the path, thinking. "I could spend the rest of my life reading through the books of that library and still may never find the treasures you seek. Not looking the way I have to. But there are secrets I have discovered, research we have found..."

"We?" he stopped.

"Your brother and I, Your Highness." She did not have to look at him to feel the jealous tension that created. Even Tempest fidgeted on her shoulder. "He is a friend, and has been a great help. Between the pair of us we have found what you seek and more. Every night we discover new things."

"Night?"

"Night, Your Highness," she admitted, finally meeting his cold eyes. "The true secrets in the books we have found are only yielded at night."

"If you are trying to rouse me to jealousy, my lady, I must warn you…"

She shook her head, let go of his arm and took a few steps away from him, leaning back against the nearby wall. Her own anger was rising and she was not sure if it was all her or part him, and she needed the separation to manage it. "I am not one of those empty-headed young girls playing courtly games, Your Highness," she snapped. "I am neither foolish nor mad nor quite that ambitious. My family is well seated enough that I could go home and marry one of my father's vassals quite easily and have no impact upon our fortunes. I am not so insecure that I must test the affections of the men about me. If I wish to know your feelings in a matter, I assure you I will outright ask. And as long as I am being forthright, let me tell Your Highness that I think you are a fool for not trusting your brother with this."

She watched the eyes darkening, the two guards eyeing each other, wondering if they should intervene. Even Tempest started to fluff up a little. "He is a friend, a dear friend, and unlikely to be anything more. But he and I have talked, extensively. And even were he to come to hate you, he would always have your back, no matter what, because you are the other half of him. You don't trust him, for whatever reason, and you are a fool for doing so. There are things I will not tell my brothers because I do not need them doing something foolish. But I trust them with the important things, even when I am angry with them. So do whatever you will do to me, for speaking so to you, but that, at least, you needed to hear."

She waited, watching him like a animal watches a predator at the end of a hunt, resigned yet determined.

"There it is," he said finally, softly.

"There is what?"

"The fire you promised me."

She felt as if her legs had been cut out from beneath her, and was grateful for the support of the wall.

He glanced down slightly, scratched the bridge of his nose thoughtfully. "So, the two of you have conspired against me for my own good?"

She sighed. "No, my prince. We merely came at similar purposes and met in the middle. His research is along the same vein as yours but perhaps for different reasons, seeking a different answer. Though it has helped me. ...I have this book, you see."

"Book?"

"An old one, faery tales. I'd spoken of it with him before the tourney. He asked to see it, to have it copied if he could. I agreed. But then I made a discovery the night of the attack on Stag's Hall. I owe that man a debt for what his death revealed to me." She looked around, at the high hedges surrounding them and asked softly, "How secure is this location? From eavesdropping? What I would tell you must not be repeated."

He nodded, moved to take her hand again and led her through the simple hedge maze to the bower that Liliwyn had planted for her betrothed. He ordered the guards to stand at the entrance, one facing in, the other out, then led her down the shadowed corridor to the bench at the end. He sat her down and leaned back against one of the posts with his arms crossed over his chest, putting a little distance between them. "Please, continue. No one will hear you here."

"There really is no dancing around this," she said. "So I am just going to say it. I think the late king was a shift."

"Go on," he said, showing no emotion.

"What is more, I think you are too." No reaction from those dark blue eyes. She plunged ahead, rising and pacing as she laid out what she had discovered, from the purpose of the moonsilver to the influences of the moons. Tempest flew off. "There is more out there, I am sure of it. It's just buried or hidden in plain sight," she went on. "I want to know why shifts became just nursery stories, why they aren't part of the stories of the Firstborn. Why the Eldest is suddenly trying to change the way our faith has been expressed for millennia. And what in the world is a sympath?"

He chuckled. "Is that all?"

She stopped, turned to look at him. "What?"

He tossed his ragged locks out of his eyes as he looked up at her from under his brow. "I said, is that all?"

"Is it not quite enough to be going on with?" she asked, exasperated.

"Exactly what I mean. I have a few questions of my own."

"Ask away," she sighed. "You've allowed me to rant."

He rolled off the pole and stepped closer. "Is being a shift a good thing or a bad thing? If all the ones we've so far encountered are mad, perhaps they died back for a reason. Which begs the question 'why now'?"

"I am suffering from not enough information, and not enough moonlight to read by," she explained. "I think they are being driven mad by the pain, and the fear of not understanding what is going on, what is happening to them. The stories tell that the Firstborn took the clans of man under their wing according to their natures, and shared with them their gifts. It never really says what those gifts were, but what if the shift was it?"

"What would be the point?"

Her eyes lit up. She turned around, spreading her arms as she gestured to everything around them. "What would be the point?" she echoed. "Imagine being able to fly, to scout ahead in safety. To go from one place to another in the time it takes a bird. To have the strength and stamina of the mighty horse, or the cunning and stealth of a wolf? Full or half, there are advantages," she exclaimed. "My family has always hunted deer, even though we answer to Stag for our strength and protection. We respect his grace and beauty even as we sacrifice him to feed our families. To that end, we are taught to understand and respect him as prey, and to be wary of him should he stand and fight. I've seen men killed by stags they'd cornered. I've also ended up galloping beside one in a breathtaking chase that ended with me not shooting and coming home empty handed. If the Mother made us so, why should we not embrace it?"

"The Eldest would have us believe it sorcery," he warned.

She stepped closer. "So what if it is? Is not magic as natural as breathing and in everything around us?"

"How so?"

"That this lump of flesh heals," she said, squeezing his arm, "that it can make another of itself within it, that it lives at all!" She gathered a handful of blossoms and let the petals fall away in her hand. "That these beautiful and fragrant petals fade to become swollen fruit that can feed or procreate. That if you eat of its leaves, it will help chase away disease but eat of its roots and you will sicken and die. Need you even ask?"

He chuckled, "I guess not. There are others who would not believe it so. Every one so far encountered has been ravening mad," he added seriously.

"I believe it is because they are fighting the change. Whether because they are not dressed for it, bear no moonsilver... there could be a hundred reasons and none of them could be right. The bearsarker who attacked my home was a bull. I don't remember what family answers to that particular of the second born, but... it might help us identify him or to whom he answered. When he began to shift, he was tearing out of steel gauntlets. The pain had to be excruciating."

She was so close to him she could feel the warmth of his body even though they were not touching.

"And what have the moons to do with it all?" he asked softly.

"Did you not feel more calm when you stepped out of the light?" she whispered.

His hand reached up to brush aside a stray lock from her face. "How much of that was the maiden taming the dragon? That is really what is happening, in those stories," he grinned. "They steal maidens to soothe them."

She just gazed, lost in his eyes. "Meet me at the astronomy tower tonight, around moonrise. I will show you. We don't know how it works yet, only that it does."

"If anyone can figure it out, it will be my brother," he said, his voice far too tender for the words spoken.

"It is a secret for now," she breathed. "Only the five of us know."

"Five?"

"You, me...," her breath caught in her throat, saying those two words together, "Bal, Jan and Fern."

"Who is Fern?"

"My maid. I trust her with all my secrets. And well, Jan knew before any of us."

He was closer, too close. It seemed there was a conversation going on below the words spoken that had an entirely different context. They were inches apart when Tempest shrilled as she dropped out of the sky and onto the bower roof, showering them with lavender petals. Startled, they pulled apart, glaring up at her as she stuck her head down between the vines, cried again.

"Jelma, tyet," she growled.

The bird would not be calm, continued fussing. When the prince moved, she scolded him too.

"They were not kidding about her being an excellent chaperone," he grumbled, backing away. He saw the guards looking over in question and shook his head at them, telling them not to worry.

Tempest swung down and hopped to the ground, grabbed the hem of Cae's gown and began to walk away, holding it like a leash. "My prince," she began. "I do not think that is her problem."

He looked over, and both eyebrows shot up as he watched the spectacle. "Does she do this often?"

"Never," she breathed. She stopped, tugging her skirt free and holding out her leather-bound wrist. Tempest flew to the perch. "Jelma, is it Vyncet? Janem? ...Will?"

At his name, she began to flap her wings and cried.

"Oh my."

He was beside her again. "What do you think is the matter?"

"I don't know, but I think he may have gone and done something foolish. I have to go to him. If you will please excuse me, Your Highness?"

"Back to that are we?" he growled, but did not explain. "No, I will not excuse you."

She looked at him, too shocked to speak.

"I am coming with you." When she relaxed he asked, "Can she lead you to him?"

"Yes," she breathed. "Jelma is he inside the Citadel?" The bird shook herself. "Did he go home?" she asked, dreading the answer. Again, Tempest shook. "Oh, no. He went to the training grounds, didn't he?" she groaned. Tempest chirped.

"Why is that a bad thing?" asked the prince.

She began rushing down the path. "In his current mood, and based on what I think your sister said to him? He's liable to kill someone."

He caught up with her quickly, hooked her elbow and pulled her back. "Wait. We mustn't be seen to hurry." He placed her arm on his and began to escort her up the shortest path to the castle. The first servant he saw he sent with an order to have horses saddled and waiting. As they continued past, she heard hurried footsteps down another route. She looked up at him in question.

"Servants can run," he said.

Cae was surprised at how quickly they did manage to get out of the gardens and through the Citadel, coming out a side door she had never seen before. Four horses were just being brought out, one of them her own. Unfortunately, Wraith wore a side-saddle. The prince lifted her into place and she settled herself quickly. As he turned to mount his own horse, she spoke to the groom holding Wraith's head. "Next time, please use a regular saddle. Unless I ask for it, and I likely won't, I don't ride side-saddle."

"Um, yes, my lady," he stammered. "We weren't told. Just that your horse was wanted."

"Thank you for being so quick," she said, turning Wraith's head towards the gate. Tempest flew on ahead.

It was all she could do not to gallop out, to settle for a brisk trot along the street. Once they cleared the gate to the training grounds, she urged her to a run. It was a rough ride in the side-saddle, but she did not care. The prince caught up, though his guards were further behind. She did not wait for him to help her down, but practically threw herself from the saddle when they reached the fence to the sparring field.

Willam was alone in the middle of the area, stripped to the waist. Though he did not wield his war hammer, he had a maul in hand, and was pulverizing a wooden training dummy. The dummy had shield and a mace and chain, and swivelled freely with each blow. Will dodged most of it, and ignored the rest. Harlan and several other squires were sitting on the fence, and the others who had been training had vacated the field and were watching with trepidation.

Harlan saw them approach, noticed the prince and slid immediately off the fence, bowing deeply. "Your Highness, my lady," he stammered.

Tempest walked the rail over to them, chirped pitifully.

"How long has he been like this?" she asked the squire.

"Since no one would get in the ring with him."

"No one?" the prince asked.

The boy gulped. "Not since he nearly stove Fen's head in, Your Highness," he said, jerking his thumb towards a man with a bandage on his head, looking forlornly at a severely dented suit of armour.

"He was the only one dumb enough to accept the challenge," said another squire. "When a man challenges a man in armour while not wearing any of his own? The look in his eye warned the smart ones off."

"Was it a Challenge?" Valan asked, his eyes narrowed.

Harlan shook his head quickly. "No, sire. Just more of an …offer to take all comers? No more of a challenge than any you'll get here."

"How long?" she asked again.

The boy shrugged. "About an hour? When no one else would fight him, he stripped down and went after the dummies. That's the third one."

Cae sighed. "At least no one has gotten seriously hurt yet." She glanced at the man called Fen. "He isn't serious, is he?"

Harlan chuckled. "Naw. Knocked some sense into him, though."

Cae turned to say something to the prince, but he was no longer beside her. She looked around, was startled to see him selecting a shield and an arming sword. She hurried over to him. "My prince, are you mad?" she whispered.

"No, but he is. He needs to get out his aggression and his hurt, and inanimate objects are no substitute. I know," he said flatly, trying to put a spaulder on his shoulder.

With a low growl, she moved to help him. "You are going to face him unarmoured while he is using a maul?" she fussed as she buckled the straps.

"Hence the shield," he answered.

"The spaulder is smart, but he is still going to crush you. You cannot responsibly risk it," she insisted.

His guards seemed at complete loss what to do, were clearly debating on trying to stop him. One of them finally spoke up. "Your Highness, at least let one of us fight him if it must be done."

He gave a snort. "That would be a waste of a man."

While the prince stood discussing matters with his men, Cae stared out at her brother. She snatched up a shield and arming sword and pushed her way past those watching and entered the arena, stomping over to her brother.

"WILL!" she shouted.

He turned. She was standing there with the shield on her arm and the sword in her off hand, just hanging there. "I will not fight you, sister," he said, his voice deep in his chest.

"They aren't for me," she snapped, throwing the sword at his feet.

He scowled. "Why would I want to destroy the edge on a wooden dummy?"

She stepped closer. "What dummy?" she snarled, shoving the shield into his chest.

He glanced over his shoulder. The last blow had finally cracked the pole it was attached to and it had been slowly listing.

"I'm still not going to fight you, and no one else will," he began.

"I will fight you."

They turned, saw the prince standing there with a determined look, holding shield and sword, the only armour on his shoulder to protect from slips against the shield.

"Your Highness," Will began.

"It is not wise, I know," Valan said, cutting him off. "But apparently it is necessary."

"Give me the maul," Cae insisted.

He scowled down at her.

She held out her hands. "It is the only way you're getting me off this field and out of the way."

He growled, but put it across her hands. The weight staggered her for a moment, but she held her stance and did not drop it. "Do not kill each other!" she snarled, glaring at both of them, pointing to each in turn. "You hear me?"

The prince gave a feral grin as he adjusted his grip on the sword in his hand, not taking his eyes from Willam. "Yes, ma'am," he quipped.

Finally Will slid the shield on his arm and bent to pick up the sword.

Cae backed off a few feet, still watching the two men who had yet to move. It wasn't until she was on the far side of the fence that they began circling each other.

"Oh, Mother, this is not going to be good," she moaned, worried sick.

"Are you kidding?" crowed Harlan. "This is going to be epic!"

"Legendary," grinned the other squire.

The air rang with the clash of metal on metal as they began to feel each other out. Cae could not tear her eyes from the field, even though she was aware of the crowd growing around her. Failing to be able to protect their charge, the prince's two guards stepped up to flank her, keeping everyone but young Harlan at a distance as she had set a hand on the boy's shoulder.

The fight began with Willam testing the prince's reach and strength, and the prince trying to draw him out. Both men were almost of a height, but Will had the mass, being broader across shoulders and chest, making him seem the larger man. The prince however, was no lightweight, as Cae had seen the day of the grand melee. His muscle was all whipcord and speed. Will preferred blunt surface weapons with crushing weight, the prince a pair of swords. Both were at disadvantage, using weapons and a style they did not prefer, but they both understood that it was best since they fought without armour.

The prince kept his shield up, luring all of Willam's blows to its surface. It was easy to tell that the strength behind Will's strikes were growing as he warmed to the fight, and the prince was very much feeling it. He did not just dance around and take the hits, though. Biding his time, he would pick the moment to snake out and strike unexpectedly, and just as often turning out of the way of a blow to throw his opponent off balance and get a strike in.

It was clear they were drawing out the fight, neither of them really closing to engage or quickly end it. Will now had an active and devious opponent and had to keep his wits about him. Valan had to make certain he did not take too hard a blow or deal too much damage. Cae had been right that this was not the wisest thing they could have done. Either of them taking serious harm from this 'friendly spar' would be a political nightmare and Caelerys prayed that both of them continued to remember that.

Her hand tightened on Harlan's shoulder as a particularly fierce exchange was made. Will came away with a ribbon of blood on his sword arm and the prince had a tear in his trousers just over the thigh. They paused only long enough to assess themselves, then closed again in a flurry of steel. Will shoved his shoulder into Val's slighter frame, forcing him to turn out of the coming blow, rolling off Will's side and slamming his shield into his bared back. Will staggered forward, back arched from the sting and turned. He shook himself out, reloosening his limbs and waited until the prince had regained his footing and stance.

They went at each other for nearly an hour, neither really gaining the advantage. The prince was too quick and light and used to dart and flurry attacks, and Will was too strong and massive, used to simply overbearing and crushing his opponents. Both knew the other's style and knew better than to allow the other the advantage of theirs.

Cae feared that both men were tiring, though neither showed signs of it. Will kept having to reach slightly farther to make contact, and the lighter weapon kept causing him to over extend, wasting his energy. However, the near steady rain of heavy blows had to be exhausting Valan's shield arm.

Their exchanges became fierce and rapid fire. They ended up in a blade lock, shields pressed together, both men trying to gain the upper hand as they pushed against one another. Will had strength and weight on his side, but the prince had managed some trick of footing or hand that not only had him holding his own, but gaining inches. Finally, Will threw back his head with a roar that made Cae flinch, knowing what was coming, as he rammed his forehead into that of the prince. Valan was thrown to the torn up turf onto his backside.

He dropped his shield and held up his fist, pressing his sword hand to his temple. Willam stepped back.

The crowd held its breath.

Prince Valan finally dropped his fist and his sword arm onto his lap, staring up at Willam with a small trickle of blood running down the side of his nose. "Have you had enough, yet?" he asked. "Because I can keep this up, oh... another half hour before my shield arm is useless."

Will just stared at him for a long moment before he burst out laughing. He stepped up and held out his hand, helping the prince to his feet. "No, I think I'm good now." He pulled the prince closer. "Though had I my choice of weapon, that would have been a very different fight."

Valan nodded solemnly, even as he wiped away the line of blood. "No doubt. Thankfully, your sister has more wisdom than is really good for either of us."

He glanced over his shoulder to where Cae stood amid the shouting and crowing crowd. "That does not make me worry about her any less." He looked back at the prince. "Do we need to have a conversation?"

Cae did not hear his response as Harlan slipped from her grasp and entered the field, wincing as he rubbed his shoulders where she had gripped them. Around her, men were cheering, some of them exchanging money and promises of bought drinks in good humour. As the crowd thinned, she noticed a group of women, no doubt fresh back from a ride through the wood, watching the two men with open desire and admiration.

Cae grabbed a couple of drying cloths from nearby and crossed the field to the two of them. Harlan was gathering up the weapons, accepting even the prince's as it was handed to him. Cae threw one cloth at her brother and handed the other to the prince with slightly more decorum. He kept his eyes on her as he first wiped the blood from his face, then dabbed at the mark on his leg.

"Will that need stitching, do you think?" she asked, concerned and trying to discreetly determine if he took any other damage.

He glanced down at it, peeling away part of the cloth to look. He shook his head. "I don't think so."

"Good. You should both probably head inside though," she said, gesturing towards the out-building nearby. "Get your wounds looked at and cleaned at the very least."

Will tried to swipe at an itch on his back that he could not reach. He half turned so that Cae could see. "Is that blood that is driving me mad back there?" he asked.

She looked. "Yes," she snapped, grabbing the cloth and wiping it away and not being gentle about it. "And the rest of it is black and blue. Again. I repeat, you should go inside."

The prince grinned. "Will my lady be attending to both our wounds?"

"Does his highness think that wise?" she countered. "What with the audience you two have drawn," she added, flicking her eyes towards the women still staring at Will's half naked body.

He glanced over there and groaned, "Great. By this afternoon, it will be all over court that we were fighting over you." He sighed, looking at the prince and tilting his head in deference. "Shall we, Your Highness?"

Valan made an exaggerated bow to Caelerys. "I bow to the lady's superior wisdom."

Will chuckled at that and the three of them walked back to the building. Tempest flew out to land on her wrist and walk up to her shoulder, chirping her question if everything was all right.

Cae soothed her as she walked behind the two of them. She noticed the prince was moving a little less gracefully and more stiffly than before, and even Willam was beginning to slow down. They headed into the open door and looked back when she did not follow.

"Are you not coming to serve Physician?" Will asked.

She crossed her arms over her chest and glared at him. "In light of the audience? No. Besides," she turned her gaze onto Valan, "someone has reminded me that I should not be left alone with him. If you don't want the rumours to grow worse, best I avoid both of you for the time being. Harlan can play Physician if there isn't one inside."

"What are you going to do?" Will frowned.

"I need a gallop along the beach. I have not had the opportunity in quite some time and I am going to take it while I can." She looked back to where her horse stood waiting, eyed the dreaded saddle. "After I get her re-saddled."

"You cannot go alone," Will insisted.

"Queen's orders," Valan added.

"They'll have to catch us first," she growled, beginning to feel very irritated with the whole situation and tempted to just go.

The prince called to the men trailing along behind her. "Go with her," he ordered.

She looked up at him. "And leave you without a guard? How will that look?"

He sighed. "Fine, Larch, go with her. Ralen, stay with me."

The two men nodded and moved closer to their new charges. Cae growled again, "Fine, Your Highness. Thank you," she said curtly, dropping into a sharp curtsey and turning away. As she walked back to the horses she heard a low exchange between the prince and her brother.

"Whatever happened to the quiet, frightened doe I first met?" asked the prince.

Will snorted, "Whatever you did, you may live to regret it. There is just as much ca'theryn as mouse in her."

"The mouse who roars," he chuckled as she moved out of earshot.

Cae felt the blush rising from her throat as she took Wraith's reins and began to walk to the stables just down the path. Once there, she found the nearest stable hand and requested the change of saddle. The man gave her a funny look, but noting the crest and tabard of the guard with her, he said nothing and led Wraith off.

Cae paced idly along the first row of stalls as she waited, ignoring the guard watching over her. She did make sure not to get too far away from him out of courtesy. There were only two horses on the row currently, and both of them poked their heads out, whickering at her. She stopped to stroke their broad noses and to scratch in favourite places. Their presence helped to calm her until Tempest grabbed a lock of her hair and tugged, trying to draw her attention to something.

She turned and felt everything grow cold. As lord Aldane walked over with a smile upon his thin lips, she drew herself up, calling back her earlier irritation and putting on an imperious manner. She figured, if she could 'take tone' with the crown prince, she could manage with the Kaladen heir.

"My lady," he purred, bowing and reaching out to take her hand.

She left her hands upon the horse's face, keeping them unavailable. "Lord Aldane," she replied coldly. Tempest puffed up on her shoulder, holding her wings loosely and her head down.

He did not seem overly concerned at her manner or tone, though he withdrew his hand. "I have been trying to reach you since my return. The staff at your hall in town assured me you are not at home, but would not say where you had gone. I searched the gardens, hoping to find you among the princess's ladies, but you are no where to be found. I had begun to fear you had gone home to the Reach."

"My people are loyal to their House and Lord," she said, turning to face the horse as she stroked him, but still keeping Aldane in her peripheral vision. "They do not reveal our locations to any who ask."

"Ah, but I am not just anyone," he said. "I take it you liked your gift?" He glanced at her throat. "Though I am sad that you are not wearing it. I am sure there will be occasion enough when the princess is wed."

She looked at him. "Were you not informed?"

The smile did not leave his lips, but vanished quickly from his eyes. "Informed of what, my beauty?"

"First of all, I am not *your* anything. Second, the gift was stolen the day before it was to be returned to you."

"Stolen?" he repeated, standing straighter.

"Have you not yet heard any of the news? Whilst you men were away gallantly saving Folk, the Griff Harvest ship was attacked by pirates at the very mouth of the Desiter, and Stag Hall was attacked that night. I was nearly killed." She watched the tightening around his eyes at that.

"Were you harmed, my lady?" he asked.

She chose to ignore his question, "Unfortunately, your gift was stolen by the few that managed to escape."

"No matter," he said, smiling again and taking a step closer, "I shall simply send another that will pale the first."

She was now tired of this game, hearing the approaching hoof-beats of Wraith an aisle away. She gave him her most stern look. "Please save me the trouble of having to arrange its return as well, lord Aldane." He paused, having finally understood her meaning. "No gift or request from you or your House will be welcomed by mine. I am sorry for having to be so blunt, but you seem a little hard of hearing on the matter."

"I am the heir to a Lordly House," he began, only barely hiding his growing anger. "There is no reason for your father to refuse my suit."

"Then why have you not asked my father yet? Or is it because you know what he'll say and only hope to sway me first so that I will convince him?"

Out of the corner of her eye, she saw the guard coming closer, hand upon his hilt. She saw what had drawn him, was not blind to Aldane's reaction. She looked him in his flat grey eyes, unflinching. Out of courtesy, she lowered her voice so that it would not carry. "I would light my candle for yon stable hand before I would light it for you. Now you will excuse me, sir."

She turned her back on him, walking around him as if he were insignificant and accepted her horse from the groom. She thanked him with the utmost courtesy and allowed him to give her a leg up. Without a thought, she settled herself into the saddle, twitching her skirts into place and turning to Larch who had moved to stand between her and the

Kaladen heir. "When you are ready, Sir Larch," she said.

The man nodded to lord Aldane and turned, taking Wraith's bridle and walking out of the stable at her side. He said nothing until they reached his own horse and he had mounted up beside her. "It is Mester Larch, if it pleases my lady," he said.

She looked over at him, studying him thoughtfully. "It does not please me," she said simply. "I believe sir to fit you better. I may have to have words with your master about that." Hiding her smile, she tapped Wraith with her heels and Tempest took to the sky even as the mare leapt forward with joy. Larch managed to keep up.

Supper was served in their private apartments, and Cae did not join her brothers. In fact, she did not even know if Will had gone back to Stag Hall or not. He most likely had. She rushed through her own meal, informing Coral that she and Fern would be spending a large part of the evening in the library and for them to not wait up for her. Since she had already established this pattern, no comment was made beyond wishing her luck in finding whatever it was that drove her.

Cae actually did spend a few minutes in the library itself, recollecting two of the books she had referred the prince to, and letting Fern carry them into the secret passage with her.

When Cae peered out of the peep-hole at their exit, she could see a glimmer of light near the tower door and smiled. She blew out their light and slipped out of the passage, closing it quickly and softly as the prince was trying the door to the tower. She bade Fern wait in silence and padded down the stone corridor, her eyes on the dark tunic of the prince's back.

She pulled the iron key from her pocket and stopped a few feet away. "Would my prince like the key?" she asked softly, holding it up.

He turned, the flash in his eye banking quickly as he recognized her in the dim light of his candle. He looked behind her, down the corridor, and the way he had come, seeing no way she could have sneaked up on him. "Dare I ask how you found your way here without a light or anyone seeing you?"

She bobbed a shallow curtsey, giving him a sly look. "It's a secret, my prince."

He narrowed his eyes as he studied her. "I see you have not wasted your time here," he finally said, stepping aside and sweeping his hand towards the door, gesturing for her to do the honours.

She smiled as she brushed past him, unlocking the door and preceding him into the room. Fern followed behind him, carrying the books. Cae was careful to lock the door behind her.

Valan used his candle to light the lamp in the centre of the room and looked around. "You two have made things rather cosy. I believe the last time I was up here was just before my aunt banished the astronomer." He gave a soft chuckle, running his fingers along the edge of an empty but dust-free shelf. "In fact, our last visit might have been what prompted her to remove him."

"Were you both trouble in your youth?" she smiled, crossing to the cord hanging from the ceiling.

"Some," he shrugged. "I was always the more serious of the two. Yet somehow, Bal was always the more studious."

She frowned, "I do not believe that. Your Highness is well versed in many subjects which can only come with careful study."

He leaned against the shelf, staring at her, his arms crossed. Finally, he conceded. "I studied practical things, strategy, history, politics, law. Bal prefers more esoteric subjects."

"Ah," she said, reaching up and pulling the cord, dancing out of the way of the ladder as it slid to the floor. Moonlight slanted into the room, turning the pale green gown she wore to rippling silver.

She turned, picking up the heavy volume from the shelf near the trapdoor and daintily pulled her hems out of the way, walking up the ladder as if it were a mere staircase. Stepping up onto the roof, she looked back down the hole. He was looking up after her, clearly not knowing what to think. She beckoned and finally he mounted the ladder to join her. Fern followed behind with the books from the library and set them on the table beside her mistress's book.

The prince looked around at the top of the tower, carefully avoiding the open trap door. He took in the single comfortable chair and table. "You worked together up here?"

She shook her head, opening the book to the two page illustration. "We did the first night, but after that we alternated. It was your brother's idea, to protect my reputation. In fact, as far as anyone is concerned, I am currently in the library."

"The worms will know better."

"And they will not speak but that I enter the library and leave it. Which I do, and always in the company of Fern."

He nodded, pleased with the intelligence of the arrangement. "I take it there is a secret passage at the end of that hall which leads to the library?" he grinned.

"I did say it was a secret, my prince," she smiled, her eyes glinting. "Just not whose."

He moved to join her at the table and she watched his eyes widen, seeing the gleam of gold and silver upon the pages. Cautiously, he turned the page, reading the sub-story buried within the ordinary tale. "Where did you get this book?"

She shook her head. "It has been in the family for a very long time," she said. "I do not know its origins. But the whole book is like this. There are stories of the Firstborn and the original clans of men in here that tell more than they ever used to when read in this light. Here is where we discovered what moonsilver is for, we think. I think shifting can be safely done while wearing it. I don't know if it changes with the body or prevents that portion from changing, because there isn't a story in here about moonsilver itself, just what we've been able to glean from the pictures. And there is poetic license to consider."

He snorted lightly, "Artists rarely allow the facts to get in the way of a good yarn."

"And there is nothing wrong with that for mere stories," she said. "This book was for entertainment. It is not a history book."

He turned to the front of the book, looking through the first story. "Or maybe it is, and we have no way of knowing."

"I will warn you, I do believe the author to be Maral, or hired thereby," she said, perching on the edge of the chair. "Most of the stories deal with our neck of the woods and that of our neighbours. Any mention of other families is only where they encounter mine, or something that was so well known at the time that it crossed those lines. It even speaks of the death of the Leviathan and the destruction of

House Levitau."

He looked over at her. "Why was that? I never knew. I mean, I knew what they were accused of, but the actual event that prompted a military extinction?"

"It's the third story. It speaks of atrocities committed by the House and suggests that the Leviathan itself was pushing it. The other Houses rose up and wiped them out. The final battle was somewhere north of that, near other Levitau properties, but where isn't clear. The attack on the Eastern Isles itself is fairly detailed."

He raised an eyebrow, "Too detailed for a nursery book?"

"Maybe."

He reached over and picked up one of the other tomes, scanning the pages for glints of silver and gold. "I take it you know or suspect these to have hidden writing as well?"

"The bottom one should, it is old enough. The other two I grabbed for their content."

He looked at their spines and frowned at the one now on top. "This is a book of the Eldest."

She nodded slowly, not taking her eyes from his face. "I grabbed it one afternoon to 'know my enemy'? And I was shocked at what it contains. Have you ever read it? Or been to a service?"

He shook his head. "I have no patience with or time for formal religion. I see no need for it. The Mother provides the means, Man provides the will and the muscle."

"You should read it. There are significant changes between that and the history of the world as we were taught," she said pointedly. "If you do not wish this absurd new faith to take over, you would do well to know what they are preaching and why. I am not liking the contradictions."

He thought about it, then nodded, setting the book aside and looking through the older of the three, eventually carrying it to the battlement to lean against the wall and read.

Enjoying the simple, quiet time with him, she took out the notes that Balaran had left for her on his own discoveries.

Several hours had passed when she felt a shift in the wind, stifled a shiver. She stretched, glancing up at the sky and realized that they would not have much more time to read. The moons were almost gone. Bonfire night was coming, when the night sky was empty and the people lit bonfires to fill the gap and guard their souls. It was another practice that the Eldest was trying to usurp. The book she had recommended to Valan claimed that the bonfires were lit to prove the dominance of man over the demesne of this world and to light the way for the worthy to the other.

She sighed. Thoughts of the new religion depressed her.

She felt eyes on her and looked up, saw the prince just watching her from the other side of the tower. She blushed. "What, Your Highness?"

A flash of irritation crossed his face, fading quickly. "You are a contradiction. A fey thing I am trying to figure out. Staring helps."

This caused her to choke on a laugh. "Well," she said when she could finally speak, "if you ever manage to do so, my brothers will pay handsomely for the secret."

A shadow of a smile danced on his face, quickly hidden as the wind blew his hair into his face. He did not move to brush it away. She felt a shift in his mood, but could not read it. "You've managed to impress my guardsman," he said.

She shrugged, sitting back in the chair to ease her back. "He impressed me," she said simply. "Not many will allow a lady to fight her own battles. He knew when to interfere and when to stand aside but present. And completely proper; he didn't bat an eye at the sight of my ankles. That and he's not a bad rider."

She saw the arched brow, felt a breath of angry jealousy. "He saw your ankles?" he asked.

She blushed further. "Well, I wasn't dressed for riding. I doubt he even looked," she shrugged.

"What do you wear when you ride?"

She looked up at him, tipping her head. "Was my prince not paying attention when I rode against his brother in the tourney?"

"Your prince was trying very hard to not pay attention to anyone of the delicate persuasion," he said, his eyes glinting through his windblown hair. Still, he did not move.

"Well, I sincerely hope I have dissuaded you of the notion that I am in any way delicate... or persuadable," she added lightly, arching her brow.

"You are beginning to," he said with a faint tip of his head. His gaze locked once more on her own. "But the stag's daughter has a softer side as well. And I grow fond of that, too."

She felt everything go cold with a little shiver, could not find the breath to respond. He was suddenly closer than she remembered him standing, a finger reaching out to brush aside a curl.

"Fire has its place and purpose and ignites passion, but a dragon likes a soft place to lay his head now and again."

She felt something drop away from under her, not unlike her dreams of flight and throwing her body to the wind. A sense of worry followed it. She pulled herself out of the prince's gaze, frowning slightly. She glanced off to the east and saw a flicker of white growing out of the night. A second later, Tempest landed on the battlement with a shriek. She turned her beaded eye warningly on the prince who growled even as he backed off.

"Tempest," Cae sighed, holding out her hand. The bird landed on her wrist, accepting her caress. "What are you doing flying at night?" She chirped and Cae groaned. "Someone must be looking for me. I should go. I've been here much longer than I should have." A flick of her wrist sent Tempest flying back the way she had come.

Valan reached out and lifted her hand to his lips. "Go. I shall return things to their places when I am done."

She rose, bobbed a curtsey, trying not to allow the feelings rising up within her at his touch overwhelm her or show. "Thank you, my prince." She pulled the key from her pocket. "You will need this. Janem made the copy. Your brother has the original."

She slipped from his hand and glided down the ladder, waking Fern at the table with a gentle hand. "We need to go."

Fern woke completely, fetching the candle. The prince followed her down and unlocked the door, holding it open for them. Fern led the way with the light.

Before she set foot in the hall, Cae looked up at him. "How did your conversation with my brother go?" she asked, searching for her answers in his face.

His smile was enigmatic. "As expected."

As he said nothing else, she curtseyed again and swept off down the hall after her maid and into the waiting passage. She glanced back once more as Fern lit the lamp from the candle. He was still in the doorway, watching her. Finally she closed the secret door and hurried down the passage.

She had barely closed the bookcase when she was approached by young Ward who looked a little worried. He seemed relieved when he saw her.

"I was hoping I wouldn't have to go in there hunting you, my lady," he sighed. "Your brother was here looking for you."

"Which one?" she asked.

"The smith."

She was surprised by the response. "Janem? Did he say why?"

"No, my lady. Only that when you were found you were to be sent to Stag's Hall. He implied that finding you was a priority," he apologized.

She felt worry rising within her breast. "Thank you, Ward. I'll go straight to the stables. Fern," she began, turning to the girl.

"I'll go with you, my lady. It will stem any questions," she said, shaking her head. "My lady still has her knife on her?" she asked softly.

Cae's hand drifted to her thigh, felt the hardness of the slim hilt strapped there. She nodded. "Just in case," she said.

Ward began to lead them out of the stacks. "Good luck, my lady," he said as he saw them to the library door.

Cae hurried through the ground floor of the Citadel, surprised at how quiet and empty it seemed at this hour. She was afraid she would have difficulty explaining things to the guards at the door, but they opened the side door for her on sight. "The stable master is waiting for you, Lady Caelerys," he said. "I hope everything is well."

This caused her even more worry and she barely thanked him as she swept past. She flew down the front steps and ran towards the lighted stable. A groom was walking out of the building leading three horses. Wraith whickered when she saw Cae, pulling herself free and coming to her. Cae breathed a sigh of relief when she noticed the simple riding saddle. The groom, the same one from that afternoon, gave her a nodding smile and moved to help Fern into the side-saddle on the other palfrey. Cae did not wait for assistance, but vaulted up and cursorily adjusted her skirts. She frowned when the groom swung up onto the third horse and was passed a short sword by a sleepy stable boy.

"That is..."

"Absolutely necessary," he finished, began to lead them across the courtyard to the gateway.

Cae was actually surprised at the relief she felt that he was going with them. She told herself that it was better than the fully armed escort she would have gotten if the queen or Prince Valan had known what was afoot.

Tempest flew down to rest on her shoulder, even as Cae urged the mare into a swifter pace than was perhaps wise for the narrow streets.

The gates of the Hall were standing open, waiting for her, and the courtyard was well lit for servants who were busy loading a small cart. She only spared a glance at the activity, jumping down from the saddle before the grooms even had a chance to hold the bridle. It was all she could to do stop herself from running into the house.

Once in the open doors, she was at a loss which way to go. Most of the activity seemed to be coming from upstairs, so she headed to the living floor. She had barely crested the top of the stair when Janem saw her and shouted her name.

"What in the name of the First is going on?" she demanded.

"This way," he said, leading her down to Will's chambers. "I looked all over for you. Your maids said you were in the library, but the worms couldn't find you."

"I was... what is going on?" she asked again as they stepped into the hive of activity that was Willam's room.

"Where were you?" Will asked, turning at the sound of her voice. She could feel the tension roiling off him like waves.

"I was ...with the prince," she said in a lower voice, instead of the prepared lie.

He scowled. "Which one?"

"The crown," she answered shortly.

He actually growled. "Are you mad? There is scandal enough trying to cling to this House without you...."

"Nothing untoward happened and no one should know we were together," she snapped, cutting him off, his own anger beginning to ignite hers.

Fern stepped forward with a half curtsey. "Nothing untoward happened, my lord," she said. "I was with them the whole time."

"And what were they doing at this hour of the night?" he demanded.

"Reading, my lord."

"Reading?"

Cae let her worry and anger take full rein and moved to block her maid from her brother. "Yes, reading! Since when have my study habits been of any concern to you and what in the name of all that is sacred is going on here!?"

SHIFT: Stag's Heart

"He's leaving," said Vyncet, hobbling in from the balcony on his cane. "Running like a dog with his tail between his legs."

Will shot him a threatening glare. "The princess has asked that I make myself scarce until she has left the City. In order for her to be able to do as she must, I cannot be near. I happen to agree. I do not trust myself right now."

"Is this what you and Valan spoke of?" she asked, her fists on her hips.

If Will caught her intimate use of the crown prince's name, he gave no indication, though Vynce and Janem exchanged a glance. "No. Though it is merely further reasoning to go. Also, Father needs one of us to come home. That cannot be you, and Vynce," he glanced over at his brother, "will be useless in this matter."

"Hey!" he started, but a glare from Will silenced him.

"The three of us have had the chance to talk. You were mysteriously unavailable," Will ground.

"What I was doing was as important as anything else," she snapped. "You could have sent word earlier. Asked me to supper. But no, I'm sure the 'men' wanted to discuss things on their own. What could possibly prompt you to rush out of town like a thief in the night? You think reputations are at stake now? How do you think it's going to look with you having a fight with the crown prince in front of a full quarter of the court and then disappearing that very night?"

Vyncet's head came up at that, as did Janem. "You had a fight with royalty?"

"An argument or a fight?" Jan clarified.

Will was growling his frustration as things had gotten well out of hand. Fed up with the activity rushing around them, he stormed out onto the balcony, crossing to the Mistress's door with the three of them trailing along behind. Once in the relative quiet, he closed the door, not caring that it put them in the dark. Thankfully Janem had the wits to grab and light the lamp he had seen on a table just before the door closed.

"It was neither," Will snapped. "I was exercising my frustrations and the prince offered to spar."

Cae crossed her arms over her chest and met his glare. "That's not how I remember it."

"It doesn't matter what really happened," Vynce interrupted. "It only matters how things will be seen."

"I'll leave the rumour mill to you, Vynce. Your charm will serve us well there."

Cae began to pace, oblivious to the bird following in her footsteps on the floor behind her. "None of this explains why you have to rush off tonight. Why you could not tell me this over breakfast and leave at a far more reasonable hour. Why you had to scare me half to death with desperate searches without leaving me so much as a note!"

"Father is ill," said Janem quietly.

She stopped dead, all colour draining from her face. She looked from one brother to the other. The differences in the three men were worlds apart, but the similarities were consistent and all of them the shadow of their father. "Then I need to..."

"Stay here," Will interrupted.

She started to protest but he stepped up to her, set gentle hands on her arms. "You cannot leave right now, Cae," he said softly. "The princess will be wed a week after Bonfire night. You are to be there. You and

Vynce must represent the House. Jan will have the gift ready by then, yes?" he glanced over, seeking confirmation.

Jan nodded. "It is not that difficult for all I make it out to be."

"And that is why you are the best," Will said, giving him a tight smile.

Jan just shrugged, sitting down on a padded ottoman.

"I have to go. There are House matters he needs handled and cannot at the moment," Willam continued.

"Is this why he couldn't come to the coronation?"

"Partly," he evaded. "If he takes a turn for the worst, I will notify you immediately. I know how fast you can ride. But you have to stay here. Things are too close, our enemies everywhere. Who knows what damage can be done in the time you would be gone, what prospects could vanish into the wind? You must keep yourself in everyone's eye, and yet give them nothing untoward to speak of."

At the far end of the balcony, they heard Harlan's voice calling.

Will opened the door and looked out.

"My lord, the Captain says the tide turns in the hour. You need to be aboard before then."

Will nodded, grunting his frustration. "Send the baggage on now," he ordered. He turned back to his sister, bent to kiss her forehead. "I will write. Please, do not worry. We survive."

"We survive," she whispered, hugging him tightly. She had forgotten how tightly he hugged. She was going to miss this.

He turned and embraced both of his brothers, said something to each in their turn, before crossing to his squire to take his leave.

Cae stepped out onto the balcony, watching the sleeping city and wondering how they were going to weather the coming storm. She did not move until she heard the hoof-beats of her brother's horse leaving the Hall for the docks, followed by what was most likely his squire.

She heard her brothers come up behind her.

"You think it serious?" Vynce asked Jan as softly as he could.

"He's taking a ship," she growled. "Of course it's serious. Why else would he not ride?" She felt hands on her shoulders and sighed. "I am sorry. You do not deserve the brunt of my frustration. I had not realized how much I had come to depend upon him."

"He was gone for more than a fortnight," Vynce frowned.

"Yes, and so was nearly everyone else. Every one was in the same boat. Now it's just us."

"We're to stay here tonight," Janem said, moving to practical matters.

"What about the forge?" she asked.

"I've someone watching it," he said. "I'll be back there tomorrow night."

She nodded, leaning back against him, glad that he was there.

"You're to go back to the Citadel in the morning," Vyncet told her, leaning on the rail and fiddling with Tempest's feathers to get her to move over.

She looked at him. "Just me? What about you?"

He shook his head. "I have to stay here. We cannot risk the Hall standing empty at this time. Marko will go back with you to supervise my things being moved."

"How will you manage your flirting from the Hall?" she asked, giving him a sad smile.

He shrugged. "May not need the gardens any more. Father's business is not the only business he's on," he said, nodding off towards Will's room.

"Good luck. I'm glad you finally found something you like."

He laughed. "One rarely knows what one is really looking for until it slaps you."

She eyed him. "She slapped you?"

"No, it's an expression," he grumbled. "...Though she has beat the hide off me at Castle," he added with a grin.

Caelerys had not realized how tired she was until she found herself stifling a yawn. Tempest did not bother to hide hers, opening wide with a tiny squeak.

Jan took that as a signal to usher her off to her old room, where Fern had already turned down the bed and gotten her nightdress ready.

She was half asleep before Fern had taken her hair down and put it in a nightbraid, and fully unconscious before her head hit the pillow.

In her dreams she could feel the golden dragon breathing beside her, but could not see him no matter how she tried. In the distance she could see a massive stag, his head bowed beneath the weight of his antlers. She lost count at thirty-two points. There were other things moving in the mists of the wood, other stags, other creatures, and something bellowing in anger or pain at a great distance. So much was going on around her that the world began to spin. It was like being caught up in a whirlwind or a water spout. She was falling, no sensation of anything around her, not sky or sea or ground. The last thing she felt before she woke, was the coiling of a scaled body around hers.

17

It felt odd, waking in her bed in Stag's Hall. By virtue of their late night, she slept almost 'til dinner. She wasted no time getting dressed and out of the house. Janem was still asleep and Vyncet was busy with House business, so she did not bother to say goodbye. She knew the servants would let them know. The groom from the castle returned with her and Fern.

As soon as she reached the citadel, she hurried up to her room to change. The old riding skirt they had found for her at the Hall was slightly outgrown, being both too tight and too loose in all the wrong places. Seeing it cast off onto the clothes press, she got the idea that it might fit Onelle, and told the maids to have it wrapped up and set aside just in case. If nothing else, it would serve for a pattern. Finally ready in a pearl grey gown and her hair simply dressed, she headed down to the gardens with Pansy in tow, steeling herself for the ordeal she knew would be coming.

When she arrived, she discovered she was not the only one arriving late. Lady Malyna and her cluster of ladies were parading in, all of them in simpler gowns than their usual wont, and all in shades of iron or black with veils covering their hair. Malyna's eyes lit up when she saw Cae coming down another path. She fluttered over to her, looking overjoyed, which surprised Cae completely.

"Greetings, lady Malyna," she said, unsure what else to say or do.

"Oh, Caelerys!" she exclaimed. "You've finally gone! We didn't see you at the grand hall in town but perhaps you just attended here at the Citadel. I am so happy for you! It must be such a comfort to you in your time of need."

Caelerys frowned. "What are you talking about?"

She gestured to Cae's gown in confusion. "It's Fourth Day and you are wearing... coming late. I thought... you'd gone to church like the rest of us." She looked crestfallen as she slowly realized she'd been wrong in her assumptions.

"Of course she didn't go," sneered one of the other ladies in a low voice. "She's one of those heathen sigil worshippers."

Cae's eyes darkened, but she held her tongue. "I am late because I had a family emergency last night."

The older of Malyna's ladies spoke up, not bothering to hide her disdain. "Her brother was banished yesterday," she explained.

Malyna looked shocked. "Oh no, which one? Not the younger one?" she asked hopefully. She looked at Caelerys with eyes full of sympathy. "What happened?"

Her friend sneered, "All I know is that the crown prince fought a duel with him over something he said to the princess,"

"And what gave you that hare-brained idea?" Caelerys demanded.

"It's all over the court," she simpered in her defence, not reading the warning in Cae's manner. "The princess left the gardens in tears after a conversation with Lord Willam and next thing anyone knows, the two of them are at it on the training grounds. I'd heard the prince tracked him down and challenged him right there, didn't even bother to don armour."

A familiar voice purred from behind Caelerys, "Well, if it had been a duel, lady Haria, the fact that the prince lost stood Lord Willam in the right and to continue to gossip about whatever he is supposed to have done is a gross violation of etiquette."

Cae turned around and smiled, nodding gratefully to lady Sigourney. She was surprised to see Liliwyn standing beside her.

"If you wish to know what really happened, it would be wiser to ask the princess directly, wouldn't you think?" Lili asked sweetly. "I mean, she would know."

Lady Haria started to backtrack. "That would be rude, to bring up a tender subject."

"So is discussing it behind her back," Cae snapped. "Malyna, you really need better friends," she added before turning to Sigourney and Lili. She forced herself to smile. "Shall we go on to the terrace? I feel a need to watch the river in pleasant company."

Lili and Sigourney split up and turned, each taking an arm and walked down a different path with Cae to the pavilioned terrace. They found seating that faced the river where they had a good view. Lili sat on the bench beside Cae and Sigourney took the corner chair. Lady Sigourney set a hand on Cae's, gave her a reassuring smile.

"How are you holding up, dear?"

She sighed. "I was fine until I ran into those... hens," she said finally, settling on the most polite of her word choices.

"Jealousy becomes no one," Lili sighed. "So, what have you heard about your father? Is it serious?"

She took a deep breath, shook her head. "I don't know. Will is being tight-lipped as always. But it may be that he doesn't know and won't until he gets home. He's going to miss bonfire night."

"We'll light a torch for him and your father," Sigourney said. "So, if we are going to put any of these rumours properly to bed, we'll need to know the truth," she said pointedly, keeping her voice low enough to not carry.

Cae gave her hand a squeeze, told the pair of them what had happened yesterday.

"Well, I can see where they are getting their ideas," sniffed Sigourney.

Liliwyn nodded. "What with Princess Syera leaving the gardens so soon after their conversation, and I can attest, she was indeed in tears. I know what happened, and why she's not going to want to talk about it. It would not do for her reasons to get back to her betrothed or his family," she whispered.

"I know," Cae nodded. "It seems like the harder one tries to keep something from the court the more they are intent upon spreading it and in the worst possible light."

"That is the nature of court, I'm afraid," sighed Sigourney.

Liliwyn nodded. "My sister is right. I, at least, was prepared for it, you... Sai? Neither of you were really expecting to have to deal with the viper's nest court politics can be."

Cae frowned. "Sister?" she asked, looking from one to the other. Now that she knew, the similarities were so obvious she wondered how she could have missed them.

Liliwyn frowned. "You didn't know?"

Sigourney looked resigned. "I have tried very hard to distance myself from the family for your sake, Lili. I am quite happy with the way my life has turned out, but I will not have it be a millstone around your neck."

"I wouldn't care," Lili protested.

"I do," she insisted. "Just as well I'm the elder by a good decade and a half. By the time you were of age, I'd been so far out of the picture most had people forgotten all about me." She turned to Cae with a conspiratory smile. "I was never half the beauty our Lili is."

Liliwyn blushed and made a retort that Cae didn't hear. Other voices nearby caught her attention. Across the terrace, nearer a curved shrub full of bright orange blooms, was Malyna and her mother. The other ladies had drifted a little ways away from them, to grant the appearance of privacy. Malyna, at least, was trying to keep her voice down. Her mother had no such qualms. Malyna was clearly upset. "...be so mean?" Cae heard.

Lady Asparadane had her narrow nose in the air. "Because she is no better than Folk, with her rough country ways and irreligious manner! She never had a mother to teach her to be a proper lady, and was raised in a house full of men. It is no wonder she does not know how to react to kindness."

Sigourney and Lili, like most of the terrace's scattered population, had now stopped talking and discreetly begun to pay attention. Everyone saw the queen approaching. No one moved. She came to a stop a few yards away, her presence shielded from both Asparadanes by the curve of the hedge the Lady had chosen mostly likely for the amplification properties it apparently possessed.

"But mother," Malyna began, "maybe it is just she's had so much..."

"No excuse, Malyna," she snapped. "She should be ashamed to even show her face right now. One brother banished for whatever he said to the princess, and then actually duelling a member of the royal family? Her father too above himself to even come to the coronation? Herself out at all hours of the night without proper reason or escort...."

"That will be quite enough, Semelle." The cold, quiet tone of the queen's normally warm and buoyant voice caused the woman to draw up stiffly before she turned and followed her daughter into a deep curtsey.

She stared at the two bowing before her, every inch the queen of the realm. "It is not enough that you are trying to suborn my husband to your whims and slither your bony fingers into the arrangements of my children, but that you must bring others down with base lies to accomplish this. Now you are spreading rumours you know very well are false that cast both my daughter and my eldest son into scandals?"

She paused. Still no one moved and no one spoke, and the queen left the two of them bent in their positions. Finally she raised her voice enough to carry throughout the terrace and to everyone now obviously listening, not that she had been unable to be heard before. "No one has yet been banished from the capitol. If ever anyone is, everyone will know, for it will happen in open and formal court, as well as the reasons for it," she said, her eyes boring into Lady Asparadane. "No duels were fought. 'Twas a friendly spar between two men with no other purpose but to test each others' skill."

SHIFT: Stag's Heart

She dropped her volume and stepped closer so that she was looking down at the top of Semelle's platinum head. "Lady Caelerys has been busy at all hours at royal request. Something you would do well not to question, Semelle. Duke Maral has fallen ill, and his son has rushed to his side as any dutiful child should. I would suggest you take your daughter and leave whilst you still have a shred of dignity left. If I see you in my house again, I will have you in chains. You are quite done spreading your venom in this place of peace and beauty."

"Malyna?" Lady Asparadane dared, not raising her eyes.

"Provided she fails to follow your example and speaks no ill nor spreads no gossip, she may return after Bonfire Night. As for yourself, you would do well to ensure I never lay eyes upon you again." She bent and whispered something in the lady's ear that made her go pale. Finally she rose and stepped back. "Now go before I banish the both of you."

She stood still as a statue and more imposing than Caelerys had ever seen her as the two women rose and walked out of the gardens at a sedate pace. A couple of Malyna's friends started to follow, but a gesture from Lady Asparadane's hand stopped them. As they passed where Cae and the two Cygent women were sitting, she saw tears on Malyna's cheeks.

Everyone seemed to come to their senses at once and bowed to the queen. She took a deep, calming breath and seemed to shrink back into the dowdy, motherly woman Caelerys had come to know. When her voice called out, it was once more firm and maternal. "Caelerys, I would have you walk with me," she said.

"Yes, Your Majesty," she answered demurely. Cae rose, giving both her companions a squeeze of her hands in theirs, excused herself and trailed after the queen who turned and began walking back the way she had come.

The queen only glanced at her. "I would ask how you are doing, but I have my answers to that already," she said mysteriously, but not unkindly. "That woman is the worst kind of poison and I am done with her. ...Even though I know that is not the end of this," she sighed, frowning. "I just wish I knew how...." Her brow smoothed out almost immediately. "Syera wishes to see you, so I came to get you."

Cae glanced up at the queen in confusion. "You came yourself, Your Majesty?" she asked. "Why not send a servant?"

"I felt like a walk," was all she would say on the matter. "I am quite aware of Syera's feelings on the matter, and I wish to thank you for taking care of her that night. In spite of how," she added with a slightly reproving glance. "Though I dare say she will never over-indulge again."

"Neither will I, Your Majesty," she smiled ruefully.

"So, what were my son and your brother fighting over?" she asked suddenly, as they left the gardens and entered a side door of the Citadel.

Cae looked up. "You do not know, Your Majesty?"

"I, too, have heard the rumours." When Cae scowled as she tried to rein in her anger at the maliciousness and wicked minds of others, the queen added, "One of which was that my son had said something disparaging about **you**, causing your brother to challenge him. Val, of course, insists there was no duel. I do hope that is the truth."

Cae blushed. "Whatever the Crown says is the truth."

"Hmm, yes. But it does the Crown no service if it is often or obviously wrong."

Cae nodded. "My brother was... upset, I think, by his conversation with the princess. He never told me why, I only assumed. He has known about father longer than any of us, which might have added to matters. He went to the grounds to exercise his ...frustrations. Wisely, no one would spar with him, ...after the first idiot," she added with a roll of her eyes. "I had run to the grounds to try and talk some sense into him, afraid he might suddenly take further after father and slip into the battle rage. I've seen him come close before. Prince Valan accompanied me. When he realized destroying practice dummies was not helping Will, he volunteered." She sighed, "I at least made them fight with weapons that wouldn't result in one of them broken."

"Well, you ask me those two have been dying to test one other," the queen said with a conspiratory tip of her head.

Cae giggled at that, covering her mouth with her hand.

The queen smiled. "There. I am pleased to see you smiling again. It will do my daughter a world of good," she said as she opened the door to Syera's apartments.

The princess was standing on a low table in the middle of the receiving chamber being pinned into yards of gold fabric. "You found her!" she cried, resisting the urge to leap off the table and run to her. She flinched as a pin found something other than fabric to pierce.

"Was I missing?" Cae smiled.

"Yes!" She stopped as her mother just looked at her. "Well, I wanted to share breakfast with you and have you help with," she gestured to the women pinning, cutting and sewing all around her, "this. But your women said your brother had come looking for you to return to the Hall. When Tempest was gone this morning too, we assumed you'd remained there overnight. I was worried when you didn't come back."

Cae came as close as she could, reached up to take the princess's hand and give it a companionable squeeze. "I was up until nearly dawn. I slept late for once."

"Is everything... all right?" she asked hesitantly, glancing at the ladies around them.

"As well as can be. We'll know more after Bonfire Night."

"Do you know what... the matter is?"

She shook her head, "Will did not have time to tell me what he did know, just that if father takes a turn for the worst I'll be sent for."

"W... Lord Willam has left then?" she asked, trying to be indifferent and more regal.

Cae nodded. "On this morning's tide."

"A ship? Why didn't he ride?" she asked, surprised.

"Day and a half faster if you're lucky enough to have a ship going the right way."

She glanced up at the queen. "The Mother knows best," she sighed.

Caelerys sat down beside one of the seamstresses and looked over the embroidery she was doing. "So, will this be an Eldest or a Candle ceremony?"

She smiled as the princess looked offended by the mere thought. "Candle," she grimaced. "Like I would throw myself away with a church wedding? Not after what Lili told us."

"So have you decided who will stand and who will walk with you?" she asked evasively. In a Candle ceremony, each partner was brought to the altar by their closest friends, and chose one person to stand for them. Those who walked with them brought the assurances that they come willingly to the candle. The person who stood for them made the promise to stand behind them should anything go wrong in the marriage, to avenge or steal back a candle if necessary. This person could not be family.

"Well, you and Lili will walk with me, if you want to," she added. "I would have asked Lord Willam to stand for me, but that is not possible. I'm considering Vyncet, but not sure for a number of reasons."

The queen sat and picked up a small embroidery frame and began to sew. "There is a great deal of politics to consider," she advised.

Syera sighed. "I know. If I decide to do the political thing and asked another family, it will look as if yours has indeed fallen out of favour."

"Surely my walking with you will alleviate that enough?" Cae asked, looking over at the queen for confirmation.

"It might," Syera mused when her mother did not reply. "Wouldn't it, mother?"

The queen finally relented. "It should. If you chose carefully."

"Then I think I'll ask Lili's brother, Lord Selgan Cygent, to stand for me."

The queen smiled and Cae nodded. "I like that," said Cae. "It keeps us on the carpet but not so heavily in the light. I really think that if you had our House stand for you it would come across as too heavy handed."

The princess frowned. "But having Liliwyn walk with me **and** her brother standing... won't that do the same thing?"

Cae shook her head. "There are no rumours of a falling out between House Cygent and the throne. Also, it's not like you have any other choice unless you want to ask one of your vassal houses, and you really shouldn't. A royal wedding calls for a Great House."

They made idle chatter until the seamstresses had what they needed.

Then Syera ran them off, maids included, leaving only her, her mother and Cae. She sat down in the most comfortable chair in the room next to the one her mother was in.

Cae looked over at her. "So how are you *really* doing?" she asked softly.

She took a second to hold back the urge for tears. "Wretched," she muttered. At the moment, she did not look like a princess, merely an utterly miserable sixteen year old girl about to be wed, and not to the man she wanted. "I felt truly awful when I found out about the fight. I know it was all because of what I asked of him."

Cae moved closer, set her hand on hers and squeezed. "Even Will told me he agreed it was for the best, even though he did not elaborate. Just that you couldn't do what you needed to if he was around and that he didn't trust himself not to put up a fight if he stayed."

"It still hurt him," she sniffled.

"And you, too, from what I've heard."

"Yes, well, I didn't go pick a fight."

"I wouldn't call it picking a fight exactly," Cae demurred. Then she sighed. "Yeah, no. He was looking for something to work out his agony on. It is his way. Your brother merely volunteered to be the sacrifice."

This caused a laugh to burst from the princess's mouth. "So how badly did Will beat him?"

"Well," she breathed, drawing the word out and she leaned back in her chair, "It was a long, drawn out, close thing. But only because neither man had their preferred weapons in hand."

Syera thought about it. "That wouldn't have guaranteed a short, decisive fight. Just more injuries."

"Which we couldn't have. I knew what I was doing when I forced sword and shield on him. Your brother wanted to face him with only those weapons while Will was stripped to the waist and carried a maul."

Syera yielded to a slight shiver at that, though at the thought of Will without a shirt or her brother against a maul, Cae could not really tell. "At least Val thought to use a shield," she sighed. "He was initially just trying to give him something more active to vent his frustrations on. I don't think he realized what would happen."

"Or he didn't care."

"I told you," said the queen, tying off a thread. "Those two have been thinking about how that would play out ever since the grand melee at the very least."

"At least," Cae sighed. "What man could resist that kind of challenge? It was why Will went after Uncle in the melee. He'd been dying to test himself against what he considers the best."

The queen chuckled. "Yes, well, men are often fools when their egos become concerned." Her expression darkened as she thought of another implication of those words.

Syera turned to Cae, leaning over to rest her head upon her shoulder. "How are you doing? I know the rumours have to be killing you."

Cae snorted. "I'm not careful they might kill someone else. I've gone armed since the attack at the Hall."

Syera sat up and looked over at her. "Armed?"

Cae patted her thigh. "Right next to my pocket. A pretty little dagger Jan made me. I've used it hunting, but never against a person as yet. I get the feeling that may change."

"Sad state of affairs, but that is life," Syera sighed.

A maid entered the room with a light knock, curtseyed before them.

"If Your Majesty pleases, supper is ready."

The queen set aside her sewing and rose. "Thank you, Sallie. Girls, I shall see you both shortly. Liliwyn should be joining us." With that she left with the maid.

Cae and Syera rushed to make each other presentable, and arrived in the family dining hall not long after the princes.

The queen must have had words with the menfolk before they had joined them, as no one mentioned the rumours going around or what had happened in the gardens. The two brothers sat across the table from one another and often exchanged glances that Cae could not decide were hostile or not. They were certainly studying. Whenever she would notice, inevitably Valan would turn his gaze onto her, which would cause her to immediately find some other location for her eyes.

After supper, Liliwyn joined Cae in her room to talk about the coming wedding and to check up on her.

"You know, I actually feel sorry for Malyna," Cae sighed, after the wedding topic was exhausted.

"I know what you mean. I don't think she's really cut from the same cloth as her mother, but I'm not certain she will escape her meddling. She'll turn into her just to survive."

"She really didn't deserve being shamed with her mother, and I'm quite certain that woman will take it all out on her."

Lili nodded. "It's her own fault. Malyna was trying to be discreet. Lady Asparadane chose that spot deliberately, knowing it would not shield anyone from the conversation. I don't think she counted on the queen showing up."

"It has been a long time since the queen was in the gardens," Cae conceded. "But it was spectacular," she added with widened eyes.

"Oh, they were talking of nothing but, after you left," Lili said, her eyes lighting up. "You know Malyna's women whom her mother waved off?"

"Saw that did you?" Cae smiled.

"Oh, yes. She left them to do a bit of spying and attempted recovery."

"What could they do to recover from that?" Cae exclaimed. "She was clearly in the wrong."

She shook her head. "Oh, they were slyly going on here and there at how it all got started. How you were mean to Malyna when she was just trying to comfort you," she said dramatically.

Cae ground her teeth angrily.

"Oh, don't worry, Signy and I fixed most of that. Explaining exactly what had happened and lady Haria's part in it all. It really was her vicious remarks that made you unkind, justifiably too."

"I take it from Sigourney's presence that the Lord Mendicant will be performing for the wedding?" Cae asked her, feeling relieved to have the two women in her corner.

"Absolutely," she smiled.

"I rather like your sister," Cae said. "She was a great help to me when I first got here."

"Oh, she's great busybody," she laughed. "She's like one of those maiden aunts who can get away with saying just about anything to anybody and knows practically everyone. Not to mention all their dirty laundry. I'm still a little sore about Duke Griff's handling of the situation," she frowned. "After all, it's not like Avondyl cared. Everything would have been just fine if he hadn't made such a big deal of it."

"Can I ask what happened?"

Liliwyn sighed. "It's not really remembered much any more and we'd like to keep it that way but... let us just say that lord Remlock caught her in a secluded area of the gardens and ...well, forced his suit."

Cae's eyes grew wide. "How I think?"

She nodded.

"Wait, lord Remlock? You don't mean Lord Kaladen? Aldane's father?"

Again, she nodded. "He wasn't Lord Kaladen back then. Granted, he was shortly after that, not that it did any good. When Lord Griff cancelled the betrothal, father asked her if she would accept Remlock's proposal."

Cae gasped. "What? What did she do?"

"I don't think I've ever been afraid of my sister until that moment. I didn't know if she intended to stab father or herself with that knife, but she ended up throwing it instead. When the scandal began to circulate... and I'm sure Remlock made sure that it did..."

"I'm sure Lord Griff was no help there. He'd need to save face in light of the broken betrothal," Cae said.

Lili nodded. "That's when she ran away. A few years later we found out she was with the Lord Mendicant's show and father quietly... well, he never formally disowned her, but they've got some agreement that she's never really mentioned. He's respecting her choice to protect me."

Cae sighed sadly, "The things we do for family."

Lili shrugged. "Sometimes those things end up making us happy."

This made Cae look more closely at her friend. "How are you doing? Everyone's asking about me, but you're the one being forced onto the market when you're probably still mourning."

"That part still hurts," she said. She reached out and squeezed Cae's hand. "But I have plenty of friends helping me deal with it. Like you and your brothers say: 'We survive'."

Cae chuckled. "That is practically our House motto. Though there is a story that it was suggested ages ago, but a wise ancestor thought it would imply that we'll do anything to do so and would cast us in a darker light."

Lili gave her a wicked grin, "Oh, like the Asparadane motto should be 'We shall rise... at all cost'?"

Cae nodded vigorously. "I think uncle would have us 'Even our does have antlers'!"

This left the girls in giggles that, once they began coming up with mottoes for other Houses, became almost hysterical. Everything was funny, and no sooner had they gotten themselves partly under control, something would start it all over again. When they finally got to the stage where even breathing hurt, they managed, in tears, to calm down and bid their farewells.

However, as Lili was hugging her good night, she whispered in her ear in the old tongue, "You have a spy in your household."

As she was pulling away, Cae held onto her with widened eyes and broad smile as if she had just imparted half a delicious secret. "Oh, you must tell me who!"

Lily smiled mysteriously and shook her head coyly. "I'm not sure yet. You'll be the first to know, I promise."

When Liliwyn left, Cae kept her smile of secret joy upon her face even though she did not feel it. One of the ladies assigned to her was a spy. Some of the rumours made sense now.

Her ladies began to come out of their retiring chamber.

"Will my lady be going to the library tonight or be abed early?" asked Coral.

"I... I am staying in tonight, thank you," she said. There was really no point in any of them going to the tower tonight as the moons were nearly non-existent and would not yield enough light.

The younger maids were sent for bathwater and Cae pulled out an old bit of lacing with a scrap of fur tied to it. She attracted Tempest's attention on the floor and spent the time playing a game of cat and mouse with her until Fern came to tell her the bath was ready.

Seeing Fern was alone, she asked her to bring her the bag of scraps for the bird as she lured Tempest onto her wrist. When Fern brought it and held it open for her, Cae took the opportunity to whisper what Lili had warned her of as she fed a few titbits to her greedy companion. "So watch what you say but don't seem to be. Say only what is safely repeated. Mayhap we can use this to our advantage."

Fern nodded, putting the bag back on its hook and leading Cae into the warm dressing chamber to undress her for the bath waiting in there. There was chatter about tomorrow night, and excitement at the inevitable show. Gowns were chosen for day and the evening's festivities: green for the morning and a rich russet and gold for Bonfire Night.

"Will my lady be returning to the library after tomorrow?" Fern asked casually.

Cae shook her head before tipping back to wet her hair for washing. "I am not sure yet. The queen said I could take a break for a little while. I've been working very hard. I will go back, I just don't know when."

"Of course, my lady."

Pansy could not help herself as she began the process of washing Cae's long dark hair. "Is it true that Lady Liliwyn has had an offer?" she asked. "I am so excited for her if it is true. She does seem less ...morose of late."

"She does seem less unhappy," Cae mused. "She hinted there might be, but she wouldn't tell me. She may not know yet. Of course, until the princess is wed, no one else will really be settled."

"I might be able to find out for you, my lady," said Coral. "I know quite a few influential and well placed people. It is a harmless bit of information that might still be useful to you. If the young Cygent does not herself know, perhaps she would appreciate knowing?"

She glanced at the older woman, wondering what information she herself might have slipped and to what 'harmless' purpose. She decided that if she could find out whether the ruse was even true, it would at least warn Liliwyn there were spies in her own household. "I think that would be very kind if you could manage it," she said. "But please, discretion. It would not do for anyone else to know, or to know we are asking."

"My lady, I am the soul of discretion," she said, with a look in her eye that Cae could not decipher.

"But of course," Cae answered, and sank back under Pansy's ministrations.

"Do you think Lord Willam will send a messenger or a toomi when he gets home and learns more about the duke's health?" Fern asked, setting out drying cloths on a stool near where Tempest paced the edge of the tub.

"Toomi, probably. He knows I'm worried. And he took some of our husbands back home with him, so there are plenty of messenger birds. We could know as early as the day after tomorrow, when he gets off the ship."

"A pair of Toomi might be a good wedding gift," Coral offered as they rinsed her hair with pitchers of warm water.

"I am sure that someone will be gifting her a set of birds," she answered. "Though I might make sure she has a few of our husbands before she leaves. The wedding present is already being made."

They got her out of the bath and dried off, getting her into her nightdress. As they were turning down the bed for her, Cae found a book on the night table that she did not remember putting there. "Where did this come from?" she asked.

Sorrel smiled. "Oh, that was delivered by a worm earlier, my lady. Forgive me, it came so early I forgot to tell you."

She nodded, and climbed into the bed, letting them light the canopy lamp. She intended to stay up for several hours, and even Tempest snuggled down next to her. When she opened the front, unmarked cover, she found a small note in old Vermian. 'Compliments of your research partner. Now comparing notes with my other half who said this might interest you. Also, have located the telescope. Will alert you when it arrives.'

It was unsigned, but then it did not need to be, she knew the hand from her notes and 'research partner' could only be Balaran. She hoped she understood his message correctly, and that he and Val were indeed comparing notes. Curious as to what Val could have thought would interest her, she began to read the book. It was a history of faith and cultural comparisons for Elanthus and beyond, with a whole chapter on

Alumet and mentions even of Telmar and her neighbours across the sea.

That night she had a nightmare of sharks attacking something large at the surface of the water. She could not tell what it was, as it was night and there was little light to see anything beyond a vague shape. But the beasts tore at her heart even as they tore at their prey. It left her feeling like she was drowning, and, when she woke, she was covered in sweat.

18

Waking as she did, Cae started her day with yet another bath. This one not quite as immersive, as the very thought of submerging her body in water made her ill. No one said anything about it, and only Fern quietly asked for assurances that she was well.

As she sat to breakfast, she was delighted to have Janem drop in for a visit. She offered to share her breakfast with him, which he did not refuse. She knew it would likely be his supper. He was slowly losing some of his tan.

She smiled. "Have you gone completely nocturnal?"

"Whooo, me?" he quipped with a grin. "Just about. Hear you've almost done the same."

"Not quite," she countered. "And I've been smart and taking naps."

"I am not old enough yet to subject myself to naps," he frowned. As he ate he reached into the pocket of his jerkin and set a box on the table. "Daph said to deliver this."

She picked it up eagerly, not caring that her occupied hands meant he had unimpeded access to her plate. "I'd go easy on the sweets and heavy foods if you are going to bed when you leave," she warned, but let him as she opened the box. Inside was a pretty rose-gold bat in flight, winging across the face of a silver moon. It was realistically rendered with chips of onyx for its eyes. The pin-back was thin enough not to damage fine fabrics, but sturdy enough to hold even damask without bending or coming open. "It is beautiful. I hope she likes it. Please tell Daph it is everything I was looking for."

Mouth full, he merely nodded. "Bonfiring?" he asked when he swallowed.

"Here in the gardens. I assume you'll be out on the fairgrounds with the rest of the city?"

"Yup. Far be it for me to mingle with my betters," he quipped.

"But surely they are your best customers?" she said, eyeing him.

"Yeah," he smirked. "Exactly why I'm not going to spend my free time among them. It wouldn't be free for long."

She played with the edge of her napkin. "Some of the ladies have expressed an interest in you."

He paled. "What?" he choked, her mug of small ale halfway to his mouth.

"Very interested," she smiled, nodding as she teased. She shrugged. "Not sure they're your type though."

"If they have a title of any kind they're very much 'not my type'," he growled.

SHIFT: Stag's Heart

"You are hardly Folk, Jan," she admonished, threatening him with a sweet roll which he snatched from her.

"Half," he said.

She held her hand out flat.

"What?" he asked, taking a large bite.

"Half," she demanded.

He grumbled, "Not what I meant and you know it," even as he ripped the roll in two and handed her the part he had not bitten.

"Well, if that's your criteria, I can always see if Fern is of a mind," she smiled. "That way I can always keep track of you."

"Not a chance. She's too... slender. I'd break her in half."

Fern came in with a second mug of ale which she set in front of him with a humph, taking Cae's from his hand and returning it to her. "I'd like to see you try it," she growled. "My lady, if you wish to see the queen this morning, I would suggest you not dally over long. She usually leaves her chambers in about a half hour." As she sauntered away from the table, she called over her shoulder, "Skinny girls are more limber."

Cae blushed and giggled as Janem turned to stare at her maid's retreating form. He finally turned back to the table. "Nope," he said firmly, as if convincing himself. "Not interested in your little spy, no matter how tempting that..." he cut himself off, glaring at his sister's smirk. He pointed a finger at her, "Tyet," he growled in Vermian.

Tempest's head came up at that and she stopped trying to sidle closer to the plate.

Cae laughed. "I think she has her eyes on a young man here at the Citadel. Servant named Roan. I'll have to ask how that's going, if it even is." She shrugged, "Then again, she may surprise us both." She rose, bent to pick up the box and kiss his cheek. "I have to go," she said. "You two can have the rest."

She left the room with her brother and her bird both making grabs for the last sausage.

She was admitted to the queen's rooms shortly after she was announced. The queen was indeed getting ready to leave her apartments for the day. She smiled as Cae was led in. "How are you this morning, my dear?" she asked warmly.

"Well enough, Your Majesty," she answered with a curtsey.

"Suitably vague," she commented. "You are not well but managing. You are learning. Anything new troubling you?" she asked as if she knew there was. And with the queen, she very well could.

"Oh, nothing really. Just bad dreams."

The queen eyed her. "Bad dreams are very often our minds trying to tell us what we are afraid of. Do not dismiss them out of hand. Especially if they repeat themselves."

She bowed her head. "Thank you for the advice, Your Majesty. You have far too much to do today to waste time with my dreams. Perhaps some afternoon when you are not so much in demand, if you truly wish to know. Today I come bearing a gift."

"A gift?" she asked, surprised. "What ever for? This is the time of presents for my daughter, not me."

Cae blushed. "I had it made for you well before the announcement, to thank you for everything you have done for me and my family. I know that I am only aware of part it, and I wish my gratitude and loyalty known, at least to you." She held out the gift.

A maid crossed over and accepted the small wooden box. Opening it, she gasped. She lifted the brooch from the box, turned it over, opened the pin deftly. She surreptitiously ran her fingers along the length, testing for burrs, then tapped the point. She winced only a little as the sharp tip drew blood and slipped the wounded finger into her mouth. Only then did she turn and hand it, once more closed, to the queen on her open palm.

The queen was delighted. She fondled the gleaming bat, her eyes moist and lost in thought. "How did you know that I have been thinking of my family?"

Cae was surprised and quick to deny it. "Oh, I am not like you, Your Majesty. The Mother does not guide me, not nearly so directly. I merely... the talk of weddings in general has had me thinking of my own, and how I shall miss my home and family and crest wherever I end up. It is always so much harder upon the women, isn't it, Your Majesty?"

The queen nodded. "Sometimes," she said softly.

"So I thought some small token of your House, as a reminder that ours has not forgotten."

The queen looked up a few seconds before lady Caena entered the room. She nodded before the lady could speak, knowing she was being hurried. She handed her the pin. "Please set that out with my gown for this evening. I will wear it to the Bonfire."

"Of course, my queen," she curtseyed, eyeing the pin as she placed it back in the box the first maid handed her.

The queen then allowed herself to be led from the room, but paused in the hall. "You and Liliwyn will be attending the performance and the lighting tonight with Syera. Please do not be late."

Cae sank into a deep curtsey. "Of course, Your Majesty."

Everywhere that Cae went that day she saw signs of preparation for the coming night. Servants swarmed the grounds and castle proper, setting up the holders for the slim, ceremonial torches that would be lit from the bonfire later as prayers and wishes. What courtiers were in the gardens were making small straw poppets, effigies of their troubles to burn.

Sigourney was seated with Lili instructing a group of other younger women and a few young men who were far more interested in the ladies than learning to make the dolls. Cae joined them. It took her a little practice to get the neat twist and tuck Sigourney was showing them.

There were baskets of scrap paper all over the terrace with pen and ink available to write one's troubles and wishes. Cae made four of them, writing upon each in the Old Vermian. One for her family's health, Vyncet and their father. One for Willam's trouble and protection. One for Syera, and one which she could not make up her mind what she wanted it for. It was more she could not put into words what was needed: answers, guidance, help for the afflicted. Finally she wrote simply: Understanding.

Before Liliwyn slipped one of her papers into her doll, she showed Cae what it read. It was a simple wish for Malyna to wake up and get free of her mother's wickedness before it ruined her. Cae nodded, pleased that Lili had thought of it, a little disappointed in herself that she hadn't.

"A lot of wishes," grinned Lord Avondyl as she sauntered up and saw the array of dolls on the table. "Or am I to believe that the very flowers of Elanthus are so deeply troubled?"

"There has been a great deal of trouble of late," Cae said with a sad smile, tucking her tiny dolls into her pocket. "What with the attacks on the villages and the treasure ship. People are worried."

He eyed her carefully, "Least of all about a young girl's future?" he asked.

She shook her head. "My future will be what it will be. It is my family that worry me."

"I am sorry to hear about your father," he said, taking a serious tone. "You have my sincerest wishes that he will get well."

"Thank you, my lord. Your kindness is appreciated."

He glanced down at Sigourney. "I don't know what they mean at all," he exclaimed. "She seems perfectly capable of seeing and appreciating kindness when it is properly and sincerely offered." He looked back up at Caelerys and flashed her a mischievous smile. "I don't think you have a mean bone in your body. Any one who can train a gauvan to curtsey can't possibly."

She blushed, mumbling a second thank you for his vote of confidence.

"By the way," he added, "I believe my brother is looking for you."

"Me?" she asked, surprised.

"Yes, you. Seeing as you are the only Maral currently available," he mused, wandering off again.

"Well, where would I find him?" she called.

He turned, walking backwards. "Oh, I am certain he'll find you eventually. It's not like he's in a hurry. Oh, wait, he is!" he laughed, turning back around.

"Oh, that man!" Sigourney snarled playfully.

This brought a laugh from the present company and conversation turned to more pleasant subjects.

Lord Rorik found her on her way back into the Citadel to get ready.

He was very formal in his approach, bowing and greeting her appropriately. "May I speak with you a moment?" he asked.

She stopped and smiled, returning his greeting, "Of course."

He offered her his arm to walk her to wherever she was bound. She made sure the pace was slow enough that they might talk without ending up standing outside her door. "I am in a bit of a quandary, my lady."

"Surely not," she demurred.

He gave her a slightly embarrassed smile which looked out of place on his rugged face. "You see, I need someone to stand for me, and I would like very much for Willam to be the one, but I had heard he was called home." There was something in the way he said it that hinted that he had heard at least some of the rumours.

She gave him a reassuring smile, "I thank you for being so circumspect. Are you certain you wish my family in light of ...things?"

He shook his head. "I pay little heed to rumours, especially when they seem out of character with what I know of a person. I have fought with your brother, and I know he is fair and will ride Death itself down where his friends and family are concerned. I count him a friend and sincerely hope he does as well."

She gave him a small nod. "I cannot speak for my brother's mind, but I know he does not count you an enemy."

Rorik chuckled. "That's a relief. I've seen what he does to those. Which is why I cannot countenance anything I have heard about the training grounds," he added with a frown.

"Our father is ill and merely needed his heir to help him with Ducal business," she said. "Sadly, I do not think he can be back in time for the wedding. I have no idea what he was called home for or how long it will take, and it is a four day trip to the capitol. I am sorry."

He sighed, resigned. "I feared as much. I would ask you, but," he smiled, "you are walking with my bride and that would be..."

"Awkward?" she offered.

"I would have said a conflict, but then I think in terms of conflict," he apologized.

She patted his arm. "That is nothing for a warrior to be ashamed of, unless he allows it to consume all his affairs. That might lead to marital trouble," she grinned.

"Ah, yes. Would your other brother, Lord Vyncet be available or inclined? He'll just have to stand, no walking required."

"Available, yes, inclined? You'll have to ask him. He has returned to Stag Hall, though he will be here tonight. And if you must have a Maral behind you, and he cannot, my subsequent brother cleans up nicely, though he will be harder to convince."

"I'm sure if you asked, he would tackle armies," he said, flattering her.

"He would certainly arm them," she responded wryly.

This gave him pause. "Oh yes, the moonsilver smith! It is hard to remember him as a noble son," he said ruefully.

She nodded. "No need to apologize. He works very hard to cultivate his Folk image. If I remember correctly, he speaks Rustic as fluently as anything else he speaks, and twice as fast," she chuckled.

Reaching her door, Rorik turned to face her, bowed over her hand. "Well, I shall leave you to get ready. I should go and do the same. I thank you for your time and care, Lady Caelerys. I shall seek Lord Vyncet out tonight. My sincerest wishes for your father's health."

She gave a shallow curtsey. "Thank you, Lord Rorik. I wish you good fortune."

He smiled at her and then took his leave. Pansy opened the door for her, and ushered her into the flurry that was her preparations for one of the most anticipated nights of the year.

※

Caelerys stepped out into the hall with Fern and Pansy flanking her, both in their holiday best: Pansy in green and Fern in blue. Cae was a vision in a russet damask with an underdress and accents of harvest gold. Her hair was braided into a coronet and left to fall in rich, dark curls down her back. The braid was graced by tiny white and yellow flowers tucked here and there, and a small pair of carved wooden antlers accented in gold leaf ringed the back half of her head.

Before she could take more than a few steps, Liliwyn came out of her room, a scintillating dream in yellow that rippled with cross threads of gold and red and orange. Even her hair had been done up with strips of veiling in oranges and reds, turning her honey tresses into a simulated bonfire. Only one of her ladies came with her, the others hurried off down the hall to get to the fairgrounds to enjoy what they could of the evening.

Lili looked her over, began to fuss over how fetching Caelerys looked. Tempest chirped at her from the floor, wanting admiration too. Even she was decked out with small bells on her ankles and shook a leg to show them off. Lili made sure to fuss over the bird as well.

Cae was marvelling at how they had managed Lili's hair when they reached the princess's suite on the floor above them. Syera was resplendent in emerald with a flame coloured underdress, and her hair looped into a standing halo-like crown of braids entwined with cloth-of-gold ribbons. The princess added two more handmaids to their entourage and together they swept down the grand staircase to the gardens for the lighting ceremony.

It was already dusk by the time they reached the wide terrace where the pavilions were always set up. The sun was gone and the remaining light was fading fast. The pavilion was absent and in its place stood a stack of firewood that was twice the height of a man, and easily four across at the base. The bonfire in the fairgrounds would dwarf this one. Cae knew that deep in the heart of the bonfire were bales of straw to help it catch.

People had already begun to gather well back from the possible reach of the flames, and servants were doing last minute prep work: setting out buckets of water near the plants at the edges of the terrace and crates filled with the slender torches.

The princess's group stood at the outer edge of the cleared area, at the head of one of the paths. They did not wait long before the twin princes and their retinues came to stand at the head of a different path. The king and queen, with the two youngest princes approached from yet a third point, standing in such a way that all three groups could see the others. Everyone all but held their breath as it grew darker and the stars came out in the heavens, the only lights anywhere to be seen.

Then a piece of that night seemed to materialize out of the darkness in front of the tower of wood. A stream of fire streaked from a narrow point to a wide blaze at the kindling igniting it in a burst of colours: green, red and blue. The light flared revealing a hooded man in a starry cloak with the head of a dragon blowing across his open palm from whence came the flames. The audience reacted first with screams, then gasps of delight.

Cae leaned over to Lili to whisper, "That's going to go over well with the church crowd."

Liliwyn grinned, "That's the best thing about Bonfire Night. The church crowd are in the churchyard, gathered around a sanctioned fire. They'll not involve themselves in our pagan revelry."

"All hail the barbarian," Cae laughed.

The Lord Mendicant turned with a swirl of his cloak and swept off the dragon's head mask as he bowed flamboyantly, revealing his usual black silk mask. He crossed to the princess and executed another florid turning of his hands in the air as he went to one knee like an ardent suitor. From nothing in his hands materialized a glittering glass rose, with a tiny coiled dragon wrapped around it to bury its face within the gilt edged petals.

She almost squealed with delight, but remembered herself and where she was. She smiled, giving him a graceful nod and a gracious thank you as she accepted the gift. She looked it over in the growing firelight, watching the light glint through the petals and the ungilded parts of the dragon with fascination. Finally, she turned to one of her maids and bade her to see the gift safely to her chambers. The girl took the glass rose with all due care and slipped away down a less used path.

Syera turned back to the still kneeling master performer and glanced over towards her parents. Her father merely nodded at her to get on with it. She smiled down at the man, offering him her hand. He kissed the air over her fingertips. "My Lord Mendicant, you are ever a surprise and a delight. I can think of no more appropriate way to begin this Bonfire Night. May the darkness of the sky hide away all your faults, the fire burn away all your cares and the light of the returning moons illuminate your good fortune."

He smiled at her, bowing his head once more before he rose. He stepped back and turned with a dramatic flair. "Where are my goblins? My fey things, my beasts?" he called.

There was a cough and answering roar of the great spotted cat from somewhere nearby in the gardens, and the jingling of bells and the chatter of birds. Tempest poked around Cae's skirts where she had hidden when the fire had been lit. Cae offered her wrist and the bird flew up, watched the tumblers cavorting in among the revellers, each in elaborate costumes, some scattering little flowers twisted from the dried leaves of harvested plants.

Liliwyn recognized her sister in a dress made of a rainbow of scarves, almost every available surface of her arms, shoulders and head covered with colourful and chatty birds. She only smiled.

Folk mingled for a while, taking their turns going to the fire to toss in their poppets and light their torches. One of the performers was walking about with the ca'theryn on a leash. Most people were giving them a wide berth, even as they stared with delight.

Cae's group did not move much, though Liliwyn stepped back a little to give them room to pass, and Tempest crawled up to Cae's shoulder warily. Fern held her ground, though terrified, and the other maids all backed away. Syera's attempted to get her to back up with them, but the princess stayed put. The handler tried to give them a respectable distance while still providing a good view of the animal, but the creature had other ideas.

Cae flicked her shoulder in a gesture that sent Tempest into the air. The bird flew as far as one of the torchless stands and clung there, looking worried and pitiful as the great spotted cat crept slowly closer to her mistress. Cae was careful to stand still.

"He will not harm you," the handler said quietly, still trying to convince the cat otherwise. "Just do not make any sudden moves."

The cat stretched to the limit of his leash and sniffed at her skirts, his mouth open as he tasted the air, tried to reach her. Cautiously, Cae extended her hand, let the cat touch it with his stiff but tickly whiskers. She smiled, slowly knelt until she was face to face with it. "Sensen," she said gently.

Behind her, she heard one of the ladies ask, "What did she call it?"

"She told it 'softly'," Liliwyn translated in a low voice.

Cae was delighted as the cat first sniffed her face, then licked her nose, before lowering his head and headbutting her in the chest. He was strong enough to knock her off balance, causing her to fall back onto her rear, laughing as he tried to climb over her to reach her still. "Tyet, tyet. Sensen," she laughed, even as the handler began pulling back on the leash, calling for it to stop in Alumet.

The cat cocked his head at her, but stepped back, sitting down, pretty as you please. Cae sat up and looked into the flickering green eyes for a moment. No one moved. Then she reached up and began to run her fingers over the surprisingly soft and thick fur. The cat was understandably happy with this, even more so when the princess dared to touch him too.

"He's so soft," Syera breathed.

"Your Highness, is that wise?" quivered one of her ladies.

"It won't be if you cause the beast to start," she said with a smile that was not echoed in her voice. "If you are too nervous, you can return to the Citadel, or go to the fairgrounds with the others."

The girl closed her mouth and slinked even further back.

Liliwyn, not to be left out, joined on the other side of Cae. "Oooh, he smells... like spice flowers."

Cae bent closer and sniffed, got herself licked for her trouble. "He does! Aren't you just beautiful?" she purred to the cat. He rubbed his head against her cheek, purring so hard she felt the vibrations to her bones. "I didn't know they purred like cats," she commented to the handler.

"They do. They have a great deal in common with their tiny cousins," he said, still trying to understand what had come over his animal. "He's not usually this friendly."

"Well, most people shy away from him, don't they?" Liliwyn said, adding the last to the cat as her nails found a spot behind his ear that had him over the moons.

"This is true. You do not fear him?" he asked Cae.

She shook her head. "Why should I? You have deemed him safe enough to walk through the royal gardens, and I know that they can be trained as hunting companions, much like we train hounds."

"You know of the ca'theryn?"

"Of," she smiled. "I do not know much. His Highness, Prince Cyran Onkelan was kind enough to tell me a little."

He gave her a doubtful look when she said the word kind which caused her to smile. "Well, he was more bragging than anything. But one must be polite where Royalty is concerned, anan?"

He gave a toothy, understanding smile. "Dasa," he nodded.

"That means 'yes'?"

He nodded again.

"I will learn Alumet eventually," she chuckled.

"Ooo, teach me?" Liliwyn asked. "When you know enough?"

Cae laughed. "Why don't I just find us both a tutor?" She gave the cat one last scratch and pressed a kiss to his cheek. "*No more, my sweet,*" she said in Vermian, and slowly stood.

The cat stepped back to give her room, and Lili and the princess stood with her.

"Thank you for allowing us such a close look at this magnificent animal," the princess said. "It was a worthy experience."

The man bowed in the style of the North. "Consider it a wedding gift from a humble and unworthy supplicant, princess," he said, the pause and hitch of his native accent becoming more pronounced. He turned to the other two and bowed again, "And may the light of Love and Justice shine favourably upon both of you upon their return."

Cae curtseyed, "And upon you, most noble and worthy keeper of cats."

His white teeth flashed in his dark face as he clucked to his charge and began to lead him away. Those who had seen the exchange did not move quite so far away this time.

The moment the cat was out of reach, Tempest flew to Cae's shoulder and began scolding her.

Liliwyn laughed, reaching up to stroke her head feathers. "Oh, hush.

Jealousy does not become you, young lady."

Tempest huffed, but began to settled down with feigned indifference as Cae began to pet and croon sweet words to her. The other two laughed.

Cae looked away from the bird to see Prince Valan a few dozen yards away, watching her.

He looked very sharp in an embroidered, green velvet cote so dark it looked black. His hair, still uncut, hung in loosely curling, gold locks to his shoulders, held back from his face only by the gold circlet on his brow.

She could feel his gaze deep inside her, and knew that one of them needed to look away soon or who knew what she might do. She felt a little faint.

She was thankfully distracted by one of the performers cavorting in front of her, offering her and her companions torches from the bucket he carried. When he realized it was the princess he was before, he performed a bow so violent, it turned into a somersault.

The ladies laughed and Syera and Liliwyn moved to select torches from his trove. When Cae looked up to see the prince again, he was gone. Sighing, she selected two torches. The performer handed them wood wrapped graphite sticks to write names upon the torches and waited until they were done to reclaim them.

Liliwyn noticed that Cae had written both her father and Willam's names in old Vermian.

Cae looked over her shoulder to her maids, asking if either of them desired to light a torch for someone. Fern accepted one, but showed no one the name she wrote.

Once they were done, they approached the bonfire, amazed by the amount of heat it gave off. Before they lit them, their maids handed them their poppets to throw in. Fern had been carrying Cae's, not trusting any of the other ladies to do so. Each of them held the straw dolls for a moment in their hands, concentrating on their desires, and then cast them into the blaze, committing them to the Mother's will and care. Liliwyn threw two, the princess only one. Cae sent hers into the fire one by one, sending her prayers with them. The last she held up to Tempest who had watched the activity with curiosity. Cae had not often felt the need to cast poppets. The bird took the doll in her beak and flew up, circling the fire before dropping her cargo into the highest point. She stayed there a while, riding the thermals high into the sky, watching the world below.

Cae could almost feel the contradiction of cool breeze and hot, rising wind.

Lili jostled her back to attention, stepped forward to light her torch. Like most people doing the same thing, she reached her arm as far as she could, trying to keep clothing and hair out of danger. When Cae and Syera had followed suit, they waited for Fern to light hers before carrying the slim, lit flambeaus through the gardens until they found torch stands not yet occupied in a location they felt right.

They were down by the wall that overlooked the river. After setting their torches upon the stands, they paused to gaze out over the harbour. They could easily see the ships out on the river by the glittering of torches on the water. The sounds of revelry drifted ashore.

It was a quiet, pleasant, private moment. Even the maids hung back, trying their best to be invisible.

"So what did you throw in?" Liliwyn asked Syera.

SHIFT: Stag's Heart

"My love for Willam," she whispered.

"Oh, ketava," Cae breathed. She leaned against the princess, taking her hand in hers. On the other side, Lili did the same. The three of them stood like that until a deep, gonging sound reverberated throughout the gardens.

"The Lord Mendicant," gasped one of the princess's ladies excitedly.

Syera gave their hands a last squeeze before letting go and turning. "Yes, that is our signal to head in if we wish to see the show."

"Same place as last time?" Cae asked.

The princess nodded.

Lili's eyes lit up. "You've had the opportunity to see them perform?"

"At the coronation," she nodded.

"I'm so glad. They are a wonder, are they not?"

"Absolutely. Even Tempest enjoyed herself," she added as the bird fluttered down to her shoulder to tell her to hurry.

They rushed through the now well-lit gardens. In darker corners they could hear the playful antics of men and women enjoying the advantages and novelty of the royal gardens at night. They exchanged knowing smiles and kept going.

They arrived just before the final gong, calling patrons to their seats. Syera sat next to Balaran and pulled young Janniston onto her lap to enjoy the show. Cae and Lili were seated beside her, and Tempest remained upon her shoulder, the better to see now that she knew some of what to expect.

It was just as spectacular as before, but by no means the same. Sigourney's performance held the same form but the songs were different. The lady and the dragon went largely unchanged because it was always so popular, though the fire tricks were altered for variety. Even the skit with the fat man being chased by the ca'theryn looked more like a sequel to the first, as both parties seemed to know what to expect, having gone through it before. The merchant was prepared with a long, wobbly spear which the cat amused everyone by dancing around, over and under. He finally grabbed the spear and took it away from the man and chased him down. Only this time, when he pounced and gutted him, instead of butterflies, a child midget in spotted, yellow motley popped out to everyone's surprise. She looked startled to see the cat and tried to run, only to have the ca'theryn grab her by the scruff of her costume and carry her offstage like a cub.

There were other acts of wonder and magic. The final performance took place against a black backdrop before which two costumed actors portrayed the moons: golden justice and silver compassion, turning slowly in their dance across the skies. The backs of their costumes were black, so that, as they turned, they seemed to roll through their phases. Cae suspected that the pattern of their dance was carefully choreographed so that any astronomer would find them intensely familiar. The dance ended with both promenading towards the back of the stage area, where they disappeared.

The show ended to a thunderous applause, with even Tempest shrilling her pleasure. Once folk began to wander away after the performance, musicians started to play in various places throughout the gardens.

They found themselves once more on the terrace, watching the dancing flames, when Lord Rorik found them, and asked Syera to dance. She could find no reason to deny him, and, after a long glance into the fire, nodded.

SHIFT: Stag's Heart

Lili and Cae stood side by side, watching their friend with a mix of sadness and joy, wishing her only the best, knowing how hard it was going to be. They were so distracted, they did not notice when the two princes slipped up, one on either side of them like a pair of bookends, sliding their hands along their lower arms and raising them until the ladies' hands were perched upon theirs as they walked forward, drawing the surprised women along with them. Just like that, they found themselves dancing around the bonfire. Tempest made herself scarce.

The twin princes were dressed similarly. In the dim light, at a distance, one would only tell them apart by Valan's shorter, loose curls, and Balaran's flying braid, bound neatly from the nape of his neck. Cae caught glimpses of Liliwyn as they whirled by, saw the soft smile on her face and smiled herself. Then she was captivated by the fierce expression with which Valan watched her.

"What is it that my prince finds so fascinating about my face?" she asked.

"If my lady does not own a mirror, perhaps I shall make her a gift of one."

She blushed. "There are other faces more fair," she insisted.

"Ah, but none that confuse me half so much as you."

She swallowed, not sure what to say to that, how to take it or the feelings that were beginning creep unbidden into her heart from where the two of them touched. As they turned, palm to palm, eyes locked, she felt his hand like a firebrand against her skin and wondered if he found hers cool to the touch.

"How goes your research?" she asked, as much to distract her mind as to gain an answer.

"Frustrated by the dark," he said, a glimmer of a smile on his lips.

"Ah. But partners can make even dark nights fruitful." She regretted her wording the moment it was out of her mouth, and blushed furiously, turning her eyes from his. "That was not..." she tried to say, but couldn't get the words out.

"I know what you meant. Granted, my 'other half' would not have let you off nearly so lightly."

She smiled ruefully, knowing full well where the conversation would have ended with the party in question. "No, he would not."

"But I am glad the two of you are speaking again," she added.

"For once, our studies coincide."

She glanced once more to Balaran and Lili. "Will he ask for her, do you think?" she asked.

"I would hardly think them well matched," he said, watching her. She could not feel the other moving at all beneath the gaze, though his questions were leading.

"Couples do not have to be similar in every way to be perfectly in tandem. The Marrok brothers aside. Yes, he is bright and gregarious and full of life and she is still in mourning, sedate and sad and beautiful. But he will draw her out and fill her with life, and she will help him focus and take life just a little more seriously. Intellectually, they are well matched."

"In short, not for me," he said.

"Ah, I fear she would leave you too much to your deepness, understanding it too well, and neither of you will find that contented middle where you are whole people," she answered.

"So have you found any candidates among your associates?" he asked, reminding her of her promise once upon a different dance.

She sighed. "So far, only Liliwyn is suitable who remains unmarried."

"But you mean her for my brother."

"I did not say she was not for you. Only that she and your brother were better off together. Lady Balyra is a match for you in mindset, strong willed and determined to do the best for her people. Alas, I also think she is too much like you in temperament and would therefore allow you to overindulge those traits I think need a little tempering, for your own good, of course," she said, softening her words with a smile. "She would have to give up the heirship to her sister if you were to choose her, which might not be in the best interests of House Roshan. But, I believe she would set aside hopes for my brother if you asked for her."

He shook his head, "No, I quite think the crown has taken enough from your brothers to last a few generations." He watched the changes of emotion ripple across her face, unable to read any of them. "Are you telling me, that with all the flowers of Elanthian maidenhood gathered here, there are none more suited?"

She shook her head. "Among the maidens, no. Unless you wish an empty-headed trinket, or one not capable of handling the stress and responsibilities."

He drew her close, his voice rumbling possessively in his chest. "And what if I fly in the face of your recommendations and merely take where my desire leads?"

She felt a chill from one direction and an inexplicable warmth from another, reacting violently where they met somewhere in her middle. "That... that would be entirely between Your Highness and His Majesty your father,... and the kingdom," she breathed. "Though I would advise my prince to remember the tale of Isildar and Denan before you steal yourself a bride."

He leaned down to her ear and whispered, "I am no thief who takes what is not on offer. If the maiden be willing... I think I am quite to the point where fathers be damned."

Her breath caught in her throat at that. Her mind chastised her body for wishful thinking, but her body was just not listening. She thought, for a second, that she felt scales writhe against her hand, but when she looked, it was as smooth as ever. His pulse was noticeable, however, as she was sure was hers.

Balaran bumped into them. When he was certain he had his brother's attention, he cut in, deftly passing Liliwyn off to Val and snatching Cae up. "Getting too close there, brother. Wouldn't do to tip our hands too early," he said cryptically as he whirled away with Cae for a more energetic saltation.

"What are you up to?" she accused him.

"Nothing I'm ready to reveal," he grinned. "Though I do want to thank you."

"For?" she sighed, allowing him the diversion.

"For telling him." She gave him a nod of acceptance. "We're almost as close as we were before he went... weird. Though now we know why, eh?" he grinned.

She blushed. "That is just a theory."

"And as good as any we've got."

They danced for almost the entire song without saying much of anything else. Cae was thoroughly enjoying herself. She enjoyed her times with Bal, he made her laugh, and really exert herself. Though his brother caused her to feel things she didn't even understand.

The song was almost over when he said, "I'm sorry about this, really."

"Sorry about what?" she asked.

"This," he said. And the next thing she knew, she had a different partner and he was dancing off with another lady who was surprised and delighted.

Cae made the best of her partner, changing several times throughout the next dance, even ending up with the young Lord Avondyl, at one point.

"Enjoying yourself?" he grinned.

"In fits and starts," she laughed. "Though I must know, who is the man in the dark purple cote?"

"That would be lord Maddox, lady Lucelle Roshan's older brother. Why? Interested?" he smirked.

"Not really, he...," she tried to think of something she could say to explain her discomfort with the man.

"Is a little too eager?" he chuckled. "You would not be the first lady to complain of it. Paid it no mind and stay alert. I don't think he even realizes he does it. Op, here we go!" he exclaimed, spinning her off into the arms of another partner. This one was the brightly attired Lord Carlan Araan, the Telman merchant who married into Elanthian nobility.

She suppressed a shudder and did her best to keep her distance in the dance. He smelled strongly of some herby oil that might have been pleasant in moderation. She managed a smile and clever deflections of his leading questions about her brothers. This man was very much 'anything for a profit', and she had a very good idea where his loyalties lay in the realms outside of his coffers.

Thankfully, her turn with him was short, as the song came to an end.

She made her excuses not to accept a second, longer dance, explaining that she really needed to find the princess as she was supposed to be part of her entourage tonight. He bowed, unable to protest such an excuse.

She found the princess easily enough, and her brother as well, seated with lady Balyra and her sister. She smiled, greeting them. "Where is your cousin, Lucelle?" she asked. She had all but taken for granted the idea that where you found one, you found all three.

Onelle just pointed to the dancers, where Lucelle was cavorting with Lord Edler. She smiled and shrugged.

Tempest landed, snuggling up to her, feeling left out.

Vyncet groaned, rubbing his leg. Cae glared at him. "Did you go against Physician orders and dance?"

"Just one," he complained. "It wasn't very... energetic. Not like what you were doing with Prince Balaran, that's for sure." He looked like he was about to say something else but stopped when she gave him a warning look. "Lord Rorik spoke to me earlier," he said.

"And?"

"And he wants me to stand for him."

"Are you going to?" Syera asked.

He nodded respectfully to the princess. "I will, Your Highness. It is in the best interests of everyone involved that I do. And it's not like he has many other choices," he added.

"Stop while you're ahead," Cae warned.

"Well, he doesn't," he complained.

"Oh, I'm going to find something to drink," she growled. She turned to the princess and curtseyed, "If my princess doesn't mind?"

Syera turned to gesture to the maids that should have been standing behind her. "Why don't you get one of …oh." She sighed. "Well, it is Bonfire Night. It was bound to happen eventually. Go ahead. I'll be fine. I'm sure lady Balyra will not object to taking your place for a while."

"Of course not, Your Highness," she smiled.

Cae nodded and drifted off, keeping an eye out for her maids, certain that Fern was trying to track Pansy down. Of all her maids, Pansy was the one most likely to have gotten distracted. Especially if someone smiled at her. She sent Tempest to go see if she could find Fern. The bird flew off dutifully. Alone, she stayed to the wider, better lit, more popular paths.

Cae found the refreshment table not far from the dragon fountain, got herself a glass of a fine Cygent white and moved off to sit and enjoy it where she could watch the movements and life in the gardens. She found a bench just out of the direct light of the torches, and away from the direct heat. She had a fragrant breeze up from the river through the roses behind her that were heavy with the last blooms of the season, drinking up the colder air and milder late-Harvest sun.

As she sat, she sipped and took note of the comings and goings. Couples were slipping off into the more shadowed, less travelled paths that led to dead ends and private bowers. Not all of them were wholly noble. She thought she saw a minor lady slipping off with a servant.

She smiled. It was not often that both moons were dark at once. Somehow it became a night of license, during which all manner of inappropriate behaviours were overlooked as the golden light of Justice had his back turned. Similar things happened when the Southern Moon was new and the Eastern Lady was still overlooking the world, as inappropriate passions were indulged without judgement. For one idle moment, she allowed herself to wonder what it would be like to be one of those women, running, giggling, through moon-shadowed gardens pursued by an ardent lover. She did not entertain the thought for long.

Voices came up the path beside her. Not unusual, she'd been hearing various conversations most of the night, but the tones caught her attention. The speaker was feminine and complaining. "It is so frustrating. He might as well announce his decision already. The Eastern Lady knows his mind is already made up."

"How can you tell?" asked her friend.

A third lady snapped, "It's easy if you just pay attention."

The first lady spoke again, explaining. "With any other woman, he's his usual stiff, distant self, ill-tempered. Like he doesn't even want to be here."

"Or he doesn't like women at all," added the third in what was supposed to be a whisper.

"Oh, he likes *her* well enough," First snarled. "The moment he lays eyes on her ...hell, the moment she enters the same room, he calms down."

"Goes all soft," said Third.

"I wouldn't say soft," corrected First. "He's never soft. But he softens. And he doesn't even have to see her. He knows. It's like he can smell her."

"Who knows, maybe he can," offered Second. "I've heard rumours she uses no scents whatsoever. Not even in her talc. Her odour has to precede her. Though why that would calm him, I don't know."

Third sighed. "My brother-in-law has the most awful body odour. Especially after he's been... exercising. No one else can stand it, but it drives my sister mad with desire for him. One never knows."

"It can't be that," mused First in frustration. "But there has to be something. Maybe some magic she holds over him?"

"She certainly charms beasts," simpered Second. "I saw that ca'theryn rubbing itself all over her like it was a lapdog. And she's not afraid of anything."

"Just people," Third sneered. "Lady Haria claims she is a terrible snob, but my maid's heard from hers that she's just shy... like terrified."

"Wouldn't have known it toight," said Second with scorn as they began to move away.

The three of them walked right past where Cae sat and never noticed her. The shadows also protected their identities. Once they were safely on their way to the refreshments, Cae rose, leaving her goblet on the bench beside her and walked away.

She didn't know where she was going at first. In the end, she turned towards the Citadel and found her way to her room, which was where Fern found her, led there by a concerned Tempest.

"My lady, why have you..."

"I just didn't feel much like socializing any more," she sighed.

"Begging your pardon, my lady, but that is so much horse apples," she snapped. "Something is bothering you."

"A number of things, Fern, but there is nothing for some of them." Fern waited, hands on her hips. "Am I a snob?" Cae asked suddenly.

"What?"

Caelerys repeated the question.

"Lady Haria is a snob," Fern huffed. "Daia, the princess's chief lady, is a snob. You are most certainly not a snob. You are the kindest, most considerate and friendly woman I know." She softened. "You remind me a lot of your mother, actually. What I remember of her."

"We were both so young," Cae sighed.

Fern sat beside her. "What gave you the impression you're thought to be a snob?"

"Something overheard. Considering some of their information came from Haria, I can dismiss it. That's not... what I have to figure out."

"Did something else happen tonight? With someone of the masculine persuasion?" she suggested, watching Cae's expression. "A certain dragon?"

Cae glared at her. "We aren't certain of that."

"Certain enough. He was dancing awfully close with you. He say something?"

She leaned back in her chair. "A few things, none of which made any sense."

"What'd you talk about?"

"I'd told him once, ...the last time we danced, in fact... that I'd keep an eye out among the ladies for anyone suitable for him. He asked me if I'd found anyone."

"You spent that dance talking about other prospective brides for him?" she asked, incredulous.

"Well, yes. He asked."

She eyed her lady in a way she never would have in the presence of Coral or the others. "What exactly did he say? I mean the last part, the part that made you miss a step."

She blushed afresh as she thought about the words that had confused her. "I reminded him of Denan and Isildar and he said... something about father's be damned."

"Oooo."

"Don't even try to go there, Fern," Cae sighed, tired to the bone. "I can't even think about it right now."

"Are afraid to, you mean."

"Maybe. Yes. Irrelevant." She pulled herself to her feet. "Get me out of this gown and the antlers from my hair and go back out to enjoy Bonfire Night. Maybe go see if you can track down Roan? Or Jan if you really want to know if he can break you in half," she laughed.

Fern had the dignity to look shocked at the implication, more so that her lady had understood what had been meant. Then a thoughtful look crossed her face. "Might be as I will," she said, moving to help Cae get ready for bed. Deft fingers swiftly unbound the coronet braid and brushed out her hip length tresses, whipping them almost immediately back into a nightbraid.

She pulled back the covers and tucked Cae into bed, even humouring the bird by tucking her in, too. "Are you certain, my lady? I don't think even Coral is in the anteroom."

"Lock the door, then. Coral should have a key, and so do you." She put her arm around the mound of bird under the coverlet. "I have my guard dog. Go, have fun."

"Good night, my lady," she sighed, closing the curtains.

Cae was awake only long enough to hear the key turn in the lock of the outer room.

Her dreams were too chaotic to remember or make sense of.

19

Cae rose much closer to her normal time, close to dawn. She rolled out of bed, put on her dressing gown and went into the outer room, opening the window to gaze out. She was contemplating going up to the astronomy tower to watch Tempest fly in the pale dawn when she remembered she no longer had the key.

She looked over her shoulder at the maids entering the room, smiled. "Good morning," she said cheerfully. "Everyone enjoy themselves last night?"

Sorrel and Pansy both blushed, and Fern had the confidence to reveal nothing in her manner as she crossed to the dressing room to set out clothes for the day. Coral bowed her head respectfully, "It was very kind of you to grant us the night, my lady. And kind of Fern to remain on duty so that we might participate. It has been a number of years since

I have been free to attend more than a quick trip to the fire and back. Thank you."

Cae nodded, joining the others in the dressing room and let them lace her into the pale green gown that had swiftly become one of her favourites.

After a brief breakfast, Cae felt the need to just get out of doors, so she took Tempest down to the gardens with a book. When she entered the gardens, she was disappointed to see the bustle that was post-event clean up. She sank onto the edge of the dragon fountain, clutching the book to her chest and just stared out at the early morning activity.

She heard a soft chuckle coming up beside her around the fountain's edge. "It would appear that the gardens are ...indisposed?"

She looked up to see Prince Valan, in a simple, dark, sleeveless tunic over a white shirt. She smiled at him. "Apparently it is expected that the nobility will all be sleeping in after a night of extreme indulgence. I am surprised everyone wasn't in masks last night."

He sat beside her on the fountain's wide rim. "That's not a bad idea. Perhaps I will suggest a masquerade next Bonfire Night."

She laughed, "Oh, that would just make it worse."

"Perhaps," he said, crossing his arms over his chest and stretching out his long legs in front of him.

"And what are you doing up so early, my prince?" she asked, flicking a light spray of water at the falcon pacing the rim watching the ripples on the surface.

"Well," he began, "I went looking for a maiden, but it turned out she had fled the festivities." Cae blushed slightly, hugging the book tighter to her chest. "I followed her inside. When she vanished to a place I should not go, I decided I, too, had had my fill of the evening."

"So we both got an early night?" she said, not looking at him.

"Earlier than everybody else," he grinned. "This is a far cry from the last Bonfire Night held here a couple years ago."

Cae suddenly remembered. "Oh, right, your aunt would have had a more... church styled evening."

He nodded. "Much more staid."

"In other words, boring?"

"Even for me," he chuckled.

She bumped her shoulder companionably into his, smiling shyly. "Not that you are the revelling kind," she teased.

"Not like my brother, no. But I think you cannot say that I cannot dance," he said.

Her blush grew. "No, I cannot," she agreed.

They watched the industry quietly for a bit.

"So has the book been enlightening?" he asked.

She looked down, realizing what book she had brought with her. "Oh, very. A lot of it I already knew, but I am finding the mentions of other cultures fascinating. It makes me far more worried about the rise of the church and the lies they are spreading, the oppression they are encouraging, all in the name of the 'divinity of man'."

He nodded. "Later in the book you'll begin to understand why they use that phrase and how they've twisted it. The old faith has the concept of the divinity of man at its core, but the meaning is very different. The old faith says that we are part of the divine, and thereby have responsibilities to the world around us, not that we are divine beings with license to lay claim to superiority."

"The man part is definitely being warped," she sighed.

"And that's what confuses me most, that some of the most devout followers are women."

"That's what confuses you? What confuses me is that none of the other First or Second born, nor even the Mother herself, demand formal worship. And then the Eldest up and decides to build a church."

"I think it might have to do with the fact that, of all the Mother's children, the Eldest is the only human. For all we know, this is not the doing of the Eldest, but of men, seeking more power than they warrant. No good will come of it, of that I am certain. If we abandon our First..."

"Then they will abandon us and all that means." She looked at him, a thought suddenly striking her. "What if... that's already happening?" she whispered.

His dark blue eyes bored into hers, flicking almost imperceptibly at the servants moving about, though none were close enough to overhear. "Explain."

"Well, most of the ...incidents... have been when the moons were high. The Southern Lord specifically. That's the light you were in the night after you returned."

"Lord Justice," he nodded.

"What if he is the reason? Punishing the neglect? Protesting the corruption of the faith and the rise of the church?"

"But wouldn't he then target the priesthood?"

She shook her head. "What if you can only trigger those prone to it? It would be the Mother who would make one person a ...target... or not," she said, trying hard to be circumspect. "And She never directly interferes."

He gave a snort of agreement. "What She does to mother is anything but direct."

"And if the Southern Lord is pushing, then the victims are likely being driven mad by the pressure and impulses. And since the Fair Sister craves peace and harmony as well as love and beauty, maybe she's adding weight to the opposite fulcrum, causing," she waved her hand in a see-sawing motion.

"Causing the push-pull that is driving the victims to rage," he breathed. He looked up to the empty sky, the colours of sunrise already fading to a pale blue day. "Well, we shall see how your theory holds soon enough. The Lady will show her face more slowly, be less able to counter the Lord's actions. If you are right, we may see more... victims... in the coming days."

"And the strength of the church's reaction," she shivered.

"That is not likely to end well," he sighed. He looked up, slightly irritated by the interruption of Fern. "Yes?" he growled.

She curtseyed, gesturing silently behind her to a young man Cae recognized immediately. "Colt?" she asked, handing Fern the book and crossing to where the young man stood miserably, cradling something in his hands. "What is it?"

It was a toomi wife, looking weak and listless. She seemed to be having trouble breathing. "Is she sick?"

When he spoke, his voice was hoarse as if from much weeping or trying not to do so. "She be the last. T'others be all dead."

She paled, felt the prince approaching to stand at her back. "Poisoned you think?" she asked. "Who would kill our wives?" The implication terrified her.

"Not all," he said, placing the dying bird in her hands as his were suddenly trembling too much. "Just what..."

"Out with it, man," Valan barked.

But he did not need to tell Cae which ones. At first all she felt was an intense sadness and an overwhelming sense of aloneness, the feeling that the one soul in all the world who understood you and completed you was suddenly no more and would never return. That was crippling enough. But then came the approaching darkness, the shrilling of his companions, the crushing cold of water in the lungs followed by the piercing, jagged teeth over and over again.

As the bird died in her hands, the pain and the sorrow and the cold and the breathlessness overwhelmed her. She heard shouting, felt something slither around her, so hot it burned in the icy depths, and then the abyss consumed her.

༺

Her dreams had a hold of her again. The dragon was near, she could feel him, smell him. There was a tiny, still heart in her hand, broken in half, it's other fraction miles away in a fog she could never penetrate. There were wolves in the water she had drowned in, in a frenzy of feeding. She was terrified, felt like she was still drowning even as she knew she was above the water, wrapped in a warm embrace that was slowly thawing her out as she slipped out of the dreams' grip.

She blinked, found herself gazing into a pair of intense, dark blue eyes. She took a gasping breath of dry air. The arms that cradled her held her tightly as she began to cough out water that simply wasn't there.

When she could breathe easily again, she merely yielded to the warmth that held her and wept. At last, her tears were exhausted and someone was offering her water. She sipped the cool liquid before handing it back, allowed the hands to wipe her face with a soft kerchief. She then took stock of where she was and who she was with. She was cradled upon Valan's lap in one of the retiring rooms near the banquet hall, with the queen herself kneeling in front of them, watching her with her warm, but worried, hazel eyes.

"I think it time you told me your dreams, my little bird," she said gently.

"What... what happened?" she asked, fighting the urge to weep again. She was beginning to feel a little awkward.

"You were handed a toomi," said the prince. "When she died in your hands, you fainted. I caught you, but then you went into convulsions. Neither your maid nor your servant could find the words to explain."

"Where?" she asked, starting to look around for them.

"Fern has him in hand. The boy is a wreck," said the queen, standing. She gestured for Valan to set her on the couch. Reluctantly, he slid her from his lap onto the thick cushions beside him and the queen sat beside her, taking her hand in hers. "Now, please explain. The toomi's band said Taluscliff."

Cae threatened to choke on her words. "Her husband was on the ship with my brother. Colt said they were all dead, the ones..." her voice dropped to a hoarse whisper, "the ones whose husbands Will was taking home with him. If they're all dead, then the husbands are... and that means..."

Valan's arm went around her and the queen's hand tightened. She took Cae's cheek gently and turned her face to look into her eyes. "Tell me your dreams."

Cae did not understand how this could help beyond maybe distracting her enough to think straight. "I've been dreaming of strange things," she said, and began telling about them, starting with the first, the one of shifting perspectives and the first time she saw the dragon. She ended with the last one she could remember, with the pack of sea-wolves swarming and devouring whatever had floated above them.

"And then when I held her, felt what she was feeling, and she was reliving her husband's death, over and over and over again," she sobbed. "I couldn't... I could see it, feel it. I wanted to die too, to just fade away and make all that stop."

The queen glanced over at her son. "Just as well you wouldn't let go of her."

He sighed, "I do occasionally have good instincts, mother."

She gave him an indulgent, half-smile. "Of course you do. I raised you."

"What is happening to me?" she pleaded.

The queen looked at her with a mix of sadness and joy in her eyes. "Nothing, my dear," she smiled, cradling her face like a favoured child. "You are what you are. And you are coming into your power."

"Power?" both Cae and Valan asked, frowning.

"What you have in your arms, darling son, is the fabled sympath."

Cae gasped, and all Valan could do was repeat the word numbly.

"Ah, you've heard of it. Well, you have been researching," she sighed. "I would like very much to know what you've found, but now is not the time."

"What is a sympath?" she pleaded, reaching out to take the queen's hand. "Please? I've seen the word, the references. But I can't find what it is and I am not even sure I am translating the word right."

"You are. It is the root of our word for sympathy. I do not know everything about them, but I know a little. I used to have a book a long time ago. I will write my brother and see if it is still at Echo Hall, have it sent to you. You're going to need it."

She went to a side table and poured a goblet of strong wine, tasted it herself before bringing it over and making Cae drink it. "Now, a sympath," she said, sitting down again, "is the companion of the shift. They are far more rare, only a handful, if that, in any generation. They can feel the emotions of those around them. The untrained are often unaware they are even doing it. And, if they touch someone, they can feel their pain, see the sources of the emotions. Or other things. They understand the beast, and are understood by them, and thus are very in tune with any shifts around them. They are often plagued by dreams, especially at first."

"Prophetic?" Cae asked timidly, feeling the wine beginning to affect her.

"No," the queen said, shaking her head. "More... experiential." She frowned. "Experiential? Is that even a word?" she mused, then shook it off.

"But the shipwreck, I know that's what it was," Cae insisted.

The queen shrugged. "You could have gotten that from the dying bird. I think this explains why they're so in tune with each other. They're sympathic themselves."

Cae shook her head. "I dreamed of it *before* it happened."

"If that is even what happened. We won't know until reports come in. I will send out riders at once, armed with toomi of their own to send us word swiftly," said Valan, pulling her close.

"There could be a number of reasons," the queen said. "The Mother has her eye on you. And knowing you are a sympath, I understand it now. There hasn't been one we know of in easily a hundred years. There is much we do not know of them."

"I think you might be the only person who knows what they are any more," Cae sighed. She bent forward, burying her face in her hands. "I just know that was Will's ship," she sobbed. "It's the only connection I can think of that I have to a ship."

She felt hands set comfortingly on her back. "We do not know as of yet," the queen insisted gently. "All we know is that the toomi drowned. They could have gone overboard in a storm and there are other survivors. There is no sense in borrowing trouble until we know for certain."

"It is so hard not to," she whispered.

"Son, why don't you take her to the queen of the forest. It will help."

Sigrun rose as Valan pulled Cae into his arms again. She went to the door and opened it, intending to call for a servant and found a white gauvan sitting outside it instead, patiently waiting. With a chirp of thanks and a polite bow, Tempest walked around the queen and hopped up onto the couch next to Cae, butting her head against her leg in sympathy.

"Well, that explains that," the queen said. "And so much more," she added, signalling to the nearest servant.

In short order, Cae was taken to her room where Fern quickly redressed her for riding. Cae paused long enough to spend a few minutes just holding Fern, both for the maid's comfort and her own.

"We don't know anything yet, my lady," she whispered hoarsely.

Cae nodded. "They are sending messengers," she said, pulling away and crossing to where Colt sat numbly in the sitting room, still holding the dead wife. She knelt, cradling the hands cradling the bird. "We will know what happened soon, Colt. It will be all right."

"They died in agony," he whispered.

"And there is still a whole flock for you to take care of," she said. "Wives probably terrified out of their wits right now."

He looked at her finally, his sense of responsibility starting to overcome his grief.

"Are there any Taluscliff wives left?" she asked.

Numbly, he nodded. "One or two. Ones whose husbands were Reach-wise before."

"Send a message to Taluscliff, then. Tell them what happened and ask for information. Unless Vynce has already done so?"

Colt looked shocked. "I... I forgot."

Cae stopped, paling. "You... haven't told Vyncet?" she asked.

The boy swallowed, shaking his head slowly. "I be ... 's been so long no master at Hall-wise, I be forgetting. You and young lord been here so long and with Lord Willam awaying again... it be's slippin' my brain."

He stood, wiping his face and straightening his shirt. "I... I go the nowing, my lady. Please be forgiving?"

She smiled sadly and hugged him. It took him a minute before he relaxed into the embrace, timidly returning it. When she finally released him, both seemed to have found some of their spine, or, at the very least, enough to get what needed to be done, done.

She saw him to the door. "Please tell my brother that if he wishes to see me, to take his time. I am going riding to clear my head. I should be back by dinner," she said quietly. "Tell no one else."

He nodded and trotted off down the hall, pausing to bow as the prince strode by.

Cae stepped out of the room to meet him, curtseyed.

"You are looking a little better," Valan said.

"The needs of others exceed my own," she sighed. "I am ready when you are, Your Highness."

He extended his arm to her. "Balaran has found out already and wished to know if you would mind more company? Perhaps Lady Liliwyn as well?"

"The princess?" she asked, surprised she had not been included.

"Is locked in her bedchamber. If Liliwyn can get her out, she might very well join us."

Cae sighed. "I need a little time first," she pleaded. "If they would give me at least part of an hour out there alone...?"

He met her eyes. "Alone?" he asked, the second half of his question unsaid and not needing to be.

"Without others," she amended with a light pressure on his hand.

Mollified, he turned to one of the two menservants following behind him, sent him to deliver the message to his brother.

Wraith was standing primly beside the prince's smoky black steed, who comported himself a perfect gentleman. Only four guards were with them. Valan gave her a leg up, hung on to the ankle of her boot perhaps a hair longer than he should have. He smirked up at her, causing her to blush as she remembered the comment about her ankles a few nights before. He vaulted into his own saddle and they rode out and around the Citadel. Tempest flew off.

Valan did not not lead them down the path she expected him to. She had thought they would go straight to the queen by the most direct route.

Instead, they entered the wood where the race had emerged and rode about halfway through. Just before they reached the fallen tree, he brought them to a halt in front of a narrow path that was little more than a game trail. "Ralen, take the lead. You know the way," he said. "Larch, rear guard, please."

Once Ralen turned his horse up the path, Valan followed, gesturing for her to come behind him. The other three fell into place with Larch at the rear. The trail opened up after a little ways to a cleaner ground cover, more widely spaced trees. Still, they kept to single file and the path shortly was over-grown again. They emerged onto the path on the far side of the queen's glen.

Entering the canopy of the great tree, the guards scattered. One guarding each path, and the other two slipping into the wooded area off the trail, to provide privacy and yet be able to deal with trouble before it reached them.

Cae felt the weight of her pain fall away as she dismounted and stepped closer to the great tree. Tempest was already dozing on a lower branch, only opened one eye as Valan joined Caelerys on the ground. She moved carefully, trying to mind her footing, but her riding boots were too unyielding. She sat down on a ridge of root and began to pull them off, setting them neatly side by side. She then more nimbly crossed the rippled ground that was the queen's root system. When she finally got close enough to reach up and touch the spicy-sweet bark, she leaned her forehead against the roughness of it, breathing deep.

Then she remembered that she was not alone, or with her father's men, and looked over her shoulder. The guards were no where to be seen, and the prince stood beside the horses, watching her not unlike a cat watches a mouse hole, but with a hint of amusement. Embarrassed, she put her back to the tree, hiding her bare toes beneath the hem of her riding skirt. "What?" she mumbled. "You can't climb trees in boots."

His eyebrow rose. "Does my lady plan on climbing the queen?"

She blushed. "No, though I wouldn't refuse the challenge were I inclined. But the roots... one might as well be climbing," she added.

He stepped closer. "Why do I get the feeling you've once been challenged?"

"Because I have?" she winced.

He smiled as if he were not really surprised. "Which?"

"The great queen of the Reach. Brothers," she shrugged. "She made me feel safe."

"That is their purpose, after all," he smiled, coming slowly closer. "Which brother?"

She leaned her head back against the bark and gazed up into the feathery leaves. "Will." She took a deep breath and slowly let it out. "He was eighteen and didn't think I would. I was eight and afraid of nothing." Another deep breath. "And now I am afraid of everything."

"When did that start?" he asked softly. He had moved to right beside her without her noticing.

"I don't know really. Not until after mother died. I guess strangers... wanted things of me I wasn't willing to give."

She felt her grief and worry seeping out of her into the tree behind her, felt nothing but the love and patience of The Mother in the rough, rippled wood.

"Maybe," he said tenderly, resting his head beside hers on the tree. He wanted to touch her, but restrained himself for reasons she understood less than why she ached for him to do so. "Maybe you were starting to bloom and strangers were emotions and desires from unknown sources. It didn't feel familiar, so it felt uncomfortable."

She turned to look at him, gazing into the depths of his eyes, taking in every scar and nick and plane of his face. "I never really thought of it that way." She blinked slowly. "It feels right though. And some people I feel more than others. You for instance," she breathed. "I was always uneasy around you, uncertain of myself, afraid of …doing something wrong and thus dangerous, but what I was feeling was your own fear of yourself, fear of letting it out even for a moment. I always felt so formal around you."

"And now?"

She smiled softly. "Now I feel... like there's hope? I find myself drawn to your inner torment. I...." She moved her fingers against the bark, looked up in to the branches again and smiled more openly. "I feel more as she must feel, the queen. Like I am drawing all of your tension and anger and unease and turning it into something more productive, something comforting. Like what she is doing to me now."

She felt the heat of him, so close to her. She leaned just a little, pressing her cheek against his.

"What am I feeling now?" he asked hoarsely.

"Oh," she quivered, "all sorts of improper things. ...and with an intensity I think would set me afire right now."

"Would that be so bad?" She could feel his breath on her neck, the petal soft of his lips just brushing her skin.

"In so many ways, with so much uncertain. What I want and what I can have may not be the same thing," she whispered, unable to speak any louder.

"What if I..."

"You won't," she sighed. "You want to. But you won't. Because you are in the same boat as I... waiting on the will of others."

"I ache..."

"As do I... my prince."

He took a deep breath, his nose just at the hollow behind her earlobe. "Honey and leather," he exhaled. "Always, they end in honey and leather."

"Spice." He pulled far enough away to see her eyes. "Mine end in spice," she said. "Warm and rich, musky. And scales."

He turned around, managing to do so without his head leaving the tree. "What kind? Lizard? Serpent? ...Fish?"

She laughed at the last. "They shift like a fish's. I think they are connected to the skin like bird feathers, but they feel more like the skin of the small lizards you find on the garden walls during Planting."

"Does it scare you?"

She shook her head. "Not any more. Sometimes I am afraid for it, but usually... it is protecting me."

"When I've dreamed... there's always something," he said. "There's a dune and one of the Northern cats killing a gazelle. I'm so angry and everything just burns. Sometimes there's a figure, or an animal, and it hurts or is in trouble and I have to catch it, or protect it. But no matter what it was, in the end it always smells of honey and leather. It is never the same except for that."

"I wonder if what I've been doing is witnessing the dreams of shifts?"

"Anything is possible at this point," he said. "We'll have to get hold of mother's book." He grinned, "Find out if it has any hidden text."

She did not smile. "If that is the case," she continued, "then the dream I had the night before Bonfire... was the dreams or minds of shifts planning the attack."

They stared at each other in silence a long moment.

"You are not to blame," he said. "You could not know."

She continued to stare at him. "You should know better than anyone that does not change self-blame."

He sighed, knowing she was right. He reached out and brushed her cheek with the back of his fingers. "Let the queen take that, too."

"I am going to worry."

"I know. But don't let it cripple you. Giving in too much to anything is a destructive thing."

She managed a soft smile. "Oh? And who told you that?"

"Oh, some maiden I danced with forever ago," he said dismissively. "I don't think I even remember what she looked like."

"I'll bet you remember what she smelled like," she countered.

He smiled. "That is very possible."

Before he could creep in for another tempting sniff, one of the guards gave a quiet warning, "Your Highness?"

He raised his head, and she could see the frustration he fought to control. She pressed the back of her fingers to his temple, easing him back. "I love my brother," he sighed. "But I hate his timing."

She gave him a rueful smile. "Would you really have been able to stop yourself if you had done what you were thinking?"

He growled. "Doesn't make me like it any less. Let them through!" he called.

She eyed him. "You can't be sure that's your brother."

He raised an eyebrow. "Oh, can't I?"

She groaned. "Oh, right. Twins."

Liliwyn and Balaran rode in, doubling the contingent of guards. Bal dismounted, but Lili remained upon her side-saddle. He crossed to them, looking concerned.

"Syera?" Valan asked.

"She's inconsolable," he grumbled, frustrated. "Lili thinks Cae might be able to do something."

"Why?" she asked. "She's as close to her as I am. Why me?"

He shook his head, throwing up his hands helplessly. "Not a clue."

"Because I believe you two have a common grief," Lili called. "Because I think there's more to it than just his loss." Cae stepped past the princes to see her better. "I think it has to do with the Bonfire," she said pointedly.

It took Cae a moment before she remembered what Syera had said she had wished for. "Oh. Oh, dear."

"Wait, are you barefoot?" Lili asked, frowning.

Caelerys was suddenly self-conscious. "Yes," she blushed. "I'll explain later," she said, making her way towards Wraith.

"You, too?" Balaran exclaimed, suddenly looking at his brother's feet.

The heat went to Cae's ears. She had not even noticed. She picked her boots up, but before she could even try and put them on, she was lifted up and set sideways on the saddle. She yelped, dropping her boots in an attempt to grab something to steady herself. She looked down as Valan picked up her boots.

She could only watch him as he took each foot in hand in its turn, brushing off the soles with care before sliding on her socks, then her boots. When he was done, he reached up and lifted her to the ground again. She opened her mouth, trying to articulate her confusion when he bent to offer his hands to assist her to mount properly.

She set her boot upon his palms and allowed him to boost her up. As she swung her leg over, she felt him grasp her foot at sole and ankle, holding firmly. Skirts settled, she looked down at him, wiggling it lightly to ask for its freedom.

The look he gave her was almost predatory. "I assure you, my lady," he said softly, "I looked."

Her only response was to blush furiously, adjusting her seat in the wake of the strange sensations his words caused.

Valan moved to mount his own horse, but his brother held him back. "Let them go. I assure you, we will be very much surplus to requirement. You and I need to take a ride and talk."

He met his twin's eyes for a moment, then nodded, assigning Larch and one of the other of his guards to join two of Bal's and escort the ladies back to the Citadel.

Cae was very aware of Valan's eyes on her as they rode away, flanked fore and aft by guards.

Before they got too far, Lili asked, "You took your shoes off?"

"They were making crossing the root system difficult. It's easier as the Mother made us."

"Ha, a lot of things are easier as the Mother made us," she quipped suggestively. "Him, too?"

Cae fidgeted. "I didn't know he had...."

"And you let him put them back on for you," said Lili.

"I don't think I could have told him no if I wanted to," she answered uncomfortably.

Lili grinned. "Aye, but did you want to?"

"It was..." she squirmed, "a bit thrilling," she admitted.

"I'll bet. And his comment about looking?" Lili asked, pinning Cae with her violet-blue eyes.

"That went back to my wild ride the night Will left. I'd made a comment," she lowered her voice so Larch would not hear, "that the guard with me didn't even bat an eye at the sight of my ankles, that I doubted he even looked."

"Oh, he was jealous," she mused.

This made Cae blush even more, causing her system to go even more haywire.

Liliwyn did not look at her, but grinned and with her hand made a slow falling gesture.

When they reached Syera's apartments, Liliwyn just walked unannounced into the receiving room and straight back to the bedchamber door. She knocked, pressing her ear to the wood. "Caelerys is here," she called, listening.

She then turned to the maids hovering at the edges of the room, held out her hand in the direction of the senior of them. "Daia, the key," she said, with every confidence that it would be handed over.

Reluctantly, the maid complied, passing over the small brass key.

Lili handed it to Cae. "Here. Let us know when it's safe."

Cae gave her a look as she accepted the key, fitting it into the lock. Slipping quietly into the room, she closed the door behind her. The chamber was dark. The curtains were drawn on both window and bed, but some light filtered through. The room was in disarray, as if Syera had thrown things. Her boots crunched on something and she looked down to see the remains of a broken vase and it's unfortunate contents, and a matching, wet stain on the back of the door. She sighed, slipping the key into her pocket.

"Sai, it's Cae," she said, not moving. She waited for a response and got none, though she heard movement on the bed. She crossed cautiously. "Sweetling?" She peeked inside the curtains, saw the lump of a body curled up in the middle.

Unwilling to climb into the bed with her riding boots on, she bent and slid them off, leaving the short stockings on. She then climbed up into the bed, coming as close to the lump of blankets as she dared. "We don't know anything for certain, and it may be days yet."

Silence.

"We cannot let it be known, Sai. Until there is word, you and I both are going to have to act as if everything is as it should be."

A sob.

She set her hand on the tallest part of the blanket. "Sai, please. Come with us to the queen of the forest. It will help, I promise."

There were muffled words from the depths of cloth.

"What?" she asked, pulling lightly on the shoulder she was sure was what she had her hand on.

"You must hate me!" came the sobbed exclamation, perhaps a little louder than intended.

"What?" she said again. "Why, ever would I hate you? It's not like you've stolen the love of my life."

"Worse," came the mumbled sobs. "I killed your brother."

Now Cae pulled her onto her back, not caring about resistance or rank. "What in the Abyss are you talking about?" she exclaimed. "That is the most ridiculous..."

The wisteria eyes looked up at her. They were tortured. "I wished to destroy my love for him. In the end I destroyed *him*," she sobbed.

The sight and the words roused her anger. "Now you listen here," she snapped. The princess's eyes grew wide in the dim light. "You made a wish to the Mother to burn away your love to ease your pain. You did not wish for my brother to go away, that you asked of him, and just for a little while. The Mother would never destroy one person at the whim of another, or misread a wish that way. The Eldest, maybe, but never Caelyrima!" She softened her voice. "She never interferes that much. You should know this. No, this has the hands of man written all over it. And the hands of pirates at that," she said bitterly.

The princess rolled over and buried her head in Cae's lap, her arms going around her waist, and sobbing her heart out. Caelerys let her, one hand gently rubbing her back like a child, the other softly stroking her hair. It was a long time before Syera pulled herself together enough to sit up. Cae tenderly brushed her hair from her face. "You know what?" she mused, trying not to grin. "You are not one of those women who are more beautiful when they cry."

Syera froze for a half second, then burst out laughing, wiping away tears with the heel of her hand. "Not when I go all out like this," she laughed. "Bet you Lili is," she added warmly.

Cae smiled. "Yes, well, Lili isn't human. She's some fey thing from the mists."

They giggled.

The curtain opened and Liliwyn poked her head in. "Is it safe? We heard laughing."

"It's safe," Cae smiled.

"What were you laughing about?" she asked.

This only made them laugh harder. "Only," gasped the princess, "how you were just too good to be true."

"Or real," Cae added.

"What?" Lili laughed, climbing into the bed with them.

Cae shook her head. "Oh, just being jealous little wildcats about how beautiful and good we're not compared to you."

Lili blushed with embarrassment. "Really," she chastised. She caught sight of Syera's face and clucked, pulling out a kerchief to clean her up. "Oh, you are a right mess."

This only made the two of them laugh more.

Liliwyn frowned at both of them, tried to divert them before they went into hysterics. "Why don't we go down to the queen for a picnic?"

Syera shook her head, getting her laughing under control. "I don't think I need to. Cae here was queen enough for my needs."

Cae looked at her, confused. "How do you mean?" she asked, remembering something said between her and Valan under the sacred branches.

She plucked at Cae's skirts. "I can smell her all over you."

"Oh," she breathed, relieved. "Well, we need to get ourselves presentable."

"For what?" Syera asked. "No one is coming to court today. I mean, under my aunt they did, but that was because Bonfire Night was less debauchery and more ...churchy. But, even father's nursing his head this morning."

"Then what are we going to do with our day?" Liliwyn asked.

Cae's eyes lit up. "Let's find ourselves an Alumet tutor."

Lili seemed in agreement, but the princess frowned. "Only you two would think filling a day off with lessons is fun," she griped. "Besides, I'm not going to be here much longer. I would start the lessons and then have to end them."

"How about a trip on the river?" Lili suggested. "A boat ride is always relaxing."

Cae shivered at that thought, shook her head.

"Oh, right," Lili sighed.

"Why don't you come spend some time with me?" came a voice.

Lili peered out of the bed curtains and then quickly scrambled off and curtseyed. "My queen," she said.

The curtain drew back as she waved Lili up. She peer into the bed at her daughter, drawing her to the edge to stroke her face and hair. "Oh, my joy," she sighed. "Why didn't you come to me?"

She shrugged numbly. "You were busy. And I,... I thought you would be disappointed in me for wishing as I did... I thought... my wish caused..."

The queen crooned softly, bent to kiss her forehead. "You have never been a disappointment to me." She looked down at Syera's nightdress and clucked her tongue. "It is time to get dressed, my child. The day has begun and I would like to spend some time with you before I lose you to the Southern Coast."

She turned to Cae and Lili, who both bowed from their respective positions. "Would the two of you be so kind as to help her, then find something to occupy your time? I am afraid I must steal her away."

"Of course, Your Majesty," they said.

The queen drifted out of the room.

"Is it my imagination," began Lili, watching the queen leave, "but does she seem more subdued than normal?"

"She's about to lose her daughter, who is grieving over a lost possibility," Cae shrugged.

"That's not it."

She looked at Lili, then closed her eyes and thought about the queen. She opened them again. "You're right, it's not." They turned back to the now open curtains and the princess beginning to climb out of the great bed. "What's going on with your mother?"

Syera looked startled by that, then looked towards the open door of the main chamber and her mother's figure drifting out into the hall beyond. "Oh, I think her and father are having issues."

Lili shook her head. "They were always so loving," she commented. "What's going on?"

Cae drew the group of them towards the dressing room to find clothes.

The princess sighed. "I'll give you one guess."

"Semelle," Liliwyn scowled.

Cae was a little surprised that Lili did not use the woman's full title. "Has she found a way to get to the king?"

Syera shook her head, letting them slip her out of her nightgown. "Not directly. But she has people loyal to her."

"Or blackmailed, or beholden," Lili sneered, pulling a pretty, lavender gown out of the press and shaking it out.

"Father's not happy that she's been banished from the Citadel, but he can't argue. He can't go out to meet her with causing a scandal, but she's managing to get word to him and thereby influence him. She's trying to convert him, I think, whispering about how a man should take control of his household and not be bent to his wife's will, or some such rot. My parents were such a complete partnership before, but now that father's the king and not the archduke, Semelle's after him for all its worth."

"I don't think she really cares for him," Liliwyn said. "She's just using him. She didn't care a wit about him when he was just a high noble living out his life, or his sons when they were just a Captain of the Watch and a scholar."

"But father doesn't see that," Syera protested, shifting herself inside the dress as her friends started to lace her into it. "She's flattering him."

"The weakness of most men," Cae sighed.

"Mother is still holding firm. And her warnings from supper that night are still sticking in his mind, so he's reluctant to chance it."

"Even whilst he's picking away at it? Feeling her out?" Cae snarked.

"She's rarely wrong. That's one of the reasons their partnership has worked so well. And she rarely interferes, so when she does,..." Syera said, drifting off.

"He tends to listen," Lili finished. "What is he trying to push for?"

Syera didn't want to say. She sat at the vanity while Cae brushed her hair out and Lili gathered pins and ties. Lili had started dressing her hair before she answered. "Mostly for brides," she finally answered.

"Anyone in particular?" Cae asked.

"Both of them. I think he'd find someone for Janniston if he thought he could. But there's no need for childhood betrothals, not with two older brothers. Liliwyn is a surety," she said, watching the woman in question in the mirror. Lili showed no reaction as she swiftly braided and pinned. "Who to is the question. He likes your family, Cae, but the more trouble that falls upon your House, the more ammunition Lady Asparadane has to weaken your case."

"My case?" Cae asked. "So he is actually considering me?"

Syera nodded, earning her a reprimand from Liliwyn who was trying to pin a braid into a tricky rosette. "Why else do you think you were put up at the Citadel?"

"Your mother liked me? Foresaw the trouble at Stag's Hall? I was being groomed for your lady in waiting?" Cae rattled off, fighting hope.

"No. Mother is certain she wants both of you in the family, but... why father is fighting it, I don't know." She threw the comb she was fiddling with onto the table. "If he doesn't... I'll have been sold off to Griff for nothing," she spat.

Cae set her hand on her shoulder, trying to calm her. "Never for nothing."

"Exactly for nothing," she countered. "It's not like he wants me to provide him heirs. He has plenty of those, and a daughter he's just married off to House Selkan. And of course, if I outlive him, they'll cast me off just as quickly as they can hand me the candle."

"If they don't try to marry you off to one of his sons," Liliwyn mused.

"Or his brother. Avondyl is not married yet," Cae added.

"That is if I'll have any of them," she grumped. She sighed, gazing at her face in the mirror and applying a little powder to try and smooth out the redness around her eyes. "Don't get your hopes up too much," she warned. "You aren't the only candidates."

"We didn't..." they both answered at once.

"But you are the strongest. Father is waiting until after my wedding and then he's going to start pushing harder. He'll make a decision before the Fair sister sees her first quarter."

Neither girl could think of anything to say to that.

They had no time to speak of anything else before lady Caena came to fetch the princess to join her mother.

Cae and Lili went to the first place they could think of: the library.

They ended up going their separate ways to seek out their chosen reading materials, and as Cae passed by the stack containing the complete works of Waller, she thought of her nights on the astronomy tower with fond longing. Getting an idea, she found the nearest worm and asked where the oldest volumes in the library were found.

He led her to the desk of the Master Librarian who smiled fondly at the boy and gave her a deferential nod. He appeared to be an ancient man, with long, twisted fingers gnarled with age. He was tall, in spite of the bend in his back from too many years of bending over dusty volumes, and a squint from reading too often in poor light. His white hair was bound in a long tail down his back. He wore a robe of warm brown whose wide sleeves ended at his elbows, leaving the fitted sleeves of his tunic exposed, a colour not unlike the yellowing pages of his charges. He smelled of paper and ink and leather and binding glue.

Cae told him what she was looking for.

He eyed her for a long moment, his grey eyes reading her as he would have a book. Finally, "Do you know how to handle such documents, my lady? The care their delicacy requires?" His voice was weathered like his face, but kind.

"I love books too much to treat them unkindly, Master," she said politely. "I know to be gentle, but if there is special care you wish taken, I am willing to learn."

He smiled and stepped away from his desk, waving off the worm by throwing him an apple. He gestured for her to follow him and led her deep in to the left-hand stacks of the first floor.

It was a labyrinth back here. Carefully bound records were ordered upon their shelves by year, and that was as much as Cae could decipher of their sequence. She was amazed to see two worms shifting a shelf, records and all, gliding it along the floor on hidden wheels to move it out of the way of the desired stack just behind its original position.

The Master Librarian smiled at her wondrous expression. "How else are we to keep every record in the kingdom and still have room for more? There is well over a thousand years of records here."

They passed through a room where ten worms were bent to copying and making bindings for new record books. "We are coming to the end of this year," he said. "When Fallow ends, this year's records will be closed out, bound and filed."

"This is amazing. An important aspect of government no one ever thinks about," she said.

"Alas, it is getting harder and harder to get copies of everything to be filed from the new church," he sighed, leading her deeper beyond that room to a barred door with three locks. "They want to keep their own records and often forget to add to the official one. Deliberately, I suspect."

He pulled out a ring of keys and selected a golden one and a silver one, and a smaller one that could only have been made of moonsilver. Like the golden key, it was still as bright and gleaming as the day it was cast. The silver key was tarnished, though slightly less so where it was most often handled. Removing them from the ring, one by one, he slipped them into the locks, then swiftly turned them in order.

When he set his shoulder to the door and pushed it open, Cae felt the change of the air at once, slightly chill, like a wine cellar. And while the air was not dry, neither was it damp. And it was clean. Entering the room, he very carefully pushed the door closed behind them.

The room was in darkness, its dimensions lost in the shadows beyond the Master's light. The stacks were closer together, and those nearest her were filled with books whose age she could smell from the door. She was distracted by the Master handing her a pair of soft gloves. "First rule, my lady. You will not bring the bird."

She blushed immediately. "Of course, Master," she said, with a bob of her head. "I had not intended to bring her the first time, but... then the worms said it was all right so long as there were no territorial spats with the cats."

"And so it is, out there," he said patiently. "Second rule: you wear these or you touch nothing. And try not to breathe over much onto the pages. Third: these are the only lamps permitted," he added, showing her a glow lamp he had brought with him. It was a neat little contraption, a hinged glass ball on a stand that was filled with a phosphorescent fungus like that found on cave walls. It illuminated the room enough to read by, though the light did not stretch too far. "The worms will provide them. You will leave when it starts to dim. A worm will always be in here with you, to assist you as needed, but he will be working whilst you do what you are here to."

"What kind of work?" she asked.

"Likely dusting," he said wryly. "The further back you go, the older the documents. Some are merely scrolls, which must be unrolled very carefully. Always put a document back exactly where it was taken from." He handed her an enamelled white rod. "Place this upon the shelf or in the scroll's place when you take it down. That way you always know where you've taken it from."

"Thank you, Master. Will the worms in here know the contents of the shelves?"

"Some might. What is it you seek?" His grey eyes watched her intently.

She blushed under the scrutiny. "I mean no disrespect, Great Worm, but... the nature of my research is as delicate as that which it is written upon, and none may know of what I seek. I would greatly appreciate your wisdom and guidance if only I can be assured of secrecy."

"Illegal?" he asked with a slight arch of brow.

"Not yet," she quipped. "Something the royal family have requested. I only thought of looking in the oldest books today."

"While I may recommend and even deliver unrequested books from time to time pertaining to an individual's particulars, I never reveal who is looking for what, or who is reading which," he said staidly.

She felt he was not offended, in fact, was pleased by her circumspection. "Thank you. I seek any references to the old days and the old ways. The farther back the better. I need to know how people lived, what they believed."

"You've been researching the moons," he commented, beginning to lead her into the room. "The First and Second born."

"I have," she nodded. "I seek more. I seek... information upon... shifts and sympaths. And moonsilver," she added.

He smiled at that. Somehow she knew it was the moonsilver that had caused the response. The soul of discretion, he said nothing, but led her to a back shelf not quite a rack of scrolls. He gestured to a single shelf of the bookcase, at her eye level. "Concentrate here, and may the Eldest guide you to the knowledge you seek."

She looked at him suddenly, frowning. "I think the Eldest would frown upon what I seek. I had not taken you for a churchman."

"I am not," he said simply. "But the Eldest was a seeker of knowledge in the beginning. Made in his image, it is why we seek answers with all our being. May the Mother grant you understanding in what you find," he said, bowing as he passed her the orb.

"How will you..." she asked, but he had already turned and walked away.

She sighed, raised the ball to read the titles and was disappointed to find that they either lacked them or they had faded to oblivion. Resigned, she traded the first book for the rod and carried it gently to the nearest reading table at the end of the stack.

The first few books were on Caelyrima and her children, creation stories from several regions and they mostly agreed with each other. Nothing contradicted what she had learned at her mother's knee about the faith and their place in the world, but it provided her with insights she had not before known. She had read three books, cover to cover before she realized the light was beginning to dim.

Before she could panic, the room got slightly brighter. She turned, saw the approach of a worm carrying a fresh globe and a dusting cloth.

He bowed as he saw her. "My lady, if you would follow this lowly worm?"

"I would like a fresh light, if I may?" she asked. "I am only just getting started."

He smiled ruefully. "I am afraid not, my lady. There are rules. When the light dims, you must leave. You may return another day."

"Why?" she asked, not arguing, just wanting to know.

His smile was warmer. "My lady perhaps has a lovely singing voice she would like to keep?"

Cae blushed. "Oh, I warble about as well as my gauvan," she demurred. "But I take it that it would not benefit my health to breathe the air more than the time it takes a lamp to dim?"

He nodded. "And the closeness of the dark can ...start to get to you," he added.

He waited patiently as she rose from her chair, carefully closing her book and carrying it to its place. She started to pull the rod and looked back at the worm. "May I leave this here? To help me find where I was?"

"Only if you do not care if any who come know where someone is reading," he shrugged.

She paused. "Do any often come here?"

"From time to time," he evaded.

"Fine," she sighed, pulling the rod. "I shall just have to remember my way back." She turned to grab her slowly fading light and push her chair in. With a flash of cleverness, she turned the chair just a hair off-centre, and followed the worm out. She counted turns and stacks as they passed them, trying to commit the way to memory. "When I return, who do I request entry from?"

"The Master," he answered as if she should have known.

"Ah, yes. Thank you."

When she finally emerged from the stacks, she found the light coming in through the windows very dim and the activity in the great reading room almost non-existent. She found herself a little grateful for the lowered light, having become accustomed to the lack. "Oh, Mother," she breathed. "What time is it?" she asked the worm.

"Well past supper," he said. "Ward said to tell you that the lady you came in with was told only that you were deep in research and would see her when you emerged. She left to tender your excuses to the royal family at supper."

Cae felt a little faint, and not just because she realized she had missed two meals. "Oh what must he think of me now?" she groaned. "Thank you, worm. I will perhaps see you tomorrow or the next day."

He bowed and saw her to the door.

Cae went to Lili's room first, knocking upon the door. One of her ladies answered it, and Cae was swiftly admitted. "I am so sorry," she exclaimed the moment she saw Lili in her dressing gown and nightbraid.

"I figured you lost track of time," she smiled. "Where were you? They said you could not be disturbed."

"I was in the deep stacks. An archive, I think, where the oldest books are kept. I was literally locked in," she laughed. "It is more secure than the treasury! But apparently it's the rules that you go in and stay until the light they give you dims, and not a moment longer or I'd still be there."

"Is it dark there?" she asked, knowingly.

Cae nodded. "Like the Abyss."

"That's why. You can lose track of yourself if you stay too long. Not to mention the damage to your eyes. Was it worth it?"

Caelerys smiled. "It will be."

Lili nodded, trying not to yawn. "Good. Now, you might wish to go earlier, the next time you decide to go in."

"I will."

"And you might want to head to your own room and see if they can get you anything for supper. Neither of us had dinner," Lili advised gently.

"That is a good idea," she groaned, feeling her stomach protesting its neglect. "I didn't ...mess things up too badly not making it to supper?" she asked, really wanting to know if the king was angry with her.

Lili shook her head. "I tendered your excuses. The queen looked at me funny for a moment, but then didn't say anything. She guided the conversation well away from you for the most part. You're alright. ...Though you may have to explain yourself to the others," she grinned.

"Syera?" she winced.

Lili nodded. "And her brothers," she added, teasing.

Cae moaned in despair as she kissed her friend goodnight and headed towards the door.

Liliwyn called her back, suddenly remembering something. Cae turned back as Lili picked up Cae's boots from under a table. "You just can't keep your shoes on today, can you?" she smirked.

Cae looked down at her stockinged feet in horror, having never once noticed she'd left the princess's room and gone to the library unshod. "I'm never going to live this down, am I?" she groaned, taking her shoes.

Lili only gave her an enigmatic smile for an answer and turned towards her bedchamber.

Cae could only hurry down the hall to her own room, praying no one had noticed.

Fern was the only one still up, waiting with a still warm tray that smelled delicious. She promptly guided Caelerys to a chair and made her eat.

"How did you know...." she protested.

"I didn't," Fern said simply. "The queen had it sent just a little while ago."

"The Mother bless her," Cae sighed, beginning to eat the light but filling meal.

Once she had eaten, Fern helped her undress and get ready for bed. Tempest did not even bother to fuss from her perch on the headboard, merely opening one eye to glare at her and falling back asleep at once. Cae was not far behind her.

20

The week snowballed by. Between preparations for the looming wedding and private worries at no word, they barely had time to blink before it was Fourth Day. Cae was only able to get to the archives once more and her reading was, while fruitful, not quite as immediately helpful as she would have liked. Moonlight reading was not yet possible, as there was just not enough of the Southern Lord showing and it would be another week before the Eastern Lady began to turn.

They were taking a rare afternoon to rest in the gardens, basking in the slanting sun and the heavy fragrance of late harvest blooms, when Valan joined the ladies. Several of them made attempts to gain his attentions, but he was his usual curt self. He headed straight for his sister and her friends. He reached out his hand to Caelerys and she accepted it without a word, allowing him to draw her off to the entrance of one of the paths.

There he stopped, turning her to face him. He retained hold of her hand, letting his own relief and calm bleed through to her.

She could tell he had important news which both angered and soothed him. She looked up into his face with confused question.

"We've received a toomi from one of the messengers I sent," he began. Cae held her breath. "Please know that my father is watching," he warned. "The message read 'Pirates not shipwreck. Heir survives. Not on ship'."

She tensed, her entire being humming with relief and the desire to jump for joy, to hug him fiercely or to just faint. She allowed herself to do none of those things, merely tightening her grip on his hand. She managed to curtsey, bowing her head with a smile, "Thank you, my prince."

"Do you know why he might not have been on the ship?"

She started to shake her head, then did some swift, mental calculations. "Might be as he wished to check on Benhurst. That is within a half day's sail from where the ship would have been when they were attacked," she said softly. "Though that tells me that someone knew he was on that ship, just not any sudden plan changes."

"I have already come to that conclusion, my lady. Investigations proceed apace."

She smiled to cover her concern. "Liliwyn told me I have a spy among my maids."

"I will be discreet."

"Ask your brother," she suggested. "He is much better suited to the subtle inquest. Like as not, they will not realize he is investigating."

"Seduction is good for that." He bent over the hand still in his possession. "I will leave you to tell my sister and Lady Liliwyn. A walk will give you time to react unobserved."

"Thank you. For everything," she added as she slipped into a curtsey again.

He left her company and crossed back to the group, pausing there only long enough to speak to his sister. "The lady has received some news from home. You and Lili might wish to walk with her."

Both women untangled themselves from their conversations and left to join Caelerys. Valan made himself scarce after that, not wishing to stay and be subjected to the fawning efforts of noblewomen.

Two days later, a letter was delivered. Janem brought it, as Vyncet was not ready as yet to sit a horse and had no desire to ride in a carriage. He availed himself of breakfast whilst she perused what he and Vynce had already read.

Willam had apparently seen the village from the ship early in the day of Bonfire Night and asked for himself, his squire and their horses to be put ashore, but for their belongings to be carried down to Taluscliff. He had intended to spend Bonfire Night in the village, to help with morale, and then to ride hard for home. He didn't find out about the attack on the ship until word came that the salvage crews were out and had found survivors. The news had arrived less than an hour after he had.

There were three survivors, and at least one of them was able to give a good description of the pirate captain. They were known pirates in the region, believed to have ties with House Kaladen, but no one had yet been able to prove it.

Father was getting better, or at the very least no worse, and was asking after her. There were words for Vyncet regarding standing for Lord Rorik which Cae skimmed, and words to Janem regarding the attack on the forge and willingness to provide assistance. For Cae, he tendered words of pride for standing up to a bearsarker and alerting the house to the danger.

Cae was understandably relieved, and shared the news with the royal family over supper that night. Valan did not say much, but his eyes strayed often to her; a studying gaze that touched her to the core but that she found a little difficult to read, mostly because she was afraid to. It would require her to admit to something that might very easily put her into Syera's shoes.

Cae's presence was requested at every supper that week, and each was slightly more uncomfortable than the last, as the king asked her and Lili a great many questions that were clearly testing their suitability as royal wives. A handful of the suppers had included other unmarried ladies amongst the court, who were put to similar questions. It seemed the king was telling the two of them that they were by no means certain. The queen remained mostly silent those nights and retired alone, which only seemed to further sour the king's mood.

Once, lady Malyna was even present, but she fared worse than any of the others. The queen said absolutely nothing the entire meal and only smiled on the occasions of Malyna's worst blunders. That evening had been supremely awkward for everyone, even though Malyna had arrived fairly glowing with her excitement. The king had left that meal early and scowling.

Going back to their rooms that night, Lili had leaned in to Cae to whisper: "Semelle had best accept one of those 'numerous' offers for that poor girl, because she is never going to be married into the Citadel," she sighed.

"I really feel sorry for that girl," Cae said, agreeing. "She'll be lucky to land Sir Trent at this rate."

The wedding was upon them almost before they could blink with all the events and preparations that came with the royal adjective. There was a grand feast the night before which was far more what Cae had expected of a royal banquet. The great table they had been having their quiet suppers at was full to capacity with members and relatives of the wedding party.

The royal family was seated at the head of the table, as usual, with a few major differences. The queen sat beside the king and not at the corner from him as she usually preferred. The youngest sons were not present, having been fed in their nurseries. The twin princes sat beside them on opposite sides. Then came Lord Selgan Cygent, with Lili and Cae flanking Syera in their middle. Vyncet was seated beside Valan, then Lord Rorik Griff, flanked by two of his own friends whom Cae had seen about but never formally met. Arrayed beyond this were the Duke and Duchess, Lord Avondyl then Rorik's sons and their wives. He had two married daughters that were not present. On the princess's side were Master Olen, as the king's subsequent brother, and a few outlying cousins. The Griffs had certainly brought more bodies to the table.

Cae found the meal very disconcerting, though she tried to put a brave face upon everything. Master Olen, seated beside her, helped, engaging her in distracting conversation about one of her favourite subjects. But while it smoothed some of it over, it did not quite dispel the conflict of emotions of which she was beginning to become aware.

As she was drifting off, concentrating on the sensations and trying to decipher them and their individual sources, her focus was ripped away by Master Olen's hand on her wrist. "You were missed at the hunt for this feast," he said, smiling broadly as she blinked at him, something knowing behind his eyes. "I tried to make the arrangements but I was duly informed that you were too busy and the risk too great."

"I am truly sorry. I so want to go. I really could have used it."

He nodded, keeping his voice low. "I heard. I am glad that things ended well. It might have been too much to take, to lose two heirs in a lifetime."

"The master is well informed," she said, knowing better, by now, than to address him as 'my lord'.

He merely shrugged. "I try to stay abreast of current events. Also... I have some charge of the toomi," he added with a grin.

"You remind me very much of my own subsequent brother," she smiled.

"The smith? That, my lady, is high praise indeed."

Cae laughed. She felt eyes upon her that made her blush, and she refused to look up, knowing whose eyes they were. She could not afford to reveal too much emotion tonight of all nights.

The night dragged on, filled with idle chatter and little real conversation. Between her and Lili, they kept the princess distracted and entertained, preventing her from thinking overmuch of the upcoming ceremony. They made sure to keep her wine glass filled, so that she would not toss and turn all night and come to the candle unrested.

It was late when they rose, making the excuse of beauty sleep, and escorted the princess off to bed for one last chance to express regrets.

It had been planned that all three of them would be sleeping in the princess's great bed, to keep her safe that last night. Even Tempest had insisted on joining the party, taking up her perch on the headboard and doing her best to make Syera feel better, both by nuzzling her and by acting the fool to make her laugh. Just before Lili blew out the candle, they asked Syera the ritual question.

"Are you sure you are willing to do this?" Lili asked.

Cae held tight to her hand as the princess answered with a deep sigh, "It is for the best. I... I'll get used to it in time." She looked around her at the bed. "Next time I lay my head upon a pillow, it won't be my own."

"He's been married before," Lili said. "He knows what he's doing. He should be gentle."

Cae nodded. "He doesn't strike me as the rutting kind."

She threw herself back onto the pillows. "I wasn't even thinking about that!"

"And now you are," Lili groaned, chagrined.

Cae looked over the princess's body at Lili, gave her a sly grin. "Well... we could," she began slowly, drawing her fingertips lightly up the top of Syera's thigh, "find something else... to take her mind... off it." Her fingers reached Sai's belly, and just as the princess was looking up at them with a confused and partially horrified look, both of them began tickling.

The evening ended with a battering of pillows, retaliating tickles and squealing laughter until they were too tired to do more than flop under the blankets, blow out the light and pass out.

Cae's dreams began as a frightened young thing in a strange place, surrounded by strangers she could not see clearly or understand and all of them were larger than she and had a say in everything she did. She was pushed and pulled in all sorts of directions, finally tossed onto something large and soft in a dark place. Cae felt adrift for a moment, alone until something moved into the darkness towards her, sinuous and warm. The smell of spice and musk enveloped her and she embraced it, letting it pull her further into the darkness that was sleep.

21

The next morning they rose earlier than they really wanted to. Breakfast was light and quick, and Syera was put into a scented bath. Cae tried to help Lili with it, but the perfumes were too strong for her, and she had to bow out, settling for helping to lay out the golden gown that had been made for Syera to begin her new life in. She would wear that later, first came the simple green undergown that she would wear that morning.

Liliwyn attended to her hair, being better at it than Cae. Caelerys watched her twist and braid and pin with swift efficiency and smiled. "When it's your turn, Lili, you'd better pick someone other than me to walk with you," she chuckled. "I am utterly hopeless with hair."

"She's not kidding," Syera smirked. "I'm just glad it's you two and not my maids. I've seen the last of Daia and that's a fact."

"She can't be that bad," Lili began.

"Yes, she can," Caelerys attested.

Dressed simply in her house colours and wearing a dragon pin over her heart, a strand of pearls at her throat and a belt of gold at her hips, Syera led the two of them downstairs to the royal study.

It was a large room, big enough to serve as a war room if necessary and was fairly crowded with courtiers and family come to witness the contract. Both the king and Duke Griff sat at opposite ends of a map table whilst the herald read the contract out loud. Syera stood behind her father's chair, as Rorik stood behind his, even though, as a grown man and a widower, he had the right to negotiate for himself.

Cae and Lili stood behind the princess.

Once the reading was done, the herald asked if this was what both parties had agreed to. They swore that it was. He then asked the bride and groom if this was acceptable to both of them, and if they fully understood their responsibilities as they had been delineated. They, too, swore.

A white swan's feather quill was brought out with a golden nib, and the king signed his name with it, applying a double ring of wax, green around a pool of gold, and pressed his seal into it. Duke Griff did the same, in gold and red. Then the bride and groom, affixing their own seals beside their signatures, her in green and him in red. Then came the candle seal.

Syera's candle was the width of a woman's thumb and the length of a man's hand. Cae knew the inner wax would be green around the red/brown wick. But the whole had been dipped in a thin layer of gold leaf. The Alvermian seal had pressed the dragon deep enough into the candle to reveal the green beneath. Above this, Duke Griff affixed a blob of red wax and impressed his own House seal.

This done, the direct parties involved shared a toast.

Syera headed right back to her chambers afterwards, where she had another glass of a stronger wine. "I can do this, I can do this," she repeated quietly to herself. "Lesser women than I wed men they've never met, and some they outright detest. I can do this."

Lili and Cae exchanged glances but said nothing as they sat her to a light dinner before getting her ready. They made certain she ate.

The two of them put the golden overgown on the princess, making certain everything was just right. Her slippers were cloth-of-gold. Whilst Lili once more went to work on her hair, Cae went to supervise handmaids over the last of the packing.

Before they left to go down for the ceremony, Syera fetched a small box she had not allowed the maids to pack. She opened it and held it out to her friends. Inside were two emerald drops with golden, dragon claw clasps on fine gold chains. Cae recognized the pendants. "Sai... these... these were your favourite earrings!"

There were tears in her eyes as she nodded. "You are my two favourite people, and I wanted you to always have me near you, even when I am far to the South, frozen and lonely."

They both hugged her, unable to promise her that she would not be lonely. "We will visit when we can," Cae said.

"And write often," Lili added.

Daia appeared in the doorway, looking rather subdued.

Syera wiped her eyes, made sure she was perfect whilst Cae and Lili helped each other put on the necklaces. The pendants rest at just the perfectly tantalizing height, though Lili's had a much more profound setting.

Smiling, they lead Syera out of the room and down to the throne room. Entering from the door to the right of the throne, they came down the carpeted path before the dais. Rorik approached from the other door. Both parties stopped in the middle and Cae tried very hard not to pay any attention to the crowd of courtiers and nobles filling the rest of the throne room.

They turned to face the dais. The thrones had been moved to the back wall, standing mute sentinel to the proceedings. And, indeed, both the king and queen's crowns were resting upon their respective cushions, declaring that they come not as monarchs but merely parents. A small brazier was set up before them, burning some fragrant wood. Before that was a small table upon which stood Syera's candle. Selgan and Vyncet stood on either side of the table, like two sentries, each holding a taper, one of red, the other green.

Cae and Lili took Syera's cold hands in theirs and led her up the steps to stand before Selgan who asked in his deep voice, "Do you bring this maid to the candle of her own free will?"

"So we are assured," they answered.

He turned to the princess. "Do you concur?"

She did not hesitate, though she trembled just a little. "I do."

Cae let her go, and Lili passed her hand up into that of her brother before the pair of them turned to go and stand against the wall with the royal family to watch.

The ritual was performed again by Lord Griff before Vyncet. When asked if he concurred, he glanced at Syera with such inner joy that Cae could feel it tickling through her.

Then the seconds handed their charges their tapers and the couple moved behind the table to the brazier, lighting the tapers and bringing them to the candle. They looked at one another a brief moment, and then together touched their flames to the wick.

There was a tiny spark, and then the soft glow and the crowd shouted their joy, being as loud as possible to drive away any ill will or bad feelings.

The couple clasped hands and walked opposite directions around the table, lifting their arms so as not to burn themselves, extinguish the candle or let go, and then began a stately walk out of the throne room.

The rest of the audience waited just a few moments before following, all headed for the ballroom and gardens for a celebratory feast. Once the majority had left, the two families went out the side doors nearest the ballroom entrance, though the king and queen paused to fetch their crowns. Cae glanced back to where Selgan and Vyncet had taken up guard positions on either side of the candle, where they would remain for one hour before extinguishing the candle and boxing it up. They would place the box within the couple's belongings themselves. She mouthed the question to her brother, asking if he would be all right. He just nodded and gestured for her to get on with it, winking at her.

She sighed, following the families out of the throne room.

The ballroom was set up much like it had been the night of the tourney ball, complete with the thrones on the back dais. Although this time they were at the very back and spread apart, and the two smaller thrones set forward for Rorik and Syera. As before, people approached and paused to pay their respects and to deliver wedding gifts.

Someone grabbed Cae's arm as she drifted past. She turned suddenly to look and relaxed, recognizing her brother, Janem. Then she took a second look. He had cleaned up, was wearing a midnight blue cote he had no doubt borrowed from one brother's coffer or another, and wore his hair pulled back in a neat queue at the nape of his neck. At his breast was a small silver pin, a stag leaping over an anvil. She had never seen it before and reached up to touch it.

"Your sigil?" she asked.

He looked down and growled. "It was. Then the church started using an anvil in their rites and as a symbol and now it gives folk a completely wrong-headed idea. Leave it to the wormy bastards to usurp the very symbol of our trade."

As he looped his arm through hers and began to lead her closer to the dais, she mused, "What if you leave it as it is, but inscribe moons on the anvil? Something no Pontifex would condone. Speaking of which," she added under her breath, spying a pair of them not far away looking even more sour than ever.

"I think they're in a twist because they were not asked to handle the wedding," Janem smiled.

"I've heard them saying the union's not proper blessed, bein' a pagan thing," piped up Robin from behind them.

She turned to look at him, found him brushed and cleaned up better than he had been at the coronation, and carrying a rather large, long box. She looked up at Jan. "Wait, what are you doing here and all dressed up? You look practically noble!"

"Don't rub it in," he snarled, then smiled suddenly to a group of lords he was eeling their way past. "Vynce can't exactly present our gift, now can he? He's watching the candle."

"Oh, I... I didn't think about that."

He shook his head, softening. "It's all right. You've never been to a high ranking wedding like this before."

"And you have?" she asked, stunned.

"Not this high," he shook his head. "But close," he evaded, pulling her to a stop. "Not quite royalty," he added. "Bow to the couple, but make sure you acknowledge the crowns behind them," he advised quietly. Then they were before the dais and bowing.

Janem handed a smaller box to Cae and turned to take the larger one from Rob. In tandem, they stepped forward towards the dais, stopping just in front of it and bowing again, though less deeply. "A gift from House Maral, and our wishes of good fortune and happiness," Caelerys said, because even though she was younger than Janem, she outranked him.

They opened the boxes to the delights of the recipients. Janem's held a longsword, with a golden, griffin hilt and ruby eyes. Cae's held a beautifully ornate dagger with a gilded scabbard embellished with green velvet, and the hilt a pretty little dragon's head with eyes of emerald.

Syera lifted hers out with a tiny gasp, looking it over briefly before folding it to her breast for a long moment. She and Cae exchanged a long, heartfelt gaze in which no words needed to be said. Rorik rose and removed the sword from the box, turning it over in his hands before pulling it out only a hand span to see the etching at the base of the channel. He smiled at the maker's mark.

"The Singing Forge?" he asked.

Janem bowed. "House Maral never gives less. By the Master's hand," he added.

Rorik offered Janem his arm. It took Janem a moment to get over his shock, then clasped arms with the Lord. "Our thanks. If ever your House has need, it has but to call." He tightened his grasp a second, looked Janem pointedly in the eye, added, "Any part of it."

Janem nodded, then the three of them stepped back and bowed again, then again to acknowledge the monarchs behind them, and then slipped off into the crowd to permit the lordly houses their turn.

Janem headed straight for the drinks table, fetching himself an ale. Rob was drawn like a magnet to the food. Jan drank half the tankard before he breathed, and turned to his sister who was smirking at him. "What? It was a rush job," he growled.

"Nothing. Nothing at all."

"Liar," he mumbled, though in a slightly better mood, drank the rest of the ale before requesting a refill. "At the very least, the ale is top barrel," he sighed. "I will let the boy stuff himself for a bit and then I am out of here."

"What? Why?" she asked, shocked, accepting a glass of wine.

He tipped his head over his shoulder at a group of minor ladies staring in their direction. "That."

She glanced over and tried hard not to giggle. She was a little less than successful. "Aw, it seems everyone is after a set of antlers for their hall."

"Yeah, well, I don't have enough points to make it worth their while," he snapped, pointing at his head. "And they're ...not going to be happy as a smith's wife."

She tilted her head. "That's the first time I've heard you refer to yourself as a 'smith' and not a 'blacksmith'."

SHIFT: Stag's Heart

He sighed. "Not fitting any more. I smith more than iron. I still make the best swords in the kingdom, but... I'm getting to be known as more. I'm just trying to put off being called a moonsmith or moonsilversmith," he grumbled.

She swayed in place as she ran both words through her mind. "I like moonsmith best. Will you at least think about the moonmark on your anvil?"

"I'll think about it," he sighed, drawing her towards the food as an excuse to get farther from the ladies watching him like hawks.

They found a quiet place in the gardens to eat, whilst they waited for the receiving line to end. They were joined by the Roshans, though Lucelle was on the arm of Edler Marrok. "See," grinned Edler, "I told you he cleaned up nice."

Jan set his plate aside and clasped the man's hand. "Didn't you have enough fun torturing my brother Vynce?"

"Torture?" he protested. "He was a willing participant!"

Janem laughed. "All right, corrupted," he amended.

Edler laughed. "All right, I'll give you that one."

"Where's the other book end?" he asked.

Edler rolled his eyes, "Trying to find himself a maid half as fair as this rabbit I've caught."

Lucelle blushed on his arm and Cae covered her smile with her hand.

"So you've asked?" Jan eyed him.

"Oh, asked and granted!" he crowed. "There's only the ... you know, the messy stuff," he shrugged.

Cae cleared her throat and introduced Janem to the ladies. "As some of you have no manners."

They stood around talking until Lucelle heard the strains of music playing and tugged on Edler's arm. "They're dancing."

He turned with a grin, offered her his arm. "Well, then let us join them, by all means. Teach them how it's done!"

The pair of them rolled off as Vyncet limped up on his cane. He sank immediately onto the bench, elbowing Cae over. She graciously rose and moved to let Balyra sit with him.

"Thank you for doing this, Jan," he breathed, pulling a small flask from a pocket and picking up Cae's half drunk glass of wine, pouring a measure in.

Jan shrugged. "Duty swings both ways."

Cae watched how much of the medicine he poured into the goblet, nodded when he stopped just short. "You'll want to eat with that."

He nodded, drinking the wine down in one swallow. "I'll get food in a minute. I need to sit for a while."

"I'll get you food," Balyra offered.

"You don't have to..." he protested weakly.

"I want to," she shrugged.

"I'll help," Cae said, not wanting to spend the whole party with her brothers. She gestured from Jan to Vynce, "Watch him," she asked. Jan just grinned, nodding. She turned her finger back at Vynce as she began walking backwards after Balyra, "No dancing!"

"Not a chance," he groaned, rubbing his leg.

As Cae turned around and went with Balyra to the buffet, Balyra asked her, "*Can* he dance?"

Cae smiled. "Better than Balaran."

"Really?" she smiled. "Challenge accepted. ...Another night, of course. When he's well," she added.

The two of them laughed on their way inside. She helped Balyra make him a plate, telling her his favourites. She was just pointing out a sweetmeat that he was particularly fond of when she felt someone approaching her from behind. She turned just in time to find herself staring up into Prince Valan's eyes, gasped as she had not expected him to be so close so quickly.

"My lady," he said, taking a half step back so that he might bow over her hand. "*The beast needs soothing*," he rumbled softly so that only she heard the Vermian words.

She curtseyed her agreement, and he took her in arm and swept her out onto the floor. The dance was a blend of semi-aggressive spins and turns, in and out and under, and of close pressed, slower, more possessive steps. Part of the dance required the ladies to spin out, turn and walk away only to be caught and snatched back. When she made the attempt, she could have sworn she heard an actual growl from him and he swung her in so possessively that she actually collided with his chest.

When she could find the breath to speak, she said softly, "This is not helping, my prince."

"No, it is not," he grumbled. "It is making it worse." A few steps later, "We could disappear into the gardens... find the bower..."

"Not a chance," she breathed. "Lady Asparadane is not here herself, but her son is among your father's guards and her daughter and her ladies are about somewhere."

"Blast appearances to the depths of the Abyss," he said flatly, sending a chill down her back, starting from where his hand was placed.

When the dance was over, a more stately waltz was played and this did far more to soothe his savage breast. By the end, he was calmer.

"Better," she said. "But now you know you must dance with other women."

"Must I?" he challenged.

She nodded gently. "I have troubles enough without being singled out by the crown prince himself."

"Am I trouble?" he smiled.

"Always and absolutely, my prince," she said with a serious face.

"I think you have me confused with my twin, my lady," he said.

She smiled. "Oh, I don't think I could ever make that mistake. Besides, you are two very different kinds of trouble."

He bowed to her wisdom and escorted her off the floor and over to where her brother and lady Balyra were sitting watching the dancing whilst he ate. He bowed to Vyncet once he had released Caelerys's hand. "Good evening, Lord Vyncet," he said. "How's the leg?"

"Keeping me sidelined and out of sorts, but mending, Your Highness," he said bowing from his chair when the prince gestured for him not to rise.

"Ah, well, then I apologize for this."

"Apologize for what?" he asked, frowning.

Val then turned to Balyra and offered her his hand. "Lady Balyra? Would you care to dance?"

She glanced over at Vyncet, laughed at his martyred look and accepted. "One of us needs to stay in shape," she quipped with a grin.

Cae laughed at her brother's reaction, even as she watched his interest dancing off with hers. She could not deny it now, she was interested. As she watched the court whirling by in a flare of colour, she spotted Janem over by the ale. She leaned in to her brother and asked, "Why is he still here? I would have thought he'd have escaped the moment he thought he could."

Vynce craned his head to look around a group of dancers, saw Jan talking with a tanned, dark-haired woman in a flowing, embroidered tunic over billowy pantaloons gathered at the ankles, all in peacock colours; vivid teals and rich purples. She was laughing and keeping up with Janem pint for pint. "Who in the world?" he asked.

"The lady with the dangly hair-pins?" asked Reled Marrok, sliding up to the table. "That'd be a Telmar by the name of... oh, I'll remember it... Altima, Altama... Altessa!" he crowed. "That was it."

"A mercari? Here?" Vyncet asked. "How'd she get an invitation?"

"Merit of her countryman expatriated. You might remember Lord Carlan Araan?"

She nodded with a shudder of distaste. "Should I be worried?"

He shook his head, "Nah, nothing like the ..." he bit his tongue on the word he'd been about to say in her presence.

She just laughed. "Thank you for the consideration, but I've probably heard worse."

"According to Jan, you've said worse," Vynce quipped, earning him an elbow in the ribs.

"Well, he would know," she admitted, sipping the last of her brother's ale.

He looked at her, confounded. "You swore around him but not me?"

She gave him a look that said the answer should have been obvious.

"Why?"

She shrugged. "Easy. He'd never tell on me. Besides, he knows better words than you do."

"Does not!"

She grinned wolfishly. "He knows a few that have made Uncle whistle."

Reled looked from one sibling to the other and laughed, coming around and holding his hand out to Cae. "A woman as strong and colourful as my lady Maral? I must, must have this dance!"

Cae happily joined him, needing to feel something more upbeat. She could sense Valan chaffing at the duty of dancing at his sister's wedding.

Reled was an enthusiastic dancer if not a graceful one, and she found she had to be quick on her feet to keep them up and out of the way. Still, she enjoyed herself and she could feel the prince strangely calming. When she caught sight of him again, he was standing on the sidelines, watching with a faint smile and all but ignoring the chatty young lady beside him.

The next dance was a partner trade, only mildly energetic, but the partner swaps happened outside the four couple circles, turning to change with the groups around them. She had a couple of good partners, a few bad ones, one she could not stand the touch of, and one she would have dropped her brother's anvil on if she could have lifted it. The set ended with her in the grasp of lord Aldane, and there was a determination in his eyes she did not like.

"Was I not clear enough, lord Aldane?" she asked, when he held onto her into the next dance. It was another waltz and he kept a tight enough grasp of her that she could not break free without making a scene she was not yet willing to make.

"You were. But I like fire, and I do not back down when I see something I want."

She rolled her eyes. "Surely there are other women who'd be happy to marry the heir to a Lordly House as wealthy as you, now that the wealthiest is no longer available."

His eyes were focused and insistent, pulling her tighter. "You are the only woman here worth pursuing."

She could smell his breath as she was pressed to his chest. It reeked of garlic and ale and something stronger, like Balaran's bottle of spirits but sweeter. She met his flat grey eyes with fire in her sapphires. "If you do not unhand me at once, I shall embarrass you in front of everyone here."

He actually laughed. "And what can my lady do to embarrass me?" he crowed.

Her eyes hardened as she leaned in just enough that only he heard the words she spoke through her teeth. "Best you."

He was startled not just by her vehemence but her conviction. He did not get the chance to retort as a heavy hand landed on his shoulder. He turned, eyes flashing, anger spiking so strongly it felt like needles puncturing her skin where he touched her. It was all ripped back in a heartbeat, leashed by an intense resentment as he saw who stood behind him.

"I am cutting in," said Valan and Cae could see the dragon moving behind his eyes, itching to be released here and now.

For a half second, Cae thought Aldane would refuse. She twisted her hand out of his grasp and attempted to curtsey, forcing him to let go as he bowed or reveal to everyone what had really transpired. Valan barely gave him time to get out of the way before he lightly took Cae's hand in his and swept her away from the scene.

Once out of the incident, she began to tremble. Valan held her as close as he properly could, trying to soothe her this time, taking sweeping steps and turns that would cover her trembling. It did not take very long for her to get herself under control. "Don't ever turn your back to him like that again," she warned. "Next time he'll have a dagger."

"Next time I'll have claws," he said tightly. "Are you all right?"

"I will be," she said, suppressing a shiver. "I do not know what has possessed him."

He watched her closely. "Probably the same thing that has possessed me."

She looked up, "You don't think he's... 'a victim', do you?" She shook her head. "And I refuse to believe this something so base as possession. It's more of ...an awakening."

His look told her there was something else in what he had said that she had missed. She had no time to fathom it as Aldane caught her eye again, this time dancing with lady Malyna who looked almost as uncomfortable as she had. The poor girl had only her twin to rescue her and he was no more gentle than Kaladen.

"Is this really wise, my prince?" she asked, finally letting go of the last vestiges of her discomfort.

"Dancing with you?"

"Again. Taking me so obviously from another man."

His eyes flashed. "Where you are concerned, my lady, I fear I no longer possess wisdom. Only instinct."

Abruptly, he swept her out of the dance, continuing the promenade steps off the dance floor, through the crowd and out of the doors into the garden. He ignored everyone, his hand locked on hers, guiding her through the gardens to the head of one particular path where he stopped, turned to face her. He seemed to be fighting for control and it was bleeding into her from their contact. "Last chance," he said in a husky voice.

"I fear it is far too late for that," she breathed, and let him lead her down to the bower.

Every step they took filled the air with a symphony of fragrance, even as the music from the ballroom drifted faintly to them on the breeze. He brought her to a single spot under the latticework where an opening had been left and what little light of the Southern Lord there was could bathe them. There he took her face in his hands and, drawing her to him, kissed her.

The touch was searing, as soft and sweet as rose petals, but burning like the sands of the northern deserts. The heat sank into her from her mouth to her roots, scorching the soles of her feet until she could no longer feel the ground beneath them, and sending ripples of weakness back upwards to her heart and beyond, leaving her light-headed and out of air. The hunger that fed from that caress was oceans deep and not likely to be sated with just one, burning kiss.

Fear entered her mind, and duty reared its head. She did not want to stop any more than he did, but she knew they should. Nothing was certain yet and the whole thing could be unhinged by a single, errant word.

He pulled back, releasing her lips to take a long, painful breath.

She slowly became aware again, realized she had put her arms around his neck and that her feet were no longer on the ground. His arms were tight around her, holding her up and crushing her to him as if unwilling to let go even though his own mind was telling him the same thing as hers.

He set his forehead against hers, gazing down into her eyes. They had no need to speak, as each could imagine the conversation already. For the moment, the beast lurking within lay calm, even though both knew that had only whet its appetite.

Cae blinked for a second. On a whim, she tilted her head back and looked up into the opening above them to see a black beaded eye on a white face lightly gilded by the southern moon. She laughed, causing the prince to look up from the tempting expanse of her golden throat. Tempest tipped her head to look at him from another angle, uncertain if any of this was a problem.

Valan glared at her for a moment, hardly able to believe he was jealous of a bird. Then a stray thought struck him. He looked back down into Cae's star-filled eyes. "She's not sounding the alarm," he said softly. "Does this mean I can kiss you again?"

She let go of his neck and he took that as a signal to put her down. He sighed, disappointed but understanding. "You are right," he said. "I wouldn't be able to stop a second time."

She began brushing at the shoulders of his coat and straightening his hems in silence, attempting to get her body under control as much as trying to make sure he did not look as if he had been kissing in the bower. He set his hands upon hers to stop her. "Please."

She withdrew, saddened but understanding. It was incredibly intimate. She turned, started to walk away. She stopped halfway down the trellis arch and looked over her shoulder at him. He was still standing in the light, watching her with hungry eyes. She smiled softly. "Are you coming, my prince?" she asked.

"There will be so many questions," he said, afraid to join her.

"There will be more if we are not together when we reappear."

"Truth," he nodded. He moved slowly to join her. He held out his hand to her.

She set her fingertips on his and he curled his hand, pulling hers into his fist. He slowly bowed over it, pressing a kiss, feather-light, upon the valley between her knuckles which sent a very improper flutter through her deepest core. He then straightened, setting her hand upon his arm and escorted her formally out of the bower and labyrinth. He glanced back at the bird now flying back to her rooms. "Some chaperone she turned out to be," he muttered.

She smiled. "Maybe she thinks we've been wasting enough time."

He looked at her. "Does she?"

She shook her head. "She was confused. Probably because I looked like I was in distress, but wasn't."

"Ah."

"Have you even been into the archives?" she asked suddenly.

"No. Bal might have," he said. "Why?"

"There is a shelf there, not the oldest books in the collection, but close, which tell stories of the First in ways I have never heard, granting insights you won't believe. There is so much to be understood there, and I wonder... if anything glows there," she said, looking pointedly up at him.

"I will have to see what can be done. First an experiment with mirrors and the writing," he mused.

"Something to leave to Bal, I would guess. He'd be thrilled to play with it."

"Yes, he would."

They walked in silence, listening to the strains of the music and the laughter and various conversations both intimate and otherwise. It was not long before it was time for Cae and Lili to go get Syera ready for bed. Rorik's friends were doing the same for him.

A servant with a lantern led each group to a pair of doors on the upper guest floor. It was not Syera's room. The women entered one door to the lady's dressing chamber and the men another. They carefully undressed her, and Cae pulled a small leather bag out of her pocket. "This is my last wedding present to you," she said, pulling out the fur wand and lightly dusting her body with it before they put her in her nightdress.

"What was that?" she asked as they sat her down and brushed out her hair.

Cae smiled. "My secret. Lick your fingers."

Frowning, Syera did, then opened her eyes wide in delight.

"See. It keeps your skin silky, helps the complexion. It also helps to put it in areas you tend to sweat more. But tonight..." she left it unsaid, just as they left her hair unbraided, falling in waves of honey-gold down her back. "I'll make sure it goes into your things."

Syera kissed her cheek. "I should have liked to have had you for a sister."

"Maybe soon," she smiled, touching her own lips lightly, still feeling the warmth of his on them. "Just... give him a chance?" she asked, leading her into the next room where a great canopy bed lay waiting.

SHIFT: Stag's Heart

She and Lili offered what words of soothing wisdom they could, but in the end, Cae just held her hand, drawing off her nervousness as the tree had shown her, and the books she had found told her, and tucked her in. She carried that nervousness out of the room with her. Lili paused to ring the small bell just inside the door to tell the men that the husband was allowed to enter the room. Then the two women left their friend alone with her new husband.

They walked together, arm in arm down to their own floor and their own rooms. They paused outside Cae's room, the first on the hall. They hugged each other tightly, whispering prayers that Syera would be treated gently tonight and not be disappointed with married life.

Fern and Pansy were the only ones still up, and they put Cae to bed with quiet efficiency.

Cae's dreams were clearly not her own, influenced by what she knew must be happening floors above her with her closest friend, but the parties involved in her dreams were herself and her dragon. The kiss carried them farther, exploring each other's bodies until dawn woke them cruelly.

To be continued in

SHIFT

Book 2

"Dragon's Bride"

Other Books By
S.L.Thorne

Love In Ruins
The Speaker
Mercy's Ransom
The Gryphon's Rest Series:
Lady of the Mist
The Gloaming

SHIFT Books 1 & 2
Stag's Heart
Dragon's Bride

*All Available in both paperback and ebook
at:
Thornewoodstudios.com/books*

Made in the USA
Columbia, SC
10 October 2023